Elric of Melniboné

Michael Moorcock

ELRIC OF MELNIBONÉ

MILLENNIUM
An Orion Book
LONDON

This collected edition first published
in Great Britain in 1993 by
Millennium
An imprint of Orion Books Ltd
Orion House, 5 Upper St Martin's Lane
London WC2H 9EA

A CIP catalogue record for this book is available
from the British Library

ISBN: (Csd) 1 85798 037 9
(Ppr) 1 85798 038 7

Millennium
Book Fifteen

Printed and bound in Great Britain by
Clays Ltd, St Ives Plc

Dear Reader

Elric is often described as an anti-hero, but I prefer to think of him simply as a hero. When I was growing up my favourite heroes (William, Tarzan, Mord Em'ly, Zenith the Albino, Jo March, The Continental Op) all seemed people struggling for liberty and identity, forced to rely on their own wits and values but ready, at some point, to make a serious, if reluctant, sacrifice in the common interest. There is a level at which the hero becomes fairly ridiculous, often because he never fundamentally questions his society. John Wayne was always basically in favour of old-fashioned paternalism, no matter how much a rugged individualist he claimed to be.

Later, I became fascinated by the kind of book examining the myths which make such heroes attractive (*Lord Jim*, for instance) and came to understand that there is a level at which heroism can be used as mere manipulative propaganda designed, for instance, to make young women sacrifice their futures in unjust marriages or young men sacrifice their lives in unjust wars.

The 'alienated' hero or heroine is often able to stand back a little and work out what's really going on. The fiction in which they are protagonists allows them the power (often against terrible odds) to take dramatic action and run the kinds of risks most of us would be prepared to if we had their resources or their friends. In real life such power only comes through group action and the ballot box, yet we're all familiar with examples of local heroism, the courage of ordinary individuals in terrifying conditions.

I see nothing wrong with heroes who reflect the best that we would wish to be and do. I still have unashamed affection for my own heroes who remain sceptical of authority and its pronouncements.

I began the Elric stories in the mid-1950s. They evolved gradually, often in correspondence with Jim Cawthorn, who sent me his ideas in pictures, until in 1959 I was asked to write the series for Ted Carnell's SCIENCE FANTASY magazine.

Elric was created in conscious opposition to the macho tendencies of the day. He first appeared in *The Dreaming City* and only later did I go back and write some of his earlier adventures. Elric, as I've written elsewhere, reflected the person I was when I first wrote about him. His conflicts and searches had a great deal in common with my own and in some ways still do.

Elric was my first born hero to grow beyond infancy and it's with him I most identify. While I've put his adventures in this final order and made some minor revisions, I've made only a few changes to the prose, which has lasted like some hardy mongrel through the ups and downs of a good few literary seasons, and does the job it's meant to do with, I hope, a bit of diverting gusto.

My debt to Anthony Skene (*Monsieur Zenith*), Fletcher Pratt (*Well of the Unicorn*), James Branch Cabell (*Jurgen*), Lord Dunsany, Fritz Leiber and Poul Anderson, as well as *The Castle of Otranto, Ivanhoe, Melmoth* and others, has been acknowledged elsewhere. The first Elric book came out in 1963 and was dedicated to my mother. This edition I dedicate with considerable thanks to John Davey, whose help with it has proven invaluable.

Yours,
Michael Moorcock

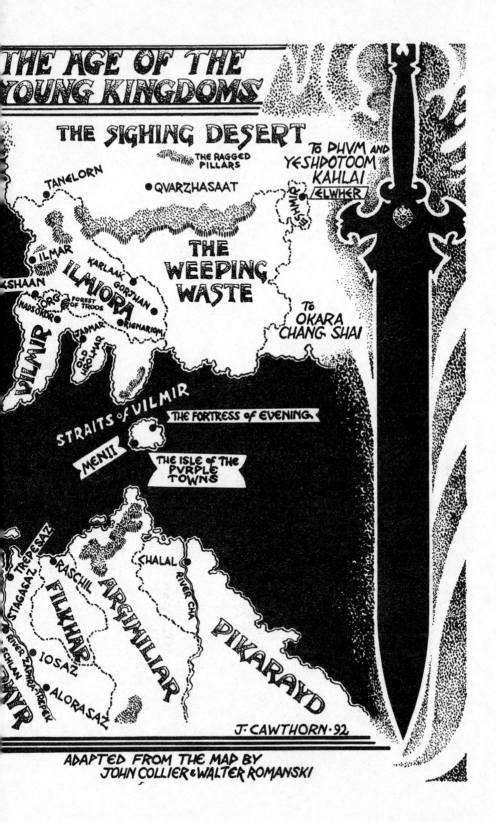

ELRIC OF MELNIBONÉ

To Poul Anderson for The Broken Sword *and* Three Hearts
and Three Lions. *To the late Fletcher Pratt for* The Well of the
Unicorn. *To the late Bertolt Brecht for* The Threepenny Opera
*which, for obscure reasons, I link with the other books as
being one of the chief influences on the first Elric stories*

ONE

On the island kingdom of Melniboné all the old rituals are still observed, though the nation's power has waned for five hundred years, and now her way of life is maintained only by her trade with the Young Kingdoms and by the fact that the city of Imrryr has become the meeting place of merchants. Are those rituals no longer useful; can the rituals be denied and doom avoided? One who would rule in Emperor Elric's stead prefers to think not. He says that Elric will bring destruction to Melniboné by his refusal to honour all the rituals (Elric honours many). And now opens the tragedy which will close many years from now and precipitate the destruction of this world.

1

A Melancholy King:
A Court Strives to
Honour Him

It is the colour of a bleached skull, his flesh; and the long hair which flows below his shoulders is milk-white. From the tapering, beautiful head stare two slanting eyes, crimson and moody, and from the loose sleeves of his yellow gown emerge two slender hands, also the colour of bone, resting on each arm of a seat which has been carved from a single, massive ruby.

The crimson eyes are troubled and sometimes one hand will rise to finger the light helm which sits upon the white locks: a helm made from some dark, greenish alloy and exquisitely moulded into the likeness of a dragon about to take wing. And on the hand which absently caresses the crown there is a ring in which is set a single rare Actorios stone whose core sometimes shifts sluggishly and reshapes itself, as if it were sentient smoke and as restless in its jewelled prison as the young albino on his Ruby Throne.

He looks down the long flight of quartz steps to where his court disports itself, dancing with such delicacy and whispering grace that it might be a court of ghosts. Mentally he debates moral issues and in itself this activity divides him from the great majority of his subjects, for these people are not human.

These are the people of Melniboné, the Dragon Isle, which ruled the world for ten thousand years and has ceased to rule it for less than five hundred years. And they are cruel and clever and to them 'morality' means little more than a proper respect for the traditions of a hundred centuries.

To the young man, four hundred and twenty-eighth in direct line of descent from the first Sorcerer Emperor of Melniboné, their assumptions seem not only arrogant but foolish; it is plain that the Dragon Isle has lost most of her power and will soon be threatened, in another century or two, by a direct conflict with the emerging human nations whom they call, somewhat patronizingly, the Young Kingdoms. Already pirate fleets have made unsuccessful attacks on Imrryr the Beautiful, the Dreaming City, capital of the Dragon Isle of Melniboné.

Yet even the emperor's closest friends refuse to discuss the prospect of Melniboné's fall. They are not pleased when he mentions the idea, considering his remarks not only unthinkable, but also a singular breach of good taste.

So, alone, the emperor broods. He mourns that his father, Sadric the Eighty-Sixth, did not sire more children, for then a more suitable monarch might have been available to take his place on the Ruby Throne. Sadric has been dead a year; seeming to whisper glad welcome to that which came to claim his soul. Through most of his life Sadric had never known another woman than his wife, for the Empress had died bringing her sole thin-blooded issue into the world. But, with Melnibonéan emotions (oddly different from those of the human newcomers), Sadric had loved his wife and had been unable to find pleasure in any other company, even that of the son who had killed her and who was all that was left of her. By magic potions and the chanting of runes, by rare herbs had her son been nurtured, his strength sustained artifically by every art known to the Sorcerer Kings of Melniboné. And he had lived – still lives – thanks to sorcery alone, for he is naturally lassitudinous and, without his drugs, would barely be able to raise his hand from his side through most of a normal day.

If the young emperor has found any advantage in his lifelong weakness it must be in that, perforce, he has read much. Before he was fifteen he had read every book in his father's library, some more than once. His sorcerous powers, learned initially from Sadric, are now greater than any possessed by his ancestors for many a generation. His knowledge of the world beyond the shores of Melniboné is profound, though he has as yet had little direct experience of it. If he wished he could resurrect the Dragon Isle's former might and rule both his own land and the Young Kingdoms as an invulnerable tyrant. But his reading has also taught him to question the uses to which power is put, to question his motives, to question whether his own power should be used at all, in any cause. His reading has led him to this 'morality', which, still, he barely understands. Thus, to his subjects, he is an enigma and, to some, he is a threat, for he neither thinks nor acts in accordance with their conception of how a true Melnibonéan (and a Melnibonéan emperor, at that) should think and act. His cousin Yyrkoon, for instance, has been heard more than once to voice strong doubts concerning the emperor's right to rule the people of Melniboné. 'This feeble scholar will bring doom to us all,' he said one night to

Dyvim Tvar, Lord of the Dragon Caves.

Dyvim Tvar is one of the emperor's few friends and he had duly reported the conversation, but the youth had dismissed the remarks as 'only a trivial treason', whereas any of his ancestors would have rewarded such sentiments with a very slow and exquisite public execution.

The emperor's attitude is further complicated by the fact that Yyrkoon, who is even now making precious little secret of his feelings that he should be emperor, is the brother of Cymoril, a girl whom the albino considers the closest of his friends, and who will one day become his empress.

Down on the mosaic floor of the court Prince Yyrkoon can be seen in all his finest silks and furs, his jewels and his brocades, dancing with a hundred women, all of whom are rumoured to have been mistresses of his at one time or another. His dark features, at once handsome and saturnine, are framed by long black hair, waved and oiled, and his expression, as ever, is sardonic while his bearing is arrogant. The heavy brocade cloak swings this way and that, striking other dancers with some force. He wears it almost as if it is armour or, perhaps, a weapon. Amongst many of the courtiers there is more than a little respect for Prince Yyrkoon. Few resent his arrogance and those who do keep silent, for Yyrkoon is known to be a considerable sorcerer himself. Also his behaviour is what the court expects and welcomes in a Melnibonéan noble; it is what they would welcome in their emperor.

The emperor knows this. He wishes he could please his court as it strives to honour him with its dancing and its wit, but he cannot bring himself to take part in what he privately considers a wearisome and irritating sequence of ritual posturings. In this he is, perhaps, somewhat more arrogant than Yyrkoon who is, at least, a conventional boor.

From the galleries, the music grows louder and more complex as the slaves, specially trained and surgically operated upon to sing but one perfect note each, are stimulated to more passionate efforts. Even the young emperor is moved by the sinister harmony of their song which in few ways resembles anything previously uttered by the human voice. Why should their pain produce such marvellous beauty? he wonders. Or is all beauty created through pain? Is that the secret of great art, both human and Melnibonéan?

The Emperor Elric closes his eyes.

There is a stir in the hall below. The gates have opened and the dancing courtiers cease their motion, drawing back and bowing low as soldiers enter. The soldiers are clad all in light blue, their ornamental helms cast in fantastic shapes, their long, broad-bladed lances decorated with jewelled ribbons. They surround a young woman whose blue dress matches their uniforms and whose bare arms are encircled by five or six bracelets of diamonds, sapphires and gold. Strings of diamonds and sapphires are wound into her hair. Unlike most of the women of the court, her face has no designs painted upon the eyelids or cheekbones. Elric smiles. This is Cymoril. The soldiers are her personal ceremonial guard who, according to tradition, must escort her into the court. They ascend the steps leading to the Ruby Throne. Slowly Elric rises and stretches out his hands.

'Cymoril. I thought you had decided not to grace the court tonight.'

She returns his smile. 'My emperor, I found that I was in the mood for conversation, after all.'

Elric is grateful. She knows that he is bored and she knows, too, that she is one of the few people of Melniboné whose conversation interests him. If protocol allowed, he would offer her the throne, but as it is she must sit on the topmost step at his feet.

'Please sit, sweet Cymoril.' He resumes his place upon the throne and leans forward as she seats herself and looks into his eyes with a mixed expression of humour and tenderness. She speaks softly as her guard withdraws to mingle at the sides of the steps with Elric's own guard. Her voice can be heard only by Elric.

'Would you ride out to the wild region of the island with me tomorrow, my lord?'

'There are matters to which I must give my attention . . . ' He is attracted by the idea. It is weeks since he left the city and rode with her, their escort keeping a discreet distance away.

'Are they urgent?'

He shrugs. 'What matters are urgent in Melniboné? After ten thousand years, most problems may be seen in a certain perspective.' His smile is almost a grin, rather like that of a young scholar who plans to play truant from his tutor. 'Very well – early in the morning, we'll leave, before the others are up.'

'The air beyond Imrryr will be clear and sharp. The sun will be warm for the season. The sky will be blue and unclouded.'

Elric laughs. 'Such sorcery you must have worked!'

Cymoril lowers her eyes and traces a pattern on the marble of the dais. 'Well, perhaps a little. I am not without friends among the weakest of the elementals . . . '

Elric stretches down to touch her fine, fair hair. 'Does Yyrkoon know?'

'No.'

Prince Yyrkoon has forbidden his sister to meddle in magical matters. Prince Yyrkoon's friends are only among the darker of the supernatural beings and he knows that they are dangerous to deal with; thus he assumes that all sorcerous dealings bear a similar element of danger. Besides this, he hates to think that others possess the power that he possesses. Perhaps this is what, in Elric, he hates most of all.

'Let us hope that all Melniboné needs fine weather for tomorrow,' says Elric. Cymoril stares curiously at him. She is still a Melnibonéan. It has not occurred to her that her sorcery might prove unwelcome to some. Then she shrugs her lovely shoulders and touches her lord lightly upon the hand.

'This "guilt",' she says. 'This searching of the conscience. Its purpose is beyond my simple brain.'

'And mine, I must admit. It seems to have no practical function. Yet more than one of our ancestors predicted a change in the nature of our earth. A spiritual as well as a physical change. Perhaps I have glimmerings of this change when I think my stranger, un-Melnibonéan, thoughts?'

The music swells. The music fades. The courtiers dance on, though many eyes are upon Elric and Cymoril as they talk at the top of the dais. There is speculation. When will Elric announce Cymoril as his empress-to-be? Will Elric revive the custom that Sadric dismissed, of sacrificing twelve brides and their bridegrooms to the Lords of Chaos in order to ensure a good marriage for the rulers of Melniboné? It was obvious that Sadric's refusal to allow the custom to continue brought misery upon him and death upon his wife; brought him a sickly son and threatened the very continuity of the monarchy. Elric must revive the custom. Even Elric must fear a repetition of the doom which visited his father. But some say that Elric will do nothing in accordance with tradition and that he threatens not only his own life, but the existence of Melniboné itself and all it stands for. And those who speak thus are often seen to be on good terms with Prince Yyrkoon who dances on, seemingly unaware of their conversation or, indeed, unaware that his sister talks quietly with the cousin who sits on the Ruby Throne; who sits on the edge of the seat, forgetful of his dignity, who exhibits none of the ferocious and disdainful pride which has, in the past, marked virtually every other emperor of Melniboné; who chats animatedly, forgetful that the court is supposed to be dancing for his entertainment.

And then suddenly Prince Yyrkoon freezes in mid-pirouette and raises his dark eyes to look up at his emperor. In one corner of the hall, Dyvim Tvar's attention is attracted by Yyrkoon's calculated and dramatic posture and the Lord of the Dragon Caves frowns. His hand falls to where his sword would normally be, but no swords are worn at a court ball. Dyvim Tvar looks warily and intently at Prince Yyrkoon as the tall nobleman begins to ascend the stairs to the Ruby Throne. Many eyes follow the emperor's cousin and now hardly anyone dances, though the music grows wilder as the masters of the music slaves goad their charges to even greater exertions.

Elric looks up to see Yyrkoon standing one step below that on which Cymoril sits. Yyrkoon makes a bow which is subtly insulting.

'I present myself to my emperor,' he says.

2

An Upstart Prince: He Confronts His Cousin

'And how do you enjoy the ball, cousin?' Elric asked, aware that Yyrkoon's melodramatic presentation had been designed to catch him off-guard and, if possible, humiliate him. 'Is the music to your taste?'

Yyrkoon lowered his eyes and let his lips form a secret little smile. 'Everything is to my taste, my liege. But what of yourself? Does something displease you? You do not join the dance.'

Elric raised one pale finger to his chin and stared at Yyrkoon's hidden eyes. 'I enjoy the dance, cousin, nonetheless. Surely it is possible to take pleasure in the pleasure of others?'

Yyrkoon seemed genuinely astonished. His eyes opened fully and met Elric's. Elric felt a slight shock and then turned his own gaze away, indicating the music galleries with a languid hand. 'Or perhaps it is the pain of others which brings me pleasure. Fear not, for my sake, cousin. I am pleased. I am pleased. You may dance on, assured that your emperor enjoys the ball.'

But Yyrkoon was not to be diverted from his object. 'Surely, if his subjects are not to go away saddened and troubled that they have not pleased their ruler, the emperor should demonstrate his enjoyment . . .?'

'I would remind you, cousin,' said Elric quietly, 'that the emperor has no duty to his subjects at all, save to rule them. Their duty is to him. That is the tradition of Melniboné.'

Yyrkoon had not expected Elric to use such arguments against him, but he rallied with his next retort. 'I agree, my lord. The emperor's duty is rule his subjects. Perhaps that is why so many of them do not, themselves, enjoy the ball as much as they might.'

'I do not follow you, cousin.'

Cymoril had risen and stood with her hands clenched on the step above her brother. She was tense and anxious, worried by her brother's bantering tone, his disdainful bearing.

'Yyrkoon . . . ' she said.

He acknowledged her presence. 'Sister. I see you share our emperor's reluctance to dance.'

'Yyrkoon,' she murmured, 'you are going too far. The emperor is tolerant, but . . . '

'Tolerant? Or is he careless? Is he careless of the traditions of our great race? Is he contemptuous of that race's pride?'

Dyvim Tvar was now mounting the steps. It was plain that he, too, sensed that Yyrkoon had chosen this moment to test Elric's power.

Cymoril was aghast. She said urgently: 'Yyrkoon. If you would live . . . '

'I would not care to live if the soul of Melniboné perished. And the guardianship of our nation's soul is the responsibility of the emperor. And what if we should have an emperor who failed in that responsibility? An emperor who was weak? An emperor who cared nothing for the greatness of the Dragon Isle and its folk?'

'A hypothetical question, cousin.' Elric had recovered his composure and his voice was an icy drawl. 'For such an emperor has never sat upon the Ruby Throne and such an emperor never shall.'

Dyvim Tvar came up, touching Yyrkoon on the shoulder. 'Prince, if you value your dignity and your life . . . '

Elric raised his hand. 'There is no need for that, Dyvim Tvar. Prince Yyrkoon merely entertains us with an intellectual debate. Fearing that I was bored by the music and the dance – which I am not – he thought he would provide the subject for a stimulating discourse. I am certain that we are most stimulated, Prince Yyrkoon.' Elric allowed a patronizing warmth to colour his last sentence.

Yyrkoon flushed with anger and bit his lips.

'But go on, dear cousin Yyrkoon,' Elric said. 'I am interested. Enlarge further on your argument.'

Yyrkoon looked around him, as if for support. But all his supporters were on the floor of the hall. Only Elric's friends, Dyvim Tvar and Cymoril, were nearby. Yet Yyrkoon knew that his supporters were hearing every word and that he would lose face if he did not retaliate. Elric could tell that Yyrkoon would have preferred to have retired from this confrontation and choose another day and another ground on which to continue the battle, but that was not possible. Elric, himself, had no wish to continue the foolish banter which was, no matter how disguised, a little better than the quarrelling of two little girls over who should play with the slaves first. He decided to make an end of it.

Yyrkoon began: 'Then let me suggest that an emperor who was

physically weak might also be weak in his will to rule as befitted . . . '

And Elric raised his hand. 'You have done enough, dear cousin. More than enough. You have wearied yourself with this conversation when you would have preferred to dance. I am touched by your concern. But now I, too, feel weariness steal upon me.' Elric signalled for his old servant Tanglebones who stood on the far side of the throne dais, amongst the soldiers. 'Tanglebones! My cloak.'

Elric stood up. 'I thank you again for your thoughtfulness, cousin.' He addressed the court in general. 'I was entertained. Now I retire.'

Tanglebones brought the cloak of white fox fur and placed it around his master's shoulders. Tanglebones was very old and much taller than Elric, though his back was stooped and all his limbs seemed knotted and twisted back on themselves, like the limbs of a strong, old tree.

Elric walked across the dais and through the door which opened onto a corridor which led to his private apartments.

Yyrkoon was left fuming. He whirled round on the dais and opened his mouth as if to address the watching courtiers. Some, who did not support him, were smiling quite openly. Yyrkoon clenched his fists at his sides and glowered. He glared at Dyvim Tvar and opened his thin lips to speak. Dyvim Tvar coolly returned the glare, daring Yyrkoon to say more.

Then Yyrkoon flung back his head so that the locks of his hair, all curled and oiled, swayed against his back. And Yyrkoon laughed.

The harsh sound filled the hall. The music stopped. The laughter continued.

Yyrkoon stepped up so that he stood on the dais. He dragged his heavy cloak round him so that it engulfed his body.

Cymoril came forward. 'Yyrkoon, please do not . . . ' He pushed her back with a motion of his shoulder.

Yyrkoon walked stiffly towards the Ruby Throne. It became plain that he was about to seat himself in it and thus perform one of the most traitorous actions possible in the code of Melniboné. Cymoril ran the few steps to him and pulled at his arm.

Yyrkoon's laughter grew. 'It is Yyrkoon they would wish to see on the Ruby Throne,' he told his sister. She gasped and looked in horror at Dyvim Tvar whose face was grim and angry.

Dyvim Tvar signed to the guards and suddenly there were two ranks of armoured men between Yyrkoon and the throne.

Yyrkoon glared back at the Lord of the Dragon Caves. 'You had best hope you perish with your master,' he hissed.

'This guard of honour will escort you from the hall,' Dyvim Tvar said evenly. 'We were all stimulated by your conversation this evening, Prince Yyrkoon.'

Yyrkoon paused, looked about him, then relaxed. He shrugged. 'There's time enough. If Elric will not abdicate, then he must be deposed.'

Cymoril's slender body was rigid. Her eyes blazed. She said to her brother:

'If you harm Elric in any way, I will slay you myself, Yyrkoon.'

He raised his tapering eyebrows and smiled. At that moment he seemed to hate his sister even more than he hated his cousin. 'Your loyalty to that creature has ensured your own doom, Cymoril. I would rather you died than that you should give birth to any progeny of his. I will not have the blood of our house diluted, tainted – even touched – by his blood. Look to your own life, sister, before you threaten mine.'

And he stormed down the steps, pushing through those who came up to congratulate him. He knew that he had lost and the murmurs of his sycophants only irritated him further.

The great doors of the hall crashed together and closed. Yyrkoon was gone from the hall.

Dyvim Tvar raised both his arms. 'Dance on, courtiers. Pleasure yourselves with all that the hall provides. It is what will please the emperor most.'

But it was plain there would be little more dancing done tonight. Courtiers were already deep in conversation as, excitedly, they debated the events.

Dyvim Tvar turned to Cymoril. 'Elric refuses to understand the danger, Princess Cymoril. Yyrkoon's ambition could bring disaster to all of us.'

'Including Yyrkoon.' Cymoril sighed.

'Aye, including Yyrkoon. But how can we avoid this, Cymoril, if Elric will not give orders for your brother's arrest?'

'He believes that such as Yyrkoon should be allowed to say what they please. It is part of his philosophy. I can barely understand it, but it seems integral to his whole belief. If he destroys Yyrkoon, he destroys the basis on which his logic works. That at any rate, Dragon Master, is what he has tried to explain to me.'

Dyvim Tvar sighed and he frowned. Unable to understand Elric, he was afraid that he could sometimes sympathize with Yyrkoon's viewpoint. At least Yyrkoon's motives and arguments were relatively straightforward. He knew Elric's character too well, however, to believe that Elric acted from weakness or lassitude. The paradox was that Elric tolerated Yyrkoon's treachery because he was strong, because he had the power to destroy Yyrkoon whenever he cared. And Yyrkoon's own character was such that he must constantly be testing that strength of Elric's, for he knew instinctively that if Elric did weaken and order him slain, then he would have won. It was a complicated situation and Dyvim Tvar dearly wished that he was not embroiled in it. But his loyalty to the royal line of Melniboné was strong and his personal loyalty to Elric was great. He considered the idea of having Yyrkoon secretly assassinated, but he knew that such a plan would almost certainly come to nothing. Yyrkoon was a sorcerer of immense power and doubtless would be forewarned of any attempt on his life.

'Princess Cymoril,' said Dyvim Tvar, 'I can only pray that your brother swallows so much of his rage that it eventually poisons him.'

'I will join you in that prayer, Lord of the Dragon Caves.'

Together, they left the hall.

3

Riding Through the Morning: A Moment of Tranquillity

The light of the early morning touched the tall towers of Imrryr and made them scintillate. Each tower was of a different hue; there were a thousand soft colours. There were rose pinks and pollen yellows, there were purples and pale greens, mauves and browns and oranges, hazy blues, whites and powdery golds, all lovely in the sunlight. Two riders left the Dreaming City behind them and rode away from the walls, over the green turf towards a pine forest where, among the shadowy trunks, a little of the night seemed to remain. Squirrels were stirring and foxes crept homeward; birds were singing and forest flowers opened their petals and filled the air with delicate scent. A few insects wandered sluggishly aloft. The contrast between life in the nearby city and this lazy rusticity was very great and seemed to mirror some of the contrasts existing in the mind of at least one of the riders who now dismounted and led his horse, walking knee-deep through a mass of blue flowers. The other rider, a girl, brought her own horse to a halt but did not dismount. Instead, she leaned casually on her high Melnibonéan pommel and smiled at the man, her lover.

'Elric? Would you stop so near to Imrryr?'

He smiled back at her, over his shoulder. 'For the moment. Our flight was hasty. I would collect my thoughts before we ride on.'

'How did you sleep last night?'

'Well enough, Cymoril, though I must have dreamed without know-ing it, for there were – there were little intimations in my head when I awoke. But then, the meeting with Yyrkoon was not pleasant . . . '

'Do you think he plots to use sorcery against you?'

Elric shrugged. 'I would know if he brought a large sorcery against me. And he knows my power. I doubt if he would dare employ wizardry.'

'He has reason to believe you might not use your power. He has worried at your personality for so long – is there not a danger he will begin to worry at your skills? Testing your sorcery as he has tested your patience?'

Elric frowned. 'Yes, I suppose there is that danger. But not yet, I should have thought.'

'He will not be happy until you are destroyed, Elric.'

'Or is destroyed himself, Cymoril.' Elric stooped and picked one of the flowers. He smiled. 'Your brother is inclined to absolutes, is he not? How the weak hate weakness.'

Cymoril took his meaning. She dismounted and came towards him. Her thin gown matched, almost perfectly, the colour of the flowers through which she moved. He handed her the flower and she accepted it, touching its petals with her perfect lips. 'And how the strong hate strength, my love. Yyrkoon is my kin and yet I give you this advice – use your strength against him.'

'I could not slay him. I have not the right.' Elric's face fell into familiar, brooding lines.

'You could exile him.'

'Is not exile the same as death to a Melnibonéan?'

'You, yourself, have talked of travelling in the lands of the Young Kingdoms.'

Elric laughed somewhat bitterly. 'But perhaps I am not a true Melnibonéan. Yyrkoon has said as much – and others echo his thoughts.'

'He hates you because you are contemplative. Your father was contemplative and no one denied that he was a fitting emperor.'

'My father chose not to put the results of his contemplation into his personal actions. He ruled as an emperor should. Yyrkoon, I must admit, would also rule as an emperor should. He, too, has the opportunity to make Melniboné great again. If he were emperor, he would embark on a campaign of conquest to restore our trade to its former volume, to extend our power across the earth. And that is what the majority of our folk would wish. Is it my right to deny that wish?'

'It is your right to do what you think, for you are the emperor. All who are loyal to you think as I do.'

'Perhaps their loyalty is misguided. Perhaps Yyrkoon is right and I will betray that loyalty, bring doom to the Dragon Isle.' His moody, crimson eyes looked directly into hers. 'Perhaps I should have died as I left my mother's womb. Then Yyrkoon would have become emperor. Has Fate been thwarted?'

'Fate is never thwarted. What has happened has happened because Fate willed it thus – if, indeed, there is such a thing as Fate and if men's actions are not merely a response to other men's actions.'

Elric drew a deep breath and offered her an expression tinged with irony. 'Your logic leads you close to heresy, Cymoril, if we are to believe the traditions of Melniboné. Perhaps it would be better if you forgot your friendship with me.'

She laughed. 'You begin to sound like my brother. Are you testing my love for you, my lord?'

He began to remount his horse. 'No, Cymoril, but I would advise you to test your love yourself, for I sense there is tragedy implicit in our love.'

As she swung herself back into her saddle she smiled and shook her head. 'You see doom in all things. Can you not accept the good gifts granted you? They are few enough, my lord.'

'Aye. I'll agree with that.'

They turned in their saddles, hearing hoofbeats behind them. Some distance away they saw a company of yellow-clad horsemen riding about in confusion. It was their guard, which they had left behind, wishing to ride alone.

'Come!' cried Elric. 'Through the woods and over yonder hill and they'll never find us!'

They spurred their steeds through the sun-speared wood and up the steep sides of the hill beyond, racing down the other side and away across a plain where noidel bushes grew, their lush, poison fruit glimmering a purplish blue, a night-colour which even the light of day could not disperse. There were many such peculiar berries and herbs on Melniboné and it was to some of them that Elric owed his life. Others were used for sorcerous potions and had been sown generations before by Elric's ancestors. Now few Melnibonéans left Imrryr even to collect these harvests. Only slaves visited the greater part of the island, seeking the roots and the shrubs which made men dream monstrous and magnificent dreams, for it was in their dreams that the nobles of Melniboné found most of their pleasures; they had ever been a moody, inward-looking race and it was for this quality that Imrryr had come to be named the Dreaming City. There, even the meanest slaves chewed berries to bring them oblivion and thus were easily controlled, for they came to depend on their dreams. Only Elric himself refused such drugs, perhaps because he required so many others simply to ensure his remaining alive.

The yellow-clad guards were lost behind them and once across the plain where the noidel bushes grew they slowed their flight and came at length to cliffs and then the sea.

The sea shone brightly and languidly washed the white beaches below the cliffs. Seabirds wheeled in the clear sky and their cries were distant, serving only to emphasize the sense of peace which both Elric and Cymoril now had. In silence the lovers guided their horses down steep paths to the shore and there they tethered the steeds and began to walk across the sand, their hair – his white, hers jet black – waving in the wind which blew from the east.

They found a great, dry cave which caught the sounds the sea made and replied in a whispering echo. They removed their silken garments and made love tenderly in the shadows of the cave. They lay in each other's arms as the day warmed and the wind dropped. Then they went to bathe in the waters, filling the empty sky with their laughter.

When they were dry and were dressing themselves they noticed a darkening of the horizon and Elric said: 'We shall be wet again before we return to Imrryr. No matter how fast we ride, the storm will catch us.'

'Perhaps we should remain in the cave until it is past?' she suggested, coming close and holding her soft body against him.

'No,' he said. 'I must return soon, for there are potions in Imrryr I must take if my body is to retain its strength. An hour or two longer and I shall begin to weaken. You have seen me weak before, Cymoril.'

She stroked his face and her eyes were sympathetic. 'Aye. I've seen you weak before, Elric. Come, let's find the horses.'

By the time they reached the horses the sky was grey overhead and full of boiling blackness not far away in the east. They heard the grumble of thunder and the crash of lightning. The sea was threshing as if infected by the sky's hysteria. The horses snorted and pawed at the sand, anxious to return. Even as Elric and Cymoril climbed into their saddles large spots of rain began to fall on their heads and spread over their cloaks.

Then, suddenly, they were riding at full tilt back to Imrryr while the lightning flashed around them and the thunder roared like a furious giant, like some great old Lord of Chaos attempting to break through, unbidden, into the Realm of Earth.

Cymoril glanced at Elric's pale face, illuminated for a moment by a flash of sky-fire, and she felt a chill come upon her then and the chill had nothing to do with the wind or the rain, for it seemed to her in that second that the gentle scholar she loved had been transformed by the elements into a hell-driven demon, into a monster with barely a semblance of humanity. His crimson eyes had flared from the whiteness of his skull like the very flames of the Higher Hell; his hair had been whipped upward so that it had become the crest of a sinister warhelm and, by a trick of the stormlight, his mouth had seemed twisted in a mixture of rage and agony.

And suddenly Cymoril knew.

She knew, profoundly, that their morning's ride was the last moment of peace the two of them would ever experience again. The storm was a sign from the gods themselves – a warning of storms to come.

She looked again at her lover. Elric was laughing. He had turned his face upward so that the warm rain fell upon it, so that the water splashed into his open mouth. The laughter was the easy, unsophisticated laughter of a happy child.

Cymoril tried to laugh back, but then she had to turn her face away so that he should not see it. For Cymoril had begun to weep.

She was weeping still when Imrryr came in sight – a black and grotesque silhouette against a line of brightness which was the as yet-untainted western horizon.

4

Prisoners: Their Secrets Are Taken from Them

The men in yellow armour saw Elric and Cymoril as the two approached the smallest of the eastern gates.

'They have found us at last,' smiled Elric through the rain, 'but somewhat belatedly, eh, Cymoril?'

Cymoril, still embattled with her sense of doom, merely nodded and tried to smile in reply.

Elric took this as an expression of disappointment, nothing more, and called to his guards: 'Ho, men! Soon we shall all be dry again!'

But the captain of the guard rode up urgently, crying: 'My lord emperor is needed at Monshanjik Tower where spies are held.'

'Spies?'

'Aye, my lord.' The man's face was pale. Water cascaded from his helm and darkened his thin cloak. His horse was hard to control and kept sidestepping through pools of water, which had gathered wherever the road was in disrepair. 'Caught in the maze this morning. Southern barbarians, by their chequered dress. We are holding them until the emperor himself can question them.'

Elric waved his hand. 'Then lead on, captain. Let's see the brave fools who dare Melniboné's sea-maze.'

The Tower of Monshanjik had been named for the wizard-architect who had designed the sea-maze millennia before. The maze was the only means of reaching the great harbour of Imrryr and its secrets had been carefully guarded, for it was their greatest protection against sudden attack. The maze was complicated and pilots had to be specially trained to steer ships through it. Before the maze had been built, the harbour had been a kind of inland lagoon, fed by the sea which swept in through a system of natural caverns in the towering cliff which rose between lagoon and ocean. There were five separate routes through the sea-maze and any individual pilot knew but one. In the outer wall of the cliff there were five entrances. Here Young Kingdom ships waited until a pilot came aboard. Then one of the gates to one of the entrances would be lifted, all aboard the ship would be blindfolded and sent below save for the oar-master and the steersman who would also be masked in heavy steel helms so that they could see nothing, do nothing but obey the complicated instructions of the pilot. And if a Young Kingdom ship should fail to obey any of those instructions and should crush itself against the rock walls, Melniboné did not mourn for it and any survivors from the crew would be taken as slaves. All who sought to trade with the Dreaming City understood the risks, but scores of merchants came every month to dare the dangers of the maze and trade their own poor goods for the splendid riches of Melniboné.

The Tower of Monshanjik stood overlooking the harbour and the massive mole which jutted out into the middle of the lagoon. It was a sea-green tower and was squat compared with most of those in Imrryr, though still a beautiful and tapering construction, with wide windows so that the whole of the harbour could be seen from it. From Monshanjik Tower most of the business of the harbour was done and in its lower cellars were kept any prisoners who had broken any of the myriad rules governing the functioning of the harbour. Leaving Cymoril to return to the palace with a guard, Elric entered the tower, riding through the great archway at the base, scattering not a few merchants who were waiting for permission to begin their bartering, for the whole of the ground floor was full of sailors, merchants and Melnibonéan officials engaged in the business of trade, though it was not here that the actual wares were displayed. The great echoing babble of a thousand voices engaged in a thousand separate aspects of bargaining slowly stilled as Elric and his guard rode arrogantly through to another dark arch at the far end of the hall. This arch opened onto a ramp which sloped and curved down into the bowels of the tower.

Down this ramp clattered the horsemen, passing slaves, servants and officials who stepped hastily aside, bowing low as they recognized the emperor. Great brands illuminated the tunnel, guttering and smoking and casting distorted shadows onto the smooth obsidian walls. A chill was in the air now, and a dampness, for water washed about the outer walls below the quays of Imrryr. And still the emperor rode on and still the ramp struck lower through the glassy rock. And then a wave of heat rose to meet them and shifting light could be seen ahead and they passed into a chamber that was full of smoke and the scent of fear. From the low ceiling hung chains and from eight of the chains, swinging by their feet, hung four people. Their clothes had been torn from them, but their bodies were clothed in blood from tiny wounds, precise but severe, made by the artist who stood, scalpel in hand, surveying his handiwork.

The artist was tall and very thin, almost like a skeleton in his stained, white garments. His lips were thin, his eyes were slits, his fingers were thin, his hair was thin and the scalpel he held was thin, too, almost invisible save when it flashed in the light from the fire which erupted from a pit on the far side of the cavern. The artist was named Doctor Jest and the art he practised was a performing art rather than a creative one (though he could argue otherwise with some conviction): the art of drawing secrets from those who kept them. Doctor Jest was the Chief Interrogator of Melniboné. He turned sinuously as Elric entered, the scalpel held between the thin thumb and the thin forefinger of his right hand; he stood poised and expectant, almost like a dancer, and then bowed from the waist.

'My sweet emperor!' His voice was thin. It rushed from his thin throat as if bent on escape and one was inclined to wonder if one had heard the words at all, so quickly had they come and gone.

'Doctor. Are these the southlanders caught this morning?'

'Indeed they are, my lord.' Another sinuous bow. 'For your pleasure.'

Coldly Elric inspected the prisoners. He felt no sympathy for them. They were spies. Their actions had led them to this pass. They had known what would happen to them if caught. But one of them was a boy and another a woman, it appeared, though they writhed so in their chains it was quite difficult to tell at first. It seemed a shame. Then the woman snapped what remained of her teeth at him and hissed: 'Demon!' And Elric stepped back, saying:

'Have they informed you of what they were doing in our maze, doctor?'

'They still tantalize me with hints. They have a fine sense of drama. I appreciate that. They are here, I would say, to map a route through the maze which a force of raiders might then follow. But they have so far withheld the details. That is the game. We all understand how it must be played.'

'And when will they tell you, Doctor Jest?'

'Oh, very soon, my lord.'

'It would be best to know if we are to expect attackers. The sooner we know, the less time we shall lose dealing with the attack when it comes. Do you not agree, doctor?'

'I do, my lord.'

'Very well.' Elric was irritated by this break in his day. It had spoiled the pleasure of the ride, it had brought him face to face with his duties too quickly.

Doctor Jest returned to his charges and, reaching out with his free hand, expertly seized the genitals of one of the male prisoners. The scalpel flashed. There was a groan. Doctor Jest tossed something onto the fire. Elric sat in the chair prepared for him. He was bored rather than disgusted by the rituals attendant upon the gathering of information and the discordant screams, the clash of the chains, the thin whisperings of Doctor Jest, all served to ruin the feeling of well-being he had retained even as he reached the chamber. But it was one of his kingly duties to attend such rituals and attend this one he must until the information was presented to him and he could congratulate his Chief Interrogator and issue orders as to the means of dealing with any attack and even when that was over he must confer with admirals and with generals, probably through the rest of the night, choosing between arguments, deciding on the deposition of men and ships. With a poorly disguised yawn he leaned back and watched as Doctor Jest ran fingers and scalpel, tongue, tongs and pincers over the bodies. He was soon thinking of other matters: philosophical problems which he had still failed to resolve.

It was not that Elric was inhumane; it was that he was, still, a Melnibonéan. He had been used to such sights since childhood. He could not have saved the prisoners, even if he had desired, without going against every tradition of the Dragon Isle. And in this case it was a simple matter of a threat being met by the best methods available. He had become used to shutting off those feelings which conflicted with his duties as emperor. If there had been any point in freeing the four who danced now at Doctor Jest's pleasure he would have freed them, but there was no point and the four would have been astonished if they had received any other treatment than this. Where moral decisions were concerned Imrryr was, by and large, practical. He would make his decision in the context of what action he could take. In this case, he could take no action. Such a reaction had become second nature to him. His desire was not to reform Melniboné but to reform himself, not to initiate action but to know the best way of responding to the actions of others. Here, the decision was easy to make. A spy was an aggressor. One defended oneself against aggressors in the best possible way. The methods employed by Doctor Jest were the best methods.

'My lord?'

Absently, Elric looked up.

'We have the information now, my lord.' Doctor Jest's thin voice whispered across the chamber. Two sets of chains were now empty and slaves were gathering things up from the floor and flinging them on the fire. The two remaining shapeless lumps reminded Elric of meat carefully prepared by a chef. One of the lumps still quivered a little, but the other was still.

Doctor Jest slid his instruments into a thin case he carried in a pouch at his belt. His white garments were almost completely covered in stains.

'It seems there have been other spies before these,' Doctor Jest told his master. 'These came merely to confirm the route. If they do not return in time, the barbarians will still sail.'

'But surely they will know that we expect them?' Elric said.

'Probably not, my lord. Rumours have been spread amongst the Young Kingdom merchants and sailors that four spies were seen in the maze and were speared – slain whilst trying to escape.'

'I see.' Elric frowned. 'Then our best plan will be to lay a trap for the raiders.'

'Aye, my lord.'

'You know the route they have chosen?'

'Aye, my lord.'

Elric turned to one of his guards. 'Have messages sent to all our generals and admirals. What's the hour?'

'The hour of sunset is just past, my liege.'

'Tell them to assemble before the Ruby Throne at two hours past sunset.'

Wearily, Elric rose. 'You have done well, as usual, Doctor Jest.'

The thin artist bowed low, seeming to fold himself in two. A thin and somewhat unctuous sigh was his reply.

5

A Battle: The King
Proves His War-Skill

Yyrkoon was the first to arrive, all clad in martial finery, accompanied by two massive guards, each holding one of the prince's ornate war-banners.

'My emperor!' Yyrkoon's shout was proud and disdainful. 'Would you let me command the warriors? It will relieve you of that care when, doubtless, you have many other concerns with which to occupy your time.'

Elric replied impatiently: 'You are most thoughtful, Prince Yyrkoon, but fear not for me. I shall command the armies and the navies of Melniboné, for that is the duty of the emperor.'

Yyrkoon glowered and stepped to one side as Dyvim Tvar, Lord of the Dragon Caves, entered. He had no guard whatsoever with him and it seemed he had dressed hastily. He carried his helmet under his arm.

'My emperor – I bring news of the dragons . . . '

'I thank you, Dyvim Tvar, but wait until all my commanders are assembled and impart that news to them, too.'

Dyvim Tvar bowed and went to stand on the opposite side of the hall to that on which Prince Yyrkoon stood.

Gradually the warriors arrived until a score of great captains waited at the foot of the steps which led to the Ruby Throne where Elric sat. Elric himself still wore the clothes in which he had gone riding that morning. He had not had time to change and had until a little while before been consulting maps of the mazes – maps which only he could read and which, at normal times, were hidden by magical means from any who might attempt to find them.

'Southlanders would steal Imrryr's wealth and slay us all,' Elric began. 'They believe they have found a way through our sea-maze. A fleet of a hundred warships sails on Melniboné even now. Tomorrow it will wait below the horizon until dusk, then it will sail to the maze and enter. By midnight it expects to reach the harbour and to have taken the Dreaming City before dawn. Is that possible, I wonder?'

'No!' Many spoke the single word.

'No.' Elric smiled. 'But how shall we best enjoy this little war they offer us?'

Yyrkoon, as ever, was first to shout. 'Let us go to meet them now, with dragons and with battle-barges. Let us pursue them to their own land and take their war to them. Let us attack their nations and burn their cities! Let us conquer them and thus ensure our own security!'

Dyvim Tvar spoke up again:

'No dragons,' he said.

'What?' Yyrkoon whirled. 'What?'

'No dragons, prince. They will not be awakened. The dragons sleep in their caverns, exhausted by their last engagement on your behalf.'

'Mine?'

'You would use them in our conflict with the Vilmirian pirates. I told you that I would prefer to save them for a larger engagement. But you flew them against the pirates and you burned their little boats and now the dragons sleep.'

Yyrkoon glowered. He looked up at Elric. 'I did not expect . . . '

Elric raised his hand. 'We need not use our dragons until such a time as we really need them. This attack from the southlander fleet is nothing. But we will conserve our strength if we bide our time. Let them think we are unready. Let them enter the maze. Once the whole hundred are through, we close in, blocking off all routes in or out of the maze. Trapped, they will be crushed by us.'

Yyrkoon looked pettishly at his feet, evidently wishing he could think of some flaw in the plan. Tall, old Admiral Magum Colim in his sea-green armour stepped forward and bowed. 'The golden battle-barges of Imrryr are ready to defend their city, my liege. It will take time, however, to manoeuvre them into position. It is doubtful if all will fit into the maze at once.'

'Then sail some of them out now and hide them around the coast, so that they can wait for any survivors that may escape our attack,' Elric instructed him.

'A useful plan, my liege.' Magum Colim bowed and sank back into the crowd of his peers.

The debate continued for some time and then they were ready and about to leave. But then Prince Yyrkoon bellowed once more:

'I repeat my offer to the emperor. His person is too valuable to risk in battle. My person – it is worthless. Let me command the warriors of both land and sea while the emperor may remain at the palace, untroubled by the battle, confident that it will be won and the south-landers trounced – perhaps there is a book he wishes to finish?'

Elric smiled. 'Again I thank you for your concern, Prince Yyrkoon. But an emperor must exercise his body as well as his mind. I will command the warriors tomorrow.'

When Elric arrived back at his apartments it was to discover that Tanglebones had already laid out his heavy, black wargear. Here was the armour which had served a hundred Melnibonéan emperors; an armour which was forged by sorcery to give it a strength unequalled on the Realm of Earth, which could, so rumour went, even withstand the bite of the mythical runeblades, Stormbringer and Mournblade, which had been wielded by the wickedest of Melniboné's many wicked rulers before being seized by the Lords of the Higher Worlds and hidden forever in a realm where even those Lords might rarely venture.

The face of the tangled man was full of joy as he touched each piece of armour, each finely balanced weapon, with his long, gnarled fingers. His seamed face looked up to regard Elric's care-ravaged features. 'Oh, my lord! Oh, my king! Soon you will know the joy of the fight!'

'Aye, Tanglebones – and let us hope it will be a joy.'

'I taught you all the skills – the art of the sword and the poignard – the art of the bow – the art of the spear, both mounted and on foot. And you learned well, for all they say you are weak. Save one, there's no better swordsman in Melniboné.'

'Prince Yyrkoon could be better than me,' Elric said reflectively. 'Could he not?'

'I said "save one", my lord.'

'And Yyrkoon is that one. Well, one day perhaps we'll be able to test the matter. I'll bathe before I don all that metal.'

'Best make speed, master. From what I hear, there is much to do.'

'And I'll sleep after I've bathed.' Elric smiled at his old friend's consternation. 'It will be better thus, for I cannot personally direct the barges into position. I am needed to command the fray – and that I will do better when I've rested.'

'If you think it good, lord king, then it is good.'

'And you are astonished. You are too eager, Tanglebones, to get me into all that stuff and see me strut about in it as if I were Arioch himself . . . '

Tanglebones's hand flew to his mouth as if he had spoken the words, not his master, and he was trying to block them. His eyes widened.

Elric laughed. 'You think I speak bold heresies, eh? Well, I've spoken worse without any ill befalling me. On Melniboné, Tanglebones, the emperors control the demons, not the reverse.'

'So you say, my liege.'

'It is the truth.' Elric swept from the room, calling for his slaves. The war-fever filled him and he was jubilant.

Now he was in all his black gear: the massive breastplate, the padded jerkin, the long greaves, the mail gauntlets. At his side was a five-foot broadsword which, it was said, had belonged to a human hero called Aubec. Resting on the deck against the golden rail of the bridge was the great round warboard, his shield, bearing the sign of the swooping dragon. And a helm was on his head; a black helm, with a dragon's head craning over the peak, and dragon's wings flaring backward above it, and a dragon's tail curling down the back. All the helm was black, but within the helm there was a white shadow from which glared two crimson orbs, and from the sides of the helm strayed wisps of milk-white hair, almost like smoke escaping from a burning building. And, as the helm turned in what little light came from the lantern hanging at the base of the mainmast, the white shadow sharpened to reveal features – fine, handsome features – a straight nose, curved lips, up-slanting eyes. The face of Emperor Elric of Melniboné peered into the gloom of the maze as he listened for the first sounds of the sea-raider's approach.

He stood on the high bridge of the great golden battle-barge which, like all its kind, resembled a floating ziggurat equipped with masts and sails and oars and catapults. The ship was called *The Son of the Pyaray* and it was the flagship of the fleet. The Grand Admiral Magum Colim stood beside Elric. Like Dyvim Tvar, the admiral was one of Elric's few close friends. He had known Elric all his life and had encouraged him to learn all he could concerning the running of fighting ships and fighting fleets. Privately Magum Colim might fear that Elric was too scholarly and introspective to rule Melniboné, but he accepted Elric's right to rule and was made angry and impatient by the talk of the likes of Yyrkoon. Prince Yyrkoon was also aboard the flagship, though at this moment he was below, inspecting the war-engines.

The Son of the Pyaray lay at anchor in a huge grotto, one of hundreds built into the walls of the maze when the maze itself was built, and designed for just this purpose – to hide a battle-barge. There was just enough height for the masts and enough width for the oars to move freely. Each of the golden battle-barges was equipped with banks of oars, each bank containing between twenty and thirty oars on either side. The banks were four, five or six decks high and, as in the case of *The Son of the Pyaray*, might have three independent steering systems, fore and aft. Being armoured all in gold, the ships were virtually in-destructible, and, for all their massive size, they could move swiftly and manoeuvre delicately when occasion demanded. It was not the first time they had waited for their enemies in these grottoes. It would not be the last (though when next they waited it would be in greatly different circumstances).

The battle-barges of Melniboné were rarely seen on the open seas these days, but once they had sailed the oceans of the world like fearsome floating mountains of gold and they had brought terror whenever they were sighted. The fleet had been larger then, comprising hundreds of craft. Now there were less than forty ships. But forty would suffice. Now, in damp darkness, they awaited their enemies.

Listening to the hollow slap of the water against the sides of the ship, Elric wished that he had been able to conceive a better plan than this. He was sure that this one would work, but he regretted the waste of lives, both Melnibonéan and barbarian. It would have been better if some way could have been devised of frightening the barbarians away rather than trapping them in the sea-maze. The southlander fleet was not the first to have been attracted by Imrryr's fabulous wealth. The southlander crews were not the first to entertain the belief that the Melnibonéans, because they never now ventured far from the Dreaming City, had become decadent and unable to defend their treasures. And so the southlanders must be destroyed in order to make the lesson clear. Melniboné was still strong. She was strong enough, in Yyrkoon's view, to resume her former dominance of the world — strong in sorcery if not in soldiery.

'Hist!' Admiral Magum Colim craned forward. 'Was that the sound of an oar?'

Elric nodded. 'I think so.'

Now they heard regular splashes, as of rows of oars dipping in and out of the water, and they heard the creak of timbers. The southlanders were coming. *The Son of the Pyaray* was the ship nearest to the entrance and it would be the first to move out, but only when the last of the southlanders' ships had passed them. Admiral Magum Colim bent and extinguished the lantern, then, quickly, quietly, he descended to inform his crew of the raiders' coming.

Not long before, Yyrkoon had used his sorcery to summon a peculiar mist, which hid the golden barges from view, but through which those on the Melnibonéan ships could peer. Now Elric saw torches burning in the channel ahead as carefully the reavers negotiated the maze. Within the space of a few minutes ten of the galleys had passed the grotto. Admiral Magum Colim rejoined Elric on the bridge and now Prince Yyrkoon was with him. Yyrkoon, too, wore a dragon helm, though less magnificent than Elric's, for Elric was chief of the few surviving Dragon Princes of Melniboné. Yyrkoon was grinning through the gloom and his eyes gleamed in anticipation of the bloodletting to come. Elric wished that Prince Yyrkoon had chosen another ship than this, but it was Yyrkoon's right to be aboard the flagship and he could not deny it.

Now half the hundred vessels had gone past.

Yyrkoon's armour creaked as, impatiently, he waited, pacing the bridge, his gauntletted hand on the hilt of his broadsword. 'Soon' he kept saying to himself. 'Soon.'

And then their anchor was groaning upwards and their oars were plunging into the water as the last southland ship went by and they shot from the grotto into the channel ramming the enemy galley amidships and smashing it in two.

A great yell went up from the barbarian crew. Men were flung in all directions. Torches danced erratically on the remains of the deck as men tried to save themselves from slipping into the dark, chill waters of the channel. A few brave spears rattled against the sides of the Melnibonéan flag-galley as it began to turn amongst the debris it had created. But Imrryrian archers returned the shots and the few survivors went down.

The sound of this swift conflict was the signal to the other battle-barges. In perfect order they came from both sides of the high rock walls and it must have seemed to the astonished barbarians that the great golden ships had actually emerged from solid stone – ghost ships filled with demons who rained spears, arrows and brands upon them. Now the whole of the twisting channel was confusion and a medley of war-shouts echoed and boomed and the clash of steel upon steel was like the savage hissing of some monstrous snake, and the raiding fleet itself resembled a snake which had been broken into a hundred pieces by the tall, implacable golden ships of Melniboné. These ships seemed almost serene as they moved against their enemies, their grappling irons flashing out to catch wooden decks and rails and draw the galleys nearer so that they might be destroyed.

But the southlanders were brave and they kept their heads after their initial astonishment. Three of their galleys headed directly for *The Son of the Pyaray*, recognizing it as the flagship. Fire arrows sailed high and dropped down into the decks which were wooden and not pro-tected by the golden armour, starting fires wherever they fell, or else bringing blazing death to the men they struck,

Elric raised his shield above his head and two arrows struck it, bouncing, still flaring, to a lower deck. He leapt over the rail, following the arrows, jumping down to the widest and most exposed deck where his warriors were grouping, ready to deal with the attacking galleys.

Catapults thudded and balls of blue fire swished through the blackness, narrowly missing all three galleys. Another volley followed and one mass of fire struck the far galley's mast and then burst upon the deck, scattering huge flames wherever it touched. Grapples snaked out and seized the first galley, dragging it close and Elric was amongst the first to leap down onto the deck, rushing forward to where he saw the southland captain, dressed all in crude, chequered armour, a chequered surcoat over that, a big sword in both his huge hands, bellowing at his men to resist the Melnibonéan dogs.

As Elric approached the bridge three barbarians armed with curved swords and small, oblong shields ran at him. Their faces were full of fear, but there was determination there as well, as if they knew they must die but planned to wreak as much destruction as they could before their souls were taken.

Shifting his war-board onto his arm, Elric took his own broadsword in both hands and charged the sailors, knocking one off his feet with the lip of the shield and smashing the collar-bone of another. The remaining barbarian skipped aside and thrust his curved sword at Elric's face. Elric barely escaped the thrust and the sharp edge of the sword grazed his cheek, bringing out a drop or two of blood. Elric swung the broadsword like a scythe and it bit deep into the barbarian's waist, almost cutting him in two. He struggled for a moment, unable to believe that he was dead but then, as Elric yanked the sword free, he closed his eyes and dropped. The man who had been struck by Elric's shield was staggering to his feet as Elric whirled, saw him, and smashed the broadsword into his skull. Now the way was clear to the bridge. Elric began to climb the ladder, noting that the captain had seen him and was waiting for him at the top.

Elric raised his shield to take the captain's first blow. Through all the noise he thought he heard the man shouting at him.

'Die, you white-faced demon! Die! You have no place in this earth any longer!'

Elric was almost diverted from defending himself by these words. They rang true to him. Perhaps he really had no place on the earth. Perhaps that was why Melniboné was slowly collapsing, why fewer children were born every year, why the dragons themselves were no longer breeding. He let the captain strike another blow at the shield, then he reached under it and swung at the man's legs. But the captain had anticipated the move and jumped backwards. This, however, gave Elric time to run up the few remaining steps and stand on the deck, facing the captain.

The man's face was almost as pale as Elric's. He was sweating and he was panting and his eyes had misery in them as well as a wild fear.

'You should leave us alone,' Elric heard himself saying. 'We offer you no harm, barbarian. When did Melniboné last sail against the Young Kingdoms?'

'You offer us harm by your very presence, Whiteface. There is your sorcery. There are your customs. And there is your arrogance.'

'Is that why you came here? Was your attack motivated by disgust for us? Or would you help yourselves to our wealth? Admit it, captain – greed brought you to Melniboné.'

'At least greed is an honest quality, an understandable one. But you creatures are not human. Worse – you are not gods, though you behave as if you were. Your day is over and you must be wiped out, your city destroyed, your sorceries forgotten.'

Elric nodded. 'Perhaps you are right, captain.'

'I am right. Our holy men say so. Our seers predict your downfall. The Chaos Lords whom you serve will themselves bring about that downfall.'

'The Chaos Lords no longer have any interest in the affairs of Melniboné. They took away their power nearly a thousand years since.' Elric watched the captain carefully, judging the distance between them. 'Perhaps that is why our own power waned. Or perhaps we merely became tired of power.'

'Be that as it may,' the captain said, wiping his sweating brow, 'your time is over. You must be destroyed once and for all.' And then he groaned, for Elric's broadsword had come under his chequered breastplate and gone up through his stomach and into his lungs.

One knee bent, one leg stretched behind him, Elric began to withdraw the long sword, looking up into the barbarian's face which had now assumed an expression of reconciliation. 'That was unfair, Whiteface. We had barely begun to talk and you cut the conversation short. You are most skilful. May you writhe forever in the Higher Hell. Farewell.'

Elric hardly knew why, after the captain had fallen face down on the deck, he hacked twice at the neck until the head rolled off the body, rolled to the side of the bridge and was then kicked over the side so that it sank into the cold, deep water.

And then Yyrkoon came up behind Elric and he was still grinning.

'You fight fiercely and well, my lord emperor. That dead man was right.'

'Right?' Elric glared at his cousin. 'Right?'

'Aye – in his assessment of your prowess.' And, chuckling, Yyrkoon went to supervise his men who were finishing off the few remaining raiders.

Elric did not know why he had refused to hate Yyrkoon before. But now he did hate Yyrkoon. At that moment he would gladly have slain him. It was as if Yyrkoon had looked deeply into Elric's soul and expressed contempt for what he had seen there.

Suddenly Elric was overwhelmed by an angry misery and he wished with all his heart that he was not a Melnibonéan, that he was not an emperor and that Yyrkoon had never been born.

6

Pursuit: A Deliberate Treachery

Like haughty Leviathans the great golden battle-barges swam through the wreckage of the reaver fleet. A few ships burned and a few were still sinking, but most had sunk into the unplumbable depths of the channel. The burning ships sent strange shadows dancing against the dank walls of the sea-caverns, as if the ghosts of the slain offered a last salute before departing to the sea-depths where, it was said, a Chaos king still ruled, crewing his eerie fleets with the souls of all who died in conflict upon the oceans of the world. Or perhaps they went to a gentler doom, serving Straasha, Lord of the Water Elementals, who ruled the upper reaches of the sea.

But a few had escaped. Somehow the southland sailors had got past the massive battle-barges, sailed back through the channel and must even now have reached the open sea. This was reported to the flagship where Elric, Magum Colim and Prince Yyrkoon now stood together again on the bridge, surveying the destruction they had wreaked.

'Then we must pursue them and finish them,' said Yyrkoon. He was sweating and his dark face glistened; his eyes were alight with fever. 'We must follow them.'

Elric shrugged. He was weak. He had brought no extra drugs with him to replenish his strength. He wished to go back to Imrryr and rest. He was tired of bloodletting, tired of Yyrkoon and tired, most of all, of himself. The hatred he felt for his cousin was draining him still further – and he hated the hatred; that was the worst part. 'No,' he said. 'Let them go.'

'Let them go? Unpunished? Come now, my lord king! That is not our way!' Prince Yyrkoon turned to the aging admiral. 'Is that our way, Admiral Magum Colim?'

Magum Colim shrugged. He, too, was tired, but privately he agreed with Prince Yyrkoon. An enemy of Melniboné should be punished for daring even to think of attacking the Dreaming City. Yet he said: 'The emperor must decide.'

'Let them go,' said Elric again. He leant heavily against the rail. 'Let them carry the news back to their own barbarian land. Let them say how the Dragon Princes defeated them. The news will spread. I believe we shall not be troubled by raiders again for some time.'

'The Young Kingdoms are full of fools,' Yyrkoon replied. 'They will not believe the news. There will always be raiders. The best way to warn them will be to make sure that not one southlander remains alive or uncaptured.'

Elric drew a deep breath and tried to fight the faintness which threatened to overwhelm him. 'Prince Yyrkoon, you are trying my patience . . . '

'But, my emperor, I think only of the good of Melniboné. Surely you do not want your people to say that you are weak, that you fear a fight with but five southland galleys?'

This time Elric's anger brought him strength. 'Who will say that Elric is weak? Will it be you, Yyrkoon?' He knew that his next statement was senseless, but there was nothing he could do to stop it. 'Very well, let us pursue these poor little boats and sink them. And let us make haste. I am weary of it all.'

There was a mysterious light in Yyrkoon's eyes as he turned away to relay the orders.

The sky was turning from black to grey when the Melnibonéan fleet reached the open sea and turned its prows south towards the Boiling Sea and the southern continent beyond. The barbarian ships would not sail through the Boiling Sea – no mortal ship could do that, it was said – but would sail around it. Not that the barbarian ships would even reach the edges of the Boiling Sea, for the huge battle-barges were fast-sailing vessels. The slaves who pulled the oars were full of a drug which increased their speed and their strength for a score or so of hours, before it slew them. And now the sails billowed out, catching the breeze. Golden mountains, skimming rapidly over the sea, these ships; their method of construction was a secret lost even to the Melnibonéans (who had forgotten so much of their lore). It was easy to imagine how men of the Young Kingdoms hated Melniboné and its inventions, for it did seem that the battle-barges belonged to an older, alien age, as they bore down upon the fleeing galleys now sighted on the horizon.

The Son of the Pyaray was in the lead of the rest of the fleet and was priming its catapults well before any of its fellows had seen the enemy. Perspiring slaves gingerly manhandled the viscous stuff of the fireballs, getting them into the bronze cups of the catapults by means of long, spoon-ended tongs. It flickered in the pre-dawn gloom.

Now slaves climbed the steps to the bridge and brought wine and food on platinum platters for the three Dragon Princes who had remained there since the pursuit had begun. Elric could not summon the strength to eat, but he seized a tall cup of yellow wine and drained it. The stuff was strong and revived him a trifle. He had another cup poured and drank that as swiftly as the other. He peered ahead. It was almost dawn. There was a line of purple light on the horizon. 'At the first sign of the sun's disc,' Elric said, 'let loose the fireballs.'

'I will give the order,' said Magum Colim, wiping his lips and putting down the meat bone on which he had been chewing. He left the bridge. Elric heard his feet striking the steps heavily. All at once the albino felt surrounded by enemies. There had been something strange in Magum Colim's manner during the argument with Prince Yyrkoon. Elric tried to shake off such foolish thoughts. But the weariness, the self-doubt, the open mockery of his cousin, all succeeded in increasing the feeling that he was alone and without friends in the world. Even Cymoril and Dyvim Tvar were, finally, Melnibonéans and could not understand the peculiar concerns which moved him and dictated his actions. Perhaps it would be wise to renounce everything Melnibonéan and wander the world as an anonymous soldier of fortune, serving whoever needed his aid?

The dull red semicircle of the sun showed above the black line of the distant water. There came a series of booming sounds from the forward decks of the flagship as the catapults released their fiery shot; there was a whistling scream, fading away, and it seemed that a dozen meteors leapt through the sky, hurtling towards the five galleys which were now little more than thirty ship-lengths away.

Elric saw two galleys flare, but the remaining three began to sail a zig-zag course and avoided the fireballs which landed on the water and burned fitfully for a while before sinking (still burning) into the depths.

More fireballs were prepared and Elric heard Yyrkoon shout from the other side of the bridge, ordering the slaves to greater exertions. Then the fleeing vessels changed their tactics, evidently realizing that they could not save themselves for long, and, spreading out, sailed towards *The Son of the Pyaray*, just as the other ships had done in the sea-maze. It was not merely their courage that Elric admired but their manoeuvring skill and the speed at which they had arrived at this logical, if hopeless, decision.

The sun was behind the southland ships as they turned. Three brave silhouettes drew nearer to the Melnibonéan flagship as scarlet stained the sea, as if in anticipation of the bloodletting to come.

Another volley of fireballs was flung from the flagship and the leading galley tried to tack round and avoid it, but two of the fiery globes spattered directly on its deck and soon the whole ship was alive with flame. Burning men leapt into the water. Burning men shot arrows at the flagship. Burning men fell slowly from their positions in the rigging. The burning men died, but the burning ship came on; someone had lashed the steering arm and directed the galley at *The Son of the Pyaray*. It crashed into the golden side of the battle-barge and some of the fire splashed on the deck where the main catapults were in position. A cauldron containing the firestuff caught and immediately men were running from all quarters of the ship to try to douse the flame. Elric grinned as he saw what the barbarians had done. Perhaps that ship had deliberately allowed itself to be fired. Now the majority of the flagship's complement was engaged with putting out the blaze – while the southland ships drew alongside, threw up their own grapples, and began to board.

''Ware boarders!' Elric shouted, long after he might have warned his crew. 'Barbarians attack.'

He saw Yyrkoon whirl round, see the situation, and rush down the steps from the bridge. 'You stay there, my lord king,' he flung at Elric as he disappeared. 'You are plainly too weary to fight.'

And Elric summoned all that was left of his strength and stumbled after his cousin, to help in the defense of the ship.

The barbarians were not fighting for their lives – they knew those to be taken already. They were fighting for their pride. They wanted to take one Melnibonéan ship down with them and that ship must be the flagship itself. It was hard to be contemptuous of such men. They knew that even if they took the flagship the other ships of the golden fleet would soon overwhelm them.

But the other ships were still some distance away. Many lives would be lost before they reached the flagship.

On the lowest deck Elric found himself facing a pair of tall barbarians, each armed with a curved blade and a small, oblong shield. He lunged forward, but his armour seemed to drag at his limbs, his own shield and sword were so heavy that he could barely lift them. Two swords struck his helm, almost simultaneously. He lunged back and caught a man in the arm, rammed the other with his shield. A curved blade clanged on his backplate and he all but lost his footing. There was choking smoke everywhere, and heat, and the tumult of battle. Desperately he swung about him and felt his broadsword bite deep into flesh. One of his opponents fell, gurgling, with blood spouting from his mouth and nose. The other lunged. Elric stepped backwards, fell over the corpse of the man he had slain, and went down, his broadsword held out before him in one hand. And as the triumphant barbarian leapt forward to finish the albino, Elric caught him on the point of the broadsword, running him through. The dead man fell towards Elric who did not feel the impact, for he had already fainted. Not for the first time had his deficient blood, no longer enriched by drugs, betrayed him.

He tasted salt and thought at first it was blood. But it was sea water. A wave had risen over the deck and momentarily revived him. He struggled to crawl from under the dead man and then he heard a voice he recognized. He twisted his head and looked up.

Prince Yyrkoon stood there. He was grinning. He was full of glee at Elric's plight. Black, oily smoke still drifted everywhere, but the sounds of the fight had died.

'Are – are we victorious, cousin?' Elric spoke painfully.

'Aye. The barbarians are all dead now. We are about to sail for Imrryr.'

Elric was relieved. He would begin to die soon if he could not get to his store of potions.

His relief must have been evident, for Yyrkoon laughed. 'It is as well the battle did not last longer, my lord, or we should have been without our leader.'

'Help me up, cousin.' Elric hated to ask Prince Yyrkoon any favour, but he had no choice. He stretched out his empty hand. 'I am fit enough to inspect the ship.'

Yyrkoon came forward as if to take the hand, but then he hesitated, still grinning. 'But, my lord, I disagree. You will be dead by the time this ship turns eastward again.'

'Nonsense. Even without the drugs I can live for a considerable time, though movement is difficult. Help me up, Yyrkoon, I command you.'

'You cannot command me, Elric. I am emperor now, you see.'

'Be wary, cousin. I can overlook such treachery, but others will not. I shall be forced to . . . '

Yyrkoon swung his legs over Elric's body and went to the rail. Here were bolts which fixed one section of the rail in place when it was not used for the gangplank. Yyrkoon slowly released the bolts and kicked the section of rail into the water.

Now Elric's efforts to free himself became more desperate. But he could hardly move at all.

Yyrkoon, on the other hand, seemed possessed of unnatural strength. He bent and easily flung the corpse away from Elric.

39

'Yyrkoon,' said Elric, 'this is unwise of you.'

'I was never a cautious man, cousin, as well you know.' Yyrkoon placed a booted foot against Elric's ribs and began to shove. Elric slid towards the gap in the rail. He could see the black sea heaving below. 'Farewell, Elric. Now a true Melnibonéan shall sit upon the Ruby Throne. And, who knows, might even make Cymoril his queen? It has not been unheard of . . . '

And Elric felt himself rolling, felt himself fall, felt himself strike the water, felt his armour pulling him below the surface. And Yyrkoon's last words drummed in Elric's ears like the persistent booming of the waves against the sides of the golden battle-barge.

TWO

Less certain of himself or his destiny than ever, the albino king must perforce bring his powers of sorcery into play, conscious of embarking on actions which will make of his life something other than he might have wished it to be. And now matters must be settled. He must begin to rule. He must become cruel. But even in this he will find himself thwarted.

1

The Caverns of the Sea King

Elric sank rapidly, desperately trying to keep the last of his breath in his body. He had no strength to swim and the weight of the armour denied any hope of his rising to the surface and being sighted by Magum Colim or one of the others still loyal to him.

The roaring in his ears gradually faded to a whisper so that it sounded as if little voices were speaking to him, the voices of the water elementals with whom, in his youth, he had had a kind of friendship. and the pain in his lungs faded; the red mist cleared from his eyes and he thought he saw the face of his father, Sadric of Cymoril and, fleetingly, of Yyrkoon. Stupid Yyrkoon: for all that he prided himself that he was a Melnibonéan, he lacked the Melnibonéan subtlety. He was as brutal and direct as some of the Young Kingdom barbarians he so much despised. And now Elric began to feel almost grateful to his cousin. His life was over. The conflicts which tore his mind would no longer trouble him. His fears, his torments, his loves and his hatreds all lay in the past and only oblivion lay before him. As the last of his breath left his body, he gave himself wholly to the sea; to Straasha, Lord of all the Water Elementals, once the comrade of the Melnibonéan folk. And as he did this he remembered the old spell which his ancestors had used to summon Straasha. The spell came unbidden into his dying brain.

> Waters of the sea, thou gave us birth
> And were our milk and mother both
> In days when skies were overcast
> You who were first shall be the last.
>
> Sea-rulers, fathers of our blood,
> Thine aid is sought, thine aid is sought,
> Your salt is blood, our blood your salt,
> Your blood the blood of Man.

Straasha, eternal king, eternal sea
Thine aid is sought by me;
For enemies of thine and mine
Seek to defeat our destiny, and drain
away our sea.

Either the words had an old, symbolic meaning or they referred to some incident in Melnibonéan history which even Elric had not read about. The words meant very little to him and yet they continued to repeat themselves as his body sank deeper and deeper into the green waters. Even when blackness overwhelmed him and his lungs filled with water, the words continued to whisper through the corridors of his brain. It was strange that he should be dead and still hear the incantation.

It seemed a long while later that his eyes opened and revealed swirling water and, through it, huge, indistinct figures gliding towards him. Death, it appeared, took a long time to come and, while he died, he dreamed. The leading figure had a turquoise beard and hair, pale green skin that seemed made of the sea itself and, when he spoke, a voice that was like a rushing tide. He smiled at Elric.

'*Straasha answers thy summons, mortal. Our destinies are bound together. How may I aid thee, and, in aiding thee, aid myself?*'

Elric's mouth was filled with water and yet he still seemed capable of speech (thus proving he dreamed).

He said:

'King Straasha. The paintings in the Tower of D'a'rputna – in the library. When I was a boy I saw them, King Straasha.'

The sea-king stretched out his sea-green hands. '*Aye. You sent the summons. You need our aid. We honour our ancient pact with your folk.*'

'No. I did not mean to summon you. The summons came unbidden to my dying mind. I am happy to drown, King Straasha.'

'*That cannot be. If your mind summoned us it means you wish to live. We will aid you.*' King Straasha's beard streamed in the tide and his deep, green eyes were gentle, almost tender, as they regarded the albino.

Elric closed his own eyes again. 'I dream,' he said. 'I deceive myself with fantasies of hope.' He felt the water in his lungs and he knew he no longer breathed. It stood to reason, therefore, that he was dead. 'But if you were real, old friend, and you wished to aid me, you would return me to Melniboné so that I might deal with the usurper, Yyr-

44

koon, and save Cymoril, before it is too late. That is my only regret – the torment which Cymoril will suffer if her brother becomes Emperor of Melniboné.'

'*Is that all you ask of the water elementals?*' King Straasha seemed almost disappointed.

'I do not even ask that of you. I only voice what I would have wished, had this been reality and I was speaking, which I know is impossible. Now I shall die.'

'*That cannot be, Lord Elric, for our destinies are truly intertwined and I know that it is not yet your destiny to perish. Therefore I will aid you as you have suggested.*'

Elric was surprised at the sharpness of detail of this fantasy. He said to himself. 'What a cruel torment I subject myself to. Now I must set about admitting my death . . . '

'*You cannot die. Not yet.*'

Now it was as if the sea-king's gentle hands had picked him up and bore him through twisting corridors of a delicate coral pink texture, slightly shadowed, no longer in water. And Elric felt the water vanish from his lungs and stomach and he breathed. Could it be that he had actually been brought to the legendary plane of the elemental folk – a plane which intersected that of the earth and in which they dwelled, for the most part?

In a huge, circular cavern, which shone with pink and blue mother-of-pearl, they came to rest at last. The sea-king laid Elric down upon the floor of the cavern, which seemed to be covered with fine, white sand which was yet not sand for it yielded and then sprang back when he moved.

When King Straasha moved, it was with a sound like the tide drawing itself back over shingle. The sea-king crossed the white sand, walking towards a large throne of milky jade. He seated himself upon this throne and placed his green head on his green fist, regarding Elric with puzzled, yet compassionate, eyes.

Elric was still physically weak, but he could breathe. It was as if the sea water had filled him and then cleansed him when it was driven out. He felt clear-headed. And now he was much less sure that he dreamed.

'I still find it hard to know why you saved me, King Straasha,' he murmured from where he lay on the sand.

'*The rune. We heard it on this plane and we came. That is all.*'

'Aye. But there is more to sorcery-working than that. There are chants, symbols, rituals of all sorts. Previously that has always been true.'

'*Perhaps the rituals take the place of urgent need of the kind which* sent out your summons to us. Though you say you wished to die, it was evident that this was not your true desire or the summoning would not have been so clear nor reached us so swiftly. Forget all this now. When you have rested, we shall do what you have requested of us.'

Painfully, Elric raised himself into a sitting position. 'You spoke earlier of "intertwined destinies". Do you, then, know something of my destiny?'

'A little, I think. Our world grows old. Once the elementals were powerful on your plane and the people of Melniboné all shared that power. But now our power wanes, as does yours. Something is changing. There are intimations that the Lords of the Higher Worlds are again taking an interest in your world. Perhaps they fear that the folk of the Young Kingdoms have forgotten them. Perhaps the folk of the Young Kingdoms threaten to bring in a new age, where gods and beings such as myself no longer shall have a place. I suspect there is a certain unease upon the planes of the Higher Worlds.'

'You know no more?'

King Straasha raised his head and looked directly into Elric's eyes. 'There is no more I can tell you, son of my old friends, save that you would be happier if you gave yourself up entirely to your destiny when you understand it.'

Elric sighed. 'I think I know of what you speak, King Straasha. I shall try to follow your advice.'

'And now that you have rested, it is time to return.'

The sea-king rose from his throne of milky jade and flowed towards Elric, lifting him up in strong, green arms.

'We shall meet again before your life ends, Elric. I hope that I shall be able to aid you once more. And remember that our brothers of the air and of fire will try to aid you also. And remember the beasts – they, too, can be of service to you. There is no need to suspect their help. But beware of gods, Elric. Beware of the Lords of the Higher Worlds and remember that their aid and their gifts must always be paid for.'

These were the last words Elric heard the sea-king speak before they rushed again through the sinuous tunnels of this other plane, moving at such a speed that Elric could distinguish no details and, at times, did not know whether they remained in King Straasha's kingdom or had returned to the depths of his own world's sea.

A New Emperor and an Emperor Renewed

Strange clouds filled the sky and the sun hung heavy and huge and red behind them and the ocean was black as the golden galleys swept homeward before their battered flagship *The Son of the Pyaray* which moved slowly with dead slaves at her oars and her tattered sails limp at their masts and smoke-begrimed men on her decks and a new emperor upon her war-wrecked bridge. The new emperor was the only jubilant man in the fleet and he was jubilant indeed. It was his banner now, not Elric's, which took pride of place on the flagmast, for he had lost no time in proclaiming Elric slain and himself ruler of Melniboné.

To Yyrkoon, the peculiar sky was an omen of change, of a return to the old ways and the old power of the Dragon Isle. When he issued orders, his voice was a veritable croon of pleasure, and Admiral Magum Colim, who had ever been wary of Elric but who now had to obey Yyrkoon's orders, wondered if, perhaps, it would not have been preferable to have dealt with Yyrkoon in the manner in which (he suspected) Yyrkoon had dealt with Elric.

Dyvim Tvar leaned on the rail of his own ship, *Terhali's Particular Satisfaction*, and he also paid attention to the sky, though he saw omens of doom, for he mourned for Elric and considered how he might take vengeance on Prince Yyrkoon, should it emerge that Yyrkoon had murdered his cousin for possession of the Ruby Throne.

Melniboné appeared on the horizon, a brooding silhouette of crags, a dark monster squatting in the sea, calling her own back to the heated pleasures of her womb, the Dreaming City of Imrryr. The great cliffs loomed, the central gate to the sea-maze opened, water slapped and gasped as the golden prows disturbed it and the golden ships were swallowed into the murky dankness of the tunnels where bits of wreckage still floated from the previous night's encounter; where white, bloated corpses could still be seen when the brandlight touched them. The prows nosed arrogantly through the remains of their prey, but there was no joy aboard the golden battle-barges, for they brought news of their old emperor's death in battle (Yyrkoon had told them what had happened). Next night and for seven nights in all the Wild Dance of Melniboné would fill the streets. Potions and petty spells would ensure that no-one slept, for sleep was forbidden to any Melnibonéan, old or young, while a dead emperor was mourned. Naked, the Dragon Princes would prowl the city, taking any young woman they found and filling her with their seed for it was traditional that if an emperor died then the nobles of Melniboné must create as many children of aristocratic blood as was possible. Music-slaves would howl from the top of every tower. Other slaves would be slain and some eaten. It was a dreadful dance, the Dance of Misery, and it took as many lives as it created. A tower would be pulled down and a new one erected during those seven days and the tower would be called for Elric VIII, the Albino Emperor, slain upon the sea, defending Melniboné against the southland pirates.

Slain upon the sea and his body taken by the waves. That was not a good portent, for it meant that Elric had gone to serve Pyaray, the Tentacled Whisperer of Impossible Secrets, the Chaos Lord who commanded the Chaos Fleet – dead ships, dead sailors, forever in his thrall – and it was not fitting that such a fate should befall one of the Royal Line of Melniboné. Ah, but the mourning would be long, thought Dyvim Tvar. He had loved Elric, for all that he had sometimes disapproved of his methods of ruling the Dragon Isle. Secretly he would go to the Dragon Caves that night and spend the period of mourning with the sleeping dragons who, now that Elric was dead, were all he had left to love. And Dyvim Tvar then thought of Cymoril, awaiting Elric's return.

The ships began to emerge into the half-light of the evening. Torches and braziers already burned on the quays of Imrryr which were deserted save for a small group of figures who stood around a chariot which had been driven out to the end of the central mole. A cold wind blew. Dyvim Tvar knew that it was the Princess Cymoril who waited, with her guards, for the fleet.

Though the flagship was the last to pass through the maze, the rest of the ships had to wait until it could be towed into position and dock first. If this had not been the required tradition, Dyvim Tvar would have left his ship and gone to speak to Cymoril, escort her from the quay and tell her what he knew of the circumstances of Elric's death. But it was impossible. Even before *Terhali's Particular Satisfaction* had dropped anchor, the main gangplank of *The Son of the Pyaray* had been lowered and the Emperor Yyrkoon, all swaggering pride, had stepped down it, his arms raised in triumphant salute to his sister who

48

could be seen, even now, searching the decks of the ships for a sign of her beloved albino.

Suddenly Cymoril knew that Elric was dead and she suspected that Yyrkoon had, in some way, been responsible for Elric's death. Either Yyrkoon had allowed Elric to be borne down by a group of southland reavers or else he had managed to slay Elric himself. She knew her brother and she recognized his expression. He was pleased with himself as he always had been when successful in some form of treachery or another. Anger flashed in her tear-filled eyes and she threw back her head and shouted at the shifting, ominous sky:

'Oh! Yyrkoon has destroyed him!'

Her guards were startled. The captain spoke solicitously. 'Madam?'

'He is dead – and that brother slew him. Take Prince Yyrkoon, captain. Kill Prince Yyrkoon, captain.'

Unhappily, the captain put his right hand on the hilt of his sword. A young warrior, more impetuous, drew his blade, murmuring: 'I will slay him princess, if that is your desire.' The young warrior loved Cymoril with considerable and unthinking intensity.

The captain offered the warrior a cautionary glance, but the warrior was blind to it. Now two others slid swords from scabbards as Yyrkoon, a red cloak wound about him, his dragon crest catching the light from the brands guttering in the wind, stalked forward and cried:

'Yyrkoon is emperor now!'

'No!' shrieked Yyrkoon's sister. 'Elric! Elric! Where are you?'

'Serving his new master, Pyaray of Chaos. His dead hands pull at the sweep of a Chaos ship, sister. His dead eyes see nothing at all. His dead ears hear only the crack of Pyaray's whips and his dead flesh cringes, feeling nought but that unearthly scourge. Elric sank in his armour to the bottom of the sea.'

'Murderer! Traitor!' Cymoril began to sob.

The captain, who was a practical man, said to his warriors in a low voice: 'Sheath your weapons and salute your new emperor.'

Only the young guardsman who loved Cymoril disobeyed. 'But he slew the emperor! My lady Cymoril said so!'

'What of it? He is emperor now. Kneel or you'll be dead within the minute.'

The young warrior gave a wild shout and leapt towards Yyrkoon, who stepped back, trying to free his arms from the folds of his cloak. He had not expected this.

But it was the captain who leapt forward, his own sword drawn, and hacked down the youngster so that he gasped, half-turned, then fell at Yyrkoon's feet.

This demonstration of the captain's was confirmation of his real power and Yyrkoon almost smirked with satisfaction as he looked down at the corpse. The captain fell to one knee, the bloody sword still in his hand. 'My emperor,' he said.

'You show a proper loyalty, captain.'

'My loyalty is to the Ruby Throne.'

'Quite so.'

Cymoril shook with grief and rage, but her rage was impotent. She knew now that she had no friends.

Leering, the Emperor Yyrkoon presented himself before her. He reached out his hand and he caressed her neck, her cheek, her mouth. He let his hand fall so that it grazed her breast. 'Sister,' he said, 'thou art mine entirely now.'

And Cymoril was the second to fall at his feet, for she had fainted.

'Pick her up,' Yyrkoon said to the guard. 'Take her back to her own tower and there be sure she remains. Two guards will be with her at all times, in even her most private moments they must observe her, for she may plan treachery against the Ruby Throne.'

The captain bowed and signed to his men to obey the emperor. 'Aye, my lord. It shall be done.'

Yyrkoon looked back at the corpse of the young warrior. 'And feed that to her slaves tonight, so that he can continue serving her.' He smiled.

The captain smiled, too, appreciating the joke. He felt it was good to have a proper emperor in Melniboné again. An emperor who knew how to behave, who knew how to treat his enemies and who accepted unswerving loyalty as his right. The captain fancied that fine, martial times lay ahead for Melniboné. The golden battle-barges and the warriors of Imrryr could go a-spoiling again and instil in the barbarians of the Young Kingdoms a sweet and satisfactory sense of fear. Already, in his mind, the captain helped himself to the treasures of Lormyr, Argimiliar and Pikarayd, of Ilmiora and Jadmar. He might even be made governor, say, of the Isle of the Purple Towns. What luxuries of torment would he bring to those upstart sealords, particularly Count Smiorgan Baldhead who was even now beginning to try to make the isle a rival to Melniboné as a trading port! As he escorted the limp body of the Princess Cymoril back to her tower, the captain looked on that body and felt the swellings of lust within him. Yyrkoon would reward his loyalty, there was no doubt of that. Despite the cold wind, the captain began to sweat in his anticipation. He, himself, would guard the Princess Cymoril. He would relish it.

*

Marching at the head of his army, Yyrkoon strutted for the Tower of D'a'rputna, the Tower of Emperors, and the Ruby Throne within. He preferred to ignore the litter which had been brought for him and to go on foot, so that he might savour every small moment of his triumph. He approached the tower, tall among its fellows at the very centre of Imrryr, as he might approach a beloved woman. He approached it with a sense of delicacy and without haste, for he knew that it was his.

He looked about him. His army marched behind him. Magum Colim and Dyvim Tvar led the army. People lined the twisting streets and bowed low to him. Slaves prostrated themselves. Even the beasts of burden were made to kneel as he strode by. Yyrkoon could almost taste the power as one might taste a luscious fruit. He drew deep breaths of the air. Even the air was his. All Imrryr was his. All Melniboné. Soon would all the world be his. And he would squander it all. How he would squander it! Such a grand terror would he bring back to the earth; such a munificence of fear! In ecstasy, amost blindly, did the Emperor Yyrkoon enter the tower. He hesitated at the great doors of the throne room. He signed for the doors to be opened and as they opened he deliberately took in the scene tiny bit by tiny bit. The walls, the banners, the trophies, the galleries, all were his. The throne room was empty now, but soon he would fill it with colour and celebration and true, Melnibonéan entertainments. It had been too long since blood had sweetened the air of this hall. Now he let his eyes linger upon the steps leading up to the Ruby Throne itself, but, before he looked at the throne, he heard Dyvim Tvar gasp behind him and his gaze went suddenly to the Ruby Throne and his jaw slackened at what he saw. His eyes widened in incredulity.

'An illusion!'

'An apparition,' said Dyvim Tvar with some satisfaction.

'Heresy!' cried the Emperor Yyrkoon, staggering forward, finger pointing at the robed and cowled figure which sat so still upon the Ruby Throne. 'Mine! Mine!'

The figure made no reply.

'Mine! Begone! The throne belongs to Yyrkoon. Yyrkoon is emperor now! What are you? Why would you thwart me thus?'

The cowl fell back and a bone-white face was revealed, surrounded by flowing, milk-white hair. Crimson eyes looked coolly down at the shrieking, stumbling thing which came towards them.

'You are dead, Elric! I know that you are dead!'

The apparition made no reply, but a thin smile touched the white lips.

'You *could* not have survived. You drowned. You cannot come back. Pyaray owns your soul!'

'There are others who rule in the sea,' said the figure on the Ruby Throne. 'Why did you slay me, cousin?'

Yyrkoon's guile had deserted him, making way for terror and confusion. 'Because it is my right to rule! Because you were not strong enough, nor cruel enough, nor humorous enough . . . '

'Is this not a good joke, cousin?'

'Begone! Begone! Begone! I shall not be ousted by a spectre! A dead emperor cannot rule Melniboné!'

'We shall see,' said Elric, signing to Dyvim Tvar and his soldiers.

3

A Traditional Justice

'**N**ow indeed I shall rule as you would have had me rule, cousin.' Elric watched as Dyvim Tvar's soldiers surrounded the would-be usurper and seized his arms, relieving him of his weapons.

Yyrkoon panted like a captured wolf. He glared around him as if hoping to find support from the assembled warriors, but they stared back at him either neutrally or with open contempt.

'And you, Prince Yyrkoon, will be the first to benefit from this new rule of mine. Are you pleased?'

Yyrkoon lowered his head. He was trembling now. Elric laughed. 'Speak up, cousin.'

'May Arioch and all the Dukes of Hell torment you for eternity,' growled Yyrkoon. He flung back his head, his wild eyes rolling, his lips curling: 'Arioch! Arioch! Curse this feeble albino! Arioch! Destroy him or see Melniboné fall!'

Elric continued to laugh. 'Arioch does not hear you. Chaos is weak upon the earth now. It needs a greater sorcery than yours to bring the Chaos Lords back to aid you as they aided our ancestors. And now, Yyrkoon, tell me – where is the Lady Cymoril?'

But Yyrkoon had lapsed, again, into a sullen silence.

'She is at her own tower, my emperor,' said Magum Colim.

'A creature of Yyrkoon's took her there,' said Dyvim Tvar. 'The captain of Cymoril's own guard, he slew a warrior who tried to defend his mistress against Yyrkoon. It could be that Princess Cymoril is in danger, my lord.'

'Then go quickly to the tower. Take a force of men. Bring both Cymoril and the captain of her guard to me.'

'And Yyrkoon, my lord?' asked Dyvim Tvar.

'Let him remain here until his sister returns.'

Dyvim Tvar bowed and, selecting a body of warriors, left the throne room. All noticed that Dyvim Tvar's step was lighter and his expression less grim than when he had first approached the throne room at

Prince Yyrkoon's back.

Yyrkoon straightened his head and looked about the court. For a moment he seemed like a pathetic and bewildered child. All the lines of hate and anger had disappeared and Elric felt sympathy for his cousin growing again within him. But this time Elric quelled the feeling.

'Be grateful, cousin, that for a few hours you were totally powerful, that you enjoyed domination over all the folk of Melniboné.'

Yyrkoon said in a small, puzzled voice: 'How did you escape? You had no time for making a sorcery, no strength for it. You could barely move your limbs and your armour must have dragged you deep to the bottom of the sea so that you should have drowned. It is unfair, Elric. You should have drowned.'

Elric shrugged, 'I have friends in the sea. They recognize my royal blood and my right to rule if you do not.'

Yyrkoon tried to disguise the astonishment he felt. Evidently his respect for Elric had increased, as had his hatred for the albino emperor. 'Friends.'

'Aye,' said Elric, with a thin grin.

'I – I thought, too, you had vowed not to use your powers of sorcery.'

'But you thought that a vow which was unbefitting for a Melnibonéan monarch to make did you not? Well, I agree with you. You see, Yyrkoon, you have won a victory, after all.'

Yyrkoon stared narrowly at Elric, as if trying to divine a secret meaning behind Elric's words. 'You will bring back the Chaos Lords?'

'No sorcerer, however powerful, can summon the Chaos Lords or, for that matter, the Lords of Law, if they do not wish to be summoned. That you know. You must know it, Yyrkoon. Have you not, yourself, tried? And Arioch did not come, did he? Did he bring you the gift you sought – the gift of the two black swords?'

'You know that?'

'I did not. I guessed. Now I know.'

Yyrkoon tried to speak but his voice would not form words, so angry was he. Instead, a strangled growl escaped his throat and for a few moments he struggled in the grip of his guards.

Dyvim Tvar returned with Cymoril. The girl was pale but she was smiling. She ran into the throne room. 'Elric!'

'Cymoril! Are you harmed?'

Cymoril glanced at the crestfallen captain of her guard who had been brought with her. A look of disgust crossed her fine face. Then she shook her head. 'No. I am not harmed.'

The captain of Cymoril's guard was shaking with terror. He looked pleadingly at Yyrkoon as if hoping that his fellow prisoner could help him. But Yyrkoon continued to stare at the floor.

'Have that one brought closer.' Elric pointed at the captain of the guard. The man was dragged to the foot of the steps leading to the Ruby Throne. He moaned. 'What a petty traitor you are,' said Elric. 'At least Yyrkoon had the courage to attempt to slay me. And his ambitions were high. Your ambition was merely to become one of his pet curs. So you betrayed your mistress and slew one of your own men. What is your name?'

The man had difficulty speaking, but at last he murmured, 'It is Valharik, my name. What could I do? I serve the Ruby Throne, whoever sits upon it.'

'So the traitor claims that loyalty motivated him. I think not.'

'It was, my lord. It was.' The captain began to whine. He fell to his knees. 'Slay me swiftly. Do not punish me more.'

Elric's impulse was to heed the man's request, but he looked at Yyrkoon and then remembered the expression on Cymoril's face when she had looked at the guard. He knew that he must make a point now, whilst making an example of Captain Valharik. So he shook his head. 'No. I will punish you more. Tonight you will die here according to the traditions of Melniboné, while my nobles feast to celebrate this new era of my rule.'

Valharik began to sob. Then he stopped himself and got slowly to his feet, a Melnibonéan again. He bowed low and stepped backward, giving himself into the grip of his guards.

'I must consider a way in which your fate may be shared with the one you wished to serve,' Elric went on. 'How did you slay the young warrior who sought to obey Cymoril?'

'With my sword. I cut him down. It was a clean stroke. But one.'

'And what became of the corpse.'

'Prince Yyrkoon told me to feed it to Princess Cymoril's slaves.'

'I understand. Very well, Prince Yyrkoon, you may join us at the feast tonight while Captain Valharik entertains us with his dying.'

Yyrkoon's face was almost as pale as Elric's. 'What do you mean?'

'The little pieces of Captain Valharik's flesh which our Doctor Jest will carve from his limbs will be the meat on which you feast. You may give instructions as to how you wish the captain's flesh prepared. We should not expect you to eat it raw, cousin.'

Even Dyvim Tvar looked astonished at Elric's decision. Certainly it was in the spirit of Melniboné and a clever irony improving on Prince Yyrkoon's own idea, but it was unlike Elric – or at least, it was unlike

55

the Elric he had known up until a day earlier.

As he heard his fate, Captain Valharik gave a great scream of terror and glared at Prince Yyrkoon as if the would-be usurper were already tasting his flesh. Yyrkoon tried to turn away, his shoulders shaking.

'And that will be the beginning of it,' said Elric. 'The feast will start at midnight. Until that time, confine Yyrkoon to his own tower.'

After Prince Yyrkoon and Captain Valharik had been led away, Dyvim Tvar and Princess Cymoril came and stood beside Elric who had sunk back in his great throne and was staring bitterly into the middle-distance.

'That was a clever cruelty,' Dyvim Tvar said.

Cymoril said: 'It is what they both deserve.'

'Aye,' murmured Elric. 'It is what my father would have done. It is what Yyrkoon would have done had our positions been reversed. I but follow the traditions. I no longer pretend that I am my own man. Here I shall stay until I die, trapped upon the Ruby Throne – serving the Ruby Throne as Valharik claimed to serve it.'

'Could you not kill them both quickly?' Cymoril asked. 'You know that I do not plead for my brother because he is my brother. I hate him most of all. But it might destroy you, Elric, to follow through with your plan.'

'What if it does? Let me be destroyed. Let me merely become an unthinking extension of my ancestors. The puppet of ghosts and memories, dancing to strings which extend back through time for ten thousand years.'

'Perhaps if you slept . . . ' Dyvim Tvar suggested.

'I shall not sleep, I feel, for many nights after this. But your brother is not going to die, Cymoril. After his punishment – after he has eaten the flesh of Captain Valharik – I intend to send him into exile. He will go alone into the Young Kingdoms and he will not be allowed to take his grimoires with him. He must make his way as best he can in the lands of the barbarian. That is not too severe a punishment, I think.'

'It is too lenient,' said Cymoril. 'You would be best advised to slay him. Send soldiers now. Give him no time to consider counterplots.'

'I do not fear his counterplots.' Elric rose wearily. 'Now I should like it if you would both leave me, until an hour or so before the feasting begins. I must think.'

'I will return to my tower and prepare myself for tonight,' said Cymoril. She kissed Elric lightly upon his pale forehead. He looked up, filled with love and tenderness for her. He reached out and touched her hair and her cheek. 'Remember that I love you, Elric,' she said.

'I will see that you are safely escorted homeward,' Dyvim Tvar said to her. 'And you must choose a new commander of your guard. Can I assist in that?'

'I should be grateful, Dyvim Tvar.'

They left Elric still upon the Ruby Throne, still staring into space. The hand that he lifted from time to time to his pale head shook a little and now the torment showed in his strange, crimson eyes.

Later, he rose up from the Ruby Throne and walked slowly, head bowed, to his own apartments, followed by his guards. He hesitated at the door which led onto the steps going up to the library. Instinctively he sought the consolation and forgetfulness of a certain kind of know-ledge, but at that moment he suddenly hated his scrolls and his books. He blamed them for his ridiculous concerns regarding 'morality' and 'justice'; he blamed them for the feelings of guilt and despair which now filled him as a result of his decision to behave as a Melnibonéan monarch was expected to behave. So he passed the door to the library and went on to his apartments, but even his apartments displeased him now. They were austere. They were not furnished according to the luxurious tastes of all Melnibonéans (save for his father) with their delight in lush mixtures of colour and bizarre design. He would have them changed as soon as possible. He would give himself up to those ghosts who ruled him. For some time he stalked from room to room, trying to push back that part of him which demanded he be merciful to Valharik and to Yyrkoon – at very least to slay them and be done with it or, better, to send them both into exile. But it was impossible to reverse his decision now.

At last he lowered himself to a couch which rested beside a window looking out over the whole of the city. The sky was still full of turbu-lent cloud, but now the moon shone through, like the yellow eye of an unhealthy beast. It seemed to stare with a certain triumphant irony at him, as if relishing the defeat of his conscience. Elric sank his head into his arms.

Later the servants came to tell him that the courtiers were as-sembling for the celebration feast. He allowed them to dress him in his yellow robes of state and to place the dragon crown upon his head and then he returned to the throne room to be greeted by a mighty cheer, more wholehearted than any he had ever received before. He acknowledged the greeting and then seated himself in the Ruby Throne, looking out over the banqueting tables which now filled the hall. A table was brought and set before him and two extra seats were brought, for Dyvim Tvar and Cymoril would sit beside him. But Dyvim Tvar and Cymoril were not yet here and neither had the renegade Valharik been brought. And where was Yyrkoon? They should, even now, be at the centre of the hall – Valharik in chains and Yyrkoon seated beneath him. Doctor Jest was there, heating his brazier on which rested his cooking pans, testing and sharpening his knives. The hall was filled with excited talk as the court waited to be entertained. Already the food was being brought in, though no one might eat until the emperor ate first.

Elric signed to the commander of his own guard. 'Has the Princess Cymoril or Lord Dyvim Tvar arrived at the tower yet?'

'No, my lord.'

Cymoril was rarely late and Dyvim Tvar never. Elric frowned. Perhaps they did not relish the entertainment.

'And what of the prisoners?'

'They have been sent for, my lord.'

Doctor Jest looked up expectantly, his thin body tensed in anticipation.

And then Elric heard a sound above the din of the conversation. A groaning sound which seemed to come from all around the tower. He bent his head and listened closely.

Others were hearing it now. They stopped talking and also listened intently. Soon the whole hall was in silence and the groaning increased.

Then, all at once, the doors of the throne room burst open and there was Dyvim Tvar, gasping and bloody, his clothes slashed and his flesh gashed. And following him in came a mist – a swirling mist of dark purples and unpleasant blues and it was this mist that groaned.

Elric sprang from his throne and knocked the table aside. He leapt down the steps towards his friend. The groaning mist began to creep further into the throne room, as if reaching out for Dyvim Tvar.

Elric took his friend in his arms. 'Dyvim Tvar! What is this sorcery?'

Dyvim Tvar's face was full of horror and his lips seemed frozen until at last he said:

'It is Yyrkoon's sorcery. He conjured the groaning mist to aid him in his escape. I tried to follow him from the city but the mist engulfed me and I lost my senses. I went to his tower to bring him and his accessory here, but the sorcery had already been accomplished.'

'Cymoril? Where is she?'

'He took her, Elric. She is with him. Valharik is with him and so are a hundred warriors who remained secretly loyal to him.'

'Then we must pursue him. We shall soon capture him.'

'You can do nothing against the groaning mist. Ah! It comes!'

And sure enough the mist was beginning to surround them. Elric tried to disperse it by waving his arms, but then it had gathered thickly around him and its melancholy groaning filled his ears, its hideous colours blinded his eyes. He tried to rush through it, but it remained with him. And now he thought he heard words amongst the groans. 'Elric is weak. Elric is foolish. Elric must die!'

'Stop this!' he cried. He bumped into another body and fell to his knees. He began to crawl, desperately trying to peer through the mist. Now faces formed in the mist – frightful faces, more terrifying than any he had ever seen, even in his worst nightmares.

'Cymoril!' he cried. 'Cymoril!'

And one of the faces became the face of Cymoril – a Cymoril who leered at him and mocked him and whose face slowly aged until he saw a filthy crone and, ultimately, a skull on which the flesh rotted. He closed his eyes, but the image remained.

'*Cymoril,*' whispered the voices. '*Cymoril.*'

And Elric grew weaker as he became more desperate. He cried out for Dyvim Tvar, but heard only a mocking echo of the name, as he had heard Cymoril's. He shut his lips and he shut his eyes and, still crawling, tried to free himself from the groaning mist. But hours seemed to pass before the groans became whines and the whines became faint strands of sound and he tried to rise, opening his eyes to see the mist fading, but then his legs buckled and he fell down against the first step which led to the Ruby Throne. Again he had ignored Cymoril's advice concerning her brother – and again she was in danger. Elric's last thought was a simple one:

'I am not fit to live,' he thought.

4

To Call the Chaos Lord

As soon as he recovered from the blow which had knocked him unconscious and thus wasted even more time, Elric sent for Dyvim Tvar. He was eager for news. But Dyvim Tvar could report nothing. Yyrkoon had summoned sorcerous aid to free him, sorcerous aid to effect his escape. 'He must have had some magical means of leaving the island, for he could not have gone by ship,' said Dyvim Tvar.

'You must send out expeditions,' said Elric. 'Send a thousand detachments if you must. Send every man in Melniboné. Strive to wake the dragons that they might be used. Equip the golden battle-barges. Cover the world with our men if you must, but find Cymoril.'

'All those things I have already done,' said Dyvim Tvar, 'save that I have not yet found Cymoril.'

A month passed and Imrryrian warriors marched and rode through the Young Kingdoms seeking news of their renegade countrymen.

'I worried more for myself than for Cymoril and I called that "morality",' thought the albino. 'I tested my sensibilities, not my conscience.'

A second month passed and Imrryrian dragons sailed the skies to South and East, West and North, but though they flew across mountains and seas and forests and plains and, unwittingly, brought terror to many a city, they found no sign of Yyrkoon and his band.

'For, finally, one can only judge oneself by one's actions,' thought Elric. 'I have looked at what I have done, not at what I meant to do or thought I would like to do, and what I have done has, in the main, been foolish, destructive and with little point. Yyrkoon was right to despise me and that was why I hated him so.'

A fourth month came and Imrryrian ships stopped in remote ports and Imrryrian sailors questioned other travellers and explorers for news of Yyrkoon. But Yyrkoon's sorcery had been strong and none had seen him (or remembered seeing him).

'I must now consider the implications of all these thoughts,' said

Elric to himself.

Wearily, the swiftest of the soldiers began to return to Melniboné, bearing their useless news. And as faith disappeared and hope faded, Elric's determination increased. He made himself strong, both physically and mentally. He experimented with new drugs which would increase his energy. He read much in the library, though this time he read only certain grimoires and he read those over and over again.

These grimoires were written in the High Speech of Melniboné – the ancient language of sorcery with which Elric's ancestors had been able to communicate with the supernatural beings they had summoned. And at last Elric was satisfied that he understood them fully, though what he read sometimes threatened to stop him in his present course of action.

And when he was satisfied – for the dangers of misunderstanding the implications of the things described in the grimoires were catastrophic – he slept for three nights in a drugged slumber.

And then Elric was ready. He ordered all slaves and servants from his quarters. He placed guards at the doors with instructions to admit no one, no matter how urgent their business. He cleared one great chamber of all furniture so that it was completely empty save for one grimoire which he had placed in the very centre of the room. Then he seated himself beside the book and began to think.

When he had meditated for more than five hours Elric took a brush and a jar of ink and began to paint both walls and floor with complicated symbols, some of which were so intricate that they seemed to disappear at an angle to the surface on which they had been laid. At last this was done and Elric spreadeagled himself in the very centre of his huge rune, face down, one hand upon his grimoire, the other (with the Actorios upon it) stretched palm down. The moon was full. A shaft of its light fell directly upon Elric's head, turning the hair to silver. And then the Summoning began.

Elric sent his mind into twisting tunnels of logic, across endless plains of ideas, through mountains of symbolism and endless universes of alternate truths; he sent his mind out further and further and as it went he sent with it the words which issued from his writhing lips – words that few of his contemporaries would understand, though their very sound would chill the blood of any listener. And his body heaved as he forced it to remain in its original position and from time to time a groan would escape him. And through all this a few words came again and again.

One of these words was a name. 'Arioch'.

Arioch, the patron demon of Elric's ancestors; one of the most powerful of all the Dukes of Hell, who was called Knight of the Swords, Lord of the Seven Darks, Lord of the Higher Hell and many more names besides.

'Arioch!'

It was on Arioch whom Yyrkoon had called, asking the Lord of Chaos to curse Elric. It was Arioch whom Yyrkoon had sought to summon to aid him in his attempt upon the Ruby Throne. It was Arioch who was known as the Keeper of the Two Black Swords – the swords of unearthly manufacture and infinite power which had once been wielded by emperors of Melniboné.

'Arioch! I summon thee.'

Runes, both rhythmic and fragmented, howled now from Elric's throat. His brain had reached the plane on which Arioch dwelt. Now it sought Arioch himself.

'Arioch! It is Elric of Melniboné who summons thee.'

Elric glimpsed an eye staring down at him. The eye floated, joined another. The two eyes regarded him.

'Arioch! My Lord of Chaos! Aid me!'

The eyes blinked – and vanished.

'Oh, Arioch! Come to me! Come to me! Aid me and I will serve you.'

A silhouette that was not a human form, turned slowly until a black, faceless head looked down upon Elric. A halo of red light gleamed behind the head.

Then that, too, vanished.

Exhausted, Elric let the image fade. His mind raced back through plane upon plane. His lips no longer chanted the runes and the names. He lay exhausted upon the floor of his chamber, unable to move, in silence.

He was certain that he had failed.

There was a small sound. Painfully he raised his weary head.

A fly had come into the chamber. It buzzed about erratically, seeming almost to follow the lines of the runes Elric had so recently painted.

The fly settled first upon one rune and then on another.

It must have come in through the window, thought Elric. He was annoyed by the distraction but still fascinated by it.

The fly settled on Elric's forehead. It was a large, black fly and its buzz was loud, obscene. It rubbed its forelegs together, and it seemed to be taking a particular interest in Elric's face as it moved over it. Elric shuddered, but he did not have the strength to swat it. When it came into his field of vision, he watched it. When it was not visible he felt its legs covering every inch of his face. Then it flew up and, still buzzing loudly, hovered a short distance from Elric's nose. And then Elric could see the fly's eyes and recognize something in them. They were the eyes – and yet not the eyes – he had seen on that other plane.

It began to dawn on him that this fly was no ordinary creature. It had features that were in some way faintly human.

The fly smiled at him.

From his hoarse throat and through his parched lips Elric was able to utter but one word:

'Arioch?'

And a beautiful youth stood where the fly had hovered. The beautiful youth spoke in a beautiful voice – soft and sympathetic and yet manly. He was clad in a robe that was like a liquid jewel and yet which did not dazzle Elric, for in some way no light seemed to come from it. There was a slender sword at the youth's belt and he wore no helm, but a circlet of red fire. His eyes were wise and his eyes were old and when they were looked at closely they could be seen to contain an ancient and confident evil.

'Elric.'

That was all the youth said, but it revived the albino so that he could raise himself to his knees.

'Elric.'

And Elric could now stand. He was filled with energy.

The youth was taller, now, than Elric. He looked down at the Emperor of Melniboné and he smiled the smile that the fly had smiled. 'You alone are fit to serve Arioch. It is long since I was invited to this plane, but now that I am here I shall aid you, Elric. I shall become your patron. I shall protect you and give you strength and the source of strength, though master I be and slave you be.'

'How must I serve you, Duke Arioch?' Elric asked, having made a monstrous effort of self-control, for he was filled with terror by the implications of Arioch's words.

'You will serve me by serving yourself for the moment. Later a time will come when I shall call upon you to serve me in specific ways, but (for the moment) I ask little of you, save that you swear to serve me.'

Elric hesitated.

'You must swear that,' said Arioch reasonably, 'or I cannot help you in the matter of your cousin Yyrkoon or his sister Cymoril.'

'I swear to serve you,' said Elric. And his body was flooded with ecstatic fire and he trembled with joy and he fell to his knees.

'Then I can tell you that, from time to time, you can call on my aid and I will come if your need is truly desperate. I will come in whichever form is appropriate, or no form at all if that should prove appropriate. And now you may ask me one question before I depart.'

'I need the answers to two questions.'

'Your first question I cannot answer. I will not answer. You must accept that you have now sworn to serve me. I will not tell you what the future holds. But you need not fear, if you serve me well.'

'Then my second question is this: 'Where is Prince Yyrkoon?'

'Prince Yyrkoon is in the south, in a land of barbarians. By sorcery and by superior weapons and intelligence he has effected the conquest of two mean nations, one of which is called Oin and the other of which is called Yu. Even now he trains the men of Oin and the men of Yu to march upon Melniboné, for he knows that your forces are spread thinly across the earth, searching for him. Ask a third.'

'How has he hidden?'

'He has not. But he has gained possession of the Mirror of Memory – a magical device whose hiding place he discovered by his sorceries. Those who look into this mirror have their memories taken. The mirror contains a million memories: the memories of all who have looked into it. Thus anyone who ventures into Oin or Yu or travels by sea to the capital which serves both is confronted by the mirror and forgets that he has seen Prince Yyrkoon and his Imrryrians in those lands. It is the best way of remaining undiscovered.'

'It is.' Elric drew his brows together. 'Therefore it might be wise to consider destroying the mirror. But what would happen then, I wonder?'

Arioch raised his beautiful hand. 'Although I have answered further questions which are, one could argue, part of the same question, I will answer no more. It could be in your interest to destroy the mirror, but it might be better to consider other means of countering its effects, for it does, I remind you, contain many memories, some of which have been imprisoned for thousands of years. Now I must go. And you must go – to the lands of Oin and Yu which lie several months' journey from here, to the south and well beyond Lormyr. They are best reached by the Ship Which Sails Over Both Land and Sea. Farewell, Elric.'

And a fly buzzed for a moment upon the wall before vanishing.

Elric rushed from the room, shouting for his slaves.

5

The Ship Which Sails Over Land and Sea

'And how many dragons still sleep in the caverns?' Elric paced the gallery overlooking the city. It was morning, but no sun came through the dull clouds which hung low upon the towers of the Dreaming City. Imrryr's life continued unchanged in the streets below, save for the absence of the majority of her soldiers who had not yet returned home from their fruitless quests and would not be home for many months to come.

Dyvim Tvar leaned on the parapet of the gallery and stared unseeingly into the streets. His face was tired and his arms were folded on his chest as if he sought to contain what was left of his strength.

'Two perhaps. It would take a great deal to wake them and even then I doubt if they'd be useful to us. What is this "Ship Which Sails Over Land and Sea" which Arioch spoke of?'

'I've read of it before – in the Silver Grimoire and in other tomes. A magic ship. Used by a Melnibonéan hero even before there was Melniboné and the empire. But where it exists, and if it exists, I do not know.'

'Who would know?' Dyvim Tvar straightened his back and turned it on the scene below.

'Arioch?' Elric shrugged. 'But he would not tell me.'

'What of your friends the Water Elementals? Have they not promised you aid? And would they not be knowledgeable in the matter of ships?'

Elric frowned, deepening the lines which now marked his face. 'Aye – Straasha might know. But I'm loath to call on his aid again. The Water Elementals are not the powerful creatures that the Lords of Chaos are. Their strength is limited and, moreover, they are inclined to be capricious, in the manner of the elements. What is more, Dyvim Tvar, I hesitate to use sorcery, save where absolutely imperative . . .'

'You are a sorceror, Elric. You have but lately proved your greatness in that respect, involving the most powerful of all sorceries, the summoning of a Chaos Lord – and you still hold back? I would suggest, my lord king, that you consider such logic and that you judge it unsound. You decided to use sorcery in your pursuit of Prince Yyrkoon. The die is already cast. It would be wise to use sorcery now.'

'You cannot conceive of the mental and physical effort involved . . . '

'I can conceive of it, my lord. I am your friend. I do not wish to see you pained – and yet . . . '

'There is also the difficulty, Dyvim Tvar, of my physical weakness,' Elric reminded his friend. 'How long can I continue in the use of these overstrong potions that now sustain me? They supply me with energy, aye – but they do so by using up my few resources. I might die before I find Cymoril.'

'I stand rebuked.'

But Elric came forward and put his white hand on Dyvim Tvar's butter-coloured cloak. 'But what have I to lose, eh? No. You are right. I am a coward to hesitate when Cymoril's life is at stake. I repeat my stupidities – the stupidities which first brought this pass upon us all. I'll do it. Will you come with me to the ocean?'

'Aye.'

Dyvim Tvar began to feel the burden of Elric's conscience settling upon him also. It was a peculiar feeling to come to a Melnibonéan and Dyvim Tvar knew very well that he liked it not at all.

Elric had last ridden these paths when he and Cymoril were happy. It seemed a long age ago. He had been a fool to trust that happiness. He turned his white stallion's head towards the cliffs and the sea beyond them. A light rain fell. Winter was descending swiftly on Melniboné.

They left their horses on the cliffs, lest they be disturbed by Elric's sorcery-working, and clambered down to the shore. The rain fell into the sea. A mist hung over the water little more than five ship lengths from the beach. It was deathly still and, with the tall, dark cliffs behind them and the wall of mist before them, it seemed to Dyvim Tvar that they had entered a silent netherworld where might easily be encountered the melancholy souls of those who, in legend, had committed suicide by a process of slow self-mutilation. The sound of the two men's boots on shingle was loud and yet was at once muffled by the mist which seemed to suck at noise and swallow it greedily as if it sustained its life on sound.

'Now,' Elric murmured. He seemed not to notice the brooding and depressive surroundings. 'Now I must recall the rune which came so easily, unsummoned, to my brain not many months since.' He left Dyvim Tvar's side and went down to the place where the chill water lapped the land and there, carefully, he seated himself, cross-legged.

His eyes stared, unseeingly, into the mist.

To Dyvim Tvar the tall albino appeared to shrink as he sat down. He seemed to become like a vulnerable child and Dyvim Tvar's heart went out to Elric as it might go out to a brave, nervous boy, and he had it in mind to suggest that the sorcery be done with and they seek the lands of Oin and Yu by ordinary means.

But Elric was already lifting his head as a dog lifts its head to the moon. And strange, thrilling words began to tumble from his lips and it became plain that, even if Dyvim Tvar did speak now, Elric would not hear him.

Dyvim Tvar was no stranger to the High Speech – as a Melnibonéan noble he had been taught it as a matter of course – but the words seemed nonetheless strange to him, for Elric used peculiar inflections and emphases, giving the words a special and secret weight and chanting them in a voice which ranged from bass groan to falsetto shriek. It was not pleasant to listen to such noises coming from a mortal throat and now Dyvim Tvar had some clear understanding of why Elric was reluctant to use sorcery. The Lord of the Dragon Caves, Melnibonéan though he was, found himself inclined to step backward a pace or two, even to retire to the cliff-tops and watch over Elric from there, and he had to force himself to hold his ground as the summoning continued.

For a good space of time the rune-chanting went on. The rain beat harder upon the pebbles of the shore and made them glisten. It dashed most ferociously into the still, dark sea, lashed about the fragile head of the chanting, pale-haired figure, and caused Dyvim Tvar to shiver and draw his cloak more closely about his shoulders.

'Straasha – Straasha – Straasha . . . '

The words mingled with the sound of the rain. They were now barely words at all but sounds which the wind might make or a language which the sea might speak.

'Straasha . . . '

Again Dyvim Tvar had the impulse to move, but this time he desired to go to Elric and tell him to stop, to consider some other means of reaching the lands of Oin and Yu.'

'Straasha!'

There was a cryptic agony in the shout.

'Straasha!'

Elric's name formed on Dyvim Tvar's lips, but he found that he could not speak it.

'Straasha!'

The cross-legged figure swayed. The word became the calling of the wind through the Caverns of Time.

'Straasha!'

It was plain to Dyvim Tvar that the rune was, for some reason, not working and that Elric was using up all his strength to no effect. And yet there was nothing the Lord of the Dragon Caves could do. His tongue was frozen. His feet seemed frozen to the ground.

He looked at the mist. Had it crept closer to the shore? Had it taken on a strange, almost luminous, green tinge? He peered closely.

There was a massive disturbance of the water. The sea rushed up the beach. The shingle crackled. The mist retreated. Vague lights flickered in the air and Dyvim Tvar thought he saw the shining silhouette of a gigantic figure emerging from the sea and he realized that Elric's chant had ceased.

'King Straasha,' Elric was saying in something approaching his normal tone. 'You have come. I thank you.'

The silhouette spoke and the voice reminded Dyvim Tvar of slow, heavy waves rolling beneath a friendly sun.

'We elementals are concerned, Elric, for there are rumours that you have invited Chaos Lords back to your plane and the elementals have never loved the Lords of Chaos. Yet I know that if you have done this it is because you are fated to do it and therefore we hold no enmity against you.'

'The decision was forced upon me, King Straasha. There was no other decision I could make. If you are therefore reluctant to aid me, I shall understand that and call on you no more.'

'I will help you, though helping you is harder now, not for what happens in the immediate future but what is hinted will happen in years to come. Now you must tell me quickly how we of the water can be of service to you.'

'Do you know ought of the Ship Which Sails Over Land and Sea? I need to find that ship if I am to fulfil my vow to find my love, Cymoril.'

'I know much of that ship, for it is mine. Grome also lays claim to it. But it is mine. Fairly, it is mine.'

'Grome of the Earth?'

'Grome of the Land Below the Roots. Grome of the Ground and all that lives under it. My brother. Grome. Long since, even as we elementals count time, Grome and I built that ship so that we could travel between the realms of Earth and Water whenever we chose. But we quarrelled (may we be cursed for such foolishness) and we fought. There were earthquakes, tidal waves, volcanic eruptions, typhoons and battles in which all the elementals joined, with the result that new

continents were flung up and old ones drowned. It was not the first time we had fought each other, but it was the last. And finally, lest we destroy each other completely, we made a peace. I gave Grome part of my domain and he gave me the Ship Which Sails Over Land and Sea. But he gave it somewhat unwillingly and thus it sails the sea better than it sails the land, for Grome thwarts its progress whenever he can. Still, if the ship is of use to you, you shall have it.'

'I thank you, King Straasha. Where shall I find it?'

'It will come. And now I grow weary, for the further from my own realm I venture, the harder it is to sustain my mortal form. Farewell, Elric – and be cautious. You have a greater power than you know and many would make use of it to their own ends.'

'Shall I wait here for the Ship Which Sails Over Land and Sea?'

'No . . .' the Sea King's voice was fading as his form faded. Grey mist drifted back where the silhouette and the green lights had been. The sea again was still. *'Wait. Wait in your tower . . . It will come . . .'*

A few wavelets lapped the shore and then it was as if the king of the Water Elementals had never been there at all. Dyvim Tvar rubbed his eyes. Slowly at first he began to move to where Elric still sat. Gently he bent down and offered the albino his hand. Elric looked up in some surprise. 'Ah, Dyvim Tvar. How much time has passed?'

'Some hours, Elric. It will soon be night. What little light there is begins to wane. We had best ride back for Imrryr.'

Stiffly Elric rose to his feet, with Dyvim Tvar's assistance. 'Aye . . .' he murmured absently. 'The Sea King said . . .'

'I heard the Sea King, Elric. I heard his advice and I heard his warning. You must remember to heed both. I like too little the sound of this magic boat. Like most things of sorcerous origin, the ship appears to have vices as well as virtues, like a double-bladed knife which you raise to stab your enemy and which, instead, stabs you . . .'

'That must be expected where sorcery is concerned. It was you who urged me on, my friend.'

'Aye,' said Dyvim Tvar almost to himself as he led the way up the cliff-path towards the horses. 'Aye. I have not forgotten that, my lord king.'

Elric smiled wanly and touched Dyvim Tvar's arm. 'Worry not. The summoning is over and now we have the vessel we need to take us swiftly to Prince Yyrkoon and the lands of Oin and Yu.'

'Let us hope so.' Dyvim Tvar was privately sceptical about the benefits they would gain from the Ship Which Sails Over Land and Sea. They reached the horses and he began to wipe the water off the flanks of his own roan. 'I regret,' he said, 'that we have once again allowed the dragons to expend their energy on a useless endeavour. With a squadron of my beasts, we could do much against Prince Yyrkoon. And it would be fine and wild, my friend, to ride the skies again, side by side, as we used to.'

'When all this is done and Princess Cymoril brought home, we shall do that,' said Elric, hauling himself wearily into the saddle of his white stallion. 'You shall blow the Dragon Horn and our dragon brothers will hear it and you and I shall sing the *Song of the Dragon Masters* and our goads shall flash as we straddle Flamefang and his mate Sweetclaw. Ah, that will be like the days of old Melniboné, when we no longer equate freedom with power, but let the Young Kingdoms go their own way and be certain that they let us go ours!'

Dyvim Tvar pulled on his horse's reins. His brow was clouded. 'Let us pray that day will come, my lord. But I cannot help this nagging thought which tells me that Imrryr's days are numbered and that my own life nears its close . . . '

'Nonsense, Dyvim Tvar. You'll survive me. There's little doubt of that, though you be my elder.'

Dyvim Tvar said, as they galloped back through the closing day: 'I have two sons. Did you know that, Elric?'

'You have never mentioned them.'

'They are by old mistresses.'

'I am happy for you.'

'They are fine Melnibonéans.'

'Why do you mention this, Dyvim Tvar?' Elric tried to read his friend's expression.

'It is that I love them and would have them enjoy the pleasures of the Dragon Isle.'

'And why should they not?'

'I do not know.' Dyvim Tvar looked hard at Elric. 'I could suggest that it is your responsibility, the fate of my sons, Elric.'

'Mine?'

'It seems to me, from what I gathered from the Water Elemental's words, that your decisions could decide the fate of the Dragon Isle. I ask you to remember my sons, Elric.'

'I shall, Dyvim Tvar. I am certain they shall grow into superb Dragon Masters and that one of them shall succeed you as Lord of the Dragon Caves.'

'I think you miss my meaning, my lord emperor.'

And Elric looked solemnly at his friend and shook his head. 'I do not miss your meaning, old friend. But I think you judge me harshly if you fear I'll do ought to threaten Melniboné and all she is.'

'Forgive me, then.' Dyvim Tvar lowered his head. But the expression in his eyes did not change.

In Imrryr they changed their clothes and drank hot wine and had spiced food brought. Elric, for all his weariness, was in better spirits than he had been for many a month. And yet there was still a tinge of something behind his surface mood which suggested he encouraged himself to speak gaily and put vitality into his movements. Admittedly, thought Dyvim Tvar, the prospects had improved and soon they would be confronting Prince Yyrkoon. But the dangers ahead of them were unknown, the pitfalls probably considerable. Still, he did not, out of sympathy for his friend, want to dispel Elric's mood. He was glad, in fact, that Elric seemed in a more positive frame of mind. There was talk of the equipment they would need in their expedition to the mysterious lands of Yu and Oin, speculation concerning the capacity of the Ship Which Sails Over Land and Sea – how many men it would take, what provisions they should put aboard and so on.

When Elric went to his bed, he did not walk with the dragging tiredness which had previously accompanied his step and again, bidding him goodnight, Dyvim Tvar was struck by the same emotion which had filled him on the beach, watching Elric begin his rune. Perhaps it was not by chance that he had used the example of his sons when speaking to Elric earlier that day, for he had a feeling that was almost protective, as if Elric were a boy looking forward to some treat which might not bring him the joy he expected.

Dyvim Tvar dismissed the thoughts, as best he could, and went to his own bed. Elric might blame himself for all that had occurred in the question of Yyrkoon and Cymoril, but Dyvim Tvar wondered if he, too, were not to blame in some part. Perhaps he should have offered his advice more cogently – more vehemently, even – earlier and made a stronger attempt to influence the young emperor. And then, in the Melnibonéan manner, he dismissed such doubts and questions as pointless. There was only one rule – seek pleasure however you would. But had that always been the Melnibonéan way? Dyvim Tvar wondered suddenly if Elric might not have regressive rather than deficient blood. Could Elric be a reincarnation of one of their most distant ancestors? Had it always been in the Melnibonéan character to think only of oneself and one's own gratification?

And again Dyvim Tvar dismissed the questions. What use was there in questions, after all? The world was the world. A man was a man. Before he sought his own bed he went to visit both his old mistresses, waking them up and insisting that he see his sons, Dyvim Slorm and

Dyvim Mav and when his sons, sleepy-eyed, bewildered, had been brought to him, he stared at them for a long while before sending them back. He had said nothing to either, but he had brought his brows together frequently and rubbed at his face and shaken his head and, when they had gone, had said to Niopal and Saramal, his mistresses, who were as bewildered as their offspring, 'Let them be taken to the Dragon Caves tomorrow and begin their learning.'

'So soon, Dyvim Tvar?' said Niopal.

'Aye. There's little time left, I fear.'

He would not amplify on this remark because he could not. It was merely a feeling he had. But it was a feeling that was fast becoming an obsession with him.

In the morning Dyvim Tvar returned to Elric's tower and found the emperor pacing the gallery above the city, asking eagerly for any news of a ship sighted off the coast of the island. But no such ship had been seen. Servants answered earnestly that if their emperor could describe the ship, it would be easier for them to know for what to look, but he could not describe the ship, and could only hint that it might not be seen on water at all, but might appear on land. He was all dressed up in his black war gear and it was plain to Dyvim Tvar that Elric was indulging in even larger quantities of the potions which replenished his blood. The crimson eyes gleamed with a hot' vitality, the speech was rapid and the bone-white hands moved with unnatural speed when Elric made even the lightest gesture.

'Are you well this morning, my lord?' asked the Dragon Master.

'In excellent spirits, thank you, Dyvim Tvar.' Elric grinned. 'Though I'd feel even better if the Ship Which Sails Over Land and Sea were here now.' He went to the balustrade and leaned upon it, peering over the towers and beyond the city walls, looking first to the sea and then to the land. 'Where can it be? I wish that King Straasha had been able to be more specific.'

'I'll agree with that.' Dyvim Tvar, who had not breakfasted, helped himself from the variety of succulent foods laid upon the table. It was evident that Elric had eaten nothing.

Dyvim Tvar began to wonder if the volume of potions had not affected his old friend's brain; perhaps madness, brought about by his involvement with complicated sorcery, his anxiety for Cymoril, his hatred of Yyrkoon, had begun to overwhelm Elric.

'Would it not be better to rest and to wait until the ship is sighted?' he suggested quietly as he wiped his lips.

'Aye – there's reason in that,' Elric agreed. 'But I cannot. I have an urge to be off, Dyvim Tvar, to come face to face with Yyrkoon, to have my revenge on him, to be united with Cymoril again.'

'I understand that. Yet, still . . . '

Elric's laugh was loud and ragged. 'You fret like Tanglebones over my well-being. I do not need two nursemaids, Lord of the Dragon Caves.'

With an effort Dyvim Tvar smiled. 'You are right. Well, I pray that this magical vessel – what is that?' He pointed out across the island. 'A movement in yonder forest. As if the wind passes through it. But there is no sign of wind elsewhere.'

Elric followed his gaze. 'You are right. I wonder . . . '

And then they saw something emerge from the forest and the land itself seemed to ripple. It was something which glinted white and blue and black. It came closer.

'A sail,' said Dyvim Tvar. 'It is your ship, I think, my lord.'

'Aye,' Elric whispered, craning forward. 'My ship. Make yourself ready, Dyvim Tvar. By midday we shall be gone from Imrryr.'

6

What the Earth God Desired

The ship was tall and slender and she was delicate. Her rails, masts and bulwarks were exquisitely carved and obviously not the work of a mortal craftsman. Though built of wood, the wood was not painted but naturally shone blue and black and green and a kind of deep smoky red; and her rigging was the colour of sea-weed and there were veins in the planks of her polished deck, like the roots of trees, and the sails on her three tapering masts were as fat and white and light as clouds on a fine summer day. The ship was everything that was lovely in nature; few could look upon her and not feel a delight like that which comes from sighting a perfect view. In a word, the ship radiated harmony, and Elric could think of no finer vessel in which to sail against Prince Yyrkoon and the dangers of the lands of Oin and Yu.

The ship sailed gently in the ground as if upon the surface of a river and the earth beneath the keel rippled as if turned momentarily to water. Wherever the keel of the ship touched, and a few feet around it, this effect became evident, though, after the ship had passed, the ground would return to its usual stable state. This was why the trees of the forest had swayed as the ship passed through them, parting before the keel as the ship sailed towards Imrryr.

The Ship Which Sails Over Land and Sea was not particularly large. Certainly she was considerably smaller than a Melnibonéan battle-barge and only a little bigger than a southern galley. But the grace of her; the curve of her line; the pride of her bearing – in these, she had no rival at all.

Already her gangplanks had been lowered to the ground and she was being made ready for her journey. Elric, hands on his slim hips, stood looking up at King Straasha's gift. From the gates of the city wall slaves were bearing provisions and arms and carrying them up the gangways. Meanwhile Dyvim Tvar was assembling the Imrryrian warriors and assigning them their ranks and duties while on the expedition. There were not many warriors. Only half the available strength could come with the ship, for the other half must remain behind under the command of Admiral Magum Colim and protect the city. It was unlikely that there would be any large attack on Melniboné after the punishment meted out to the barbarian fleet, but it was wise to take precautions, particularly since Prince Yyrkoon had vowed to conquer Imrryr. Also, for some strange reason that none of the onlookers could divine, Dyvim Tvar had called for volunteers – veterans who shared a common disability – and made up a special detachment of these men who, so the onlookers thought, could be of no use at all on the expedition. Still, neither were they of use when it came to defending the city, so they might as well go. These veterans were led aboard first.

Last to climb the gangway was Elric himself. He walked slowly, heavily, a proud figure in his black armour, until he reached the deck. Then he turned, saluted his city, and ordered the gangplank raised.

Dyvim Tvar was waiting for him on the poop-deck. The Lord of the Dragon Caves had stripped off one of his gauntlets and was running his naked hand over the oddly coloured wood of the rail. 'This is not a ship made for war, Elric,' he said. 'I should not like to see it harmed.'

'How can it be harmed?' Elric asked lightly as Imrryrians began to climb the rigging and adjust the sails. 'Would Straasha let it be destroyed? Would Grome? Fear not for the Ship Which Sails Over Land and Sea, Dyvim Tvar. Fear only for our own safety and the success of our expedition. Now, let us consult the charts. Remembering Straasha's warning concerning his brother Grome, I suggest we travel by sea for as far as possible, calling in here . . . ' he pointed to a seaport on the western coast of Lormyr – 'to get our bearings and learn what we can of the lands of Oin and Yu and how those lands are defended.'

'Few travellers have ever ventured beyond Lormyr. It is said that the edge of the world lies not far from that country's most southerly borders.' Dyvim Tvar frowned. 'Could not this whole mission be a trap, I wonder? Arioch's trap? What if he is in league with Prince Yyrkoon and we have been completely deceived into embarking upon an expedition which will destroy us?'

'I have considered that,' said Elric. 'But there is no other choice. We must trust Arioch.'

'I suppose we must.' Dyvim Tvar smiled ironically. 'Another matter now occurs to me. How does the ship move? I saw no anchors we could raise and there are no tides that I know of that sweep across the land. The wind fills the sails – see.' It was true. The sails were billowing and the masts creaked slightly as they took the strain.

Elric shrugged and spread his hands. 'I suppose we must tell the ship,' he suggested. 'Ship – we are ready to sail.'

Elric took some pleasure in Dyvim Tvar's expression of astonishment as, with a lurch, the ship began to move. It sailed smoothly, as over a calm sea, and Dyvim Tvar instinctively clutched the rail, shouting: 'But we are heading directly for the city wall!'

Elric crossed quickly to the centre of the poop where a large lever lay, horizontally attached to a ratchet which in turn was attached to a spindle. This was almost certainly the steering gear. Elric grasped the lever as one might grasp an oar and pushed it round a notch or two. Immediately the ship responded – and turned towards another part of the wall! Elric hauled back on the lever and the ship leaned, protesting a little as she yawed around and began to head out across the island. Elric laughed in delight. 'You see, Dyvim Tvar, it is easy. A slight effort of logic was all it took!'

'Nonetheless,' said Dyvim Tvar suspiciously, 'I'd rather we rode dragons. At least they are beasts and may be understood. But this sorcery, it troubles me.'

'Those are not fitting words for a noble of Melniboné!' Elric shouted above the sound of the wind in the rigging, the creaking of the ship's timbers, the slap of the great white sails.

'Perhaps not,' said Dyvim Tvar. 'Perhaps that explains why I stand beside you now, my lord.'

Elric darted his friend a puzzled look before he went below to find a helmsman whom he could teach how to steer the ship.

The ship sped swiftly over rocky slopes and up gorse-covered hills; she cut her way through forests and sailed grandly over grassy plains. She moved like a low-flying hawk which keeps close to the ground but progresses with incredible speed and accuracy as it searches for its prey, altering its course with an imperceptible flick of a wing. The soldiers of Imrryr crowded her decks, gasping in amazement at the ship's progress over the land, and many of the men had to be clouted back to their positions at the sails or elsewhere about the ship. The huge warrior who acted as bosun seemed the only member of the crew unaffected by the miracle of the ship. He was behaving as he would normally behave aboard one of the golden battle-barges; going solidly about his duties and seeing to it that all was done in a proper seamanly manner. The helmsman Elric had selected was, on the other hand, wide-eyed and somewhat nervous of the ship he handled. You could see that he felt he was, at any moment, going to be dashed against a slab of rock or smash the ship apart in a tangle of thick-trunked pines. He was forever wetting his lips and wiping sweat from his brow, even though the air was sharp and his breath steamed as it left his throat. Yet he was a good helmsman and gradually he became used to handling the ship, though his movements were, perforce, more rapid, for there was little time to deliberate upon a decision, the ship travelled with such speed over the land. The speed was breathtaking; they sped more swiftly than any horse – were swifter, even, than Dyvim Tvar's beloved dragons. Yet the motion was exhilarating, too, as the expressions on the faces of all the Imrryrians told.

Elric's delighted laughter rang through the ship and infected many another member of the crew.

'Well, if Grome of the Roots is trying to block our progress, I hesitate to guess how fast we shall travel when we reach water!' he called to Dyvim Tvar.

Dyvim Tvar had lost some of his earlier mood. His long, fine hair streamed around his face as he smiled at his friend. 'Aye – we shall all be whisked off the deck and into the sea!'

And then, as if in answer to their words, the ship began suddenly to buck and at the same time sway from side to side, like a ship caught in powerful cross-currents. The helmsman went white and clung to his lever, trying to get the ship back under control. There came a brief, terrified yell and a sailor fell from the highest cross-tree in the main mast and crashed onto the deck, breaking every bone in his body. And then the ship swayed once or twice and the turbulence was behind them and they continued on their course.

Elric stared at the body of the fallen sailor. Suddenly the mood of gaiety left him completely and he gripped the rail in his black gauntleted hands and he gritted his strong teeth and his crimson eyes glowed and his lips curled in self-mockery. 'What a fool I am. What a fool I am to tempt the gods so!'

Still, though the ship moved almost as swiftly as it had done, there seemed to be something dragging at it, as if Grome's minions clung on to the bottom as barnacles might cling in the sea. And Elric sensed something around him in the air, something in the rustling of the trees through which they passed, something in the movement of the grass and the bushes and the flowers over which they crossed, something in the weight of the rocks, of the angle of the hills. And he knew that what he sensed was the presence of Grome of the Ground – Grome of the Land Below the Roots – Grome, who desired to own what he and his brother Straasha had once owned jointly, what they had made as a sign of the unity between them and over which they had then fought. Grome wanted very much to take back the Ship Which Sails Over Land and Sea. And Elric, staring down at the black earth, became afraid.

7

King Grome

But at last, with the land tugging at their keel, they reached the sea, sliding into the water and gathering speed with every moment, until Melniboné was gone behind them and they were sighting the thick clouds of steam which hung forever over the Boiling Sea. Elric thought it unwise to risk even this magic vessel in those peculiar waters, so the vessel was turned and headed for the coast of Lormyr, sweetest and most tranquil of the Young Kingdom nations, and the port of Ramasaz on Lormyr's western shore. If the southern barbarians with whom they had so recently fought had been from Lormyr, Elric would have considered making for some other port, but the barbarians had almost certainly been from the South-East on the far side of the continent, beyond Pikarayd. The Lormyrians, under their fat, cautious King Fadan, were not likely to join a raid unless its success were completely assured. Sailing slowly into Ramasaz, Elric gave instructions that their ship be moored in a conventional way and treated like any ordinary ship. It attracted attention, nonetheless, for its beauty, and the inhabitants of the port were astonished to find Melnibonéans crewing the vessel. Though Melnibonéans were disliked throughout the Young Kingdoms, they were also feared. Thus, outwardly at any rate, Elric and his men were treated with respect and were served reasonably good food and wine in the hostelries they entered.

In the largest of the waterfront inns, a place called *Heading Outward and Coming Safely Home Again*, Elric found a garrulous host who had, until he bought the inn, been a prosperous fisherman and who knew the southernmost shores reasonably well. He certainly knew the lands of Oin and Yu, but he had no respect for them at all.

'You think they could be massing for war, my lord.' He raised his eyebrows at Elric before hiding his face in his wine-mug. Wiping his lips, he shook his red head. 'Then they must war against sparrows. Oin and Yu are barely nations at all. Their only halfway decent city is Dhoz-Kam – and that is shared between them, half being on one side of the River Ar and half being on the other. As for the rest of Oin and Yu – it is inhabited by peasants who are for the most part so ill-educated and superstition-ridden that they are poverty stricken. Not a potential soldier among 'em.'

'You've heard nothing of a Melnibonéan renegade who has conquered Oin and Yu and set about training these peasants to make war?' Dyvim Tvar leaned on the bar next to Elric. He sipped fastidiously from a thick cup of wine. 'Prince Yyrkoon is the renegade's name.'

'Is that whom you seek?' The innkeeper became more interested. 'A dispute between the Dragon Princes, eh?'

'That's our business,' said Elric haughtily.

'Of course, my lords.'

'You know nothing of a great mirror which steals men's memories?' Dyvim Tvar asked.

'A magical mirror!' The innkeeper threw back his head and laughed heartily. 'I doubt if there's one decent mirror in the whole of Oin or Yu! No, my lords, I think you are misled if you fear danger from those lands!'

'Doubtless you are right,' said Elric, staring down into his own untasted wine. 'But it would be wise if we were to check for ourselves – and it would be in Lormyr's interests, too, if we were to find what we seek and warn you accordingly.'

'Fear not for Lormyr. We can deal easily with any silly attempt to make war from that quarter. But if you'd see for yourselves, you must follow the coast for three days until you come to a great bay. The River Ar runs into that bay and on the shores of the river lies Dhoz-Kam – a seedy sort of city, particularly for a capital serving two nations. The inhabitants are corrupt, dirty and disease-ridden, but fortunately they are also lazy and thus afford little trouble, especially if you keep a sword by you. When you have spent an hour in Dhoz-Kam, you will realize the impossibility of such folk becoming a menace to anyone else, unless they should get close enough to you to infect you with one of their several plagues!' Again the innkeeper laughed hugely at his own wit. As he ceased shaking, he added: 'Or unless you fear their navy. It consists of a dozen or so filthy fishing boats, most of which are so unseaworthy they dare only fish the shallows of the estuary.'

Elric pushed his wine-cup aside. 'We thank you, landlord.' He placed a Melnibonéan silver piece upon the counter.

'This will be hard to change,' said the innkeeper craftily.

'There is no need to change it on our account,' Elric told him.

80

'I thank you, masters. Would you stay the night at my establishment? I can offer you the finest beds in Ramasaz.'

I think not,' Elric told him. 'We shall sleep aboard our ship tonight, that we might be ready to sail at dawn.'

The landlord watched the Melnibonéans depart. Instinctively he bit at the silver piece and then, suspecting he tasted something odd about it, removed it from his mouth. He stared at the coin, turning it this way and that. Could Melnibonéan silver be poisonous to an ordinary mortal? he wondered. It was best not to take risks. He tucked the coin into his purse and collected up the two wine-cups they had left behind. Though he hated waste, he decided it would be wiser to throw the cups out lest they should have become tainted in some way.

The Ship Which Sails Over Land and Sea reached the bay at noon on the following day and now it lay close inshore, hidden from the distant city by a short isthmus on which grew thick, near-tropical foliage. Elric and Dyvim Tvar waded through the clear, shallow water to the beach and entered the forest. They had decided to be cautious and not make their presence known until they had determined the truth of the inn-keeper's contemptuous description of Dhoz-Kam. Near the tip of the isthmus was a reasonably high hill and growing on the hill were several good-sized trees. Elric and Dyvim Tvar used their swords to clear a path through the undergrowth and made their way up the hill until they stood under the trees, picking out the one most easily climbed. Elric selected a tree whose trunk bent and then straightened out again. He sheathed his sword, got his hands onto the trunk and hauled him-self up, clambering along until he reached a succession of thick branches which would bear his weight. In the meantime Dyvim Tvar climbed another nearby tree until at last both men could get a good view across the bay where the city of Dhoz-Kam could be clearly seen. Certainly the city itself deserved the innkeeper's description. It was squat and grimy and evidently poor. Doubtless this was why Yyrkoon had chosen it, for the lands of Oin and Yu could not have been hard to conquer with the help of a handful of well-trained Imrryrians and some of Yyrkoon's sorcerous allies. Indeed, few would have bothered to conquer such a place, since its wealth was plainly virtually non-existent and its geographical position of no strategic importance. Yyrkoon had chosen well, for purposes of secrecy if nothing else. But the landlord had been wrong about Dhoz-Kam's fleet. Even from here Elric and Dyvim Tvar could make out at least thirty good-sized war-ships in the harbour and there seemed to be more anchored up-river. But the ships did not interest them as much as the thing which flashed and glittered above the city – something which had been mounted on huge pillars which supported an axle which, in turn, supported a vast, circular mirror set in a frame whose workmanship was as plainly non-mortal as that of the ship which had brought the Melnibonéans here. There was no doubt that they looked upon the Mirror of Memory and that any who had sailed into the harbour after it had been erected must have had their memory of what they had seen stolen from them instantly.

'It seems to me, my lord,' said Dyvim Tvar from his perch a yard or two away from Elric, 'that it would be unwise of us to sail directly into the harbour of Dhoz-Kam. Indeed, we could be in danger if we entered the bay. I think that we look upon the mirror, even now, only because it is not pointed directly at us. But you notice there is machinery to turn it in any direction its user chooses – save one. It cannot be turned inland, behind the city. There is no need for it, for who would approach Oin and Yu from the wastelands beyond their borders and who but the inhabitants of Oin or Yu would need to come overland to their capital?'

'I think I take your meaning, Dyvim Tvar. You suggest that we would be wise to make use of the special properties of our ship and . . .'

' . . . and go overland to Dhoz-Kam, striking suddenly and making full use of those veterans we brought with us, moving swiftly and ignoring Prince Yyrkoon's new allies – seeking the prince himself, and his renegades. Could we do that, Elric? Dash into the city – seize Yyrkoon, rescue Cymoril – then speed out again and away?'

'Since we have too few men to make a direct assault, it is all we can do, though it's dangerous. The advantage of surprise would be lost, of course, once we had made the attempt. If we failed in our first attempt it would become much harder to attack a second time. The alternative is to sneak into the city at night and hope to locate Yyrkoon and Cymoril alone, but then we should not be making use of our one important weapon, the Ship Which Sails Over Land and Sea. I think your plan is the best one, Dyvim Tvar. Let us turn the ship inland, now, and hope that Grome takes his time in finding us – for I still worry lest he try seriously to wrest the ship from our possession.' Elric began to climb down towards the ground.

Standing once more upon the poop-deck of the lovely ship, Elric ordered the helmsman to turn the vessel once again towards the land. Under half-sail the ship moved gracefully through the water and up the curve of the bank and the flowering shrubs of the forest parted before its prow and then they were sailing through the green dark of the jungle, while startled birds cawed and shrilled and little animals paused in astonishment and peered down from the trees at the Ship Which Sails Over Land and Sea and some almost lost their balance as the graceful boat progressed calmly over the floor of the forest, turning aside for only the thickest of the trees.

And thus they made their way to the interior of the land called Oin, which lay to the north of the River Ar, which marked the border between Oin and the land called Yu with which Oin shared a single capital.

Oin was a country consisting largely of unforested jungle and infertile plains where the inhabitants farmed, for they feared the forest and would not go into it, even though that was where Oin's wealth might be found.

The ship sailed well enough through the forest and out over the plain and soon they could see a large lake glinting ahead of them and Dyvim Tvar, glancing at the crude map with which he had furnished himself in Ramasaz, suggested that they begin to turn towards the south again and approach Dhoz-Kam by means of a wide semi-circle. Elric agreed and the ship began to tack round.

It was then that the land began to heave again and huge waves of grassy earth this time rolled around the ship and blotted out the surrounding view. The ship pitched wildly up and down and from side to side. Two more Imrryrians fell from the rigging and were killed on the deck below. The bosun was shouting loudly – though in fact all this upheaval was happening in silence – and the silence made the situation seem that much more menacing. The bosun yelled to his men to tie themselves to their positions. 'And all those not doing anything – get below at once!' he added.

Elric had wound a scarf around the rail and tied the other end to his wrist. Dyvim Tvar had used a long belt for the same purpose. But still they were flung in all directions, often losing their footing as the ship bucked this way and that, and every bone in Elric's body seemed about to crack and every inch of his flesh seemed bruised. And the ship was creaking and protesting and threatening to break up under the awful strain of riding the heaving land.

'Is this Grome's work, Elric?' Dyvim Tvar panted. 'Or is it some sorcery of Yyrkoon's?'

Elric shook his head. 'Not Yyrkoon. It is Grome. And I know no way to placate him. Not Grome, who thinks least of all the Kings of the Elements, yet, perhaps, is the most powerful.'

'But surely he breaks his bargain with his brother by doing this to us?'

'No. I think not. King Straasha warned us this might happen. We can only hope that Grome expends all his energy and that the ship survives, as it might survive a natural storm at sea.'

'This is worse than a sea-storm, Elric!'

Elric nodded his agreement but could say nothing, for the deck was tilting at a crazy angle and he had to cling to the rails with both hands in order to retain any kind of footing.

And now the silence stopped.

Instead they heard a rumbling and a roaring that seemed to have something of the character of laugher.

'King Grome!' Elric shouted. 'King Grome! Let us be! We have done you no harm!'

But the laughter increased and it made the whole ship quiver as the land rose and fell around it, as trees and hills and rocks rushed towards the ship and then fell away again, never quite engulfing them, for Grome doubtless wanted his ship intact.

'Grome! You have no quarrel with mortals!' Elric cried again. 'Let us be! Ask a favour of us if you must, but grant us this favour in return!'

Elric was shouting almost anything that came into his head. Really, he had no hope of being heard by the earth god and he did not expect King Grome to bother to listen even if the elemental did hear. But there was nothing else to do.

'*Grome! Grome! Grome!* Listen to me!'

Elric's only response was in the louder laughter which made every nerve in him tremble. And the earth heaved higher and dropped lower and the ship spun round and round until Elric was sure he would lose his senses entirely.

'*King Grome! King Grome!* Is it just to slay those who have never done you harm?'

And then, slowly, the heaving earth subsided and the ship was still and a huge, brown figure stood looking down at the ship. The figure was the colour of earth and looked like a vast, old oak. His hair and his beard were the colour of leaves and his eyes were the colour of gold ore and his teeth were the colour of granite and his feet were like roots and his skin seemed covered in tiny green shoots in place of hair and he smelled rich and musty and good and he was King Grome of the Earth Elementals. He sniffed and he frowned and he said in a soft, mighty voice that was yet coarse and grumpy: 'I want my ship.'

'It is not our ship to give, King Grome,' said Elric.

Grome's tone of petulance increased. 'I want my ship,' he said slowly. 'I want the thing. It is mine.'

'Of what use is it to you, King Grome?'

'Use? It is mine.'

Grome stamped and the land rippled.

Elric said desperately: 'It is your brother's ship, King Grome. It is King Straasha's ship. He gave you part of his domain and you allowed him to keep the ship. That was the bargain.'

'I know nothing of a bargain. The ship is mine.'

'You know that if you take the ship then King Straasha will have to take back the land he gave you.'

'I want my ship.' The huge figure shifted its position and bits of earth fell from it, landing with distinctly heard thuds on the ground below and on the deck of the ship.

'Then you must kill us to obtain it,' Elric said.

'Kill? Grome does not kill mortals. He kills nothing. Grome builds. Grome brings to life.'

'You have already killed three of our company,' Elric pointed out. 'Three are dead, King Grome, because you made the land-storm.'

Grome's great brows drew together and he scratched his great head, causing an immense rustling noise to sound. 'Grome does not kill,' he said again.

'King Grome has killed,' said Elric reasonably. 'Three lives lost.'

Grome grunted. 'But I want my ship.'

'The ship is lent to us by your brother. We cannot give it to you. Besides, we sail in it for a purpose – a noble purpose, I think. We ... '

'I know nothing of "purposes" – and care nothing for you. I want my ship. My brother should not have lent it to you. I had almost forgotten it. But now that I remember it, I want it.'

'Will you not accept something else in place of the ship, King Grome?' said Dyvim Tvar suddenly. 'Some other gift.'

Grome shook his monstrous head. 'How could a mortal give me something? It is mortals who take from me all the time. They steal my bones and my blood and my flesh. Could you give me back all that your kind has taken?'

'Is there not one thing?' Elric said.

Grome closed his eyes.

'Precious metals? Jewels?' suggested Dyvim Tvar. 'We have many such in Melniboné.'

'I have plenty,' said King Grome.

Elric shrugged in despair. 'How can we bargain with a god, Dyvim Tvar?' He gave a bitter smile. 'What can the Lord of the Soil desire? More sun, more rain? These are not ours to give.'

'I am a rough sort of god,' said Grome, 'if indeed god I am. But I did not mean to kill your comrades. I have an idea. Give me the bodies of the slain. Bury them in my earth.'

Elric's heart leapt. 'That is all you wish of us?'

'It would seem much to me.'

'And for that you will let us sail on?'

'On water, aye,' growled Grome. 'But I do not see why I should allow you to sail over my land. It is too much to expect of me. You can go to yonder lake, but from now this ship will only possess the properties bestowed upon it by my brother Straasha. No longer shall it cross my domain.'

'But, King Grome, we need this ship. We are upon urgent business. We need to sail to the city yonder.' Elric pointed in the direction of Dhoz-Kam.

'You may go to the lake, but after that the ship will sail only on water. Now give me what I ask.'

Elric called down to the bosun who, for the first time, seemed amazed by what he was witnessing. 'Bring up the bodies of the three dead men.'

The bodies were brought up from below. Grome stretched out one of his great, earthy hands and picked them up.

'I thank you,' he growled. 'Farewell.'

And slowly Grome began to descend into the ground, his whole huge frame becoming, atom by atom, absorbed with the earth until he was gone.

And then the ship was moving again, slowly towards the lake, on the last short voyage it would ever make upon the land.

'And thus our plans are thwarted,' said Elric.

Dyvim Tvar looked miserably towards the shining lake. 'Aye. So much for that scheme. I hesitate to suggest this to you, Elric, but I fear we must resort to sorcery again if we are to stand any chance of achieving our goal.'

Elric sighed.

'I fear we must,' he said.

8

The City and the Mirror

Prince Yyrkoon was pleased. His plans went well. He peered through the high fence which enclosed the flat roof of his house (three storeys high and the finest in Dhoz-Kam); he looked out towards the harbour at his splendid, captured fleet. Every ship which had come to Dhoz-Kam and which had not flown the standard of a powerful nation had been easily taken after its crew had looked upon the great mirror which squatted on its pillars above the city. Demons had built those pillars and Prince Yyrkoon had paid them for their work with the souls of all those in Oin and Yu who had resisted him. Now there was one last ambition to fulfil and then he and his new followers would be on their way to Melniboné . . .

He turned and spoke to his sister. Cymoril lay on a wooden bench, staring unseeingly at the sky, clad in the filthy tatters of the dress she had been wearing when Yyrkoon abducted her from her tower.

'See our fleet, Cymoril! While the golden barges are scattered we shall sail unhampered into Imrryr and declare the city ours. Elric cannot defend himself against us now. He fell so easily into my trap. He is a fool! And you were a fool to give him your affection!'

Cymoril made no response. Through all the months she had been away, Yyrkoon had drugged her food and drink and produced in her a lassitude which rivalled Elric's undrugged condition. Yyrkoon's own experiments with his sorcerous powers had turned him gaunt, wild-eyed and somewhat mangy; he ceased to take any pains with his physical appearance. But Cymoril had a wasted, haunted look to her, for all that beauty remained. It was as if Dhoz-Kam's rundown seediness had infected them both in different ways.

'Fear not for your own future, however, my sister,' Yyrkoon continued. He chuckled. 'You shall still be empress and sit beside the emperor on his Ruby Throne. Only I shall be emperor and Elric shall die for many days and the manner of his death will be more inventive than anything he thought to do to me.'

Cymoril's voice was hollow and distant. She did not turn her head when she spoke, 'You are insane, Yyrkoon.'

'Insane? Come now, sister, is that a word that a true Melnibonéan should use? We Melnibonéans judge nothing sane or insane. What a man is – he is. What he does – he does. Perhaps you have stayed too long in the Young Kingdoms and its judgments are becoming yours. But that shall soon be righted. We shall return to the Dragon Isle in triumph and you will forget all this, just as if you yourself had looked into the Mirror of Memory.' He darted a nervous glance upwards, as if he half-expected the mirror to be turned on him.

Cymoril closed her eyes. Her breathing was heavy and very slow; she was bearing this nightmare with fortitude, certain that Elric must eventually rescue her from it. That hope was all that had stopped her from destroying herself. If the hope went altogether, then she would bring about her own death and be done with Yyrkoon and all his horrors.

'Did I tell you that last night I was successful? I raised demons, Cymoril. Such powerful, dark demons. I learned from them all that was left for me to learn. And I opened the Shade Gate at last. Soon I shall pass through it and there I shall find what I seek. I shall become the most powerful mortal on earth. Did I tell you all this, Cymoril?'

He had, in fact, repeated himself several times that morning, but Cymoril had paid no more attention to him than she did now. She felt so tired. She tried to sleep. She said slowly, as if to remind herself of something: 'I hate you, Yyrkoon.'

'Ah, but you shall love me soon, Cymoril. Soon.'

'Elric will come . . . '

'Elric! Ha! He sits twiddling his thumbs in his tower, waiting for news that will never come – save when I bring it to him!'

'Elric will come,' she said.

Yyrkoon snarled. A brute-faced Oinish girl brought him his morning wine. Yyrkoon seized the cup and sipped the stuff. Then he spat it at the girl who, trembling, ducked away. Yyrkoon took the jug and empt-ied it onto the white dust of the roof. 'This is Elric's thin blood. This is how it will flow away!'

But again Cymoril was not listening. She was trying to remember her albino lover and the few sweet days they had spent together since they were children.

Yyrkoon hurled the empty jug at the girl's head, but she was adept at dodging him. As she dodged, she murmured her standard response to all his attacks and insults. 'Thank you, Demon Lord,' she said. 'Thank you, Demon Lord.'

Yyrkoon laughed. 'Aye. Demon Lord. Your folk are right to call me that, for I rule more demons than I rule men. My power increases every day!'

The Oinish girl hurried away to fetch more wine, for she knew he would be calling for it in a moment. Yyrkoon crossed the roof to stare through the slats in the fence at the proof of his power, but as he looked upon his ships he heard sounds of confusion from the other side of the roof. Could the Yurits and the Oinish be fighting amongst themselves? Where were their Imrryrian centurions? Where was Captain Valharik?

He almost ran across the roof, passing Cymoril who appeared to be sleeping, and peered down into the streets.

'Fire?' he murmured. 'Fire?'

It was true that the streets appeared to be on fire. And yet it was not an ordinary fire. Balls of fire seemed to drift about, igniting rush-thatched roofs, doors, anything which would easily burn – as an invading army might put a village to the torch.

Yyrkoon scowled, thinking at first that he had been careless and some spell of his had turned against him, but then he looked over the burning houses at the river and he saw a strange ship sailing there, a ship of great grace and beauty, that somehow seemed more a creation of nature than of man – and he knew they were under attack. But who would attack Dhoz-Kam? There was no loot worth the effort. It could not be Imrryrians . . .

It could not be Elric.

'It must not be Elric,' he growled. 'The Mirror. It must be turned upon the invaders.'

'And upon yourself, brother?' Cymoril had risen unsteadily and leaned against a table. She was smiling. 'You were too confident, Yyrkoon. Elric comes.'

'Elric! Nonsense! Merely a few barbarian raiders from the interior. Once they are in the centre of the city, we shall be able to use the Mirror of Memory upon them.' He ran to the trapdoor which led down into his house. 'Captain Valharik! Valharik where are you?'

Valharik appeared in the room below. He was sweating. There was a blade in his gloved hand, though he did not seem to have been in any fighting as yet.

'Make the mirror ready, Valharik. Turn it upon the attackers.'

'But, my lord, we might . . . '

'Hurry! Do as I say. We'll soon have these barbarians added to our own strength – along with their ships.'

'Barbarians, my lord? Can barbarians command the fire elementals?

These things we fight are flame spirits. They cannot be slain any more than fire itself can be slain.'

'Fire can be slain by water,' Prince Yyrkoon reminded his lieutenant. 'By water, Captain Valharik. Have you forgotten?'

'But, Prince Yyrkoon, we have tried to quench the spirits with water – and the water will not move from our buckets. Some powerful sorcerer commands the invaders. He has the aid of the spirits of fire *and* water.'

'You are mad, Captain Valharik,' said Yyrkoon firmly. 'Mad. Prepare the mirror and let us have no more of these stupidities.'

Valharik wetted his dry lips. 'Aye, my lord.' He bowed his head and went to do his master's bidding.

Again Yyrkoon went to the fence and looked through. There were men in the streets now, fighting his own warriors, but smoke obscured his view, he could not make out the identities of any of the invaders. 'Enjoy your petty victory,' Yyrkoon chuckled, 'for soon the mirror will take away your minds and you will become my slaves.'

'It is Elric,' said Cymoril quietly. She smiled. 'Elric comes to take vengeance on you, brother.'

Yyrkoon sniggered. 'Think you? Think you? Well, should that be the case, he'll find me gone, for I still have a means of evading him – and he'll find you in a condition which will not please him (though it will cause him considerable anguish). But it is not Elric. It is some crude shaman from the steppes to the east of here. He will soon be in my power.'

Cymoril, too, was peering through the fence.

'Elric,' she said. 'I can see his helm.'

'What?' Yyrkoon pushed her aside. There, in the streets, Imrryrian fought Imrryrian, there was no longer any doubt of that. Yyrkoon's men – Imrryrian, Oinish and Yurit – were being pushed back. And at the head of the attacking Imrryrians could be seen a black dragon helm such as only one Melnibonéan wore. It was Elric's helm. And Elric's sword, that had once belonged to Earl Aubec of Malador, rose and fell and was bright with blood which glistened in the morning sunshine.

For a moment Yyrkoon was overwhelmed with despair. He groaned. 'Elric. Elric. Elric. Ah, how we continue to underestimate each other! What curse is on us?'

Cymoril had flung back her head and her face had come to life again. 'I said he would come, brother!'

Yyrkoon whirled on her. 'Aye – he has come – and the mirror will rob him of his brain and he will turn into my slave, believing anything I care to put in his skull. This is even sweeter than I planned, sister.

Ha!' He looked up and then flung his arms across his eyes as he realized what he had done. 'Quickly – below – into the house – the mirror begins to turn.' There came a great creaking of gears and pulleys and chains as the terrible Mirror of Memory began to focus on the streets below. 'It will be only a little while before Elric has added himself and his men to my strength. What a splendid irony!' Yyrkoon hurried his sister down the steps leading from the roof and he closed the trapdoor behind him. 'Elric himself will help in the attack on Imrryr. He will destroy his own kind. He will oust himself from the Ruby Throne!'

'Do you not think that Elric has anticipated the threat of the Mirror of Memory, brother?' Cymoril said with relish.

'Anticipate it, aye – but resist it he cannot. He must see to fight. He must either be cut down or open his eyes. No man with eyes can be safe from the power of the mirror.' He glanced around the crudely furnished room. 'Where is Valharik? Where is the cur?'

Valharik came running in. 'The mirror is being turned, my lord, but it will affect our own men, too. I fear . . . '

'Then cease to fear. What if our own men are drawn under its influence? We can soon feed what they need to know back into their brains – at the same time as we feed our defeated foes. You are too nervous, Captain Valharik.'

'But Elric leads them . . . '

'And Elric's eyes *are* eyes – though they look like crimson stones. He will fare no better than his men.'

In the streets around Prince Yyrkoon's house Elric, Dyvim Tvar and their Imrryrians pushed on, forcing back their demoralised opponents. The attackers had lost barely a man, whereas many Oinish and Yurits lay dead in the streets, beside a few of their renegade Imrryrian commanders. The flame elementals, whom Elric had summoned with some effort, were beginning to disperse, for it cost them dear to spend so much time entirely within Elric's plane, but the necessary advantage had been gained and there was now little question of who would win as a hundred or more houses blazed throughout the city, igniting others and requiring attention from the defenders lest the whole squalid place burn down about their ears. In the harbour, too, ships were burning.

Dyvim Tvar was the first to notice the mirror beginning to swing into focus on the streets. He pointed a warning finger, then turned, blowing on his war-horn and ordering forward the troops who, up to now, had played no part in the fighting. 'Now you must lead us!' he cried, and he lowered his helm over his face. The eyeholes of the helm had been blocked so that he could not see through.

Slowly Elric lowered his own helm until he was in darkness. The sound of fighting continued however, as the veterans who had sailed with them from Melniboné, set to work in their place and the other troops fell back. The leading Imrryrians had not blocked their eyeholes.

Elric prayed that the scheme would work.

Yyrkoon, peeking cautiously through a chink in a heavy curtain, said querulously: 'Valharik? They fight on. Why is that? Is not the mirror focussed?'

'It should be, my lord.'

'Then, see for yourself, the Imrryrians continue to forge through our defenders – and our men are beginning to come under the influence of the mirror. What is wrong, Valharik? What is wrong?'

Valharik drew air between his teeth and there was a certain admiration in his expression as he looked upon the fighting Imrryrians.

'They are blind,' he said. 'They fight by sound and touch and smell. They are blind, my lord emperor – and they lead Elric and his men whose helms are so designed they can see nothing.'

'Blind?' Yyrkoon spoke almost pathetically, refusing to understand. 'Blind?'

'Aye. Blind warriors – men wounded in earlier wars, but good fighters nonetheless. That is how Elric defeats our mirror, my lord.'

'Agh! No! No!' Yyrkoon beat heavily on his captain's back and the man shrank away. 'Elric is not cunning. He is not cunning. Some powerful demon gives him these ideas.'

'Perhaps, my lord. But are there demons more powerful than those who have aided you?'

'No,' said Yyrkoon. 'There are none. Oh, that I could summon some of them now! But I have expended my powers in opening the Shade Gate. I should have anticipated . . . I could not anticipate . . . Oh Elric! I shall yet destroy you, when the runeblades are mine!' Then Yyrkoon frowned. 'But how could he have been prepared? What demon . . . ? Unless he summoned Arioch himself? But he has not the power to summon Arioch. I could not summon him . . . '

And then, as if in reply, Yyrkoon heard Elric's battle song sounding from the nearby streets. And that song answered the question.

'Arioch! Arioch! Blood and souls for my lord Arioch!'

'Then I must have the runeblades. I must pass through the Shade Gate.

There I still have allies – supernatural allies who shall deal easily with Elric, if need be. But I need time . . . ' Yyrkoon mumbled to himself as he paced about the room. Valharik continued to watch the fighting.

'They come closer,' said the captain.

Cymoril smiled. 'Closer, Yyrkoon? Who is the fool now? Elric? Or you?'

'Be still! I think. I think . . . ' Yyrkoon fingered his lips.

Then a light came into his eye and he looked cunningly at Cymoril for a second before turning his attention to Captain Valharik.

'Valharik, you must destroy the Mirror of Memory.'

'Destroy it? But it is our only weapon, my lord?'

'Exactly – but is it not useless now?'

'Aye.'

'Destroy it and it will serve us again.' Yyrkoon flicked a long finger in the direction of the door. 'Go. Destroy the mirror.'

'But, Prince Yyrkoon – emperor, I mean – will that not have the effect of robbing us of our only weapon?'

'Do as I say, Valharik! Or perish!'

'But how shall I destroy it, my lord?'

'Your sword. You must climb the column *behind* the face of the mirror. Then, without looking into the mirror itself, you must swing your sword against it and smash it. It will break easily. You know the precautions I have had to take to make sure that it was not harmed.'

'Is that all I must do?'

'Aye. Then you are free from my service – you may escape or do whatever else you wish to do.'

'Do we not sail against Melniboné?'

'Of course not. I have devised another method of taking the Dragon Isle.'

Valharik shrugged. His expression showed that he had never really believed Yyrkoon's assurances. But what else had he to do but follow Yyrkoon, when fearful torture awaited him at Elric's hands? With shoulders bowed, the captain slunk away to do his prince's work.

'And now, Cymoril . . . ' Yyrkoon grinned like a ferret as he reached out to grab his sister's soft shoulders. 'Now to prepare you for your lover, Elric.'

One of the blind warriors cried: 'They no longer resist us, my lord. They are limp and allow themselves to be cut down where they stand. Why is this?'

'The mirror has robbed them of their memories,' Elric called, turning his own blind head towards the sound of the warrior's voice. 'You can lead us into a building now – where, with luck, we shall not glimpse the mirror.'

At last they stood within what appeared to Elric, as he lifted his helm, to be a warehouse of some kind. Luckily it was large enough to hold their entire force and when they were all inside Elric had the doors shut while they debated their next action.

'We should find Yyrkoon,' Dyvim Tvar said. 'Let us interrogate one of those warriors . . . '

'There'll be little point in that, my friend,' Elric reminded him. 'Their minds are gone. They'll remember nothing at all. They do not at present remember even what they are, let alone who. Go to the shutters yonder, where the mirror's influence cannot reach, and see if you can see the building most likely to be occupied by my cousin.'

Dyvim Tvar crossed swiftly to the shutters and looked cautiously out. 'Aye – there's a building larger than the rest and I see some movement within, as if the surviving warriors were regrouping. It's likely that's Yyrkoon's stronghold. It should be easily taken.'

Elric joined him. 'Aye. I agree with you. We'll find Yyrkoon there. But we must hurry, lest he decides to slay Cymoril. We must work out the best means of reaching the place and instruct our blind warriors as to how many streets, how many houses and so forth, we must pass.'

'What is that strange sound?' One of the blind warriors raised his head. 'Like the distant ringing of a gong.'

'I hear it too,' said another blind man.

And now Elric heard it. A sinister noise. It came from the air above them. It shivered through the atmosphere.

'The mirror!' Dyvim Tvar looked up. 'Has the mirror some property we did not anticipate?'

'Possibly . . . ' Elric tried to remember what Arioch had told him. But Arioch had been vague. He had said nothing of this dreadful, mighty sound, this shattering clangour as if . . . ' He is breaking the mirror!' he said. 'But why?' There was something more now, something brushing at his brain. As if the sound were, itself, sentient.

'Perhaps Yyrkoon is dead and his magic dies with him,' Dyvim Tvar began. And then he broke off with a groan.

The noise was louder, more intense, bringing sharp pain to his ears.

And now Elric knew. He blocked his ears with his gauntleted hands. The memories in the mirror. They were flooding into his mind. The mirror had been smashed and was releasing all the memories it had stolen over the centuries – the aeons, perhaps. Many of those memories were not mortal. Many were the memories of beasts and intelligent creatures which had existed even before Melniboné. And the

94

memories warred for a place in Elric's skull – in the skulls of all the Imrryrians – in the poor, tortured skulls of the men outside whose pitiful screams could be heard rising from the streets – and in the skull of Captain Valharik, the turncoat, as he lost his footing on the great column and fell with the shards from the mirror to the ground far below.

But Elric did not hear Captain Valharik scream and he did not hear Valharik's body crash first to a roof-top and then into the street where it lay all broken beneath the broken mirror.

Elric lay upon the stone floor of the warehouse and he writhed, as his comrades writhed, trying to clear his head of a million memories that were not his own – of loves, of hatreds, of strange experiences and ordinary experiences, of wars and journeys, of the faces of relatives who were not his relatives, of men and women and children, of animals, of ships and cities, of fights, of lovemaking, of fears and desires – and the memories fought each other for possession of his crowded skull, threatening to drive his own memories (and thus his own character) from his head. And as Elric writhed upon the ground, clutching at his ears, he spoke a word over and over again in an effort to cling to his own identity.

'Elric. Elric. Elric.'

And gradually, by an effort which he had experienced only once before when he had summoned Arioch to the plane of the Earth, he managed to extinguish all those alien memories and assert his own until, shaken and feeble, he lowered his hands from his ears and no longer shouted his own name. And then he stood up and looked about him.

More than two thirds of his men were dead, blind or otherwise. The big bosun was dead, his eyes wide and staring, his lips frozen in a scream, his right eye-socket raw and bleeding from where he had tried to drag his eye from it. All the corpses lay in unnatural positions, all had their eyes open (if they had eyes) and many bore the marks of self-mutilation, while others had vomited and others had dashed their brains against a wall. Dyvim Tvar was alive, but curled up in a corner, mumbling to himself and Elric thought he might be mad. Some of the other survivors were, indeed, mad, but they were quiet, they afforded no danger. Only five, including Elric, seemed to have resisted the alien memories and retained their own sanity. It seemed to Elric, as he stumbled from corpse to corpse, that most of the men had had their hearts fail.

'Dyvim Tvar?' Elric put his hand on his friend's shoulder. 'Dyvim Tvar?'

Dyvim Tvar took his head from his arm and looked into Elric's eyes. In Dyvim Tvar's own eyes was the experience of a score of millennia and there was irony there, too. 'I live, Elric.'

'Few of us live now.'

A little later they left the warehouse, no longer needing to fear the mirror, and found that all the streets were full of the dead who had received the mirror's memories. Stiff bodies reached out hands to them. Dead lips formed silent pleas for help. Elric tried not to look at them as he pressed through them, but his desire for vengeance upon his cousin was even stronger now.

They reached the house. The door was open and the ground floor was crammed with corpses. There was no sign of Prince Yyrkoon.

Elric and Dyvim Tvar led the few Imrryrians who were still sane up the steps, past more imploring corpses, until they reached the top floor of the house.

And here they found Cymoril.

She was lying upon a couch and she was naked. There were runes painted on her flesh and the runes were, in themselves, obscene. Her eyelids were heavy and she did not at first recognize them. Elric rushed to her side and cradled her body in his arms. The body was oddly cold.

'He – he makes me – sleep . . . ' said Cymoril. 'A sorcerous sleep – from which – only he can wake me . . . ' She gave a great yawn. 'I have stayed awake – this long – by an effort of – will – for Elric comes . . . '

'Elric is here,' said her lover, softly. 'I am Elric, Cymoril.'

'Elric?' She relaxed in his arms. 'You – you must find Yyrkoon – for only he can wake me . . . '

'Where has he gone?' Elric's face had hardened. His crimson eyes were fierce. 'Where?'

'To find the two black swords – the runeswords – of – our ancestors – Mournblade . . . '

'And Stormbringer,' said Elric grimly. 'Those swords are cursed. But where has he gone, Cymoril? How has he escaped us?'

'Through – through – through the – Shade Gate – he conjured it – he made the most fearful pacts with demons to go through . . . The – other – room . . . '

Now Cymoril slept, but there seemed to be a certain peace on her face.

Elric watched as Dyvim Tvar crossed the room, sword in hand, and flung the door open. A dreadful stench came from the next room, which was in darkness. Something flickered on the far side.

'Aye – that's sorcery, right enough,' said Elric. 'And Yyrkoon has thwarted me. He conjured the Shade Gate and passed through it into some netherworld. Which one, I'll never know, for there is an infinity of them. Oh, Arioch, I would give much to follow my cousin!'

'*Then follow him you shall,*' said a sweet, sardonic voice in Elric's head.

At first the albino thought it was a vestige of a memory still fighting for possession of his head, but then he knew that Arioch spoke to him.

'*Dismiss your followers that I may speak with thee,*' said Arioch.

Elric hesitated. He wished to be alone – but not with Arioch. He wished to be with Cymoril, for Cymoril was making him weep. Tears already flowed from his crimson eyes.

'*What I have to say could result in Cymoril being restored to her normal state,*' said the voice. '*And, moreover, it will help you defeat Yyrkoon and be revenged upon him. Indeed, it could make you the most powerful mortal there has ever been.*'

Elric looked up at Dyvim Tvar, 'Would you and your men leave me alone for a few moments?'

'Of course.' Dyvim Tvar led his men away and shut the door behind him.

Arioch stood leaning against the same door. Again he had assumed the shape and poise of a handsome youth. His smile was friendly and open and only the ancient eyes belied his appearance.

'It is time to seek the black swords yourself, Elric,' said Arioch. 'Lest Yyrkoon reach them first. I warn you of this – with the runeblades Yyrkoon will be so powerful he will be able to destroy half the world without thinking of it. That is why your cousin risks the dangers of the world beyond the Shade Gate. If Yyrkoon possesses those swords before you find them, it will mean the end of you, of Cymoril, of the Young Kingdoms and, quite possibly, the destruction of Melniboné, too. I will help you enter the netherworld to seek for the twin rune-swords.'

Elric said musingly: 'I have often been warned of the dangers of seeking the swords – and the worse dangers of owning them. I think I must consider another plan, my lord Arioch.'

'There is no other plan. Yyrkoon desires the swords if you do not. With Mournblade in one hand and Stormbringer in the other, he will be invincible, for the swords give their user power. Immense power.' Arioch paused.

'You must do as I say. It is to your advantage.'

'And to yours, Lord Arioch?'

'Aye – to mine. I am not entirely selfless.'

Elric shook his head. 'I am confused. There has been too much of

97

the supernatural about this affair. I suspect the gods of manipulating us . . . '

'The gods serve only those who are willing to serve them. And the gods serve destiny, also.'

'I like it not. To stop Yyrkoon is one thing, to assume his ambitions and take the swords myself – that is another thing.'

'It is your destiny.'

'Cannot I change my destiny?'

Arioch shook his head. 'No more than can I.'

Elric stroked sleeping Cymoril's hair. 'I love her. She is all I desire.'

'You shall not wake her if Yyrkoon finds the blades before you do.'

'And how shall I find the blades?'

'Enter the Shade Gate – I have kept it open, though Yyrkoon thinks it closed – then you must seek the Tunnel Under the Marsh which leads to the Pulsing Cavern. In that chamber the runeswords are kept. They have been kept there ever since your ancestors relinquished them . . . '

'Why were they relinquished?'

'Your ancestors lacked courage.'

'Courage to face what?'

'Themselves.'

'You are cryptic, my lord Arioch.'

'That is the way of the Lords of the Higher Worlds. Hurry. Even I cannot keep the Shade Gate open long.'

'Very well. I will go.'

And Arioch vanished immediately.

Elric called in a hoarse, cracking voice for Dyvim Tvar who entered at once.

'Elric? What has happened in here? Is it Cymoril? You look . . . '

'I am going to follow Yyrkoon – alone, Dyvim Tvar. You must make your way back to Melniboné with those of our men who remain. Take Cymoril with you. If I do not return in reasonable time, you must declare her empress. If she still sleeps, then you must rule as regent until she wakes.'

Dyvim Tvar said softly. 'Do you know what you do, Elric?'

Elric shook his head.

'No, Dyvim Tvar, I do not.'

He got to his feet and staggered towards the other room where the Shade Gate waited for him.

THREE

And now there is no turning back at all. Elric's destiny has been forged and fixed as surely as the hellswords were forged and fixed aeons before. Was there ever a point where he might have turned off this road to despair, damnation and destruction? Or has he been doomed since before his birth? Doomed through a thousand incarnations to know little else but sadness and struggle, loneliness and remorse – eternally the champion of some unknown cause?

1

Through the Shade Gate

And Elric stepped into a shadow and found himself in a world of shadows. He turned, but the shadow through which he had entered now faded and was gone. Old Aubec's sword was in Elric's hand, the black helm and the black armour were upon his body and only these were familiar, for the land was dark and gloomy as if contained in a vast cave whose walls, though invisible, were oppressive and tangible. And Elric regretted the hysteria, the weariness of brain, which had given him the impulse to obey his patron demon Arioch and plunge through the Shade Gate. But regret was useless now, so he forgot it.

Yyrkoon was nowhere to be seen. Either Imrryr's cousin had had a steed awaiting him or else, more likely, he had entered this world at a slightly different angle (for all the planes were said to turn about each other) and was thus either nearer or farther from their mutual goal. The air was rich with brine — so rich that Elric's nostrils felt as if they had been packed with salt — it was almost like walking under water and just being able to breathe the water itself. Perhaps this explained why it was so difficult to see any great distance in any direction, why there were so many shadows, why the sky was like a veil which hid the roof of a cavern. Elric sheathed his sword, there being no evident danger present at that moment, and turned slowly, trying to get some kind of bearing.

It was possible that there were jagged mountains in what he judged the east, and perhaps a forest to the west. Without sun, or stars, or moon, it was hard to gauge distance or direction. He stood on a rocky plain over which whistled a cold and sluggish wind, which tugged at his cloak as if it wished to possess it. There were a few stunted, leafless trees standing in a clump about a hundred paces away. It was all that relieved the bleak plain, save for a large, shapeless slab of rock which stood a fair way beyond the trees. It was a world which seemed to have been drained of all life, where Law and Chaos had once battled and, in their conflict, destroyed all. Were there many planes such as this one? Elric wondered. And for a moment he was filled with a dreadful presentiment concerning the fate of his own rich world. He shook this mood off at once and began to walk towards the trees and the rock beyond.

He reached the trees and passed them, and the touch of his cloak on a branch broke the brittle thing which turned almost at once to ash which was scattered on the wind. Elric drew the cloak closer about his body.

As he approached the rock he became conscious of a sound which seemed to emanate from it. He slowed his pace and put his hand upon the pommel of his sword.

The noise continued – a small, rhythmic noise. Through the gloom Elric peered carefully at the rock, trying to locate the source of the sound.

And then the noise stopped and was replaced by another – a soft scuffle, a padding footfall, and then silence. Elric took a pace backward and drew Aubec's sword. The first sound had been that of a man sleeping. The second sound was that of a man waking and preparing himself either for attack or to defend himself.

Elric said: 'I am Elric of Melniboné. I am a stranger here.'

And an arrow slid past his helm almost at the same moment as a bowstring sounded. Elric flung himself to one side and sought about for cover, but there was no cover save the rock behind which the archer hid.

And now a voice came from behind the rock. It was a firm, rather bleak voice. It said:

'That was not meant to harm you but to display my skill in case you considered harming me. I have had my fill of demons in this world and you look like the most dangerous demon of all, Whiteface.'

'I am mortal,' said Elric, straightening up and deciding that if he must die it would be best to die with some sort of dignity.

'You spoke of Melniboné. I have heard of the place. An isle of demons.'

'Then you have not heard enough of Melniboné. I am mortal as are all my folk. Only the ignorant think us demons.'

'I am not ignorant, my friend. I am a Warrior Priest of Phum, born to that caste and the inheritor of all its knowledge and, until recently, the Lords of Chaos themselves were my patrons. Then I refused to serve them longer and was exiled to this plane by them. Perhaps the same fate befell you, for the folk of Melniboné serve Chaos, do they not?'

'Aye. And I know of Phum – it lies in the unmapped East – beyond the Weeping Waste, beyond the Sighing Desert, beyond even Elwher. It is one of the oldest of the Young Kingdoms.'

'All that is so – though I dispute that the East is unmapped, save by the savages of the West. So you are, indeed, to share my exile, it seems.'

'I am not exiled. I am upon a quest. When the quest is done, I shall return to my own world.'

'Return, say you? That interests me, my pale friend. I had thought return impossible.'

'Perhaps it is and I have been tricked. And if your own powers have not found you a way to another plane, perhaps mine will not save me either.'

'Powers? I have none since I relinquished my servitude to Chaos. Well, friend, do you intend to fight me?'

'There is only one upon this plane I would fight and it is not you, Warrior Priest of Phum.' Elric sheathed his sword and at the same moment the speaker rose from behind the rock, replacing a scarlet-fletched arrow in a scarlet quiver.

'I am Rackhir,' said the man. 'Called the Red Archer for, as you see, I affect scarlet dress. It is a habit of the Warrior Priests of Phum to choose but a single colour to wear. It is the only loyalty to tradition I still possess.' He had on a scarlet jerkin, scarlet breeks, scarlet shoes and a scarlet cap with a scarlet feather in it. His bow was scarlet and the pommel of his sword glowed ruby-red. His face, which was aquiline and gaunt, as if carved from fleshless bone, was weather-beaten, and that was brown. He was tall and he was thin, but muscles rippled on his arms and torso. There was irony in his eyes and something of a smile upon his thin lips, though the face showed that it had been through much experience, little of it pleasant.

'An odd place to choose for a quest,' said the Red Archer, standing with hands on hips and looking Elric up and down. 'But I'll strike a bargain with you if you're interested.'

'If the bargain suits me, archer, I'll agree to it, for you seem to know more of this world than do I.'

'Well – you must find something here and then leave, whereas I have nothing at all to do here and wish to leave. If I help you in your quest, will you take me with you when you return to our own plane?'

'That seems a fair bargain, but I cannot promise what I have no power to give. I will say only this – if it is possible for me to take you back with me to our own plane, either before or after I have finished my quest, I will do it.'

'That is reasonable,' said Rackhir the Red Archer. 'Now – tell me what you seek.'

'I seek two swords, forged millennia ago by immortals, used by my ancestors but then relinquished by them and placed upon this plane. The swords are large and heavy and black and they have cryptic runes carved into their blades. I was told that I would find them in the Pulsing Cavern which is reached through the Tunnel Under the Marsh. Have you heard of either of these places?'

'I have not. Nor have I heard of the two black swords.' Rackhir rubbed his bony chin. 'Though I remember reading something in one of the Books of Phum and what I read disturbed me . . . '

'The swords are legendary. Many books make some small reference to them – almost always mysterious. There is said to be one tome which records the history of the swords and all who have used them – and all who will use them in the future – a timeless book which contains all time. Some call it the Chronicle of the Black Sword and in it, it is said, men may read their whole destinies.'

'I know nothing of that, either. It is not one of the Books of Phum. I fear, Comrade Elric, that we shall have to venture to the City of Ameeron and ask your questions of the inhabitants there.'

'There is a city upon this plane?'

'Aye – a city. I stayed but a short time in it, preferring the wilderness. But with a friend, it might be possible to bear the place a little longer.'

'Why is Ameeron unsuited to your taste?'

'Its citizens are not happy. Indeed, they are a most depressed and depressing group, for they are all, you see, exiles or refugees or travellers between the worlds who lost their way and never found it again. No one lives in Ameeron by choice.'

'A veritable City of the Damned.'

'As the poet might remark, aye.' Rackhir offered Elric a sardonic wink. 'But I sometimes think all cities are that.'

'What is the nature of this plane where are, as far as I can tell, no planets, no moon, no sun? It has something of the air of a great cavern.'

'There is, indeed, a theory that it is a sphere buried in an infinity of rock. Others say that it lies in the future of our own Earth – a future where the universe has died. I heard a thousand theories during the short space of time I spent in the City of Ameeron. All it seemed to me, were of equal value. All, it seemed to me, could be correct. Why not? There are some who believe that everything is a Lie. Conversely, everything could be the Truth.'

It was Elric's turn to remark ironically: 'You are a philosopher, then, as well as an archer, friend Rackhir of Phum?'

Rackhir laughed. 'If you like! It is such thinking that weakened my loyalty to Chaos and led me to this pass. I have heard that there is a city called Tanelorn which may sometimes be found on the shifting shores of the Sighing Desert. If I ever return to our own world, Comrade Elric, I shall seek that city, for I have heard that peace may be found there – that such debates as the nature of Truth are considered meaningless. That men are content merely to exist in Tanelorn.'

'I envy those who dwell in Tanelorn,' said Elric.

Rackhir sniffed. 'Aye. But it would probably prove a disappointment, if found. Legends are best left as legends and attempts to make them real are rarely successful. Come – yonder lies Ameeron and that, sad to say, is more typical of most cities one comes across – on any plane.'

The two tall men, both outcasts in their different ways, began to trudge through the gloom of that desolate wasteland.

2

In the City of Ameeron

The city of Ameeron came in sight and Elric had never seen such a place before. Ameeron made Dhoz-Kam seem like the cleanest and most well-run settlement there could be. The city lay below the plain of rocks, in a shallow valley over which hung perpetual smoke: a filthy, tattered cloak meant to hide the place from the sight of men and gods.

The buildings were mostly in a state of semi-ruin or else were wholly ruined and shacks and tents erected in their place. The mixture of architectural styles – some familiar, some most alien – was such that Elric was hard put to see one building which resembled another. There were shanties and castles, cottages, towers and forts, plain, square villas and wooden huts heavy with carved ornamentation. Others seemed merely piles of rock with a jagged opening at one end for a door. But none looked well – could not have looked well in that landscape under that perpetually gloomy sky.

Here and there red fires sputtered, adding to the smoke, and the smell as Elric and Rackhir reached the outskirts was rich with a great variety of stinks.

'Arrogance, rather than pride, is the paramount quality of most of Ameeron's residents,' said Rackhir, wrinkling his hawklike nose. 'Where they have any qualities of character left at all.'

Elric trudged through filth. Shadows scuttled amongst the close-packed buildings. 'Is there an inn, perhaps, where we can enquire after the Tunnel Under the Marsh and its whereabouts?'

'No inn. By and large the inhabitants keep themselves to themselves . . . '

'A city square where folk meet?'

'This city has no centre. Each resident or group of residents built their own dwelling where they felt like it, or where there was space, and they come from all planes and all ages, thus the confusion, the decay and the oldness of many of the places. Thus the filth, the hopelessness, the decadence of the majority.'

'How do they live?'

'They live off each other, by and large. They trade with demons who occasionally visit Ameeron from time to time . . . '

'Demons?'

'Aye. And the bravest hunt the rats which dwell in the caverns below the city.'

'What demons are these?'

'Just creatures, mainly minor minions of Chaos, who want something that the Ameeronese can supply – a stolen soul or two, a baby, perhaps (though few are born here) – you can imagine what else, if you've knowledge of what demons normally demand from sorcerers.'

'Aye. I can imagine. So Chaos can come and go on this plane as it pleases?'

'I'm not sure it's quite as easy. But it is certainly easier for the demons to travel back and forth here than it would be for them to travel back and forth in our plane.'

'Have you seen any of these demons?'

'Aye. The usual bestial sort. Coarse, stupid and powerful – many of them were once human before electing to bargain with Chaos. Now they are mentally and physically warped into foul, demon shapes.'

Elric found Rackhir's words not to his taste. 'Is that ever the fate of those who bargain with Chaos?' he said.

'You should know, if you come from Melniboné. I know that in Phum it is rarely the case. But it seems that the higher the stakes the subtler are the changes a man undergoes when Chaos agrees to trade with him.'

Elric sighed. 'Where shall we enquire of our Tunnel Under the Marsh?'

'There was an old man . . . ' Rackhir began, and then a grunt behind him made him pause.'

Another grunt.

A face with tusks in it emerged from a patch of darkness formed by a fallen slab of masonry. The face grunted again.

'Who are you?' said Elric, his sword-hand ready.

'Pig,' said the face with tusks in it. Elric was not certain whether he was being insulted or whether the creature was describing himself.

'Pig.'

Two more faces with tusks in them came out of the patch of darkness. 'Pig,' said one.

'Pig,' said another.

'Snake,' said a voice behind Elric and Rackhir. Elric turned while Rackhir continued to watch the pigs. A tall youth stood there. Where his head would have been sprouted the bodies of about fifteen good-sized snakes. The head of each snake glared at Elric. The tongues flickered and they all opened their mouths at exactly the same moment to say again:

'Snake.'

'Thing,' said another voice. Elric glanced in that direction, gasped, drew his sword and felt nausea sweep through him.

Then Pigs, Snake and Thing were upon them.

Rackhir took one Pig before it could move three paces. His bow was off his back and strung and a red-fletched arrow nocked and shot, all in a second. He had time to shoot one more Pig and then drop his bow to draw his sword. Back to back he and Elric prepared to defend themselves against the demons' attack. Snake was bad enough, with its fifteen darting heads hissing and snapping with teeth which dripped venom, but Thing kept changing its form – first an arm would emerge, then a face would appear from the shapeless, heaving flesh which shuffled implacably closer.

'Thing!' it shouted. Two swords slashed at Elric who was dealing with the last Pig and missed his stroke so that instead of running the Pig through the heart, he took him in a lung. Pig staggered backward and slumped to the ground in a pool of muck. He crawled for a moment, but then collapsed. Thing had produced a spear and Elric barely managed to deflect the cast with the flat of his sword. Now Rackhir was engaged with Snake and the two demons closed on the men, eager to make a finish of them. Half the heads of Snake lay writhing on the ground and Elric had managed to slice one hand off Thing, but the demon still seemed to have three other hands ready. It seemed to be created not from one creature but from several. Elric wondered if, through his bargaining with Arioch, this would ultimately be his fate, to be turned into a demon – a formless monster. But wasn't he already something of a monster? Didn't folk already mistake him for a demon?

These thoughts gave him strength. He yelled as he fought. 'Elric!'

And: 'Thing!' replied his adversary, also eager to assert what he regarded as the essence of his being.

Another hand flew off as Aubec's sword bit into it. Another javelin jabbed out and was knocked aside; another sword appeared and came down on Elric's helm with a force which dazed him and sent him reeling back against Rackhir who missed his thrust at Snake and was almost bitten by four of the heads. Elric chopped at the arm and the tentacle which held the sword and saw them part from the body but then become reabsorbed again. The nausea returned. Elric thrust his sword into the mass and the mass screamed: 'Thing! Thing! Thing!'

Elric thrust again and four swords and two spears waved and clashed and tried to deflect Aubec's blade.

'Thing!'

'This is Yyrkoon's work,' said Elric, 'without a doubt. He has heard that I have followed him and seeks to stop us with his demon allies.' He gritted his teeth and spoke through them. 'Unless one of these is Yyrkoon himself! Are you my cousin Yyrkoon, Thing?'

'Thing . . . ' The voice was almost pathetic. The weapons waved and clashed but they no longer darted so fiercely at Elric.

'Or are you some other old, familiar friend?'

'Thing . . . '

Elric stabbed again and again into the mass. Thick, reeking blood spurted and fell upon his armour. Elric could not understand why it had become so easy to take the attack to the demon.

'Now!' shouted a voice from above Elric's head. 'Quickly!'

Elric glanced up and saw a red face, a white beard, a waving arm. 'Don't look at me you fool! Now – strike!'

And Elric put his two hands above his sword hilt and drove the blade deep into the shapeles creature which moaned and wept and said in a small whisper 'Frank . . . ' before it died.

Rackhir thrust at the same moment and his blade went under the remaining snake heads and plunged into the chest and thence into the heart of the youth-body and his demon died, too.

The white-haired man came clambering down from the ruined arch-way on which he had been perched. He was laughing. 'Niun's sorcery still has some effect, even here, eh? I heard the tall one call his demon friends and instruct them to set upon you. It did not seem fair to me that five should attack two – so I sat upon that wall and I drew the many-armed demon's strength out of it. I still can. I still can. And now I have his strength (or a fair part of it) and feel considerably better than I have done for many a moon (if such a thing exists).'

'It said "Frank",' said Elric frowning. 'Was that a name, do you think? Its name before?'

'Perhaps,' said old Niun, 'perhaps. Poor creature. But still, it is dead now. You are not of Ameeron, you two – though I've seen you here before, red one.'

'And I've seen you,' said Rackhir with a smile. He wiped Snake's blood from his blade, using one of Snake's heads for the purpose. 'You are Niun Who Knew All.'

'Aye. Who Knew All but who now knows very little. Soon it will be over, when I have forgotten everything. Then I may return from this awful exile. It is the pact I made with Orland of the Staff. I was a fool who wished to know everything and my curiosity led me into an adventure concerning this Orland. Orland showed me the error of my ways and sent me here to forget. Sadly, as you noticed, I still remember some of my powers and my knowledge from time to time. I know you seek the Black Swords. I know you are Elric of Melniboné. I know what will become of you.'

'You know my destiny?' said Elric eagerly. 'Tell me what it is, Niun Who Knew All.'

Niun opened his mouth as if to speak but then firmly shut it again. 'No,' he said. 'I have forgotten.'

'No!' Elric made as if to seize the old man. 'No! You remember! I can see that you remember!'

'I have forgotten.' Niun lowered his head.

Rackhir took hold of Elric's arm. 'He has forgotten, Elric.'

Elric nodded. 'Very well.' Then he said, 'But have you remembered where lies the Tunnel Under the Marsh?'

'Yes. It is only a short distance from Ameeron, the Marsh itself. You go that way. Then you look for a monument in the shape of an eagle carved in black marble. At the base of the monument is the entrance to the tunnel.' Niun repeated this information parrot-fashion and when he looked up his face was clearer. 'What did I just tell you?'

Elric said: 'You gave us instructions on how to reach the entrance to the Tunnel Under the Marsh.'

'Did I?' Niun clapped his old hands. 'Splendid. I have forgotten that now, too. Who are you?'

'We are best forgotten,' said Rackhir with a gentle smile. 'Farewell, Niun and thanks.'

'Thanks for what?'

'Both for remembering and for forgetting.'

They walked on through the miserable City of Ameeron, away from the happy old sorcerer, sighting the odd face staring at them from a doorway or a window, doing their best to breathe as little of the foul air as possible.

'I think perhaps that I envy Niun alone of all the inhabitants of this desolate place,' said Rackhir.

'I pity him,' said Elric.

'Why so?'

'It occurs to me that when he has forgotten everything, he may well forget that he is allowed to leave Ameeron.'

Rackhir laughed and slapped the albino upon his black armoured back. 'You are a gloomy comrade, friend Elric. Are all your thoughts so hopeless?'

'They tend in that direction, I fear,' said Elric with a shadow of a smile.

The Tunnel Under the Marsh

And on they travelled through that sad and murky world until at last they came to the marsh.

The marsh was black. Black spiky vegetation grew in clumps here and there upon it. It was cold and it was dank; a dark mist swirled close to the surface and through the mist sometimes darted low shapes. From the mist rose a solid black object which could only be the monument described by Niun.

'The monument,' said Rackhir, stopping and leaning on his bow. 'It's well out into the marsh and there's no evident pathway leading to it. Is this a problem, do you think, Comrade Elric?'

Elric waded cautiously into the edge of the marsh. He felt the cold ooze drag at his feet. He stepped back with some difficulty.

'There must be a path,' said Rackhir, fingering his bony nose. 'Else how would your cousin cross?'

Elric looked over his shoulder at the Red Archer and he shrugged. 'Who knows? He could be travelling with sorcerous companions who have no difficulty where marshes are concerned.'

Suddenly Elric found himself sitting down upon the damp rock. The stink of brine from the marsh seemed for a moment to have overwhelmed him. He was feeling weak. The effectiveness of his drugs, last taken just as he stepped through the Shade Gate, was beginning to fade.

Rackhir came and stood by the albino. He smiled with a certain amount of bantering sympathy. 'Well, Sir Sorcerer, cannot you summon similar aid?'

Elric shook his head. 'I know little that is practical concerning the raising of small demons. Yyrkoon has all his grimoires, his favourite spells, his introductions to the demon worlds. We shall have to find a path of the ordinary kind if we wish to reach yonder monument, Warrior Priest of Phum.'

The Warrior Priest of Phum drew a red kerchief from within his tunic and blew his nose for some time. When he had finished he put down a hand, helped Elric to his feet, and began to walk along the rim of the marsh, keeping the black monument ever in sight.

It was some time later that they found a path at last and it was not a natural path but a slab of black marble extending out into the gloom of the mire, slippery to the feet and itself covered with a film of ooze.

'I would almost suspect this of being a false path – a lure to take us to our death,' said Rackhir as he and Elric stood and looked at the long slab, 'but what have we to lose now?'

'Come,' said Elric, setting foot on the slab and beginning to make his cautious way along it. In his hand he now held a torch of sorts, a bundle of sputtering reeds which gave off an unpleasant yellow light and a considerable amount of greenish smoke. It was better than nothing.

Rackhir, testing each footstep with his unstrung bow-stave, followed behind, whistling a small, complicated tune as he went along. Another of his race would have recognized the tune as the *Song of the Son of the Hero of the High Hell who is about to Sacrifice his Life*, a popular melody in Phum, particularly amongst the caste of the Warrior Priest.

Elric found the tune irritating and distracting, but he said nothing, for he concentrated every fragment of his attention on keeping his balance upon the slippery surface of the slab, which now appeared to rock slightly, as if it floated on the surface of the marsh.

And now they were halfway to the monument whose shape could be clearly distinguished: a great eagle with spread wings and a savage beak and claws extended for the kill. An eagle in the same black marble as the slab on which they tried to keep their balance. And Elric was reminded of a tomb. Had some ancient hero been buried here? Or had the tomb been built to house the Black Swords – imprison them so that they might never enter the world of men again and steal men's souls?

The slab rocked more violently. Elric tried to remain upright but swayed first on one foot and then the other, the brand waving crazily. Both feet slid from under him and he went flying into the marsh and was instantly buried up to his knees.

He began to sink.

Somehow he had managed to keep his grip on the brand and by its light he could see the red-clad archer peering forward.

'Elric?'

'I'm here, Rackhir.'

'You're sinking?'

'The marsh seems intent on swallowing me, aye.'

'Can you lie flat?'

'I can lie forward, but my legs are trapped.' Elric tried to move his body in the ooze which pressed against it. Something rushed past him in front of his face, giving voice to a kind of muted gibbering. Elric did his best to control the fear which welled up in him. 'I think you must give me up, friend Rackhir.'

'What? And lose my means of getting out of this world? You must think me more selfless than I am, Comrade Elric. Here . . . ' Rackhir carefully lowered himself to the slab and reached out his arm towards Elric. Both men were now covered in clinging slime; both shivered with cold. Rackhir stretched and stretched and Elric leaned forward as far as he could and tried to reach the hand, but it was impossible. And every second dragged him deeper into the stinking filth of the marsh.

Then Rackhir took up his bow-stave and pushed that out.

'Grab the bow, Elric. Can you?'

Leaning forward and stretching every bone and muscle in his body, Elric just managed to get a grip on the bow-stave.

'Now, I must – Ah!' Rackhir, pulling at the bow, found his own feet slipping and the slab beginning to rock quite wildly. He flung out one arm to grab the far lip of the slab and with his other hand kept a grip on the bow. 'Hurry, Elric! Hurry!'

Elric began painfully to pull himself from the ooze. The slab still rocked crazily and Rackhir's hawklike face was almost as pale as Elric's own as he desperately strove to keep his hold on both slab and bow. And then Elric, all soaked in mire, managed to reach the slab and crawl onto it, the brand still sputtering in his hand, and lie there gasping.

Rackhir, too, was short of breath, but he laughed. 'What a fish I've caught!' he said. 'The biggest yet, I'd wager!'

'I am grateful to you, Rackhir the Red Archer. I am grateful, Warrior Priest of Phum. I owe you my life,' said Elric after a while. 'And I swear that whether I'm successful in my quest or not I'll use all my powers to see you through the Shade Gate and back into the world from which we have both come.'

Rackhir shrugged and grinned. 'Now I suggest we continue towards yonder monument on our knees. Undignified it might be, but safer it is also. And it is but a short way to crawl.'

Elric agreed.

Not much more time had passed in that timeless darkness before they had reached a little moss-grown island on which stood the Monument of the Eagle, huge and heavy and towering above them into the greater gloom which was either the sky or the roof of the cavern. And at the base of the plinth they saw a low doorway. And the doorway was open.

'A trap?' mused Rackhir.

'Or does Yyrkoon assume us perished in Ameeron?' said Elric, wiping himself free of slime as best he could. He sighed. 'Let's enter and be done with it.'

And so they entered.

They found themselves in a small room. Elric cast the faint light of a brand about the place and saw another doorway. The rest of the room was featureless – each wall made of the same faintly glistening black marble. The room was filled with silence.

Neither man spoke. Both walked unfalteringly towards the next doorway and, when they found steps, began to descend the steps, which wound down and down into total darkness.

For a long time they descended, still without speaking, until eventually they reached the bottom and saw before them the entrance to a narrow tunnel which was irregularly shaped so that it seemed more the work of nature than of some intelligence. Moisture dripped from the roof of the tunnel and fell with the regularity of heartbeats to the floor, seeming to echo a deeper sound, far away, emanating from somewhere in the tunnel itself.

'This is without doubt a tunnel,' said the Red Archer, 'and it, unquestionably leads under the marsh.'

Elric felt that Rackhir shared his reluctance to enter the tunnel. He stood with the guttering brand held high, listening to the sound of the drops falling to the floor of the tunnel, trying to recognize that other sound which came so faintly from the depths.

And then he forced himself forward, almost running into the tunnel, his ears filled with a sudden roaring which might have come from within his head or from some other source in the tunnel. He heard Rackhir's footfalls behind him. He drew his sword, the sword of the dead hero Aubec, and he heard the hissing of his own breath echo from the walls of the tunnel which was now alive with sounds of every sort.

Elric shuddered, but he did not pause.

The tunnel was warm. The floor felt spongy beneath his feet, the smell of brine persisted. And now he could see that the walls of the tunnel were smoother, that they seemed to shiver with quick, regular movement. He heard Rackhir gasp behind him as the archer, too, noted the peculiar nature of the tunnel.

'It's like flesh,' murmured the Warrior Priest of Phum. 'Like flesh,'

Elric could not bring himself to reply. All his attention was required to force himself forward. He was consumed by terror. His whole body shook. He sweated and his legs threatened to buckle under him. His grip was so weak that he could barely keep his sword from falling to the floor. And there were hints of something in his memory, something which his brain refused to consider. Had he been here before? His trembling increased. His stomach turned. But he still stumbled on, the brand held before him.

And now the soft, steady thrumming sound grew louder and he saw ahead a small, almost circular aperture at the very end of the tunnel. He stopped, swaying.

'The tunnel ends,' whispered Rackhir. 'There is no way through.'

The small aperture was pulsing with a swift, strong beat.

'The Pulsing Cavern,' Elric whispered. 'That is what we should find at the end of the Tunnel Under the Marsh. That must be the entrance, Rackhir.'

'It is too small for a man to enter, Elric,' said Rackhir reasonably.

'No . . . '

Elric stumbled forward until he stood close to the opening. He sheathed his sword. He handed the brand to Rackhir and then, before the Warrior Priest of Phum could stop him, he had flung himself headfirst through the gap, wriggling his body through – and the walls of the aperture parted for him and then closed behind him, leaving Rackhir on the other side.

Elric got slowly to his feet. A faint, pinkish light now came from the walls and ahead of him was another entrance, slightly larger than the one through which he had just come. The air was warm and thick and salty. It almost stifled him. His head throbbed and his body ached and he could barely act or think, save to force himself onward. On faltering legs he flung himself towards the next entrance as the great, muffled pulsing sounded louder and louder in his ears.

'Elric!'

Rackhir stood behind him, pale and sweating. He had abandoned the brand and followed Elric through.

Elric licked dry lips and tried to speak.

Rackhir came closer.

Elric said thickly: 'Rackhir. You should not be here.'

'I said I would help.'

'Aye, but . . . '

'Then help I shall.'

Elric had no strength for arguing, so he nodded and with his hands forced back the soft walls of the second aperture and saw that it led into a cavern whose round wall quivered to a steady pulsing. And in the centre of the cavern, hanging in the air without any support at all were two swords. Two identical swords, huge and fine and black.

And standing beneath the swords, his expression gloating and greedy, stood Prince Yyrkoon of Melniboné, reaching up for them, his lips moving but no words escaping from him. And Elric himself was able to voice but one word as he climbed through and stood upon that shuddering floor. 'No,' he said.

Yyrkoon heard the word. He turned with terror in his face. He snarled when he saw Elric and then he, too, voiced a word which was at once a scream of outrage.

'No!'

With an effort Elric dragged Aubec's blade from its scabbard. But it seemed too heavy to hold upright, it tugged his arm so that it rested on the floor, his arm hanging straight at his side. Elric drew deep breaths of heavy air into his lungs. His vision was dimming. Yyrkoon had become a shadow. Only the two black swords, standing still and cool in the very centre of the circular chamber, were in focus. Elric sensed Rackhir enter the chamber and stand beside him.

'Yyrkoon,' said Elric at last, 'those swords are mine.'

Yyrkoon smiled and reached up towards the blades. A peculiar moaning sound seemed to issue from them. A faint, black radiance seemed to emanate from them. Elric saw the runes carved into them and he was afraid.

Rackhir fitted an arrow to his bow. He drew the string back to his shoulder, sighting along the arrow at Prince Yyrkoon. 'If he must die, Elric, tell me.'

'Slay him,' said Elric.

And Rackhir released the string.

But the arrow moved very slowly through the air and then hung halfway between the archer and his intended target.

Yyrkoon turned, a ghastly grin on his face. 'Mortal weapons are useless here,' he said.

Elric said to Rackhir. 'He must be right. And your life is in danger, Rackhir. Go . . . '

Rackhir gave him a puzzled look. 'No, I must stay here and help you . . . '

Elric shook his head. 'You cannot help, you will only die if you stay. Go.'

Reluctantly the Red Archer unstrung his bow, glanced suspiciously up at the two black swords, then squeezed his way through the doorway and was gone.

'Now, Yyrkoon,' said Elric, letting Aubec's sword fall to the floor. 'We must settle this, you and I.'

4

Two Black Swords

And then the runeblades Stormbringer and Mournblade were gone from where they had hung so long.

And Stormbringer had settled into Elric's right hand. And Mournblade lay in Prince Yyrkoon's right hand.

And the two men stood on opposite sides of the Pulsing Cavern and regarded first each other and then the swords they held.

The swords were singing. Their voices were faint but could be heard quite plainly. Elric lifted the huge blade easily and turned it this way and that, admiring its alien beauty.

'Stormbringer,' he said.

And then he felt afraid.

It was suddenly as if he had been born again and that this runesword was born with him. It was as if they had never been separate.

'Stormbringer.'

And the sword moaned sweetly and settled even more smoothly into his grasp.

'Stormbringer!' yelled Elric and he leapt at his cousin.

'Stormbringer!'

And he was full of fear – so full of fear. And the fear brought a wild kind of delight – a demonic need to fight and kill his cousin, to sink the blade deep into Yyrkoon's heart. To take vengeance. To spill blood. To send a soul to hell.

And now Prince Yyrkoon's cry could be heard above the thrum of the sword-voices, the drumming of the pulse of the cavern.

'Mournblade!'

And Mournblade came up to meet Stormbringer's blow and turn that blow and thrust back at Elric who swayed aside and brought Stormbringer round and down in a sidestroke which knocked Yyrkoon and Mournblade backward for an instant. But Stormbringer's next thrust was met again. And the next thrust was met. And the next. If the swordsmen were evenly matched, then so were the blades, which seemed possessed of their own wills.

And the clang of the metal upon metal turned into a wild, metallic song which the swords sang. A joyful song as if they were glad at last to be back to battling, though they battled each other.

And Elric barely saw his cousin, Prince Yyrkoon, at all, save for an occasional flash of his dark, wild face. Elric's attention was given entirely to the two black swords, for it seemed that the swords fought with the life of one of the swordsmen as a prize (or perhaps the lives of both, thought Elric) and that the rivalry between Elric and Yyrkoon was nothing compared with the brotherly rivalry between the swords who seemed full of pleasure at the chance to engage again after many millennia.

And this observation, as he fought – and fought for his soul as well as his life – gave Elric pause to consider his hatred of Yyrkoon.

Kill Yyrkoon he would, but not at the will of another power. Not to give sport to these alien swords.

Mournblade's point darted at his eyes and Stormbringer rose to deflect the thrust once more.

Elric no longer fought his cousin. He fought the will of the two black swords.

Stormbringer dashed for Yyrkoon's momentarily undefended throat. Elric clung to the sword and dragged it back, sparing his cousin's life. Stormbringer whined almost petulantly, like a dog stopped from biting an intruder.

And Elric spoke through clenched teeth. 'I'll not be your puppet, runeblade. If we must be united, let it be upon a proper understanding.'

The sword seemed to hesitate, to drop its guard, and Elric was hard put to defend himself against the whirling attack of Mournblade which, in turn, seemed to sense its advantage.

Elric felt fresh energy pour up his right arm and into his body. This was what the sword could do. With it, he needed no drugs, would never be weak again. In battle he would triumph. At peace, he could rule with pride. When he travelled, it could be alone and without fear. It was as if the sword reminded him of all these things, even as it returned Mournblade's attack.

And what must the sword have in return?

Elric knew. The sword told him, without words of any sort. Stormbringer needed to fight, for that was its reason for existence. Stormbringer needed to kill, for that was its source of energy, the lives and the souls of men, demons – even gods.

And Elric hesitated, even as his cousin gave a huge, cackling yell and dashed at him so that Mournblade glanced off his helm and he was flung backwards and down and saw Yyrkoon gripping his moaning black sword in both hands to plunge the runeblade into Elric's body.

And Elric knew he would do anything to resist that fate – for his soul to be drawn into Mournblade and his strength to feed Prince Yyrkoon's strength. And he rolled aside, very quickly, and got to one knee and turned and lifted Stormbringer with one gauntleted hand upon the blade and the other upon the hilt to take the great blow Prince Yyrkoon brought upon it. And the two black swords shrieked as if in pain, and they shivered, and black radiance poured from them as blood might pour from a man pierced by many arrows. And Elric was driven, still on his knees, away from the radiance, gasping and sighing and peering here and there for sight of Yyrkoon who had disappeared.

And Elric knew that Stormbringer spoke to him again. If Elric did not wish to die by Mournblade, then Elric must accept the bargain which the Black Sword offered.

'He must not die!' said Elric. 'I will not slay him to make sport for you!'

And through the black radiance ran Yyrkoon, snarling and snapping and whirling his runesword.

Again Stormbringer darted through an opening, and again Elric made the blade pull back and Yyrkoon was only grazed.

Stormbringer writhed in Elric's hands.

Elric said: 'You shall not be my master.'

And Stormbringer seemed to understand and become quieter, as if reconciled. And Elric laughed, thinking that he now controlled the runesword and that from now on the blade would do his bidding.

'We shall disarm Yyrkoon,' said Elric. 'We shall not kill him.'

Elric rose to his feet.

Stormbringer moved with all the speed of a needle-thin rapier. It feinted, it parried, it thrust. Yyrkoon, who had been grinning in triumph, snarled and staggered back, the grin dropping fron his sullen features.

Stormbringer now worked for Elric. It made the moves that Elric wished to make. Both Yyrkoon and Mournblade seemed disconcerted by this turn of events. Mournblade shouted as if in astonishment at its brother's behaviour. Elric struck at Yyrkoon's sword-arm, pierced cloth – pierced flesh – pierced sinew – pierced bone. Blood came, soaking Yyrkoon's arm and dripping down onto the hilt of the sword. The blood was slippery. It weakened Yyrkoon's grip on his runesword. He took it in both hands, but he was unable to hold it firmly.

Elric, too, took Stormbringer in both hands. Unearthly strength surged through him. With a gigantic blow he dashed Stormbringer against Mournblade where blade met hilt. The runesword flew from Yyrkoon's grasp. It sped across the Pulsing Cavern.

Elric smiled. He had defeated his own sword's will and, in turn, had defeated the brother sword.

Mournblade fell against the wall of the Pulsing Cavern and for a moment was still.

A groan then seemed to escape the defeated runesword. A high-pitched shriek filled the Pulsing Cavern. Blackness flooded over the eery pink light and extinguished it.

When the light returned Elric saw that a scabbard lay at his feet. The scabbard was black and of the same alien craftsmanship as the runesword. Elric saw Yyrkoon. The prince was on his knees and he was sobbing, his eyes darting about the Pulsing Cavern seeking Mournblade, looking at Elric with fright as if he knew he must now be slain.

'Mournblade?' Yyrkoon said hopelessly. He knew he was to die.

Mournblade had vanished from the Pulsing Cavern.

'Your sword is gone,' said Elric quietly.

Yyrkoon whimpered and tried to crawl towards the entrance of the cavern. But the entrance had shrunk to the size of a small coin. Yyrkoon wept.

Stormbringer trembled, as if thirsty for Yyrkoon's soul. Elric stooped.

Yyrkoon began to speak rapidly. 'Do not slay me, Elric – not with that runeblade. I will do anything you wish. I will die in any other way.'

Elric said: 'We are victims, cousin, of a conspiracy – a game played by gods, demons and sentient swords. They wish one of us dead. I suspect they wish you dead more than they wish me dead. And that is the reason why I shall not slay you here.' He picked up the scabbard. He forced Stormbringer into it and at once the sword was quiet. Elric took off his old scabbard and looked around for Aubec's sword, but that, too, was gone. He dropped the old scabbard and hooked the new one to his belt. He rested his left hand upon the pommel of Stormbringer and he looked not without sympathy upon the creature that was his cousin.

'You are a worm, Yyrkoon. But is that your fault?'

Yyrkoon gave him a puzzled glance.

'I wonder, if you had all your desire, would you cease to be a worm, cousin?'

Yyrkoon raised himself to his knees. A little hope began to show in his eyes.

Elric smiled and drew a deep breath. 'We shall see,' he said. 'You must agree to wake Cymoril from her sorcerous slumber.'

'You have humbled me, Elric,' said Yyrkoon in a small pitiful voice. 'I will wake her. Or would . . . '

'Can you not undo your spell?'

'We cannot escape from the Pulsing Cavern. It is past the time . . . '

'What's this?'

'I did not think you would follow me. And then I thought I would easily finish you. And now it is past the time. One can keep the entrance open for only a little while. It will admit anyone who cares to enter the Pulsing Cavern, but it will let no-one out after the power of the spell dies. I gave much to know that spell.'

'You have given too much for everything,' said Elric. He went to the entrance and peered through. Rackhir waited on the other side. The Red Archer had an anxious expression. Elric said: 'Warrior Priest of Phum, it seems that my cousin and I are trapped in here. The entrance will not part for us.' Elric tested the warm, moist stuff of the wall. It would not open more than a tiny fraction. 'It seems that you can join us or else go back. If you do join us, you share our fate.'

'It is not much of a fate if I go back,' said Rackhir. 'What chances have you?'

'One,' said Elric. 'I can invoke my patron.'

'A Lord of Chaos?' Rackhir made a wry face.

'Exactly,' said Elric. 'I speak of Arioch.'

'Arioch, eh? Well, he does not care for renegades from Phum.'

'What do you choose to do?'

Rackhir stepped forward. Elric stepped back. Through the opening came Rackhir's head, followed by his shoulders, followed by the rest of him. The entrance closed again immediately. Rackhir stood up and untangled the string of his bow from the stave, smoothing it. 'I agreed to share your fate – to gamble all on escaping from this plane,' said the Red Archer. He looked surprised when he saw Yyrkoon. 'Your enemy is still alive?'

'Aye.'

'You are merciful indeed.'

'Perhaps. Or obstinate. I would not slay him merely because some supernatural agency used him as a pawn, to be killed if I should win. The Lords of the Higher Worlds do not as yet control me completely – nor will they if I have any power at all to resist them.'

Rackhir grinned. 'I share your view – though I'm not optimistic about its realism. I see you have one of those black swords at your belt. Will that not hack a way through the cavern?'

'No,' said Yyrkoon from his place against the wall. 'Nothing can harm the stuff of the Pulsing Cavern.'

'I'll believe you,' said Elric, 'for I do not intend to draw this new sword of mine often. I must learn how to control it first.'

'So Arioch must be summoned.' Rackhir sighed.

'If that is possible,' said Elric.

'He will doubtless destroy me,' said Rackhir, looking to Elric in the hope that the albino would deny this statement.

Elric looked grave. 'I might be able to strike a bargain with him. It will also test something.'

Elric turned his back on Rackhir and on Yyrkoon. He adjusted his mind. He sent it out through vast spaces and complicated mazes. And he cried:

'Arioch! Arioch! Aid me, Arioch!'

He had a sense of something listening to him.

'Arioch!'

Something shifted in the places where his mind went.

'Arioch . . . '

And Arioch heard him. He knew it was Arioch.

Rackhir gave a horrified yell. Yyrkoon screamed. Elric turned and saw that something disgusting had appeared near the far wall. It was black and it was foul and it slobbered and its shape was intolerably alien. Was this Arioch? How could it be? Arioch was beautiful. But perhaps, thought Elric, this was Arioch's true shape. Upon this plane, in this peculiar cavern, Arioch could not deceive those who looked upon him.

But then the shape had disappeared and a beautiful youth with ancient eyes stood looking at the three mortals.

'You have won the sword, Elric,' said Arioch, ignoring the others. 'I congratulate you. And you have spared your cousin's life. Why so?'

'More than one reason,' said Elric. 'But let us say he must remain alive in order to wake Cymoril.'

Arioch's face bore a little, secret smile for a moment and Elric realized that he had avoided a trap. If he had killed Yyrkoon, Cymoril would never have woken again.

'And what is this little traitor doing with you?' Arioch turned a cold eye on Rackhir who did his best to stare back at the Chaos Lord.

'He is my friend,' said Elric. 'I made a bargain with him. If he aided me to find the Black Sword, then I would take him back with me to our own plane.'

'That is impossible. Rackhir is an exile here. That is his punishment.'

'He comes back with me,' said Elric. And now he unhooked the scabbard holding Stormbringer from his belt and he held the sword out before him. 'Or I do not take the sword with me. Failing that, we all three remain here for eternity.'

'That is not sensible, Elric. Consider your responsibilities.'

'I have considered them. That is my decision.'

Arioch's smooth face had just a tinge of anger. 'You must take the sword. It is your destiny.'

'So you say. But I now know that the sword may only be borne by me. You cannot bear it, Arioch, or you would. Only I – or another mortal like me – can take it from the Pulsing Cavern. Is that not so?'

'You are clever, Elric of Melniboné.' Arioch spoke with sardonic admiration. 'And you are a fitting servant of Chaos. Very well – that traitor can go with you. But he would be best warned to tread warily. The Lords of Chaos have been known to bear malice . . . '

Rackhir said hoarsely: 'So I have heard, My Lord Arioch.'

Arioch ignored the archer. 'The man of Phum is not, after all, important. And if you wish to spare your cousin's life, so be it. It matters little. Destiny can contain a few extra threads in her design and still accomplish her original aims.'

'Very well then,' said Elric. 'Take us from this place.'

'Where to?'

'Why, to Melniboné, if you please.'

With a smile that was almost tender Arioch looked down on Elric and a silky hand stroked Elric's cheek. Arioch had grown to twice his original size. 'Oh, you are surely the sweetest of all my slaves,' said the Lord of Chaos.

And there was a whirling. There was a sound like the roar of the sea. There was a dreadful sense of nausea. And three weary men stood on the floor of the great throne room in Imrryr. The throne room was deserted, save that in one corner a black shape, like smoke, writhed for a moment and then was gone.

Rackhir crossed the floor and seated himself carefully upon the first step to the Ruby Throne. Yyrkoon and Elric remained where they were, staring into each other's eyes. Then Elric laughed and slapped his scabbarded sword. 'Now you must fulfil your promises to me, cousin. Then I have a proposition to put to you.'

'It is like a market place,' said Rackhir, leaning on one elbow and inspecting the feather in his scarlet hat. 'So many bargains!'

5

The Pale King's Mercy

Yyrkoon stepped back from his sister's bed. He was worn and his features were drawn and there was no spirit in him as he said: 'It is done.' He turned away and looked through the window at the towers of Imrryr, at the harbour where the returned golden battle-barges rode at anchor, together with the ship which had been King Straasha's gift to Elric. 'She will wake in a moment,' added Yyrkoon absently.

Dyvim Tvar and Rackhir the Red Archer looked inquiringly at Elric who knelt by the bed, staring into the face of Cymoril. Her face grew peaceful as he watched and for one terrible moment he suspected Prince Yyrkoon of tricking him and of killing Cymoril. But then the eyelids moved and the eyes opened and she saw him and she smiled. 'Elric? The dreams . . . You are safe?'

'I am safe, Cymoril. As you are.'

'Yyrkoon . . . ?'

'He woke you.'

'But you swore to slay him . . . '

'I was as much subject to sorcery as you. My mind was confused. It is still confused where some matters are concerned. But Yyrkoon is changed now. I defeated him. He does not doubt my power. He no longer lusts to usurp me.'

'You are merciful, Elric.' She brushed hair from her face.

Elric exchanged a glance with Rackhir.

'It might not be mercy which moves me,' said Elric. 'It might merely be a sense of fellowship with Yyrkoon.'

'Fellowship? Surely you cannot feel . . . '

'We are both mortal. We were both victims of a game played between the Lords of the Higher Worlds. My loyalty must, finally, be to my own kind – and that is why I ceased to hate Yyrkoon.'

'And that is mercy,' said Cymoril.

Yyrkoon walked towards the door. 'May I leave, my lord emperor?'

Elric thought he detected a strange light in his defeated cousin's eyes.

But perhaps it was only humility or despair. He nodded. Yyrkoon went from the room, closing the door softly.

Dyvim Tvar said: 'Trust Yyrkoon not at all, Elric. He will betray you again.' The Lord of the Dragon Caves was troubled.

'No,' said Elric. 'If he does not fear me, he fears the sword I now carry.'

'And you should fear that sword,' said Dyvim Tvar.

'No,' said Elric. 'I am the master of the sword.'

Dyvim Tvar made to speak again but then shook his head almost sorrowfully, bowed and, together with Rackhir the Red Archer, left Elric and Cymoril alone.

Cymoril took Elric in her arms. They kissed. They wept.

There were celebrations in Melniboné for a week. Now almost all the ships and men and dragons were home. And Elric was home, having proved his right to rule so well that all his strange quirks of character (this 'mercy' of his was perhaps the strangest) were accepted by the populace.

In the throne room there was a ball and it was the most lavish ball any of the courtiers had ever known. Elric danced with Cymoril, taking a full part in the activities. Only Yyrkoon did not dance, preferring to remain in a quiet corner below the gallery of the music-slaves, ignored by the guests. Rackhir the Red Archer danced with several Melnibonéan ladies and made assignations with them all, for he was a hero now in Melniboné. Dyvim Tvar danced, too, though his eyes were often brooding when they fell upon Prince Yyrkoon.

And later, when people ate, Elric spoke to Cymoril as they sat together on the dais of the Ruby Throne.

'Would you be empress, Cymoril?'

'You know I will marry you, Elric. We have both known that for many a year, have we not?'

'So you would be my wife?'

'Aye.' She laughed for she thought he joked.

'And not be empress? For a year at least?'

'What mean you, my lord?'

'I must go away from Melniboné, Cymoril, for a year. What I have learned in recent months has made me want to travel the Young Kingdoms – see how other nations conduct their affairs. For I think Melniboné must change if she is to survive. She could become a great force for good in the world, for she still has much power.'

'For good?' Cymoril was surprised and there was a little alarm in her voice, too. 'Melniboné has never stood for good or for evil, but for

126

herself and the satisfaction of her desires.'

'I would see that changed.'

'You intend to alter everything?'

'I intend to travel the world and then decide if there is any point to such a decision. The Lords of the Higher Worlds have ambitions in our world. Though they have given me aid, of late, I fear them. I should like to see if it is possible for men to rule their own affairs.'

'And you will go?' There were tears in her eyes. 'When?'

'Tomorrow – when Rackhir leaves. We will take King Straasha's ship and make for the Isle of the Purple Towns where Rackhir has friends. Will you come?'

'I cannot imagine – I cannot. Oh, Elric, why spoil this happiness we now have?'

'Because I feel that the happiness cannot last unless we know completely what we are.'

She frowned. 'Then you must discover that, if that is what you wish,' she said slowly. 'But it is for you to discover alone, Elric, for I have no such desire. You must go by yourself into those barbarian lands.'

'You will not accompany me?'

'It is not possible. I – I am Melnibonéan . . . ' She sighed. 'I love you, Elric.'

'And I you, Cymoril.'

'Then we shall be married when you return. In a year.'

Elric was full of sorrow, but he knew that his decision was correct. If he did not leave, he would grow restless soon enough and if he grew restless he might come to regard Cymoril as an enemy, someone who had trapped him.

'Then you must rule as empress until I return,' he said.

'No, Elric. I cannot take that responsibility.'

'Then, who . . . ? Dyvim Tvar . . . '

'I know Dyvim Tvar. He will not take such power. Magum Colim, perhaps . . . '

'No.'

'Then you must stay, Elric.'

But Elric's gaze had travelled through the crowd in the throne room below. It stopped when it reached a lonely figure seated by itself under the gallery of the music-slaves. And Elric smiled ironically and said:

'Then it must be Yyrkoon.'

Cymoril was horrified. 'No, Elric. He will abuse any power . . . '

'Not now. And it is just. He is the only one who wanted to be emperor. Now he can rule as emperor for a year in my stead. If he rules well, I may consider abdicating in his favour. If he rules badly, it will prove, once and for all, that his ambitions were misguided.'

'Elric,' said Cymoril. 'I love you. But you are a fool — a criminal, if you trust Yyrkoon again.'

'No,' he said evenly. 'I am not a fool. All I am is Elric. I cannot help that, Cymoril.'

'It is Elric that I love!' she cried. 'But Elric is doomed. We are all doomed unless you remain here now.'

'I cannot. Because I love you, Cymoril, I cannot.'

She stood up. She was weeping. She was lost.

'And I am Cymoril,' she said. 'You will destroy us both.' Her voice softened and she stroked his hair. 'You will destroy us, Elric.'

'No,' he said. 'I will build something that will be better. I will discover things. When I return we shall marry and we shall live long and we shall be happy, Cymoril.'

And now, Elric had told three lies. The first concerned his cousin Yyrkoon. The second concerned the Black Sword. The third concerned Cymoril. And upon those three lies was Elric's destiny to be built, for it is only about things which concern us most profoundly that we lie clearly and with profound conviction.

Epilogue

There was a port called Menii which was one of the humblest and friendliest of the Purple Towns. Like the others on the isle it was built mainly of the purple stone which gave the towns their name. And there were red roofs on the houses and there were bright-sailed boats of all kinds in the harbour as Elric and Rackhir the Red Archer came ashore in the early morning when just a few sailors were beginning to make their way down to their ships.

King Straasha's lovely ship lay some way out beyond the harbour wall. They had used a small boat to cross the water between it and the town. They turned and looked back at the ship. They had sailed it themselves, without crew, and the ship had sailed well.

'So, I must seek peace and mythic Tanelorn,' said Rackhir, with a certain amount of self-mockery. He stretched and yawned and the bow and the quiver danced on his back.

Elric was dressed in simple costume that might have marked any soldier-of-fortune of the Young Kingdoms. He looked fit and relaxed. He smiled into the sun. The only remarkable thing about his garb was the great, black runesword at his side. Since he had donned the sword, he had needed no drugs to sustain him at all.

'And I must seek knowledge in the lands I find marked upon my map,' said Elric. 'I must learn and I must carry what I learn back to Melniboné at the end of a year. I wish that Cymoril had accompanied me, but I understand her reluctance.'

'You will go back?' Rackhir said. 'When a year is over?'

'She will draw me back!' Elric laughed. 'My only fear is that I will weaken and return before my quest is finished.'

'I should like to come with you,' said Rackhir, 'for I have travelled in most lands and would be as good a guide as I was in the netherworld. But I am sworn to find Tanelorn, for all I know it does not really exist.'

'I hope that you find it, Warrior Priest of Phum,' said Elric.

'I shall never be that again,' said Rackhir. Then his eyes widened a little. 'Why, look – your ship!'

And Elric looked and saw the ship that had once been called The Ship Which Sails Over Land and Sea, and he saw that slowly it was sinking. King Straasha was taking it back.

'The elementals are friends, at least,' he said. 'But I fear their power wanes as the power of Melniboné wanes. For all that we of the Dragon Isle are considered evil by the folk of the Young Kingdoms, we share much in common with the spirits of Air, Earth, Fire and Water.'

Rackhir said, as the masts of the ship disappeared beneath the waves: 'I envy you those friends, Elric. You may trust them.'

'Aye.'

Rackhir looked at the runesword hanging on Elric's hip. 'But you would be wise to trust nothing else.' he added.

Elric laughed. 'Fear not for me, Rackhir, for I am my own master – for a year at least. And I am master of this sword now!'

The sword seemed to stir at his side and he took firm hold of its grip and slapped Rackhir on the back and he laughed and shook his white hair so that it drifted in the air and he lifted his strange, red eyes to the sky and he said:

'I shall be a new man when I return to Melniboné.'

THE FORTRESS OF
THE PEARL

To Dave Tate

And when Elric had told his three lies to Cymoril, his betrothed, and had set his ambitious cousin Yyrkoon as Regent on the Ruby Throne of Melniboné, and when he had taken leave of Rackhir the Red Archer, he set off into lands unknown, to seek knowledge which he believed would help him rule Melniboné as she had never been ruled before.

But Elric had not reckoned with a destiny already determining that he should learn and experience certain things which would have a profound effect upon him. Even before he encountered the blind captain and the Ship Which Sailed the Seas of Fate he was to find his life, his soul and all his idealism in jeopardy.

In Ufych-Sormeer he was delayed over a matter involving a misunderstanding between four unworldly wizards who amiably and inadvertently threatened the destruction of the Young Kingdoms before they had served the Balance's ultimate purpose; and in Filkhar he experienced an affair of the heart which he would never again speak about; he was learning, at some cost, the power and the pain of bearing the Black Sword.

But it was in the desert city of Quarzhasaat that he began the adventure which was to help set the course of his weird for years to come . . .

THE CHRONICLE OF THE BLACK SWORD

ONE

Is there a madman with a brain
To turn the stuff of nightmare sane
And demons crush and Chaos tame,
Who'll leave his realm, forsake his bride
And, tossed by contradictory tides,
Give up his pride for pain?

THE CHRONICLE OF THE BLACK SWORD

1

A Doomed Lord Dying

It was in lonely Quarzhasaat, destination of many caravans but terminus of few, that Elric, hereditary Emperor of Melniboné, last of a bloodline more than ten thousand years old, sometime conjuror of terrible resource, lay ready for death. The drugs and herbs which usually sustained him had been used in the final days of his long journey across the southern edge of the Sighing Desert and he had been able to acquire no replacements for them in this fortress city which was more famous for its treasure than for its sufficiency of life.

The albino prince stretched, slowly and feebly, his bone-coloured fingers to the light and brought to vividness the bloody jewel in the Ring of Kings, the last traditional symbol of his ancient responsibilities; then he let the hand fall. It was as if he had briefly hoped the Actorios would revive him, but the stone was useless while he lacked energy to command its powers. Besides, he had no great desire to summon demons here. His own folly had brought him to Quarzhasaat; he owed her citizens no vengeance. They, indeed, had cause to hate him, had they but known his origins.

Once Quarzhasaat had ruled a land of rivers and lovely valleys, its forests verdant, its plains abundant with crops, but that had been before the casting of certain incautious spells in a war with threatening Melniboné more than two thousand years earlier. Quarzhasaat's empire had been lost to both sides. It had been engulfed by a vast mass of sand which swept over it like a tide, leaving only the capital and her traditions, which in time became the prime reason for her continuing existence. Because Quarzhasaat had always stood there she must be sustained, her citizens believed, at any cost throughout eternity. Though she had no purpose or function still her masters felt a heavy obligation to continue her existence by whichever means they found expedient. Fourteen times had armies attempted to cross the Sighing Desert to loot fabulous Quarzhasaat. Fourteen times had the desert itself defeated them.

Meanwhile the city's chief obsessions (some would say her chief industry) were the elaborate intrigues amongst her rulers. A republic, albeit in name only, and hub of a vast inland empire, albeit entirely covered by sand, Quarzhasaat was ruled by her Council of Seven, whimsically known as The Six and One Other, who controlled the greater part of the city's wealth and most of her affairs. Certain other potent men and women, who chose not to serve in this Septocracy, wielded considerable influence while displaying none of the trappings of power. One of these, Elric had learned, was Narfis, Baroness of Kuwai'r, who dwelled in a simple yet beautiful villa at the city's southern extreme and gave most of her attention to her notorious rival, the old Duke Ral, patron of Quarzhasaat's finest artists, whose own palace on the northern heights was as unostentatious as it was lovely. These two, Elric was told, had elected three members each to the Council, while the seventh, always nameless and simply called the Sexocrat (who ruled the Six), maintained a balance, able to sway any vote one way or the other. The ear of the Sexocrat was most profoundly desired by all the many rivals in the city, even by Baroness Narfis and Duke Ral.

Uninterested in Quarzhasaat's ornate politics, as he was in his own, Elric's reason for being here was curiosity and the fact that Quarzhasaat was clearly the only haven in a great wasteland lying north of the nameless mountains dividing the Sighing Desert from the Weeping Waste.

Moving his exhausted bones on the thin straw of his pallet, Elric wondered sardonically if he would be buried here without the people ever knowing that the hereditary ruler of their nation's greatest enemies had died amongst them. He wondered if this had after all been the fate his gods had in store for him: nothing as grandiose as he had dreamed of and yet it had its attractions.

When he had left Filkhar in haste and some confusion, he had taken the first ship out of Raschil and it had brought him to Jadmar, where he had chosen wilfully to trust an old Ilmioran drunkard who had sold him a map showing fabled Tanelorn. As the albino had half-guessed, the map proved a deception, leading him far from any kind of human habitation. He had considered crossing the mountains to make for Kaarlaak by the Weeping Waste but on consulting his own map, of more reliable Melnibonéan manufacture, he had discovered Quarzhasaat to be significantly closer. Riding north on a steed already half-dead from heat and starvation, he had found only dried river-beds and exhausted oases, for in his wisdom he had chosen to cross the desert in a time of drought. He had failed to find fabled Tanelorn and, it seemed, would not even catch sight of a city which, in his people's histories, was almost as fabulous.

As was usual for them, Melnibonéan chroniclers showed only a passing interest in defeated rivals, but Elric remembered that Quarzhasaat's own sorcery was said to have contributed to her extinction as a threat to her half-human enemies: A misplaced rune, he understood, uttered by Fophean Dals, the Sorcerer Duke, ancestor to the present Duke Ral, in a spell meant to flood the Melnibonéan army with sand and build a bulwark about the entire nation. Elric had still to discover how this accident was explained in Quarzhasaat now. Had they created myths and legends to rationalize the city's ill-luck entirely as a result of evil emanating from the Dragon Isle?

Elric reflected how his own obsession with myth had brought him to almost inevitable destruction. 'In my miscalculations,' he murmured, turning dull crimson eyes again towards the Actorios, 'I have shown that I share something in common with these people's ancestors.' Some forty miles from his dead horse, Elric had been discovered by a boy out searching for the jewels and precious artefacts occasionally flung up by those sandstorms which constantly came and went over this part of the desert and were partially responsible for the city's survival, as well as for the astonishing height of Quarzhasaat's magnificent walls. They were also the origin of the desert's melancholy name.

In better health Elric would have relished the city's monumental beauty. It was a beauty derived from an aesthetic refined over centuries and bearing no signs of outside influence. Though so many of the curving ziggurats and palaces were of gigantic proportions there was nothing vulgar or ugly about them; they had an airy quality, a peculiar lightness of style which made them seem, in their terracotta reds and glittering silver granite, their whitewashed stucco, their rich blues and greens, as if they had been magicked out of the very air. Their luscious gardens filled marvellously complex terraces, their fountains and water courses, drawn from deep-sunk wells, gave tranquil sound and wonderful perfume to her old cobbled ways and wide tree-lined avenues; yet all this water, which might have been diverted to growing crops, was used to maintain the appearance of Quarzhasaat as she had been at the height of her imperial power and was more valuable than jewels, its use rationed and its theft punishable by the severest of laws.

Elric's own lodgings were in no way magnificent, consisting as they did of a truckle bed, straw-strewn flagstones, a single high window, a plain earthenware jug and a basin containing a little brackish water which had cost him his last emerald. Water permits were not available to foreigners and the only water on general sale was Quarzhasaat's single most expensive commodity. Elric's water had almost certainly been stolen from a public fountain. The statutory penalties for such thefts were rarely discussed, even in private.

Elric required rare herbs to sustain his deficient blood but their cost, even had they been available, would have proven far beyond his present means, which had been reduced to a few gold coins, a fortune in Kaarlaak but of virtually no worth in a city where gold was so common it was used to line the city's aqueducts and sewers. His expeditions into the streets had been exhausting and depressing.

Once a day the boy who had found Elric in the desert, and brought him to this room, paid the albino a visit, staring at him as if at a curious insect or captured rodent. The boy's name was Anigh and, though he spoke the Melnibonéan-derived *lingua franca* of the Young Kingdoms, his accent was so thick it was sometimes impossible to understand all he said.

Once more Elric tried to lift his arm only to let it fall. That morning he had reconciled himself to the fact that he would never again see his beloved Cymoril and would never sit upon the Ruby Throne. He knew regret, but it was of a distant kind, for his illness made him oddly euphoric.

'I had hoped to sell you.'

Elric peered, blinking, into the shadows of the room on the far side of a single ray of sunlight. He recognized the voice but could make out little more than a silhouette near the door.

'But now it seems all I have to offer in next week's market will be your corpse and your remaining possessions.' It was Anigh, almost as depressed as Elric at the prospect of his prize's death. 'You are still a rarity, of course. Your features are those of our ancient enemies but whiter than bone and those I have never seen before in a man.'

'I'm sorry to disappoint your expectations.' Elric rose weakly on his elbow. He had deemed it imprudent to reveal his origins but instead had said he was a mercenary from Nadsokor, the Beggar City, which sheltered all manner of freakish inhabitants.

'Then I had hoped you might be a wizard and reward me with some bit of arcane lore which would set me on the path to becoming a wealthy man and perhaps a member of the Six. Or you might have been a desert spirit who would confer on me some useful power. But I have wasted my waters, it seems. You are merely an impoverished mercenary. Have you no wealth left at all? Some curio which might prove of value, for instance?' And the boy's eyes went towards a bundle which, long and slender, rested against the wall near Elric's head.

'That's no treasure, lad,' Elric informed him grimly. 'He who possesses it could be said to bear a curse impossible to exorcize.' He smiled at
the thought of the boy trying to find a buyer for the Black Sword
which, wrapped in a torn cassock of red silk, occasionally gave out a
murmur, like a senile man attempting to recall the power of speech.

'It's a weapon, is it not?' said Anigh, his thin, tanned features
making his vivid blue eyes seem large.

'Aye,' Elric agreed. 'A sword.'

'An antique?' The boy reached under his striped brown djellabah
and picked at the scab on his shoulder.

'That's a fair description.' Elric was amused but found even this
brief conversation tiring.

'How old?' Now Anigh took a step forward so that he was entirely
illuminated by the ray of sunlight. He had the perfect look of a creature adapted to dwell amongst the tawny rocks and the dusky sands of
the Sighing Desert.

'Perhaps ten thousand years.' Elric found that the boy's startled
expression helped him forget, momentarily, his almost certain fate.
'But probably more than that . . . '

'Then it's a rarity, indeed! Rarities are prized by Quarzhasaat's
lords and ladies. There are those amongst the Six, even, who collect
such things. His honour the Master of Unicht Shlur, for instance, has
the armour of a whole Ilmioran army, each piece arranged on the
mummified corpses of the original warriors. And my Lady Talith possesses a collection of war-instruments numbering several thousands,
each one different. Let me take that, Sir Mercenary, and I'll discover a
buyer. Then I'll seek the herbs you need.'

'Whereupon I'll be fit enough for you to sell me, eh?' Elric's amusement increased.

Anigh's face became exquisitely innocent. 'Oh, no, sir. Then you
will be strong enough to resist me. I shall merely take a commission on
your first engagement.'

Elric felt affection for the boy. He paused, gathering strength before
he spoke again. 'You expect I'll interest an employer, here in Quarzhasaat?'

'Naturally.' Anigh grinned. 'You could become a bodyguard to one
of the Six, perhaps, or at least one of their supporters. Your unusual
appearance makes you immediately employable! I have already told
you what great rivals and plotters our masters are.'

'It is encouraging – ' Elric paused for breath – 'to know that I can
look forward to a life of worth and fulfilment here in Quarzhasaat.' He
tried to stare directly into Anigh's brilliant eyes, but the boy's head

turned out of the sunlight so that only part of his body was exposed. 'However, I understood from you that the herbs I described grew only in distant Kwan, days from here – in the foothills of the Ragged Pillars. I will be dead before even a fit messenger could be half-way to Kwan. Do you try to comfort me, boy? Or are your motives less noble?'

'I told you, sir, where the herbs grew. But what if there are some who have already gathered Kwan's harvest and returned?'

'You know of such an apothecary? But what would one charge me for such valuable medicines? And why did you not mention this before?'

'Because I did not know of it before.' Anigh seated himself in the relative cool of the doorway. 'I have made enquiries since our last conversation. I am a humble boy, your worship, not a learned man, nor yet an oracle. Yet I know how to banish my ignorance and replace it with knowledge. I am ignorant, good sir, but not a fool.'

'I share your opinion of yourself, Master Anigh.'

'Then shall I take the sword and find a buyer for you?' He came again into the light, hand reaching towards the bundle.

Elric fell back, shaking his head and smiling a little. 'I, too, young Anigh, have much ignorance. But, unlike you, I think I might also be a fool.'

'Knowledge brings power,' said Anigh. 'Power shall take me into the entourage of the Baroness Narfis, perhaps. I could become a captain in her guard. Maybe a noble!'

'Oh, one day you'll surely be more than either.' Elric drew in stale air, his frame shuddering, his lungs enflamed. 'Do what you will, though I doubt Stormbringer will go willingly.'

'May I see it?'

'Aye.' With painful awkward movements Elric rolled to the bed's edge and plucked the wrappings free of the huge sword. Carved with runes which seemed to flicker unsteadily upon the blade of black, glowing metal, decorated with ancient and elaborate work, some of mysterious design, some depicting dragons and demons intertwined as if in battle, Stormbringer was clearly no mundane weapon.

The boy gasped and drew back, almost as if regretting his suggested bargain. 'Is it alive?'

Elrich contemplated his sword with a mixture of loathing and something akin to sensuality. 'Some would say it possessed both a mind and a will. Others would claim it to be a demon in disguise. Some believe it composed of the vestigial souls of all damned mortals, trapped within as once, in legend, a great dragon was said to dwell inside another pommel than that which the sword now bears.' To his own faint distaste, he found that he was taking a certain pleasure in the boy's growing dismay. 'Have you never looked upon an artefact of Chaos before, Master Anigh? Or one who is wedded to such a thing? Its slave perhaps?' He let his long, white hand descend into the dirty water and raised it to wet his lips. His red eyes flickered like dying embers. 'During my travels I have heard this blade described as Arioch's own battlesword, able to slice down the walls between the very Realms. Others, as they die upon it, believe it to be a living creature. There is a theory that it is but one member of an entire race, living in our dimension but capable, should it desire, of summoning a million brothers. Can you hear it speaking, Master Anigh? Will that voice delight and charm the casual buyers in your market?' And a sound came from the pale lips that was not a laugh yet contained a desolate kind of humour.

Anigh withdrew hastily into the sunlight again. He cleared his throat. 'You called the thing by a name?'

'I called the sword *Stormbringer* but the peoples of the Young Kingdoms sometimes have another name, both for myself and for the blade. The name is *Soulstealer*. It has drunk many souls.'

'You're a dreamthief!' Anigh's eyes remained on the blade. 'Why are you not employed?'

'I do not know the term and I do not know who would employ a "dreamthief".' Elric looked to the boy for further explanation.

But Anigh's gaze did not leave the sword. 'Would it drink my soul, master?'

'If I chose. To restore my energy for a while, all I would have to do would be to let Stormbringer kill you and perhaps a few more and then she'd pass her energy on to me. Then, doubtless, I could find a steed and ride away from here. Possibly to Kwam.'

Now the black sword's voice grew more tuneful, as if approving of this notion.

'Oh, Gamek Idianit!' Anigh got to his feet, ready to flee if necessary. 'This is like that story on Mass'aboon's walls. This is what those who brought about our isolation were said to wield! Aye, the leaders bore identical swords to these. The teachers at the school tell of it. I was there. Oh, what did they say!' And he frowned deeply, an object lesson to anyone wishing to point a moral concerning the benefits of attending at classes.

Elric regretted frightening the boy. 'I am not disposed, young Anigh, to maintain my own life at the expense of others who have offered me no harm. That is partly the reaon why I find myself in this specific predicament. You saved my life, child. I would not kill you.'

'Oh, master. Thou art dangerous!' In his panic he spoke a tongue more ancient than Melnibonéan and Elric, who had learned such things to aid his studies, recognized it.

'Where came you by that language, by that Opish?' the albino asked.

Even in his terror the boy was surprised. 'They call it the gutter cant, here in Quarzhasaat. The thieves' secret. But I suppose it is common enough to hear it in Nadsokor.'

'Aye, indeed. In Nadsokor, true.' Elric was again intrigued by this minor turn of events. He reached towards the boy, to reassure him.

The motion caused Anigh to jerk up his head and make a noise in his throat. Clearly he set no store by Elric's attempt to regain his confidence. Without further remark, he left the room, his bare feet pattering down the long corridor and the steps into the narrow street.

Convinced that Anigh was now gone for good, Elric knew a sudden pang of sadness. He regretted only one thing now, that he would never be reunited with Cymoril and return to Melniboné to keep his promise to wed her. He understood that he had always been and probably would always be reluctant to ascend the Ruby Throne again, yet he knew it was his duty to do so. Had he deliberately chosen this fate for himself, to avoid that responsibility?

Elric knew that though his blood was tainted by his strange disease, it was still the blood of his ancestors and it would not have been easy to deny his birthright or his destiny. He had hoped he might, by his rule, turn Melniboné from the introverted, cruel and decadent vestige of a hated empire into a reinvigorated nation capable of bringing peace and justice to the world, of presenting an example of enlightenment which others might use to their own advantage.

For a chance to return to Cymoril he would more than willingly trade the Black Sword. Yet secretly he had little hope that this was possible. The Black Sword was more than a source of sustenance, a weapon against his enemies. The Black Sword bound him to his race's ancient loyalties, to Chaos, and he could not see Lord Arioch willingly allowing him to break that particular bond. When he considered these matters, these hints at a greater destiny, he found his mind growing confused and he preferred to ignore the questions whenever possible.

'Well, perhaps in folly and in death, I shall break that bond and thwart Melniboné's bad old friends.'

The breath in his lungs seemed to grow thin and no longer burned. Indeed, it felt cool. His blood moved more sluggishly in his veins as he turned to rise and stagger to the rough wooden table where his few provisions lay. But he could only stare at the stale bread, the vinegary wine, the wizened pieces of dried meat whose origins were best not speculated upon. He could not get up; he could not summon the will to move. He had accepted his dying if not with equanimity then at least with a degree of dignity. Falling into a languorous reverie, he recalled his deciding to leave Melniboné, his cousin Cymoril's trepidation, his ambitious cousin Yyrkoon's secret glee, his pronouncements made to Rackhir the Warrior Priest of Phum, who had also sought Tanelorn.

Elric wondered if Rackhir the Red Archer had been any more successful in his quest or whether he lay somewhere in another part of this vast desert, his scarlet costume reduced to rags by the forever sighing wind, his flesh drying on his bones. Elric hoped with all his heart that Rackhir had succeeded in discovering the mythical city and the peace it promised. Then he found that his longing for Cymoril was growing and he believed that he wept.

Earlier he had considered calling upon Arioch, his patron Duke of Chaos, to save him, yet had continued to feel a deep reluctance even to contemplate the possibility. He feared that by employing Arioch's assistance once more he would lose far more than his life. Each time that powerful supernatural agreed to help, it further strengthened an agreement both implicit and mysterious. Not that the debate was anything more than notional, Elric reflected ironically. Of late Arioch had shown a distinct reluctance to come to his aid. Possibly Yyrkoon had superseded him in every way . . .

This thought brought Elric back to pain, to his longing for Cymoril. Again he tried to rise. The sun's position had changed. He thought he saw Cymoril standing before him. Then she became an aspect of Arioch. Was the Duke of Chaos playing with him, even now?

Elric moved his gaze to contemplate the sword, which seemed to shift in its loose silk wrappings and whisper some kind of warning, or possibly a threat.

Elric turned his head away. 'Cymoril?' He peered into the shaft of sunlight, following it until he looked through the window at the intense desert sky. Now he believed he saw shapes moving there, shadows that were almost the forms of men, of beasts and demons. As these shapes grew more distinct they came to resemble his friends. Cymoril was there again. Elric moaned in despair. 'My love!'

He saw Rackhir, Dyvim Tvar, even Yyrkoon. He called out to them all.

At the sound of his own cracked speech he realized he had grown feverish, that his remaining energy was being dissipated by his fantasies, that his body was feeding on itself and that death must be close.

Elric reached to touch his own brow, feeling the sweat pouring from it. He wondered how much each bead might fetch on the open market. He found it amusing to speculate on this. Could he sweat enough to buy himself more water, or at least a little wine? Or was this production of liquid in itself against Quarzhasaat's bizarre water laws?

He looked again beyond the sunlight, thinking he saw men there, perhaps the city's guard come to inspect his premises and demand to see his licence to perspire.

Now it seemed that the desert wind, which was never very far away, came sliding through the room, bringing with it some elemental gathering, perhaps a force which was to bear his soul to its ultimate destination. He felt relief. He smiled. He was glad in several ways that his struggle was over. Perhaps Cymoril would join him soon?

Soon? What could Time mean in that intemporal Realm? Perhaps he must wait for Eternity before they could be together? Or a mere passing moment? Or would he never see her? Was all that lay ahead for him an absence, a nothingness? Or would his soul enter some other body, perhaps as sickly as his present one, and be faced again with the same impossible dilemmas, the same terrible moral and physical challenges which had plagued him since his emergence into adulthood?

Elric's mind drifted further and further from logic, like a drowning mouse swept away from the shore, spinning ever more crazily before death brought oblivion. He chuckled, he wept; he raved and occasionally slept as his life dissipated its last with the vapours now pouring from his strange, bone-white flesh. Any uninformed onlooker would have seen that some misborn diseased beast, not a man at all, lay in its final agonies upon that rough bed.

Darkness came and with it a brilliant panoply of people from the albino's past. He saw again the wizards who had educated him in all the arts of sorcery; he saw the strange mother he had never known and his stranger father; the cruel friends of his childhood with whom, bit by bit, he could no longer enjoy the luscious, terrible sports of Melniboné; the caverns and secret glades of the Dragon Isle, the slim towers and hauntingly intricate palaces of his unhuman people, whose ancestors were only partially of this world and who had arisen as beautiful monsters to conquer and rule before, with a deep weariness which he could appreciate all the better now, declining into self-examination and morbid fantasies. And he cried out, for in his mind he saw Cymoril, her body as wasted as his own while Yyrkoon, giggling with horrible pleasure, practised upon it the foulest of abominations. And then, again, he wanted to live, to return to Melniboné, to save the woman he loved so deeply that often he refused to let himself be conscious of the intensity of his passion. But he could not. He knew, as the visions passed and he saw only the dark blue sky through his window, that soon he would be dead and there would be nobody to save the woman he had sworn to marry.

By morning the fever was gone and Elric knew he was but a short hour or two from the end. He opened misted eyes to see the shaft of sunlight, soft and golden now, no longer glaring directly in as it had the previous day, but reflected from the glittering walls of the palace beside which his hovel had been built.

Feeling something suddenly cool upon his cracked lips he jerked his head away and tried to reach for his sword, for he feared that steel was being positioned against him, perhaps to cut his throat.

'Stormbringer . . . '

His voice was feeble and his hand was too weak to leave his side, let alone grip his murmuring blade. He coughed and realized that liquid was being dripped into his mouth. It was not the filthy stuff he had bought with his emerald but something fresh and clean. He drank, trying hard to focus his eyes. Immediately before him was an ornamental silver flash, a golden, soft hand, an arm clothed in exquisitely delicate brocade, a humorous face which he did not recognize. He coughed again. The liquid was more than ordinary water. Had the boy found some sympathetic apothecary? The potion was like one of his own sustaining distillations. He drew a ragged, grateful breath and stared in wary curiosity at the man who had resurrected him, however briefly. Smiling, his temporary saviour moved with studied elegance in his heavy, unseasonable robes.

'Good morning to you, Sir Thief. I trust I'm not insulting you. I gather you're a citizen of Nadsokor where all kinds of robbery are practised with pride?'

Elric, conscious of the delicacy of his situation, saw fit not to contradict him. The albino prince nodded slowly. His bones still ached.

The tall, clean-shaven man slipped a stopper into his flask. 'The boy Anigh tells me you have a sword to sell?'

'Perhaps.' Certain now that his recovery was only temporary Elric continued to exercise caution. 'though I would guess 'tis the kind of purchase most would regret making . . . '

'But your sword is not representative of your main trade, eh? You have lost your crooked staff, no doubt. Sold for water?' A knowing expression.

Elric chose to humour the man. He allowed himself to hope for life again. The liquid had revived him enough to bring back his wits, together with a proportion of his usual strength. 'Aye,' he said, appraising his visitor. 'Maybe.'

'So ho? What? Do you advertise your own incompetence? Is this the way of the Nadsokor Thieves' Company? Thou art a subtler felon than thy guise suggests, eh?' This last was delivered in the same canting tongue Anigh had used on the previous day.

Now Elric realized that this wealthy person had formed an opinion of his status and powers which, while at odds with any actuality, could provide him with a means of escape from his immediate predicament. Elric grew more alert. 'You'd buy my services, is that it? My special prowess? That of myself and possibly my sword?'

The man affected carelessness. 'If you like.' But it was clear he suppressed some urgency. 'I have been told to inform you that the Blood Moon must soon burn over the Bronze Tent.'

'I see.' Elric pretended to be impressed by what to him was pure gibberish. 'Then we must move swiftly, I suppose.'

'So my master believes. The words mean nothing to me, but they have significance for you. I was told to offer you a second draft if you appeared to respond positively to that knowledge. Here.' And he held out, smiling more broadly, the silver flask, which Elric accepted, drank sparingly and feeling still more strength return, his aches gradually dissipating.

'Your master would commission a thief? What does he wish stolen that the thieves of Quarzhasaat cannot steal for him?'

'Aha, sir, you affect a literal-mindedness I cannot believe in now.' He took back the flask. 'I am Raafi as-Keeme and I serve a great man of this Empire. He has, I believe, a commission for you. We have heard much of the Nadsokorian skills and for some while have been hoping one of your folk might wander this way. Did you plan to steal from us? None is ever successful. Better to steal *for* us, I think.'

'Wise advice, I would guess.' Elric rose in his bed and put his feet upon the flagging. Already the liquid's strength was ebbing. 'Perhaps you would outline the nature of the task you have for me, sir?' He reached for the flask but it was withdrawn into Raafi as-Keeme's sleeve.

'By all means, sir,' said the newcomer, 'when we have discussed a little of your background. You steal more than jewels, the boy says. Souls, I hear.'

Elric felt some alarm and looked suspiciously at the man whose expression remained bland. 'In a manner of speaking . . . '

'Good. My master wishes to make use of your services. If you're successful you'll have a cask of this elixir to carry you back to the Young Kingdoms or anywhere else you desire to go.'

'You are offering me my life, sir,' said Elric slowly, 'and I am willing to pay only so much for that.'

'Ah, sir, you have a streak of the merchant's bartering instinct I see. I am sure a good bargain can be struck. Will you come with me now to a certain place?'

Smiling, Elric took Stormbringer in his two hands and flung himself back across the bed, his shoulders against the wall and the source of the sunlight. Placing the sword upon his lap he waved his hand in mockery of lordly hospitality. 'Would you not prefer to stay and sample what I have to offer, Sir Raafi as-Keeme?'

The richly-clad man shook his head deliberately. 'I think not. You have doubtless become used to this stink and to the stink of your own body, but I can assure you it is not pleasant to one who is unfamiliar with it.'

Elric laughed as he accepted this. He rose to his feet, hooking his scabbard to his belt and slipping the murmuring runesword into the black leather. 'Then lead on, sir. I must admit I'm curious to discover what considerable risks I am to take that would make one of your own thieves refuse the kind of rewards a lord of Quazhasaat can offer.'

And in his mind he had already made a bargain: that he would not allow his life to slip away so easily a second time. He owed that much, he had decided, to Cymoril.

'The Pearl at the Heart of the World'

In a room through which mellow sunlight slanted in dusty bands from a massive grille set deep into the ornately painted roof of a palace called Goshasiz whose complicated architecture was stained by something more sinister than time, Lord Gho Fhaazi entertained his guest to further draughts of the mysterious elixir and food which, in Quarzhasaat, was at least as valuable as the furnishings.

Bathed and wearing fresh robes, Elric possessed a new vitality, the dark blues and greens of his silks emphasizing the whiteness of his skin and long, fine hair. The scabbarded runesword leaned against the carved arm of his chair and he was prepared to draw it and use it should this audience prove an elaborate trap.

Lord Gho Fhaazi was modishly coiffed and clad. His black hair and beard were teased into symmetrical ringlets, the long moustachios were waxed and pointed, the heavy brows bleached blond above pale green eyes and a skin artificially whitened until it resembled Elric's own. The lips were painted a vivid red. He sat at the far end of a table which slanted down subtly towards his guest, his back to the light so that he almost resembled a magistrate sitting in judgement on a felon.

Elric recognized the deliberateness of the arrangement and was not put out by it. Lord Gho was still relatively young, in his early thirties, and had a pleasant, slightly high-pitched voice. He waved plump fingers at the plates of figs and dates in mint leaves, of honeyed locusts, which lay between them, pushed the silver flask of elixir in Elric's direction with an awkward display of hospitality, his movements revealing that he performed tasks he would usually have reserved for his servants.

'My dear fellow. More. Have more.' He was unsure of Elric, almost wary of him, and it grew clear to the albino that there was some urgency involved in the matter, which Lord Gho had not yet proposed, nor revealed through the courier he had sent to the hovel. 'Is there perhaps some favourite food we have not provided?'

Elric raised yellow linen to his lips. 'I'm obliged to you, Lord Gho. I have not eaten so well since I left the lands of the Young Kingdoms.'

'Aha, just so. Food is plentiful there, I hear.'

'As plentiful as diamonds in Quarzhasaat. You have visited the Young Kingdoms?'

'We of Quarzhasaat have no need to travel.' Lord Gho spoke in some surprise. 'What is there abroad that we could possibly desire?'

Elric reflected that Lord Gho's people had a good deal in common with his own. He reached and took another fig from the nearest dish and as he chewed it slowly, savouring its sweet succulence, he stared frankly at Lord Gho. 'How came you to learn of Nadsokor?'

'We do not travel ourselves – but, naturally, travellers come to us. Some of them have taken caravans to Kaarlaak and elsewhere. They bring back the occasional slave. They tell us such astonishing lies!' He laughed tolerantly. 'But there's a grain of truth, no doubt, in some of what they say. While dreamthieves, for instance, are secretive and circumspect about their origins, we have heard that thieves of every kind are welcomed in Nadsokor. It takes little intelligence to draw the obvious conclusion . . . '

'Especially if one is blessed with only the barest information concerning other lands and peoples.' Elric smiled.

Lord Gho Fhaazi did not recognize the albino's sarcasm, or perhaps he ignored it. 'Is Nadsokor your home city or did you adopt it?' he asked.

'A temporary home at best,' Elric told him truthfully.

'You have superficial looks in common with the people of Melniboné, whose greed led us to our present situation.' Lord Gho informed him. 'Is there Melnibonéan blood in your ancestry, perhaps?'

'I have no doubt of it.' Elric wondered why Lord Gho failed to draw the most obvious conclusion. 'Are the folk of the Dragon Isle still hated for what they did?'

'Their attempt upon our empire, you mean? I suppose so. But the Dragon Isle has long-since sunk beneath the waves, a victim of our sorcerous revenge, and her puny empire with her. Why should we give much thought to a dead race which was duly punished for its infamy?'

'Indeed.' Elric realized that so thoroughly had Quarzhasaat explained away her defeat and provided herself with a reason for taking no action, that she had consigned his entire people to oblivion in her legends. He could not therefore be a Melnibonéan, for Melniboné no longer existed. On that score, at least, he could know some peace of mind. Moreover, so uninterested were these people in the rest of the world and its denizens that Lord Gho Fhaazi had no further curiosity about him. The Quarzhasaatim had decided who and what Elric was and were satisfied. The albino reflected on the power of the human mind to build a fantasy and then defend it with complete determination as a reality.

Elric's chief dilemma now lay in the fact that he had no clear notion at all of the profession he was thought to practise or of the task Lord Gho wished him to perform.

The Quarzhasaati nobleman lowered his hands into a bowl of scented water and washed his beard, ostentatiously letting the liquid fall upon the geometrical mosaics of the floor.

'My servant tells me you understood his references,' he said, drying himself upon a gauzy towel. Again it was clear he usually employed slaves for this task but had chosen to dine alone with Elric, perhaps for fear of his secrets being overhead. 'The actual words of the prophecy are a little different. You know them?'

'No,' said Elric with immediate frankness. He wondered what would happen if Lord Gho realized that he was here under false pretences.

'When the Blood Moon makes fire of the Bronze Tent, then the Path to the Pearl will be opened.'

'Aha,' said Elric. 'Just so.'

'And the nomads tell us that the Blood Moon will appear over the mountains in little less than a week. And will shine upon the Waters of the Pearl.'

'Exactly,' said Elric.

'And so the path to the Fortress shall, of course, be revealed.'

Elric nodded with gravity and as if in confirmation.

'And a man such as yourself, with a knowledge at once supernatural and not supernatural, who can tread between reality and unreality, who knows the ways along the borders of dreams and waking, may break through the defences, overwhelm the guardians, and steal the Pearl!' Lord Gho's voice was a mixture both lascivious, venal and hotly excited.

'Indeed,' said the Emperor of Melniboné.

Lord Gho took Elric's reticence for discretion. 'Would you steal that Pearl for me, Sir Thief?'

Elric gave the matter apparent consideration before he spoke. 'There is considerable danger in the stealing, I would guess.'

'Of course. Of course. Our people are now convinced that none but one of your craft is able even to enter the Fortress, let alone reach the Pearl itself!'

'And where lies this Fortress of the Pearl?'

'I suppose at the Heart of the World.'

Elric frowned.

'After all,' said Lord Gho with some impatience, 'the jewel is known as the Pearl at the Heart of the World is it not?'

'I follow your reasoning,' said Elric, and resisted an urge to scratch the back of his head. Instead he considered a further draught of the marvellous elixir, although he was growing increasingly disturbed, both by Lord Gho's conversation and the fact that the pale liquid was so delicious to him. 'But surely there is some other clue . . . ?'

'I had thought such things your sphere, Sir Thief. You must go, of course, to the Silver Flower Oasis. It is the time when the nomads hold one of their gatherings. Some significance, no doubt, concerning the Blood Moon. It is most likely that at the Silver Flower Oasis the path will be opened to you. You have heard of the oasis, naturally.'

'I have no map, I fear,' Elric informed him, a little lamely.

'That will be provided. You have never travelled the Red Road?'

'As I've explained, I'm a stranger to your empire, Lord Gho.'

'But your geographies and histories must concern themselves with us!'

'I fear we are a little ignorant, my lord. We of the Young Kingdoms, so long in the shadow of wicked Melniboné, had not the opportunity to discover the joys of learning.'

Lord Gho raised his unnatural eyebrows. 'Yes,' he said, 'that would be the case, of course. Well, well, Sir Thief, we'll provide you with a map. But the Red Road's easy enough to follow since it leads from Quarzhasaat to the Silver Flower Oasis and beyond are only the mountains the nomads called the Ragged Pillars. They're of no interest to you, I think. Unless the Path of the Pearl takes you through them. That's a mysterious road and not, you'll appreciate, marked on any conventional map. At least none that we possess. And our libraries are the most sophisticated in the world.'

So determined was Elric to get the best from his reprieve that he was prepared to continue with this farce until he was clear of Quarzhasaat and riding for the Young Kingdoms again. 'And a steed, I hope. You'll give me a mount?'

'The finest. Will you need to redeem your crooked staff? Or is that merely a kind of sign of your calling?'

'I can find another.'

Lord Gho put his hand to his peculiar beard. 'Just as you say, Sir Thief.'

Elric determined to change the subject. 'You have said little about the nature of my fee.' He drained his goblet and clumsily Lord Gho filled it again.

'What would you usually ask?' said the Quarzhasaati.

'Well, this is an unusual commission.' Elric grew amused again at the situation. 'You understand that there are very few of my skill or indeed standing, even in the Young Kingdoms, and fewer still who come to Quarzhasaat . . . '

'If you bring me that specific Pearl, Sir Thief, you will have all manner of wealth. At least enough to make you one of the most powerful men in the Young Kingdoms. I would furnish you with an entire nobleman's household. Clothes, jewels, a palace, slaves. Or, if you wished to continue your travels, a caravan capable of purchasing a whole nation in the Young Kingdoms. You could become a prince there, possibly even a king!'

'A heady prospect,' said the albino sardonically.

'Add to that what I have already paid and shall be paying and I think you'll judge the reward handsome enough.'

'Aye. Generous, no doubt.' Elric frowned, glancing around the great room, with its hangings, its rich gem-work, its mosaics of precious stones, its elaborately ornamental cornices and pillars. He had it in mind to bargain further, because he guessed it was expected of him. 'But if I have a notion of the Pearl's worth to you, Lord Gho – what it will purchase for you here – you'll admit that the price you offer is not necessarily a large one.'

Lord Gho Fhaazi grew amused in turn. 'The Pearl will buy me the place on the Council of Six which shall shortly be vacated. The Nameless Seventh has given the Pearl as her price. It is why I must have it so soon. It is already promised. You have guessed this. There are rivals, but none who has offered so much.'

'And do these rivals know of your offer?'

'Doubtless there are rumours. But I would warn you to keep silent on the nature of your task . . . '

'You do not fear that I could look for a better bargain elsewhere in your city?'

'Oh, there will be those who would offer you more, if you were so greedy and so disloyal. But they could not offer you what I offer, Sir Thief.' And Lord Gho Fhaazi let his mouth form a terrible grin.

'Why so?' Elric felt suddenly trapped and his instinct was to reach for Stormbringer.

'They do not possess it.' Lord Gho pushed the flask towards the albino and Elric was a little surprised to see that he had already drunk another goblet of the elixir. He filled his cup once more and drank thoughtfully. Some of the truth was coming to him and he feared it.

'What can be as rare as the Pearl?' The albino put down his goblet.

154

He believed he had an idea of the answer.

Lord Gho was staring at him intently. 'You understand, I think.' Lord Gho smiled again.

'Aye.' Elric felt his spirits drop and he knew a frisson of deep terror mixed with a growing anger. 'The elixir, I suppose . . . '

'Oh, that's relatively easy to make. It is, of course, a poison – a drug which feeds off its user, giving him only an appearance of vitality. Eventually there is nothing left for the drug to feed upon and the death which results is almost always unpleasant. What a wretch the stuff makes of men and women who only a week or so earlier believed themselves powerful enough to rule the world!' Lord Gho began to laugh, his little ringlets bobbing at his face and on his head. 'Yet, dying, they will beg and beg for the thing which has killed them. Is that not an irony, Sir Thief? What's so rare as the Pearl? you ask. Why, the answer must be clear to you now, eh? An individual's life, is it not?'

'So I am dying. Why then should I serve you?'

'Because there is, of course, an antidote. Something which replaces everything the other drug steals, which does not cause a craving in the one who drinks it, which restores the user to full health in a matter of days and drives out the need for the original drug. So you see, Sir Thief, my offer to you was by no means an empty one. I can give you enough of the elixir to let you complete your task and, so long as you return here in good time, I can give you the antidote. You'll have gained much, eh?'

Elric straightened himself in his chair and put his hand upon the pommel of the Black Sword. 'I have already informed your courier that my life has only limited worth to me. There are certain things I value more.'

'I understood as much,' said Lord Gho Fhaazi with cruel joviality, 'and I respect you for your principles, Sir Thief. Your point's well put. But there's another life to consider, is there not? That of your accomplice?'

'I have no accomplice, sir.'

'Have you not? Have you not, Sir Thief? Would you come with me?'

Elric, mistrustful of the man, still saw no reason not to follow him when he strode arrogantly through the huge, curving doorway of the hall. At his belt once more Stormbringer grumbled and stirred like a suspicious hound.

The passages of the palace, lined in green, brown and yellow marble to give the feeling of a cool forest, scented with the most exquisite flowering shrubs, led them past rooms of retainers, menageries, tanks of fish and reptiles, a seraglio and an armoury, until Lord Gho arrived at a wooden door guarded by two soldiers in the impractically baroque armour of Quarzhasaat, their own beards oiled and forked into fantastically exaggerated shapes. They presented their engraved halberds as Lord Gho approached.

'Open this,' he ordered. And one took a massive key from within his breastplate, inserting it into the lock.

The door opened upon a small courtyard containing a defunct fountain, a little cloister and a set of living quarters on the far side.

'Where are you? Where are you, my little one? Show yourself! Quickly now!' Lord Gho was impatient.

There was a clink of metal and a figure emerged from the doorway. It had a piece of fruit in one hand, a loop or two of chain in the other and it walked with difficulty for the links were attached to a metal band riveted around its waist. 'Ah, master,' it said to Elric, 'you have not served me as I would have hoped.'

Elric's smile was grim. 'But maybe as you deserve, eh, Anigh?' He let his anger show. 'I did not imprison you, boy. I think the choice, in reality, was probably your own. You tried to deal with a power which clearly recognizes no decencies.'

Lord Gho was unmoved. 'He approached Raafi as-Keeme's manservant,' he said, staring at the boy with a certain interest, 'and offered your services. He said he was acting as your agent.'

'Well, so he was,' agreed Elric, his smile more sympathetic in view of Anigh's evident discomfiture. 'But that surely is not against your laws?'

'Certainly not. He showed excellent enterprise.'

'Then why is he imprisoned here?'

'That's a matter of expediency. You appreciate that, Sir Thief?'

'In other circumstances I would suspect some minor infamy,' said Elric carefully. 'But I know you, Lord Gho, to be a nobleman. You would not hold this boy in order to threaten me. It would be beneath you.'

'I hope I am a nobleman, sir. Yet in such times as these not all nobles in this city are bound by the old codes of honour. Not when such stakes are played for. You appreciate that, even though you are not yourself a nobleman. Or even, I suppose, a gentleman.'

'In Nadsokor I am thought one,' said Elric quietly.

'Oh, but of course. In Nadsokor.' Lord Gho pointed at Anigh, who smiled uncertainly from one to the other, not following this exchange at all. 'And in Nadsokor, I am sure, they would hold a convenient hostage if they could.'

'But this is unfair, sir.' Elric's voice was trembling with rage and he had to control himself not to reach his right hand towards the Black

Sword on his left hip. 'If I am killed in pursuit of my goal, the boy dies, just as if I had made my escape.'

'Well, yes, that is true, dear Thief. But I expect you to return, you see. If not – well, the boy will still be useful to me, both alive and dead.'

Anigh no longer smiled. Terror came slowly into his eyes. 'Oh, masters!'

'He'll not be harmed.' Lord Gho placed a cold, powdered hand on Elric's shoulders. 'For you will return with the Pearl at the Heart of the World, will you not?'

Elric breathed deeply, controlling himself. He felt a need deep within him, a need he could not readily identify. Was it bloodlust? Did he want to draw the Black Sword and suck the soul from this scheming degenerate? He spoke evenly. 'My lord, if you would release the boy, I will assure you of my best efforts . . . I will swear . . . '

'Good Thief, Quarzhasaat is full of men and women who give the most fulsome reassurances and who, I am sure, are sincere when they do so. They will swear great, important oaths upon all that is most holy to them. Yet should circumstances change, they forget those oaths. Some security, I find, is always useful to remind them of obligations undertaken. We are, you will appreciate, playing for the very highest stakes. There are really none higher in the whole world. A seat upon the Council.' This last sentence was emphasized without mockery. Clearly Lord Gho Fhaazi could see no greater goal.

Disgusted by the man's sophistry and contemptuous of his provincialism, Elric turned his back on Lord Gho. He addressed the lad. 'You'll observe, Anigh, that little luck befalls those who league themselves with me. I warned you of this. Yet still I shall endeaovur to return to save you.' His next sentence was uttered in the thievish cant. 'Meanwhile do not trust this filthy creature and make every sensible effort to escape on your own.'

'No gutter patois here!' cried Lord Gho, suddenly alarmed, 'or you both die at once!' Evidently he did not understand the cant as his courier had done.

'Best not to threaten me, Lord Gho.' Elric returned his hand to the hilt of his sword.

The nobleman laughed. 'What? Such belligerence! Understand you not, Sir Thief, that the elixir you drink is already killing you? You have three weeks before only the antidote will save you! Do you not feel the gnawing need for the drug? If such an elixir were harmless, why, sir, we should all use it and become gods!'

Elric could not be sure if it were his mind or his body which felt the pangs. He realized that even as his instincts drove him to kill the Quarzhasaati nobleman his craving for the drug threatened to dominate him. Even close to death when his own drugs failed him he had never craved anything so much. He stood with his whole body trembling as he sought to master it again. His voice was icy. 'This is more than minor infamy, Lord Gho. I congratulate you. You are a man of the cruellest and most unpleasant cunning. Are all those who serve upon the Council as corrupt as yourself?'

Lord Gho grew still more genial. 'This is unworthy of you, Sir Thief. All I am doing is assuring myself that you'll follow my interests for a while.' Again he chuckled. 'I have assured myself, in fact, that for this period of time your interests become mine. What is so wrong with that? I would not think it fitting in a self-confessed thief, to insult a noble of Quarzhasaat merely because he knows how to strike a good bargain!'

Elric's hatred for the man, whom originally he had only disliked, still threatened to consume him. But a new, colder mood took him as his hold over his own emotions returned. 'So you are saying that I am your slave, Lord Gho.'

'If you wish to put it so. At least until you bring me back the Pearl at the Heart of the World.'

'And should I find this Pearl for you, how do I know you will supply me with the poison's antidote?'

Lord Gho shrugged. 'That is for you to determine. You are an intelligent man for an outlander, and have survived this long, I'm sure, on your wits. But make no mistake. This potion is brewed for me alone and you'll not find the identical recipe anywhere else. Best hold to our bargain, Sir Thief, and depart from here ultimately a rich man. With your little friend all in one piece.'

Elric's mood had changed to one of grim humour. With his strength returned, no matter how artificially, he could wreak considerable destruction to Lord Gho and, indeed, the whole city if he chose. As if reading his mind, Stormbringer seemed to stir against his hip and Lord Gho permitted himself a small, nervous glance towards the great runesword.

Yet Elric did not want to die and neither did he desire Anigh's death. He decided to bide his time; to pretend, at least, to serve Lord Gho until he discovered more about the man and his ambitions, and found out more, if possible, of the nature of the drug he so longed for. Possibly the elixir did not kill. Possibly it was a potion common to Quarzhasaat and many possessed the antidote. But he had no friends here, other than Anigh, not even allies serving interests prepared to help him against Lord Gho as a common enemy.

'Perhaps,' said Elric, 'I do not care what becomes of the boy.'

'Oh, I think I read your character well enough, Sir Thief. You are like the nomads. And the nomads are like the people of the Young Kingdoms. They place unnaturally high values on the lives of those with whom they associate. They have a weakness for sentimental loyalties.'

Elric could not help considering the irony of this, for Melnibonéans thought themselves equally above such loyalties and he was one of the few who cared what happened to those not of his own immediate family. It was the reason he was here now. Fate, he reflected, was teaching him some strange lessons. He sighed. He hoped they did not kill him.

'If the boy is harmed when I return, Lord Gho – if he is harmed in any way – you will suffer a fate a thousand times worse than any you bestow on him. Or, I'll add, on me!' He turned blazing red eyes upon the aristocrat. It seemed that the fires of hell raged inside that skull.

Lord Gho shuddered, then smiled to hide his fear. 'No, no, no!' His unnatural brow clouded. 'It is not for you to threaten me! I have explained the terms. I am unused to this, Sir Thief, I warn you.'

Elric laughed and the fire in his eyes did not fade. 'I will make you used to everything you have accustomed others to, Lord Gho. Whatever happens. Do you follow me? This boy will not be harmed!'

'I have told you . . . '

'And I have warned you.' Elric's lids fell over his terrible eyes, as if he closed a door on a Realm of Chaos, yet still Lord Gho took a step backward. Elric's voice was a cold whisper. 'By all the power I command, I will be revenged upon you. Nothing will stop that vengeance. Not all your wealth. Not death itself.'

This time when Lord Gho made to smile he failed.

Anigh grinned suddenly, like the happy child he had been before these events. Evidently he believed Elric's words.

The albino prince moved like a hungry tiger towards Lord Gho. Then he staggered a little and drew a sharp breath. Clearly the elixir was losing its strength, or demanding more of him; he could not tell. He had experienced nothing like this before. He longed for another draught. He felt pains in his belly and chest, as if rats chewed him from within. He gasped.

Now Lord Gho found a vestige of his former humour. 'Refuse to serve me and your death's inevitable. I would caution you to greater politeness, Sir Thief.'

Elric drew himself up with some dignity. 'You should know this,

Lord Gho Fhaazi. If you betray any part of our bargain I will keep my oath and bring such destruction upon you and your city you will regret you ever heard my name. And you will only hear who I am, Lord Gho Fhaazi, before you die, your city and all its degenerate inhabitants dying with you.'

The Quarzhasaati made to reply then bit back his words, saying only, 'You have three weeks.'

With his remaining strength, Elric dragged Stormbringer from its scabbard. The black metal pulsed, black light pouring from it while the runes carved upon the blade twisted and danced and a hideous, anticipatory song began to sound in that courtyard, echoing through all the old towers and minarets of Quarzhasaat. 'This sword drinks souls, Lord Gho. It could drink yours now and give me more strength than any potion. But you have a minor advantage over me for the moment. I'll agree to your bargain. But if you lie . . . '

'I do not lie!' Lord Gho had retreated to the other side of the barren fountain. 'No, Sir Thief, I do not lie! You must do as I say. Bring me the Pearl at the Heart of the World and I will repay you with all the wealth I promised, with your own life and that of the boy!'

The Black Sword growled, clearly demanding the nobleman's soul there and then.

With a yelp, Anigh disappeared into the little room.

'I'll leave in the morning.' Reluctantly Elric sheathed the sword. 'You must tell me which of the city's gates I must use to travel upon the Red Road to the Silver Flower Oasis. And I will want your honest advice on how best to ration that poisoned elixir'

'Come.' Lord Gho spoke with nervous eagerness. 'There is more in the hall. It awaits you. I had no wish to spoil our encounter with bad manners . . . '

Elric licked lips already growing unpleasantly dry. He paused, looking towards the doorway from which the boy's face could just be seen.

'Come, Sir Thief.' Lord Gho's hand again went to Elric's arm. 'In the hall, More elixir. Even now. You long for it, do you not?'

He spoke the truth, but Elric let his hatred control his lust for the potion. He called: 'Anigh! Young Anigh!'

Slowly the boy emerged. 'Aye, master.'

'I swear you'll suffer no harm from any action of mine. And this foul degenerate now understands that if he hurts you in any way while I am gone he will die in the most terrible torment. And yet, boy, you must remember all I've said, for I know not where this adventure will lead me.' And Elric added in the cant, 'Perhaps to death.'

'I hear you,' said Anigh in the same tongue. 'But I would beg you, master, not to die yourself. I have some interest in your remaining alive.'

'No more!' Lord Gho strode across the courtyard signalling for Elric to accompany him. 'Come. I'll supply you with all you need to find the Fortress of the Pearl.'

'And I would be most grateful if you did not let me die. I would be a most grateful boy, master,' said Anigh from behind them as the door closed.

3

On the Red Road

So it was that morning Elric of Melniboné left ancient Quarzhasaat not knowing what he sought or where to find it; knowing only that he must take the Red Road to the Silver Flower Oasis and there find the Bronze Tent where he would learn how he might continue on the path to the Pearl at the Heart of the World. And if he failed in this numinous quest, his own life at very least would be forfeit.

Lord Gho Fhaazi had offered no further illumination and it was evident the ambitious politician knew no more than he had repeated.

'The Blood Moon must make fire of the Bronze Tent before the Pathway to the Pearl shall be revealed.'

Knowing nothing of Quarzhasaat's legends or history and very little of her geography, Elric had decided to follow the map he had been given. It was simple enough. It showed a trail stretching for at least a hundred miles between Quarzhasaat and the oddly-named oasis. Beyond this were the Ragged Pillars, a range of low mountains. The Bronze Tent was not named and neither was there any reference to the Pearl.

Lord Gho believed the nomads to be better informed but had not been able to guarantee that they would be prepared to talk to Elric. He hoped that, once they understood who he was, and with a little of Lord Gho's gold to reassure them, they would be friendly, but he knew nothing of the Sighing Desert's hinterland, nor its people. He knew only that Lord Gho despised the nomads as primitives and resented occasionally admitting them into the city to trade. Elric hoped the nomads would be better mannered than those who still believed this whole continent to be under their rule.

The Red Road was well-named, dark as half-dried blood, cutting through the desert between high banks which suggested it had once been the river on whose sides Quarzhasaat had originally been built. Every few miles the banks descended to reveal the great desert in all directions – a sea of rolling dunes which stirred in a breeze whose voice was faint here but still resembled the sighing of some imprisoned lover.

The sun climbed slowly into a glaring indigo sky as still as an actor's backdrop and Elric was grateful for the local costume provided him by Raafi as-Keeme before he left, a white cowl, loose white jerkin and britches, white linen shoes to the knee and a visor which protected his eyes. His horse, a bulky, graceful beast capable of great speed and endurance, was similarly clothed in linen, to protect it from both the sun and the sand which blew in constant gentle drifts across the landscape. Clearly some effort was made to keep the Red Road free of the drifts which gathered against its banks and gradually built them into walls.

Elric had lost none of his hatred either of his situation or of Lord Gho Fhaazi; neither had he lost his determination to remain alive and rescue Anigh, return to Melniboné and be reunited with Cymoril. Lord Gho's elixir had proved as addictive as he had claimed and Elric carried two flasks of it in his saddle-bags. Now he truly believed it must indeed kill him eventually and that only Lord Gho possessed an antidote. This belief reinforced his determination to be revenged upon that nobleman at the earliest possible opportunity.

The Red Road seemed endless. The sky shivered with heat as the sun climbed higher. And Elric, who disapproved of useless regret, found himself wishing he had never been foolish enough to buy the map from the Ilmioran sailor or to venture so badly prepared into the desert.

'To summon supernaturals to aid me now would compound the folly,' he said aloud to the wilderness. 'What's more I might need that aid when I reach the Fortress of the Pearl.' He knew that his self-disgust had not merely caused him to commit further foolishness, but still dictated his actions. Without it, his thoughts might have been clearer and he might better have anticipated Lord Gho's trickery.

Even now he doubted his own instincts. For the past hour he had guessed that he was being followed but had seen no one behind him on the Red Road. He had taken to glancing back suddenly, to stopping without warning, to riding back a few yards. But he was apparently as alone now as he had been when he began the journey.

'Perhaps that damned elixir addles my senses also,' he said, patting the dusty cloth of his horse's neck. The great bulwarks of the road were falling away here, becoming little more than mounds on either side of him. He reined in the horse, for he fancied he could see movement that was more than drifting sand. Little figures ran here and there on long legs, upright like so many tiny manikins. He peered hard at them but then they were gone. Other, larger, creatures moving with far slower speeds, seemed to creep just below the surface of the sand while a cloud of something black hovered over them, following them as they made their ponderous way across the desert.

Elric was learning that, in this part of the Sighing Desert at least, what appeared to be a lifeless wilderness was actually no such thing. He hoped that the large creatures he detected did not regard Man as a worthwhile prey.

Again he received a sense of something behind him and turning suddenly thought he glimpsed a flash of yellow, perhaps a cloak, but it had disappeared in a slight bend behind him. His temptation was to stop, to rest for an hour or two before continuing, but he was anxious to reach the Silver Flower Oasis as soon as possible. There was little time to achieve his goal and return with the Pearl to Quarzhasaat.

He sniffed the air. The breeze brought a new smell. If he had not known better he would have thought someone was burning kitchen waste; it was the same acrid stink. Then he peered into the middle-distance and detected a faint plume of smoke. Were there nomads so close to Quarzhasaat? He had understood that they did not like coming within a hundred miles or more of the city unless they had specific reasons to do so. And if people were camped here, why did they not set their tents closer to the road? Nothing had been said of bandits, so he did not fear attack, but he remained curious, continuing his journey with a certain caution.

The walls rose up again and blocked his view of the desert, but the stink of burning grew stronger and stronger until it was almost unbearable. He felt the stuff clogging his lungs. His eyes began to stream. It was a most noxious smell, almost as if someone were burning putrefying corpses.

Again the walls sank a little until he could see over them. Less than a mile away, as best he could judge, he saw about twenty plumes of smoke, darker now, while other clouds danced and zig-zagged about them. He began to suspect that he had come upon a tribe who kept their cooking fires alight as they travelled in waggons of some kind. Yet it was hard to know what kind of waggons would easily cross the deep drifts. And again he wondered why they were not on the Red Road.

Tempted to investigate he knew he would be a fool to leave the road. He might again become lost and be in even worse condition than when Anigh had found him all those days ago on the far side of Quarzhasaat.

He was about to dismount and rest his mind and eyes, if not his body, for an hour, when the wall nearest him began to heave and quake and large cracks appeared in it. The terrible smell of burning was even closer now and he cleared his throat, coughing to rid himself of the stench while his horse began to whinny and refuse the rein as Elric tried to drive him forward.

Suddenly a flock of creatures ran directly across his path, bursting from the newly-made holes in the walls. These were what he had mistaken for tiny men. Now that he saw them more closely he realized they were some kind of rat, but a rat which ran on long hind-legs, its forelegs short and held up high against its chest, its long, grey face full of sharp little teeth, its huge ears making it seem like some flying creature attempting to leave the ground.

There came a great rumbling and cracking. Black smoke blinded Elric and his horse reared. He saw a shape moving out of the broken banks – a massive, flesh-coloured body on a dozen legs, its mandibles clattering as it chased the rats, which were clearly its natural prey. Elric let the horse have its head and looked back to get a clearer view of a creature he had thought existed only in ancient times. He had read of such beasts but had believed them extinct. They were called firebeetles. By some trick of biology the gigantic beetles secreted oily pools in their heavy carapaces. These pools, exposed to the sunlight and the flames already burning on other backs, would catch fire so that sometimes as many as twenty spots on the beetles' impervious backs would be burning at any one time and would only be extinguished when a beast dug its way deep underground during its breeding season. This was what he had seen in the distance.

The firebeetles were hunting.

They moved with awful speed now. At least a dozen of the gigantic insects were closing in on the road and Elric realized to his horror that he and his horse were about to be trapped in a sweep designed to catch the man-rats. He knew that the firebeetles would not discriminate where flesh was concerned and he could well be eaten by purest accident by a beast which was not known for making prey of men. The horse continued to rear and snort and only put all hooves on the ground when Elric forced it under his control, drawing Stormbringer and considering how useless even that sorcerous sword would be against the pink-grey carapaces from which flames now leapt and guttered. Stormbringer drew scant energy from natural creatures like these. He could only hope for a lucky blow splitting a back, perhaps, and breaking through the tightening circle before he was completely trapped.

He swung the great black battle-blade down and severed a waving appendage. The beetle hardly noticed and did not pause for a second in its progress. Elric yelled and swung again and fire scattered. Hot oil was flung into the air as he struck the firebeetle's back and again failed to do it any significant harm. The shrieking of the horse and the wailing of the blade now mingled and Elric found himself yelling as he turned the horse this way and that in search of escape while all around his horse's feet the man-rats scurried in terror, unable to burrow easily into the hard clay of that much-travelled road. Blood spattered against Elric's legs and arms, against the linen which clad his horse to below its knees. Little spots of flaming oil flared on cloth and burned holes. The beetles were feasting, moving more slowly as they ate. There was nowhere in the circle a gap large enough for horse and rider to escape.

Elric considered trying to ride the horse over the backs of the great beetles, though it seemed their shells would be too slippery for purchase. There was no other hope. He was about to force the horse forward when he heard a peculiar humming in the air around him, saw the air suddenly fill with flies and knew that these were the scavengers which always followed the firebeetles, feeding off whatever scraps they left and upon the dung they scattered as they travelled. Now they were beginning to settle on him and his horse, adding to his horror. He slapped at the things, but they formed a thick coat, crawling on every part of him, their noise both sickening and deafening, their bodies half-blinding him.

The horse cried out again and stumbled. Elric desperately tried to see ahead. The smoke and the flies were too much for either himself or his horse. Flies filled his mouth and nostrils. He gagged, trying to brush them from him, spitting them down to where the little man-rats squealed and died.

Another sound came dimly to him and miraculously the flies began to rise. Through watering eyes he saw the beetles start to move all in one direction, leaving a space through which he might ride. Without another thought he spurred his horse towards the gap, dragging great gasps of air into his lungs, as yet unsure if he had escaped or whether he had merely moved into a wider circle of firebeetles, for the smoke and the noise were still confusing him.

Spitting more flies from his mouth, he adjusted his visor and peered ahead. The beetles were no longer in sight, though he could hear them behind him. There were new shapes in the dust and smoke.

They were riders, moving on either side of the Red Road, driving the beetles back with long spears which they hooked under the carapaces and used as goads, doing the creatures no real harm but giving them enough pain to make them move, where Elric's blade had failed. The riders wore flowing yellow robes which were caught by the breeze of their own movement and lifted about them like wings as, systematically, they herded the firebeetles away from the road and out into the desert while the remainder of the man-rats, perhaps grateful for this unexpected salvation, scattered and found burrows in the sand.

Elric did not sheath Stormbringer. He knew enough to understand that these warriors might well be saving him only incidentally and might even blame him for being in their way. The other possibility, which was stronger, was that these men had been following him for some time and did not wish the firebeetles to cheat them of their prey.

Now one of the yellow-clad riders detached himself from the throng and galloped up to Elric, hailing him with spear raised.

'I thank you mightily,' the albino said. 'You have saved my life, sir. I trust I did not disrupt your hunt too much.'

The rider was taller than Elric, very thin, with a gaunt dark face and black eyes. His head was shaved and both his lips were decorated, apparently with tiny tattoos, as if he wore a mask of fine, multicoloured lace across his mouth. The spear was not sheathed and Elric prepared to defend himself, knowing that his chances against even so many human beings were greater than they had been against the firebeetles.

The man frowned at Elric's statement, puzzled for a moment. Then his brow cleared. 'We did not hunt the firebeetles. We saw what was happening and realized that you did not know enough to get out of the creatures' way. We came as quickly as we could. I am Manag Iss of the Yellow Sect, kinsman to Councillor Iss. I am of the Sorcerer Adventurers.'

Elric had heard of these sects, who had been the chief warrior caste of Quarzhasaat and had been largely responsible for the spells which inundated the Empire with sand. Had Lord Gho, not trusting him completely, set them to following him? Or were they assassins instructed to kill him?

'I thank you, nonetheless, Manag Iss, for your intervention. I owe you my life. I am honoured to meet one of your sect. I am Elric of Nadsokor in the Young Kingdoms.'

'Aye, we know of you. We were trailing you, waiting until we were far enough from the city to speak to you safely.'

'Safely? You're in no danger from me, Master Sorcerer Adventurer.'

Manag Iss was evidently not a man who smiled often and when he smiled now it was a strange contortion of the face. Behind them, other members of the sect were beginning to ride back, rehousing their long spears in the scabbards attached to their saddles. 'I did not think we were, Master Elric. We come to you in peace and we are your friends, if you will have us. My kinswoman sends her greetings. She is the wife of Councillor Iss. Iss remains, however, our family name. We all tend to marry the same blood, our clan.'

'I am glad to make your acquaintance.' Elric waited for the man to speak further.

Manag Iss waved a long, brown hand whose nails had been removed and replaced with the same tattoos as those on his mouth. 'Would you dismount and talk, for we come with messages and the offer of gifts.'

Elric slipped Stormbringer back into the scabbard and swung his leg over his saddle, sliding to the dust of the Red Road. He watched as the beetles lurched slowly away, perhaps in search of more man-rats, their smoking backs reminding him of the fires of the leper camps on the outskirts of Jadmar.

'My kinswoman wishes you to know that she, as well as the Yellow Sect, are all at your service, Master Elric. We are prepared to give you whatever aid you require in seeking out the Pearl at the Heart of the World.'

Now Elric felt a certain amusement. 'I fear you have me at a disadvantage, Sir Manag Iss. Do you journey in quest of treasure?'

Manag Iss let an expression of mild impatience cross his strange face. 'It is known that your patron Lord Gho Fhaazi has promised the Pearl at the Heart of the World to the Nameless Seventh and she, in turn, has promised him the new place on the Council in return. We have discovered enough to know that only an exceptional thief could have been commissioned to this task. And Nadsokor is famous for her exceptional thieves. It is a task which, I am sure you know, all Sorcerer Adventurers have failed in completing. For centuries members of every sect have tried to find the Pearl at the Heart of the World, whenever the Blood Moon rises. Those few who ever survived to return to Quarzhasaat were raving mad and died soon after. Only recently have we received some little knowledge and evidence that the Pearl does actually exist. We know, therefore, that you are a dreamthief, though you disguise your profession by not carrying your hooked staff, for we do know that only a dreamthief of the greatest skill could reach the Pearl and bring it back.'

'You tell me more than I knew, Manag Iss,' said Elric seriously. 'And it is true that I am commissioned by Lord Gho Fhaazi. But know you this also – I go upon this journey reluctantly.' And Elric trusted his instincts enough to reveal to Manag Iss the hold that Lord Gho had over him.

Manag Iss plainly believed him. His tattooed fingertips brushed lightly over the tattoos of his lips as he considered this information.

'That elixir is well-known to the Sorcerer Adventurers. We have distilled it for millennia. It is true that it feeds the very substance of the user back to him. The antidote is much harder to prepare. I am surprised that Lord Gho claims to possess it. Only certain sects of the Sorcerer Adventurers own small quantities. If you would return with us to Quarzhasaat we shall, I know, be able to administer the antidote to you within a day at the most.'

Elric considered this carefully. Manag Iss was employed by one of Lord Gho's rivals. This made him suspicious of any offer, no matter how generous it seemed. Councillor Iss, or the Lady Iss, or whoever it was desired to place their own candidate upon the Council, would no doubt be prepared to stop at nothing to achieve that end. For all Elric knew, Manag Iss's offer might merely be a means of lulling him out of his wariness so that he might be the more easily murdered.

'You'll forgive me if I am blunt,' said the albino, 'but I have no means of trusting you, Manag Iss. I know already that Quarzhasaat is a city whose chief sport is intrigue and I have no wish to be involved in that game of plots and counter-plots which your fellow citizens seem to enjoy so thoroughly. If the antidote to the elixir exists, as you say, I would be better disposed to consider your claims if, for instance, you were to meet me at the Silver Flower Oasis in, say, six days from today. I have enough elixir to last me three weeks, which is the time of the Blood Moon plus the time of my journey from and to your city. This will convince me of your altruism.'

'I shall also be frank,' said Manag Iss, his voice cool. 'I am commissioned and bound both by my blood oath, my sect contract and my honour as a member of our holy guild. That commission is to convince you, by any means, either to relinquish your quest or to sell the Pearl. If you will not relinquish the quest, then I will agree to purchase the Pearl from you at any price save, of course, a position on our Council. Therefore I will match Lord Gho's offer and add to it anything else you desire.'

Elric spoke with some regret. 'You cannot match his offer, Manag Iss. There is the matter of the boy whom he will kill.'

'The boy is of little importance, surely.'

'Little, doubtless, in the great scheme of things as they are played out in Quarzhasaat.' Elric grew weary.

Realizing he had made a tactical mistake, Manag Iss said hastily: 'We'll rescue the boy. Tell us how to find him.'

'I think I'll keep to my original bargain,' said Elric. 'There seems little to choose between the offers.'

'What if Lord Gho were assassinated?'

Elric shrugged and made to remount. 'I'm grateful for your intervention, Manag Iss. I'll consider your offer as I ride. You'll appreciate I have little time to find the Fortress of the Pearl.'

'Master, Thief, I would warn you – ' At this Manag Iss broke off. He looked behind him, along the Red Road. There was a faint cloud of dust to be seen. Out of it emerged dim shapes, their robes pale green and flowing behind them as they rode. Manag Iss cursed. But he was smiling his peculiar smile as the leaders galloped up.

It was clear to Elric, from their garb, that these men were also members of the Sorcerer Adventurers. They, too, had tattoos, but upon the eyelids and the wrists, and their billowing surcoats, which reached to their ankles, bore an embroidered flower upon them while the trimming of sleeves had the same design in miniature. The leader of these newcomers jumped from his horse and approached Manag Iss. He was a short man, handsome and clean-shaven save for a tiny goatee which was oiled in the fashion of Quarzhasaat and drawn to an exaggerated point. Unlike the Yellow Sect members, he carried a sword, unscabbarded in a simple leather harness. He made a sign which Manag Iss imitated.

'Greetings, Oled Alesham and peace upon you. The Yellow Sect wishes great successes to the Foxglove Sect and is curious as to why you travel so far along the Red Road.' All this was spoken rapidly, a formality. Manag Iss doubtless was as aware as Elric why Oled Alesham and his men followed.

'We ride to give protection to this thief,' said the leader of the Foxglove Sect with a nod of acknowledgement to Elric. 'He is a stranger to our land and we would offer him help, as is our ancient custom.'

Elric himself smiled openly at this. 'And are you, Master Oled Alesham, related, by any chance, to some member of the Six and One Other?'

Oled Alesham's sense of humour was better developed than that of Manag Iss. 'Oh, we are all related to everyone in Quarzhasaat, Sir Thief. We are on our way to the Silver Flower Oasis and thought you might require assistance with your quest.'

'He has no quest,' said Manag Iss, then instantly regretted the stupidity of the lie. 'No quest, that is, save the one he shares with his friends of the Yellow Sect.'

'Since we are bound by our guild loyalties not to fight, we are not, I hope, going to quarrel over who is to escort our guest to the Silver Flower Oasis,' said Oled Alesham with a chuckle. He was greatly amused by the situation. 'Are we all to journey together, perhaps? And each receive a little piece of the Pearl?'

'There is no Pearl,' said Elric, 'and shall not be if I am further hindered in my journey. I thank you, gentlemen, for your concern, and I bid you all good afternoon.'

This caused some consternation amongst the two rival sects and they were attempting to decide what to do when over the rubble created by the firebeetles there rode about half-a-dozen black-clad, heavily veiled and cowled warriors, their swords already drawn.

Elric, guessing these to mean him no good, withdrew so that Manag Iss and Oled Alesham and their men were surrounding him. 'More of your kind, gentlemen?' he asked, his hand on the hilt of his own sword.

'They are the Moth Brotherhood,' said Oled Alesham, 'and they are assassins. They do nothing but kill, Sir Thief. You would best throw in with us. Evidently somone has determined that you should be murdered before you even see the Blood Moon rising.'

'Will you help me defend myself?' asked the albino, mounting and getting ready to fight.

'We cannot,' said Manag Iss and he sounded genuinely regretful. 'We cannot do battle with our own kind. But they will not kill us if we surround you. You would be best advised to accept our offer, Sir Thief.'

Then the impatient rage which was a mark of his ancient blood took hold of Elric and he drew Stormbringer without further ado. 'I am tired of these little bargains,' he said. 'I would ask you to stand aside from me, Manag Iss, for I mean to do battle.'

'There are too many!' Oled Alesham was shocked. 'You'll be butchered. These are skilled killers!'

'Oh, so am I, master Sorcerer Adventurer. So am I.' And with that Elric drove his horse forward, through the startled ranks of Yellow and Foxglove Sects, directly at the leader of the Moth Brotherhood.

The runesword began to howl in unison with its master and the white face glowed with the energy of the damned while the red eyes blazed and the Sorcerer Adventurers realized for the first time that an extraordinary creature had come amongst them and that they had underestimated him.

Stormbringer rose in Elric's gloved hand, its black metal catching the rays of the glaring sun and seeming to absorb them. The black blade fell, almost as if by accident, and split the skull of the Moth Brotherhood's leader, clove him to his breastbone and howled as it sucked the man's soul from him in the very split second of his dying. Elric turned in his saddle, the sword swinging to bury its edge in the side of the assassin riding up on his left. The man shrieked. 'It has me! Ah, no!'

And he, too, died.

Now the other veiled riders were warier, circling the albino at some distance while they determined their strategy. They had thought they would need none, that all they must do was ride a Young Kingdom thief down and destroy him. There were five of the black riders left. They were calling on their fellow guild members for aid, but neither Manag Iss nor Oled Alesham was ready to give orders to his own people which could result in the unholy death they had already witnessed.

Elric showed no such prudence. He rode directly at the next assassin, who parried with great cleverness and even struck under Elric's guard for a second before his arm was severed and he fell back in his saddle, blood gouting from the stump. Another graceful movement, half Elric's, half his sword's, and that man, too, had his soul drawn from him. Now the others fell back amongst the yellow and green robes of their brothers. There was panic in their eyes. They recognized sorcery, even if this was something more powerful than they had ever anticipated.

'Hold! Hold!' cried Manag Iss. 'There is no need for any more of us to die! We are here to make the thief an offer. Did old Duke Ral send you here?'

'He wants no more intrigue around the Pearl,' growled one of the veiled men. 'He said clean death was the best solution. But these deaths are not clean for us.'

'Those who commission us have set the pattern,' said Oled Alesham. 'Thief! Put up your sword. We do not wish to fight you!'

'I believe that.' Elric was grim. The blood-lust was still upon him and he fought to control it. 'I believe you merely wish to slay me without a fight. You are fools all. I have already warned Lord Gho of this. I have the power to destroy you. It is your good fortune that I am sworn to myself not to use my power merely to make others perform my will to my own selfish ends. But I am not sworn to let myself die at the hands of hired slaughterers! Go back! Go back to Quarzhasaat!'

This last was almost screamed and the sword echoed it as he lifted the great black blade into the sky, to warn them of what would befall them if they did not obey.

Manag Iss said softly to Elric, 'We cannot, Sir Thief. We can only pursue our commissions. It is the way of our Guild, of all the Sorcerer Adventurers. Once we have agreed to perform a task, then the task must be performed. Death is the only excuse for failure.'

'Then I must kill you all,' said Elric simply. 'Or you must kill me.'

'We can still make the bargain I spoke of,' said Manag Iss. 'I was not deceiving you, Sir Thief.'

'My offer, too, is sound,' said Oled Alesham.

'But the Moth Brotherhood is sworn to kill me,' Elric pointed out, almost amused, 'and you cannot defend me against them. Nor, I would guess, can you do anything but aid them against me.'

Manag Iss was trying to draw back from the black-robed assassins but it was clear they were determined to retain the safety of their guild ranks.

Then Oled Alesham murmured something to the leader of the Yellow Sect which made Manag Iss thoughtful. He nodded and signed to the remaining members of the Moth Brotherhood. For a few moments they were in conference, then Manag Iss looked up and addressed Elric.

'Sir Thief, we have found a formula which will leave you in peace and allow us to return with honour to Quarzhasaat. If we retreat now, will you promise not to follow us?'

'If I have your word you'll not let those Moths attack me again.' Elric was calmer now. He laid the crooning runeblade across his arm.

'Put away your swords, brothers!' cried Oled Alesham and the Moths obeyed at once.

Next Elric sheathed Stormbringer. The unholy energy which he had drawn from those who sought to slay him was filling him now and he felt all the old heightened sensibility of his race, all the arrogance and all the power of his ancient blood. He laughed at his enemies. 'Know you not whom you would kill, gentlemen?'

Oled Alesham scowled a little. 'I am beginning to guess a little of your origins, Sir Thief. 'Tis said that the lords of the Bright Empire carried such blades as yours once, in a time before this time. In a time before history. 'Tis said those blades are living things, a race allied to your own. You have the look of our long-lost enemies. Does this mean that Melniboné did not drown?'

'I'll leave that for you to think on, Master Oled Alesham.' Elric suspected that they plotted some trick but was almost careless. 'If your people spent less time maintaining their own devalued myths about themselves and more upon studying the world as it is I think your city would have a greater chance of surviving. As it is, the place is crumbling beneath the weight of its own degraded fictions. The legends which offer a race their sense of pride and history eventually become putrid. If Melniboné drowns, Master Sorcerer Adventurer, it will be as Quarzhasaat drowns now . . . '

'We are unconcerned with matters of philosophy,' Manag Iss said with evident poor temper. 'We do not question the motives or the ideas of those who employ us. That is written in our charters.'

'And must therefore be obeyed!' Elric smiled. 'Thus you celebrate your decadence and resist reality.'

'Go now,' said Oled Alesham. 'It is not your business to instruct us in moral matters and not ours to listen. We have left our student days behind.'

Elric accepted this mild rebuke and turned his tiring horse again towards the Silver Flower Oasis. He did not look back once at the Sorcerer Adventurers but guessed them to be deeper than ever in conversation. He began to whistle as the Red Road stretched before him and the stolen energy of his enemies filled him with euphoria. His thoughts were on Cymoril and his return to Melniboné where he hoped to ensure his nation's survival by bringing about in her the very changes he had spoken of to the Sorcerer Adventurers. At this moment, his goal seemed a little closer, his mind clearer than it had been for several months.

Night seemed to come swiftly and with it a rapid descent in temperature which left the albino shivering and robbed him of some of his good humour. He drew heavier robes from his saddle-bags and donned them as he tethered his horse and prepared to build a fire. The elixir on which he had depended had not been touched since his encounter with the Sorcerer Adventurers and he was beginning to understand its nature a little better. The craving had faded, although he was still conscious of it, and he could now hope to free himself of his dependency without need of further bargaining with Lord Gho.

'All I have to do,' he said to himself as he ate sparingly of the food provided him, 'is to make sure that I am attacked at least once a day by members of the Moth Brotherhood . . . ' And with that he put away his figs and bread, wrapped himself in the night-cloak and prepared to sleep.

His dreams were formal and familiar. He was in Imrryr, the Dreaming City, and Cymoril sat beside him as he lay back upon the Ruby Throne, contemplating his court. Yet this was not the court which the emperors of Melniboné had kept for the thousands of years of their rule. This was a court to which had come men and women of all nations, from each of the Young Kingdoms, from Elwher and the Unmapped East, from Phum, from Quarzhasaat even. Here information and philosophies were exchanged, together with all manner of goods. This was a court whose energies were not devoted to maintaining itself unchanged for eternity, but to every kind of new idea and lively, humane discussion, which welcomed fresh thought not as a threat to its existence but as a very necessity to its continued well-being whose wealth was devoted to experiment in the arts and sciences, to supporting those who were needy, to aiding thinkers and scholars. The Bright Empire's brightness would come no longer from the glow of putrefaction but from the light of reason and good will.

This was Elric's dream, more coherent now than it had ever been. This was his dream and it was why he travelled the world, why he refused the power which was his, why he risked his life, his mind, his love and everything else he valued, for he believed that there was no life worth living that was not risked in pursuit of knowledge and justice. And this was why his fellow countrymen feared him. Justice was not obtained, he believed, by administration but by experience. One must know what it was to suffer humiliation and powerlessness; at least to some degree, before one could entirely appreciate its effect. One must give up power if one was to achieve true justice. This was not the logic of Empire, but it was the logic of one who truly loved the world and desired to see an age dawn when all people would be free to pursue their ambitions in dignity and self-respect.

'Ah, Elric,' said Yyrkoon, crawling like a serpent from behind the Ruby Throne, 'thou art an enemy of your own race, an enemy of her gods and an enemy of all I worship and desire. That is why you must be destroyed and why I must possess all you own. All . . . '

At this, Elric woke up. His skin was clammy. He reached for his sword. He had dreamed of Yyrkoon as a serpent and now he could swear he heard something slithering over the sand not far off. The horse smelled it and grunted, displaying increasing agitation. Elric rose, the night-cloak falling from him. The horse's breath was steaming in the air. There was a moon overhead, casting a faintly blue light over the desert.

The slithering came closer. Elric peered at the high banks of the road but could make out nothing. He was sure that the firebeetles had not returned. And what he heard next confirmed this certainty. It was a great outpouring of foetid breath, a rushing sound, almost a shriek, and he knew some gigantic beast was nearby.

Elric knew also that the beast was not of this desert, nor indeed of this world. He could sniff the stink of something supernatural, something which had been raised from the pits of Hell, summoned to serve his enemies, and he knew suddenly why the Sorcerer Adventurers had called off their attack so readily, what they had planned when they had let him go.

Cursing his own euphoria, Elric drew Stormbringer and crept back into the darkness, away from the horse.

The roar came from behind him. He whirled and there it was!

It was a huge cat-like thing, save that its body resembled that of a baboon with an arching tail and there were spines along its back. Its claws were extended and it reared up, reaching for him as he yelled and jumped to one side, slashing at it. The thing flickered with peculiar colours and lights, as if not quite of the material world. He was in no doubt of its origin. Such things had been summoned more than once by the sorcerers of Melniboné to help them against those they sought to destroy. He searched his mind for some spell, something which would drive it back to the regions from which it had been summoned, but it had been too long since he had practised any kind of sorcery himself.

The thing had got his scent now and was moving in pursuit as he ran rapidly and erratically away from it across the desert, attempting to put as much space between himself and the creature as possible.

The beast screamed. It was hungry for more than Elric's flesh. Those who had summoned it had promised it his soul at very least. It was the usual reward to a supernatural beast of that kind. He felt its claws whistle in the air behind him as it again attempted to seize him and he turned, slashing at the creature's forepaws with his sword. Stormbringer caught one of the pads and drew something like blood. Elric felt a sickening wave of energy pour into him. He stabbed this time and the beast shrieked, opening a red mouth in which rainbow-coloured teeth glittered.

'By Arioch,' gasped Elric, 'you're an ugly creature. 'Tis almost a duty to send you back to hell . . . ' And Stormbringer leapt out again, slashing at the same wounded paw. But this time the cat-thing saved itself and began to gather itself for a spring which Elric knew he had little chance of surviving. A supernatural beast was not as easily slain as the warriors of the Moth Brotherhood.

It was then he heard a yell and turning saw an apparition moving towards him in the moonlight. It was man-like, riding on an oddly humped animal which galloped more rapidly than any horse.

The cat-creature paused uncertainly and turned, spitting and growling, to deal with this distraction before finishing the albino.

Realizing that this was not a further threat but some passing traveller attempting to come to his assistance, Elric shouted: 'Best save yourself, sir. That beast is supernatural and cannot easily be killed by familiar means!'

The voice which replied was deep and vibrant, full of good humour. 'I'm aware of that, sir, and would be obliged if you would deal with the thing while I draw its attention to myself.' Whereupon the rider turned his odd mount and began to ride at a reduced pace in the opposite direction. The supernatural creature was not, however, deceived. Clearly those who had raised it had instructed it as to its prey. It scented at the air, seeking out Elric again.

The albino lay behind a dune, gathering his strength. He remembered a minor spell which, given the extra energy he had drawn already from the demon, he might be able to employ. He began to sing in the old, beautiful, musical language they called High Melnibonéan, and as he did so he took up a handful of sand and passed it through the air with strange, graceful movements. Gradually, from the grains of the dunes, a spiral of sand began to move upwards, whistling as it spun faster and faster in the oddly-coloured moonlight.

The cat-beast growled and rushed forward. But Elric stood between it and the whirling spiral. Then, at the last moment, he moved aside. The spiral's voice rose still higher. It was no more than a simple trick taught to young sorcerers by way of encouragement, but it had the effect of blinding the cat-thing long enough for Elric to charge and with his sword duck under the claws to plunge the blade deep into the beast's vitals.

At once the energy began to drain into the blade and from the blade into Elric. The albino screamed and raved as the stuff filled him. Demon-energy was not unfamiliar to him, but it threatened to make a demon of him, too, for it was all but impossible to control.

'Aah! It is too much. Too much!' He writhed in agony while the daemonic life-essence poured into him and the cat-thing roared and died.

Then it was gone and Elric lay gasping on the sand as the beast's corpse gradually faded into nothingness returning to the realm from which it had been summoned. For a few seconds Elric wanted to follow the thing into its home regions, for the stolen energy threatened to spill out of his body, burst its way from his blood and his bones; but old habits fought to control this lust until at last he once again had a rein upon himself. He began slowly to rise from the ground only to hear the approach of hooves.

He whirled, the sword ready, but saw it was the traveller who had earlier sought to help him. Stormbringer felt no sentiment in the matter and stirred in his hand, ready to take the soul of this friend as readily as it had stolen the souls of Elric's enemies.

No!' The albino forced the blade back into its scabbard. He felt almost sick with the energy leeched from the demon but he made himself take a grave bow as the rider joined him. 'I thank you for your help, stranger. I had not expected to find a friend this close to Quarzhasaat.'

The young man regarded him with some sympathy and good will. He had startlingly handsome features with dark, humorous eyes in his gleaming black flesh. On his short, curly hair he wore a skull cap decorated with peacock feathers and his jacket and breeches seemed to be of black velvet stiched with gold thread, over which was thrown a pale-coloured hooded cloak of the pattern usually worn by desert peoples in these parts. He rode up slowly on the loping, bovine mount which had cloven hoofs and a broad head, a massive hump above its shoulders, like that of certain cattle Elric had seen in scrolls depicting the Southern Continent.

At the young man's belt was a richly carved stick of some kind with a crooked handle, about half his height, and on his other hip he wore a simple flat-hilted sword.

'I had not expected to find an emperor of Melniboné in these parts, either!' said the man with some amusement. 'Greetings, Prince Elric. I am honoured to make your acquaintance.'

'We have not met? How do you know my name?'

'Oh, such tricks are nothing to one of my craft, Prince Elric. My name is Alnac Kreb and I am making my way to the oasis they call the Silver Flower. Shall we return to your camp and your horse? I am glad to say he is unharmed. What powerful enemies you have, to send such a foul demon against you! Have you given offence to the Sorcerer Adventurers of Quarzhasaat?'

'It would seem so.' Elric walked beside the newcomer as they made their way back towards the Red Road. 'I am grateful to you, Master Alnac Kreb. Without your help, I should now be absorbed body and soul in that creature and borne back to whatever hell gave birth to it. But I must warn you, there is some danger that I shall be attacked again by those who sent it.'

'I think not, Prince Elric. They were doubtless confident of their success and, what's more, wanted no further business with you, once they realized that you were no ordinary mortal. I saw a pack of them – from three separate sects of that unpleasant guild – riding rapidly back to Quarzhasaat not an hour since. Curious as to what they fled from, I came this way. And so found you. I was glad to be of some minor service.'

'I, too, am riding for the Silver Flower Oasis, though I know not what to expect there.' Elric had taken a strong liking to this young man. 'I would be glad of your company on the journey.'

'Honoured, sir. Honoured!' Smiling, Alnac Kreb dismounted from his odd beast and tethered it close to Elric's horse which was yet to recover from its terror, though it was now quieter.

'I will not ask you to weary yourself further tonight, sir,' Elric added, 'but I'm mightily curious to know how you guessed my name and my race. You spoke of a trick of your craft. What would that trade be, may I ask?'

'Why, sir,' said Alnac Kreb, dusting sand from his velvet breeches, 'I'd thought you guessed. I am a dreamthief.'

4

A Funeral at the Oasis

'The Silver Flower Oasis is rather more than a simple clearing in the desert as you'll discover,' said Alnac Kreb, dabbing delicately at his beautiful face with a kerchief trimmed with glittering lace. 'It is a great meeting place for all the nomad nations and much wealth comes to it to be traded. It is frequented by kings and princes. Marriages are arranged and often take place there, as do other ceremonies. Great political decisions are made. Alliances are maintained and fresh ones struck. News is exchanged. Every manner of thing is bartered. Not everything is conventional, not everything – material. It is a vital place, unlike Quarzhasaat, which the nomads visit reluctantly only when necessity – or greed – demands.'

'Why have we seen none of these nomads, friend Alnac?' Elric asked.

'They avoid Quarzhasaat. For them the place and its people are the equivalent of Hell. Some even believe that the souls of the damned are sent to Quarzhasaat. The city represents everything they fear and everything that is at odds with what they most value.'

'I'd be inclined to see eye to eye with those nomads.' Elric allowed himself a smile. Still free of the elixir, his body was again craving it. The energy his sword had given him would normally have sustained him for a considerably longer time. This was further proof that the elixir, as explained by Manag Iss, fed off his very life-force to give him temporary physical strength. He was beginning to suspect that as well as feeding his own vitality he was also feeding the elixir. The distillation had come almost to represent a sentient creature, like the sword. Yet the Black Sword had never given him the same sense of being invaded. He kept his mind free of such thoughts as much as he could. 'I feel a certain kinship with them already,' he added.

'Your hope, Prince Elric, is that they find you acceptable!' And Alnac laughed. 'Though an ancient enemy of the Lords of Quarzhasaat must have certain credentials. I have acquaintances amongst some of the clans. You must let me introduce you, when the time comes.'

'Willingly,' said Elric, 'though you have yet to explain how you came to know me.'

Alnac nodded as if he had forgotten the matter. 'It is not complicated and yet it is remarkably complex, if you do not understand the fundamental workings of the multiverse. As I told you, I'm a dreamthief. I know more than most because I am familiar with so many dreams. Let's merely say that I heard of you in a dream and that it is sometimes my destiny to be your companion – though not for long, I'd guess, in my present guise.'

'In a dream? You have yet to tell me what a dreamthief does.'

'Why, steal dreams, of coure. Twice a year we take our booty to a certain market to trade, just as the nomads trade.'

'You trade in dreams?' Elric was disbelieving.

Alnac enjoyed his astonishment. 'There are dealers at the market who'll pay for certain dreams. In turn they sell them to those unfortunates who either cannot dream or who have such banal dreams they desire something better.'

Elric shook his head. 'You speak in parables, surely?'

'No, Prince Elric, I speak the exact truth.' He dragged the oddly hooked staff from his belt. It reminded Elric of a shepherd's crook, though it was shorter. 'One does not acquire this without having studied the basic skills of the dreamthief's craft. I am not the best in my trade, nor am I likely ever to be, but in this realm, in this time, this is my destiny. There are few in this realm, for reasons you shall no doubt learn, and only the nomads and the folk of Elwher recognize our craft. We are not known, save to a few wise people, in the Young Kingdoms.'

'Why do you not venture there?'

'We are not asked to do so. Have you ever heard of anyone seeking the services of a dreamthief in the Young Kingdoms?'

'Never. But why should that be?'

'Perhaps because Chaos has so much influence in the West and South. There, the most terrible nightmares can readily become reality.'

'You fear Chaos?'

'What rational being does not? I fear the dreams of those who serve her.' Alnac Kreb looked away towards the desert. 'Elwher and what you call "the unmapped East" have in the main less complicated inhabitants, Melniboné's influence was never so strong. Nor was it, of course, in the Sighing Desert.'

'So it is my folk whom you fear?'

'I fear any race which gives itself over to Chaos, which makes pacts with the most powerful of supernaturals, with the very Dukes of

Chaos, with the Sword Rulers themselves! I do not regard such dealings as wholesome or sane. I am opposed to Chaos.'

'You serve Law?'

'I serve myself. I serve, I suppose, the Balance. I believe that one can live and let live and celebrate the world's variety.'

'Such philosophy is enviable, Master Alnac. I aspire to it myself, though I suppose you do not believe me.'

'Aye, I believe you, Prince Elric. I am party to many dreams and you occur in some of them. And dreams are reality and vice versa in other realms.' The dreamthief glanced sympathetically at the albino. 'It must be hard for one who has known millennia of power to attempt a relinquishing of such power.'

'You understand me well, Sir Dreamthief.'

'Oh, my understanding is only ever of the broadest kind in such matters.' Alnac Kreb shrugged and made a self-deprecating gesture.

'I have spent much time in seeking the meaning of justice, in visiting lands where it is said to exist, in trying to discover how best it may be accomplished, how it may be established so that all the world shall benefit. Have you heard of Tanelorn, Alnac Kreb? There justice is said to rule. There the Grey Lords, those who keep charge of the world's equilibrium, are said to have their greatest influence.'

'Tanelorn exists,' said the dreamthief quietly. 'And it has many names. Yet in some realms, I fear, it is no more than an idea of perfection. Such ideas are what maintain us in hope and fuel our urge to make reality of dreams. Sometimes we are successful.'

'Justice exists?'

'Of course it does. But it is not an abstraction. It must be worked for. Justice is your demon, I think, Prince Elric, more than any Lord of Chaos. You have chosen a cruel and an unhappy road.' He smiled delicately as he stared ahead of them at the long, red trail stretching out to the horizon. 'Crueller, I think, than the Red Road to the Silver Flower Oasis.'

'You're not encouraging, Master Alnac.'

'You must know yourself that there's precious little justice in the world that is not hard fought for, hard won and hard held. It is in our mortal nature to give that responsibility to others. Yet poor creatures like yourself continue to try to relinquish power while acquiring more and more responsibility. Some would say that it is admirable to do as you do, that it builds character and strength of purpose, that it reaches towards a higher form of sanity . . . '

'Aye. And some would say it is the purest form of madness, at odds with all natural impulses. I do not know what it is I long for, Sir

Dreamthief, but I know I hope for a world where the strong do not prey on the weak like mindless insects, where mortal creatures may attain their greatest possible fulfilment, where all are dignified and healthy, never victims of a few stronger than themselves . . . '

'Then you serve the wrong masters in Chaos, Prince. For the only justice recognized by the Dukes of Hell is the justice of their own unchallenged existence. They are like fresh-born babes in this. They are opposed to your every ideal.'

Elric grew disturbed and spoke softly when he replied. 'But can one not use such forces to defeat them – or at least challenge their power and adjust the Balance?'

'Only the Balance gives you the power you desire. And it is a subtle, sometimes exceptionally delicate power.'

'Not strong enough in my world, I fear.'

'Strong only when sufficient numbers believe in it. Then it is stronger than Chaos and Law combined.'

'Well, I shall work for that day when the power of the Balance holds sway, Master Alnac Kreb, but I am not sure I will live to see it.'

'If you live,' said Alnac quietly. 'I suspect it will not come. But it will be many years before you are called upon to blow Roland's horn.'

'A horn? What horn is that?' But Elric's question was casual. He believed that the dreamthief was making another allegorical allusion.

'Look!' Alnac pointed ahead. 'See in the far distance? There is the first sign of the Silver Flower Oasis.'

To their left the sun was going down. It cast deep shadows across the dunes and the high banks of the Red Road while the sky was darkening to a deep amber on the horizon. Yet almost at the limit of his vision Elric made out another shape, something that was neither a shadow nor a sand-dune but which might have been a group of rocks.

'What is it? What do you recognize?'

'The nomads call it "kashbeh". In our common tongue we would say it was a castle, perhaps, or a fortified village. We have no exact word for such a place, for we have no need of them. Here, in the desert, it is a necessity. The Kashbeh Moulor Ka Riiz was built long before the extinction of the Quarzhasaatin Empire and is named for a wise king, founder of the Aloum'rit dynasty which still holds the place in charge for the nomad clans and is respected above all other peoples of the desert. It is a kashbeh sheltering anyone in need. Anyone who is a fugitive may seek shelter there and there may be assured of a fair trial.'

'So justice exists in this desert, if nowhere else?'

'Such places exist, as I said, throughout the realms of the multiverse.

They are maintained by men and women of the purest and most humane principle . . . '

'Then is this kashbeh not Tanelorn, whose legend brought me to the Sighing Desert?'

'It is not Tanelorn, for Tanelorn is eternal. The Kashbeh Moulor Ka Riiz must be maintained through constant vigilance. It is the antithesis of Quarzhasaat and that city's lords have made many attempts to destroy it.'

Elric felt the pangs of craving and he resisted reaching for one of his silver flasks. 'Is that also called The Fortress of the Pearl?'

At this, Alnac Kreb laughed suddenly. 'Oh, my good prince, clearly you have only the haziest notion of the place and the thing you seek. Let me now say that the Fortress of the Pearl may well exist within that kashbeh and that the kashbeh could also have an existence within the Fortress. But they are in no way the same!'

'Please, Master Alnac, do not confuse me further! I pretended to know something of this, first because I wished to extend my own life and then because I needed to purchase the life of another. I would be grateful for some illumination. Lord Gho Fhaazi thought me a dreamthief, after all, which supposes that a dreamthief would know of the Blood Moon, the Bronze Tent and the location of the Place of the Pearl.'

'Aye, well. Some dreamthieves are better informed than others. And if a dreamthief is required for this task, Prince, if, as you've told me, Quarzhasaat's Sorcerer Adventurers cannot achieve it, then I would guess the Fortress of the Pearl is more than mere stones and mortar. It has to do with realms familiar only to a trained dreamthief – but one probably more sophisticated than myself'

'Know you, Master Alnac, that I have already travelled to strange realms in pursuit of my various goals. I am not completely unsophisticated in such matters . . . '

'These realms are denied to most.' Alnac seemed reluctant to say more but Elric pressed him.

'Where lie these realms?' He stared ahead, straining his eyes to see more of the Kashbeh Moulor Ka Riiz but failing, for the sun was now almost below the horizon. 'In the East? Beyond Elwher? Or in another part of the multiverse altogether?'

Alnac Kreb was regretful. 'We are sworn to speak as little as we can of our knowledge, save in the most crucial and specific of circumstances. But I should inform you that those realms are at once closer and more distant than Elwher. I promise you that I will not mystify you any more than I have done so already. And if I can illuminate you and help you in your quest, that I will do also.' He made to laugh, to lighten his own mood. 'Best ready yourself for company, Prince. We shall have a great deal of it by nightfall, if I'm not mistaken.'

The moon had risen before the last rays of the sun had vanished and its silver bore a pinkish sheen, like that of a rare pearl itself, as they reached a rise in the Red Road and looked down now upon a thousand fires. Silhouetted against them were as many tall tents, settled on the sand so as to resemble gigantic winged insects stretched out to catch the warmth from above. Within these tents burned lamps while men, women and children wandered in and out. A delicious smell of mingled herbs, spices, vegetables and meats drifted up towards them and the soft smoke of the fires rose and curled into the sky above the great rocks on which perched the Kashbeh Moulor Ka Riiz, a massive tower about which had grown a collection of buildings, some of wonderfully imaginative architecture, the whole surrounded by a crenellated wall of irregular but equally monumental proportions, all of the same red rock so that it seemed to grow out of the very earth and sand that surrounded it.

At intervals around those battlements great torches blazed, revealing men who were evidently guards patrolling the walls and roofs, while through tall gates a steady stream of traffic came and went across a bridge carved from the living rock.

This was, as Alnac Kreb had warned him, not the simple resting place of primitive caravans Elric had expected to find on the Red Road.

They were not challenged as they descended towards the wide sheet of water around which blossomed a rich variety of palms, cypresses, poplars, fig trees and cactus, but many looked at them with open curiosity. And not all the curious eyes were friendly.

Their horses were of a similar build to Elric's own, while others of the nomads rode the bovine creatures favoured by Alnac. The sounds of bellowing, grunting and spitting rose from every quarter and Elric could see that beyond the field of tents lay corrals in which riding beasts as well as sheep, goats and other creatures were penned.

But the sight which dominated this extraordinary scene was that of some hundred or more torches blazing in a semi-circle at the water's edge.

Each torch was held by a cloaked and cowled figure and each burned with a bright, white steady flame which cast the same strong light upon a dais of carved wood at the very centre of the gathering.

Elric and his companion reined in their mounts to watch, as fascinated by this vision as the scores of other nomads who walked slowly to the edge of the semi-circle to witness what was clearly a ceremony of some magnitude. The witnesses stood in attitudes of respect, their various robes and costumes identifying their clan. The nomads were of a variety of colours, some as black as Alnac Kreb, some almost as white-skinned as Elric, with every shade in between, yet in features they were similar, with strong-boned faces and deep-set eyes. Both men and women were tall and bore themselves with considerable grace. Elric had never seen so many handsome people and he was as impressed by their natural dignity as he had been disgusted by the extremes of arrogance and degradation he had witnessed in Quarzhasaat.

Now a procession approached down the hill and Elric saw that six men bore a large, domed chest on their shoulders, proceeding with grave slowness until they came to the dais.

The white light showed every detail of the scene. The men were drawn from different clans, though all of the same height and all of middle age. A single drum began to sound, its beat sharp and clear in the night air. Then another joined it, then another, until at least twenty drums were echoing across the waters of the oasis and the rooftops of Kashbeh Moulor Ka Riiz, their voices at once slow and obeying complicated rhythmic patterns whose subtlety Elric gradually came to marvel at.

'Is it a funeral?' the albino asked his new friend.

Alnac nodded. 'But I know not who they bury.' He pointed to a series of symmetrical mounds in the distance beyond the trees. 'Those are the nomad burial grounds.'

Now another, older man, his beard and brows grey beneath his cowl, stepped forward and began to read from a scroll he produced from his sleeve, while two others opened the lid of the elaborate coffin and, to Elric's astonishment, spat into it.

Now Alnac gasped. He stood on his toes and peered, for the brands clearly illuminated the coffin's contents. He turned, still more mystified, to Elric. ''Tis empty, Prince Elric. Or else the corpse is invisible.'

The rhythm of the drums increased in tempo and complexity. Voices began to chant, rising and falling like waves in an ocean. Elric had never heard such music before. He found that it was moving him to obscure emotions. He felt rage. He felt sorrow. He found that he was close to weeping. And still the music continued, growing in intensity. He longed to join in, but could understand nothing of the language they used. It seemed to him that the words were older by far than the speech of Melniboné, which was the oldest in the Young Kingdoms.

And then, suddenly, the singing and the drumming ended.

The six men took the coffin from the dais and began to march away with it, towards the mounds, and the men with the torches followed, the light casting strange shadows amongst the trees, illuminating sudden patches of shining whiteness which Elric could not identify.

As suddenly as they had stopped the drumming and the chanting began again, but this time they had a celebratory, triumphant note to them. Slowly the crowd lifted their heads and from several hundred throats came a high-pitched ululation, clearly a traditional response.

Then the nomads began to drift back towards their tents. Alnac stopped one, a woman wearing richly decorated green and gold robes, and pointed to the disappearing procession. 'What is this funeral, sister? I saw no corpse.'

'The corpse is not here,' she said, and she was smiling at his confusion. 'It is a ceremony of revenge, taken by all our clans at the instigation of Raik Na Seem. The corpse is not present because its owner will not know he is dead, perhaps for several months. We bury him now because we cannot reach him. He is not one of us, not of the desert. He is dead, however, but merely unaware of that fact. There is no mistake, though. We lack only the physical body.'

'He is an enemy of your people, sister?'

'Aye, indeed. He is an enemy. He sent men to steal our greatest treasure. They failed, but they have done us profound harm in their failing. I know you, do I not? You are the one Raik Na Seem hoped would return. He sent for a dreamthief.' And she looked back to the dais where, beneath the light of a single torch, a huge figure stood, bowed as if in prayer. 'You are our friend, Alnac Kreb, who aided us once before.'

'I have been privileged to do your people a trifling service in the past, aye.' Alnac Kreb acknowledged her recognition with his habitual grace.

'Raik Na Seem waits upon you,' she said. 'Go in peace and peace be with your family and friends.'

Puzzled, Alnac Kreb turned to Elric. 'I know not why Raik Na Seem should have sent for me but I feel obliged to find out. Will you stay here or accompany me, Prince Elric?'

'I am growing curious about this whole affair,' said Elric, 'and would know more, if that's possible.'

They made their way through the trees until they stood on the banks of the great oasis, waiting respectfully while the old man remained in the position he had assumed since the coffin had been carried off. Eventually he turned and it was clear that he had been weeping. When he saw them he straightened up and, as he recognized Alnac Kreb, he smiled, making a gesture of welcome. 'My dear friend!'

'Peace be upon you, Raik Na Seem.' Alnac stepped forward and embraced the old man, who was at least a head and shoulders taller than himself. 'I bring with me a friend. His name is Elric of Melniboné, of that same people who were the great enemies of the Quarzhasaatim.'

'The name has substance in my heart,' said Raik Na Seem. 'Peace be upon you, Elric of Melniboné. You are welcome here.'

'Raik Na Seem is First Elder to the Bauradi Clan,' Alnac said, 'and a father to me.'

'I am blessed by a good, brave son.' Raik Na Seem gestured back towards the tents. 'Come. Take refreshment in my tent.'

'Willingly,' said Alnac. 'I would learn why you are burying an empty casket and who your enemy is that he should merit such elaborate ceremony.'

'Oh, he is the worst of villains, make no mistake of that.' A deep sigh escaped the old man as he led them through the throngs of tents until he reached a massive pavilion into which they followed him, their feet treading on richly patterned carpets. The pavilion was actually a series of compartments, one leading into another, each occupied by members of Raik Na Seem's family, which seemed vast enough to be almost a tribe in itself. The smell of delicious food came through to them as they were seated on cushions and offered bowls of scented water with which to wash themselves.

Eventually, as they ate, the old man told his story and, while it unfolded, Elric came to realize that Fate had brought him to the Silver Flower Oasis at an auspicious time, for he slowly recognized the significance of what was being said. At the time of the last Blood Moon, said Raik Na Seem, a group of men had come to the Silver Flower Oasis asking after the road to the Place of the Pearl. The Bauradim had recognized the name, for it was in their literature, but they understood the references to be poetic metaphor, something for scholars and other poets to discuss and interpret. They had told the newcomers this and hoped that they would leave, for they were Quarzhasaatim, members of the Sparrow Sect of Sorcerer Adventurers and as such notorious for their murky wizardry and cruelty. The Bauradim wanted no quarrel, however, with any Quarzhasaatim, with whom they traded. The men of the Sparrow Sect did not leave, though, but continued to ask anyone they could about the Place of the Pearl, which was how they came to learn of Raik Na Seem's daughter.

'Varadia?' Alnac Kreb knew alarm. 'They surely did not think she knew anything of this jewel?'

'They heard that she was our Holy Girl, the one we believe will grow to be our spiritual leader and bring wisdom and honour to our clan. They believed that, because we say that our Holy Girl is the receptacle of all our knowledge, she must know where this pearl was to be found. They attempted to steal her.'

Alnac Kreb growled with sudden anger. 'What did they do, father?'

'They drugged her, then made to ride away with her. We learned of their crime and followed them. We caught them before they had completed half the length of the Red Road back to Quarzhasaat and in their terror they threatened us with the power of their master, the man who had commissioned them to seek out the Pearl and use any means to bring it back to him.'

'Was his name Lord Gho Fhaazi?' asked Elric softly.

'Aye, prince, it was.' Raik Na Seem looked at him with new curiosity. 'Do you know him?'

'I know him. And I know him for what he is. Is that the man you buried?'

'It is.'

'When do you plan his death?'

'We do not plan it. We have been promised it. The Sorcerer Adventurers attempted to use their arts against us, but we have such people of our own and they were easily countered. It is not something we like to use, that power, but sometimes it is necessary. A certain creature was summoned from the netherworld. It devoured the men of the Sparrow Sect and before it left it granted us a prophecy, that their master would die within the year, before the next Blood Moon had faded.'

'But Varadia?' said Alnac Kreb urgently. 'What became of your daughter, your Holy Girl?'

'She had been drugged, as I said, but she lived. We brought her back.'

'And she recovered?'

'She half-wakes, perhaps once a month,' said Raik Na Seem, controlling his sadness. 'But the sleep will not lift from her. Shortly after we found her she opened her eyes and told us to take her to the Bronze Tent. There she sleeps, as she has slept for almost a year, and we know that only a dreamthief may save her. That was why I have sent word by every traveller and caravan we have encountered, asking for a dreamthief. We are fortunate, Alnac Kreb, that a friend heard our prayer.'

The dreamthief shook his handsome head. 'It was not your message which brought me hither, Raik Na Seem.'

'Still,' said the old man philosophically, 'you are here. You can help us.'

Alnac Kreb seemed disturbed, but disguised his emotions quickly. 'I will do my best, that I swear. In the morning we shall visit the Bronze Tent.'

'It is well guarded now, for more Quarzhasaatim have come since those first evil ones, and we have been forced to defend our Holy Girl against them. That has been a simple enough matter. But you spoke of the enemy we have buried, Prince Elric. What do you know of him?'

Elric paused for only a few seconds before he spoke. He told Raik Na Seem everything which had happened: how he had been tricked by Lord Gho, what he had been told to find, the hold which Lord Gho had over him. He refused to lie to the old man and the respect he showed Raik Na Seem was apparently reciprocated, for though the First Elder's face darkened with anger at the tale he reached out with a firm hand when it was finished and gripped Elric's arm in a gesture of sympathy.

'The irony is, my friend, that the Place of the Pearl exists only in our poetry and we have never heard of the Fortress of the Pearl.'

'You must know that I would do your Holy Girl no further harm,' said Elric, 'and that if I can help you and yours in any way that is what I shall do. My quest is ended here and now.'

'But Lord Gho's potion will kill you unless you can find the antidote. Then he'll kill your friend, too. No, no. Let us look more positively at these problems, Prince Elric. We have them in common, I think, for we are all victims of that soon-dead lord. We must consider how to defeat his schemes. It is possible that my daughter does indeed know something about this fabulous Pearl, for she is the vessel of all our wisdom and has already learned more than ever my poor head could hold . . . '

'Her knowledge and her intelligence are as breathtaking as her beauty and her amiability,' said Alnac Kreb, still fuming at the story of what the Quarzhasaatim had done to Varadia. 'If you had known her, Elric . . . ' He broke off, his voice shaking.

'We are all in need of rest, I think,' said the First Elder of the Bauradim. 'You shall be our guests and in the morning I shall take you to the Bronze Tent, there to look upon my sleeping daughter and hope, perhaps with the sum of all our wisdom, to find a means of bringing her waking mind back to this realm.'

That night, sleeping in the luxury only a wealthy nomad tent could provide, Elric dreamed again of Cymoril, trapped in a drugged slumber by his cousin Yyrkoon, and it seemed that he slept beside her, that they were one and the same, as he had always felt when they lay together. But now he saw the dignified figure of Raik Na Seem standing over him and he knew that this was his father, not the neurotic tyrant, the

distant figure of his childhood, and he understood why he was obsessed with questions of morality and justice, for it was this Bauradi
who was his true ancestor. He knew a kind of peace, then, as well as
some kind of new, disturbing emotion, and when he awoke in the
morning he was reconciled to the fact that he was craving the elixir
which at once brought him life and death, and he reached for his flask
and took a small sip before rising, washing himself and joining Alnac
and Raik Na Seem at the morning meal.

When this was done, the old man called for the fleet, sturdy mounts
for which the Bauradim were famous, and the three of them rode away
from the Silver Flower Oasis, which bustled with every kind of activity,
where comedians, jugglers and snake-charmers were already
performing their skills and story-tellers had gathered groups of children whose parents had sent them there while they went about their
business, and they rode towards the Ragged Pillars seen faintly on the
morning horizon. These mountains had been eroded by the winds of
the Sighing Desert until they did, indeed, resemble huge columns of
ragged red stone, as if they should have supported the roof of the sky
itself. Elric had thought at first he observed the ruins of some ancient
city. But Alnac Kreb had told him the truth.

'There are, indeed, many ruins in these parts. Farms, small villages,
whole towns, which the desert sometimes reveals, all engulfed by the
sand summoned by the foolish wizards of Quarzhasaat. Many built
here, even after the sands came, in the belief that they would disperse
after a while. Forlorn dreams, I fear, like so many of the things built by
men.'

Raik Na Seem continued to lead them across the desert, though he
used no map or compass. Apparently he knew the way by habit and
instinct alone.

They stopped once at a spot where a tiny growth of cacti had been
all but covered by the sand and here Raik Na Seem took his long knife
and sliced the plants close to their roots, peeling them swiftly and
handing the juicy parts to his friends. 'There was once a river here,' he
said, 'and a memory of it remains, far below the surface. The cactus
remembers.'

The sun had reached zenith. Elric began to feel the heat sapping him
and was forced again to drink a little of the elixir, merely in order to
keep pace with the other two. And it was not until evening, when the
Ragged Pillars were considerably closer, that Raik pointed to something which flashed and glittered in the last rays of the sun. 'There is
the Bronze Tent, where the peoples of the desert go when they must
meditate.'

'It is your temple?' said Elric.

'It is the nearest thing we have to a temple. And there we debate with our inner selves. It is also the nearest thing we have to the religions of the West. And it is there we keep our Holy Girl, the symbol of all our ideals, the vessel of our race's wisdom.'

Alnac was surprised. 'You keep her there always?'

Raik Na Seem shook his head, almost amused. 'Only while she sleeps in this unnatural slumber, my friend. As you know, before this she was a normal little child, a joy to all who met her. Perhaps with your help she will be that child again.'

Alnac's brow clouded. 'You must not expect too much of me, Raik Na Seem. I am an inexpert dreamthief at best. There are those with whom I learned my craft who would tell you so.'

'But you are our dreamthief.' Raik Na Seem smiled sadly and put his hand on Alnac Kreb's shoulder. 'And our good friend.'

The sun had set by the time they approached the great tent, which resembled those Elric had seen at the Silver Flower Oasis but was several times the size, its walls of pure bronze.

Now the moon made its appearance in the sky almost directly overhead. It seemed that the sun's rays reached for it even as they began to sink beneath the horizon, touching it with their colour, for it glowed with a richness Elric had never seen in Melniboné or the lands of the Young Kingdoms. He gasped in surprise, realizing the specific nature of the prophecy.

A Blood Moon had risen over the Bronze Tent. Here he would find the path to the Fortress of the Pearl.

Though it meant that his own life might now be saved, the Prince of Melniboné discovered that he was only disturbed by this revelation.

5

The Dreamthief's Pledge

'Here is our treasure,' said Raik Na Seem. 'Here is what greedy Quarzhasaat would steal from us.' And there was sorrow as well as anger in his voice.

At the very centre of the Bronze Tent's cool interior, in which tiny lamps burned over hundreds of heaped cushions and carpets occupied by men and women in attitudes of deep contemplation, was a raised level and on this a bed carved with intricate designs of exquisite delicacy, set with mother-of-pearl and pale turquoise, with milky jade and silver filigree and blond gold. Upon this, her little hands folded on her chest, which rose and fell with profound regularity, lay a young girl of about thirteen years. She had the strong beauty of her people and her hair was the colour of honey against her tawny skin. She might have been sleeping as naturally as any child of her age save for the single startling fact that her eyes, blue as the wonderful Vilmirian sea, stared upwards towards the roof of the Bronze Tent and were unblinking.

'My people believed that Quarzhasaat destroyed herself forever,' said Elric. 'Would that they had or that Melniboné had shown less arrogance and completed what their wizards began!' He rarely betrayed such ferocious emotions towards those his race had defeated but now he knew only loathing for Lord Gho, whose men, he was sure, had done this terrible thing. He recognized the nature of the sorcery, for it was not unlike that he had learned himself, though his cousin Yyrkoon had shown more interest in those specific arts and cared to practise them where Elric did not.

'But who can save her now?' said Raik Na Seem softly, perhaps a little embarrassed by Elric's outburst in this place of meditation.

The albino recovered himself and made a gesture of apology. 'Are there no potions which will rouse her from this slumber?' he asked.

Raik Na Seem shook his head. 'We have consulted everyone and everything. The spell was cast by the leader of the Sparrow Sect and he was killed when we took our premature revenge.'

In deference to those who sat within the Bronze Tent, Raik Na Seem now led them out into the desert again. Here guards stood, their lamps and torches casting great shadows across the sand, while the rays of the ruby moon drenched everything with crimson, so it was almost as if they drowned in a tide of blood. Elric was reminded how, as a youth, he had peered into the depths of his Actorios, imagining the gem as a gateway into other lands, each facet representing a different realm, for by then he had already read much of the multiverse and how it was thought to be constituted.

'Steal the dream which entraps her,' Raik Na Seem was saying, 'and you know that all we have will be yours, Alnac Kreb.'

The handsome black man shook his head. 'To save her would be all the reward I wanted, father. Yet I fear I have not the skills . . . Has no other tried?'

'We have been deceived more than once. Sorcerer Adventurers from Quarzhasaat, either believing themselves possessed of your knowledge or thinking they could accomplish what only a dreamthief can accomplish, have come to us, pretending to be members of your craft. We have seen them all go mad before our eyes. Several died. Some we let run back to Quarzhasaat in the hope they would be a warning to others not to waste their lives and our time.'

'You sound very patient, Raik Na Seem,' said Elric, remembering what he had already heard and clearer now as to why Lord Gho so desperately sought a dreamthief for this work. The news brought back to Quarzhasaat by the maddened Sorcerer Adventurers had been garbled. What little Lord Gho had made of it, he had passed on to Elric. But now the albino saw that it was the child herself who possessed the secret of the path to the Pearl at the Heart of the World. Doubtless, as the recipient of all her people's wisdom, she had learned of its location. Perhaps it was a secret she must keep to herself. Whatever the reason, it was obvious that the girl, Varadia, must wake from her sorcerous sleep before any further progress could be made. And Elric knew that even if she did wake it was not in his nature to question her, to beg for a secret which was not his to know. His only hope would be if she offered the knowledge freely to him but he knew that no matter what occurred he would never be able to ask.

Raik Na Seem seemed to understand a little of the albino's dilemma. 'My son, you are a friend of my son,' he said in the formal manner of his people. 'We know that you are not our enemy and that you did not come here willingly to steal what was ours. We know, too, that you had no intention of taking from us any treasure to which we are guardian. Know this, Elric of Melniboné, that if Alnac Kreb can save our Holy Girl, we shall do all we can to put you on the path to the Fortress of the Pearl. The only reason for hindering you would be if Varadia, awakened, warned us against giving this aid. Then, at least, you will be told as much.'

'There could be no fairer promise,' said Elric gratefully. 'Meanwhile, I pledge myself to you, Raik Na Seem, to help guard your daughter against all those who would harm her and to watch over her until Alnac should bring her back to you.'

Alnac had moved a little away from the other two and was standing in deep thought on the edge of the torchlight, his white night-cloak drenched a dark pinkish hue by the rays of the Blood Moon. From his belt he had drawn his hooked staff and was holding it in his two hands, looking at it and murmuring to it, much as Elric might speak to his own runesword.

At length the dreamthief turned back to them, his face full of great seriousness. 'I will do my best,' he said. 'I will call upon every resource within myself and upon everything I have been taught, but I should warn you that I have weaknesses of character I have not yet overcome. These are weaknesses which I can control if called upon to exorcize an old merchant's nightmares or a boy's love-trance. What I see here, however, might defeat the cleverest dreamthief, the most experienced of my calling. There can be no partial success. I succeed or I fail. I am willing, because of the circumstances, because of our old friendship, because I loathe everything that the Sorcerer Adventurers represent, to attempt the task.'

'It is all I would hope,' said Raik Na Seem sombrely. He was impressed by Alnac's tone.

'If you succeed you bring the child's soul back to the world where it belongs,' said Elric. 'What do you lose if you fail, Master Dreamthief?'

Alnac shrugged. 'Nothing of any great value, I suppose.'

Elric, looking hard into his new friend's face, saw that he lied. But he saw, too, that he wished to be questioned no further in the matter.

'I must rest,' said Alnac. 'And eat.' He wrapped himself in the folds of his night-cloak, his dark eyes staring back at Elric as if he wished for all the world to share some secret which he felt in his heart should never be shared. Then he turned away suddenly, laughing. 'If Varadia should wake as a result of my efforts and if she knows the whereabouts of your terrible pearl, why then, Prince Elric, I'll have done most of your work for you. I'll expect part of your reward, you know.'

'My reward will be the slaying of Lord Gho,' said Elric quietly.

'Aye,' said Alnac, moving towards the Bronze Tent, which shifted and shimmered like some half-materialized artefact of Chaos, 'that is exactly what I hope to share!'

The Bronze Tent consisted of the great central chamber and then a series of smaller chambers, where travellers could rest and revive themselves, and it was to one of these that the three men went to lay themselves down and, still wakeful, consider the work which must begin the next day. They did not talk, but it was several hours before all were eventually asleep.

In the morning, while Elric, Raik Na Seem and Alnac Kreb approached the place where the Holy Girl still lay, those who still remained in the Bronze Tent drew back respectfully. Alnac Kreb held his dreamwand gently in his right hand, balancing it rather than gripping it, as he stared down into the face of the child he loved almost as his own daughter. A long sigh escaped him and Elric saw that his sleep had not apparently refreshed him. He looked drawn and unhappy. He turned, smiling to the albino. 'When I saw you partaking of the contents of that silver flask earlier, I had half a mind to ask you for a little . . . '

'The drug's poison and it's addictive,' said Elric, shocked. 'I thought I had explained as much.'

'You had.' Alnac Kreb again revealed by his expression that he possessed thoughts he felt unable to share. 'I had merely thought that, in the circumstances, there would be little point in fearing its power.'

'That is because you do not know it,' said Elric forcefully. 'Believe me, Alnac, if there was any way in which I could help you in this task I would do so. But to offer you poison would not, I think, be an act of friendship . . . '

Alnac Kreb smiled a little. 'Indeed. Indeed.' He slid his dreamwand from hand to hand. 'But you said that you would watch over me?'

'I promise that, aye. And as you asked, the moment you tell me to carry the dreamwand from the Bronze Tent, I shall do so.'

'That is all you can do and I thank you for that,' said the dreamthief. 'Now I'll begin. Farewell for the moment, Elric. I think we are fated to meet again, but perhaps not in this existence.'

And with those mysterious words Alnac Kreb approached the sleeping girl, placing his dreamwand over her unblinking eyes, laying his ear against her heart, his own gaze growing distant and strange, as if he entered a trance himself. He straightened, swaying, then took the girl in his arms and lowered her gently to the carpets. Next he lay down beside her, putting her lifeless hand within his own, his dreamwand in the other. His breathing grew slower and deeper and Elric almost thought he heard a faint song coming from within the dreamthief's throat.

Raik Na Seem bent forward, peering into Alnac's face, but Alnac did not see him. With his other hand he brought up the dreamwand so that the hook passed over their clasped hands, as if to secure them, to bind them together.

To his surprise, Elric saw that the dreamwand was beginning to glow faintly and to pulse a little. Alnac's breathing grew deeper still, his lips opening, his eyes staring directly above him, just as Varadia's stared.

Elric thought he heard the child murmur and it was no illusion that a tremor passed between Alnac and the Holy Girl while the dreamwand pulsed in tempo with their mutual breathing and glowed brighter.

Then suddenly the dreamwand was curling and writhing, moving with astonishing speed between the two, as if it had entered their very veins and was following the blood itself. Elric had the impression of a tangle of arteries and nerves, all touched by the strange light from the dreamwand, then Alnac gave a single cry and his breathing was no longer the steady movement it had been. Instead it had become shallow, almost non-existent, while the child continued to breathe with the same slow, deep, steady rhythm.

The dreamwand had returned to Alnac. It seemed to burn from within his body, almost as if it had become fused with his spine and cortex. The hook end appeared to glow from within his brain, flooding his flesh with indescribable luminance, displaying every bone, every organ, every vein.

The child herself seemed unchanged until Elric looked at her more closely, seeing almost with horror that her eyes had turned from vibrant blue to jet black. Reluctantly he looked from Varadia's face to Alnac's and saw what he had not wished to see. The dreamthief's own eyes were now bright blue. It was as if the two of them had exchanged souls.

The albino, with all his experience of sorcery, had never witnessed anything like this and he found it disturbing. Gradually he was beginning to understand the strange nature of a dreamthief's calling, why it could be so dangerous, why there were so few who could practise the trade and why fewer still would wish to.

Now a further change began to take place. The crooked staff seemed to writhe again and begin to absorb the dreamthief's very substance, taking the blood and the vitality of flesh and bones and brain into itself.

Raik Na Seem groaned with terror. He stepped backwards, unable to control himself. 'Ah, my son! What have I asked of thee!'

Soon all that remained of Alnac's splendid body seemed little more than a husk, like the discarded skin of some transmuted dragonfly. But the dreamwand lay where Alnac had first placed it upon his own hand and Varadia's, though it seemed larger and glowed with an impossible brilliance, its colours constantly moving through a spectrum part natural, part supernatural.

'I think he is giving much in his attempt to save my daughter,' said Raik Na Seem. 'Perhaps more than anyone should give.'

'He would give everything,' Elric said. 'I think that it is in his nature. That is why you call him your son and why you trust him.'

'Aye,' said Raik Na Seem. 'but now I fear that I lose a son as well as a daughter.' And he sighed and was troubled, perhaps wondering if, after all, he had been wise in begging this service of Alnac Kreb.

For more than a day and a night Elric sat with Raik Na Seem and the men and women of the Bauradim within the shelter of the Bronze Tent, their eyes fixed upon the strangely wizened body of Alnac the Dreamthief, which occasionally stirred and murmured yet still seemed as lifeless as the mummified goats which the sand-dunes sometimes revealed. Once Elric thought he heard the Holy Girl make a sound and once Raik Na Seem rose to put his hand on his daughter's brow, then returned shaking his head.

'This is not the time to despair, father of my friend,' said Elric.

'Aye.' The First Elder of the Bauradim drew himself up, then settled down again beside Elric. 'We set high store by prophecies here in the desert. It seems that our longing for help might have coloured our reason.'

They looked out of the tent into the morning. Smoke from the still burning brands drifted across the lilac-coloured sky, borne upward and to the north by the light breeze. Elric found the smell almost sickening now, but his concern for his new friend made him forgetful of his own health. Occasionally he drank sparingly of Lord Gho's elixir, unable to do more than control his craving, and when Raik Na Seem offered him water from his own flask Elric shook his head. Within him there were still many conflicts. He felt a strong comradeship with these people, a liking for Raik Na Seem which he valued. He had grown to care for Alnac Kreb, who had helped save his life in an action clearly as generous as the man's general character. Elric was grateful for the Bauradim's trust of him. Having heard his tale they would have been within their rights to banish him at very least from the Silver Flower Oasis. Rather they had taken him to the Bronze Tent when the Blood Moon burned, allowing him to follow Lord Gho's instructions, trusting him not to abuse their action. He was bound to them now by a loyalty he could never break. Perhaps they knew this. Perhaps they read his character as easily as they read Alnac's. This sense of their trust heartened him, though it made his task all the more difficult, and he was determined in no way, however inadvertently, to betray it.

Raik Na Seem sniffed the wind and looked back towards the distant oasis. A column of black smoke marched into the sky, growing taller and taller, mingling with the smoke closer at hand: some released afrit joining its fellows. Elric would not have been surprised if it had taken shape before his eyes, so familiar had he become with strange events in the past days.

'There has been another attack,' said Raik Na Seem. He spoke unconcernedly. 'Let us hope it is the last. They are burning the bodies.'

'Who attacks you?'

'More men of the Sorcerer Adventurer societies. I suspect their decisions have something to do with the internal politics of the city. Dozens of them are battling for some favour or other – perhaps the seat on the Council you mentioned. From time to time their machinations involve us. This is familiar to us. But I suppose the Pearl at the Heart of the World has become the only price which will pay for the seat, eh? So as the story spreads, more and more of those warriors are sent here to find it!' Raik Na Seem spoke with fierce humour. 'Let us hope they must soon run out of inhabitants and eventually only the scheming lords themselves will be left, squabbling for non-existent power over a non-existent people!'

Elric watched as a whole tribe of nomads rode past, keeping some distance away from the Bronze Tent in order to show their respect. These tanned, white-skinned people had burning blue eyes as bright as those which stared into nothing within the tent and when their hoods were thrown back, startlingly blond hair, also like Varadia's. Their clothing distinguished them, however, from the Bauradim. It was predominantly of a rich lavender shade with gold and dark green trimming. They were heading towards the Silver Flower Oasis, driving herds of sheep and riding the odd humped bull-like beasts which, as Alnac had declared, were so well-adapted to the desert.

'The Waued Nii,' said Raik Na Seem. 'They are amongst the last at any gathering. They come from the very edge of the desert and they trade with Elwher, bringing that lapis lazuli and jade carving we all value so much. In the winter, when the storms grow too intense for them, they even raid across the plains and into the cities. Once, they boast, they looted Phum, but we believe it was some other, smaller place which they mistook for Phum.' This was clearly a joke the desert peoples enjoyed at the expense of the Waued Nii.

'I had a friend who was once of Phum,' said Elric. 'His name was Rackhir and he sought Tanelorn.'

'Rackhir I know. A good bowman. He travelled with us for a few weeks last year.'

Elric was strangely pleased by this news. 'He was well?'

'In excellent health.' Raik Na Seem was glad of a subject to draw his mind away from the fate of his daughter and his adoptive son. 'He was a welcome guest and hunted for us when we went close to the Ragged Pillars, for there's game there which we lack the skill to find. He spoke of his friend. A friend who has many thoughts and whose thoughts led him to many quandaries. That was you, no doubt. I remember now. He must have been joking. He said that you were a little on the pale side. He wondered what had become of you. He cared for us, I think.'

'And I for him. We had something in common. As I feel a bond with your folk and with Alnac Kreb.'

'You shared dangers together, I gather.'

'We had many strange experiences. He, however, was tired of the quest for such things and hoped to retire, to find peace. Know you where he went from here?'

'Aye. As you say, he was searching for legendary Tanelorn. When he had learned all he could from us, he bade us farewell and rode on to the West. We counselled him not to waste himself in pursuit of a myth, but he believed he knew enough to continue. Did you not wish to journey with your friend?'

'I have other duties which call me, though I, too, have sought Tanelorn.' He would have added more but thought better of it. Any further explanation would have led him into memories and problems he had no wish to contemplate at present. His main concern was for Alnac Kreb and the girl.

'Ah, yes. Now I recall. You are a king in your own country, of course. But a reluctant one, eh? The duties are hard for a young man. Much is expected of you and you bear upon your shoulders the weight of the past, the ideals and loyalties of an entire people. It is difficult to rule well, to make good judgements, to dispense justice fairly. We have no kings here amongst the Bauradim, merely a group of men and women elected to speak for the whole clan, and I think it is better to share those burdens. If all share the burden, if all are responsible for themselves, then no single individual has to carry a weight that is too much for them.'

'The reason I travel is to learn more of such means of administering justice,' said Elric. 'But I will tell you this, Raik Na Seem, my people are as cruel as any in Quarzhasaat, and have more real power. We have a scanty notion of justice and the obligations of rule involve little more than inventing new terrors by which we may cow and control others. Power, I think, is a habit as terrible as the potion I must now sip in order to sustain myself. It feeds upon itself. It is a hungry beast, devouring those who would possess it and those who hate it – devouring even those who own it.'

'The hungry beast is not power itself,' said the old man. 'Power is neither good nor evil. It is the use one makes of it which is good or evil. I know that Melniboné once ruled the world, or that part of it she could find and the part she did not destroy.'

'You seem to know more of my nation than my nation knows of you!' The albino smiled.

'It is said by our folk that we all came to the desert because we fled first Melniboné and then Quarzhasaat. Each was as cruel as the other, each as corrupting, and it did not matter to us which destroyed which. We had hoped they would extinguish each other of course, but that was not to be. The second best thing occurred – Quarzhasaat almost destroyed herself and Melniboné forgot all about her – and us! I believe that soon after their war, Melniboné became bored with expansion and withdrew to rule only the Young Kingdoms. Now I hear she rules even less.'

'Only the Dragon Isle now.' Elric found that his thoughts were going back to Cymoril and he tried to stop himself thinking of her. 'But many a reaver's sought to sail against her and loot her wealth. They discover, however, that she remains too powerful for them. They must continue to trade with her instead.'

'Trade was ever War's superior,' said Raik Na Seem and looked suddenly back over his shoulder at Alnac's withered body. The golden outline of the dreamwand was glowing again and throbbing, as it had done from time to time since Alnac had first lain down beside the girl.

''Tis a strange organ,' said Raik Na Seem softly. 'Almost a second spine.'

He was about to say more when there was a faint movement in Alnac's features and a dreadful, desolate groan escaped the bloodless lips.

They turned and went to kneel beside him. Alnac's eyes still blazed blue and Varadia's were still black.

'He is dying,' whispered the First Elder. 'Is it so, Prince Elric?'

Elric knew no more than the Bauradi.

'What can we do for him?' asked Raik Na Seem.

Elric touched the cold, leathery carcass. He lifted an almost weightless wrist and could feel no pulse beating. It was at this moment, startlingly, that Alnac's eyes turned from blue to black and looked at Elric with all their old intelligence. 'Ah, you have come to help me. I have learned where the Pearl lies. But it is too well protected.'

The voice was a whisper from the dusty-dry mouth.

Elric cradled the dreamthief in his arms. 'I will help you, Alnac. Tell me how.'

'You cannot. There are caverns . . . These dreams are defeating me. They are drowning me. They are drawing me in. I am doomed to join those already doomed. Poor company for one such as me, Prince Elric. Poor company . . . '

The dreamwand pulsed and glowed white as bleached bones. The dreamthief's eyes turned to blue again, then back to black. The thin air stirred in the leathery remains of his throat. Suddenly there was horror in his face. 'Ah, no! I must find the will!'

The dreamwand moved like a snake through his body, then slithered into Varadia, then returned. 'Oh, Elric,' said the tiny voice, 'help me if you can. Oh, I am trapped. This is the worst I have ever known . . . '

His words seemed to Elric to call to him directly from the grave, as if his friend was already dead. 'Elric, if there is some way . . . '

Then the body shuddered, filled as if with a single huge breath while the dreamwand flickered and writhed again and then grew still, lying as it had first done with the crook upon the two clasped hands.

'Ah, my friend, I was a fool even to consider myself able to survive this . . . ' The tiny voice faded. 'Would that I had understood the nature of her mind. It is so strong! So strong!'

'Who does he speak of?' asked Raik Na Seem. 'My child? That which holds her? My daughter is of the Sarangli women. Her grandmother could charm whole tribes to believe they died of disease. I told him as much. What does he not understand?'

'Oh, Elric, she has destroyed me!' There was a tremor in the frail hand as it reached towards the albino.

Then, suddenly, all the colour and life came flooding back into Alnac's body. It seemed to expand to its former size and vitality. The hooked staff became nothing more than the artefact Elric had originally seen at Alnac's belt.

The handsome dreamthief grinned. He was surprised. 'I live! Elric, I live!'

He took a firmer grip on his staff and made to rise. Then he coughed and something disgusting oozed from his lips, like a gigantic, half-digested worm. It was as if he regurgitated his own rotten organs. He wiped the stuff away. For a moment he was bewildered, the terror returning to his eyes.

'No.' Alnac seemed reconciled suddenly. 'I was too proud. I die, of course.' He collapsed backward on to the sheet as Elric again tried to hold him. With his old irony the dreamthief shook his head. 'A little too late, I think. It's not my fate, after all, to be your companion, Sir Champion, in this plane.'

Elric, to whom the words made no sense, believed Alnac to be raving and sought to quieten him.

Then the staff fell from the dreamthief's grasp and he rolled on to his side before a wavering, sickly scream came out of him, then a stink which threatened to drive Elric and Raik Na Seem from the Bronze Tent. It was as if his body putrefied before their eyes even as the dreamthief tried to speak again and failed.

And then Alnac Kreb was dead.

Elric, mourning a brave, good man, felt then that his own doom and that of Anigh had been determined. The dreamthief's death suggested forces at work of which the albino understood nothing, for all his sorcerous wisdom. He had come across no grimoire which even hinted of such a fate. He had seen worse befall those who meddled with sorcery, but here was a sorcery which he could not begin to interpret.

'He is gone, then,' said Raik Na Seem.

'Aye.' Elric's own breath shuddered in his throat. 'Aye. His courage was greater than any of us suspected. Including, I think, himself.'

The First Elder walked slowly to where his child still slept in her terrible trance. He looked down into her blue eyes as if he almost hoped to see the black eyes somewhere there within her.

'Varadia?'

She did not respond.

Solemnly, Raik Na Seem took the Holy Girl and placed her back upon the raised block, settling her into the cushions as if she merely slept a natural sleep and he, her father, laid her down for her nightly rest.

Elric stared at the remains of the dreamthief. He had doubtless understood the cost of failure and perhaps that was the secret he had refused to share.

'It is over,' said Raik Na Seem gently. 'Now I can think of nothing to do for her. He gave too much.' He was fighting not to lose himself either in self-mortification or despair. 'We must try to think what to do. Will you help me in this, friend of my son?'

'If I can.'

As Elric rose, shaking, to his feet he heard a sound behind him. He thought at first it was some Bauradi woman come to mourn. He looked back at the light which streamed in through the tent and saw only her outline.

It was a young woman, but she was not of the Bauradim. She entered the tent slowly and there were tears in her eyes as she stared down at Alnac Kreb's ruined body.

'I am too late, then?'

Her musical voice was full of the most intense sorrow. She reached a hand to her face. 'He should not have attempted such a task. They told me at the Silver Flower Oasis that you had come here. Why could you not have waited a little longer? Just a day more?'

It was with great effort that she controlled her grief and Elric felt a sudden, obscure kindship with her.

She took another step towards the body. She was an inch or so shorter than Elric, with a heart-shaped face framed by thick brown hair. Slender and well-muscled, she wore a padded jerkin slashed to show its red silk lining. She had soft velvet breeches, embroidered felt riding boots and over all this an almost transparent cotton dust-coat pushed back from her shoulders. At her belt was a sword while cradled above her left shoulder was a hooked staff of gold and ebony, a more elaborate version of the one which lay on the carpet beside Alnac's corpse.

'I taught him all he knew of this craft,' she said. 'But it was not enough for this. How could he ever have thought that it would be! He could never have achieved such a goal. He had not the character for it.' She turned away, brushing at her face. When she looked back her tears had gone and she stared directly back into Elric's eyes.

'I am Oone,' she said. She bowed briefly to Raik Na Seem. 'I am the dreamthief you sent for.'

TWO

Is there a daughter born in dreams
Whose flesh is snow, whose ruby eyes
Stare into realms whose substance seems
Strong as agony, soft as lies?
Is there a girlchild born of dreams
Who carries blood as old as Time,
Destined one day to blend with mine
And give new lands a newer queen?

THE CHRONICLE OF THE BLACK SWORD

1

How a Thief May Instruct an Emperor

Oone removed a date stone from her mouth and dropped it into the sand of the Silver Flower Oasis. She reached her hand towards one of the brilliant cactus flowers which gave the place its name. She stroked the petals with long, delicate fingers. She sang to herself and it seemed to Elric that her words were a lament.

Respectfully he remained silent, sitting with his back to a palm tree looking to the distant camp and its continuing activity. She had asked him to accompany her but had said little to him. He heard a calling from the kashbeh high above but when he peered in that direction he saw nothing. The breeze blew over the desert and red dust raced like water towards the Ragged Pillars on the horizon.

It was almost noon. They had returned to the Silver Flower Oasis that morning and the few remains of Alnac Kreb were to be burned with honour according to the customs of the Bauradim that night.

Oone's staff was no longer slung on her back. Now she held the dreamwand in both hands, turning it over and over, watching the light on its burnish and polish as if she had only now seen it for the first time. The other wand, Alnac's she had tucked into her belt.

'It would have made my task a little easier,' she said suddenly, 'if Alnac had not acted so precipitously. He did not realize I was coming and was doing his best to save the child, I know. But a few more hours and I could have used his help, perhaps successfully. Certainly, I might have saved him.'

'I do not understand what happened to him,' said Elric.

'Even I do not know the exact cause of his fall,' she said. 'But I will explain what I can. That is why I asked you to come with me. I would not wish to be overheard. And I must demand your word that you will be discreet.'

'I am ever that, madam.'

'Forever,' she said.

'Forever?'

'You must promise never to tell another soul what I tell you today, nor recount any event which results from the telling. You must agree to be bound by a dreamthief's code even though you are not of our kind.'

Elric was baffled. 'For what reason?'

'Would you save their Holy Girl? Avenge Alnac? Free yourself from the drug's slavery? Adjust certain wrongs in Quarzhasaat?'

'You know I would.'

'Then we may reach an agreement, for it is certain that, unless we help each other, you and the girl and perhaps myself, too, will all be dead before the Blood Moon fades.'

'Certain?' Elric was grimly amused. 'Are you an oracle, too, then, madam?'

'All dreamthieves are that, to some degree.' She was almost impatient, as if she spoke to a slow child. She caught herself. 'Forgive me. I forget that our craft is unknown in the Young Kingdoms. Indeed, it's rarely that we travel to this plane at all.'

'I have met many supernaturals in my life, my lady, but few who seem so human as yourself.'

'Human? Of course I am human!' She seemed puzzled. Then her brow cleared. 'Ah. I forget that you are at once more sophisticated and less learned than those of my own persuasion.' She smiled at him. 'I am still not recovered from Alnac's unnecessary dissolution.'

'He need not have died.' Elric's tone was flat, unquestioning. He had known Alnac long enough to care for him as a friend. He understood something of Oone's loss. 'And there is no way to revive him?'

'He lost all essence,' said Oone. 'Instead of stealing a dream he was robbed of his own.' She paused, then spoke quickly, as if she feared she would regret her words. 'Will you help me, Prince Elric?'

'Yes.' He spoke without hesitation. 'If it is to avenge Alnac and save the child.'

'Even if you risk Alnac's fate? The fate which you witnessed?'

'Even that. Can it be worse than dying in Lord Gho's power?'

'Yes,' she said simply.

Elric laughed aloud at her frankness. 'Ah, well. Just so, madam! Just so! What's your bargain?'

She moved her hand again towards the silver petals, balancing her wand between her fingers. She was frowning, still not wholly certain of the rightness of her decision. 'I think that you are one of the few mortals on this earth who could understand the nature of my profession, who'll know what I mean when I speak of the nature of dreams and reality and how they intersect. I think, too, that you have habits of mind which would make you if not a perfect ally then an ally on whom I could to some extent depend. We dreamthieves have made something of a science of a trade which logically can tolerate no consistent laws. It has enabled us to pursue our craft with some success largely, I suspect, because we are able, to a degree, to impose our own wills upon the chaos we encounter. Does this make sense to you, Prince?'

'I think so. There are philosophers of my own people who claim that much of our magic is actually the imposition of a powerful will upon the fundamental stuff of reality, an ability, if you like, to make dreams come true. Some claim our whole world was created thus.'

Oone seemed pleased. 'Good. I knew there were certain ideas I would not have to explain.'

'But what would you have me do, lady?'

'I want you to help me. Together we can find a way to what the Sorcerer Adventurers call the Fortress of the Pearl and by so doing one or both of us might steal the dream which binds the child to perpetual sleep and free her to wakefulness, return her to her people to be their seeress and their pride.'

'The two are linked then?' Elric began to rise to his feet, ignoring the call of his ever-present craving. 'The child and the Pearl?'

'I think so.'

'What is the link?'

'In discovering that we shall doubtless discover how to free her.'

'Forgive me, Lady Oone,' said Elric gently, 'but you sound almost as ignorant as I!'

'In some ways it is true that I am. Before I go further, I must ask you to swear to abide by the Dreamthief's Code.'

'I swear,' said Elric, and he held up the hand on which his Actorios glowed to show that he swore by one of his people's most revered artefacts. 'I swear by the Ring of Kings.'

'Then I will tell you what I know and what I desire of you,' said Oone. She linked her free hand in his arm and led him further into the groves of palms and cypress. Sensing the shuddering hunger in him which yearned for Lord Gho's terrible drug, she seemed to show some sympathy.

'A dreamthief,' she began, 'does exactly what the title implies. We steal dreams. Originally our guild were true thieves. We learned the trick of entering the worlds of other people's dreams and stealing those which were most magnificent or exotic. Gradually, however, people began to call upon us to steal unwanted dreams – or rather the dreams which entrapped or plagued friends or relatives. So we stole those.

Frequently the dreams themselves were in no way harmful to another, only to the one who was in their power . . . '

Elric interrupted. 'Are you saying that a dream has some material reality? That it can be seized, like a volume of verse, say, or a money purse, and slipped free of its owner?'

'Essentially, yes. Or, I should say, our guild learned the trick of making a dream sufficiently real for it to be handled thus!' She now laughed openly at his confusion and some of the care went away from her for a moment. 'There is a certain talent needed and a great deal of training.'

'But what do you do with these stolen dreams?'

'Why, Prince Elric, we sell them at the Dream Market, twice a year. There's a fine trade in almost any sort of dream, no matter how bizarre or terrifying. There are merchants who purchase them and customers who would buy them. We distil them, of course, into a form which can be transported and later translated. And because we make the dreams take substance, we are threatened by them. That substance can destroy us. You see what happened to Alnac. It takes a certain character, a certain cast of mind, a certain attitude of spirit, all combining, to protect oneself in the Dream Realms. But because we have codified these realms we have also to a degree made them our own to manipulate.'

'You must explain more to me,' said Elric, 'if I am to follow you at all, madam!'

'Very well.' She paused at the edge of the grove, where the earth grew dustier and formed a territory between oasis and desert that was a little of both and was neither. She studied the cracked earth as if the cracks were the outlines of a singularly complicated map, a geometry which only she could understand.

'We have made rules,' she said. Her voice was distant, almost as if she spoke to herself. 'And codified what we have discovered over the centuries. And yet we are still subject to the most unimaginable hazards . . . '

'Wait, madam. Are you suggesting that Alnac Kreb, by some wizardry known only to your guild, entered the world of the Holy Girl's dreams and there suffered adventures such as you or I might suffer in this material world?'

'Well put.' She turned with a strange smile on her lips. 'Aye. And his substance went into that world and was absorbed by it, strengthening the substance of her dreams . . . '

'The dreams he hoped to steal.'

'He hoped to steal only one. The one which imprisons her in that perpetual slumber.'

'And then he would sell it, you say, at your Dream Market?'

'Perhaps.' She was clearly unwilling to discuss this aspect of the matter.

'Where is that market held?'

'In a realm beyond this one, in a place where only those of our profession, or those who attend upon us, may travel.'

'You'd take me there?' Elric spoke from curiosity.

Her glance was a mixture of amusement and caution. 'Possibly. But first we must be successful. We must steal a dream so that we may trade it there. Know you, Elric, I have every desire to inform you of all you wish to learn, but there are many things hard to explain to one who has not studied with our Guild. They can only be demonstrated or experienced. I am not a native of your world, nor are most dreamthieves from this sphere. We are wanderers – nomads, you might say – between many times and many places. We have learned that a dream in one realm can be an undeniable reality in another, while what is utterly prosaic in that realm can elsewhere be the stuff of the most fantastic nightmare.'

'Is all creation so malleable?' Elric asked with a shudder.

'What we create must ever be, lest it die,' she said, her tone one of ironical finality.

'The struggle between Law and Chaos echoes that struggle within ourselves between unbridled emotion and too much caution, I suppose,' Elric mused, aware that she did not wish to pursue this particular conversation.

With her foot Oone traced the cracks in the red earth. 'To learn more you must become an apprentice dreamthief . . . '

'Willingly,' said Elric. 'I'm sufficiently curious now, madam. You spoke of your laws. What are they?'

'Some are instructive, some are descriptive. First I'll tell you that we have determined every Dream Realm shall have seven aspects, which we have named. By naming and describing we hope to shape that which has no shape and control that which few can begin to control. By such impositions we have learned to survive in worlds where others would be destroyed within minutes. Yet even when we perform such impositions, even that which our own wills define can become transmuted beyond our control. If you would accompany me and aid me in this adventure you must know that I have determined we shall pass through seven lands. The first land we call Sadanor, or the Land of Dreams-in-Common. The second land is Marador, which we call the Land of Old Desires, while the third is Paranor, the Land of Lost

Beliefs. The fourth land is known to dreamthieves as Celador, which is the Land of Forgotten Love. The fifth is Imador, the Land of New Ambition, and the sixth is Falador, the Land of Madness . . . '

'Fanciful names indeed, madam. The Guild of Dreamthieves has a penchant for poetry, I think. And the seventh? What is that named?'

She paused before she replied. Her wonderful eyes peered into his, as if exploring the recesses of his own skull. 'That has no name,' she said quietly, 'save any name the inhabitants shall give it. But there, if anywhere, you will find the Fortress of the Pearl.'

Elric felt himself trapped by that gentle yet determined gaze. 'And how may we enter these lands?' The albino forced himself to engage with these questions though by now his whole body was crying out for a draught of Lord Gho's elixir.

She sensed his tension and her hand on his arm was meant to calm and reassure him. 'Through the child,' said Oone.

Elric remembered what he had witnessed in the Bronze Tent and he shuddered. 'How is such a thing achieved?'

Oone frowned and the pressure of her hand increased. 'She is our gateway and the dreamwands are our keys. There is no way in which I will harm her, Elric. Once we have reached the seventh aspect, the Nameless Land, there we might in turn find the key to her particular prison.'

'She is a medium, then? Is that what has happened to her? Did the Sorcerer Adventurers know something of her power and in attempting to use her put her into this trance?'

Again she hesitated, then she nodded. 'Close enough, Prince Elric. It is written in our histories, of which we have many, though most are inaccessible to us in the libraries of Tanelorn, *"What lies within always has a form without and that which is without takes a shape within."* Put another way, we sometimes say that what is visible must always have an invisible aspect, just as everything invisible must be represented by the visible.'

Elric found this too cryptic for him, though he was familiar enough with such mysterious utterances from his own grimoires. He did not dismiss them, but he knew they frequently required much pondering and certain experience before they made complete sense. 'You speak of supernatural realms, madam. The worlds inhabited by the Lords of Chaos and of Law, by the elementals, by immortals and the like. I know something of such realms and have even journeyed in them some little way. But I have never heard of leaving part of one's physical substance behind and travelling into those realms by means of a sleeping child!'

She looked at him for a long moment as if she thought he was deliberately disingenuous, then she shrugged. 'You will find the realms of the dreamthief very similar. And you would do well to memorize and obey our code.'

'You are a strict order, then, madam . . . '

'If we are to survive. Alnac had the instincts of a good dreamthief but he had not acquired the full discipline. That was one of the chief reasons for his dissolution. You on the other hand are familiar with the necessary disciplines, for they were how you came by your knowledge of sorcery. Without those disciplines you, too, would have perished.'

'I have rejected much of that, Lady Oone.'

'Aye. So I believe. But you have not lost the habit, I think. Or so I hope. The first law the dreamthief obeys says: "Offers of guidance must always be accepted but never trusted". The second says: "Beware the familiar" and the third tells us: "What is strange should be cautiously welcomed". There are many others, but it is those three which encompass the fundamentals by which a dreamthief survives.' She smiled. Her smile was oddly sweet and vulnerable and Elric realized she was weary. Perhaps her grief had exhausted her.

The Melnibonéan spoke gently, looking back to the great red rocks of the Silver Flower Oasis's protection and sanctuary. The voices were stilled now. Thin lines of smoke ascended the rich blue of the sky. 'How long does it take to instruct and train one of your calling?'

She recognized his irony now. 'Five years or more,' she said. 'Alnac had been a full member of the Guild for perhaps six years.'

'And he failed to survive in the realm where the Holy Girl's spirit is held prisoner?'

'He was for all his skills, only an ordinary mortal, Prince Elric.'

'And you think I'm more than that?'

She laughed openly. 'You are the last Emperor of Melniboné. You are the most powerful of your race, which is a race whose familiarity with sorcery is legendary. True, you have left your bride-to-be waiting for you while you place your cousin Yyrkoon on the Ruby Throne to reign as regent until you return – a decision only an idealist would make – but nonetheless, my lord, you cannot pretend to me that you are in any way ordinary!'

In spite of his craving for the poisonous elixir, Elric found himself laughing back at her. 'If I am such a man of qualities, madam, how is it that I find myself in this position, contemplating death from the tricks of a second-rate provincial politician?'

'I did not say you admired yourself, my lord. But it would be foolish to deny what you have been and what you could become.'

'I prefer to consider the latter, my lady.'

'Consider, if you will, the fate of Raik Na Seem's daughter. Consider the fate of his people deprived of their history and their oracle. Consider your own doom, to perish for no good reason in a distant land, your destiny unfulfilled.'

Elric accepted this.

She continued. 'It is probable, too, that you have no rival as a sorcerer in your world. While your specific skills might be of little use to you in the adventure I propose, your experience, knowledge and understanding might make the difference between success and failure.'

Elric had become impatient as his body's demand for the drug grew unbearable. 'Very well, Lady Oone. Whatever you decide, I shall agree to.'

She took a step back from him and looked at him coolly. 'You had best return to your tent and find your elixir,' she said softly.

Familiar desperation filled the albino's mind. 'I shall, madam. I shall.' And he turned and strode swiftly back towards the gathered tents of the Bauradim.

He scarcely spoke to any of those who greeted him as he passed. Raik Na Seem had moved nothing from the tent Elric had last shared with Alnac Kreb and the albino hastily drew the flask from his saddle-bag and took a deep draught, feeling, for a short while at least, the relief, and resurgence of energy, the illusion of health which the Quarzhasaati's drug gave him. He sighed and turned towards the entrance of the tent as Raik Na Seem came up, his brow furrowed, his eyes full of pain which he tried to disguise. 'Have you agreed to help the dreamthief, Elric? Will you attempt to achieve what the prophecy predicted? Bring our Holy Girl back to us? There is now less time than there ever was. Soon the Blood Moon will be gone.'

Elric dropped the flask on to the carpet which covered the ground. He bent and picked up the Black Sword which he had unbuckled while he walked with Oone. The thing thrilled in his fingers and he felt vaguely nauseated. 'I will do whatever is required of me,' the albino said.

'Good.' The older man gripped Elric by the shoulders. 'Oone has told me that you are a great man with a great destiny and that this time is one of considerable moment in your life. We are honoured to be part of that destiny and grateful for your concern . . . '

Elric accepted Raik Na Seem's words with all his old grace. He bowed. 'I believe that the health of your Holy Girl is more important than any fate of mine. I will do whatever is possible to bring her back to you.'

Oone had entered behind the Bauradim's First Elder. She smiled at the albino. 'You are ready now?'

Elric nodded and began to buckle on the Black Sword, but Oone stopped him with a gesture. 'You'll find the weapons you need where we travel.'

'But the sword is more than a weapon, Lady Oone!' the albino knew a kind of panic.

She held out Alnac's dreamwand to him. 'This is all you need for our venture, my lord Emperor.'

Stormbringer murmured violently as Elric let the sword fall back to the cushions of the tent. It seemed almost to threaten him.

'I am dependent . . . ' he began.

She shook her head gently. 'You are not. You believe that sword to be part of your identity but it is not. It is your nemesis. It is the part of you which represents your weakness, not your strength.'

Elric sighed. 'I do not understand you, my lady, but if you do not wish me to bring the sword, I'll leave it.'

Another sound, a peculiar growl, from the blade, but Elric ignored it. He left both flask and sword in the tent and strode to where horses awaited them to carry them from the Silver Flower Oasis back to the Bronze Tent.

As they rode a little distance behind Raik Na Seem, Oone told Elric something more of what the Holy Girl meant to the Bauradim.

'As you perhaps have already realized, the child holds in trust the history and the aspirations of the Bauradim – their collected wisdom. Everything they know to be true and of value is contained within her. She is the living representation of her people's learning – what is the essence of their history – of a time before they became desert dwellers even. If they lose her there is every chance, they believe, that they must begin their history all over again – re-learn hard-won lessons, relive experience and make the mistakes and blunders which so painfully informed their people's understanding down the centuries. She is Time, if you like – their library, museum, religion and culture personified in a single human being. Can you imagine, Prince Elric, what her loss means to them? She is the very soul of the Bauradim. And that soul is imprisoned where only those of a certain skill can even find her, let alone free her.'

Elric fingered the dreamwand which now replaced his runesword at his hip. 'If she were only an ordinary child, bringing sorrow to her family through her condition, I would be inclined to help if I could,' he said. 'For I like this people and their leader.'

'Her fate and yours are intertwined,' said Oone. 'Whatever your sentiments, my lord, you probably have little real choice in the matter.'

He did not wish to hear this. 'It seems to me, madam, that you dreamthieves are altogether too familiar with myself, my family, my people and my destiny. It makes me somewhat uncomfortable. Yet I cannot deny you know more than anyone, save my betrothed, about my inner conflicts. How come you by this power of divination and prophecy?'

She spoke almost casually. 'There is a land all dreamthieves have visited. It is a place where all dreams intersect, where all that we have in common meets. And we call that land The Birthplace of the Bone, where mankind first assumed reality.'

'This is legend! And primitive legend at that!'

'Legend to you. Truth to us. As one day you'll discover.'

'If Alnac could foretell the future, why did he not wait for you to come to help him?'

'We rarely know our own destiny, only the general movements of the tides and of the figures who stand out in their world's histories. All dreamthieves, it is true, know the future, for half their lives are spent without Time. For us there is no past or future, only a changing present. We are free of those particular chains while bound as strongly by others.'

'I have read of such ideas, but they mean very little to me.'

'Because you lack experience to make sense of them.'

'You have already spoken of the Land of Dreams-in-Common. Is that the same as the Birthplace of the Bone?'

'Perhaps. Our people are undecided on the point.'

Temporarily invigorated by the drug, Elric began to enjoy the conversation, much of which he saw as mere pleasant abstraction. Free of his runesword he knew a kind of lightness of spirit which he had not experienced since the first months of his courtship of Cymoril in those relatively untroubled years before Yyrkoon's growing ambition had begun to contaminate life at the Melnibonéan Court.

He recalled something from one of his own people's histories. 'I have seen it said that the world is no more than what its denizens agree it is. I remember reading something to that effect in *The Gabbling Sphere* which said: "For who is to say which is the inner world and which the outer? What we make reality may be what will alone decides and what we define as dreams may be the greater truth." Is that a philosophy close to your own, Lady Oone?'

'Close enough,' she said. 'Though it seems a little airy.'

They rode like this, almost like two children on a picnic until they reached the Bronze Tent when the sun was setting and were led, once more, into the place where men and women sat or lay around the great raised bed on which rested the little girl who symbolized their entire existence.

It seemed to Elric that the illuminating braziers and lamps were burning lower than when last he was here, and that the child looked even paler than before, but he forced an expression of confidence when he turned to Raik Na Seem. 'This time we shall not fail her,' he said.

Oone appeared to approve of Elric's words and watched carefully as, on her instructions, Varadia's frail body was lifted from the bed and placed this time upon a huge cushion which, in its turn, was set between two other cushions, also of great size. She signed to the albino to lay his body down on the far side of the child while she herself took up her position on the girl's left.

'Grasp her hand, my lord Emperor,' said Oone ironically, 'and place the crook of the dreamwand over both yours and hers, as you saw Alnac do.'

Elric felt some trepidation as he obeyed her, but he knew no fear for himself, only for the child and her people, for Cymoril waiting for him in Melniboné, for the boy who prayed in Quarzhasaat that he would return with the jewel his jailer had demanded. His hand locked to the girl's by the dreamwand, he knew a sense of fusion that was not unpleasant, yet seemed to burn as hot as any flame. He watched as Oone did the same thing.

Immediately Elric felt a power possess him and for a moment it was as if his body grew lighter and lighter until it threatened to drift away on the slightest breeze. His vision faded, yet dimly he could still see Oone. She seemed to be concentrating.

He looked into the face of the Holy Girl and for a second thought he saw her skin turn still whiter, her eyes glow as crimson as his own and a strange thought came and went in his mind: *If I had a daughter she would look thus . . .*

And then it was as if his bones were melting, his flesh dissolving, his whole mind and spirit dissipating. He gave himself up to this sensation as he had determined he must, since he now served Oone's purpose, and now the flesh became flowing water, the veins and blood were coloured strands of air, his skeleton flowed like molten silver, mingling with the Holy Child's, becoming hers, then flowing on beyond her, into caverns and tunnels and dark places, into places where whole worlds existed in hollowed rock, where voices called to him and knew him and sought to comfort him or frighten him or tell him truths he did not wish to learn; and then the air grew bright again and he felt Oone beside him, guiding him, her hand on his, her body almost his body, her voice confident and even cheerful, like one who moves towards familiar danger; danger which she had overcome many times. Yet there was an edge to her voice which made him believe she had never faced a danger as great as this one and that there was every chance neither of them would return to the Bronze Tent or the Silver Flower Oasis.

And there was music which he understood was the very soul of this child turned into sound. Sweet, sad, lonely music. Music so beautiful he would have wept had he anything more than the airiest substance.

Then he saw blue sky before him, a red desert stretching away towards red mountains on the horizon and he had the strangest of sensations, as if he were coming home to a land he had somehow lost in his childhood and then forgotten.

2

In the Marches at the Heart's Edge

As Elric felt his bones reform and the flesh resume its familiar weight and contour he saw that the land they had entered seemed scarcely any different from that which they had left. Red desert stretched before them, red mountains lay beyond. So familiar was the landscape that Elric looked back, expecting to see the Bronze Tent, but immediately behind him now yawned a chasm so vast no further side could be seen. He knew sudden vertigo and checked his balance, somewhat to Oone's amusement.

The dreamthief was dressed in her same functional velvets and silks and seemed a little amused by his response. 'Aye, Prince Elric! Now we are indeed at the very edge of the world! We have only certain choices here and they do not include retreat!'

'I had not considered it, madam.' Looking more closely, he realized that the mountains were considerably taller and were all leaning in the same direction, as if bent by a tremendous wind.

'They are like the teeth of some ancient predator,' said Oone with the shudder of one who might actually have stared into such a maw at some time in their career. 'Doubtless the first stage of our journey takes us there. This is the land we dreamthieves always call Sadanor. The Land of Dreams-in-Common.'

'Yet you seem unfamiliar with this scenery.'

'The scenery varies. We know only the *nature* of the land. It may change in its details. But where we travel is frequently dangerous not because it is unfamiliar but because of its familiarity. That is the second rule of the dreamthief.'

'Beware the familiar.'

'You learn well.' She seemed unduly pleased by his response, as if she had doubted her own description of his qualities and was glad to have them confirmed. Elric began to realize the degree of desperation involved in this adventure and was seized by that wild carelessness, that willingness to give himself up to the moment, to any experience, which so set him apart from the other lords of Melniboné, whose lives were ruled by tradition and a desire to maintain their power at any cost.

Smiling, his eyes alight with all their old vitality, he bowed ironically. 'Then lead on, madam! Let us begin our journey towards the mountains.'

Oone, a little startled by his mood, frowned. But she began to walk through sand so light it stirred like water around her feet. And the albino followed.

'I must admit,' he said, after they had walked for perhaps an hour, without noting any shift in the position of the light, 'this place begins to disturb me more the more I am in it. I thought the sun obscured, but now I realize there is no sun in the sky at all.'

'Such abnormalities come and go in the Land of Dreams-in-Common,' said Oone.

'I would feel more secure with my sword at my side.'

'Swords are easily come by here,' she said.

'Drinkers of souls?'

'Perhaps. But do you feel the need for that peculiar form of sustenence? Do you crave Lord Gho's drug?'

Elric admitted to his own surprise that he had lost no energy. For perhaps the first time in his adult life he had the sense that he was physically as other people, able to sustain himself without calling on any form of artifice. 'It occurs to me,' he said, 'that I might be well-advised to make my home here.'

'Ah, now you begin to fall into another of this realm's traps,' she said, lightly enough. 'First there is suspicion and maybe fear. Then there is relaxation, a feeling that you have always belonged here, that this is your natural home, or your spiritual home. These are all illusions common to the traveller, as I am sure you know. Here those illusions must be resisted, for they are more than sentiment. They may be traps set to snare you and destroy you. Be grateful that you have more apparent energy than that which you normally know, but remember another rule of the dreamthief – *Every gain is paid for, either before or after the event*. Every apparent benefit could well have its contrary disadvantage.'

Privately Elric still thought the price of such a sense of well-being might be worth the paying.

It was at that moment that he saw the leaf.

It drifted down from over his head, a broad, red-gold oak leaf, falling gently as any ordinary autumn shedding, and landed upon the sand at his feet. Without at first finding this extraordinary, he bent to pick the leaf up.

Oone had seen it, too, and made as if to caution him, then changed her mind.

Elric laid the leaf on the palm of his hand. There was nothing unusual about it, save that there was not a tree visible in any direction. He was about to ask Oone to explain this phenomenon when he noticed that she was staring beyond him, over his shoulder.

'Good afternoon to you,' said a jaunty voice. 'This is luck indeed, to find some fellow mortals in such a miserable wilderness. What trick of the Wheel brought us here, do you think?'

'Greetings,' said Oone, her smile growing broad. 'You're ill-dressed, sir, for this desert.'

'I was neither told of my destination nor the fact that I was leaving . . .'

Elric turned and to his surprise saw a small man whose sharp, merry features were shadowed by an enormous turban of yellow silk. This headdress, at least as wide as the man's shoulders, was decorated with a pin containing a great green gem and from it sprouted several peacock's feathers. He seemed to be wearing many layers of clothing, all highly-coloured, of silk and linen, including an embroidered waistcoat and a long jacket of beautifully stitched blue patchwork, each shade subtly different from the one next to it. On his legs were baggy trousers of red silk and his feet sported curling slippers of green and yellow leather. The man was unarmed, but in his hands he held a startled black and white cat upon whose back were folded a pair of silky black wings.

The man bowed when he saw Elric. 'Greetings, sir. You would be the incarnation of the Champion on this plane, I take it. I am – ' he frowned as if he had for a second forgotten his own name. 'I am something beginning with "J" and something beginning with "C". It will return to me in a moment. Or another name or event will occur, I'm sure. I am your – what? – amanuensis, eh?' He peered up into the sky. 'Is this one of those sunless worlds? Are we to have no night at all?'

Elric looked to Oone, who did not seem wary of this apparition. 'I did not ask for a secretary, sir,' he said to the small man. 'Nor did I expect to be assigned one. My companion and I are on a quest in this world . . .'

'A quest, naturally. It is your role, as it is mine to accompany you. That's in order, sir. My name is – ' But again his own name eluded him. 'Yours is?'

'I am Elric of Melniboné and this is Oone the Dreamthief.'

'Then this is the Land the dreamthieves call Sadanor, I take it. Good, then I am called Jaspar Colinadous. And my cat's name is Whiskers, as always.'

At this, the cat gave voice to a small, intelligent noise, to which its owner listened carefully and nodded.

'I recognize this land now,' he said. 'You'll be seeking the Marador Gate, eh? For the Land of Old Desires.'

'You are a dreamthief yourself, Sir Jaspar?' Oone asked in some surprise.

'I have relatives who are.'

'But how came you here?' Elric asked. 'Through a medium? Did you use a mortal child, as we did?'

'Your words are mysterious to me, sir.' Jaspar Colinadous adjusted his turban, the little cat tucked carefully under one voluminous silk sleeve. 'I travel between the worlds, apparently at random, usually at the behest of some force I do not understand, frequently to find myself guiding or accompanying venturers such as yourselves. Not,' he added feelingly, 'always dressed appropriately for the realm or the moment of my arrival. I dreamed, I think, I was the sultan of some fabulous city, where I possessed the most astonishing variety of treasures. Where I was waited upon . . . ' here he coloured and looked away from Oone. 'Forgive me. It was a dream. I have awakened from it now. Unfortunately, the clothes followed me from the dream . . . '

Elric believed the man's words were close to nonsense, but Oone had no difficulty with them. 'You know a road, then, to the Marador Gate?'

'Surely, I must, if this is the Land of Dreams-in-Common.' Carefully, he placed his cat on his shoulder and then began to rummage in his sleeves, within his shirt, in the pockets of his several garments, producing all manner of scrolls and papers and little books, boxes, compacts, writing instruments, lengths of cord and reels of thread, until one of the rolled pieces of vellum caused him to cry out in relief. 'Here it is, I think! Our map.' He replaced all the other items in exactly the places he had drawn them from and unrolled the parchment. 'Indeed, indeed! This shows us the road through yonder mountains.'

'Offers of guidance . . . ' began Elric.

'And beware the familiar,' said Oone softly. Then she made a dismissive gesture. 'Here we have conflict already, you see, for what is unfamiliar to you is highly familiar to me. That is part of the nature of this land.' She turned to Jaspar Colinadous. 'Sir? May I see your map?'

Without hesitation, the small man handed it to her. 'A straight road. It's always a straightish road, eh? And only one. That's the joy of these dream realms. One can interpret and control them so simply. Unless, of course, they swallow one up completely. Which they are wont to do.'

'You have the advantage of me,' said Elric, 'for I know nothing of this world. Neither was I aware that there are others like it.'

'Aha! Then you have so much wonder to anticipate, sir! So many marvels yet to witness. I would tell you of them, but my own memory is not what it should be. I frequently have only the vaguest of recollections. But there is an infinity of worlds and some are yet unborn, some so old they have grown senile, some born of dreams, some destroyed by nightmares.' Jaspar Colinadous paused apologetically. 'I grow over-enthusiatic. I do not intend to confuse you, sir. Just know you that I am a little confused myself. I am ever that. Does my map make sense to you, Lady Dreamthief?'

'Aye.' Oone was frowning over the parchment. 'There is only one pass through those mountains, which are called the Shark's Jaws. If we assume that the mountains are lying to our north, then we must bear to the north-east and find the Shark's Gullet, as it's named here. We are much obliged to you, Master Jaspar Colinadous.' She rolled up the map and returned it to him. It disappeared into one of his sleeves and the cat crept down to lie, purring, in the crook of his arm.

For a moment, Elric had the strongest instinct that this likeable individual had been called up by Oone from her own imagination, though it was impossible to believe he did not exist in his own right, such a self-confident personality was he. Indeed, Elric had the passing fancy that perhaps he, himself, was the phantasy.

'You'll note there are dangers in that pass,' said Jaspar Colinadous casually, as he fell in beside them. 'I'll let Whiskers scout for us, if you like, when we get closer.'

'We should be much obliged to you, sir,' said Oone.

They continued their journey across the bleak landscape, with Jaspar Colinadous telling tales of previous adventures, most of which he could only half recall, of people he had known, whose names escaped him, and of great moments in the histories of a thousand worlds whose importance now eluded him. To hear him was like coming upon the old halls of Imrryr, on the Dragon isle, where once huge series of windows had told in pictures the tales of the first Melnibonéans and how they had come to their present home. Now they were mere shards, small fragments of the story, brilliant details whose context was only barely imaginable and whose information was gone forever. Elric ceased trying to follow Jaspar Colinadous's conversation but, as he had learned to do with the fragments of glass, let himself enjoy them for their texture and their colour instead.

The consistency of the light had begun to disturb him and eventually he interrupted the little man in his flow and asked him if he, too, were not made uncomfortable by it.

Jaspar Colinadous took this opportunity to stop and remove his slippers, shaking sand from them as Oone waited ahead of them, her stance impatient. 'No, sir. Supernatural worlds are frequently sunless, for they obey none of the laws we are familiar with in our own. They may be flat, half-spheres, oval, circular, even shaped like cubes. They exist only as satellites to those realms we call "real", and therefore are dependent not upon any sun or moon or planetary system for their ordering, but upon the demands – spiritual, imaginative, philosophical and so on – of worlds which do, in fact, require a sun to heat them and a moon to move their tides. There is even a theory that our worlds are the satellites and that these supernatural worlds are the birthplaces of all our realities.' His shoes again free from sand, Jaspar Colinadous began to follow Oone, who was some distance on, having refused to wait upon them.

'Perhaps this is the land ruled by Arioch, my patron Duke of Hell,' said Elric. 'The land from which the Black Sword sprang.'

'Oh, quite possibly, Prince Elric. For, see, there's a hellish sort of creature stooping on your friend at this moment and us without a weapon between us!'

The three-headed bird must have flown at such a great height it had not been seen to approach, but now it was dropping at terrifying speed from above and Oone, alerted by Elric's cry of warning, began to run, perhaps hoping to divert it in its descent upon her. It was like a gigantic crow, with two of its heads tucked deep into its neck, while the other stretched out to help its downward flight, its wings spread behind it, its claws extended, ready to seize the woman.

Elric began to run forward, screaming at the thing. He, too, hoped that this activity would disturb the creature enough and make it lose its momentum.

With a terrible cawing which seemed to fill the entire heavens, the monster slowed its descent a trifle in order to make a more accurate strike on the woman.

It was then that Jaspar Colinadous cried from behind Elric.

'Jack Three Beaks, thou naughty bird!'

The beast wavered in the air, turning all heads towards the turbaned figure who stode decisively towards it across the sand, his cat alert on his arm.

'What's this, Jack? I thought you were forbidden living meat!' Jaspar

Colinadous's voice was contemptuous, familiar. Whiskers growled and gibbered at the thing, though it was many times larger than the little cat.

With a croak of defiance the bird flopped on to the sand and began to run at some considerable speed towards Oone, who had stopped to witness this bizarre event. Now she took to her heels again, the three-headed crow in pursuit.

'Jack! Jack! Remember the punishment.'

The bird's cry was almost mocking. Elric began to stumble through the desert in its track, hoping to find a means of saving the dreamthief.

It was then that he felt something cut through the air above his head, fanning him with unexpected coolness, and a dark shape sped in pursuit of the thing Jaspar Colinadous had called Jack Three Beaks.

It was the black and white cat. The beast flung his little body at the bird's central neck and sank all four sets of claws into the feathers. With a shrill scream the gigantic three-headed crow whirled round, its other heads trying to peck at the tenacious cat and just failing to reach it.

To Elric's astonishment the cat seemed to swell larger and larger as if feeding on the lifestuff of the crow, while the crow appeared to grow smaller.

'Bad Jack Three Beaks! Wicked Jack!' The almost ridiculous figure of Jaspar Colinadous strutted up to the thing now, wagging a finger at which beaks snapped but dared not bite. 'You were warned. And now you must perish. How came you here at all? You followed me, I suppose, when I left my palace.' He scratched his head. 'Not that I recall leaving the palace. Ah, well . . . '

Jack Three Beaks cawed again, glaring with mad, frightened eyes in the direction of his original prey. Oone was approaching again.

'This creature is your pet, Master Jaspar?'

'Certainly not, madam. It is my enemy. He knew he'd had his last warning. But I think he did not expect to find me here and believed he could attack living prey with impunity. Not so, Jack, eh?'

The answering croak was almost pathetic now. The little black and white cat resembled nothing so much as a feeding vampire bat as it sucked and sucked of the monster's lifestuff.

Oone watched in horror as gradually the crow shrank to a tiny, wizened thing and Whiskers at last sat back, huge and round, and began to clean himself, purring with considerable pleasure. Clearly pleased with his pet, Jaspar Colinadous reached up to pat his head. 'Good lad, Whiskers. Now poor Jack's not even gravy for an old man's bread.' He smiled proudly at his two new friends. 'This cat has saved my life on many an occasion.'

'How had you the name of that monster?' Oone wished to know. Her lovely features were flushed and she was out of breath. Elric was reminded suddenly of Cymoril, though he could not exactly identify the similarity.

'Why, it was Jack frightened the principality I visited before this.' Jaspar Colinadous displayed his rich clothing. 'And how I came to be so favoured by the folk of that place. Jack Three Beaks always knew the power of Whiskers and was afraid of him. He had been terrorizing the people when I arrived. I tamed Jack – or strictly speaking Whiskers did – but let him live, since he was a useful carrion eater and the province was given to terrible heat in the summer. When I fell through that particular rent in the fabric of the multiverse he must have come after me, without realizing I was already here with Whiskers. There's little mystery to it, Lady Oone.'

She drew a deep breath. 'Well, I'm grateful for your aid, sir.'

He inclined his head. 'Now had we better not move on towards the Marador Gate? There are more, if less unexpected, dangers ahead of us in the Shark's Gullet. The map marks 'em.'

'Would that I had a weapon at my side,' said Elric, feelingly. 'I would be more confident, whether it were an illusion or no!' But he marched beside the others as they moved on towards the mountain.

The cat remained behind, licking his paws and cleaning himself, for all the world like an ordinary domestic creature which had killed a pantry-raiding mouse.

At last the ground began to rise as they reached the shallow foothills of the Shark's Jaws and saw ahead of them a great, dark fissure in the mountains, the Gullet which would lead them through to the next land of their journey. In the heat of the barren wilderness the pass looked cool and almost welcoming, though even from here Elric thought he could see shapes moving in it. White shadows flickered against the black.

'What manner of people live here?' he asked Oone, who had not shown him the map.

'Chiefly those who have either lost their way or become too fearful to continue the journey inwards. The other name for the pass is the Valley of Timid Souls.' Oone shrugged. 'But I suspect it is not from them that we shall be in danger. At least, not greatly. They'll ally themselves with whatever power rules the pass.'

'And the map says nothing of its nature?'

'Only that we should be wary.'

There came a noise from behind them and Elric turned, expecting threat, but it was only Whiskers, looking a little plumper, a little sleeker, but back to his normal size, who had at last caught up with them.

Jaspar Colinadous laughed and bent to let the cat leap on to his shoulder. 'We have no need of weapons, eh? Not with such a handsome beast to defend us!'

The cat licked his face.

Elric was peering into the dark pass, trying to determine what he might find there. For a moment he thought he saw a rider at the entrance, a man mounted on a silvery-grey horse, wearing strange armour of different shades of white and grey and yellow. The warrior's horse reared as he turned it and rode back into the blackness and Elric knew a sensation of foreboding, though he had never seen the figure before.

Oone and Jaspar Colinadous were apparently unaware of the apparition and continued with untiring stride in the direction of the pass.

Elric said nothing of the rider but instead asked Oone how it was that they had all walked for hours and felt neither hungry nor weary.

'It is one of the advantages of this realm,' she said. 'The disadvantages are considerable, however, since a sense of time is easily lost and one can forget direction and goals. Moreover it's wise to bear in mind that while one does not appear to lose physical energy or experience hunger, other forms of energy are being expended. Psychic and spiritual they may be, but they are just as valuable, as I'm sure you appreciate. Conserve those particular resources, Prince Elric, for you'll have urgent need of them soon enough!'

Elric wondered if she, too, had caught sight of the pale warrior but, for a reason he could not understand, was reluctant to ask her.

The hills were growing ever taller around them as, subtly, they moved into the Shark's Gullet. The light was dimmer already, blocked by the mountains, and Elric felt a chill which was not altogether the result of the shade.

He became aware of a rushing sound and Jaspar Colinadous ran towards a high bank of rocks to peer over them and look down. He turned, a little baffled. 'A deep chasm. A river. We must find a bridge before we can go on.' He murmured to his winged cat, which immediately took flight over the abyss and was soon lost in the shadows beyond.

Forced to pause, Elric knew sudden gloom. Unable to gauge his physical needs, uncertain of what events took place in the world he had left, perturbed by the knowledge that their time was running short and that Lord Gho would cerainly keep his word to torture young

Anigh to death, he began to believe that he could well be on a fool's errand, embarked on an adventure which could only end in disaster for all. He wondered why he had trusted Oone so completely. Perhaps because he had been so desperate, so shocked by the death of Alnac Kreb . . .

She touched him on the shoulder. 'Remember what I told you. Your weariness is not physical here, but it manifests itself in your moods. You must seek spiritual sustenance as assiduously as you would normally seek food and water.'

He looked into her eyes, seeing warmth and kindness there. Immediately his despair began to dissipate. 'I must admit I was beginning to know strong doubt . . . '

'When that feeling overwhelms you, try to tell me,' she said. 'I am familiar with it and might be able to help you . . . '

'So I am entirely in your hands, madam.' He spoke without irony.

'I thought you understood that when you agreed to accompany me,' she said softly.

'Aye.' He turned in time to see the little cat coming back and alighting on Jaspar Colinadous's shoulder. The turbaned man listened carefully and intelligently and Elric was certain that the cat was speaking.

At last Jaspar Colinadous nodded. 'There's a good bridge not a quarter of a mile from here and it leads to a trail winding directly into the pass. Whiskers tells me that the bridge is guarded by a single mounted warrior. We can hope, I suppose, that he will let us cross.'

They followed the course of the river as the sky overhead grew darker and Elric wished that, together with his lack of hunger and tiredness, he did not feel the rapid drop in temperature which made his body shake. Only Jaspar Colinadous was unaffected by the cold.

The rough walls of rocks at the chasm's edge gradually fell away, curving inward towards the pass, and very soon they saw the bridge ahead of them, a narrow spur of natural stone pushing outwards over the foaming river below. And they heard the echo of the water as it plunged yet deeper down the gorge. Yet nowhere was there the guard which the little cat had reported.

Elric moved cautiously in the lead now, again wishing he had a weapon to give him reassurance. He reached the bridge and set a foot upon it. Far down at the base of the chasm's granite walls grey foam leapt and danced and the river gave voice to its own peculiar song, half triumph, half despair, almost as if it were a living thing.

Elric shivered and took another step. Still he saw no figure in that deepening gloom. Another step and he was high above the water, refusing to look down lest the water call him to it. He knew the fascination of such torrents and how one could be drawn into them, hypnotized by their rush and noise.

'See you any guard, Prince Elric?' called Jaspar Colinadous.

'Nothing,' the albino cried back. And he took two more steps.

Oone was behind him now, moving as cautiously as he. He peered to the bridge's further side. Great slabs of dank rock, covered in lichen and oddly-coloured creepers, rose up and disappeared into the dark air above. The sound of the river made him think he heard voices, little skittering sounds, the scuffle of threatening limbs, but still he saw nothing.

Elric was half-way across the bridge before he detected the suggestion of a horse in the shadows of the gorge, the barest hint of a rider, perhaps wearing armour which was the colour of his own bone-white skin.

'Who's that?' The albino raised his voice. 'We come in peace. We mean no harm to anyone here.'

Again it might have been that the water made him believe he heard a faint, unpleasant chuckle.

Then it seemed the rush of water grew louder and he realized he heard the sound of hooves on rock. Formed as if by the spray, a figure suddenly appeared on the far side of the bridge, bearing down on him, its long, pale sword poised to strike.

There was nowhere to turn. The only way of avoiding the warrior was to jump from the bridge into the torrent below. Elric found his vision dimmed even as he prepared to spring forward, hoping to catch the horse's bridle and at least halt the rider in his tracks.

Then again there was a whirring of wings and something fixed itself on the attacker's helm, slashing at the face within. It was Whiskers, spitting and yowling like any ordinary alley cat engaged in a brawl over a piece of ripe fish.

The horse reared. The rider gave out a shriek of rage and pain and released the bridle in order to try to pull the little cat from him. Whiskers rushed upward into the air, out of reach. Elric glimpsed glaring, silvery eyes, a skin which glowed with the leper's mark, and then the horse, out of control, had slipped on the wet rock and fallen sideways. For a moment it tried to get back to its feet, the rider yelling and roaring as if demented, the long, white sword still in his hand. And then both had tumbled over the edge of the bridge and went falling, a chaotic mixture of arms and hooves, down into the echoing chasm to be swallowed by the distant, murky waters.

Elric was gasping for breath. Jaspar Colinadous came to grip his arm and steady him, helping him and Oone cross to the far side of the rocky slab and stand upon the bank, still scarcely aware of what had happened to them.

'I'm grateful again to Whiskers,' said Elric with an unstable grin. 'That's a valuable pet you have, Master Colinadous.'

'More valuable than you know,' said the little man feelingly. 'He has played a crucial part in more than one world's history!' He patted the cat as the beast returned to his arms, purring and pleased with himself. 'I'm glad we were able to be of service to you.'

'We're well rid of the bridge's guardian.' Elric peered down into the foam. 'Are we to encounter more such attacks, my lady?'

'Most certainly,' she said. She was frowning as if lost in some conundrum only she perceived.

Jaspar Colinadous pursed his lips. 'Here,' he said. 'Look how the gorge narrows. It becomes a tunnel.'

It was true. They could now see how the rocks leaned in upon one another so that the pass was little more than a cave barely large enough to let Elric enter without bending his head. A set of crude steps led up to it and from time to time a little flicker of yellow fire appeared within, as if the place were lit by torches.

Jaspar Colinadous sighed. 'I had hoped to journey with you further than this, but I must turn back now. I can go no further than the Marador Gate, which is what this seems to be. To do so would be to destroy me. I must find other companions now, in the Land of Dreams-in-Common.' He seemed genuinely regretful. 'Farewell, Prince Elric, Lady Oone. I wish you success in your adventure.'

And suddenly the little man had turned and walked swiftly back over the bridge, not looking behind him. He left them almost as suddenly as he had arrived and was gone back into the darkness before either could speak, his cat with him.

Oone seemed to accept this and, at Elric's questioning glance, said: 'Such people come and go here. Another rule the dreamthief learns is *"Hold on to nothing but your own soul"*. Do you understand?'

'I understand that it must be a lonely thing to be a dreamthief, madam.'

And with that Elric began to climb the great rough-hewn steps which led into the Marador Gate.

3

Of Beauty Found in Deep Caverns

The tunnel began to descend almost as soon as they had entered it. Where it had at first been cool now the air became hot and humid so that sometimes it seemed to Elric he was wading through water. The little lights which gave faint illumination were not, as he had at first thought, lamps or brands, but seemed naturally luminescent, delicate nodes of soft, glowing substance almost flesh-like in appearance. They found that they were whispering, as if unwilling to disturb any denizens of this place. Yet Elric did not feel afraid here. The tunnel had the atmosphere of a sanctuary and he noticed that Oone, too, had lost some of her normal caution, though her experience had taught her to be wary of anything as a potentially dangerous illusion.

There was no obvious transition from Sadanor to Marador, save perhaps a slight change of mood, and then the tunnel had opened up into a vast natural hall of richly glowing blues and greens and golden yellows and dark pinks, all flowing one to the other, like lava which had only recently cooled, more like exotic plants than the rock they were. Scents, like those of the loveliest, headiest flowers, made Elric feel he walked in a garden, not unlike the gardens he had known as a child, places of the greatest security and tranquillity; yet there was no doubt that the place was a cavern and that they had travelled underground to reach it.

At first delighted by the sight, Elric began to feel a certain sadness for until now he had not remembered those gardens of childhood, the innocent happiness which comes so rarely to a Melnibonéan, no matter what their age. He thought of his mother, dead in childbirth, of his infinitely mourning father, who had refused to acknowledge the son who, in his opinion, had killed his wife.

A movement from the depths of this natural hall and Elric again feared danger, but the people who began to emerge were unarmed and they had faces full of restrained melancholy.

'We have arrived in Marador,' whispered Oone with certainty.

'You are here to join us?' A woman spoke. She wore flowing robes of myriad, glistening colours, mirroring the colours of the rock on walls and roof. She had long hair of faded gold and her eyes were the shade of old pewter. She reached to touch Elric – a greeting – and her hand was cold on his. He felt himself becoming infected with the same sad tranquillity and it seemed to him that there could be worse fates than remaining here, recalling the desires and pleasures of his past, when life had been so much simpler and the world had seemed easily conquered, easily improved.

Behind him Oone said in a voice which sounded unduly harsh to his ear. 'We are travellers in your land, my lady. We mean you no harm, but we cannot stay.'

A man spoke. 'Travellers? What do you seek?'

'We seek,' said Elric, 'the Fortress of the Pearl.'

Oone was clearly displeased by his frankness. 'We have no desire to tarry in Marador. We wish only to learn the location of the next gate, the Paranor Gate.'

The man smiled wistfully. 'It is lost, I fear. Lost to all of us. Yet there is no harm in loss. There is comfort in it, even, don't you feel?' He turned dreaming, distant eyes on them. 'Better not to seek that which can only disappoint. Here we prefer to remember what we most wanted and how it was to want it . . . '

'Better, surely, to continue looking for it?' Elric was surprised by his own blunt tone.

'Why so, sir, when the reality can only prove inadequate when compared against the hope?'

'Think you so, sir?' Elric was prepared to consider this notion, but Oone's grip on his arm tightened.

'Remember the name that dreamthieves give this land,' she murmured.

Elric reflected that it was truly the Land of Old Desires. All of his own forgotten yearnings were returning to him, bringing a sense of simplicity and peace. Now he remembered how those sensations had been replaced by anger as he began to realize that there was little likelihood of his dreams ever coming true. He had raged at the injustice of the world. He had flung himself into his sorcerous studies. He had become determined to change the balance of things and introduce greater liberty, greater justice by means of the power he had in the world. Yet his fellow Melnibonéans had refused to accept his logic. The early dreams had begun to fade and with them the hope which had at first lifted his heart. Now here was the hope offered him again. Perhaps there were realms where all he desired was true? Perhaps

Marador was such a world.

'If I went back and found Cymoril and brought her here, we could live in harmony with these people, I think,' he said to Oone.

The dreamthief was almost contemptuous.

'This is called the Land of Old Desires – not the Land of Fulfilled Desire! There is a difference. The emotions you feel are easy and easily maintained – while the reality remains out of your reach, while you merely long for the unattainable. When you set out to discover fulfilment, Elric of Melniboné, then you achieved stature in the world. Turn your back on that determination – your own determination to help build a world where justice reigns – and you'll lose my respect. You'll lose respect for yourself. You'll prove yourself a liar and you'll prove me a fool for believing you could help me save the Holy Girl!'

Elric was shocked by her outburst, which seemed offensive in that pleasant mood of serenity surrounding them. 'But I think it is impossible to build such a world. Better to have the prospect, surely, than the knowledge of failure?'

'That is what all in this realm believe. Remain here, if you will, and believe what they believe forever. But I think one must always make an attempt at justice, no matter how poor the prospect of success!'

Elric felt tired and wished to settle down and rest. He yawned and stretched. 'These people seem to have a secret I would learn. I think I will talk to them for a while before continuing.'

'Do so and Anigh dies. The Holy Girl dies. And everything of yourself that you value, that dies, also.' Oone did not raise her voice. She spoke almost in a matter-of-fact tone. But her words had an urgency which broke Elric's mood. It was not for the first time that he had considered retreating into dreams. Had he done so, his people would now be ruled by him and Yyrkoon would be dead or exiled.

Thought of his cousin and his cousin's ambition, of Cymoril waiting for him to return so that they might be married, helped remind Elric of his purpose here and he shook off the mood of reconciliation, of retreat. He bowed to the people of the cavern. 'I thank you for your generosity, but my own path lies forward, through the Paranor Gate.'

Oone drew a deep breath, perhaps in relief. 'Time's not measured in any familiar way here, Prince Elric, but be assured it's passing more rapidly than I would like . . . '

It was with a sense of deep regret that Elric left the melancholy people behind him and followed her further into the glowing caverns.

Oone added: 'These lands are well-called. Be wary of the familiar.'

'Perhaps we could have rested there? Restored our energies?' said Elric.

'Aye. And died full of sweet melancholy.'

He looked at her in surprise and saw that she had not been un-affected by the atmosphere. 'Is that what befell Alnac Kreb?'

'Of course not!' She recovered herself. 'He was fully able to resist so obvious a trap.'

Elric now felt ashamed. 'I almost failed the first real test of my determination and my discipline.'

'We dreamthieves have the advantage of having been tested thus many times,' she told him. 'It gets easier to confront, though the lure remains as strong.'

'For you, too.'

'Why not? You think I have no forgotten desires, nothing I would not wish to dream of? No childhood which had its sweet moments?'

'Forgive me, madam.'

She shrugged. 'There's an attraction to that aspect of the past. To the past in general, I suppose. But we forget the other aspects – those things which forced us into fantasy in the first place.'

'You're a believer in the future, then madam?' Elric tried to joke. The rock beneath their feet became slippery and they were forced to make the gentle descent with more caution. Ahead Elric thought he heard again the sound of the river, perhaps where it now raced under-ground.

'The future holds as many traps as the past,' she said with a smile. 'I am a believer in the present, my lord. In the eternal present.' And there was an edge to her voice, as if she had not always held this view.

'Speculation and regret offer many temptations, I suppose,' said Elric; then he gasped at what he saw ahead.

Molten gold was cascading down two well-worn channels in the rock, forming a gigantic V-shaped edifice. The metal flowed unchecked and yet as they approached it became obvious that it was not hot. Some other agent had caused the effect, perhaps a chemical in the rock itself. As the gold reached the floor of the cavern it spread into a pool and the pool in turn fed a brook which bubbled, brilliant with the precious stuff, down towards another stream which seemed at first to contain ordinary water. But when Elric looked more carefully he saw that that stream was, in turn, composed of silver and the two elements blended as they met. Following the course of this stream with his eyes he saw that it met, some distance away, with a further river, this one of glistening scarlet, which might be liquid rubies. In all his travels, in the Young Kingdoms and the realms of the supernatural, Elric had seen nothing like it. He made to move towards it, to inspect it further, but she checked him.

'We have reached the next gate, she said. 'Ignore that particular wonder, my lord. Look.'

She pointed between twin streams of gold and he could just make out something shadowy beyond. 'There is Paranor. Are you ready to enter that land?'

Remembering the dreamthieves' term for it, Elric allowed himself an ironic smile. 'As ready as I shall ever be, madam.'

Then, just as he stepped towards the portal, there came the sound of galloping hooves behind them. They rang sharply on the rock of the cavern. They echoed through the gloomy roof, through a thousand chambers, and Elric had no time to turn before something heavy struck his shoulder and he was flung to one side. He had the impression of a deathly white horse, of a rider wearing armour of ivory, mother-of-pearl and pale tortoiseshell, and then it was gone through the gate of molten gold and disappearing into the shadows beyond. But there was no doubt in Elric's mind that he had encountered one of the warriors who had already attacked him on the bridge. He had the impression of the same mocking chuckle as the hooves faded and the sound was absorbed by whatever lay beyond the gate.

'We have an enemy,' said Oone. Her face was grim and she clenched her hands to her sides, clearly taking a grip on herself. 'We have been identified already. The Fortress of the Pearl does not merely defend. She attacks.'

'You know those riders? You have seen them before?'

She shook her head. 'I know their kind, that's all.'

'And we've no means of avoiding them?'

'Very few.' She was frowning to herself again, considering some problem she was not prepared to discuss. Then she seemed to dismiss it and taking his arm led him under the twin cascades of cool gold into a further cavern which this time suddenly filled with a gentle green glow, as if they walked beneath a canopy of leaves in autumn sunlight. And Elric was reminded of Old Melniboné, at the height of her power, when his people were proud enough to take the whole world for granted. When entire nations had been remoulded for their passing pleasure. As they emerged into a further cavern, so vast he did not at first realize they were still underground, he saw the spires and minarets of a city, glowing with the same warm green, which was as beautiful as his own beloved Imrryr, the Dreaming City, which he had explored throughout his boyhood.

'It is like Imrryr and yet it is not like Imrryr at all,' he said in surprise.

'No,' she said, 'it is like London. It is like Tanelorn. It is like Ras-

Paloom-Atai.' And she did not speak sarcastically. She spoke as if she really did believe the city resembled those other cities, only one of which Elric recognized.

'But you have seen it before. What is it called?'

'It has no name,' she said. 'It has all names. It is called whatever you desire to call it.' And she turned away, as if resting herself, before she led him onwards down the road past the city.

'Should we not visit it? There may be people there who can help us find our way.'

Oone gestured. 'And there may be those who would hamper us. It is now clear, Prince Elric, that our mission is suspected and that certain forces could well have the intention of stopping us at any cost.'

'You think the Sorcerer Adventurers have followed us?'

'Or preceded us. Leaving at least something of themselves here.' She was peering cautiously towards the city.

'It seems such a peaceful place,' said Elric. The more he looked at the city the more he was impressed by the architecture, all of the same greenish stone but varying from yellow to blue. There were vast buttresses and curving bridges between one tower and another; there were spires as delicate as cobwebs yet so tall they almost disappeared into the roofs of the cavern. It seemed to reflect some part of him which he could not at once recall. He longed to go there. He grew resentful of Oone's guidance, though he had sworn to follow it, and began to believe that she herself was lost, that she was not better suited to discover their goal than was he.

'We must continue,' she said. She was speaking more urgently now.

'I know I would find something within that city which would make Imrryr great again. And in her greatness I could lead her to dominate the world. But this time, instead of bringing cruelty and terror, we could bring beauty and good will.'

'You are more prone to illusion than I thought, Prince Elric,' said Oone.

He turned on her angrily. 'What's wrong with such ambitions?'

'They are unrealistic. As unreal as that city.'

'The city looks solid enough to me.'

'Solid? Aye, in its way. Once you enter its gate it will embrace you as thoroughly as any long-lost lover! Come then, sir. Come!' She seemed seized by an equally poor temper and strode on up an obsidian road which twisted along the hill towards the city.

Startled by her sudden change, Elric followed. But now his own anger was dissipating. 'I'll abide, madam, by your judgement. I am sorry . . .'

She was not listening to him. Moment by moment the city came closer until soon they were overshadowed by it, looking up at walls and domes and towers whose size was so tremendous it was almost impossible to guess at their true extent.

There's a gate,' she said. 'There! Go through and I'll say farewell. I'll try to save the child myself and you can give yourself up to lost beliefs and so lose the beliefs you currently hold!'

And now Elric looked closer at the walls, which were like jade, and he saw dark shapes within the walls and he saw that the dark shapes were the figures of men, women and children. He gasped as he stepped forward to peer at them, observing living faces, eyes which were undying, lips frozen in expressions of terror, of anguish, of misery. They were like so many flies in amber.

'That's the unchanging past, Prince Elric,' said Oone. 'That's the fate of those who seek to reclaim their lost beliefs without first experiencing the search for new ones. This city has another name. Dreamthieves call it the City of Inventive Cowardice. You would not understand the twists of logic which brought so many to this pass! Which made them force those they loved to share their fate. Would you stay with them, Prince Elric, and nurse your lost beliefs?'

The albino turned away with a shudder. 'But if they could see what had happened to earlier travellers, why did they continue into the city?'

'They blinded themselves to the obvious. That is the great triumph of mindless need over intelligence and the human spirit.'

Together the two returned to the patch below the city and Elric was relieved when the beautiful towers were far behind and they had passed through several more great caverns, each with its own city, though none as magnificent as the first. These he had felt no desire to visit, though he had detected movement in some and Oone had said she suspected not all were as dangerous as the City of Inventive Cowardice.

'You called this world the Dream Realm,' he said, 'and indeed it's well-named, madam, for it seems to contain a catalogue of dreams, and not a few nightmares. It's almost as if the place was born of a poet's brain, so strange are some of the sights.'

'I told you,' she said, speaking more warmly now that he had acknowledged the danger, 'much of what you witness here is the semi-formed stuff of realities other worlds, such as yours and mine, are yet to witness. To what extent they will come to exist elsewhere I do not know. These places have been fashioned over centuries by a succession of dreamthieves, imposing form on what is otherwise formless.'

Elric was now beginning to understand better what he had been told by Oone. 'Rather than making a map of what exists, you impose your own map upon it!'

'To a degree. We do not invent. We merely describe in a particular way. By that means we can make pathways through each of the myriad Dream Realms for, in this alone, the realms comply one with the other.'

'In reality there could be a thousand different lands in each realm?'

'If you would see it so. Or an infinity of lands. Or one with an infinity of aspects. Roads are made so that the traveller without a compass may not wander too far from their destination.' She laughed almost gaily. 'The fanciful names we give these places are not from any poetical impulse, nor from whim, but from a certain necessity. Our survival depends on accurate descriptions!'

'Your words have a profundity to them, madam. Though my survival has also tended to depend on a good, sharp blade!'

'While you depend upon your blade, Prince Elric, you condemn yourself to a singular fate.'

'You predict my death, eh, madam?'

Oone shook her head, her beautiful lips forming an expression of utmost sympathy and tenderness. 'Death is inevitable to almost all of us, in some shape or another. And I'll admit, if Chaos ever conquered Chaos, then you would be the instrument of that remarkable conquest. It would be sad indeed, Prince Elric, if in taming Chaos you destroyed yourself and all you loved into the bargain!'

'I promise you, Lady Oone, to do my best to avoid such a fate.' And Elric wondered at the look in the dreamthief's eyes and then chose not to speculate further.

They walked through a forest of stalagmites and stalactites now, all of the same glowing colours, dark greens and dark blues and rich reds, and there was a musical sound as water splashed from roof to floor. Every so often a huge drop would fall on one or the other of them but such was the nature of the caverns that they were soon dry again. They had begun to relax and walked arm in arm, almost merry, and it was only then that they saw the figures flitting between the up-ward-thrusting fangs of rock.

'Swordsmen,' murmured Elric. He added ironically, 'This is when a weapon would be useful . . . ' His mind was half with the situation, half feeling its way out through the worlds of the elementals, seeking some kind of spell, some supernatural aid, but he was baffled. It seemed that the mental paths he was used to following were blocked to him.

The warriors were veiled. They were dressed in heavy flowing cloaks and their heads were protected by helms of metal and leather. Elric had the impression of cold, hard eyes with tattooed lids and knew at once that these were members of the Sorcerer Assassin Guild from Quarzhasaat, left behind when their fellows had retreated from the Dream Realms. Doubtless they were trapped here. It was clear, however, that they did not intend to parley with Elric and Oone, but were closing in, following a familiar pattern of attack.

Elric was struck by a strangeness about these men. They lacked a certain fluidity of movement and, the closer they came, the more he realized that it was almost possible to see past their eyes and into the hollows of their skulls. These were not ordinary mortals. He had seen men like them in Imrryr once, when he had gone with his father on one of those rare times when Sadric chose to take him upon some local expedition, out to an old arena whose high walls imprisoned certain Melnibonéans who had lost their souls in pursuit of sorcerous knowledge, but whose bodies still lived. They, too, had seemed to be possessed of a cold, raging hatred against any not like themselves.

Oone cried out and moved rapidly, dropping to one knee as a sword struck at her, then clattered against one of the great pointed pillars. So close together were the stalagmites that it was difficult for the swordsmen to swing or to stab and for a while both the albino and the dreamthief ducked and dodged the blades until one cut Elric's arm and he saw, almost in surprise, that the man had drawn blood.

The Prince of Melniboné knew that it was just a matter of time before they were both killed and, as he fell back against one of the great rocky teeth, he felt the stalagmite move behind him. Some trick of the cavern had weakened the rock and it was loose. He flung all of his weight forward against it. It began to topple. Quickly he got his body in front of it, supporting the thing on his shoulder, then, with all his energy he ran with the great rocky spear at his nearest assailant.

The point of the rock drove full into the veiled man's chest. The Sorcerer Assassin uttered a bleak, agonized shout, and strange, unnatural blood began to well up around the stone, gushing down and soaking into the warrior's bones, almost reabsorbed by him. Elric sprang forward and dragged the sabre and the poignard from his hands even as another of the attackers came upon him from the rear. All his battle cunning and his war skills returned to Elric. Long before he had come by Stormbringer he had learned the arts of the sword and the dagger, of the bow and the lance, and now he had no need of an enchanted blade to make short work of the second Sorcerer Assassin, then a third. Shouting to Oone to help herself to weapons, he darted from rock to rock, taking one of the warriors at a time. They moved sluggishly, uncertainly now, yet none ran from him.

Soon Oone had joined him, showing that she was as accomplished a fighter as he. He admired the delicacy of her technique, the sureness of her hands as she parried and thrust, striking with the utmost efficiency and piling up her corpses with all the economy of a cat in a nest of rats.

Elric took time to grin over his shoulder. 'For one who so recently extolled the virtues of words over the sword, you show yourself well-accomplished with a blade, madam!'

'It is often as well to have the experience of both before one makes the choice,' she said. She despatched another of their assailants. 'And there are times, Prince Elric, I'll admit, when a decent piece of steel has a certain advantage over a neatly-turned phrase!'

They fought together like two old friends. Their techniques were complementary but not dissimilar. Both fought as the best soldiers fight, with neither cruelty nor pleasure in the killing, but with the intention of winning as quickly as possible, while causing as little pain to their opponents.

These opponents appeared to suffer no pain, as such, but every time one died he offered up the same disturbing wail of anguish and the blood which poured from the wounds was strange stuff indeed.

At last the man and the woman were done and stood leaning on their borrowed blades panting and seeking to control that nausea which so often follows a battle.

Then, as Elric watched, the corpses around them swiftly faded, leaving only a few swords behind. The blood too disappeared. There was virtually nothing to say that a fight had taken place in that great cavern.

'Where have they gone?'

Oone picked up a sheath and fitted her new sabre into it. For all her words, she clearly had no intention of proceeding any further without arms. She placed two daggers in her belt. 'Gone? Ah.' She hesitated. 'To whatever pool of half-living ectoplasm they came from.' She shook her head. 'They were almost phantasms, Prince Elric, but not quite. They were, as I told you, what the Sorcerer Adventurers left behind.'

'You mean part of them returned to our own world, as part of Alnac returned?'

'Exactly.' She drew a breath and made as if to continue.

'Then why shall we not find Alnac here? Still alive?'

'Because we do not seek him,' she said. And she spoke with all her old firmness, enough to make Elric proceed only a degree further with the subject.

'And perhaps anyway we would not find him here, as we found the Sorcerer Adventurers, in the Land of Lost Beliefs,' said the albino quietly.

'True,' she said.

Then Elric took her in his arms for a moment and they remained, embracing, for a few seconds, until they were ready to continue forward, seeking the Celador Gate. He had made no conscious decision.

Later, as Elric helped his ally across another natural bridge, below which flowed a river of dull brown stuff, Oone said to him, 'This is no ordinary adventure for me, Prince Elric. That is why I needed you to come with me.'

A little puzzled as to why she should, after all, say something which they had both taken for granted, Elric did not reply.

When the snout-faced women attacked them, with nets and spikes, it did not take them long to cut their way free and drive the cowardly creatures off and neither were they greatly inconvenienced by the vulpine things which loped on their hind-legs and had claws like birds. They even joked together as they despatched packs of snapping beasts which resembled nothing so much as horses the size of dogs and spoke a few words of a human tongue, though without any sense of the meaning.

Now at last they were reaching the borders of Paranor and saw looming ahead of them two enormous towers of carved rock, with little balconies and windows and terraces and crenellations, all covered in old ivy and climbing brambles bearing light yellow fruit.

'It is the Celador Gate,' said Oone. She seemed reluctant to approach it. Her hand on the hilt of her sword, her other arm linked with Elric's, she stopped and drew a deep, slow breath. 'It is the land of forests.'

'You called it the Land of Forgotten Love,' said Elric.

'Aye. That's the dreamthieves' name.' She laughed a little sardonically.

Elric, uncertain of her mood and not wishing to intrude upon her, held back also, looking from her to the gate and back again.

She reached a hand to his bone-white features. Her own skin was golden, still full of enormous vitality. She stared into his face. Then, with a sigh, she turned away and stepped towards the gate, taking his hand and pulling him after her.

They passed between the towers and here Elric's nostrils immediately were filled with the rich smells of leaf and turf. All around them were massive oak-trees and elms and birches and every other kind of tree, yet all of them, though they formed a canopy, grew not beneath the light of the open sky but were nurtured by the oddly glowing rocks in the cavern ceilings. Elric had thought it impossible for trees to grow underground and he marvelled at the health, the very ordinariness, of everything.

It was therefore with some astonishment that he observed a creature emerge from the wood and plant itself firmly on the path along which they must move.

'Halt! I must know your business!' His face was covered in brown fur and his teeth were so prominent, his ears so large, his eyes so large and doe-like, he resembled nothing so much as an overgrown rabbit, though he was armoured solidly in battered brass, with a brass cap upon his head and his weapons, a sword and spear of workmanlike steel, were also bound in brass.

'We seek merely to pass through this land without doing harm or being harmed,' said Oone.

The rabbit-warrior shook his head. 'Too vague,' he said, and suddenly he hefted his spear and plunged the point deep into the bole of an oak. The oak tree screamed. 'That's what he told me. And many more of these.'

'The trees were travellers?' said Elric.

'Your name, sir?'

'I am Elric of Melniboné and, like my lady Oone here, I mean you no disturbance. We travel on to Imador.'

'I know no "Elric" or "Oone". I am the Count of Magnes Doar and I hold this land as my own. By my conquest. By my ancient right. You must go back through the gate.'

'We cannot,' said Oone. 'To retreat would mean our destruction.'

'To proceed, madam, would mean the same thing. What? Shall you camp at the gates forever?'

'No, sir,' she said. She put her hand to the hilt of her sword. 'We will hack our way through your forest if need be. We are on urgent business and will accept no halt.'

The rabbit-warrior pulled the spear from the oak, which ceased to scream, and flung it into another tree. This, in turn, set up a swirling and a moaning until even the Count of Magnes Doar shook his head in irritation and drew his weapon out of the trunk. 'You must fight me, I think,' he said.

It was then that they heard a yell from the other side of the right pillar and something white and rearing appeared there. It was another of the pale riders in armour of bone, tortoiseshell and mother-of-pearl, his horrible eyes slitted with hatred, his horse's hooves beating at a barrier which had not been there when Oone and Elric passed through.

Then it was down and the warrior was charging.

The albino and the dreamthief made to defend themselves, but it was the Count of Magnes Doar who moved ahead of them and jabbed his spear up at the warrior's body. Steel was deflected by an armour stronger than it looked and the sword rose and fell, almost contemptuously, slicing down through the brass helm into the brain of the rabbit-warrior. He staggered backwards, his hands clutching at his head, his sword and spear abandoned. His round brown eyes seemed to grow still wider and he began to squeal. He turned slowly, round and round, then fell to his knees.

Elric and Oone had positioned themselves behind the bole of one of the oaks, ready to defend themselves when the rider attacked.

The horse reared again, snorting with the same mindless fury as its master, and Elric darted from his cover, seized the dropped spear and stabbed up to where the breastplate and gorget joined, sliding the spearhead expertly into the warrior's throat.

There came a choking sound which in turn grew to a familiar chuckling and the rider had turned his horse and was riding ahead of them again, along the path through the forest, his body swaying and jerking as if in its death agonies, yet still borne on by the horse.

They watched it disappear.

Elric was trembling. 'If I had not already seen him die on the bridge from Sadanor I would swear that was the same man who attacked me there. He has a puzzling familiarity.'

'You did not see him die,' said Oone. 'You saw him plunge into the river.'

'Well, I think he is dead now, after that stroke. I almost severed his head.'

'I doubt if he is,' she said. 'It's my belief he is our most powerful enemy and we shall not have to deal with him in any serious way until we near the Fortress of the Pearl itself.'

'He protects the fortress?'

'Many do.' She embraced him again, swiftly, then sank to one knee to inspect the dead Count of Magnes Doar. In death he more resembled a man, for already the hair on his face and hands was fading to grey and even his flesh seemed on the point of disappearance. The brass helm, too, had turned an ugly shade of silver. Elric was reminded of Alnac's dying. He averted his eyes.

Oone, too, stood up quickly and there were tears in her eyes. The tears were not for the Count of Magnes Doar. Elric took her in his arms. He was suddenly full of longing for someone he barely remembered from old dreams, the dreams of his youth, someone who, perhaps, had never existed.

He thought he felt a slight shudder run through Oone as he embraced her. He reached out for a memory of a little boat, of a fair-haired girl sleeping at the bottom of the vessel as it drifted out to open sea, of himself sailing a skiff towards her, full of pride that he might be her rescuer. Yet he had never known such a girl, he was sure, though Oone reminded him of that girl grown up.

With a gasp Oone moved away from him. 'I thought you were . . . It's as if I'd always known you . . . ' She put her hands to her face. 'Oh, this damned land is well-called, Elric!'

'Yet what danger is there to us?' he asked.

She shook her head. 'Who knows? Much or little. None? The dreamthieves say that it is in the Land of Forgotten Love that the most important decisions are made. Decisions which can have the most monumental consequences.'

'So one should do nothing here? Make no decisions?'

She passed her fingers through her hair. 'At least we should be aware that the consequences might not manifest themselves for a long while yet.'

Together they left the dead rabbit-warrior behind them and continued down the tunnel of trees. Now from time to time Elric thought he saw faces peering at him from the green shadows. Once he was sure he saw the figure of his dead father, Sadric, mourning for Elric's mother, the only creature he had ever truly loved. So strong was the image that Elric called out.

'Sadric! Father! Is this your Limbo?'

At this Oone cried urgently. 'No! Do not address him. Do not bring him to you. Do not make him real! It is a trap, Elric. Another trap.'

'My father?'

'Did you love him?'

'Aye. Though it was an unhappy kind of love.'

'Remember that. Do not bring him here. It would be obscene to recall him to this gallery of illusion.'

Elric understood her and used all his habits of self-discipline to rid himself of his father's shade. 'I tried to tell him, Oone, how much I grieved for him in his loss and his sorrow.' He was weeping. His body was shaking with an emotion from which he believed he had long since freed himself. 'Ah, Oone. I would have died myself to let him have his wife returned to him. Is there no way . . . ?'

'Such sacrifices are meaningless,' she said, gripping him in both her hands and holding him to her. 'Especially here. Remember your quest. We have already crossed three of the seven lands which will bring us to the Fortress of the Pearl. We have crossed half this. That means we have already accomplished more than most. Hold on to yourself, Prince of Melniboné. Remember who and what depends upon your success!'

'But if I have the opportunity to make something right that was so wrong . . . ?'

'That is to do with your own feelings, not what is and what can be. Would you invent shadows and make them play out your dreams? Would that bring happiness to your tragic mother and father?'

Elric looked over her shoulder into the forest. There was no sign of his father now. 'He seemed so real. Of such solid flesh!'

'You must believe that you and I are the only solid flesh in this entire land. And even we are – ' She stopped herself. She reached up to his face and kissed it. 'We will rest for a little, if only to restore our psychic strength.'

And Oone drew Elric down into the soft leaves at the side of the path. And she kissed him and she moved her lovely hands over his body and slowly she became all that he had lost in his love of women and he knew that he, in turn, became everything she had ever refused to allow herself to desire in a man. And he knew, without guilt or regret, that their love-making had no past and that its only future lay somewhere beyond their own lives, beyond any realm they would ever visit, and that neither would ever witness the consequences.

And in spite of this knowledge they were careless and they were happy and they gave each other the strength they would need if they ever hoped to fulfil their quest and reach the Fortress of the Pearl.

4

The Intervention of a Navigator

Surprised by his own lack of confusion, filled with an apparent clarity, Elric stepped, side by side with Oone, through the shimmering silver gateway into Imador, called mysteriously by dreamthieves the Land of New Ambition, and found himself at the top of an heroic flight of steps which curved downward towards a plain which stretched towards a horizon turned a pale, misty blue and which he could almost have mistaken for the sky. For a moment he thought that he and Oone were alone on that vast stairway and then he saw that it was crowded with people. Some were engaged in hectic conversation, some bartering, some embracing, while others were gathered around holy men, speech makers, priestesses, story-tellers, either listening avidly or arguing.

The steps down to the plain were alive with every manner of human intercourse. Elric saw snake-charmers, bear-baiters, jugglers and acrobats. They were dressed in costumes typical of the desert lands – enormous silk pantaloons of green, blue, gold, vermilion and amber – coats of brocade or velvet – turbans, burnouses and caps of the most intricate needlework – and burnished metal and silver, gold, precious jewels of every kind – animals, stalls, baskets overflowing with produce, with fabrics, with goods of leather and copper and brass.

'How handsome they are!' he remarked. It was true that though they were of all shapes and sizes the people had a beauty which was not easily defined. Their skins were all healthy, their eyes bright, their movements dignified and easy. They bore themselves with confidence and good humour and while it was clear they noticed Oone and Elric walking down the steps, they acknowledged them without making any great effort to greet them or ask them their business. Dogs, cats and monkeys ran about in the crowd and children played the cryptic games all children play. The air was warm and balmy and full of scents of fruit, flowers and the other goods being sold. 'Would that all worlds were like this,' Elric added, smiling at a young woman who offered him embroidered cloth.

Oone bought oranges from a boy who ran up to her. She handed one to Elric. 'This is a sweet realm indeed. I had not expected it to be so pleasant.' But when she bit into the fruit she spat it into her hand. 'It has no taste!'

Elric tried his own orange and he, too, found it a dry, flavourless thing.

The disappointment he felt at this was out of all proportion to the occurrence. He threw the orange from him. It struck a step below and bounced until it was out of sight.

The grey-green plain appeared unpopulated. There was a road sweeping across it, wide and well-paved, but there was not a single traveller visible, in spite of the great crowd. 'I wonder why the road is empty,' he said to Oone. 'Do all these people sleep at nights on these steps? Or do they disappear into another realm when their business here is done?'

'Doubtless that question will be answered for us soon enough, my lord.'

She linked her arm in his own. Since their love-making in the wood a sense of considerable comradeship and mutual liking had grown up between them. He knew no guilt; he knew in his heart that he had betrayed no-one and it was clear she was equally untroubled. In some strange way they had restored each other, making their combined energy something more than its sum. This was the kind of friendship he had never really known before and he was grateful for it. He believed that he had learned much from Oone and that the dreamthieves would teach him more that would be valuable to him when he returned to Melniboné to claim his throne back from Yyrkoon.

As they descended the steps it seemed to Elric that the costumes became more and more elaborate, the jewels and headdresses and weapons richer and more exotic, while the stature of the people increased and they grew still more handsome.

From curiosity he stopped to listen to a story-teller who held a crowd entranced, but the man spoke in an unfamiliar language – high and flat – which meant nothing to him. He and Oone paused again, beside a bead-seller, and he asked her politely if those gathered on the steps were all of the same nation.

The woman frowned at him and shook her head, replying in still another language. There seemed few words in it. She repeated much. Only when they were stopped by a sherbet-seller, a young boy, could they ask their question and be understood.

The lad frowned, as if translating their words in his head. 'Aye, we are the people of the steps. Each of us has a place here, one below the other.'

'You grow richer and more important as you descend, eh?' asked Oone.

He was puzzled by this. 'Each of us has a place here,' he said again and, as if alarmed by their questions, he ran off up into the dense crowd above. Here, too, there were fewer people and Elric could see that their numbers thinned increasingly as the steps neared the plain. 'Is this an illusion?' he murmured at Oone. 'It has the air of a dream.'

'It is our sense of what should be that intrudes here,' she said, 'and it colours our perception of the place, I think.'

'It is not an illusion?'

'It is not what you would call an illusion.' She made an effort to find words but eventually shook her head. 'The more it seems an illusion to us, the more it becomes one. Does that make sense?'

'I think so.'

At last they were nearing the bottom of the stairway. They were on the last few steps when they looked up to see a horseman riding towards them across the plain, creating a huge pillar of dust as he came.

There was a cry from the people behind them. Elric looked back and saw them all rushing rapidly up the stairs and his impulse was to join them, but Oone stayed him. 'Remember we cannot go back,' she said. 'We must meet this danger as best we can.'

Gradually the figure on the horse became distinguishable. It was either the same warrior in the armour of mother-of-pearl, ivory and tortoiseshell, or one who was identical. He bore a white lance tipped with a point of sharpened bone and the thing was aimed directly at Elric's heart.

The albino jumped forward in a manoeuvre designed to confuse his attacker. He was almost under the horse's hooves when he struck upwards with his swiftly drawn sword and cut at the lance. The force of the blow sent him reeling to one side while Oone, reacting with almost telepathic coordination, almost as if they were controlled by a single brain, leapt and thrust beneath the raised left arm, seeking their assailant's heart.

Her thrust was parried by a sudden movement of the rider's gauntleted right hand and he kicked out at her. Now, for the first time, Elric saw his face clearly. It was thin, bloodless, with eyes like the flesh of long-dead fish and a sneering gash of a mouth, opening now in a grimace of contempt. Yet with a shock he saw, too, something of Alnac Kreb! The lance swung to strike Oone's shoulder and send her to the ground.

Elric was up again before the lance could return, his sword slashing at the horse's girth-strap in an old trick learned from the Vilmirian bandits, but he was blocked by an armoured leg and the lance returned to thrust at him while he darted clear, giving Oone her opportunity.

Though Elric and Oone fought as a single entity, their attacker was almost prescient, seeming to guess their every move.

Elric began to believe the rider to be wholly supernatural in origin and even as he feinted again he sent his mind out into the realms of the elementals, seeking any aid which might possibly be available to him. But there was none. It was if every realm were deserted, as if, overnight, the entire world of elementals, demons and spirits had been banished to limbo. Arioch would not aid him. His sorcery was completely useless here.

Oone cried out sharply and Elric saw that she had been flung back against the lowest step. She tried to climb to her feet but something was paralysed. She could hardly move her limbs.

Again the pale rider chuckled and began to advance for the kill.

Elric roared out his old battle-shout and raced towards their opponent, trying to distract him. The albino was horrified at the possibility of harm coming to the woman for whom he felt both profound love and comradeship and he was willing to die to save her.

'Arioch! Arioch! Blood and souls!'

But he had no runesword to aid him there. Nothing save his own wits and skills.

'Alnac Kreb. Is this what remains of you?'

The rider turned, almost impatiently, and flung the lance at the running man. His answer.

Elric had not anticipated this. He tried to throw his body aside but the haft of the lance struck his shoulder and he fell heavily into the dust, losing his grip on the unfamiliar sabre. He began to scrabble towards it even as he saw the rider draw his own long blade and continue towards the helpless Oone. He raised himself to one knee and threw his poignard with desperate accuracy. The blade went true, between the plates of the rider's back armour and the lifted sword fell suddenly.

Elric reached his sabre, got to his feet and saw to his horror that the rider was rearing over Oone, the sword again raised, ignoring the wound in his shoulder.

'Alnac?'

Again Elric tried to appeal to whatever part of Alnac Kreb was there, but this time he was completely ignored. That same hideous, inhuman chuckling filled the air; the horse snorted, its hooves pawing at the woman as he struggled on the step.

Scarcely aware of his own movement, Elric reached the rider and leapt forward, dragging at his back, trying to haul him from the horse. The rider growled and managed to turn. His whistling sword was parried by Elric's and the albino had unseated him. Together the pair fell to the sand, a few inches from where Oone lay. Elric's sword-hand was crushed under his attacker's armoured back, but he managed to tug the poignard free with his left hand and would have struck at those hideous dead eyes had not the man's fingers closed on his wrist.

'You'll kill me before you harm her!' Elric's normally melodic voice was a snarl of hatred. But the warrior merely laughed again, the ghost of Alnac fading from his eyes.

They fought thus for several moments, neither gaining any true advantage. Elric could hear his own breathing, the grunting of the armoured man, the whinnying of the horse and Oone's gasp as she tried to get to her feet.

'Pearl Warrior!'

It was another voice. Not Oone's, but a woman's; and it carried considerable authority.

'Pearl Warrior! You must do no further violence to these travellers!'

The warrior grunted but ignored the woman. His teeth snapped at Elric's throat. He tried to turn the poignard towards the albino's heart. There were drops of foaming saliva on his lips now – beads of white rimming his mouth.

'Pearl Warrior!'

Suddenly the warrior began to speak, whispering to Elric as if to a fellow conspirator. 'Don't listen to her. I can aid thee. Why do you not come with us and learn to explore the Great Steppe, where all the hunting is rich? And there are melons, tasting like the most delicate cherries. I can give thee such wonderful clothing. Do not listen. Do not listen. Yes I am Alnac, thy friend. Yes!'

Elric was repelled by the insane babble, more than he had been by the creature's horrible appearance and his violence.

'Think of all the power there is. They fear thee. They fear me. Elric. I know thee. Let us not be rivals. Together we can succeed. I am not free, but thou couldst journey for us both. I am not free, but thou wouldst never bear responsibilities. I am not free, but, Elric, I have many slaves at my disposal. They are thine. I offer thee new wealth and new philosophies, new ways of fulfilling every desire. I fear thee and thou fearest me. So we will bind us together, one to the other. It is the only tie that ever means anything. They dream of thee, all of them. Even I, who do not dream. Thou art the only enemy . . . '

'Pearl Warrior!'

With a rattle of bone and ivory, of tortoiseshell and mother-of-pearl, the leprous-skinned warrior disentangled himself from Elric. 'Together we can defeat her,' he mumbled urgently. 'There would be no force to resist us. I will give thee my ferocity!'

Nauseated by all this, Elric climbed slowly to his feet, turning to stare in the same direction as Oone, who now sat on the step, nursing limbs to which life seemed to be restored.

A woman, taller either than Elric or Oone, stood there. She was veiled and hooded. Her eyes moved steadily from them to the one she called Pearl Warrior and then she raised the great staff she held in her right hand and struck at the ground with it.

'Pearl Warrior! You must obey me!'

The Pearl Warrior was furious. 'I do not wish this!' he snarled and, clattering, brushed at his breastplate. 'You anger me, Lady Sough.'

'These are my charges and under my protection. Go, Pearl Warrior. Kill elsewhere. Kill the true enemies of the Pearl.'

'I do not want you to order me!' He was surly, sulking like a child. 'All are enemies of the Pearl. You, too, Lady Sough.'

'You are a silly creature! Begone!' and she lifted the staff to point beyond the stairway, where hazy rock could be seen, rising up forever.

He said again, warningly, 'You make me angry, Lady Sough. I am the Pearl Warrior. I have the strength from the Fortress.' He turned to Elric as if to a comrade. 'Ally yourself with me and we'll kill her now. Then we shall rule – thou in thy freedom, me in my slavery. All of this and many other realms beside, unknown to dreamthieves. Safety is there forever. Be mine. We shall be married. Yes, yes, yes . . . '

Elric shuddered and turned his back on the Pearl Warrior. He went to help Oone to her feet.

Oone was able to move all her limbs but she was still dazed. She looked back at the steps which disappeared above them. Not a single one of the people who had occupied that vast staircase was visible.

Troubled, Elric glanced at the newcomer. Her robes were of different shades of blue, with silver threads running through them, hemmed with gold and dark green. She carried herself with extraordinary grace and dignity and stared back at Oone and Elric with an air of amusement. Meanwhile the Pearl Warrior climbed to his feet and stood defiantly to one side, alternately glaring at Lady Sough and offering Elric a hideous conspiratorial smile.

'Where are all the folk of the steps gone?' Elric asked her.

'They have merely returned to their home, my lord,' said Lady Sough. Her voice, when she addressed him, was warm and full, yet

251

retained all the authority with which she had ordered the Pearl Warrior to stop his attack. 'I am Lady Sough and I bid you welcome to this land.'

'We are grateful for your intervention, my lady.' Oone spoke for the first time, though with a degree of suspicion. 'Are you the ruler here?'

'I am merely a guide and a navigator.'

'That mad thing there accepts your command.' Oone rose, rubbing at her arms and legs, glaring at the Pearl Warrior who sneered, becoming shifty as Lady Sough gave him her attention.

'He is incomplete.' Lady Sough was dismissive. 'He guards the Pearl. But he has such an insubstantial intelligence, he cannot understand the nature of his task, nor who is friend or who foe. He can make only the most limited choices, poor corrupt thing. The ones who put him to this work had, themselves, only the faintest understanding of what was required in such a warrior.'

'Bad! I will not!' The Pearl Warrior began to utter his chuckle again. 'Never! It is why! *It is why!*'

'Go!' cried Lady Sough, gesturing once more with her staff, her eyes glaring above her veil. 'You have no business with these.'

'Dying is unwise, madam,' said the Pearl Warrior, lifting his shoulder in a gesture of defiant arrogance. 'Beware thine own corruption. We may all dissolve if this achieves that resolution.'

'Go, stupid brute!' She pointed at his horse. 'And leave that spear behind you. Destructive, insensate grotesque that you are.'

'Am I mistaken,' said Elric, 'or does he speak gibberish?'

'Possibly,' murmured Oone. 'But it could be he speaks more of the truth than those who would protect us.'

'Anything will come and anything will have to be resisted!' said the Pearl Warrior darkly as he mounted. He began to ride to where his lance had fallen after he had thrown it at Elric. 'This is why we are to be!'

'*Begone! Begone!*'

He leaned from his saddle, reaching towards the lance.

'No,' she said firmly, as if to a silly child. 'I told you that you should not have it. Look what you have done, Pearl Warrior! You are forbidden to attack these people again.'

'No alliance, then. Not now! But soon this freedom will be exchanged and all shall come together!' Another appalling chuckle from the half-crazed rider and he was digging his spurs into his horse's flanks, going at a gallop in the direction he had come. 'There shall be bonds! Oh, yes!'

'Do his words make sense to you, Lady Sough?' Elric asked politely, when the warrior had disappeared.

'Some of them,' she said. It seemed that she was smiling behind her veil. 'It is not his fault that his brain is malformed. There are few warriors in this world, you know. He is perhaps the best.'

'Best?'

Oone's sardonic question went unanswered. Lady Sough reached out a hand on which delicately-coloured jewels glowed and she beckoned to them. 'I am a navigator here. I can bear you to sweet islands where two lovers could be happy forever. I have a place that is hidden and safe. Can I take you there?'

Elric glanced at Oone, wondering if perhaps she was attracted by Lady Sough's invitation. For a second he forgot their purpose here. It would be wonderful to spend a short idyll in Oone's company.

'This is Imador, is it not, Lady Sough?'

'It is the place the dreamthieves call Imador, aye. We do not call it by that name.' She seemed disapproving.

'We are grateful for your help in this matter, my lady,' said Elric, thinking Oone a little brusque and seeking to apologize for his friend's manner. 'I am Elric of Melniboné and this is Lady Oone of the Dreamthieves' Guild. Do you know that we seek the Fortress of the Pearl?'

'Aye. And this road is a straight one for you. It can lead you forward to the Fortress. But it might not lead you by the best route. I will guide you by whatever route you wish.' She sounded a little distant, almost as if she were half-asleep herself. Her tone had become dreamy and Elric guessed she was offended.

'We owe you much, Lady Sough, and your advice is of value to us. What would you suggest?'

'That you raise an army first, I think. For your own safety. There are such terrible defences at the Fortress of the Pearl. Why, and before that, too. You are brave, the both of you. There are several roads to success. Death lies at the end of many other paths. Of this, you are I am sure aware . . . '

'Where could we recruit such an army?' Elric ignored Oone's warning look. He felt that she was being obstinate, overly suspicious of this dignified woman.

'There is an ocean not far from here. There is an island in it. The people of that island long to fight. They will follow anyone who promises them danger. Will you come there? It is very good. There is warmth and secure walls. Gardens and much to eat.'

'Your words have a strong degree of common-sense,' said Elric. 'It would be worth, perhaps, pausing in our quest to recruit those soldiers. And I was offered alliance by the Pearl Warrior. Will he help us? Can he be trusted?'

'For what you wish to do? Yes, I think.' Her forehead furrowed. 'Yes, I think.'

'No, Lady Sough.' Oone spoke suddenly and with considerable force. 'We are grateful for your guidance. Will you take us to the Falador Gate? Do you know it?'

'I know what you call the Falador Gate, young woman. And whatever your questions or your desires, they are mine to answer and fulfil.'

'What is your own name for this land?'

'None.' She seemed confused by Oone's question. 'There is not one. It is this place. It is here. But I can guide you through it.'

'I believe you, my lady.' Oone's voice softened. She took Elric by the arm. 'Our other name for this land is the Land of New Ambition. But new ambitions can mislead. We invent them when the old ambition seems too hard to achieve, eh?'

Elric understood her. He felt foolish. 'You offer a diversion, Lady Sough?'

'Not so.' The veiled woman shook her head. The movement had all her gracefulness in it and she seemed a little wounded by the directness of his question. 'A fresh goal is sometimes preferable when the road becomes impassable.'

'But the road is not impassable, Lady Sough,' said Oone. 'Not yet.'

'That is true.' Lady Sough bowed her head a fraction. 'I offer you all truth in this matter. Every aspect of it.'

'We shall retain the aspect of which we are most sure,' Oone continued softly, 'and thank you greatly for your help.'

'It is yours to take, Lady Oone. Come.' The woman whirled, her draperies lifting like clouds in a gale, and led them away from the steps to a place where the ground dipped and revealed, when they were closer, a shallow river. There a boat was moored. The boat had a curling prow of gilded wood, not unlike the crook of Oone's dreamwand, and its sides were covered with a thin layer of beaten gold, and bronze, and silver. Brass gleamed on rails, on the single mast, and a sail, blue with threads of silver, like Lady Sough's robes, was furled upon the yardarm. There was no visible crew. Lady Sough pointed with her staff. 'Here is the boat with which we shall find the gate you seek. I have a vocation, Lady Oone, Prince Elric, to protect you. Do not fear me.'

'My lady, we do not,' said Oone with great sincerity. Still, her voice was gentle. Elric was mystified by her manner but accepted that she had a clear notion of their situation.

'What does this mean?' Elric murmured as Lady Sough descended towards the boat.

'I think it means we are close to the Fortress of the Pearl,' said Oone. 'She tried to help us but is not altogether sure how best to do it.'

'You trust her?'

'If we trust ourselves, we can trust her I think. We must know what are the right questions to ask her.'

'I'll trust you, Oone, to trust her.' Elric smiled.

At Lady Sough's insistent beckoning they clambered into the beautiful boat which rocked only slightly on the dark waters of what seemed to Elric an entirely artificial canal, straight and deep, moving in a sweeping curve until it disappeared from sight a mile or two from them. He peered upwards, still not sure if he looked upon a strange sky or the roof of the largest cavern of all. He could just see the stairs stretching away in the distance and wondered again what had happened to the inhabitants when they had fled at the Pearl Warrior's attack.

Lady Sough took the great tiller of the boat. With a single movement she guided the craft into the centre of the waterway. Almost at once the ground levelled out so that it was possible to see the grey desert on all sides, while ahead was foliage, greenery, the suggestion of hills. There was a quality about the light which reminded Elric of a September evening. He could almost smell the early autumn roses, the turning trees, the orchards of Imrryr. Seated near the front of the boat with Oone beside him, leaning on his shoulder, he sighed with pleasure, enjoying the moment. 'If the rest of our quest is to be conducted in such a way, I shall be glad to accompany you on many such adventures, Lady Oone.'

She, too, was in good humour. 'Aye. Then all the world would desire to be dreamthieves.'

The boat rounded a bend of the canal and they were alerted by figures standing on both banks. These sad, silent people, dressed in white and yellow, regarded the sailing barge with tear-filled eyes, as if they witnessed a funeral. Elric was sure they did not weep for himself or Oone. He called out to them, but they did not seem to hear him. They were gone almost at once and they passed by gently rising terraces, cultivated for vines and figs and almonds. The air was sweet with ripening harvests and once a small, fox-like creature ran along beside them for a while before veering off into a clump of shrubs. A little later naked, brown-skinned men prowled on all fours until they, too, grew bored and disappeared into the undergrowth. The canal began to twist more and more and Lady Sough was forced to throw all her weight upon the tiller to keep the boat on course.

'Why should a canal be built so?' Elric asked her when they were once more upon a straight stretch of water.

'What was above us is now ahead and what was below is now behind,' she replied. 'That is the nature of this. I am the navigator and I know. But ahead, where it grows darker, the river is unbending. This is made to help understanding, I think.'

Her words were almost as confusing as the Pearl Warrior's and Elric tried to make sense by asking her further questions. 'The river helps us understand what, Lady Sough?'

'Their nature – her nature – what you must encounter – ah, look!'

The river was widening rapidly into a lake. There were reeds growing on the banks now, silver herons flying against the soft sky.

'It is no great distance to the island I spoke of,' said Lady Sough. 'I fear for you.'

'No,' said Oone with determined kindness. 'Take the boat across the lake towards the Falador Gate. I thank you.'

'This thanks is . . . ' Lady Sough shook her head. 'I would not have you die.'

'We shall not. We are here to save her.'

'She is afraid.'

'We know.'

'Those others said they would save her. But they made her – they made it dark and she was trapped . . . '

'We know,' said Oone, and laid a comforting hand on Lady Sough's arm as the veiled woman guided the boat out on to the open lake.

Elric said: 'Do you speak of the Holy Girl and the Sorcerer Adventurers? What imprisons her, Lady Sough? How can we release her? Bring her back to her father and her people?'

'Oh, it is a lie!' Lady Sough almost shouted, pointing to where, swimming directly towards them, came a child. But the boy's skin was metallic, of glaring silver, and his silver eyes were begging them for help. Then the child grinned, reached to pull off its own head, and submerged. 'We near the Falador Gate,' said Oone grimly.

'Those who would possess her also guard her,' said Lady Sough suddenly. 'But she is not theirs.'

'I know,' said Oone. Her gaze was fixed on what lay ahead of them. There was a mist on the lake. It was like the finest haze which forms on water in an autumn morning. There was an air of tranquillity which, clearly she mistrusted. Elric looked back at Lady Sough but the navigator's eyes were expressionless, offering no clue to what dangers they might soon be facing.

The boat turned a little and there was land just visible through the mist. Elric saw tall trees rising above a tumble of rocks. There were white pillars of limestone, shimmering faintly in that lovely light. He saw hummocks of grass and below them little coves. He wondered if Lady Sough had, after all, brought them to the island she had mentioned and was about to question her when he saw what appeared to be a massive door of carved stone and intricate mosaic bearing an air of considerable age.

'The Falador Gate,' said Lady Sough, not without a hint of trepidation.

Then the gate had opened and a horrible wind rushed out of it, tearing at their hair and clothing, clawing at their skins, shrieking and wailing in their ears. The boat rocked and Elric feared it must capsize. He ran to the stern to help Lady Sough with the tiller. Her veil had been ripped from her face. She was not a young woman, but she bore an astonishing resemblance to the little girl they had left in the Bronze Tent, the Holy Child of the Bauradim. And Elric, taking the tiller while Lady Sough replaced her veil, remembered that no mention had ever been made of Varadia's mother.

Oone was lowering the sail. The wind's initial strength had died and it was possible to tack gradually towards the dark, strangely-smelling entrance which had been revealed as the mosaic door had blown down.

Three horses appeared there. Hooves flailed at the air. Tails lashed. Then they were galloping across the water in the direction of the boat. Then they had passed it and vanished into the mist. Not one of the beasts had possessed a head.

Now Elric knew terror. But it was a familiar terror and within seconds he had regained control of himself. He knew that, whatever its name, he was about to enter a land where Chaos ruled.

It was only as the boat sailed under the carved rocks and into the grotto beyond that he recalled he had none of his familiar spells and enchantments; not one of his allies, nor his patron Duke of Hell, were available to him here. He had only experience and courage and his ordinary sensibilities. And at that moment he doubted if they were enough.

5

The Sadness of a Queen Who Cannot Rule

The mighty barrier of obsidian rock suddenly started to flow. A mass of glassy green flooded down into the water which hissed and began to stink and mountains of steam rose ahead of them. As the steam gradually dissipated another river was revealed. This one, flowing through the narrow walls of a deep canyon, appeared of natural origin and Elric, his mind now keyed to interpretation, wondered if it were not the same river they had crossed earlier, when he had fought the Pearl Warrior on the bridge.

Then the barge, which had seemed so sturdy, appeared all at once fragile as the waters tossed it, roaring steadily downwards until Elric thought they must eventually reach the very core of the world.

Standing with Lady Sough in the prow of the boat, Oone and Elric helped her use the tiller to hold a course that was almost steady. And then, ahead, the river ended without warning and they had tipped over a waterfall and before they knew it were landing heavily in calmer water, the barge bobbing like a scrap of bread on a pond and overhead they could see a diseased sky like pewter in which dark, leathery things flew and communicated with desolate cries above palms whose leaves resembled nothing so much as viridian skins stretched out to await a sun which never rose. There was a rich, rotten smell about the place and the constant splashing and distant roaring of the water filled a silence broken only by the flying creatures above the rocks and the foliage which surrounded them.

It was warm, yet Elric shivered. Oone drew up the collar of her doublet and even Lady Sough gathered her robes more tightly about herself.

'Are you familiar with this land, Lady Oone?' Elric asked. 'You have visited this realm before, I know, but you seem as surprised as I.'

'There are always new aspects. It is in the nature of the realm. Perhaps Lady Sough can tell us more.' And Oone turned courteously to their navigator.

Lady Sough had secured her veils more firmly. She seemed unhappy that Elric had seen her face. 'I am the Queen of this land,' she said, exhibiting no pride or any other emotion.

'Then you have minions who can assist us?'

'It was a Queen for me, so that I had no power over it, only the land's protection. This is the place you call Falador.'

'And is it mad?'

'It has many defences.'

'They keep out what might also wish to leave,' said Oone, almost to herself. 'Are you afraid of those who protect Falador, Lady Sough?'

'I am Queen Sough now.' A drawing up of the graceful body, but whether in parody or in earnest Elric could not tell. 'I am protected. You are not. Even I am not able to guard you here.'

The barge continued to float slowly along the watercourse. The slime of the rocks appeared to shift and move as if alive and there were shapes in the water which disturbed Elric. He would have drawn his sword if it had not seemed ill-mannered.

'What must we fear here?' he asked the queen.

Now they floated below a great spur of rock on which a horseman had positioned himself. It was the Pearl Warrior, glaring down with the same mixture of mockery and mindlessness. He lifted a long stick to which he had tied some animal's sharp, twisted horn.

Queen Sough shook her hand at him. 'Pearl Warrior shall not do this! Pearl Warrior cannot defy, even here!'

The warrior let out his hideous chuckle and turned his horse back from the rock. Then he was gone.

'Will he attack us?' Oone asked the queen.

Queen Sough was concentrating on her tiller, steering the boat subtly along a smaller water-course, away from the main river. Perhaps she already aimed to avoid any conflict. 'He is unpermitted,' she said. 'Ah!'

The water had turned a ruby red and there were now banks of glistening brown moss, gently rising towards the walls of rock. Elric was convinced he saw ancient faces staring at him both from the banks and from the cliffs, but he did not feel threatened. The red liquid looked like wine and there was a heady sweetness here. Did Queen Sough know all the secret, tranquil places of this world and was she guiding them through so as to avoid its dangers?

'Here my friend Edif has influence,' she told them. 'He is a ruler whose chief interest is poetry. Will it be now? I do not know.'

They had quickly become used to her strange speech forms and were finding her more easily understood, though they had no idea who Edif might be and had passed through his land into a place where the desert appeared suddenly on both sides of them, beyond flanking lines of palms, as if they moved towards an oasis. Yet no oasis materialised.

Soon the sky was the colour of bad liver again and the rocky walls had risen around them and there was the sickly, oppressive odour, which reminded Elric of some decadent court's anterooms. Perfume which had once been sweet but had now grown stale; food which had once made the mouth water but which was now too old; flowers which no longer enhanced but reminded one only of death.

The walls on either side now had great jagged caves in them where the water echoed and tumbled. Queen Sough seemed nervous of these and kept the barge carefully in the centre of the river. Elric saw shadows moving within the caves, both above and below the water. He saw red mouths opening and closing and saw pale, unblinking eyes staring. They had the air of Chaos-born creatures and he wished mightily then for his runesword, for his patron Duke of Hell, for his repertoire of spells and incantations.

The albino was not altogether surprised when at last a voice spoke from one of the caverns.

'I am Balis Jamon, Lord of the Blood and I wish to have some kidneys.'

'We sail on!' cried Queen Sough in response. 'I am not your food nor shall I ever be.'

'Their kidneys! Theirs!' the voice demanded implacably. 'I have fed on no true grub for so long. Some kidneys! Some kidneys!'

Elric drew his sword and his dagger. Oone did the same.

You'll not have mine, sir,' said the albino.

'Nor mine,' said Oone, seeking the source of the voice. They could not be sure which of the many caves sheltered the speaker.

'I am Balis Jamon, Lord of the Blood. You'll pay a toll here in my land. Two kidneys for me!'

'I'll take yours instead, sir, if you like!' said Elric defiantly.

'Will you now?'

There was a great movement from the furthest cave and water foamed in and out. Then something stooped and came wading into midstream, its fleshy body festooned with half-decayed plants and ruined blooms, its horned snout lifted so that it could stare at them from two tiny black eyes. The fangs in the snout were broken, yellow and black, and a red tongue licked at them, flicking little pieces of rotten meat into the water. It held one great paw over its chest and when the paw was lowered it revealed a dark, gaping hole where the heart would have been.

'I am Balis Jamon, Lord of the Blood. Look what I must fill for me to live! Have mercy, little creatures. A kidney or two and I'll let you pass. I have nothing here, while you are complete. You must make justice and share with me.'

'This is my only justice for you, Lord Balis,' said Elric, gesturing with a sword which seemed a feeble thing even to him.

'You will never be complete, Balis Jamon!' called out Queen Sough. 'Not until you know more of mercy!'

'I am fair! One kidney will do!' The paw began to reach towards Elric who cut at it but missed, then cut again and felt the sword strike the creature's hide, which scarcely showed a mark. The paw grabbed at the sword. Elric withdrew it. Balis Jamon growled with a mixture of frustration and self-pity and reached both paws towards the albino.

'Stop! Here's your kidney!' Oone held up something which dripped. 'Here it is, Balis Jamon. Now let us pass. We are agreed.'

'Agreed.' He turned, evidently mollified, delicately took what she handed up to him and popped it into the hole in his chest. 'Good. Go!' And he waded passively back towards his cave, honour and hunger both satisfied.

Elric was baffled, though grateful that she had saved his life. 'What did you do, Lady Oone?'

She smiled. 'A large bean. Some of the provisions I still carried in my purse. It looked similar to a kidney, especially when dipped in water. And I doubt if he knows the difference. He seemed a simple creature.'

Queen Sough's eyes were lifted upwards even as she steered the barge past the caves and into a wider stretch of water where buffalo lifted their heads from where they drank and stared at them with wary curiosity.

Elric followed the navigator's gaze but saw only the same lead-coloured sky. He sheathed his sword. 'These creatures of Chaos seem simple enough. Less intelligent in some ways than others I've encountered.'

'Aye.' Oone was unsurprised. 'That's likely, I think. She would be – '

The boat was lifted suddenly and for a second Elric thought Lord Balis had returned to take vengeance on them for tricking him. But they appeared to be on the crest of a huge wave. The water level rose rapidly between the slimy walls and now, on the cliffs' edges, figures appeared. They were of every kind of distorted shape and unlikely size and Elric was reminded a little of the beggar populace of Nadsokor, for these, too, were dressed in rags and bore the evidence of self-mutilation, as well as disease, wounding and ordinary neglect. They were filthy. They moaned. They looked greedily at the boat and they licked their lips.

Now, more than ever before, Elric wished he had Stormbringer with him. The runesword and a little elemental aid would have driven this rabble away in terror. But he had only the blades captured from the Sorcerer Adventurers. He must rely upon those, his alliance with Oone and their naturally complementary fighting skills. There came a juddering from the bottom of the barge and the wave receded as suddenly as it had risen, but now they were stranded on the very top of the cliff, with the misshapen horde all around them, panting and grunting and sniffing at their prey.

Elric wasted no time with parleying but jumped at once from the boat's prow and cut at the first two who grabbed for him. The blade, still sharp enough, severed their heads and he stood over their bodies grinning at them like the wolf he was sometimes called. 'I want you all,' he said. He used the battle bravado he had learned from the pirates of the Vilmirian Straits. He moved forward again and thrust, catching still another Chaos-creature in the chest. 'I must kill every one of you before I am satisfied!'

They had not expected this. They shuffled. They looked at each other. They turned their weapons in their hands, they adjusted their rags and tugged at their limbs.

Now Oone was beside Elric. 'I want my fair share of these,' she cried. 'Save them for me, Elric.' Then she, too, darted forward and cut down an ape-faced thing which carried a jewelled axe of beautiful workmanship, clearly stolen from an earlier victim.

Queen Sough called from behind them. 'They have not attacked you. They only threaten. Is this the true thing you must do?'

'It's our only choice, Queen Sough!' cried Elric over his shoulder, and feinted at two more of the half-human things.

'No! No! It is not heroic. What can the guardian do, who is no longer a hero?'

Even Oone could not follow this and when Elric met her eye in a question she shook her head.

The rabble was gaining some confidence now, closing in. Snouts sniffed at them. Tongues licked saliva from slack lips. Hot, dirty eyes full of blood and pus squinted their hatred.

Then they had begun to close and Elric felt his blade meet resistance, for he had already blunted it on the first two creatures. Yet still the neck split and the head fell to one side, glaring the while, hands clutching. Oone had her back to his and together they moved so that they were protected from one side by the boat which the rabble did not seem to wish to touch. Queen Sough, in obvious distress, wept as she watched but clearly had no authority over the Chaos-creatures. 'No! No! This does not help her to sleep! No! No! She is in need of them, I know!'

It was at that point that Elric heard the sound of hooves and saw, over the heads of the closing crowd, the white armour of the Pearl Warrior.

'They are his creatures!' he said in sudden understanding. 'This is his own army and he is to be revenged on us!'

'No!' Queen Sough's voice was distant now, as if very far away. 'This cannot be useful! It is your army. They'll be loyal. Yes.'

Hearing her, Elric knew unexpected clarity. Was it that she was not really human? Were all of these creatures merely shape-changers of some kind, disguising themselves as humans? It would explain their strange cast of mind, the peculiar logic, the strange phrasing.

But there was no time for speculation, for now the creatures were hard about him and Oone, so that it was hardly possible to swing their blades to keep them back. Blood flowed, sticky and foetid, splashing on blades and arms and making them gag. Elric felt he might be overwhelmed by the stench before he was defeated by their weapons.

It was clear they could not resist the mob and Elric was bitter, feeling that they had come very close to the object of their quest only to be cut down by the most wretched of the denizens of Chaos.

Then more bodies fell at his feet and he realized that he had not killed them. Oone, too, was astonished by this turn of events.

They looked up. They could not understand what was happening.

The Pearl Warrior was riding through the ranks of the rabble cutting this way and that, jabbing with his makeshift spear, slicing with his sword, cackling and crowing at every fresh life he took. His horrible eyes were alight with some sort of amusement and even his horse was slashing at the rabble with its hooves, nipping at them with its teeth.

'This is the proper thing!' Queen Sough clapped her hands. 'This is true. This is to ensure honour for you!'

Gradually driven back by the Pearl Warrior, by Elric and Oone as they resumed their attack, the rabble began to break up.

Soon the whole awful mob was running for the cliff edge, leaping into the abyss rather than die by the Pearl Warrior's bone spear and his silver sword.

His laughter continued as he herded the remainder to their doom. He screamed his mockery at them. He raved at them for cowards and fools. 'Ugly things. Ugly! Ugly! Go! Perish! Go! Go! Go! Banished now, they are. Banished to that! Yes!'

Elric and Oone leaned against the barge trying to catch their breaths.

'I am grateful to you, Pearl Warrior,' said the albino as the armoured rider approached. 'You have saved our lives.'

'Yes.' The Pearl Warrior nodded gravely, his eyes unusually thoughtful. 'That is so. Now we shall be equal. Then we shall know the truth. I am not free, as you. You believe this?' His last question was addressed to Oone.

She nodded. 'I believe that, Pearl Warrior. I, too, am glad you helped us.'

'I am the one who protects. This must be done. You go on? I was your friend.'

Oone looked back to where Queen Sough was nodding, her arms outstretched in some kind of offering.

'Here I am not your enemy,' said the Pearl Warrior, as if instructing the simple-minded. 'If I were complete, we three would be a trinity of greatness! Aye! Thou knowest it! I have not the personal. This words are hers, you see. I think.'

And with that particularly mystifying pronouncement he wheeled his horse and rode away over the grassy limestone.

'Too many defenders, not enough protectors, perhaps.' Oone sounded as odd as the others. Before Elric could quiz her on this she had given her attention back to Queen Sough. 'My lady? Did you summon the Pearl Warrior to our aid?'

'She called him to you, I think.' Queen Sough seemed almost in a trance. It was odd to hear her speaking of herself in the third person. Elric wondered if this were the normal mode here and again it occurred to him that all the people of this realm were not human but had assumed human shape.

They were now stranded high above the river. Going to the edge of the abyss, Elric stared down. He saw only some bodies which had been caught on the rocks, others drifting downstream. He was glad, then, that their boat was not having to negotiate waters clogged with so many corpses.

'How can we continue?' he asked Oone. He had a vision of himself and her in the Bronze Tent, of the child between them. All were dying. He knew a pang of need, as if the drug were calling to him, reminding him of his addiction. He remembered Anigh in Quarzhasaat and Cymoril, his betrothed, waiting in Imrryr. Had he been right to let Yyrkoon rule in his place? Every one of his decisions seemed now to be foolish. His self-esteem, never high, was lower than he could remember. His lack of forethought, his failures, his follies, all reminded him that not only was he physically deficient, he was also lacking in ordinary common-sense.

'It is in the nature of the hero,' said Queen Sough in relation to nothing. Then she looked at them and her eyes were maternal, kindly. 'You are safe!'

'I think there is some urgency,' said Oone. 'I sense it. Do you?'

'Aye. Is there danger in the realm we left?'

'Perhaps. Queen Sough, are we far from the Nameless Gate? How can we continue?'

'By means of the moth-steeds,' she said. 'The waters always rise here and I have my moths. We have only to wait for them. They are on their way.' Her tone was matter-of-fact. 'It was that rabble which could have been yours. No more. But I cannot anticipate, you see. Every new trap is mysterious to me, as to you. I can navigate, as you navigate. This is together, you know.'

Against the horizon there were rainbow lights winking and shimmering, like an aurora. Queen Sough sighed when she saw them. She was content.

'Good. Good. That is not late! Just the other.'

The colours filled the sky now. As they came closer Elric realized that they belonged to huge, filmy wings supporting slender bodies, more butterfly than moth, of enormous size. Without hesitation the beasts began to descend until the three of them as well as the barge were engulfed by soft wings.

'Into the boat!' cried Queen Sough. 'Quickly. We fly.'

They hurried to obey her and at once the barge was rising into the air, apparently carried on the backs of the great moths, who flew beside the canyon for a while before plunging down into the abyss.

'I watched but there was nothing,' said Queen Sough by way of explanation to Elric and Oone. 'Now we shall resume.'

With astonishing gentleness the creatures had deposited the barge on the river and were flying back up between the walls of the canyon again, filling the whole gloomy place with brilliant multi-coloured light before they vanished. Elric rubbed at his brow. 'This is truly the Land of Madness,' he said. 'I believe it is I who am mad, Lady Oone.'

'You are losing confidence in yourself, Prince Elric.' She spoke firmly. 'That is the particular trap of this land. You come to believe that it is yourself, not what surrounds you, that has little logic. Already we have imposed our sanity on Falador. Do not despair. It cannot be much longer before we reach the final gate.'

'And what is there?' He was sardonic. 'Sublime reason?' He felt the same strange sense of exhaustion. Physically he was still capable of continuing, but his mind and his spirit were depleted.

'I cannot begin to anticipate what we shall find in the Nameless

Land,' she said. 'Dreamthieves have little power over what occurs beyond the seventh gate.'

'I've noticed your considerable influence here!' But he did not mean to hurt her. He smiled to show that he joked.

From ahead they heard a howling, so painful that even Queen Sough covered her ears. It was like the baying of some monstrous hound, echoing up and down the abyss and threatening to shake the very boulders loose from the walls. As the river bore them round the bend they saw the beast standing there, a great shaggy wolf-like beast, its head lifted as it howled again. The water rushed around its huge legs, foamed against its body. As it turned its gaze upon them the beast vanished completely. They heard only the echo of its howling. The speed of the water increased. Queen Sough had removed her hands from the tiller to block her ears. The boat swung in the water and bounced as it struck a rock. She made no attempt to steer it. Elric seized the long arm but in spite of using all his strength he could do nothing with the boat. Eventually, he, too, gave up.

Down and down the river ran. Down into a gorge growing so deep that soon there was scarcely any light at all. They saw faces grinning at them. They felt hands reach out to touch them. Elric became convinced that every mortal creature who had ever died had come here to haunt him. In the dark rock he saw his own face many times, and those of Cymoril and Yyrkoon. Old battles were fought as he watched. And old, agonizing, emotions came back to him. He felt the loss of all he had ever loved, the despair of death and desertion, and soon his own voice joined the general babble and he howled as loudly as the hound had howled until Oone shook him and yelled at him and brought him back from the madness which had threatened to engulf him.

'Elric! The last gate! We are almost there! Hold on, Prince of Melniboné. You have been courageous and resourceful until now. This will require still more of you and you must be ready!'

And Elric began to laugh. He laughed at his own fate, at the fate of the Holy Child, at Anigh's fate and at Oone's. He laughed when he thought of Cymoril waiting for him on the Dragon Isle, not knowing even now if he lived or died, if he were free or a slave.

When Oone shouted at him again, he laughed in her face.

'Elric! You betray us all!'

He paused in his laughter long enough to say softly, almost in triumph, 'Aye, madam, that is so. I betray you all. Have you not heard? It is my destiny to betray!'

'You shall not betray me, sir!' She slapped at his face. She punched him. She kicked his legs. 'You shall not betray me and you shall not betray the Holy Girl!'

He knew intense pain, not from her blows but from his own mind. He cried out and then he began to sob. 'Oh, Oone. What is happening to me?'

'This is Falador,' she said simply. 'Are you recovered, Prince Elric?'

The faces still gibbered at him from the rock. The air was still alive with all he feared, all he most misliked in himself.

He was trembling. He could not meet her gaze. He realized he was weeping. 'I am Elric, last of Melniboné's royal line,' he said. 'I have looked upon horror and I have courted the Dukes of Hell. Why should I know fear now?'

She did not answer and he expected no answer from her.

The boat surged, swung again, lifted and dipped.

Suddenly he was calm. He took hold of Oone's hand in a gesture of simple affection.

'I am myself again I think,' he said.

'There is the gateway,' said Queen Sough from behind them. She had her grip on the tiller again and with her other hand was pointing ahead.

'There is the land you call the Nameless Land,' she said. She spoke plainly now, not in the cryptic phrasing she had used since they had met her. 'There you will find the Fortress of the Pearl. She cannot welcome you.'

'Who?' said Elric. The waters were calm again. They ran slowly towards a great archway of alabaster, its edges trimmed by soft leaves and shrubs. 'The Holy Girl?'

'She can be saved,' said Queen Sough. 'Only by you two, I think. I have helped her remain here, awaiting rescue. But it is all I can do. I am afraid, you see.'

'We are all that, madam,' said Elric feelingly.

The boat was caught by new currents and travelled still more slowly, as if reluctant to enter the last gate of the Dream Realm.

'But I am of no help,' said Queen Sough. 'I might even have conspired. It was those men. They came. Then more came. There was only retreat thereafter. I wish I could know such words. You would understand them if I had them. Ah, it is hard here!'

Elric, looking into her agonized eyes, realized that she was probably more of a prisoner in this world than he and Oone. It seemed to him that she longed to escape and was only kept here by her love of the Holy Girl, her protective emotions. Yet surely she had been here long before Varadia had come?

The boat had begun to pass under the alabaster arch now. There was a salty, pleasant taste to the air, as if they approached the ocean.

Elric decided he must ask the question which was on his mind.

'Queen Sough,' he said. 'Are you Varadia's mother?'

The pain in the eyes grew even more intense as the veiled woman turned away from him. Her voice was a sob of anguish and he was shocked by it.

'Oh, who knows?' she cried, *'Who knows?'*

THREE

Is there a brave lord birthed by Fate
To wield old weapons, win new estates
And tear down the walls Time sanctifies,
Raze ancient temples as hallowed lies,
His pride to break, his love to lose,
Destroying his race, his history, his muse,
And, relinquishing peace for a life of strife,
Leave only a corpse that the flies refuse?

THE CHRONICLE OF THE BLACK SWORD

1

At the Court of the Pearl

Again Elric experienced that strange frisson of recognition at the landscape before him, though he could not remember ever seeing anything like it. Pale blue mist rose around cypresses, date palms, orange trees and poplars whose shades of green were equally pale; flowing meadows occasionally revealed the rounded white of boulders and in the far distance were snow-peaked mountains. It was as if an artist had painted the scenery with the most delicate of washes, the finest of brushstrokes. It was a vision of Paradise and completely unexpected after the insanity of Falador.

Queen Sough had remained silent since she had answered Elric's question and a peculiar atmosphere had developed between the three of them. Yet all the uneasiness failed to affect Elric's delight at the world they had entered. The skies (if skies they were) were full of pearly cloud, tinged by pink and the faintest yellow, and a little white smoke rose up from the flat-roofed house some distance away. The barge had come to rest in a pool of still, sparkling water and Queen Sough gestured for them to disembark.

'You will come with us to the Fortress?' asked Oone.

'She does not know. I do not know if it is permitted,' said the Queen, her eyes hooded above her veil.

'Then I shall say farewell now.' Elric bowed and kissed the woman's soft hand. 'I thank you for your assistance, madam, and trust you will forgive me for the crudeness of my manners.'

'Forgiven, yes.' Elric, looking up, thought Queen Sough smiled.

'I thank you also, my lady.' Oone spoke almost intimately, as to one with whom she might share a secret. 'Know you how we shall find the Fortress of the Pearl?'

'That one will know.' The Queen pointed towards the distant cottage. 'Farewell, as you say. You can save her. Only you.'

'I am grateful for your confidence, also,' said Elric. He stepped almost jauntily on to the turf and followed Oone as they made their way across the fields to the little house. 'This is a great relief, my lady. A contrast, indeed to the Land of Madness!'

'Aye.' She responded a trifle cautiously, and her hand went to the hilt of her sword. 'But remember, Prince Elric, that madness takes many forms in all worlds.'

He did not allow her wariness to let him lose his enjoyment. He was determined to restore himself to the peak of his energies, in preparation for whatever might lie ahead.

Oone was first to reach the door of the white house. Outside were two chickens scratching in the gravel, an old dog, tethered to a barrel, who looked up at them over a grey muzzle and grinned, a pair of short-coated cats cleaning their silvery fur on the roof over the lintel. Oone knocked and the door was opened almost immediately. A tall, handsome young man stood there, his head covered by an old burnouse, his body clad in a light brown robe with long sleeves. He seemed pleased to see visitors.

'Greetings to you,' he said. 'I am Chamog Borm, currently in exile. Have you come with good news from the Court?'

'We have no news at all, I fear,' said Oone. 'We are travellers and we seek the Fortress of the Pearl. Is it close by here?'

'At the heart and the centre of those mountains.' He waved with his hand towards the peaks. 'Will you join me for some refreshment?'

The name the young man had given, together with his extraordinary looks, caused Elric again to rack his brains, trying to recall why all this was so familiar to him. He knew that he had only recently heard the name.

Within the cool house, Chamog Borm brewed them a herbal drink. He seemed proud of his domestic skills and it was clear he was no simple farmer. In one corner of the room was heaped a pile of rich armour, steel chased with silver and gold, a helm decorated with a tall spike, that spike decorated with ornamental snakes and falcons locked in conflict. There were spears, a long, curved sword, daggers — weapons and accoutrements of every description.

'You are a warrior by trade?' said Elric as he sipped the hot liquid. 'Your armour is very handsome.'

'I was once a hero,' said Chamog Borm sadly, 'until I was dismissed from the Court of the Pearl.'

'Dismissed?' Oone was thoughtful. 'On what charge?'

Chamog Borm lowered his eyes. 'I was charged with cowardice. Yet I believe that I was not guilty, that I was subject to an enchantment.'

And now Elric recalled where he had heard the name. When he had arrived in Quarzhasaat he had in his fever wandered in the market

272

places and listened to the storytellers. At least three of the stories he had heard had concerned Chamog Borm, hero of legend, the last brave knight of the Empire. His name was venerated everywhere, even in the camps of the nomads. Yet Elric was sure Chamog Borm had existed – if he had ever existed – at least a thousand years earlier!

'What was the action of which you were accused?' he asked.

'I failed to save the Pearl, which now lies under an enchantment, imprisoning us all in perpetual suffering.'

'What was that enchantment?' Oone asked quickly.

'It became impossible for our monarch and many of the retainers to leave the Fortress. It was for me to free them. Instead I brought a worse enchantment upon us. And my punishment is contrary to theirs. They may not leave. I may not return.' As he spoke he became increasingly melancholy.

Elric, still astonished at this conversation with a hero who should have been dead centuries before, could say little, but Oone seemed to understand completely. She made a sympathetic gesture.

'Can the Pearl be found there?' Elric asked, conscious of the bargain he had made with Lord Gho, of Anigh's impending torture and death, of Oone's predictions.

'Of course,' Chamog Borm was surprised. 'Some believe it rules the whole Court, perhaps the world.'

'Was this always so?' Oone asked softly.

'I have told you that it was not.' He looked at them both as if they were simpletons. Then he lowered his eyes, lost in his own dishonour and humiliation.

'We hope to free her,' said Oone. 'Would you come with us, to help us?'

'I cannot help. She no longer trusts me. I am banished,' he said. 'But I can let you have my armour and my weapons so that part of me, at least, can fight for her.'

'Thank you,' said Oone. 'You are generous.'

Chamog Borm grew more animated as he helped them choose from his store. Elric found that the breastplate and greaves fitted him perfectly, as did the helmet. Similar equipment was found for Oone and the straps tightened to adjust to her slightly smaller body. They looked almost identical in their new armour, and something in Elric was again struck, some deep sense of satisfaction that he could hardly understand but which he welcomed. The armour gave him not only a greater sense of security but a sense of deep recognition of his own inner strength, a strength which he knew he must call upon to the utmost in the encounter to come. Oone had warned him of subtler dangers at the Fortress of the Pearl.

Chamog Borm's gifts continued, in the shape of two grey horses which he led from their stable at the back of the house. 'These are Taron and Tadia. Brother and sister, they were twin foals. They have never been separated. Once I rode them into battle. Once I took up arms against the Bright Empire. Now the last Emperor of Melniboné will ride in my place to fulfil my destiny and end the siege of the Fortress of the Pearl.'

'You know me?' Elric looked hard at the handsome youth, seeking deception or even irony, but there was none in those steady eyes.

'A hero knows another, Prince Elric.' And Chamog Borm reached out to grip Elric's forearm in the gesture of friendship of the desert peoples. 'May you gain all you wish to gain and may you do so with honour. You, too, Lady Oone. Your courage is the greatest of all. Farewell.'

The exile watched them from the roof of his little house until they were out of sight. Now the great mountains were close, almost embracing them, and they could see a wide, white road stretching through them. The light was like that of a late summer afternoon, though Elric could still not be sure if it was sky above them or the distant roof of a vast cavern, for the sun was still not in evidence. Was the Dream Realm a limitless series of such caverns or had the dreamthieves mapped the entire world? Could they cross the mountains, cross the nameless land beyond and begin again to travel through the seven gates, ultimately arriving back at the Land of Dreams-in-Common? And would they find Jaspar Colinadous waiting for them where they had left him?

The road, when they reached it, proved to be of pure marble, but the horses' hooves were so well shod they did not slip once. The noise of their galloping began to echo through the wide pass and herds of gazelles and wild sheep looked up from their grazing to watch them pass, two silver riders on silver horses on their way to do battle with the forces who had seized power at the Fortress of the Pearl.

'You have understood these people better than I,' he said to Oone, as the road began to twist upwards towards the centre of the range and the light had grown colder, the sky a bright, hard grey. 'Do you know what we might expect to find at the Fortress of the Pearl?'

She shook her head in regret. 'It is like understanding a code without knowing what the words actually relate to,' she told him. 'The force is powerful enough to banish a hero as potent as Chamog Borm.'

'I know only the legend, and that from a little I heard in the Slave Market at Quarzhasaat.'

'He was summoned by the Holy Girl as soon as she realized that she was under further attack. That is what I believe, at any rate. She did not expect him to fail her. Somehow, indeed, he made matters worse. She felt betrayed by him and banished him to the edge of the Nameless Land, there perhaps to greet and assist others who might come to help her. That is no doubt why we are given all the appurtenances of the hero, so that we may be as much like heroes as he.'

'Yet we know this world less well. How may we succeed where he failed?'

'Perhaps because of our ignorance,' she said. 'Perhaps not. I cannot answer you, Elric.' She rode close to him, leaning from her saddle to kiss that part of his cheek exposed by the helmet. 'Only know this. I will neither betray her nor, if I can help it, you. Yet if I must betray one of you, I suppose it will be you.'

Elric looked at her in bafflement. 'Is that likely to be an issue?'

She shrugged and then she sighed. 'I do not know, Elric. Look. I think we have come to the Fortress of the Pearl!'

It was like a palace carved from the most delicate ivory. White against the silver sky it rose above the snows of the mountain, a great multitude of slender spires and turreted towers, of cupolas, of mysterious structures which seemed almost as if they had been arrested in mid-flight. There were bridges and stairways, curving walls and galleries, balconies and roof-gardens whose colours were a spectrum of pastel shades, a myriad of different plants, flowers, shrubs and trees. In all his travels Elric had only seen one place that was the equal to the Fortress of the Pearl and that was his own city, Imrryr. Yet the Dreaming City was exotic, rich, earthy in comparison, a romantic fancy compared to the complicated austerity of this palace.

As they approached on the marble road, Elric realized that the Fortress was not pure white, but contained shades of blue, silver, grey and pink, sometimes a little yellow or green, and he had the notion that the entire thing had been carved from a single gigantic pearl. Soon they had reached the fortress's only gate, a great circular opening protected by spiked grilles which came from above and below and both sides to meet at the centre. The fortress was vast but even its gate dwarfed them.

Elric could think of nothing to do but cry out, 'Open in the name of the Holy Girl! We come to do battle with those who imprison her spirit here!'

His words echoed through the towers of the fortress and through the jagged peaks of the mountains beyond and seemed to lose themselves in the heights of a cavern's roof. In the shadows beyond the gateway he saw something scarlet move and then vanish again. There came the smell of delicious perfume, mixed with the same strange ocean scent they had noticed when they first reached the Nameless Land.

Then the gates had parted, so swiftly that they seemed to melt into the air, and a rider confronted them, his humourless chuckling by now all too familiar.

'This is what should be, I think,' said the Pearl Warrior.

'League yourself with us again, Pearl Warrior,' said Oone, with all her considerable authority. 'It is what she desires!'

'No. It is so that she shall not be betrayed. You must dissolve. Now! Now! Now!' His head was flung back as he screamed these last words, for all the world like a dog gone rabid.

Elric drew a sword from its scabbard. It shone with the same silver light that poured from the Pearl Warrior's blade. Oone followed his example, though more reluctantly.

'We shall pass now, Pearl Warrior.'

'Nothing will here! I want your freedom.'

'She shall have it!' said Oone. 'It is not yours, not unless she bestows it upon you herself.'

'She says it is mine. I will be that. I will be *that*!'

Elric could not follow this strange converstion and he chose not to waste time with it. He urged his silver horse forward, the blade glaring in his hand. So balanced was this sword, so familiar to his grip, that he felt for a moment that it was somehow the natural counterpart to his runesword. Was this a sword forged by Law to serve its purposes, just as Stormbringer had, by all accounts, been forged by Chaos?

The Pearl Warrior guffawed and widened his awful eyes. Death was in them. The death of the world. He lowered the same misshapen lance he had brandished at them before and Elric saw it was encrusted with old blood. The warrior held his ground and the lance was suddenly threatening Elric's eyes so that the albino had to throw himself to one side to avoid its points, striking upwards as he did so and feeling a greater resistance to his blow than anything he had felt before. The Pearl Warrior seemed to have gained strength since their last encounter.

'Ordinary soul!' The lips twisted in this insult, clearly as disgusting as any the Pearl Warrior could conceive. And he began to chuckle again, this time because Oone was riding at him, her sword stretched out full before her, a spear held in her hand, her reins between her teeth. The sword drove forward, the spear swung back as she poised to throw. Then sword and spear struck the Pearl Warrior at the exact same moment so that his breastplate cracked like the shell of some great crustacean and was pierced by the sword.

Elric marvelled at this strategy, which he had never witnessed before. Oone's strength and coordination were almost beyond credibility. It was a feat of arms warriors would speak of for a thousand years to come, which many would try to emulate and would die in the trying.

The spear had done its work in breaking open the Pearl Warrior's armour and the sword had completed the action. But the Pearl Warrior had not been killed.

He groaned. He cackled. He floundered. His sword came up as if to protect his chest from the blow already struck. His great horse reared and its nostrils flared with fury. Oone turned her own mount away. Her sword had left its tip in the Pearl Warrior's body. She was reaching for a second spear, for her dagger.

Elric drove forward again, his own spear aimed at the cracked armour, hoping to follow her example, but the blade struck the ivory and was turned. Elric lost balance long enough for the Pearl Warrior to take the advantage. The sword struck the steel of Elric's armour with a noise that made a cacophony in his helmet and brought bright sparks like a fire. He fell on to his horse's neck, barely able to block the next thrust. Then the Pearl Warrior had shrieked, the eyes growing still wider, the mouth gaping red and the foul breath steaming from it, while blood poured from under the gorget between his helmet and his breastplate. He fell towards Elric and the albino realized that the haft of a spear was sticking from his chest in exactly the same place where Oone had broken the creature's armour.

'This will not remain so!' cried the Pearl Warrior. It was a threat. 'I cannot do that thing!'

Then he had tumbled in a heap from his horse and clattered like old bones on to the flagstones of the courtyard. From behind him an ornamental fountain, representing a fig tree in full fruit, began to spurt water, filling the surrounding trough and overflowing until it touched the body of the Pearl Warrior. The riderless horse began to scream, turning round and round, rearing, foaming, then it had galloped out through the gate and back down the marble road.

Elric turned the heavy corpse over to make sure that no life was left in the Pearl Warrior and to inspect the shattered armour. He remained admiring of Oone's manoeuvre. 'I have never seen that done before,' he said, 'and I have fought beside and against famous warriors.'

'A dreamthief must know many things,' she said, by way of acknowledgement of his praise. 'I learned such tactics from my mother, who was a greater battle-woman than I shall ever be.'

'Your mother was a dreamthief?'

'No,' said Oone absently as she inspected her ruined sword and then picked up the Pearl Warrior's, 'she was a queen.' She tested the weight of the dead creature's blade and discarded her own, trying it in her scabbard and finding that it was a little too wide. Carelessly she stuck it in her belt and unhooked the scabbard, throwing it upon the ground. The water from the fountain was around their ankles now and was disturbing their horses.

Leading the steeds they passed under a heart-shaped arch and into another courtyard. Here, too, fountains played, but these were not flooding. They seemed carved out of ivory, like so much of the fortress, and represented stylized herons, their beaks meeting at a point above their heads. Elric was reminded vaguely of the architecture of Quarzhasaat, though this had none of the decadence of that place, none of the look of senile old age which characterized the city at its worst. Had the fortress been built by the ancestors of the present Lords of Quarzhasaat, the Council of Six and One Other? Had some great king fled the city millennia before and journeyed here to the Dream Realm? Was that how the legend of the Pearl had come to Quarzhasaat?

Courtyard after courtyard, each in its own way of extraordinary beauty, followed until Elric began to wonder if this path were merely leading them through the fortress to the other side.

'For such a large building it's somewhat underpopulated,' he said to Oone.

'We shall find the inhabitants soon enough, I think,' Oone murmured. Now they ascended a spiral causeway which led around a huge central dome. Although the palace had such a mood and look of austerity, Elric did not find its architecture cold and there was something almost organic about it, as if it had been formed from flesh, then petrified.

Their horses still with them, the sound now muffled by luxurious carpet, they moved through halls and corridors whose walls were hung with tapestries and decorated with mosaics, though they saw no pictures of living things, only geometrical designs.

'We near the heart of the fortress, I think,' Oone told him in a whisper. It was as if she feared to be overheard, yet they had seen no one. She looked beyond tall columns, through a series of rooms seemingly lit by sunshine from without. Following her gaze, Elric had the impression of blue fabric wafting through a door and vanishing. 'Who was that?'

'All the same,' said Oone to herself. 'All the same.' Her sword was drawn again, however, and she signed to Elric to imitate her. They entered another courtyard. This one seemed to be open to the sky – the same grey sky they had first seen in the mountains. Gallery after gallery rose up all around them, many storeys to the top. Elric thought he saw faces peering back at him, then something liquid struck his face and he almost inhaled the sickly red stuff which covered his body. More of it was pouring down on them from every part of the gallery and already the courtyard was knee-deep in what seemed to Elric to be human blood. He heard a muttering overhead, soft laughter, a cry.

'Stop this!' he shouted, wading to the side of the chamber. 'We are here to parley. All we want is the Holy Girl! Give her spirit back to us and we shall leave!'

He was answered by a further shower of blood and he hauled his horse towards the next door. There was a gate across it. He tried to lift it. He tried to bounce it free of its mountings. He looked to Oone who, wiping the red liquid from herself, joined him. She reached out her long fingers and found some kind of button. The gate opened slowly, almost reluctantly, but it opened. She grinned at him. 'Like most men, you become a brute when you panic, my lord.'

He was hurt by her joke. 'I had no idea I should find such a means of opening the gate, my lady.'

'Think of such things in future and you will stand a better chance of survival in this fortress,' she said.

'Why will they not parley with us?'

'They probably do not believe that we are ready to bargain,' she said. Then she added: 'In reality, I can only guess at their logic. Each adventure of a dreamthief is different from the other, Prince Elric. Come.' She led them on past a series of pools full of warm water from which a little steam rose. There were no bathers in the pools. Then Elric thought he saw creatures, perhaps fish, swimming in the depths. He leaned forward to look, but Oone pulled him back. 'I warned you. Your curiosity could bring your destruction and mine.'

Something threshed and bubbled in the pool and then was gone. All at once the rooms began to shake and the water foamed. Cracks appeared in the marble floors. Their horses snorted with fear and threatened to lose their footing. Elric himself almost toppled down into one of the fissures which had opened. It was as if an earthquake had suddenly struck the mountains. Yet as they dashed hastily for the next gallery, which opened on to a peaceful lawn, all signs of the earthquake had vanished.

A man approached them. In bearing, he resembled Queen Sough, but he was shorter and older. His white beard hung upon a surcoat of gold cloth and in his hand he held a salver on which were placed two leather bags. 'Will you accept the authority of the Fortress of the

Pearl?' he said. 'I am the seneschal of this place.'

'Who do you serve?' Elric asked brusquely. His sword was still in his hand and he made no effort to disguise his readiness to use it.

The seneschal looked bewildered. 'I serve the Pearl, of course. This is the Fortress of the Pearl!'

'Who rules here, old man?' Oone asked him pointedly.

'The Pearl. I have said so.'

'Does no one rule the Pearl?' Elric was mystified.

'No longer, sir. Now, will you take this gold and go. We have no wish to expend more of our energies upon you. They flag, but they are not exhausted. I think you will be dissolved soon.'

'We have defeated all your defenders,' said Oone. 'Why should we want gold?'

'Do you not desire the Pearl?'

Before Elric could answer, Oone silenced him with a warning gesture.

'We come only to secure the release of the Holy Girl.'

The seneschal smiled. 'They have all made that claim, but what they want is the Pearl. I cannot believe you, lady.'

'How can we prove our words?'

'You cannot. We already know the truth.'

'We have no interest in bargaining with you, Sir Seneschal. If you serve the Pearl, who does the Pearl serve?'

'The child, I think.' His brow furrowed. Her question had confused him, yet to Elric it had seemed so simple. His admiration for the dreamthief's skill increased.

'You see, we can help you in this,' said Oone. 'The child's spirit is imprisoned. And while it is imprisoned, so are you held captive.'

The old man offered the bags of gold again. 'Take this and leave us.'

'I do not think we shall,' said Oone firmly and she led her horse forward, past the old man. 'Come, Elric.'

The albino hesitated. 'We should question him more, Oone, surely?'

'He could not answer more.'

The seneschal ran at her, swinging the heavy bags, the salver falling to the floor with a clang. 'She is not! It will hurt! This is not to be. Pain will come! Pain!'

Elric felt sympathy for the old man. 'Oone. We should listen to him.'

She would not pause. 'Come. You must.'

He had learned to trust her judgement. He, too, pushed past the old man who beat at his body with the bags of gold and wailed, the tears pouring down his cheeks and into his beard. It took a different courage to perform that particular action.

There was another great curving doorway ahead of them, all elaborate lattice-work and mosaic, bordered by bands of jade, blue enamel and silver. Two large doors of dark wood, hinges and studs of brass, blocked their way.

Oone did not know. She reached gently towards the doors and placed her fingertips against them. Gradually, just as with the other gate, the doors began to part. They heard a faint noise from within, almost a whimper. The doors opened wider and wider until they were completely back on their hinges.

For a moment Elric was overwhelmed by what he saw.

A grey-gold glow filled the great chamber which had been revealed to them. The glow came from a column about the height of a tall man which was topped by a globe. At the centre of the globe shone a pearl of enormous size, almost as big as Elric's fist. Short flights of steps led up to the column from all sides and around these steps were what at first appeared to be ranks of statues. Then Elric realized that they were men, women, and children, dressed in all manner of costumes, though most of them in the styles favoured in Quarzhasaat and by the desert clans.

The old man came stumbling behind them. 'Do not hurt this!'

'We defend ourelves, Sir Seneschal,' Oone told him without turning to look at him. 'That is all you need to know from us.'

Slowly, still leading the silver horses, still with their silver swords in their hands, the light from the pearl touching their silver armour and their helmets and making these, too, glow with soft radiance, they made their way into the chamber.

'This is not to destroy. This is not to defeat. This is not to despoil.'

Elric shivered when he heard the voice. He looked over towards the distant walls of the room and there was the Pearl Warrior, his armour all cracked and slimed with blood, his face a terrible bruise, the eyes seeming alternately to fade and take fire. And sometimes they were Alnac's eyes.

The warrior's next words were almost pathetic. 'I cannot fight you. No more.'

'We are not here to hurt,' said Oone again. 'We are here to free you.'

There was a movement amongst the still figures. A blue-gowned veiled woman appeared. Queen Sough's own eyes had a suggestion of tears. 'With these you come?' she indicated the swords, the horses, the armour. 'But our enemies are not here.'

'They will be here soon,' said Oone. 'Soon, I think, my lady.'

Still baffled, Elric looked behind him, as if he would see their enemies. He made a movement towards the Pearl at the Heart of the

World, merely to admire a marvel. At once all the figures came to life, blocking his path.

'You will steal!' The old man sounded even more wretched than before, even more impotent.

'No,' said Oone. 'It is not our purpose. You must understand that.' She spoke urgently. 'Raik Na Seem sent us to find her.'

'She is safe. Tell him she is safe.'

'She is not safe. Soon she will dissolve.' Oone turned her gaze on the whispering throng. 'She is separated, as we are separated. The Pearl is the cause.'

'This is a trick,' said Queen Sough.

'A trick,' echoed the wounded Pearl Warrior and there was a faint chuckle from his spoiled throat.

'A trick,' said the seneschal, and held out the bags of gold.

'We come to steal nothing. We come to defend. Look!' Oone made a circular movement with her sword to show them what they had evidently not yet seen.

Emerging through the walls of the chamber, their hands filled with every imaginable weapon, came the hooded, tattoed soldiers of Quarzhasaat. The Sorcerer Adventurers.

'We cannot fight them,' said Elric quietly to his friend. 'There are too many of them.' And he prepared himself for death.

2

The Destruction in the Fortress

Then Oone had mounted her silver horse and raised her silver sword. She called out: 'Elric, do as I do!' and had urged the stallion into a canter so that its hooves rattled like thunder in the chamber.

Prepared to die with courage, even at the moment of apparent triumph, Elric climbed into his saddle, took a spear in the hand that held the reins and with his sword already swinging charged against the invaders.

Only as they crowded around him, axes, maces, spears and swords lifted to attack, did Elric understand that Oone's action had not been one of mere desperation. These half-shades moved sluggishly, their eyes were misted, they stumbled and their blows were feeble.

The slaughter now became sickening to him. Following her example, he hacked and stabbed. from side to side, almost mechanically. Heads came away from bodies like rotten fruit; limbs were sliced as easily as leaves from a stick; torsos collapsed under the thrust of a spear or sword. Their viscous blood, already the blood of the dead, clung to weapons and armour and their cries of pain were pathetic to Elric's ears. If he had not sworn to follow Oone, he would have ridden back and let her continue the work alone. There was little danger to them as the veiled men continued to pour through the walls and be met by sharp steel and cunning intelligence.

Behind them, around the column of the Pearl, the courtiers watched. These clearly did not know what a mediocre threat the two silver-armoured warriors confronted.

At last it was done. Decapitated, limbless bodies were piled all around the hall. Elric and Oone rode out of that slaughter and they were grim, unhappy, nauseated by their own actions.

'It is done,' said Oone. 'The Sorcerer Adventurers are slain.'

'You truly are heroes!' Queen Sough came down the steps towards them, her eyes bright with admiration, her arms outstretched.

'We are who we are,' said Oone. 'We are mortal fighters and we have destroyed the threat to the Fortress of the Pearl.' Her words had taken on a ritualistic tone and Elric, trusting her, was content to listen.

'You are the children of Chamog Borm, Brother and Sister to the Bone Moon, Children of Water and Cool Breezes, Parents of the Trees . . . ' The seneschal had dropped his bags of gold and was shaken by his weeping. He wept with relief and with joy and Elric saw how much he resembled Raik Na Seem.

Oone, down from her horse again, was embraced by Queen Sough. Meanwhile, a shuffling and cackling announced the approach of the Pearl Warrior.

'There is no more for me,' he said. Alnac's dead eyes had nothing but resignation in them. 'This is for dissolution . . . ' And he fell forward on to the marble floor, his armour all broken, his limbs sprawling, and there was no longer any flesh on him, only bone, so that what was left of the Pearl Warrior resembled little more than the inedible remains of a crab, the supper of some sea-giant.

Queen Sough came towards Elric, her arms outstretched, and she seemed much smaller than when he had first encountered her. Her head hardly reached to his lowered chin. Her embrace was warm and he knew she, too, was weeping. Then her veil fell away from her face and he saw that she had lost years, that she was little more than a girl.

Behind Queen Sough the Lady Oone was smiling at him as astonished understanding filled him. Gently he touched the girl's face, the familiar folds of her hair and he drew in a sudden breath.

She was Varadia. She was the Holy Girl of the Bauradim. She was the child whose spirit they had promised to free.

Oone joined him, placing a protective hand upon Varadia's shoulder. 'You know now that we are truly your friends.'

Varadia nodded, looking about her at the courtiers who had assumed their earlier frozen stances. 'The Pearl Warrior was the best there was,' she said. 'I could summon none better. Chamog Borm failed me. The Sorcerer Adventurers were too strong for him. Now I can release him from his exile.'

'We combined his strength with our own,' said Oone. 'Your strength and our strength. That is how we succeeded.'

'We three are not shadows,' said Varadia smiling, as if at a revelation. '*That* is how we succeeded.'

Oone nodded agreement. 'That is how we succeeded, Holy Girl. Now we must consider how to bring you back to the Bronze Tent, to your people. You carry all their pride and history with you.'

'I knew that. I had to protect it. I thought I had failed.'

'You have not failed,' said Oone.

'The Sorcerer Adventurers will not attack again?'

'Never,' said Oone. 'Not here, nor anywhere. Elric and I will make sure of it.'

And then Elric realized in admiration that it had been Oone, in the end, who had summoned the Sorcerer Adventurers, summoned those shades for the last time, summoned them so that she might demonstrate their defeat.

Oone looked at him and warned him with her eyes not to say too much. But now he realized that all that they had fought, save perhaps a little of the Pearl Warrior and the Sorcerer Adventurers, had been a child's dreams. The hero of legend, Chamog Borm, could not save her because she knew he was not real. Similarly, the Pearl Warrior, chiefly her own invention, could not save her. But he and Oone were real. As real as the girl herself! In her deep dream, in which she had disguised herself as a Queen, seeking power but failing to find it, just as she had described, she had known the truth. Unable to escape from the dream, she had yet recognized the difference between her own invention and that which she had not invented – herself, Oone and Elric. But Oone had had to show that she could defeat what remained of the original threat, and in demonstrating the defeat, she freed the child.

And yet they were still within the dream, all three of them. The great Pearl pulsed as powerfully as before, the Fortress with all its mazes and intertwined passages and chambers was still their prison.

'You understood,' Elric said to Oone. 'You knew what they spoke of.' The language was a child's language – a language seeking power and failing. A child's understanding of power.'

But again Oone, with a glance, cautioned him to silence. 'Varadia knows now that power is never discovered in retreat. All one can hope to do by retreating is to let one power destroy another or hide as one hides from a storm one cannot control, until the force has passed. One cannot gain anything, save one's own self. And ultimately one must always confront the evil that would destroy one.' It was almost as if she herself were in a trance and Elric guessed that she repeated lessons learned in pursuit of her craft.

'You did not come to steal the Pearl but to save me from its prison,' said Varadia as Oone took her young hands and held them tightly. 'My father sent you to help me?'

'He asked our help and we gave it willingly,' said Elric. At last he sheathed the silver sword. He felt slightly foolish in the armour of a fairy-tale hero.

Oone recognized his discomfort. 'We shall give all this back to Chamog Borm, my lord. Is he permitted to return to the Fortress, Lady

Varadia?'

The child grinned. 'Of course!' She clapped her hands and through the doorway to the Court of the Pearl, walking proudly, still in the clothes of his banishment, came Chamog Borm, to kneel at the feet of his mistress.

'My queen,' he said. There was strong emotion in his wonderful voice.

'I return to you your armour and your weapons, your twin horses Tadia and Taron and all your honour, Chamog Borm.' Varadia spoke with warm pride.

Soon Elric and Oone had discarded the armour and again wore only their ordinary clothes. Chamog Borm was in his silver-and gold-chased breastplate and greaves, his helmet of gleaming silver, his swords and his spears in their sheaths at hip and on horse. His other armour he bound to the back of his Tadia. At last he was ready. Again he kneeled before his Queen. 'My lady. What task wouldst thou have me accomplish for thee?'

Varadia said deliberately, 'You are free to travel where you will, great Chamog Borm. But know only this – you must continue to fight evil wherever you find it and you must never again allow the Sorcerer Adventurers to attack the Fortress of the Pearl.'

'I swear.'

With a bow to Oone and Elric, the legendary hero rode slowly from the Court, his head high with pride and noble purpose.

Varadia was content. 'I have made him again what he was before I called him. I now know that legends in themselves have no power. The power comes from the uses that the living make of the legend. The legends merely represent an ideal.'

'You are a wise child,' said Oone admiringly.

'Should I not be, madam? I am the Holy Girl of the Bauradim.' Varadia spoke with considerable irony and good humour. 'Am I not the Oracle of the Bronze Tent?' She lowered her eyes, perhaps in sudden melancholy. 'I shall be a child only a little longer. I think I shall miss my palace and all its kingdoms . . . '

'Something is always lost here.' Oone placed a comforting hand on the child's shoulder. 'But much is gained, also.'

Varadia looked back at the Pearl. Following her gaze, Elric saw that the entire Court had now vanished, just as the crowds had vanished on the great staircase when they had been attacked by the Pearl Warrior just before they first met Lady Sough. He now realized that in that guise she herself had guided them to her own rescue, as best she could. She had reached out to them. She had shown them the way in which they could, with their wits and courage, accomplish her salvation.

Varadia was ascending the steps, her hands outstretched towards the Pearl. 'This is the cause of all our misfortune,' she said. 'What can we do with it?'

'Destroy it, perhaps,' said Elric.

But Oone shook her head. 'While it remains an undiscovered treasure thieves will constantly seek it. This is the cause of Varadia's imprisonment in the Dream Realm. This is what brought the Sorcerer Adventurers to her. It is why they drugged and attempted to abduct her. All the evil comes not from the Pearl itself but what evil men have made of it.'

'What shall you do?' asked Elric. 'Trade it in the Dream Market when you next go?'

'Perhaps that is what I should do. But it would not be the means of ensuring Varadia's safety in the future. Do you understand?'

'While the Pearl is a legend, there will always be those who will pursue the legend?'

'Exactly, Prince Elric. So we shall not destroy it, I think. Not here.'

Elric did not care. So absorbed had he become in the dream itself, the revealing of the levels of reality existing in the Dream Realm, that he had forgotten his original quest, the threat to his life and that of Anigh in Quarzhasaat.

It was for Oone to remind him. 'Remember, there are those in Quarzhasaat who are not only your enemies, Elric of Melniboné. They are the enemies of this girl. The enemies of the Bauradim. You have still a further task to accomplish, even when we return to the Bronze Tent.'

'Then you must advise me, Lady Oone,' said Elric simply, 'for I am a novice here.'

'I cannot advise you with any great clarity.' She turned her eyes away from him, almost in modesty, perhaps in pain. 'But I can make a decision here. We must claim the Pearl.'

'As I understand it, the Pearl did not exist before the Lords of Quarzhasaat conceived it, before someone discovered the legend, before the Sorcerer Adventurers came.'

'But it exists now,' said Oone. 'Lady Varadia, would you give the Pearl to me?'

'Willingly,' said the Holy Girl, and she ran up the remaining steps and took the globe from the plinth and threw it to the ground so that shards of milky glass shattered everywhere, mingling with the bones and the armour of the Pearl Warrior, and she took the Pearl in one hand, as an ordinary child might grasp a lost ball. And she tossed it from palm to palm in delight, fearing it no longer. 'It is very beautiful. No wonder they sought it.'

'They made it, then they used it to trap you.' Oone reached up and caught it as Varadia threw it to her. 'What a shame those who could conceive of such beauty would go to such evil lengths to own it . . . ' She frowned, looking about her in sudden concern.

The light was fading in the Court of the Pearl.

From all around them came an appalling noise, an anguished groaning; a great creaking and keening, a tortured screaming, as if all the tormented souls in all the multiverse had suddenly given voice.

It pierced their brains. They covered their ears. They stared in terror, watching as the floor of the Court erupted and undulated, as the ivory walls with all their wonderful mosaics and carvings began to rot before their eyes, crumbling and falling, like the fabric in a tomb suddenly exposed to daylight.

And then, over all the other noises, they heard the laughter.

It was sweet laughter. It was the unaffected laughter of a child.

It was the laughter of a freed spirit. It was Varadia's.

'It is dissolving at last. It is all dissolving! Oh, my friends, I am a slave no longer!'

Through all the falling filthy stuff, through all the decay and dissolution which tumbled upon them, through the destroyed carcass of the Fortress of the Pearl, Oone came towards them. She was hasty but she was careful. She held one of Varadia's hands.

'Not yet! Too soon! We could all dissolve in this!'

She made Elric take the child's hand and they led her through the crashing, shrieking darkness, out of the chamber, down through the swaying corridors, out past the courtyards where fountains now gushed detritus and where the very walls were constructed of putrefying flesh which began to rot to nothing even as they went by. Then Oone made them run, until the final gateway lay ahead of them.

They reached the causeway and the marble road. There was a bridge ahead of them. Oone almost dragged the other two towards it, running as fast as she could possibly run, with the Fortress of the Pearl tumbling into nothing, roaring like a dying beast as it did so.

The bridge seemed infinite. Elric could not see to the further side. But at length Oone stopped running and allowed them to walk, for they had reached a gateway.

The gateway was carved of red sandstone. It was decorated with geometrical tiles and pictures of gazelles, leopards and wild camels. It had an almost prosaic appearance after so many monumental doorways, yet Elric felt some trepidation in passing through it.

'I am afraid, Oone,' he said.

'You fear mortality, I think.' She pressed on. 'You have great courage, Prince Elric. Make use of it now, I beg you.'

He quelled his terrors. His grip on the child's hand was firm and reassuring.

'We go home, do we not?' said the Holy Girl. 'What is it you do not want to find there, Prince Elric?'

He smiled down at her, grateful for her question. 'Nothing much, Lady Varadia. Perhaps nothing more than myself.'

They stepped together into the gateway.

3

Celebrations at the Silver Flower Oasis

Waking beside the still sleeping child, Elric was surprised to feel so refreshed. The dreamwand, which had helped them attain substance in the Dream Realm, was still hooked over their clasped hands and, looking across the child, he saw Oone beginning to stir.

'You have failed, then?'

It was Raik Na Seem's voice, full of resigned sadness.

'What?' Oone glanced at Varadia. Even as they watched her skin began to shine with ordinary health and her eyes opened to see her anxious father staring down at her. She smiled. It was the easy, unaffected smile with which Oone and Elric were already familiar.

The First Elder of the Bauradi Clan began to weep. He wept as the seneschal of the Court of the Pearl had wept; he wept in relief and he wept in joy. He took up his daughter in his arms and he could not speak for the gladness in his heart. All he could do was reach one hand out towards his friends, the man and the woman who had entered the Dream Realm to free his child's spirit, where it had fled to escape the evil of Lord Gho's hirelings.

They touched his hand and they left the Bronze Tent. They walked together into the desert and then they stood face to face, staring into one another's eyes.

'We have a dream in common now,' said Elric. His voice was gentle, full of affection. 'I think the memory will be a good one, Lady Oone.'

She reached to hold his face in her hands. 'You are wise, Prince Elric, and you are courageous, but there is a certain kind of ordinary experience you lack. I hope that you are successful in finding it.'

'That is why I wander this world, my lady, and leave my cousin Yyrkoon as Regent on the Ruby Throne. I am aware of more than one deficiency.'

'I am glad we dreamed together,' she said.

'You lost your true love, I think,' Elric told her. 'I am glad if I helped you ease the pain of that parting.'

She was baffled for a moment, then her brow cleared. 'You speak of Alnac Kreb? I was fond of him, my lord, but he was more a brother to me than a lover.'

Elric became embarrassed. 'Forgive my presumption, Lady Oone.'

She looked up into the sky. The Blood Moon had not yet waned. It cast its red rays on to the sand, on to the gleaming bronze of the tent where Raik Na Seem welcomed his daughter back to him. 'I do not love easily in the way you mean.' Her voice was significant. She sighed. 'Do you still plan to return to Melniboné and your betrothed?'

'I must', he said. 'I love her. And my duty lies in Imrryr.'

'Sweet duty!' Her tone was sarcastic and she took a step or two away from him, her head bowed, her hand on her belt. She kicked at dust the colour of old blood.

Elric had disciplined himself against his heart's pain for too long. He could only stand and wait until she walked back to him. And now she was smiling. 'Well, Prince Elric, would you join the dreamthieves and make this your living for a while?'

Elric shook his head. 'It is a calling which requires too much of me, my lady. Yet I am grateful for what this adventure has taught me, both about myself and about the world of dreams. I still understand only a little of it. I am still not wholly sure where we travelled or what we encountered. I do not know how much in the Dream Realm was the Lady Varadia's creation and how much was yours. It was as if I witnessed a battle of inventors! And did I contribute? I do not know.'

'Oh, without you, believe me, Prince Elric, I think I would have failed. You have seen so much of other worlds! And you have read more. It does not do to analyse too closely the creatures and places one encounters in the Dream Realm, but be assured that you made your contribution. More, perhaps, than you'll ever know.'

'Can reality ever be made from the fabric of those dreams?' he wondered.

'There was an adventurer of the Young Kingdoms called Earl Aubec,' she said. 'He knew how potent a creator of reality the human mind can be. Some say he and his kind helped make the world of the Young Kingdoms.'

Elric nodded. 'I've heard that legend. But I think it is as substantial as the story of Chamog Borm, my lady.'

'You must think what you wish.' She turned away from him to look at the Bronze Tent. The old man and his daughter were emerging. From somewhere within the tent drums began to beat. There came a wonderful chanting, a dozen melodies linked together, interwoven. Slowly all the people who had remained at the Bronze Tent keeping vigil over the body of the Holy Girl began to gather around Raik Na Seem and Varadia. Their songs were songs of immense joy. Their voices filled the desert with the most gorgeous life and made even the distant mountains echo.

Oone linked her arm in Elric's, a gesture of comradeship, of reconciliation. 'Come,' she said, 'let us join the celebrations.'

They had only walked a few more paces before they were lifted on the shoulders of the crowd and soon they were borne, laughing and infected by the general joyousness, over the desert towards the Silver Flower Oasis.

The celebrations began at once, as if the Bauradim and all the other desert clans had been preparing for this moment. Every kind of delicious food was prepared until the air was rich with an enormous variety of mouth-watering smells and it seemed all the great spice warehouses of the world had been made to release their contents. Cooking fires blazed everywhere, as did great brands and lamps and candles, and from out of the Kashbeh Moulor Ka Riiz, overlooking the great oasis, rode the Aloum'rit guardians in all the glory of their ancient armour, their red-gold helmets and breastplates, their weapons of bronze and brass and steel. They had huge forked beards and massive turbans wound around the spikes of their helms. They wore surcoats of elaborate brocade and cloth-of-silver and their high boots were embroidered with designs almost as intricate as those on their shirts. They were proud, good-humoured men who rode at the sides of their wives, who were also armoured and carried bows and slender spears. All had soon mingled with the enormous crowd who had erected a large platform and placed a carved chair upon it and sat the smiling Varadia in the chair so that all could see the Holy Girl of the Bauradim restored to her clan, bringing back their history, their pride and their future.

Raik Na Seem still wept. Whenever he saw Oone and Elric he grasped them and pulled them to him, thanking them, telling them, as best he could, what it meant to him to have such friends, such saviours, such heroes.

'Your names will be remembered by the Bauradim for all time. And whatever favour you shall ask of us, so long as it be honourable, as we know it shall, then we shall grant it to you. If you are in danger ten thousand miles away you will send a message to the Bauradim and they will come to your aid. Meanwhile you must know that you have freed the spirit of a good-hearted child from dark captivity.'

'And that is our reward,' said Oone, smiling.

'Our wealth is yours,' said the old man.

'We have no need of wealth,' Oone told him. 'We have discovered better resources, I think.'

Elric agreed with her. 'Besides, there is a man in Quarzhasaat who has promised me half an Empire if I but do him a small service.'

Oone understood Elric's reference and laughed.

Raik Na Seem was a little disturbed. 'You go to Quarzhasaat? You still have business there?'

'Aye,' said Elric. 'There is a boy who is anxiously awaiting my return.'

'But you have time to celebrate with us, to talk with us, to feast with myself and Varadia? You have scarcely exhanged a word with the child!'

'I think we know her pretty well,' said Elric. 'Enough to think highly of her. She is indeed the greatest treasure of the Bauradim, my lord.'

'You were able to hold conversations in that gloomy realm where she was held prisoner?'

Elric thought to enlighten the First Elder, but Oone was quick to interrupt, so familiar was she with such questions.

'Some, my lord. We were impressed by her intelligence and her courage.'

Raik Na Seem's brow furrowed as another thought occurred to him. 'My son,' he said to Elric, 'were you able to sustain yourself in that realm without pain?'

'Without pain, aye,' said Elric. Then he realized what had been said. For the first time he understood what good had come about from his adventure. 'Aye, sir. There are benefits to assisting a dreamthief. Great benefits which I had not until now appreciated!'

With relish now Elric joined in the feasting, treasuring these hours with Oone, the Bauradim and all the other nomad clans. Again he felt as if he had come home, so welcoming were the people, and he wished that he could spend his life here, learning their ways, their philosophies and enjoying their pastimes.

Later, as he lay beneath a great date-palm, rolling one of the silver flowers between his fingers, he looked up at Oone who sat beside him and he said: 'Of all the temptations I faced in the Dream Realm, this temptation is perhaps the greatest, Oone. This is simple reality and I am reluctant to leave it. And you.'

'We have no further destiny together, I think.' She sighed. 'Not in this life, at any rate, or this world, perhaps. You shall be first a legend, then there will be none left to remember you.'

'My friends will all die? I shall be alone?'

'I believe so. While you serve Chaos.'

'I serve myself and my people.'

'If you would believe that, Elric, you must do more to achieve it. You have created a little reality and perhaps will create a little more. But Chaos cannot be a friend without it betraying you. In the end, we have only ourselves to look to. No cause, no force, no challenge, will ever replace that truth . . . '

'It is to be myself that I travel as I do, Lady Oone,' he reminded her. He looked out over the desert, over the tranquil waters of the oasis. He breathed in the cool, scented desert air.

'And you will leave here soon?' she asked.

'Tomorrow,' he said. 'I must. But I am curious to know what reality I have created.'

'Oh, I think a dream or two has come true,' she said cryptically, kissing him on the cheek. 'And another will come true soon enough.'

He did not pursue the question, for she had taken the great pearl from the pouch at her belt and held it out to him.

'It exists! It was not the chimera we believed it to be! You still have it!'

'It is for you,' she said. 'Use it how you will. That is what brought you here to the Silver Flower Oasis. It is what brought you to me. I think I will not trade it at the Dream Market. I would like you to have it. I think it might be yours by right, Elric. Be that as it may, the Holy Girl gave it to me and now I give it to you. It is what Alnac Kreb died because of, what all those assassins died to possess . . . '

'I thought you said that the Pearl did not exist before the Sorcerer Assassins sought to find it.'

'That is true. But it exists now. Here it is. The Pearl at the Heart of the World. The Great Pearl of legend. Have you no use for it?'

'You must explain to me . . . ' he began, but she cut him short.

'Ask me not how dreams take substance, Prince Elric. That is a question that concerns philosophers in all ages and all places. I ask you again – have you no use for it?'

He hesitated, then reached out to take the lovely thing. He held it in his two palms, rolling it back and forth. He wondered at its richness, its pale beauty. 'Aye,' he said, 'I think I have a use for it.'

When he had placed the jewel in his own pouch, Oone said very softly: 'I think it is an evil thing, that pearl.'

He agreed with her. 'I think so, too, But sometimes evil can be used to counter evil.'

'I cannot accept that argument.' She seemed troubled.

'I know,' he said. 'You have already said as much.' And then it was his turn to reach towards her and kiss her tenderly upon the lips. 'Fate is cruel, Oone. It would be better if it provided us with one unaltering path. Instead it forces us to make choices, never to know if those choices were for the best.'

'We are mortals,' she said with a shrug. 'That is our particular doom.'

She stroked his forehead. 'You have a troubled mind, my lord. I think I will steal a few of the smaller dreams which make you uneasy.'

'Can you steal pain, Oone, and turn it into something to sell in your market?'

'Oh, frequently,' she said.

She took his head in her lap and began to massage his temples. Her look was tender.

He said sleepily: 'I cannot betray Cymoril. I cannot . . . '

'I ask no more of you but that you sleep,' she said. 'One day you will have much to regret and you will know real remorse. Until then, I can take away a little of what is unimportant.'

'Unimportant?' His voice was slurred as she gradually stroked him into slumber.

'To you, I think, my lord. Though not to me . . . '

And the dreamthief began to sing. She sang a lullaby. She sang of a sickly child and a grieving father. She sang of happiness found in simple things.

And Elric slept. And as he slept the dreamthief performed her easy magic and took away just a few of the half-forgotten memories which had spoiled his nights in the past and might spoil those yet to come.

And when Elric awoke that next morning, it was with a light heart and an easy conscience, only the faintest memories of his adventures in the Dream Realm, a continuing affection for Oone and a determination to reach Quarzhasaat as soon as possible and take to Lord Gho what Lord Gho most desired in all the world.

His farewells to the people of the Bauradim were sincere and his sadness in parting was reciprocated. They begged him to return, to join them on their travels, to hunt with them as Rackhir, his friend, had once hunted.

'I will try to return to you one day,' he said. 'But first I have more than one oath to fulfil.'

A nervous boy brought him his great black battle-blade. As he buckled on Stormbringer the sword seemed to moan with considerable satisfaction at being reunited with him.

It was Varadia, clasping his hands and kissing them, who gave him the blessing of her clan. It was Raik Na Seem who told him that he was now Varadia's brother, his own son, and then Oone the

Dreamthief stepped forward. She had decided to remain a while as a guest of the Bauradim.

'Farewell, Elric. I hope that we may meet again. In better circumstances.'

He was amused. 'Better circumstances?'

'For me, at any rate.' She grinned, contemptuously tapping the pommel of his runesword. 'And I wish you well with your attempts to become that thing's master.'

'I am its master now, I think,' he said.

She shrugged. 'I'll ride with you a little way up the Red Road.'

'I would welcome your company, my lady.'

Side by side, as they had done in the Dream Realm, Elric and Oone rode together. And, although he did not remember how he had felt before, Elric knew a certain resonance of recognition, as if he had found his soul's satisfaction, so that it was with sadness that eventually he parted from her to go on alone towards Quarzhasaat.

'Farewell, good friend. I'll remember how you defeated the Pearl Warrior in the Fortress of the Pearl. That is one memory I do not think will ever fade.'

'I am flattered.' There was a touch of melancholy irony in her voice. 'Farewell, Prince Elric. I trust you will find all that you need and that you will know peace when you return to Melniboné.'

'It is my firm intention, madam.' A wave to her, not wishing to prolong the sadness, and he spurred his horse forward.

With eyes which refused to weep she watched him ride away up the long Red Road to Quarzhasaat.

4

Certain Matters
Resolved in Quarzhasaat

When Elric of Melniboné rode into Quarzhasaat he was limp in his saddle, hardly controlling his horse at all, and the people who gathered around him asked him if he were ill, while some feared that he brought plague to their beautiful city and would have driven him out at once.

The albino lifted his strange head long enough to gasp out the name of his patron, Lord Gho Fhaazi, and to say that all he lacked was a certain elixir which that nobleman possessed. 'I must have that elixir,' he told them, 'or I will be dead before I have accomplished my task . . .'

The old towers and minarets of Quarzhasaat were lovely in the fading rays of a huge red sun and there was a certain peace about the city which comes when the day's business is done and before it begins to take its pleasures.

A rich water-merchant, anxious to find favour with one who might soon be elected to the Council, personally led Elric's horse through the elegant alleys and impressive avenues until they came to the great palace, all golds and faded greens, of Lord Gho Fhaazi.

The merchant was rewarded by a steward's promise to mention his name to the nobleman and Elric, now mumbling and whimpering to himself, sometimes groaning a little and licking anxious lips, passed through into the lovely gardens surrounding the main palace.

Lord Gho himself came to meet the albino. He was laughing heartily at the sight of Elric in such poor condition.

'Greetings, greetings, Elric of Nadsokor! Greetings, white-faced clown-thief. Oh, you are not so proud today! You were profligate with the elixir I gave you and now you return to beg for more – in worse condition than when you first arrived here!'

'The boy . . .' whispered Elric, as servants helped him from the horse. His arms hung limply as they carried him on their shoulders. 'Does he live?'

'In better health than yourself, sir!' Lord Gho Fhaazi's pale green

297

eyes were full of exquisite malice. 'And in perfect safety. You were most adamant about that before you set off. And I am a man of my word.' The politician stroked the ringlets of his oily beard and chuckled to himself. 'And you, Sir Thief, do you also keep your word?'

'To the letter,' muttered the albino. His red eyes rolled back in his head and it appeared for a second that he died. Then he turned a painful gaze in Lord Gho's direction. 'Will you give me the antidote and all that you've promised? The water? The wealth? The boy?'

'No doubt, no doubt. But you have a poor bargaining position at present, thief. What of the Pearl? Did you find it? Or are you here to report failure?'

'I found it. And I have it hidden,' said Elric. 'The elixir has . . .'

'Yes, yes. I know what the elixir does. You must have a fundamentally strong constituion even to be able to speak by now.' The Quarzhasaati supervised the men and women who carried Elric into the cool interior of the palace and placed him on great tasselled cushions of scarlet and blue velvet and gave him water to drink and food to eat.

'The craving grows worse, does it not?' Lord Gho took considerable pleasure at Elric's discomfort. 'The elixir must feed off you, just as you appear to feed off it. You are cunning, eh, Sir Thief. You have hidden the Pearl, you say? Do you not trust me? I am a nobleman of the greatest city in the world!'

Elric sprawled on the cushions, all dusty from his long ride, and wiped his hands slowly on a cloth. 'The antidote, my lord . . .'

'You know I shall not let you have the antidote until the Pearl is in my hands . . .' Lord Gho was expansively condescending as he looked down on his victim. 'To tell you the truth, thief, I had not expected you to be as coherent as you are! Would you care for another draft of my elixir?'

'Bring it if you will.'

Elric appeared to be careless, but Lord Gho understood how desperate he must actually be. He turned to give instructions to his slaves.

Then Elric said: 'But bring the boy. Bring the boy so that I may see he has come to no harm and hear from his own lips what has taken place while I have been gone . . .'

'It's a small request. Very well.' Lord Gho Fhaazi signed to a slave. 'Bring the boy Anigh.'

The nobleman crossed to a great chair, placed on a small dais between brocaded awnings, and slumped himself down in it while they waited. 'I had scarcely expected you to survive the journey, Sir Thief, let alone succeed in finding the Pearl. Our Sorcerer Adventurers are the bravest, most skilful of warriors, trained in all the arts of sorcery and incantation. Yet those I sent, and all their brothers, failed! Oh, this is a happy day for me. I will revive you, I promise, so that you can tell me all that happened. What of the Bauradim? Did you kill many? You will recount everything so that when I present the Pearl to obtain my position I can give the story that goes with it. This will add to its value, you see. When I am elected, I shall be asked to retail such a story many times, I am sure. The Council will be so envious . . . ' He licked his painted red lips. 'Did you have to kill that child? What was the first thing you witnessed, for instance when you reached the Silver Flower Oasis?'

'A funeral, as I recall . . . ' Elric showed a little more animation. 'Aye, that was it.'

Two guards brought in a wriggling boy who did not seem greatly overjoyed when he saw Elric stretched upon the cushions. 'Oh, master! You are more wretched than before.' He stopped his struggling and tried to hide his disappointment. There were no marks of torture on him. He seemed not to have been harmed.

'Are you well, Anigh?'

'Aye. My chief problem has been in passing the time. Occasionally his lordship there has come to tell me what he will do if you fail to bring back the Pearl, but I have read such things on the walls of the lunatic stockades and they are nothing new to me.'

Lord Gho scowled. 'Be careful, boy . . . '

'You must have returned with the Pearl,' said Anigh, glancing around him. 'That is so, eh, my lord? Or you would not be here?' He was a little more relieved. 'Are we to go now?'

'Not yet!' growled Lord Gho.

'The antidote,' said Elric. 'Do you have it here?'

'You are too impatient, Sir Thief. And your cunning is matched by mine.' Lord Gho giggled and raised an admonishing finger. 'I must have some proof that you possess the Pearl. Would you give me your sword as surety, perhaps? You are, after all, too weak to wield it. It is of no further use to you.' He reached a greedy hand towards the albino's hip and Elric made a feeble movement away from him.

'Come, come, Sir Thief. Be not afraid of me. We are partners in this. Where is the Pearl? The Council congregates this evening at the Great Meeting House. If I can bring them the Pearl then . . . Oh, I shall be powerful by tonight!'

'The worm is so proud to be king of the dunghill,' said Elric.

'Do not anger him, master!' cried Anigh in alarm. 'You have still to learn where he hides the antidote!'

'I must have the Pearl!' Lord Gho grew petulant in his impatience. 'Where have you hidden it, thief? In the desert? Somewhere in the city?'

Slowly Elric raised his body on the cushions. 'The Pearl was a dream,' he said. 'It took your killers to make it real.'

Lord Gho Fhaazi frowned, scratching at his whitened forehead and showing further nervousness. He looked suspiciously at Elric. 'If you would have more elixir, you had best not insult me, thief. Nor play any game. The boy could die in an instant, and you with him, and I would be in no worse a position.'

'But you would better yourself, my lord, I think. With the price of a place on the Council, I think.' Elric seemed to gather strength and now he was upright on the luxurious velvet, signing for the boy to come towards him. The guards looked questioningly at their master, but he shrugged. Anigh walked, his brow furrowed with curiosity, towards the albino. 'You are greedy, my lord, I think. You would own the whole of your world. This pathetic monument to your race's ruined pride!'

Lord Gho glared at him. 'Thief, if you would recover yourself, if you would take the antidote to make you free of the drug I gave you, you will be more polite to me . . . '

'Ah, yes,' said Elric thoughtfully, reaching into his jerkin. He pulled out a leather pouch. 'The elixir which was to make me your slave!' He smiled. He opened the pouch.

On to his extended palm now rolled the jewel for which Gho Fhaazi had offered half his fortune, for which he had sent a hundred men to their deaths, for which he had been prepared to abduct and kill one child and imprison another.

The Quarzhasaati began to tremble. His painted eyes rounded. He gasped and bent forward, almost fainting.

'It is true,' he said. 'You have found the Pearl at the Heart of the World . . . '

'Merely a gift from a friend,' said Elric. The Pearl still displayed on his hand, he rose to his feet and put a protective arm around the boy. 'In obtaining it I found that my body lost its demand for the elixir and therefore has no need for your antidote, Lord Gho.'

Lord Gho hardly heard him. His eyes were fixed on the great Pearl. 'It is monstrous big . . . Even larger than I had heard . . . It is real. I can see it is real. The colour . . . Ah . . . ' And he stretched towards it.

Elric drew his hand back. Lord Gho frowned and looked up at the albino with eyes that were hot with greed. 'Did she die? Was it, as some said, in her body?'

Anigh shivered at Elric's side.

Full of loathing, Elric's voice was still soft. 'No one died at my hand who was not already dead. As you are already dead, my lord. It was your funeral I witnessed at the Silver Flower Oasis. I am now the agent of the Bauradi prophecy. I am to avenge all the grief you brought to them and their Holy Child.'

'What! The others all sent their soldiers, too! The entire Council and half the candidates had sects of Sorcerer Adventurers seeking the Pearl. Every one. Most of these warriors failed or were killed. Or were executed for their failure. You killed no-one, you said. Well, so there's no blood on our hands, eh? All's for the best. I'll give you what I promised, Sir Thief . . . '

Trembling with lust Lord Gho extended his plump hand to take the Pearl.

Elric smiled and to Anigh's astonishment let the nobleman lift the Pearl from his palm.

Breathing heavily, Lord Gho caressed his prize. 'Oh, it is lovely. Oh, it is so good . . . '

Elric spoke again, just as levelly as before. 'And our reward, Lord Gho?'

'What?' He looked up absently. 'Why yes, of course. Your lives. You no longer need the antidote, you say. Excellent. So you may go.'

'I believed you also offered me a large fortune. All manner of wealth. Great stature amongst the lords of Quarzhasaat?'

Lord Gho dismissed this. 'Nonsense. The antidote would have sufficed. You are not the type of person to enjoy such things. Breeding is required if they are to be used wisely and with appropriate discretion. No, no, I will let you and the boy go . . . '

'You will not keep your original bargain, my lord?'

'There was talk — but no bargain. The only bargain involved the boy's freedom and the antidote to the elixir. You were mistaken.'

'You remember nothing of your promises . . . ?'

'Promises? Certainly not.' The ringleted beard and hair quivered.

' . . . and mine?'

'No, no. You are irritating me.' His eyes were still upon the Pearl. He fondled it as another might fondle a beloved child. 'Go, sir. While I am still pleased with you.'

'I have many oaths to fulfil,' said Elric, 'and I do not break my word.'

Lord Gho looked up, his expression hardening. 'Very well. I am tired of this. By this evening I shall be a member of the Six and One Other. By threatening me you threaten the Council. You are therefore enemies of Quarzhasaat. You are traitors to the Empire and must be disposed of accordingly! Guards!'

'Oh, you are a foolish fellow,' said Elric. Then Anigh cried out, for unlike Lord Gho, he had not forgotten the power of the Black Sword.

'Do as he demands, Lord Gho!' shouted Anigh, fearing as much for himself as the nobleman. 'I beg you, great lord! Do what he says!'

'This is not how a member of the Council is addressed.' Lord Gho's tone was that of a baffled, reasonable individual. 'Guards – take them from my hall at once. Have them strangled or cut their throats – I care not . . .'

The guards knew nothing of the runesword. They saw only a slender man who might have been a leper and they saw a young, defenceless boy. They grinned, as if at a joke of their master's, and they drew their blades, advancing almost casually.

Elric pressed Anigh behind him. His hand went to Stormbringer's hilt. 'You are unwise to do this,' he told the guards. 'I have no particular wish to kill you.'

Behind the soldiers one of the servants opened the door and slipped out into the corridor. Elric watched her go. 'Best copy her,' he said. 'She has some idea, I think, of what will happen if you threaten us further . . .'

The guards laughed openly now. 'This is a madman,' said one. 'Lord Gho is well rid of him!'

They came at Elric in a rush and then the runesword was howling in the cool air of that luxurious chamber – howling like a hungry wolf freed from a cage and longing only to kill and to feed.

Elric felt the power surge through him as the blade took the first guard, splitting him from crown to breastbone. The other tried to change direction from attack to flight, stumbled forward and was impaled on the blade's tip, his eyes horrified as he felt his soul being drawn from him into the runesword.

Lord Gho cringed in his great chair, too frightened to move. In one hand he clutched the great Pearl. His other hand was held palm outwards as if he hoped to ward off Elric's blow.

But the albino, strengthened by his borrowed energy, sheathed the black blade and took five quick strides across the hall to mount the dais and stare down into Lord Gho's face which twisted in terror.

'Take the Pearl back. For my life . . .' whispered the Quarzhasaati. 'For my life, thief . . .'

Elric accepted the offered jewel, but he did not move. He reached into the pouch at his belt and drew forth a flask of the elixir Lord Gho had given him. 'Would you care for something to help you wash it down?'

Lord Gho trembled. Beneath the chalky substance on his skin his face had gone still paler. 'I do not understand you, thief.'

'I want you to eat the Pearl, my lord. If you can swallow it and live, well, it will be clear that the prophecy of your death was premature.'

'Swallow it? It is too large. I could hardly get it into my mouth!' Lord Gho sniggered, hoping that the albino joked.

'No, my lord. I think you can. And I think you can swallow it. After all, how else would it have got into the body of a child?'

'It was – they say it was a – a dream . . . '

'Aye. Perhaps you can swallow a dream. Perhaps you can enter the Dream Realm and so escape your fate. You must try, my lord, or else my runesword drinks your soul. Which would you prefer?'

'Oh, Elric. Spare me. This is not fair. We made a bargain.'

'Open your mouth, Lord Gho. Who knows if the Pearl might shrink or your throat expand like a snake's? A snake could easily swallow the Pearl, my lord. And you, surely, are superior to a snake?'

Anigh whispered from the window where he had been staring with studied gaze, unwilling to look upon a vengeance he regarded as just but distasteful. 'The servant, Lord Elric. She has alarmed the city.'

For a second a desperate hope came into Lord Gho's green eyes and then faded as Elric placed the flask on the arm of the great chair and drew the runesword part way from its scabbard. 'Your soul will help me fight those new soldiers, Lord Gho.'

Slowly, weeping and whimpering, the great Lord of Quarzhasaat began to open his mouth.

'Here is the Pearl again, my lord. Put it in. Do your best, my lord. You have some chance of life this way.'

Lord Gho's hand shook. But eventually he began to force the lovely jewel between his reddened lips. Elric took the stopper from the elixir and poured some of the liquid into the nobleman's distorted cheeks. 'Now swallow, Lord Gho. Swallow the Pearl you would have slain a child to own! And then I will tell you who I am . . . '

A few minutes later the doors crashed inward and Elric recognized the tattooed face of Manag Iss, leader of the Yellow Sect and kinsman to the Lady Iss. Manag Iss looked from Elric to the distorted features of Lord Gho. The nobleman had failed completely to swallow the Pearl.

Manag Iss shuddered. 'Elric. I heard that you had returned. They said you were close to death. Clearly this was a trick to deceive Lord Gho.'

'Aye,' said Elric. 'I had this boy to free.'

Manag Iss gestured with his own drawn sword. 'You found the Pearl?'

'I found it.'

'My Lady Iss sent me to offer you anything you desired for it.'

Elric smiled. 'Tell her I shall be at the Council Meeting House in half-an-hour. I shall bring the Pearl with me.'

'But the others will be there. She wishes to trade privately.'

'Would it not be wise to auction so valuable a thing?' said Elric.

Manag Iss sheathed his sword and smiled a little. 'You're a cunning one. I do not think they know how cunning you are. Nor who you are. I have yet to tell them that particular speculation.'

'Oh, you may tell them what I have just told Lord Gho. That I am the hereditary Emperor of Melniboné,' said Elric casually. 'For that is the truth of the matter. My Empire has survived rather more successfully than yours, I think.'

'That could incense them. I am willing to be your friend, Melnibonéan.

'Thanks, Manag Iss, but I need no more friends from Quarzhasaat. Please do as I say.'

Manag Iss looked at the slaughtered guards, at the dead Lord Gho, who had turned a strange colour, at the nervous boy, and he saluted Elric.

'The Meeting House in half-an-hour, Emperor of Melniboné.' He turned on his heel and left the chamber.

After issuing certain specific instructions to Anigh concerning travel and the products of Kwan, Elric went out into the courtyard. The sun had set and there were brands burning all over Quarzhasaat as if the city were expecting an attack.

Lord Gho's house was empty of servants. Elric went to the stables and found his horse and his saddle. He dressed the Bauradi stallion, carefully placing a heavy bundle over the pommel, then he had mounted and was riding through the streets, seeking the Meeting House where Anigh had told him it would be.

The city was unnaturally silent. Clearly some order had been given to uphold a curfew, for there was not even a city guard on the streets.

Elric rode at an easy canter along the wide Avenue of Military Success, along the Boulevard of Ancient Accomplishment and half-a-dozen other grandiosely named thoroughfares until he saw the long low building ahead of him which, in its simplicity, could only be the seat of Quarzhasaati power.

The albino paused. At his side the black runesword crooned a little, almost demanding a further letting of blood.

'You must be patient,' said Elric. 'Could be there will be no need for battle.'

He thought he saw shadows moving in the trees and shrubberies around the Meeting House but he paid them no attention. He did not care what they plotted or who spied on him. He had a mission to fulfil.

At last he had reached the doors of the building and was not surprised to find them standing open. He dismounted, threw the bundle over his shoulder and walked heavily into a large, plain room, without decoration or ostentation, in which were placed seven tall-backed chairs and a lime-washed oak table. Standing in a semi-circle at one end of the table were six robed figures wearing veils not unlike certain sects of the Sorcerer Adventurers. The seventh figure wore a tall, conical hat which completely covered the face. It was this figure who spoke. Elric was not unsurprised to hear a woman's tones.

'I am the Other,' she said. 'I believe you have brought us a treasure to add to the glory of Quarzhasaat.'

'If you believe this treasure to add to your glory then my journey has not been fruitless,' said Elric. He dropped the bundle to the ground. 'Did Manag Iss tell you all I asked him to tell you?'

One of the Councillors stirred and said, almost as an oath: 'That you are the progeny of sunken Melniboné, aye!'

'Melniboné is not sunken. Nor does she cut herself off from the world's realities quite as much as do you.' Elric was contemptuous. 'You challenged our power long ago, and defeated yourselves by your own folly. Now through your greed you have brought me back to Quarzhasaat when I would as readily have passed through your city unnoticed.'

'Do you accuse us!' A veiled woman was outraged. 'You who have caused us so much trouble? You, who are of the blood of that degenerate unhuman race which couples with beasts for its pleasure and produces – ' she pointed at Elric – 'the likes of you!'

Elric was unmoved. 'Did Manag Iss tell you to be wary of me?' he asked quietly.

'He said you had the Pearl and that you had a sorcerous sword. But he also said you were alone.' The Other cleared her throat. 'He said you brought the Pearl at the Heart of the World.'

'I have brought it and that which contains it,' said Elric. He bent down and tugged the velvet free of his bundle to reveal the corpse of Lord Gho Fhaazi, his face still contorted, the great lump in his throat making it seem as if he had an enormously enlarged adam's apple. 'Here is the one who first commissioned me to find the Pearl.'

305

'We heard you had murdered him,' said the Other with disapproval. 'But that would be a normal enough action for a Melnibonéan.'

Elric did not rise to this. 'The Pearl is in Lord Gho Fhaazi's gullet. Would you have me cut it out for you, my nobles?'

He saw at least one of them shudder and he smiled. 'You commission assassins to kill, to torture, to kidnap and to perform all other forms of evil in your name, but you would not see a little spilled blood? I gave Lord Gho a choice. He took this one. He talked so much and ate and drank so copiously I thought he might well have succeeded in getting the Pearl into his stomach. But he gagged a little and I fear that was the end of him.'

'You are a cruel rogue!' One of the men came forward to look at his would-be colleague. 'Aye, that's Gho. His colour has improved, I'd say.'

This jest did not meet with the leader's approval.

'We are to bid for a corpse, then?'

'Unless you wish to cut the Pearl free, aye.'

'Manag Iss,' said one of the veiled women, lifting her head. 'Step out, will you, sir?'

The Sorcerer Adventurer emerged from a door at the back of the hall. He looked at Elric almost apologetically. His hand went to his knife.

'We would not have a Melnibonéan spill more Quarzhasaati blood,' said the Other. 'Manag Iss will cut the Pearl free.'

The leader of the Yellow Sect drew a deep breath and then approached the corpse. Swiftly he did what he had been ordered to do. Blood poured down his arm as he held up the Pearl at the Heart of the World.

The Council was impressed. Several of the members gasped and they murmured amongst themselves. Elric believed they had suspected him of lying to them, since lies and intrigues were second nature to them.

'Hold it high, Manag Iss,' said the albino. 'It is this that you all desired so greedily that you were prepared to pay for it with what was left of your honour.'

'Be careful, sir!' cried the Other. 'We are patient with you now. Name your price and then begone.'

Elric laughed. It was not pleasant laughter. It was Melnibonéan laughter. At that moment he was a pure denizen of the Dragon Isle. 'Very well,' he said, 'I desire this city. Not its citizens, not any of its treasure, nor its animals nor even its water. I would let you leave with everything you can carry. I desire only the city itself. It is, you see, mine by hereditary right.'

'What? This is nonsense. How could we agree?'

'You must agree,' said Elric, 'or you must fight me.'

'Fight you? There is only one of you.'

'There is no question of it,' said another Councillor. 'He is mad. He must be put down like a crazed dog. Manag Iss, call in your brothers and their men.'

'I do not believe it is advisable, cousin,' said Manag Iss, clearly addressing Lady Iss. 'I think it would be wise to parley.'

'What? Have you turned coward? Has this rogue an army with him?'

Manag Iss rubbed at his nose. 'My lady . . . '

'Call in your brothers, Manag Iss!'

The captain of the Yellow Sect scratched at one silk-clad arm and he frowned. 'Prince Elric, I understand that you force us to a challenge. But we have not threatened you. The Council came here honestly to bid for the Pearl . . . '

'Manag Iss, you repeat their lies,' said Elric, 'and that is not an honourable thing to do. If they meant me no harm, why were you and all your brothers standing by? I saw almost two hundred warriors in the grounds.'

'That was a precaution only,' said the Other. She turned to her fellow councillors. 'I told you I thought it was stupid to summon so many so soon.'

Elric said evenly: 'Everything you have done, my nobles, has been stupid. You have been cruel, greedy, careless of others' lives and wills. You have been blind, thoughtless, provincial and unimaginative. It seems to me that a government so careless of anything but its own gratification should be at very least replaced. When you have all left the city I will consider electing a governor who will know better how to serve Quarzhasaat. Then, later perhaps, I will let you back into the city . . . '

'Oh, slay him!' cried the Other. 'Waste no more time on this. When that's done we can decide amongst ourselves who owns the Pearl.'

Elric sighed almost regretfully and said: 'Best parley with me now, madam, before I myself lose patience. I shall not, once I have drawn my blade, be a rational and merciful being . . . '

'Slay him!' she insisted. 'And have done with it!'

Manag Iss had the face of a man condemned to more than death. 'Madam . . . '

She strode forward, her conical hat swaying, and tugged the sword from his scabbard. She raised the blade to behead the albino.

He reached out swiftly. His arm was a striking snake. He gripped her wrist. 'No, madam! I am, I swear, giving you fair warning . . . '

Stormbringer murmured at his side and stirred.

She dropped the sword and turned away, nursing her bruised wrist.

Now Manag Iss reached for his fallen blade, making as if to sheathe it, and then, with a subtle movement, tried to bring the weapon up and take Elric in the groin, an expression of resignation crossing his terrified features as the albino, anticipating him, sidestepped and in the same action drew the Black Sword which began to sing its strange demonic song and glow with a terrible black radiance.

Manag Iss gasped as his heart was pierced. The hand that still held the Pearl seemed to stretch out, offering it back to Elric. Then the jewel had rolled from his fingers and rattled on the floor. Three Councillors rushed forward, saw Manag Iss's dying eyes, and stepped backward.

'Now! Now! Now!' cried the Other and, as Elric had expected, from every cranny of the Meeting House, members of the various sects of Sorcerer Adventurers came, their weapons at the ready.

And the albino began to grin his horrible battle-grin, and his red eyes blazed and his face was the skull of Death and his sword was the vengeance of his own people, the vengeance of the Bauradim and all those who had suffered under the injustice of Quarzhasaat over the millennia.

And he offered up the souls he took to his patron Duke of Hell, the powerful Duke Arioch who had grown sleek on many lives dedicated to him by Elric and his black blade.

'Arioch! Arioch! Blood and souls for my lord Arioch!'

Then the true slaughter began.

It was a slaughter to make all other events pale into insignificance. It was a slaughter that would never be forgotten in all the annals of the desert peoples, who would learn of it from those who fled Quarzhasaat that night – flinging themselves into the waterless desert rather than face the white laughing demon on a Bauradi horse who galloped up and down their lovely streets and taught them what the price of complacency and unthinking cruelty could be.

'Arioch! Arioch! Blood and souls!'

They would speak of a white-faced creature from Hell whose sword poured with unnatural radiance, whose crimson eyes blazed with hideous rage, who seemed possessed, himself, of some supernatural force, who was no more master of it than were his victims. He killed without mercy, without distinction, without cruelty. He killed as a mad wolf kills. And as he killed, he laughed.

That laughter would never leave Quarzhasaat. It would remain on the wind which came in from the Sighing Desert, in the music of the fountains, the clang of the metal-workers' and jewellers' hammers as they fashioned their wares. And so would the smell of blood remain, together with the memory of slaughter, that terrible loss of life which left the city without a Council and an army.

But never again would Quarzhasaat foster the legend of her own power. Never again would she treat the desert nomads as less than beasts. Never again would she know that self-destructive pride so familiar to all great empires in decline.

And when the slaughter was finished, Elric of Melniboné slumped in his saddle, sheathing a sated Stormbringer, and he gasped with the demon power which still pulsed through him and he took a great Pearl from his belt and held it to the rising sun.

'They have paid a fair price now, I think.'

He tossed the thing into a gutter where a little dog licked congealing blood.

Above, the vultures, called from a thousand miles around by the prospect of memorable feasting, were beginning to drop like a dark cloud upon the beautiful towers and gardens of Quarzhasaat.

Elric's face held no pride in his achievements as he spurred his horse for the West and the place on the road where he had told Anigh to await them with enough Kwani herbs, water, horses and food to cross the Sighing Desert and seek again the more familiar politics and sorceries of the Young Kingdoms.

He did not look back on the city which, in the name of his ancestors, had been conquered at last.

5

An Epilogue at the Waning of the Blood Moon

The celebrations at the Silver Flower Oasis had continued long after the news came of Elric's vengeance-taking on those who would have harmed the Holy Girl of the Bauradim. The news was brought by Quarzhasaatin, fleeing from the city in an action which had no precedent in all their long history.

Oone the Dreamthief, who had stayed at the Silver Flower Oasis longer than was necessary and who was yet reluctant to leave and go about her proper business, learned of Elric's vengeance without joy. The news saddened her, for she had hoped for something else to happen.

'He serves Chaos as I serve Law,' she said to herself. 'And who is to say which of us is the worse enslaved?' But she sighed and threw herself into the festivities with a force which was less than spontaneous.

The Bauradim and the other nomad clans did not notice, for their own pleasure was intensified. They were rid of a tyrant, of the only thing in the desert lands that they had ever feared.

'The cactus tears our flesh so that we shall be shown where water is,' said Raik Na Seem. 'Our troubles were great but thanks to you, Oone, and Elric of Melniboné, our troubles turned to triumphs. Soon some of us will visit Quarzhasaat and set out the terms on which we intend to trade in future. There will be a welcome equality about the transaction, I think.' He was greatly amused. 'But we will wait until the dead are decently eaten.'

Varadia took Oone's hand and they walked together beside the pools of the great oasis. The Blood Moon was waning and the silver petals of the flowers were shining brighter still. Soon the Blood Moon must wane and the flowers shed their petals and then it would be time for the people of the desert to go their different ways.

'You loved that white-faced man, did you not?' Varadia asked her friend.

'I hardly knew him, child.'

'I knew you both very well, not so long ago.' Varadia smiled. 'And I am growing rapidly, am I not? You said as much yourself.'

Oone was forced to agree. 'But there was no hope for it, Varadia. We have such different destinies. And I have scant sympathy for the choices he makes.'

'He is driven, that one. He has little in the way of ordinary volition.' She pushed a strand of honey-coloured hair away from her dark features.

'Perhaps,' said Oone. 'Yet some of us can refuse the destiny that the Lords of Law and Chaos set out for us and still survive, still create something which the gods are forbidden to touch.'

Varadia was sympathetic. 'What we create remains a mystery,' she said. 'It is still hard for me to understand how I made that Pearl, creating the very thing my enemies sought in order to escape them. And then it became real!'

'I have known this to happen,' said Oone. 'It is those creations that a dreamthief seeks and earns a living from.' She laughed. 'That Pearl would bring me a good wage for a long time if I took it to market.'

'How is it that reality is formed from dreams, Oone?'

Oone paused and looked down into the water which reflected the faint pink disc of the moon. 'An oyster, threatened by intrusion from without, seeks to isolate that threat by forming the thing around it that eventually becomes a pearl. Sometimes this is how it happens. At other times the will of humanity is so strong, the desire for something so intense, that they will bring into existence that which was thought until then to be impossible. It is not unusual, Varadia, for a dream to be made reality. This knowledge is one of the reasons why my respect for humanity is maintained, in spite of all the cruelties and injustices I witness in my travels.'

'I think I understand,' said the Holy Girl.

'Oh, you will understand all this very well in time,' Oone assured her. 'For you are one of those capable of such creation.'

A few days later Oone was ready to ride away from the Silver Flower Oasis, towards Elwher and the Unmapped East. Varadia spoke with her for the last time.

'I know you have a further secret,' she said to the dreamthief. 'Will you not share it with me?'

Oone was astonished. Her regard for the girl's sensitive intelligence increased. 'Do you want to talk more about the nature of dreams and reality?'

'I think you carry a child, Oone,' said Varadia directly. 'Is that not so?'

Oone folded her arms and leant against her horse. She shook her head in frank good humour. 'It is true that all the wisdom of your people is accumulated in you, young woman.'

'The child of one you have loved and who is lost to you?'

'Aye,' said Oone. 'A daughter, I think. Maybe even a brother and a sister, if the omens are properly interpreted. More than pearls can be conceived in dreams, Varadia.'

'And will the father ever know his offspring?' gently asked the Holy Girl.

Oone tried to speak and discovered that she could not. She looked away quickly towards distant Quarzhasaat. Then, after a few moments, she was able to force herself to answer.

'Never,' she said.

THE SAILOR ON THE
SEAS OF FATE

For Bill Butler, Mike and
Tony, and all at Unicorn
Books, Wales.

ONE
Sailing to the Future

1

In which the Prince of Ruins Embarks Upon a Mysterious Ship

It was as if the man stood in a vast cavern whose walls and roof were composed of gloomy, unstable colours which would occasionally break and admit rays of light from the moon. That these walls were mere clouds massed above mountains and ocean was hard to believe, for all that the moonlight pierced them, stained them and revealed the black and turbulent sea washing the shore on which the man now stood.

Distant thunder rolled; distant lightning flickered. A thin rain fell. And the clouds were never still. From dusky jet to deadly white they swirled slowly, like the cloaks of men and women engaged in a trance-like and formalistic minuet; the man standing on the shingle of the grim beach was reminded of giants dancing to the music of the far-away storm and felt as one must feel who walks unwittingly into a hall where the gods are at play. He turned his gaze from the clouds to the ocean.

The sea seemed weary. Great waves heaved themselves together with difficulty and collapsed as if in relief, gasping as they struck sharp rocks.

The man pulled his hood closer about his face and he looked over his leathern shoulder more than once as he trudged closer to the sea and let the surf spill upon the toes of his knee-length black boots. He tried to peer into the cavern formed by the clouds but could see only a short distance. There was no way of telling what lay on the other side of the ocean or, indeed, how far the water extended. He put his head on one side, listening carefully, but could hear nothing but the sounds of the sky and the sea. He sighed. For a moment a moonbeam touched him and from the white flesh of his face there glowed two crimson, tormented eyes; then darkness came back. Again the man turned, plainly fearing that the light had revealed him to some enemy. Making as little sound as possible, he headed towards the shelter of the rocks on his left.

Elric was tired. In the city of Ryfel in the land of Pikarayd he had naïvely sought acceptance by offering his services as a mercenary in the army of the governor of that place. For his foolishness he had been imprisoned as a Melnibonéan spy (it was obvious to the governor that Elric could be nothing else) and had but recently escaped with the aid of bribes and some minor sorcery.

The pursuit, however, had been almost immediate. Dogs of great cunning had been employed and the governor himself had led the hunt beyond the borders of Pikarayd and into the lonely, uninhabited shale valleys of a world locally called the Dead Hills, in which little grew or tried to live.

Up the steep sides of small mountains, whose slopes consisted of grey, crumbling slate, which made a clatter to be heard a mile or more away, the white-faced one had ridden. Along dales all but grassless and whose river-bottoms had seen no water for scores of years, through cave-tunnels bare of even a stalactite, over plateaus from which rose cairns of stones erected by a forgotten folk, he had sought to escape his pursuers, and soon it seemed to him that he had left the world he knew forever, that he had crossed a supernatural frontier and had arrived in one of those bleak places of which he had read in the legends of his people, where once Law and Chaos had fought each other to a stalemate, leaving their battleground empty of life and the possibility of life.

And at last he had ridden his horse so hard that its heart had burst and he had abandoned its corpse and continued on foot, panting to the sea, to this narrow beach, unable to go farther forward and fearing to return lest his enemies should be lying in wait for him.

He would give much for a boat now. It would not be long before the dogs discovered his scent and led their masters to the beach. He shrugged. Best to die here alone, perhaps, slaughtered by those who did not even know his name. His only regret would be that Cymoril would wonder why he had not returned at the end of the year.

He had no food and few of the drugs which had of late sustained his energy. Without renewed energy he could not contemplate working a sorcery which might conjure for him some means of crossing the sea and making, perhaps, for the Isle of the Purple Towns where the people were least unfriendly to Melnibonéans.

It had been only a month since he had left behind his court and his queen-to-be, letting Yyrkoon sit on the throne of Melniboné until his return. He had thought he might learn more of the human folk of the Young Kingdoms by mixing with them, but they had rejected him

318

either with outright hatred or wary and insincere humility. Nowhere had he found one willing to believe that a Melnibonéan (and they did not know he was the emperor) would willingly throw in his lot with the human beings who had once been in thrall to that cruel and ancient race. And now, as he stood beside a bleak sea feeling trapped and already defeated, he knew himself to be alone in a malevolent universe, bereft of friends and purpose, a useless, sickly anachronism, a fool brought low by his own insufficiencies of character, by his profound inability to believe wholly in the rightness or the wrongness of anything at all. He lacked faith in his race, in his birthright, in gods or men, and above all he lacked faith in himself.

His pace slackened; his hand fell upon the pommel of his black runesword Stormbringer, the blade which had so recently defeated its twin, Mournblade, in the fleshy chamber within a sunless world of Limbo. Stormbringer, seemingly half-sentient, was now his only companion, his only confidant, and it had become his neurotic habit to talk to the sword as another might talk to his horse or as a prisoner might share his thoughts with a cockroach in his cell.

'Well, Stormbringer, shall we walk into the sea and end it now?' His voice was dead, barely a whisper. 'At least we shall have the pleasure of thwarting those who follow us.'

He made a halfhearted movement toward the sea, but to his fatigued brain it seemed that the sword murmured, stirred against his hip, pulled back. The albino chuckled. 'You exist to live and to take lives. Do I exist, then, to die and bring both those I love and hate the mercy of death? Sometimes I think so. A sad pattern, if that should be the pattern. Yet there must be more to all this . . .'

He turned his back upon the sea, peering upward at the monstrous clouds forming and reforming above his head, letting the light rain fall upon his face, listening to the complex, melancholy music which the sea made as it washed over rocks and shingle and was carried this way and that by conflicting currents. The rain did little to refresh him. He had not slept at all for two nights and had slept hardly at all for several more. He must have ridden for almost a week before his horse collapsed.

At the base of a damp granite crag which rose nearly thirty feet above his head, he found a depression in the ground in which he could squat and be protected from the worst of the wind and the rain. Wrapping his heavy leather cloak tightly about him, he eased himself into the hole and was immediately asleep. Let them find him while he slept. He wanted no warning of his death.

Harsh, grey light struck his eyes as he stirred. He raised his neck,

319

holding back a groan at the stiffness of his muscles, and he opened his eyes. He blinked. It was morning – perhaps even later, for the sun was invisible – and a cold mist covered the beach. Through the mist the darker clouds could still be seen above, increasing the effect of his being inside a huge cavern. Muffled a little, the sea continued to splash and hiss, though it seemed calmer than it had on the previous night, and there were now no sounds of a storm. The air was very cold.

Elric began to stand up, leaning on his sword for support, listening carefully, but there was no sign that his enemies were close by. Doubtless they had given up the chase, perhaps after finding his dead horse.

He reached into his belt pouch and took from it a sliver of smoked bacon and a vial of yellowish liquid. He sipped from the vial, replaced the stopper, and returned the vial to his pouch as he chewed on the meat. He was thirsty. He trudged farther up the beach and found a pool of rainwater not too tainted with salt. He drank his fill, staring around him. The mist was fairly thick and if he moved too far from the beach he knew he would become immediately lost. Yet did that matter? He had nowhere to go. Those who had pursued him must have realized that. Without a horse he could not cross back to Pikarayd, the most easterly of the Young Kingdoms. Without a boat he could not venture onto that sea and try to steer a course back to the Isle of the Purple Towns. He recalled no map which showed an eastern sea and he had little idea of how far he had travelled from Pikarayd. He decided that his only hope of surviving was to go north, following the coast in the trust that sooner or later he would come upon a port or a fishing village where he might trade his few remaining belongings for a passage on a boat. Yet that hope was a small one, for his food and his drugs could hardly last more than a day or so.

He took a deep breath to steel himself for the march and then regretted it; the mist cut at his throat and his lungs like a thousand tiny knives. He coughed. He spat upon the shingle.

And he heard something, something other than the moody whisperings of the sea; a regular creaking sound, as of a man walking in stiff leather. His right hand went to his left hip and the sword which rested there. He turned about, peering in every direction for the source of the noise, but the mist distorted it. It could have come from anywhere.

Elric crept back to the rock where he had sheltered. He leaned against it so that no swordsman could take him unawares from behind. He waited.

The creaking came again, but other sounds were added. He heard a clanking; a splash; perhaps a voice, perhaps a footfall on timber; and he guessed that either he was experiencing a hallucination as a side effect of the drug he had just swallowed or he had heard a ship coming towards the beach and dropping its anchor.

He felt relieved and he was tempted to laugh at himself for assuming so readily that this coast must be uninhabited. He had thought that the bleak cliffs stretched for miles – perhaps hundreds of miles – in all directions. The assumption could easily have been the subjective result of his depression, his weariness. It occurred to him that he might as easily have discovered a land not shown on maps, yet with a sophisticated culture of its own: with sailing ships, for instance, and harbours for them. Yet still he did not reveal himself.

Instead he withdrew behind the rock, peering into the mist towards the sea. And at last he discerned a shadow which had not been there the previous night. A black, angular shadow which could only be a ship. He made out the suggestion of ropes, he heard men grunting, he heard the creak and the rasp of a yard as it travelled up a mast. The sail was being furled.

Elric waited at least an hour, expecting the crew of the ship to disembark. They could have no other reason for entering this treacherous bay. But a silence had descended, as if the whole ship slept.

Cautiously Elric emerged from behind the rock and walked down to the edge of the sea. Now he could see the ship a little more clearly. Red sunlight was behind it, thin and watery, diffused by the mist. It was a good-sized ship and fashioned throughout of the same dark wood. Its design was baroque and unfamiliar, with high decks fore and aft and no evidence of rowing ports. This was unusual in a ship either of Melnibonéan or Young Kingdoms design and it tended to prove his theory that he had stumbled upon a civilization for some reason cut off from the rest of the world, just as Elwher and the Unmapped Kingdoms were cut off by the vast stretches of the Sighing Desert and the Weeping Waste. He saw no movement aboard, heard none of the sounds one might usually expect to hear on a seagoing ship, even if the larger part of the crew was resting. The mist eddied and more of the red light poured through to illuminate the vessel, revealing the large wheels on both the foredeck and the reardeck, the slender mast with its furled sail, the complicated geometrical carvings of its rails and its figurehead, the great, curving prow which gave the ship its main impression of power and strength and made Elric think it must be a warship rather than a trading vessel. But who was there to fight in such waters as these?

He cast aside his wariness and cupped his hands about his mouth, calling out:

'Hail, the ship!'

The answering silence seemed to him to take on a peculiar hesitancy as if those on board heard him and wondered if they should answer.

'Hail, the ship!'

Then a figure appeared on the port rail and, leaning over, looked casually towards him. The figure had on armour as dark and as strange as the design of his ship; he had a helmet obscuring most of his face and the main feature that Elric could distinguish was a thick, golden beard and sharp blue eyes.

'Hail, the shore,' said the armoured man. His accent was unknown to Elric, his tone was as casual as his manner. Elric thought he smiled. 'What do you seek with us?'

'Aid,' said Elric. 'I am stranded here. My horse is dead. I am lost.'

'Lost? Aha!' The man's voice echoed in the mist. 'Lost. And you wish to come aboard?'

'I can pay a little. I can give my services in return for a passage, either to your next port of call or to some land close to the Young Kingdoms where maps are available so that I could make my own way thereafter . . . '

'Well,' said the other slowly, 'there's work for a swordsman.'

'I have a sword,' said Elric.

'I see it. A good, big battle-blade.'

'Then I can come aboard?'

'We must confer first. If you would be good enough to wait awhile . . . '

'Of course,' said Elric. He was nonplussed by the man's manner, but the prospect of warmth and food on board the ship was cheering. He waited patiently until the blond-bearded warrior came back to the rail.

'Your name, sir?' said the warrior.

'I am Elric of Melniboné.'

The warrior seemed to be consulting a parchment, running his finger down a list until he nodded, satisfied, and put the list into his large-buckled belt.

'Well,' he said, 'there was some point in waiting here, after all. I found it difficult to believe.'

'What was the dispute and why did you wait?'

'For you,' said the warrior, leaving a rope ladder over the side so that its end fell into the sea. 'Will you board now, Elric of Melniboné?'

2

The Blind Captain

Elric was surprised by how shallow the water was and he wondered by what means such a large vessel could come so close to the shore. Shoulder-deep in the sea he reached up to grasp the ebony rungs of the ladder. He had great difficulty heaving himself from the water and was further hampered by the swaying of the ship and the weight of his runesword, but eventually he had clambered awkwardly over the side and stood on the deck with the water running from his clothes to the timbers and his body shivering with cold. He looked about him. Shining, red-tinted mist clung about the ship's dark yards and rigging, white mist spread itself over the roofs and sides of the two large cabins set fore and aft of the mast, and this mist was not of the same character as the mist beyond the ship. Elric, for a moment, had the fanciful notion that the mist travelled permanently wherever the ship travelled. He smiled to himself, putting the dreamlike quality of his experience down to lack of food and sleep. When the ship sailed into sunnier waters he would see it for the relatively ordinary vessel it was.

The blond warrior took Elric's arm. The man was as tall as Elric and massively built. Within his helm he smiled, saying:

'Let us go below.'

They went to the cabin forward of the mast and the warrior drew back a sliding door, standing aside to let Elric enter first. Elric ducked his head and went into the warmth of the cabin. A lamp of red-grey glass gleamed, hanging from four silver chains attached to the roof, revealing several more bulky figures, fully dressed in a variety of armours, seated about a square and sturdy sea-table. All faces turned to regard Elric as he came in, followed by the blond warrior who said:

'This is he.'

One of the occupants of the cabin, who sat in the farthest corner and whose features were completely hidden by the shadow, nodded. 'Aye,' he said. 'That is he.'

'You know me, sir?' said Elric, seating himself at the end of the bench and removing his sodden leather cloak. The warrior nearest him passed him a metal cup of hot wine and Elric accepted it gratefully, sipping at the spiced liquid and marvelling at how quickly it dispersed the chill within him.

'In a sense,' said the man in the shadows. His voice was sardonic and at the same time had a melancholy ring, and Elric was not offended, for the bitterness in the voice seemed directed more at the owner than at any he addressed.

The blond warrior seated himself opposite Elric. 'I am Brut,' he said, 'once of Lashmar, where my family still holds land, but it is many a year since I have been there.'

'From the Young Kingdoms, then?' said Elric.

'Aye. Once.'

'This ship journeys nowhere near those nations?' Elric asked.

'I believe it does not,' said Brut. 'It is not so long, I think, since I myself came aboard. I was seeking Tanelorn, but found this craft, instead.'

'Tanelorn?' Elric smiled. 'How many must seek that mythical place? Do you know of one called Rackhir, once a warrior priest of Phum? We adventured together quite recently. He left to look for Tanelorn.'

'I do not know him,' said Brut of Lashmar.

'And these waters,' said Elric, 'do they lie far from the Young Kingdoms?'

'Very far,' said the man in the shadows.

'Are you from Elwher, perhaps?' asked Elric. 'Or from any other of what we in the west call the Unmapped Kingdoms?'

'Most of our lands are not on your maps,' said the man in the shadows. And he laughed. Again Elric found that he was not offended. And he was not particularly troubled by the mysteries hinted at by the man in the shadows. Soldiers of fortune, as he deemed these men to be, were fond of their private jokes and references; it was usually all that united them save a common willingness to hire their swords to whomever could pay.

Outside the anchor was rattling and the ship rolled. Elric heard the yard being lowered and he heard the smack of the sail as it was unfurled. He wondered how they hoped to leave the bay with so little wind available. He noticed that the faces of the other warriors, where their faces were visible, had taken on a rather set look as the ship began to move. He looked from one grim, haunted face to another and he wondered if his own features bore the same cast.

'For where do we sail?' he asked.

Brut shrugged. 'I know only that we had to stop to wait for you,

Elric of Melniboné.'

'You knew I would be there?'

The man in the shadows stirred and helped himself to more hot wine from the jug set into a hole in the centre of the table. 'You are the last one we need,' he said. 'I was the first taken aboard. So far I have not regretted my decision to make the voyage.'

'Your name, sir?' Elric decided he would no longer be at that particular disadvantage.

'Oh, names? Names? I have so many. The one I favour is Erekosë. But I have been called Urlik Skarsol and John Daker and Ilian of Garathorm to my certain knowledge. Some would have me believe that I have been Elric Womanslayer . . . '

'Womanslayer? An unpleasant nickname. Who is this other Elric?'

'That I cannot completely answer,' said Erekosë. 'But I share a name, it seems, with more than one aboard this ship. I, like Brut, sought Tanelorn and found myself here instead.'

'We have that in common,' said another. He was a black-skinned warrior, the tallest of the company, his features oddly enhanced by a scar running like an inverted V from his forehead and over both eyes, down his cheeks to his jawbones. 'I was in a land called Ghaja-Ki, a most unpleasant, swampy place, filled with perverse and diseased life. I had heard of a city said to exist there and I thought it might be Tanelorn. It was not. And it was inhabited by a blue-skinned, hermaphroditic race who determined to cure me of what they considered my malformations of hue and sexuality. This scar you see was their work. The pain of their operation gave me strength to escape them and I ran naked into the swamps, floundering for many a mile until the swamp became a lake feeding a broad river over which hung black clouds of insects which set upon me hungrily. This ship appeared and I was more than glad to seek its sanctuary. I am Otto Blendker, once a scholar of Brunse, now a hireling sword for my sins.'

'This Brunse? Does it lie near Elwher?' said Elric. He had never heard of such a place, nor such an outlandish name, in the Young Kingdoms.

The black man shook his head. 'I know naught of Elwher.'

'Then the world is a considerably larger place than I imagined,' said Elric.

'Indeed it is,' said Erekosë. 'What would you say if I offered you the theory that the sea on which we sail spans more than one world?'

'I would be inclined to believe you.' Elric smiled. 'I have studied such theories. More, I have experienced adventures in worlds other than my own.'

'It is a relief to hear it,' said Erekosë. 'Not all on board this ship are willing to accept my theory.'

'I come closer to accepting it,' said Otto Blendker, 'though I find it terrifying.'

'It is that,' agreed Erekosë. 'More terrifying than you can imagine, friend Otto.'

Elric leaned across the table and helped himself to a further mug of wine. His clothes were already drying and physically he had a sense of well-being. 'I'll be glad to leave this misty shore behind.'

'The shore has been left already,' said Brut, 'But as for the mist, it is ever with us. Mist appears to follow the ship – or else the ship creates the mist wherever it travels. It is rare that we see land at all and when we do see it, as we saw it today, it is usually obscured, like a reflection in a dull and buckled shield.'

'We sail on a supernatural sea,' said another, holding out a gloved hand for the jug. Elric passed it to him. 'In Hasghan, where I come from, we have a legend of a Bewitched Sea. If a mariner finds himself sailing in those waters he may never return and will be lost for eternity.'

'Your legend contains at least some truth, I fear, Terndrik of Hasghan,' Brut said.

'How many warriors are on board?' Elric asked.

'Sixteen other than the Four,' said Erekosë. 'Twenty in all. The crew numbers about ten and then there is the captain. You will see him soon, doubtless.'

'The Four? Who are they?'

Erekosë laughed. 'You and I are two of them. The other two occupy the aft cabin. And if you wish to know *why* we are called the Four, you must ask the captain, though I warn you his answers are rarely satisfying.'

Elric realized that he was being pressed slightly to one side. 'The ship makes good speed,' he said laconically, 'considering how poor the wind was.'

'Excellent speed,' agreed Erekosë. He rose from his corner, a broad-shouldered man with an ageless face bearing the evidence of considerable experience. He was handsome and he had plainly seen much conflict, for both his hands and his face were heavily scarred, though not disfigured. His eyes, though deep-set and dark, seemed of no particular colour and yet were familiar to Elric. He felt that he might have seen those eyes in a dream once.

'Have we met before?' Elric asked him.

'Oh, possibly – or shall meet. What does it matter? Our fates are the same. We share an identical doom. And possibly we share more than that.'

'More? I hardly comprehend the first part of your statement.'

'Then it is for the best,' said Erekosë, inching past his comrades and emerging on the other side of the table. He laid a surprisingly gentle hand on Elric's shoulder. 'Come, we must seek audience with the captain. He expressed a wish to see you shortly after you came aboard.'

Elric nodded and rose. 'This captain – what is his name?'

'He has none he will reveal to us,' said Erekosë. Together they emerged onto the deck. The mist was if anything thicker and of the same deathly whiteness, no longer tinted by the sun's rays. It was hard to see to the far ends of the ship and for all that they were evidently moving rapidly, there was no hint of a wind. Yet it was warmer than Elric might have expected. He followed Erekosë forward to the cabin set under the deck on which one of the ship's twin wheels stood, tended by a tall man in sea-coat and leggings of quilted deerskin who was so still as to resemble a statue. The red-haired steersman did not look around or down as they advanced towards the cabin, but Elric caught a glimpse of his face.

The door seemed built of some kind of smooth metal possessing a sheen almost like the healthy coat of an animal. It was reddish-brown and the most colourful thing Elric had so far seen on the ship. Erekosë knocked softly upon the door. 'Captain,' he said. 'Elric is here.'

'Enter,' said a voice at once melodious and distant.

The door opened. Rosy light flooded out, half-blinding Elric as he walked in. As his eyes adapted, he could see a very tall, pale-clad man standing upon a richly hued carpet in the middle of the cabin. Elric heard the door close and realized that Eeköse had not accompanied him inside.

'Are you refreshed, Elric?' said the captain.

'I am, sir, thanks to your wine.'

The captain's features were no more human than were Elric's. They were at once finer and more powerful than those of the Melnibonéan, yet bore a slight resemblance in that the eyes were inclined to taper, as did the face, toward the chin. The captain's long hair fell to his shoulders in red-gold waves and was kept back from his brow by a circlet of blue jade. His body was clad in buff-coloured tunic and hose and there were sandals of silver and silver-thread laced to his calves. Apart from his clothing, he was twin to the steersman Elric had recently seen.

'Will you have more wine?'

327

The captain moved towards a chest on the far side of the cabin, near the porthole, which was closed.

'Thank you,' said Elric. And now he realized why the eyes had not focused on him. The captain was blind. For all that his movements were deft and assured, it was obvious that he could not see at all. He poured the wine from a silver jug into a silver cup and began to cross towards Elric, holding the cup out before him. Elric stepped forward and accepted it.

'I am grateful for your decision to join us,' said the captain. 'I am much relieved, sir.'

'You are courteous,' said Elric, 'though I must add that my decision was not difficult to make. I had nowhere else to go.'

'I understand that. It is why we put into shore when and where we did. You will find that all your companions were in a similar position before they, too, came aboard.'

'You appear to have considerable knowledge of the movements of many men,' said Elric. He held the wine untasted in his left hand.

'Many,' agreed the captain, 'on many worlds. I understand that you are a person of culture, sir, so you will be aware of something of the nature of the sea upon which my ship sails.'

'I think so.'

'She sails between the worlds, for the most part – between the planes of a variety of aspects of the same world, to be a little more exact.' The captain hesitated, turning his blind face away from Elric. 'Please know that I do not deliberately mystify you. There are some things I do not understand and other things which I may not completely reveal. It is a trust I have and I hope you feel you can respect it.'

'I have no reason as yet to do otherwise,' replied the albino. And he took a sip of the wine.

'I find myself with a fine company,' said the captain. 'I hope that you continue to think it worthwhile honouring my trust when we reach our destination.'

'And what is that, Captain?'

'An island indigenous to these waters.'

'That must be a rarity.'

'Indeed, it is, and once undiscovered, uninhabited by those we must count our enemies. Now that they have found it and realize its power, we are in great danger.'

'We? You mean your race or those aboard your ship?'

The captain smiled. 'I have no race, save myself. I speak, I suppose, of all humanity.'

'These enemies are not human, then?'

'No. They are inextricably involved in human affairs, but this fact has not instilled in them any loyalty to us. I use "humanity", of course, in its broader sense, to include yourself and myself.'

'I understood,' said Elric. 'What is this folk called?'

'Many things,' said the captain. 'Forgive me, but I cannot continue longer now. If you will ready yourself for battle I assure you that I will reveal more to you as soon as the time is right.'

Only when Elric stood again outside the reddish-brown door, watching Erekosë advancing up the deck through the mist, did the albino wonder if the captain had charmed him to the point where he had forgotten all common sense. Yet the blind man had impressed him and he had, after all, nothing better to do than to sail on to the island. He shrugged. He could always alter his decision if he discovered that those upon the island were not, in his opinion, enemies.

'Are you more mystified or less, Elric?' said Erekosë, smiling.

'More mystified in some ways, less in others,' Elric told him. 'And, for some reason, I do not care.'

'Then you share the feeling of the whole company,' Erekosë told him.

It was only when Erekosë led him to the cabin aft of the mast that Elric realized he had not asked the captain what the significance of the Four might be.

3

Some Reference To The Three Who Are One

Save that it faced in the opposite direction, the other cabin resembled the first in almost every detail. Here, too, were seated some dozen men, all experienced soldiers of fortune by their features and their clothing. Two sat together at the centre of the table's starboard side. One was bareheaded, fair and careworn, the other had features resembling Elric's own and he seemed to be wearing a silver gauntlet on his left hand while the right hand was naked; his armour was delicate and outlandish. He looked up as Elric entered and there was recognition in his single eye (the other was covered by a brocade-work patch).

'Elric of Melniboné!' he exclaimed. 'My theories become more meaningful!' He turned to his companion. 'See, Hawkmoon, this is the one of whom I spoke.'

'You know me, sir?' Elric was nonplussed.

'You recognize me, Elric. You must! At the Tower of Voilodion Ghagnasdiak? With Erekosë – though a different Erekosë. I am Corum.'

'I know of no such tower, no name which resembles that, and this is the first I have seen of Erekosë. You know me and you know my name, but I do not know you. I find this disconcerting, sir.'

'I, too, had never met Prince Corum before he came aboard,' said Erekosë, 'yet he insists we fought together once. I am inclined to believe him. Time on the different planes does not always run concurrently. Prince Corum might well exist in what we would term the future.'

'I had thought to find some relief from such paradoxes here,' said Hawkmoon, passing his hand over his face. He smiled bleakly. 'But it seems there is none at this present moment in the history of the planes. Everything is in flux and even our identities, it seems, are prone to alter at any moment.'

'We were Three,' said Corum. 'Do you not recall it, Elric? The Three Who Are One?'

Elric shook his head.

Corum shrugged, saying softly to himself, 'Well, now we are Four. Did the captain say anything of an island we are supposed to invade?'

'He did,' said Elric. 'Do you know who these enemies might be?'

'We know no more or less than do you, Elric,' said Hawkmoon. 'I seek a place called Tanelorn and two children. Perhaps I seek the Runestaff, too. Of that I am not entirely sure.'

'We found it once,' said Corum. 'We three. In the Tower of Voilodion Ghagnasdiak. It was of considerable help to us.'

'As it might be to me,' Hawkmoon told him. 'I served it once. I gave it a great deal.'

'We have much in common,' Erekosë put in, 'as I told you, Elric. Perhaps we share masters in common, too?'

Elric shrugged. 'I serve no master but myself.'

And he wondered why they all smiled in the same strange way.

Erekosë said quietly, 'On such ventures as these one is inclined to forget much, as one forgets a dream.'

'This *is* a dream,' said Hawkmoon. 'Of late I've dreamed many such.'

'It is all dreaming, if you like,' said Corum. 'All existence.'

Elric was not interested in such philosophising. 'Dream or reality, the experience amounts to the same, does it not?'

'Quite right,' said Erekosë with a wan smile.

They talked on for another hour or two until Corum stretched and yawned and commented that he was feeling sleepy. The others agreed that they were all tired and so they left the cabin and went aft and below where there were bunks for all the warriors. As he stretched himself out in one of the bunks, Elric said to Brut of Lashmar, who had climbed into the bunk above:

'It would help to know when this fight begins.'

Brut looked over the edge, down at the prone albino. 'I think it will be soon,' he said.

Elric stood alone upon the deck, leaning upon the rail and trying to make out the sea, but the sea, like the rest of the world, was hidden by white curling mist. Elric wondered if there were waters flowing under the ship's keel at all. He looked up to where the sail was tight and swollen at the mast, filled with a warm and powerful wind. It was light, but again it was not possible to tell the hour of the day. Puzzled by Corum's comments concerning an earlier meeting, Elric wondered if there had been other dreams in his life such as this might be – dreams he had forgotten completely upon awakening. But the uselessness of such speculation became quickly evident and he turned his attention to more immediate matters, wondering at the origin of the captain and his strange ship sailing on a stranger ocean.

'The captain,' said Hawkmoon's voice, and Elric turned to bid good morning to the tall, fair-haired man who bore a strange, regular scar in the centre of his forehead, 'has requested that we four visit him in his cabin.'

The other two emerged from the mist and together they made their way to the prow, knocking on the reddish-brown door and being at once admitted into the presence of the blind captain, who had four silver wine-cups already poured for them. He gestured them towards the great chest on which the wine stood. 'Please help yourselves, my friends.'

They did so, standing there with the cups in their hands, four tall, doom-haunted swordsmen, each of a strikingly different cast of features, yet each bearing a certain stamp which marked them as being of a like kind. Elric noticed it, for all that he was one of them, and he tried to recall the details of what Corum had told him on the previous evening.

'We are nearing our destination,' said the captain. 'It will not be long before we disembark. I do not believe our enemies expect us, yet it will be a hard fight against those two.'

'Two?' said Hawkmoon. 'Only two?'

'Only two.' The captain smiled. 'A brother and a sister. Sorcerers from quite another universe than ours. Due to recent disruptions in the fabric of our worlds – of which you know something, Hawkmoon, and you, too, Corum – certain beings have been released who would not otherwise have the power they now possess. And possessing great power, they crave for more – for all the power that there is in our universe. These beings are amoral in a way in which the Lords of Law or Chaos are not. They do not fight for influence upon the earth, as those gods do; their only wish is to convert the essential energy of our universe to their own uses. I believe they foster some ambition in their particular universe which would be furthered if they could achieve their wish. At present, in spite of conditions highly favourable to them, they have not attained their full strength, but the time is not far off before they do attain it. Agak and Gagak is how they are called in human tongue and they are outside the power of any of our gods, so a more powerful group has been summoned – yourselves. The Champion Eternal in four of his incarnations (and four is the maximum number we can risk without precipitating further un-welcome disruptions among the planes of Earth) – Erekosë, Elric,

Corum, and Hawkmoon. Each of you will command four others, whose fates are linked with your own and who are great fighters in their own right, though they do not share your destinies in every sense. You may each pick the four with whom you wish to fight. I think you will find it easy enough to decide. We make landfall quite shortly now.'

'You will lead us?' Hawkmoon said.

'I cannot. I can only take you to the island and wait for those who survive – if any survive.'

Elric frowned. 'This fight is not mine, I think.'

'It is yours,' said the captain soberly. 'And it is mine. I would land with you if that were permitted me, but it is not.'

'Why so?' asked Corum.

'You will learn that one day. I have not the courage to tell you. I bear you nothing but goodwill, however. Be assured of that.'

Erekosë rubbed his jaw. 'Well, since it is my destiny to fight, and since I, like Hawkmoon, continue to seek Tanelorn, and since I gather there is some chance of my fulfilling my ambition if I am successful, I for one agree to go against these two, Agak and Gagak.'

Hawkmoon nodded. 'I go with Erekosë, for similar reasons.'

'And I,' said Corum.

'Not long since,' said Elric, 'I counted myself without comrades. Now I have many. For that reason alone I will fight with them.'

'It is perhaps the best of reasons,' said Erekosë approvingly.

'There is no reward for this work, save my assurance that your success will save the world much misery,' said the captain. 'And for you, Elric, there is less reward than the rest may hope for.'

'Perhaps not,' said Elric.

'As you say.' The captain gestured towards the jug of wine. 'More wine, my friends?'

They each accepted, while the captain continued, his blind face staring upward at the roof of the cabin.

'Upon this island is a ruin – perhaps it was once a city called Tanelorn – and at the centre of the ruin stands one whole building. It is this building which Agak and his sister use. It is that which you must attack. You will recognize it, I hope, at once.'

'And we must slay this pair?' said Erekosë.

'If you can. They have servants who help them. These must be slain, also. Then the building must be fired. This is important.' The captain paused. 'Fired. It must be destroyed in no other way.'

Elric smiled a dry smile. 'There are few other ways of destroying buildings, Sir Captain.'

The captain returned his smile and made a slight bow of

acknowledgment. 'Aye, it's so. Nonetheless, it is worth remembering what I have said.'

'Do you know what these two look like, these Agak and Gagak?' Corum asked.

'No. It is possible that they resemble creatures of our own worlds; it is possible that they do not. Few have seen them. It is only recently that they have been able to materialize at all.'

'And how may they best be overwhelmed?' asked Hawkmoon.

'By courage and ingenuity,' said the captain.

'You are not very explicit, sir,' said Elric.

'I am as explicit as I can be. Now, my friends, I suggest you rest and prepare your arms.'

As they returned to their cabins, Erekosë sighed.

'We are fated,' he said. 'We have little free will, for all we deceive ourselves otherwise. If we perish or live through this venture, it will not count for much in the overall scheme of things.'

'I think you are of a gloomy turn of mind, friend,' said Hawkmoon.

The mist snaked through the branches of the mast, writhing in the rigging, flooding the deck. It swirled across the faces of the other three men as Elric looked at them.

'A realistic turn of mind,' said Corum.

The mist massed more thickly upon the deck, mantling each man like a shroud. The timbers of the ship creaked and to Elric's ears took on the sound of a raven's croak. It was colder now. In silence they went to their cabins to test the hooks and buckles of their armour, to polish and to sharpen their weapons and to pretend to sleep.

'Oh, I've no liking for sorcery,' said Brut of Lashmar, tugging at his golden beard, 'for sorcery it was resulted in my shame.' Elric had told him all that the captain had said and had asked Brut to be one of the four who fought with him when they landed.

'It is all sorcery here,' Otto Blendker said. And he smiled wanly as he gave Elric his hand. 'I'll fight beside you, Elric.'

His sea-green armour shimmering faintly in the lantern light, another rose, his casque pushed back from his face. It was a face almost as white as Elric's, though the eyes were deep and near-black. 'And I,' said Hown Serpent-tamer, 'though I fear I'm little use on still land.'

The last to rise, at Elric's glance, was a warrior who had said little during their earlier conversations. His voice was deep and hesitant. He wore a plain iron battle-cap and the red hair beneath it was braided. At the end of each braid was a small fingerbone which rattled on the shoulders of his byrnie as he moved. This was Ashnar the Lynx, whose eyes were rarely less than fierce. 'I lack the eloquence or the breeding of you other gentlemen,' said Ashnar. 'And I've no familiarity with sorcery or those other things of which you speak, but I'm a good soldier and my joy is in fighting. I'll take your orders, Elric, if you'll have me.'

'Willingly,' said Elric.

'There is no dispute, it seems,' said Erekosë to the remaining four who had elected to join him. 'All this is doubtless preordained. Our destinies have been linked from the first.'

'Such philosophy can lead to unhealthy fatalism,' said Terndrik of Hasghan. 'Best believe our fates are our own, even if the evidence denies it.'

'You must think as you wish,' said Erekosë. 'I have led many lives, though all, save one, are remembered but faintly.' He shrugged. 'Yet I deceive myself, I suppose, in that I work for a time when I shall find this Tanelorn and perhaps be reunited with the one I seek. That ambition is what gives me energy, Terndrik.'

Elric smiled. 'I fight, I think, because I relish the comradeship of battle. That, in itself, is a melancholy condition in which to find oneself, is it not?'

'Aye.' Erekosë glanced at the floor. 'Well, we must try to rest now.'

4

Of Pain, Violence
and Loss

The outlines of the coast were dim. They waded through white water and white mist, their swords held above their heads. Swords were their only weapons. Each of the Four possessed a blade of unusual size and design, but none bore a sword which occasionally murmured to itself as did Elric's Stormbringer. Glancing back, Elric saw the captain standing at the rail, his blind face turned towards the island, his pale lips moving as if he spoke to himself. Now the water was waist-deep and the sand beneath Elric's feet hardened and became smooth rock. He waded on, wary and ready to carry any attack to those who might be defending the island. But now the mist grew thinner, as if it could gain no hold on the land, and there were no obvious signs of defenders.

Tucked into his belt, each man had a brand, its end wrapped in oiled cloth so that it should not be wet when the time came to light it. Similarly, each was equipped with a handful of smouldering tinder in a little firebox in a pouch attached to his belt, so that the brands could be instantly ignited.

'Only fire will destroy this enemy forever,' the captain had said again as he handed them their brands and their tinderboxes.

As the mist cleared, it revealed a landscape of dense shadows. The shadows spread over red rock and yellow vegetation and they were shadows of all shapes and dimensions, resembling all manner of things. They seemed cast by the huge blood-coloured sun which stood at perpetual noon above the island, but what was disturbing about them was that the shadows themselves seemed without a source, as if the objects they represented were invisible or existed elsewhere than on the island itself. The sky, too, seemed full of these shadows, but whereas those on the island were still, those in the sky sometimes moved, perhaps when the clouds moved. And all the while the red sun poured down its bloody light and touched the twenty men with its unwelcome radiance just as it touched the land.

And at times, as they advanced cautiously inland, a peculiar

336

flickering light sometimes crossed the island so that the outlines of the place became unsteady for a few seconds before returning to focus. Elric suspected his eyes and said nothing until Hown Serpent-tamer, who was having difficulty finding his land-legs, remarked:

'I have rarely been ashore, it's true, but I think the quality of this land is stranger than any other I've known. It shimmers. It distorts.'

Several voices agreed with him.

'And from whence come all these shadows?' Ashnar the Lynx stared around him in unashamed superstitious awe. 'Why cannot we see that which casts them?'

'It could be,' Corum said, 'that these are shadows cast by objects existing in other dimensions of the Earth. If all dimensions meet here, as has been suggested, that could be a likely explanation.' He put his silver hand to his embroidered eye-patch. 'This is not the strangest example I have witnessed of such a conjunction.'

'Likely?' Otto Blendker snorted. 'Pray let none give me an *unlikely* explanation, if you please!'

They pressed on through the shadows and the lurid light until they arrived at the outskirts of the ruins.

These ruins, thought Elric, had something in common with the ramshackle city of Ameeron, which he had visited on his quest for the Black Sword. But they were altogether more vast – more a collecton of smaller cities, each one in a radically different architectural style.

'Perhaps this is Tanelorn,' said Corum, who had visited the place, 'or, rather, all the versions of Tanelorn there have ever been. For Tanelorn exists in many forms, each form depending upon the wishes of those who most desire to find her.'

'This is not the Tanelorn I expected to find,' said Hawkmoon bitterly.

'Nor I,' added Erekosë bleakly.

'Perhaps it is not Tanelorn,' said Elric. 'Perhaps it is not.'

'Or perhaps this is a graveyard,' said Corum distantly, frowning with his single eye. 'A graveyard containing all the forgotten versions of that strange city.'

They began to clamber over the ruins, their arms clattering as they moved, heading for the centre of the place. Elric could tell by the introspective expressions in the faces of many of his companions that they, like him, were wondering if this were not a dream. Why else should they find themselves in this peculiar situation, unquestioningly risking their lives – perhaps their souls – in a fight with which none of them was identified?

Erekosë moved closer to Elric as they marched. 'Have you noticed,' said he, 'that the shadows now represent something?'

Elric nodded. 'You can tell from the ruins what some of the buildings looked like when they were whole. The shadows are the shadows of those buildings – the original buildings before they became ruined.'

'Just so,' said Erekosë. Together, they shuddered.

At last they approached the likely centre of the place and here was a building which was not ruined. It stood in a cleared space, all curves and ribbons of metal and glowing tubes.

'It resembles a machine more than a building,' said Hawkmoon.

'And a musical instrument more than a machine,' Corum mused.

The party came to a halt, each group of four gathering about its leader. There was no question but that they had arrived at their goal.

Now that Elric looked carefully at the building he could see that it was in fact two buildings – both absolutely identical and joined at various points by curling systems of pipes which might be connecting corridors, though it was difficult to imagine what manner of being could utilize them.

'Two buildings,' said Erekosë. 'We were not prepared for this. Shall we split up and attack both?'

Instinctively Elric felt that this action would be unwise. He shook his head. 'I think we should go together into one, else our strength will be weakened.'

'I agree,' said Hawkmoon, and the rest nodded.

Thus, there being no cover to speak of, they marched boldly towards the nearest building to a point near the ground where a black opening of irregular proportions could be discerned. Ominously, there was still no sign of defenders. The buildings pulsed and glowed and occasionally whispered, but that was all.

Elric and his party were the first to enter, finding themselves in a damp, warm passage which curved almost immediately to the right. They were followed by the others until all stood in this passage warily glaring ahead, expecting to be attacked. But no attack came.

With Elric at their head, they moved on for some moments before the passage began to tremble violently and sent Hown Serpent-tamer crashing to the floor cursing. As the man in the sea-green armour scrambled up, a voice began to echo along the passage, seemingly coming from a great distance yet nonetheless loud and irritable.

'*Who? Who? Who?*' shrieked the voice.

'*Who? Who? Who invades me?*'

The passage's tremble subsided a little into a constant quivering motion. The voice became a muttering, detached and uncertain.

'*What attacks? What?*'

The twenty men glanced at one another in puzzlement. At length Elric shrugged and led the party on and soon the passage had widened out into a hall whose walls, roof, and floor were damp with sticky fluid and whose air was hard to breathe. And now, somehow passing themselves through the walls of this hall, came the first of the defenders, ugly beasts who must be the servants of that mysterious brother and sister Agak and Gagak.

'*Attack!*' cried the distant voice. '*Destroy this. Destroy it!*'

The beasts were of a primitive sort, mostly gaping mouth and slithering body, but there were many of them oozing towards the twenty men, who quickly formed themselves into the four fighting units and prepared to defend themselves. The creatures made a dreadful slushing sound as they approached and the ridges of bone which served them as teeth clashed as they reared up to snap at Elric and his companions. Elric whirled his sword and it met hardly any resistance as it sliced through several of the things at once. But now the air was thicker than ever and a stench threatened to overwhelm them as fluid drenched the floor.

'Move on through them,' Elric instructed, 'hacking a path through as you go. Head for yonder opening.' He pointed with his left hand.

And so they advanced, cutting back hundreds of the primitive beasts and thus decreasing the breathability of the air.

'The creatures are not hard to fight,' gasped Hown Serpent-tamer, 'But each one we kill robs us a little of our own chances of life.'

Elric was aware of the irony. 'Cunningly planned by our enemies, no doubt.' He coughed and slashed again at a dozen of the beasts slithering towards him. The things were fearless, but they were stupid, too. They made no attempt at strategy.

Finally Elric reached the next passage, where the air was slightly purer. He sucked gratefully at the sweeter atmosphere and waved his companions on.

Sword-arms rising and falling, they gradually retreated back into the passage, followed by only a few of the beasts. The creatures seemed reluctant to enter the passage and Elric suspected that somewhere within it there must lie a danger which even they feared. There was nothing for it, however, but to press on and he was only grateful that all twenty had survived this initial ordeal.

Gasping, they rested for a moment, leaning against the trembling walls of the passage, listening to the tones of that distant voice, now muffled and indistinct.

'I like not this castle at all,' growled Brut of Lashmar, inspecting a rent in his cloak where a creature had seized it. 'High sorcery commands it.'

'It is only what we knew,' Ashnar the Lynx reminded him, and Ashnar was plainly hard put to control his terror. The fingerbones in his braids kept time with the trembling of the walls and the huge barbarian looked almost pathetic as he steeled himself to go on.

'They are cowards, these sorcerers,' Otto Blendker said. 'They do not show themselves.' He raised his voice. 'Is their aspect so loathsome that they are afraid lest we look upon them?' It was a challenge not taken up. As they pushed on through the passages there was no sign either of Agak or his sister Gagak. It became gloomier and brighter in turns. Sometimes the passages narrowed so that it was difficult to squeeze their bodies through, sometimes they widened into what were almost halls. Most of the time they appeared to be climbing higher into the building.

Elric tried to guess the nature of the building's inhabitants. There were no steps in the castle, no artifacts he could recognize. For no particular reason he developed an image of Agak and Gagak as reptilian in form, for reptiles would prefer gently rising passages to steps and doubtless would have little need of conventional furniture. There again it was possible that they could change their shape at will, assuming human form when it suited them. He was becoming impatient to face either one or both of the sorcerers.

Ashnar the Lynx had other reasons – or so he said – for his own lack of patience.

'They said there'd be treasure here,' he muttered. 'I thought to stake my life against a fair reward, but there's naught here of value.' He put a horny hand against the damp material of the wall. 'Not even stone or brick. What are these walls made of, Elric?'

Elric shook his head. 'That has puzzled me, also, Ashnar.'

Then Elric saw large, fierce eyes peering out of the gloom ahead. He heard a rattling noise, a rushing noise, and the eyes grew larger and larger. He saw a red mouth, yellow fangs, orange fur. Then the growling sounded and the beast sprang at him even as he raised Stormbringer to defend himself and shouted a warning to the others. The creature was a baboon, but huge, and there were at least a dozen others following the first. Elric drove his body forward behind his sword, taking the beast in its groin. Claws reached out and dug into his shoulder and waist. He groaned as he felt at least one set of claws draw blood. His arms were trapped and he could not pull Stormbringer free. All he could do was twist the sword in the wound he had already made. With all his might, he turned the hilt. The great ape shouted, its bloodshot eyes blazing, and it bared its yellow fangs as its muzzle shot towards Elric's throat. The teeth closed on his neck, the stinking breath threatened to choke him. Again he twisted the blade. Again the beast yelled in pain.

The fangs were pressing into the metal of Elric's gorget, the only thing saving him from immediate death. He struggled to free at least one arm, twisting the sword for the third time, then tugging it sideways to widen the wound in the groin. The growls and groans of the baboon grew more intense and the teeth tightened their hold on his neck, but now, mingled with the noises of the ape, he began to hear a murmuring and he felt Stormbringer pulse in his hand. He knew that the sword was drawing power from the ape even as the ape sought to destroy him. Some of that power began to flow into his body.

Desperately Elric put all his remaining strength into dragging the sword across the ape's body, slitting its belly wide so that its blood and entrails spilled over him as he was suddenly free and staggering backwards, wrenching the sword out in the same movement. The ape, too, was staggering back, staring down in stupefied awe at its own horrible wound before it fell to the floor of the passage.

Elric turned, ready to give aid to his nearest comrade, and he was in time to see Terndrik of Hasghan die, kicking in the clutches of an even larger ape, his head bitten clean from his shoulders and his red blood gouting.

Elric drove Stormbringer cleanly between the shoulders of Terndrik's slayer, taking the ape in the heart. Beast and human victim fell together. Two others were dead and several bore bad wounds, but the remaining warriors fought on, swords and armour smeared with crimson. The narrow passage stank of ape, of sweat, and of blood. Elric pressed into the fight, chopping at the skull of an ape which grappled with Hown Serpent-tamer, who had lost his sword. Hown darted a look of thanks at Elric as he bent to retrieve his blade and together they set upon the largest of all the baboons. This creature stood much taller than Elric and had Erekosë pressed against the wall, Erekosë's sword through its shoulder.

From two sides, Hown and Elric stabbed and the baboon snarled and screamed, turning to face the new attackers, Erekosë's blade quivering in its shoulder. It rushed upon them and they stabbed again together, taking the monster in its heart and its lung so that when it roared at them blood vomited from its mouth. It fell to its knees, its eyes dimming, then sank slowly down.

And now there was silence in the passage and death lay all about them.

Terndrik of Hasghan was dead. Two of Corum's party were dead. All of Erekosë's surviving men bore major wounds. One of Hawkmoon's men was dead, but the remaining three were virtually unscathed. Brut of Lashmar's helm was dented, but he was otherwise unwounded and Ashnar the Lynx was dishevelled, nothing more. Ashnar had taken two of the baboons during the fight. But now the barbarian's eyes rolled as he leaned, panting, against the wall.

'I begin to suspect this venture of being uneconomical,' he said with a half-grin. He rallied himself, stepping over a baboon's corpse to join Elric. 'The less time we take over it, the better. What think you, Elric?'

'I would agree.' Elric returned his grin. 'Come.' And he led the way through the passage and into a chamber whose walls gave off a pinkish light. He had not walked far before he felt something catch at his ankle and he stared down in horror to see a long, thin snake winding itself about his leg. It was too late to use his sword; instead he seized the reptile behind its head and dragged it partially free of his leg before hacking the head from the body. The others were now stamping and shouting warnings to each other. The snakes did not appear to be venomous, but there were thousands of them, appearing, it seemed, from out of the floor itself. They were flesh-coloured and had no eyes, more closely resembling earthworms than ordinary reptiles, but they were strong enough.

Hown Serpent-tamer sang a strange song now, with many liquid, hissing notes, and this seemed to have a calming effect upon the creatures. One by one at first and then in increasing numbers, they dropped back to the floor, apparently sleeping. Hown grinned at his success.

Elric said, 'Now I understand how you came by your surname.'

'I was not sure the song would work on these,' Hown told him, 'for they are unlike any serpents I have ever seen in the seas of my own world.'

They waded on through mounds of sleeping serpents, noticing that the next passage rose sharply. At times they were forced to use their hands to steady themselves as they climbed the peculiar, slippery material of the floor.

It was much hotter in this passage and they were all sweating, pausing several times to rest and mop their brows. The passage seemed to extend upwards forever, turning occasionally, but never levelling out for more than a few feet. At times it narrowed to little more than a tube through which they had to squirm on their stomachs and at other times the roof disappeared into the gloom over their heads. Elric had long since given up trying to relate their position to what he had seen of the outside of the castle. From time to time small, shapeless creatures rushed towards them in shoals apparently with the intention of attacking them, but these were rarely more than an irritation and were soon all but ignored by the party as it continued its climb.

For a while they had not heard the strange voice which had greeted them upon their entering, but now it began to whisper again, its tones more urgent than before.

'Where? Where? Oh, the pain!'

They paused, trying to locate the source of the voice, but it seemed to come from everywhere at once.

Grim-faced, they continued, plagued by thousands of little creatures which bit at their exposed flesh like so many gnats, yet the creatures were not insects. Elric had seen nothing like them before. They were shapeless, primitive, and all but colourless. They battered at his face as he moved; they were like a wind. Half-blinded, choked, sweating, he felt his strength leaving him. The air was so thick now, so hot, so salty, it was as if he moved through liquid. The others were as badly affected as was he; some were staggering and two men fell, to be helped up again by comrades almost as exhausted. Elric was tempted to strip off his armour, but he knew this would leave more of his flesh to the mercy of the little flying creatures.

Still they climbed and now more of the serpentine things they had seen earlier began to writhe around their feet, hampering them further, for all that Hown sang his sleeping song until he was hoarse.

'We can survive this only a little longer,' said Ashnar the Lynx, moving close to Elric. 'We shall be in no condition to meet the sorcerer if we ever find him or his sister.'

Elric nodded a gloomy head. 'My thoughts, too, yet what else may we do, Ashnar?'

'Nothing,' said Ashnar in a low voice. 'Nothing.'

'Where? Where? Where?' The word rustled all about them. Many of the party were becoming openly nervous.

5

The Meaning of
Shadows

They had reached the top of the passage. The querulous voice was much louder now, but it quavered more. They saw an archway and beyond the archway a lighted chamber.

'Agak's room, without doubt,' said Ashnar, taking a better grip on his sword.

'Possibly,' said Elric. He felt detached from his body. Perhaps it was the heat and the exhaustion, or his growing sense of disquiet, but something made him withdraw into himself and hesitate before entering the chamber.

The place was octagonal and each of its eight sloping sides was of a different colour and each colour changed constantly. Occasionally the walls became semitransparent, revealing a complete view of the ruined city (or collection of cities) far below, and also a view of the twin castle to this one, still connected by tubes and wires.

It was the large pool in the centre of the chamber which attracted most of their attention. It seemed deep and was full of evil-smelling, viscous stuff. It bubbled. Shapes formed in it. Grotesque and strange, beautiful and familiar, the shapes seemed always upon the brink of taking permanent form before falling back into the stuff of the pool. And the voice was still louder and there was no question now that it came from the pool.

'What? What? Who invades?'

Elric forced himself closer to the pool and for a moment saw his own face staring out at him before it melted.

'Who invades? Ah! I am too weak!'

Elric spoke to the pool. 'We are of those you would destroy,' he said. 'We are those on whom you would feed.'

'Ah! Agak! Agak! I am sick! Where are you?'

Ashnar and Brut joined Elric. The faces of the warriors were filled with disgust.

'Agak,' growled Ashnar the Lynx, his eyes narrowing. 'At last some sign that the sorcerer is here!'

The others had all crowded in, to stand as far away from the pool as possible, but all stared, fascinated by the variety of the shapes forming and disintegrating in the viscous liquid.

'I weaken . . . My energy needs to be replenished. . . . We must begin now, Agak . . . It took us so long to reach this place. I thought I could rest. But there is disease here. It fills my body. Agak. Awaken, Agak. Awaken!'

'Some servant of Agak's, charged with the defence of the chamber?' suggested Hown Serpent-tamer in a small voice.

But Elric continued to stare into the pool as he began, he thought, to realize the truth.

'Will Agak wake?' Brut said. 'Will he come?' He glanced nervously around him.

'Agak!' called Ashnar the Lynx. 'Coward!'

'Agak!' cried many of the other warriors, brandishing their swords.

But Elric said nothing and he noted, too, that Hawkmoon and Corum and Erekosë all remained silent. He guessed that they must be filled with the same dawning understanding.

He looked at them. In Erekosë's eyes he saw an agony, a pity both for himself and his comrades.

'We are the Four Who Are One,' said Erekosë. His voice shook.

Elric was seized by an alien impulse, an impulse which disgusted and terrified him. 'No . . . ' He attempted to sheathe Stormbringer, but the sword refused to enter its scabbard.

'Agak! Quickly!' said the voice from the pool.

'If we do not do this thing,' said Erekosë, 'they will eat all our worlds. Nothing will remain.'

Elric put his free hand to his head. He swayed upon the edge of that frightful pool. He moaned.

'We must do it, then.' Corum's voice was an echo.

'I will not,' said Elric. 'I am myself.'

'And I!' said Hawkmoon.

But Corum Jhaelen Irsei said, 'It is the only way for us, for the single thing that we are. Do you not see that? We are the only creatures of our worlds who possess the means of slaying the sorcerers – in the only manner in which they can be slain!'

Elric looked at Corum, at Hawkmoon, at Erekosë, and again he saw something of himself in all of them.

'We are the Four Who Are One,' said Erekosë. 'Our united strength is greater than the sum. We must come together, brothers. We must conquer here before we can hope to conquer Agak.'

'No . . . ' Elric moved away, but somehow he found himself standing at a corner of the bubbling, noxious pool from which the voice still murmured and complained, in which shapes still formed, reformed, and faded. And at each of the other three corners stood one of his companions. All had a set, fatalistic look to them.

The warriors who had accompanied the four drew back to the walls. Otto Blendker and Brut of Lashmar stood near the doorway, listening for anything which might come up the passage to the chamber. Ashnar the Lynx fingered the brand at his belt, a look of pure horror on his rugged features.

Elric felt his arm begin to rise, drawn upward by his sword, and he saw that each of his three companions were also lifting their swords. The swords reached out across the pool and their tips met above the exact centre.

Elric yelled as something entered his being. Again he tried to break free, but the power was too strong. Other voices spoke in his head.

'I understand . . . ' This was Corum's distant murmur. 'It is the only way.'

'Oh, no, no . . . ' And this was Hawkmoon, but the words came from Elric's lips.

'Agak!' cried the pool. The stuff became more agitated, more alarmed. 'Agak! Quickly! Wake!'

Elric's body began to shake, but his hand kept a firm hold upon the sword. The atoms of his body flew apart and then united again into a single flowing entity which travelled up the blade of the sword towards the apex. And Elric was still Elric, shouting with the terror of it, sighing with the ecstasy of it.

Elric was still Elric when he drew away from the pool and looked upon himself for a single moment, seeing himself wholly joined with his three other selves.

A being hovered over the pool. On each side of its head was a face and each face belonged to one of the companions. Serene and terrible, the eyes did not blink. It had eight arms and the arms were still; it squatted over the pool on eight legs, and its armour and accoutrements were of all colours blending and at the same time separate.

The being clutched a single great sword in all eight hands and both he and the sword glowed with a ghastly golden light.

Then Elric had rejoined this body and had become a different thing – himself and three others and something else which was the sum of that union.

The Four Who Were One reversed its monstrous sword so that the point was directed downward at the frenetically boiling stuff in the pool below. The stuff feared the sword. It mewled.

'Agak, Agak . . . '

The being of whom Elric was a part gathered its great strength and began to plunge the sword down.

Shapeless waves appeared on the surface of the pool. Its whole colour changed from sickly yellow to an unhealthy green. 'Agak, I die . . . '

Inexorably the sword moved down. It touched the surface.

The pool swept back and forth; it tried to ooze over the sides and onto the floor. The sword bit deeper and the Four Who Were One felt new strength flow up the blade. There came a moan; slowly the pool quieted. It became silent. It became still. It became grey.

Then the Four Who Were One descended into the pool to be absorbed.

It could see clearly now. It tested its body. It controlled every limb, every function. It had triumphed; it had revitalized the pool. Through its single octagonal eye it looked in all directions at the same time over the wide ruins of the city; then it focused all its attention upon its twin.

Agak had awakened too late, but he was awakening at last, roused by the dying cries of his sister Gagak, whose body the mortals had first invaded and whose intelligence they had overwhelmed, whose eye they now used and whose powers they would soon attempt to utilize.

Agak did not need to turn his head to look upon the being he still saw as his sister. Like hers, his intelligence was contained within the huge eight-sided eye.

'Did you call me, sister?'

'I spoke your name, that is all, brother.' There were enough vestiges of Gagak's life-force in the Four Who Were One for it to imitate her manner of speaking.

'You cried out?'

'A dream.' The Four paused and then it spoke again: 'A disease. I dreamed that there was something upon this island which made me unwell.'

'Is that possible? We do not know sufficient about these dimensions or the creatures inhabiting them. Yet none is as powerful as Agak and Gagak. Fear not, sister. We must begin our work soon.'

'It is nothing. Now I am awake.'

Agak was puzzled. 'You speak oddly.'

'The dream . . . ' answered the creature which had entered Gagak's body and destroyed her.

'We must begin,' said Agak. 'The dimensions turn and the time has *come. Ah, feel it. It waits for us to take it. So much rich energy. How we shall conquer when we go home!'*

'I feel it,' replied the Four, and it did. It felt its whole universe, dimension upon dimension, swirling all about it. Stars and planets and moons through plane upon plane, all full of the energy upon which Agak and Gagak had desired to feed. And there was enough of Gagak still within the Four to make the Four experience a deep, anticipatory hunger which, now that the dimensions attained the right conjunction, would soon be satisfied.

The Four was tempted to join with Agak and feast, though it knew if it did so it would rob its own universe of every shred of energy. Stars would fade, worlds would die. Even the Lords of Law and Chaos would perish, for they were part of the same universe. Yet to possess such power it might be worth committing such a tremendous crime . . . It controlled this desire and gathered itself for its attack before Agak became too wary.

'Shall we feast, sister?'

The Four realized that the ship had brought it to the island at exactly the proper moment. Indeed, they had almost come too late.

'Sister?' Agak was again puzzled. *'What . . .?'*

The Four knew it must disconnect from Agak. The tubes and wires fell away from his body and were withdrawn into Gagak's.

'What's this?' Agak's strange body trembled for a moment. *'Sister?'*

The Four prepared itself. For all that it had absorbed Gagak's memories and instincts, it was still not confident that it would be able to attack Agak in her chosen form. And since the sorceress had possessed the power to change her form, the Four began to change, groaning greatly, experiencing dreadful pain, drawing all the materials of its stolen being together so that what had appeared to be a building now became pulpy, unformed flesh. And Agak, stunned, looked on.

'Sister? Your sanity . . . '

The building, the creature that was Gagak, threshed, melted, and erupted. It screamed in agony.

It attained its form.

It laughed.

Four faces laughed upon a gigantic head. Eight arms waved in triumph, eight legs began to move. And over that head it waved a single, massive sword.

And it was running.

It ran upon Agak while the alien sorcerer was still in his static form. Its sword was whirling and shards of ghastly golden light fell away from it as it moved, lashing the shadowed landscape. The Four was as large as Agak. And at this moment it was as strong.

But Agak, realizing his danger, began to suck. No longer would this be a pleasurable ritual shared with his sister. He must suck at the energy of this universe if he were to find the strength to defend himself, to gain what he needed to destroy his attacker, the slayer of his sister. Worlds died as Agak sucked.

But not enough. Agak tried cunning.

'This is the centre of your universe. All its dimensions intersect here. Come, you can share the power. My sister is dead. I accept her death. You shall be my partner now. With this power we shall conquer a universe far richer than this!'

'No!' said the Four, still advancing.

'Very well, but be assured of your defeat.'

The Four swung its sword. The sword fell upon the faceted eye within which Agak's intelligence-pool bubbled, just as his sister's had once bubbled. But Agak was stronger already and healed himself at once.

Agak's tendrils emerged and lashed at the Four and the Four cut at the tendrils as it sought his body. And Agak sucked more energy to himself. His body, which the mortals had mistaken for a building, began to glow burning scarlet and to radiate an impossible heat.

The sword roared and flared so that black light mingled with the gold and flowed against the scarlet. And all the while the Four could sense its own universe shrinking and dying.

'Give back, Agak, what you have stolen!' said the Four.

Planes and angles and curves, wires and tubes, flickered with deep red heat and Agak sighed. The universe whimpered.

'I am stronger than you,' said Agak. *'Now.'*

And Agak sucked again.

The Four knew that Agak's attention was diverted for just that short while as he fed. And the Four knew that it, too, must draw energy from its own universe if Agak were to be defeated. So the sword was raised.

The sword was flung back, its blade slicing through tens of thousands of dimensions and drawing their power to it. Then it began to swing back. It swung and black light bellowed from its blade. It swung and Agak became aware of it. His body began to alter. Down towards the sorcerer's great eye, down towards Agak's intelligence-pool swept the black blade.

Agak's many tendrils rose to defend the sorcerer against the sword, but the sword cut through them as if they were not there and it struck the eight-sided chamber which was Agak's eyes and it plunged on down into Agak's intelligence-pool, deep into the stuff of the sorcerer's sensibility, drawing up Agak's energy into itself and thence into its master, the Four Who Were One. And something screamed through the universe and something sent a tremor through the universe. And the universe was dead, even as Agak began to die.

The Four did not dare wait to see if Agak were completely vanquished. It swept the sword out, back through the dimensions, and everywhere the blade touched the energy was restored. The sword rang round and round, round and round, dispersing the energy. And the sword sang its triumph and its glee.

And little shreds of black and golden light whispered away and were reabsorbed.

For a moment the universe had been dead. Now it lived and Agak's energy had been added to it.

Agak lived, too, but he was frozen. He had attempted to change his shape. Now he still half-resembled the building Elric had seen when he first came to the island, but part of him resembled the Four Who Were One – here was part of Corum's face, here a leg, there a fragment of sword-blade – as if Agak had believed, at the end, that the Four could only be defeated if its own form were assumed, just as the Four had assumed Gagak's form.

'We had waited so long . . . ' Agak sighed and then he was dead.

And the Four sheathed its sword.

Then there came a howling through the ruins of the many cities and a strong wind blustered against the body of the Four so that it was forced to kneel on its eight legs and bow its four-faced head before the gale. Then, gradually, it reassumed the shape of Gagak, the sorceress, and then it lay within Gagak's stagnating intelligence-pool and then it rose over it, hovered for a moment, withdrew its sword from the pool. The four beings fled apart and Elric and Hawkmoon and Erekosë and Corum stood with sword-blades touching over the centre of the dead brain.

The four men sheathed their swords. They stared for a second into each other's eyes and all saw terror and awe there. Elric turned away.

He could find neither thoughts nor emotions in him which would relate to what had happened. There were no words he could use. He stood looking dumbly at Ashnar the Lynx and he wondered why Ashnar giggled and chewed at his beard and scraped at the flesh of his own face with his fingernails, his sword forgotten upon the floor of the grey chamber.

'Now I have flesh again. Now I have flesh.' Ashnar kept saying.

Elric wondered why Hown Serpent-tamer lay curled in a ball at

Ashnar's feet, and why when Brut of Lashmar emerged from the passage he fell down and lay stretched upon the floor, stirring a little and moaning as if in disturbed slumber. Otto Blendker came into the chamber. His sword was in its scabbard. His eyes were tight shut and he hugged at himself, shivering.

Elric thought to himself: *I must forget all this or sanity will disappear forever.*

He went to Brut and helped the blond warrior to his feet. 'What did you see?'

'More than I deserved, for all my sins. We were trapped – trapped in that skull . . . ' Then Brut began to weep as a small child might weep and Elric took the tall warrior in his own arms and stroked his head and could not find words or sounds with which to comfort him.

'We must go,' said Erekosë. His eyes were glazed. He staggered as he walked.

Thus, dragging those who had fainted, leading those who had gone mad, leaving those who had died behind, they fled through the dead passages of Gagak's body, no longer plagued by the things she had created in her attempt to rid that body of those she had experienced as an invading disease. The passages and chambers were cold and brittle and the men were glad when they stood outside and saw the ruins, the sourceless shadows, the red, static sun.

Otto Blendker was the only one of the warriors who seemed to retain his sanity through the ordeal, when they had been absorbed, unknowingly, into the body of the Four Who Were One. He dragged his brand from his belt and he took out his tinder and ignited it. Soon the brand was flaming and the others lighted theirs from his. Elric trudged to where Agak's remains still lay and he shuddered as he recognized in a monstrous stone face part of his own features. He felt that the stuff could not possibly burn, but it did. Behind him Gagak's body blazed, too. They were swiftly consumed and pillars of growling fire jutted into the sky, sending up a smoke of white and crimson which for a little while obscured the red disc of the sun.

The men watched the corpses burn.

'I wonder,' said Corum, 'if the captain knew why he sent us here?'

'Or if he suspected what would happen?' said Hawkmoon. Hawkmoon's tone was near to resentful.

'Only we – only that being – could battle Agak and Gagak in anything resembling their own terms,' said Erekosë. 'Other means would not have been successful, no other creature could have the particular qualities, the enormous power needed to slay such strange sorcerers.'

'So it seems,' said Elric, and he would talk no more of it.

351

'Hopefully,' said Corum, 'you will forget this experience as you forgot – or will forget – the other.'

Elric offered him a hard stare. 'Hopefully, brother,' he said.

Erekosë's chuckle was ironic. 'Who could recall that?' And he, too, said no more.

Ashnar the Lynx, who had ceased his gigglings as he watched the fire, shrieked suddenly and broke away from the main party. He ran towards the flickering column and then veered away, disappearing among the ruins and the shadows.

Otto Blendker gave Elric a questioning stare, but Elric shook his head. 'Why follow him? What can we do for him?' He looked down at Hown Serpent-tamer. He had particularly liked the man in the sea-green armour. He shrugged.

When they moved on, they left the curled body of Hown Serpent-tamer where it lay, helping only Brut of Lashmar across the rubble and down to the shore.

Soon they saw the white mist ahead and knew they neared the sea, though the ship was not in sight.

At the edge of the mist both Hawkmoon and Erekosë paused.

'I will not rejoin the ship,' said Hawkmoon. 'I feel I've served my passage now. If I can find Tanelorn, this, I suspect, is where I must look.'

'My own feelings.' Erekosë nodded his head.

Elric looked at Corum. Corum smiled. 'I have already found Tanelorn. I go back to the ship in the hope that soon it will deposit me upon a more familiar shore.'

'That is my hope,' said Elric. His arm still supported Brut of Lashmar.

Brut whispered, 'What was it? What happened to us?'

Elric increased his grip upon the warrior's shoulder. 'Nothing,' he said.

Then, as Elric tried to lead Brut into the mist, the blond warrior stepped back, breaking free. 'I will stay,' he said. He moved away from Elric. 'I am sorry.'

Elric was puzzled. 'Brut?'

'I am sorry,' Brut said again. 'I fear you. I fear that ship.'

Elric made to follow the warrior, but Corum put a hard silver hand upon his shoulder. 'Comrade, let us be gone from this place.' His smile was bleak. 'It is what is back there that I fear more than the ship.'

They stared over the ruins. In the distance they could see the remains of the fire and there were two shadows there now, the shadows of Gagak and Agak as they had first appeared to them.

Elric drew a cold breath of air. 'With that I agree,' he told Corum.

Otto Blendker was the only warrior who chose to return to the ship with them. 'If that is Tanelorn, it is not, after all, the place I sought,' he said.

Soon they were waist-deep in the water. They saw again the outlines of the dark ship; they saw the captain leaning on the rail, his arm raised as if in salute to someone or something upon the island.

'Captain,' called Corum, 'we come aboard.'

'You are welcome,' said the captain. 'Yes, you are welcome.' The blind face turned towards them as Elric reached out for the rope ladder. 'Would you care to sail for a while into the silent places, the restful places?'

'I think so,' said Elric. He paused, halfway up the ladder, and he touched his head. 'I have many wounds.'

He reached the rail and with his own cool hands the captain helped him over. 'They will heal, Elric.'

Elric moved closer to the mast. He leaned against it and watched the silent crew as they unfurled the sail. Corum and Otto Blendker came aboard. Elric listened to the sharp sound of the anchor as it was drawn up. The ship swayed a little.

Otto Blendker looked at Elric, then at the captain, then he turned and went into his cabin, saying nothing at all as he closed the door.

The sail filled, the ship began to move. The captain reached out and found Elric's arm. He took Corum's arm, too, and led them towards his cabin. 'The wine,' he said. 'It will heal all the wounds.'

At the door of the captain's cabin Elric paused. 'And does the wine have other properties?' he asked. 'Does it cloud a man's reason? Was it that which made me accept your commission, Captain?'

The captain shrugged. 'What is reason?'

The ship was gathering speed. The white mist was thicker and a cold wind blew at the rags of cloth and metal Elric wore. He sniffed, thinking for a moment that he smelled smoke upon that wind.

He put his two hands to his face and touched his flesh. His face was cold. He let his hands fall to his sides and he followed the captain into the warmth of the cabin.

The captain poured wine into silver cups from his silver jug. He stretched out a hand to offer a cup to Elric and to Corum. They drank.

A little later the captain said, 'How do you feel?'

Elric said, 'I feel nothing.'

And that night he dreamed only of shadows and in the morning he could not understand his dream at all.

TWO
Sailing to the Present

1

Something About The Fate of Souls

His bone-white, long-fingered hand upon a carved demon's head in black-brown hardwood (one of the few such decorations to be found anywhere about the vessel), the tall man stood alone in the ship's fo'c'sle and stared through large, slanting crimson eyes at the mist into which they moved with a speed and sureness to make any mortal mariner marvel and become incredulous.

There were sounds in the distance, incongruent with the sounds of even this nameless, timeless sea: thin sounds, agonized and terrible, for all that they remained remote – yet the ship followed them, as if drawn by them; they grew louder – pain and despair were there, but terror was predominant.

Elric had heard such sounds echoing from his cousin Yyrkoon's sardonically named 'Pleasure Chambers' in the days before he had fled the responsibilities of ruling all that remained of the old Melnibonéan Empire. These were the voices of men whose very souls were under siege; men to whom death meant not mere extinction, but a continuation of existence, forever in thrall to some cruel and supernatural master. He had heard men cry so when his salvation and his nemesis, his great black battle-blade Stormbringer, drank their souls.

He did not savour the sound: he hated it, turned his back away from the source and was about to descend the ladder to the main deck when he realized that Otto Blendker had come up behind him. Now that Corum had been borne off by friends with chariots which could ride upon the surface of the water, Blendker was the last of those comrades to have fought at Elric's side against the two alien sorcerers Gagak and Agak.

Blendker's black scarred face was troubled. The ex-scholar, turned hireling sword, covered his ears with his huge palms.

'Ach! By the Twelve Symbols of Reason, Elric, who makes that din? It's as though we sail close to the shores of Hell itself!'

Prince Elric of Melniboné shrugged. 'I'd be prepared to forego an answer and leave my curiosity unsatisfied, Master Blendker, if only our ship would change course. As it is, we sail closer and closer to the source.'

Blendker grunted his agreement. 'I've no wish to encounter whatever it is that causes those poor fellows to scream so! Perhaps we should inform the captain.'

'You think he does not know where his own ship sails?' Elric's smile had little humour.

The tall black man rubbed at the inverted V-shaped scar which ran from his forehead to his jawbones. 'I wonder if he plans to put us into battle again.'

'I'll not fight another for him.' Elric's hand moved from the carved rail to the pommel of his runesword. 'I have business of my own to attend to, once I'm back on real land.'

A wind came from nowhere. There was a sudden rent in the mist. Now Elric could see that the ship sailed through rust-coloured water. Peculiar lights gleamed in that water, just below the surface. There was an impression of creatures moving ponderously in the depths of the ocean and, for a moment, Elric thought he glimpsed a white, bloated face not dissimilar to his own – a Melnibonéan face. Impulsively he whirled, back to the rail, looking past Blendker as he strove to control the nausea in his throat.

For the first time since he had come aboard the Dark Ship he was able clearly to see the length of the vessel. Here were the two great wheels, one beside him on the foredeck, one at the far end of the ship on the reardeck, tended now as always by the steersman, the captain's sighted twin. There was the great mast bearing the taut black sail, and fore and aft of this, the two deck cabins, one of which was entirely empty (its occupants having been killed during their last landfall) and one of which was occupied only by himself and Blendker. Elric's gaze was drawn back to the steersman and not for the first time the albino wondered how much influence the captain's twin had over the course of the Dark Ship. The man seemed tireless, rarely, to Elric's knowledge, going below to his quarters, which occupied the stern deck as the captain's occupied the foredeck. Once or twice Elric or Blendker had tried to involve the steersman in conversation, but he appeared to be as dumb as his brother was blind.

The cryptographic, geometrical carvings covering all the ship's wood and most of its metal, from sternpost to figure head, were picked out by the shreds of pale mist still clinging to them (and again Elric wondered if the ship actually generated the mist normally surrounding it) and, as he watched, the designs slowly turned to pale pink fire as the light from that red star, which forever followed them, permeated the overhead cloud.

A noise from below. The captain, his long red-gold hair drifting in a breeze which Elric could not feel, emerged from his cabin. The captain's circlet of blue jade, worn like a diadem, had turned to something of a violet shade in the pink light, and his buff-coloured hose and tunic reflected the hue – even the silver sandals with their silver lacing glittered with the rosy tint.

Again Elric looked upon that mysterious blind face, as unhuman, in the accepted sense, as his own, and puzzled upon the origin of the one who would allow himself to be called nothing but 'Captain.'

As if at the captain's summons, the mist drew itself about the ship again, as a woman might draw a froth of furs about her body. The red star's light faded, but the distant screams continued.

Did the captain notice the screams now for the first time, or was this a pantomime of surprise? His blind head tilted, a hand went to his ear. He murmured in a tone of satisfaction, 'Aha!' The head lifted. 'Elric?'

'Here,' said the albino. 'Above you.'

'We are almost there, Elric.'

The apparently fragile hand found the rail of the companionway. The captain began to climb.

Elric faced him at the top of the ladder. 'If it's a battle . . . '

The captain's smile was enigmatic, bitter. 'It was a fight – or shall be one.'

' . . . we'll have no part of it,' concluded the albino firmly.

'It is not one of the battles in which my ship is directly involved,' the blind man reassured him. 'Those whom you can hear are the vanquished – lost in some future which I think you will experience close to the end of your present incarnation.'

Elric waved a dismissive hand. 'I'll be glad, Captain, if you would cease such vapid mystification. I'm weary of it.'

'I'm sorry it offends you. I answer literally, according to my instincts.'

The captain, going past Elric and Otto Blendker so that he could stand at the rail, seemed to be apologizing. He said nothing for a while, but listened to the disturbing and confused babble from the mist. Then he nodded, apparently satisfied.

'We'll sight land shortly. If you would disembark and seek your own world, I should advise you to do so now. This is the closest we shall ever come again to your plane.'

Elric let his anger show. He cursed, invoking Arioch's name, and put a hand upon the blind man's shoulder. 'What? You cannot return me directly to my own plane?'

'It is too late.' The captain's dismay was apparently genuine. 'The ship sails on. We near the end of our long voyage.'

'But how shall I find my world? I have no sorcery great enough to move me between the spheres! And demonic assistance is denied me here.'

'There is one gateway to your world,' the captain told him. 'That is why I suggest you disembark. Elsewhere there are none at all. Your sphere and this one intersect directly.'

'But you say this lies in my future.'

'Be sure – you will return to your own time. Here you are timeless. It is why your memory is so poor. It is why you remember so little of what befalls you. Seek for the gateway – it is crimson and it emerges from the sea off the coast of the island.'

'Which island?'

'The one we approach.'

Elric hesitated. 'And where shall you go, when I have landed?'

'To Tanelorn,' said the captain. 'There is something I must do there. My brother and I must complete our destiny. We carry cargo as well as men. Many will try to stop us now, for they fear our cargo. We might perish, but yet we must do all we can to reach Tanelorn.'

'Was that not, then, Tanelorn, where we fought Agak and Gagak?'

'That was nothing more than a broken dream of Tanelorn, Elric.'

The Melnibonéan knew that he would receive no more information from the captain.

'You offer me a poor choice – to sail with you into danger and never see my own world again, or to risk landing on yonder island inhabited, by the sound of it, by the damned and those which prey upon the damned!'

The captain's blind eyes moved in Elric's direction. 'I know,' he said softly. 'But it is the best I can offer you, nonetheless.'

The screams, the imploring, terrified shouts, were closer now, but there were fewer of them. Glancing over the side, Elric thought he saw a pair of armoured hands rising from the water; there was foam, red-flecked and noxious, and there was yellowish scum in which pieces of frightful flotsam drifted; there were broken timbers, scraps of canvas, tatters of flags and clothing, fragments of weapons, and, increasingly, there were floating corpses.

'But where was the battle?' Blendker whispered, fascinated and horrified by the sight.

'Not on this plane,' the captain told him. 'You see only the wreckage which has drifted over from one world to another.'

'Then it was a supernatural battle?'

The captain smiled again. 'I am not omniscient. But, yes, I believe there were supernatural agencies involved. The warriors of half a world fought in the sea-battle – to decide the fate of the multiverse. It is – or will be – one of the decisive battles to determine the fate of Mankind, to fix Man's destiny for the coming Cycle.'

'Who were the participants?' asked Elric, voicing the question in spite of his resolve. 'What were the issues as they understood them?'

'You will know in time, I think.' The captain's head faced the sea again.

Blendker sniffed the air. 'Ach! It's foul!'

Elric, too, found the odour increasingly unpleasant. Here and there now the water was lighted by guttering fires which revealed the faces of the drowning, some of whom still managed to cling to pieces of blackened driftwood. Not all the faces were human, though they had the appearance of having once been human; things with the snouts of pigs and of bulls raised twisted hands to the Dark Ship and grunted plaintively for succour, but the captain ignored them and the steersman held his course.

Fires spluttered and water hissed; smoke mingled with the mist. Elric had his sleeve over his mouth and nose and was glad that the smoke and mist between them helped obscure the sights, for as the wreckage grew thicker not a few of the corpses he saw reminded him more of reptiles than of men, their pale, lizard bellies spilling something other than blood.

'If that is my future,' Elric told the captain, 'I've a mind to remain on board, after all.'

'You have a duty, as have I,' said the captain quietly. 'The future must be served, as much as the past and the present.'

Elric shook his head. 'I fled the duties of an empire because I sought freedom,' the albino told him. 'And freedom I must have.'

'No,' murmured the captain. 'There is no such thing. Not yet. Not for us. We must go through much more before we can even begin to guess what freedom is. The price for the knowledge alone is probably higher than any you would care to pay at this stage of your life. Indeed, life itself is often the price.'

'I also sought release from metaphysics when I left Melniboné,' said Elric. 'I'll get the rest of my gear and take the land that's offered. With luck this Crimson Gate will be quickly found and I'll be back among dangers and torments which will, at least, be familiar.'

'It is the only decision you could have made.' The captain's blind head turned towards Blendker. 'And you, Otto Blendker? What shall you do?'

'Elric's world is not mine and I like not the sound of those screams. What can you promise me, sir, if I sail on with you?'

'Nothing but a good death.' There was regret in the captain's voice.

'Death is the promise we're all born with, sir. A good death is better than a poor one. I'll sail on with you.'

'As you like. I think you're wise.' The captain sighed. 'I'll say farewell to you, then, Elric of Melniboné. You fought well in my service and I thank you.'

'Fought for what?' Elric asked.

'Oh, call it Mankind. Call if Fate. Call it a dream or an ideal, if you wish.'

'Shall I never have a clearer answer?'

'Not from me. I do not think there is one.'

'You allow a man little faith.' Elric began to descend the companion-way.

'There are two kinds of faith, Elric. Like freedom, there is a kind which is easily kept but proves not worth the keeping, and there is a kind which is hard-won. I agree, I offer little of the former.'

Elric strode towards his cabin. He laughed, feeling genuine affection for the blind man at that moment. 'I thought I had a penchant for such ambiguities, but I have met my match in you, Captain.'

He noticed that the steersman had left his place at the wheel and was swinging out a boat on its davits, preparatory to lowering it.

'Is that for me?'

The steersman nodded.

Elric ducked into his cabin. He was leaving the ship with nothing but that which he had brought aboard, only his clothing and his armour were in a poorer state of repair than they had been, and his mind was in a considerably greater state of confusion.

Without hesitation he gathered up his things, drawing his heavy cloak about him, pulling on his gauntlets, fastening buckles and thongs, then he left the cabin and returned to the deck. The captain was pointing through the mist at the dark outlines of a coast. 'Can you see land, Elric?'

'I can.'

'You must go quickly, then.'

'Willingly.'

Elric swung himself over the rail and into the boat. The boat struck the side of the ship several times, so that the hull boomed like the beating of some huge funeral drum. Otherwise there was silence now upon the misty waters and no sign of wreckage.

Blendker saluted him. 'I wish you luck, comrade.'

'You, too, Master Blendker.'

The boat began to sink towards the flat surface of the sea, the pulleys of the davits creaking. Elric clung to the rope, letting go as the boat hit the water. He stumbled and sat down heavily upon the seat, releasing the ropes so that the boat drifted at once away from the Dark Ship. He got out the oars and fitted them into their rowlocks.

As he pulled toward the shore he heard the captain's voice calling to him, but the words were muffled by the mist and he would never know, now, if the blind man's last communication had been a warning or merely some formal pleasantry. He did not care. The boat moved smoothly through the water; the mist began to thin, but so, too, did the light fade.

Suddenly he was under a twilight sky, the sun already gone and stars appearing. Before he had reached the shore it was already completely dark, with the moon not yet risen, and it was with difficulty that he beached the boat on what seemed flat rocks, and stumbled inland until he judged himself safe enough from any inrushing tide.

Then, with a sigh, he lay down, thinking just to order his thoughts before moving on; but, almost instantly, he was asleep.

2

Dreaming and Waking

Elric dreamed.

He dreamed not merely of the end of his world but of the end of an entire cycle in the history of the cosmos. He dreamed that he was not only Elric of Melniboné but that he was other men, too – men who were pledged to some numinous cause which even they could not describe. And he dreamed that he had dreamed of the Dark Ship and Tanelorn and Agak and Gagak while he lay exhausted upon a beach somewhere beyond the borders of Pikarayd; and when he woke up he was smiling sardonically, congratulating himself for the possession of a grandiose imagination. But he could not clear his head entirely of the impression left by that dream.

This shore was not the same, so plainly something had befallen him – perhaps he had been drugged by slavers, then later abandoned when they found him not what they expected . . . But, no, the explanation would not do. If he could discover his whereabouts, he might also recall the true facts.

It was dawn, for certain. He sat up and looked about him.

He was sprawled upon a dark, sea-washed limestone pavement, cracked in a hundred places, the cracks so deep that the small streams of foaming salt water rushing through these many narrow channels made raucous what would otherwise have been a very still morning.

Elric climbed to his feet, using his scabbarded runesword to steady himself. His bone-white lids closed for a moment over his crimson eyes as he sought, again, to recollect the events which had brought him here.

He recalled his flight from Pikarayd, his panic, his falling into a coma of hopelessness, his dreams, and, because he was evidently neither dead nor a prisoner, he could at least conclude that his pursuers had, after all, given up the chase, for if they had found him they would have killed him.

Opening his eyes and casting about him, he remarked the peculiar blue quality of the light, doubtless a trick of the sun behind the grey clouds, which made the landscape ghastly and gave the sea a dull, metallic look.

The limestone terraces which rose from the sea and stretched above him shone intermittently, like polished lead. On an impulse he held his hand to the light and inspected it. The normally lustreless white of his skin was now tinged with a faint, bluish luminosity. He found it pleasing and smiled as a child might smile, in innocent wonder.

He had expected to be tired, but he now realized that he felt unusually refreshed, as if he had slept long after a good meal, and, deciding not to question the fact of this fortunate (and unlikely) gift, he determined to climb the cliffs in the hope that he might get some idea of his bearings before he decided which direction he would take.

Limestone could be a little treacherous, but it made easy climbing, for there was almost always somewhere that one terrace met another.

He climbed carefully and steadily, finding many footholds, and seemed to gain considerable height quite quickly, yet it was noon before he had reached the top and found himself standing at the edge of a broad, rocky plateau which fell away sharply to form a close horizon. Beyond the plateau was only the sky. Save for sparse, brownish grass, little grew here and there were no signs at all of human habitation. It was now, for the first time, that Elric realized the absence of any form of wildlife. Not a single seabird flew in the air, not an insect crept through the grass. Instead, there was an enormous silence hanging over the brown plain.

Elric was still remarkably untired, so he decided to make the best use he could of his energy and reach the edge of the plateau in the hope that, from there, he would sight a town or a village. He pressed on, feeling no lack of food and water, and his stride was singularly energetic, still; but he had misjudged his distance and the sun had begun to set well before his journey to the edge was completed. The sky on all sides turned a deep, velvety blue and the few clouds that there were in it were also tinged blue, and now, for the first time, Elric realized that the sun itself was not its normal shade, that it burned blackish purple, and he wondered again if he still dreamed.

The ground began to rise sharply and it was with some effort that he walked, but before the light had completely faded he was on the steep flank of a hill, descending towards a wide valley which, though bereft of trees, contained a river which wound through rocks and russet turf and bracken.

After a short rest, Elric decided to press on, although night had fallen, and see if he could reach the river where he might at least drink and, possibly, in the morning find fish to eat.

Again, no moon appeared to aid his progress and he walked for two or three hours in a darkness which was almost total, stumbling occasionally into large rocks, until the ground levelled and he felt sure he had reached the floor of the valley.

He had developed a strong thirst by now and was feeling somewhat hungry, but decided that it might be best to wait until morning before seeking the river when, rounding a particularly tall rock, he saw, with some astonishment, the light of a camp fire.

Hopefully this would be the fire of a company of merchants, a trading caravan on its way to some civilized country which would allow him to travel with it, perhaps in return for his services as a mercenary swordsman (it would not be the first time, since he had left Melniboné, that he had earned his bread in such a way).

Yet Elric's old instincts did not desert him; he approached the fire cautiously and let no one see him. Beneath an overhang of rock, made shadowy by the flame's light, he stood and observed the group of fifteen or sixteen men who sat or lay close to the fire, playing some kind of game involving dice and slivers of numbered ivory.

Gold, bronze, and silver gleamed in the firelight as the men staked large sums on the fall of a dice and the turn of a slip of ivory.

Elric guessed that, if they had not been so intent on their game, these men must certainly have detected his approach, for they were not, after all, merchants. By the evidence, they were warriors, wearing scarred leather and dented metal, their weapons ready to hand, yet they belonged to no army – unless it be an army of bandits – for they were of all races and, oddly, seemed to be from various periods in the history of the Young Kingdoms.

It was as if they had looted some scholar's collection of relics. An axeman of the later Lormyrian Republic, which had come to an end some two hundred years ago, lay with his shoulder rubbing the elbow of a Chalalite bowman, from a period roughly contemporary with Elric's own. Close to the Chalalite sat a short Ilmioran infantryman of a century past. Next to him was a Filkharian in the barbaric dress of that nation's earliest times. Tarkeshites, Shazarians, Vilmirians, all mingled and the only thing they had in common, by the look of them, was a villainous, hungry cast to their features.

In other circumstances Elric might have skirted this encampment and moved on, but he was so glad to find human beings of any sort that he ignored the disturbing incongruities of the group; yet he remained content to watch them.

One of the men, less unwholesome than the others, was a bulky, black-bearded, baldheaded sea-warrior clad in the casual leathers and silks of the people of the Purple Towns. It was when this man produced a large gold Melnibonéan wheel – a coin not minted, as most coins, but carved by craftsmen to a design both ancient and intricate – that Elric's caution was fully conquered by his curiosity.

Very few of those coins existed in Melniboné and none, that Elric had heard of, outside; for the coins were not used for trade with the Young Kingdoms. They were prized, even by the nobility of Melniboné.

It seemed to Elric that the baldheaded man could only have acquired the coin from another Melnibonéan traveller – and Elric knew of no other Melnibonéans who shared his penchant for exploration. His wariness dismissed, he stepped into the circle.

If he had not been completely obsessed by the thought of the Melnibonéan wheel he might have taken some satisfaction in the sudden scuffle to arms which resulted. Within seconds, the majority of the men were on their feet, their weapons drawn.

For a moment, the gold wheel was forgotten. His hand upon his runesword's pommel, he presented the other in a placatory gesture.

'Forgive the interruption, gentlemen. I am but one tired fellow soldier who seeks to join you. I would beg some information and purchase some food, if you have it to spare.'

On foot, the warriors had an even more ruffianly appearance. They grinned among themselves, entertained by Elric's courtesy but not impressed by it.

One, in the feathered helmet of a Pan Tangian sea-chief, with features to match – swarthy, sinister – pushed his head forward on its long neck and said banteringly:

'We've company enough, white-face. And few here are overfond of the man-demons of Melniboné. You must be rich.'

Elric recalled the animosity with which Melnibonéans were regarded in the Young Kingdoms, particularly by those from Pan Tang who envied the Dragon Isle her power and her wisdom and, of late, had begun crudely to imitate Melniboné.

Increasingly on his guard, he said evenly, 'I have a little money.'

'Then we'll take it, demon.' The Pan Tangian presented a dirty palm just below Elric's nose as he growled, 'Give it over and be on your way.'

Elric's smile was polite and fastidious, as if he had been told a poor joke.

The Pan Tangian evidently thought the joke better than did Elric, for he laughed heartily and looked to his nearest fellows for approval.

Coarse laughter infected the night and only the bald-headed, black-bearded man did not join in the jest, but took a step or two back, while all the others pressed forward.

The Pan Tangian's face was close to Elric's own; his breath was foul and Elric saw that his beard and hair were alive with lice, yet he kept his head, replying in the same equable tone:

'Give me some decent food, a flask of water – some wine, if you have it – and I'll gladly give you the money I have.'

The laughter rose and fell again as Elric continued:

'But if you would take my money and leave me with naught – then I must defend myself. I have a good sword.'

The Pan Tangian strove to imitate Elric's irony. 'But you will note, Sir Demon, that we outnumber you. Considerably.'

Softly the albino spoke: 'I've noticed that fact, but I'm not disturbed by it,' and he had drawn the black blade even as he finished speaking, for they had come at him with a rush.

And the Pan Tangian was the first to die, sliced through the side, his vertebrae sheared, and Stormbringer, having taken its first soul, began to sing.

A Chalalite died next, leaping with stabbing javelin poised, on the point of the runesword, and Stormbringer murmured with pleasure.

But it was not until it had sliced the head clean off a Filkharian pike-master that the sword began to croon and come fully to life, black fire flickering up and down its length, its strange runes glowing.

Now the warriors knew they battled sorcery and became more cautious, yet they scarcely paused in their attack, and Elric, thrusting and parrying, hacking and slicing, needed all of the fresh, dark energy the sword passed on to him.

Lance, sword, axe, and dirk were blocked, wounds were given and received, but the dead had not yet outnumbered the living when Elric found himself with his back against the rock and nigh a dozen sharp weapons seeking his vitals.

It was at this point, when Elric had become somewhat less than confident that he could best so many, that the baldheaded warrior, axe in one gloved hand, sword in the other, came swiftly into the firelight and set upon those of his fellows closest to him.

'I thank you, sir!' Elric was able to shout, during the short respite this sudden turn produced. His morale improved, he resumed the attack.

The Lormyrian was cleaved from hip to pelvis as he dodged a feint; a Filkharian, who should have been dead four hundred years before, fell with the blood bubbling from lips and nostrils, and the corpses began to pile one upon the other. Still Stormbringer sang its sinister battle-song and still the runesword passed its power to its master so that with every death Elric found strength to slay more of the soldiers.

Those who remained now began to express their regret for their hasty attack. Where oaths and threats had issued from their mouths, now came plaintive petitions for mercy and those who had laughed with such bold braggadocio now wept like young girls, but Elric, full of his old battle-joy, spared none.

Meanwhile the man from the Purple Towns, unaided by sorcery, put axe and sword to good work and dealt with three more of his one-time comrades, exulting in his work as if he had nursed a taste for it for some time.

'Yoi! But this is worthwhile slaughter!' cried the black-bearded one.

And then that busy butchery was suddenly done and Elric realized that none were left save himself and his new ally, who stood leaning on his axe, panting and grinning like a hound at the kill, replacing a steel skullcap upon his pate from where it had fallen during the fight, and wiping a bloody sleeve over the sweat glistening on his brow, and saying, in a deep, good-humoured tone:

'Well now, it is we who are wealthy, of a sudden.'

Elric sheathed a Stormbringer still reluctant to return to its scabbard. 'You desire their gold. Is that why you aided me?'

The black-bearded soldier laughed. 'I owed them a debt and had been biding my time, waiting to pay. These rascals are all that were left of a pirate crew which slew everyone aboard my own ship when we wandered into strange waters – they would have slain me had I not told them I wished to join them. Now I am revenged. Not that I am above taking the gold, since much of it belongs to me and my dead brothers. It will go to their wives and their children when I return to the Purple Towns.'

'How did you convince them not to kill you, too?' Elric sought among the ruins of the fire for something to eat. He found some cheese and began to chew upon it.

'They had no captain or navigator, it seemed. None were real sailors at all, but coast-huggers, based upon this island. They were stranded here, you see, and had taken to piracy as a last resort, but were too terrified to risk the open sea. Besides, after the fight, they had no ship. We had managed to sink that as we fought. We sailed mine to this shore, but provisions were already low and they had no stomach for setting sail without full holds, so I pretended that I knew this coast (may the gods take my soul if I ever see it again after this business) and offered to lead them inland to a village they might loot. They had heard of no such village, but believed me when I said it lay in a hidden valley. That way I prolonged my life while I waited for the opportunity to be revenged upon them. It was a foolish hope, I know. Yet' – grinning – 'as it happened, it was well-founded after all! Eh?'

The black-bearded man glanced a little warily at Elric, uncertain of what the albino might say, hoping, however, for comradeship, though it was well known how haughty Melnibonéans were. Elric could tell that all these thoughts went through his new acquaintance's mind; he had seen many others make similar calculations. So he smiled openly and slapped the man on the shoulder.

'You saved my life, also, my friend. We are both fortunate.'

The man sighed in relief and slung his axe upon his back. 'Aye – lucky's the word. But shall our luck hold, I wonder?'

'You do not know the island at all?'

'Nor the waters, either. How we came to them I'll never guess. Enchanted waters, though, without question. You've seen the colour of the sun?'

'I have.'

'Well' – the seaman bent to remove a pendant from around the Pan Tangian's throat – 'you'd know more about enchantments and sorceries than I. How came you here, Sir Melnibonéan?'

'I know not. I fled from some who hunted me. I came to a shore and could flee no further. Then I dreamed a great deal. When next I awoke I was on the shore again, but of this island.'

'Spirits of some sort – maybe friendly to you – took you to safety, away from your enemies.'

'That's just possible,' Elric agreed, 'for we have many allies among the elementals. I am called Elric and I am self-exiled from Melniboné. I travel because I believe I have something to learn from the folk of the Young Kingdoms. I have no power, save what you see . . . '

The black-bearded man's eyes narrowed in appraisal as he pointed at himself with his thumb. 'I'm Smiorgan Baldhead, once a sea-lord of the Purple Towns. I commanded a fleet of merchantmen. Perhaps I still do. I shall not know until I return – if I ever do return.'

'Then let us pool our knowledge and our resources, Smiorgan Baldhead, and make plans to leave this island as soon as we can.'

Elric walked back to where he saw traces of the abandoned game, trampled into the mud and the blood. From among the dice and the ivory slips, the silver and the bronze coins, he found the gold Melnibonéan wheel. He picked it up and held it in his outstretched palm. The wheel almost covered the whole palm. In the old days, it had been the currency of kings.

'This was yours, friend?' he asked Smiorgan.

Smiorgan Baldhead looked up from where he was still searching the Pan Tangian for his stolen possessions. He nodded.

'Aye. Would you keep it as part of your share?'

Elric shrugged. 'I'd rather know from whence it came. Who gave it you?'

'It was not stolen. It's Melnibonéan, then?'

'Yes.'

'I guessed it.'

'From whom did you obtain it?'

Smiorgan straightened up, having completed his search. He scratched at a slight wound on his forearm. 'It was used to buy passage on our ship – before we were lost – before the raiders attacked us.'

'Passage? By a Melnibonéan?'

'Maybe,' said Smiorgan. He seemed reluctant to speculate.

'Was he a warrior?'

Smiorgan smiled in his beard. 'No. It was a woman gave that to me.'

'How came she to take passage?'

Smiorgan began to pick up the rest of the money. 'It's a long tale and, in part, a familiar one to most merchant sailors. We were seeking new markets for our goods and had equipped a good-sized fleet, which I commanded as the largest shareholder.' He seated himself casually upon the big corpse of the Chalalite and began to count the money. 'Would you hear the tale or do I bore you already?'

'I'd be glad to listen.'

Reaching behind him, Smiorgan pulled a wine-flask from the belt of the corpse and offered it to Elric, who accepted it and drank sparingly of a wine which was unusually good.

Smiorgan took the flask when Elric had finished. 'That's part of our cargo,' he said. 'We were proud of it. A good vintage, eh?'

'Excellent. So you set off from the Purple Towns?'

'Aye. Going east towards the Unknown Kingdoms. We sailed due east for a couple of weeks, sighting some of the bleakest coasts I have ever seen, and then we saw no land at all for another week. That was when we entered a stretch of water we came to call the Roaring Rocks – like the Serpent's Teeth off Shazar's coast, but much greater in expanse, and larger, too. Huge volcanic cliffs which rose from the sea on every side and around which the waters heaved and boiled and howled with a fierceness I've rarely experienced. Well, in short, the fleet was dispersed and at least four ships were lost on those rocks. At last we were able to escape those waters and found ourselves becalmed and alone. We searched for our sister ships for a while and then decided to give ourselves another week before turning for home, for we had no liking to go back into the Roaring Rocks again. Low on provisions, we sighted land at last – grassy cliffs and hospitable beaches and, inland, some signs of cultivation, so we knew we had found civilization again. We put into a small fishing port and satisfied the natives – who spoke no tongue used in the Young Kingdoms – that we were friendly. And that was when the woman approached us.'

'The Melnibonéan woman?'

'If Melnibonéan she was. She was a fine-looking woman, I'll say that. We were short of provisions, as I told you, and short of any means of purchasing them, for the fishermen desired little of what we had to trade. Having given up our original quest, we were content to head westward again.'

'The woman?'

'She wished to buy passage to the Young Kingdoms – and was content to go with us as far as Menii, our home port. For her passage she gave us two of those wheels. One was used to buy provisions in the town – Graghin, I think it was called – and after making repairs we set off again.'

'You never reached the Purple Towns?'

'There were more storms – strange storms. Our instruments were useless, our lodestones were of no help to us at all. We became even more completely lost than before. Some of my men argued that we had gone beyond our own world altogether. Some blamed the woman, saying she was a sorceress who had no intention of going to Menii. But I believed her. Night fell and seemed to last forever until we sailed into a calm dawn beneath a blue sun. My men were close to panic – and it takes much to make my men panic – when we sighted the island. As we headed for it those pirates attacked us in a ship which belonged to history – it should have been on the bottom of the ocean, not on the surface. I've seen pictures of such craft in murals on a temple wall in Tarkesh. In ramming us, she stove in half her port side and was sinking even when they swarmed aboard. They were desperate, savage men, Elric – half-starved and blood-hungry. We were weary after our voyage, but fought well. During the fighting the woman disappeared, killed herself, maybe, when she saw the stamp of our conquerors. After a long fight only myself and one other, who died soon after, were left. That was when I became cunning and decided to wait for revenge.'

'The woman had a name?'

'None she would give. I have thought the matter over and suspect that, after all, we were used by her. Perhaps she did not seek Menii and the Young Kingdoms. Perhaps it was this world she sought, and, by sorcery, led us here.'

'This world? You think it different from our own?'

'If only because of the sun's strange colour. Do you not think so, too? You, with your Melnibonéan knowledge of such things, must believe it.'

'I have dreamed of such things,' Elric admitted, but he would say no more.

'Most of the pirates thought as I – they were from all the ages of the Young Kingdoms. That much I discovered. Some were from the earliest years of the era, some from our own time – and some were from the future. Adventurers, most of them, who, at some stage in their lives, sought a legendary land of great riches which lay on the other side of an ancient gateway, rising from the middle of the ocean; but they found themselves trapped here, unable to sail back through this mysterious gate. Others had been involved in sea-fights, thought themselves drowned and woken up on the shores of the island. Many, I suppose, had once had reasonable virtues, but there is little to support life on the island and they had become wolves, living off one another or any ship unfortunate enough to pass, inadvertently, through this gate of theirs.'

Elric recalled part of his dream. 'Did any call it the "Crimson Gate"?'

'Several did, aye.'

'And yet the theory is unlikely, if you'll forgive my scepticism,' Elric said. 'As one who has passed through the Shade Gate to Ameeron . . . '

'You know of other worlds, then?'

'I've never heard of this one. And I am versed in such matters. That is why I doubt the reasoning. And yet, there was the dream . . . '

'Dream?'

'Oh, it was nothing. I am used to such dreams and give them no significance.'

'The theory cannot seem surprising to a Melnibonéan, Elric!' Smiorgan grinned again. 'It's I who should be sceptical, not you.'

And Elric replied, half to himself: 'Perhaps I fear the implications more.' He lifted his head, and with the shaft of a broken spear, began to poke at the fire. 'Certain ancient sorcerers of Melniboné proposed that an infinite number of worlds coexist with our own. Indeed, my dreams, of late, have hinted as much!' He forced himself to smile. 'But I cannot afford to believe such things. Thus, I reject them.'

'Wait for the dawn,' said Smiorgan Baldhead. 'The colour of the sun shall prove the theory.'

'Perhaps it will prove only that we both dream,' said Elric. The smell of death was strong in his nostrils. He pushed aside those corpses nearest to the fire and settled himself to sleep.

Smiorgan Baldhead had begun to sing a strong yet lilting song in his own dialect, which Elric could scarcely follow.

'Do you sing of your victory over your enemies?' the albino asked.

Smiorgan paused for a moment, half-amused. 'No, Sir Elric, I sing to keep the shades at bay. After all, these fellows' ghosts must still be lurking nearby, in the dark, so little time has passed since they died.'

'Fear not,' Elric told him. 'Their souls are already eaten.'

But Smiorgan sang on, and his voice was louder, his song more intense, than ever it had been before.

Just before he fell asleep, Elric thought he heard a horse whinny, and he meant to ask Smiorgan if any of the pirates had been mounted, but he fell asleep before he could do so.

3

Some Evidence of Sorcery

Recalling little of his voyage on the Dark Ship, Elric would never know how he came to reach the world in which he now found himself. In later years he would recall most of these experiences as dreams, and indeed they seemed dreamlike even as they occurred.

He slept uneasily, and in the morning the clouds were heavier, shining with that strange, leaden light, though the sun itself was obscured. Smiorgan Baldhead of the Purple Towns was pointing upward, already on his feet, speaking with quiet triumph:

'Will that evidence suffice to convince you, Elric of Melniboné?'

'I am convinced of a quality about the light – possibly about this terrain – which makes the sun appear blue,' Elric replied. He glanced with distaste around him at the carnage. The corpses made a wretched sight and he was filled with a nebulous misery that was neither remorse nor pity.

Smiorgan's sigh was sardonic. 'Well, Sir Sceptic, we had best retrace my steps and seek my ship. What say you?'

'I agree,' the albino told him.

'How far had you marched from the coast when you found us?'

Elric told him.

Smiorgan smiled. 'You arrived in the nick of time, then. I should have been most embarrassed by today if the sea had been reached and I could show my pirate friends no village! I shall not forget this favour you have done me, Elric. I am a count of the Purple Towns and have much influence. If there is any service I can perform for you when we return, you must let me know.'

'I thank you,' Elric said gravely. 'But first we must discover a means of escape.'

Smiorgan had gathered up a satchel of food, some water and some wine. Elric had no stomach to make his breakfast among the dead, so he slung the satchel over his shoulder. 'I'm ready,' he said.

Smiorgan was satisfied. 'Come – we go this way.'

Elric began to follow the sea-lord over the dry, crunching turf. The steep sides of the valley loomed over them, tinged with a peculiar and unpleasant greenish hue, the result of the brown foliage being stained by the blue light from above. When they reached the river, which was narrow and ran rapidly through boulders giving easy means of crossing, they rested and ate. Both men were stiff from the previous night's fighting; both were glad to wash the dried blood and mud from their bodies in the water.

Refreshed, the pair climbed over the boulders and left the river behind, ascending the slopes, speaking little so that their breath was saved for the exertion. It was noon by the time they reached the top of the valley and observed a plain not unlike the one which Elric had first crossed. Elric now had a fair idea of the island's geography: it resembled the top of a mountain, with an indentation near the centre which was the valley. Again he became sharply aware of the absence of any wildlife and remarked on this to Count Smiorgan, who agreed that he had seen nothing – no bird, fish, nor beast since he had arrived.

'It's a barren little world, friend Elric, and a misfortune for a mariner to be wrecked upon its shores.'

They moved on, until the sea could be observed meeting the horizon in the far distance.

It was Elric who first heard the sound behind them, recognizing the steady thump of the hooves of a galloping horse, but when he looked back over his shoulder he could see no sign of a rider, nor anywhere that a rider could hide. He guessed that, in his tiredness, his ears were betraying him. It had been thunder that he had heard.

Smiorgan strode implacably onward, though he, too, must have heard the sound.

Again it came. Again, Elric turned. Again he saw nothing.

'Smiorgan? Did you hear a rider?'

Smiorgan continued to walk without looking back. 'I heard,' he grunted.

'You have heard it before?'

'Many times since I arrived. The pirates heard it, too, and some believed it their nemesis – an Angel of Death seeking them out for retribution.'

'You don't know the source?'

Smiorgan paused, then stopped, and when he turned his face was grim. 'Once or twice I have caught a glimpse of a horse, I think. A tall horse – white – richly dressed – but with no man upon his back. Ignore it, Elric, as I do. We have larger mysteries with which to occupy our minds!'

'You are afraid of it, Smiorgan?'

He accepted this. 'Aye. I confess it. But neither fear nor speculation will rid us of it. Come!'

Elric was bound to see the sense of Smiorgan's statement and he accepted it; yet when the sound came again, about an hour later, he could not resist turning. Then he thought he glimpsed the outline of a large stallion, caparisoned for riding, but that might have been nothing more than an idea Smiorgan had put in his mind.

The day grew colder and in the air was a peculiar, bitter odour. Elric remarked on the smell to Count Smiorgan and learned that this, too, was familiar.

'The smell comes and goes, but it is usually here in some strength.'

'Like sulphur,' said Elric.

Count Smiorgan's laugh had much irony in it, as if Elric made reference to some private joke of Smiorgan's own. 'Oh, aye! Sulphur right enough!'

The drumming of hooves grew louder behind them as they neared the coast and at last Elric, and Smiorgan too, turned around again, to look.

And now a horse could be seen plainly – riderless, but saddled and bridled, its dark eyes intelligent, its beautiful white head held proudly.

'Are you still convinced of the absence of sorcery here, Sir Elric?' Count Smiorgan asked with some satisfaction. 'The horse was invisible. Now it is visible.' He shrugged the battle-axe on his shoulder into a better position. 'Either that, or it moves from one world to another with ease, so that all we mainly hear are its hoofbeats.'

'If so,' said Elric sardonically, eyeing the stallion, 'it might bear us back to our own world.'

'You admit, then, that we are marooned in some Limbo?'

'Very well, yes. I admit the possibility.'

'Have you no sorcery to trap the horse?'

'Sorcery does not come so easily to me, for I have no great liking for it,' the albino told him.

As they spoke, they approached the horse, but it would let them get no closer. It snorted and moved backwards, keeping the same distance between them and itself.

At last, Elric said, 'We waste time, Count Smiorgan. Let's get to your ship with speed and forget blue suns and enchanted horses as quickly as we may. Once aboard the ship I can doubtless help you with a little incantation or two, for we'll need aid of some sort if we're to sail a large ship by ourselves.'

They marched on, but the horse continued to follow them. They came to the edge of the cliffs, standing high above a narrow, rocky bay in which a battered ship lay at anchor. The ship had the high, fine lines of a Purple Towns merchantman, but its decks were piled with shreds of torn canvas, pieces of broken rope, shards of timber, torn-open bales of cloth, smashed wine-jars, and all manner of other refuse, while in several places her rails were smashed and two or three of her yards had splintered. It was evident that she had been through both storms and sea-fights and it was a wonder that she still floated.

'We'll have to tidy her up as best we can, using only the mains'l for motion,' mused Smiorgan. 'Hopefully we can salvage enough food to last us . . . '

'Look!' Elric pointed, sure that he had seen someone in the shadows near the afterdeck. 'Did the pirates leave any of their company behind?'

'None.'

'Did you see anyone on the ship, just then?'

'My eyes play filthy tricks on my mind,' Smiorgan told him. 'It is this damned blue light. There is a rat or two aboard, that's all. And that's what you saw.'

'Possibly.' Elric looked back. The horse appeared to be unaware of them as it cropped the brown grass. 'Well, let's finish the journey.'

They scrambled down the steeply sloping cliff-face and were soon on the shore, wading through the shallows for the ship, clambering up the slippery ropes which still hung over the sides, and, at last, setting their feet with some relief upon the deck.

'I feel more secure already,' said Smiorgan. 'This ship was my home for so long! He searched through the scattered cargo until he found an unbroken wine-jar, carved off the seal, and handed it to Elric. Elric lifted the heavy jar and let a little of the good wine flow into his mouth. As Count Smiorgan began to drink Elric was sure he saw another movement near the afterdeck, and he moved closer.

Now he was certain that he heard strained, rapid breathing – like the breathing of one who sought to stifle his need for air rather than be detected. They were slight sounds, but the albino's ears, unlike his eyes, were sharp. His hand ready to draw his sword, he stalked towards the source of the sound, Smiorgan now behind him.

She emerged from her hiding place before he reached her. Her hair hung in heavy, dirty coils about her pale face; her shoulders were slumped and her soft arms hung limply at her sides, and her dress was stained and ripped.

As Elric approached, she fell on her knees before him. 'Take my life,' she said humbly, 'but I beg you – do not take me back to Saxif D'Aan,

378

though I know you must be his servant or his kinsman.'

'It's she!' cried Smiorgan in astonishment. 'It's our passenger. She must have been in hiding all this time.'

Elric stepped forward, lifting up the girl's chin so that he could study her face. There was a Melnibonéan cast about her features, but she was, to his mind, of the Young Kingdoms; she lacked the pride of a Melnibonéan woman, too. 'What name was that you used, girl?' he asked kindly. 'Did you speak of Saxif D'Aan? Earl Saxif D'Aan of Melniboné?'

'I did, my lord.'

'Do not fear me as his servant,' Elric told her. 'And as for being a kinsman, I suppose you could call me that, on my mother's side – or rather my great-grandmother's side. He was an ancestor. He must have been dead for two centuries, at least!'

'No,' she said. 'He lives, my lord.'

'On this island?'

'This island is not his home, but it is in this plane that he exists. I sought to escape him through the Crimson Gate. I fled through the gate in a skiff, reached the town where you found me, Count Smiorgan, but he drew me back once I was aboard your ship. He drew me back and the ship with me. For that, I have remorse – and for what befell your crew. Now I know he seeks me. I can feel his presence growing nearer.'

'Is he invisible?' Smiorgan asked suddenly. 'Does he ride a white horse?'

She gasped. 'You see! He *is* near! Why else should the horse appear on this island?'

'He rides it?' Elric asked.

'No, no! He fears the horse almost as much as I fear him. The horse pursues him!'

Elric produced the Melnibonéan gold wheel from his purse. 'Did you take this from Earl Saxif D'Aan?'

'I did.'

The albino frowned.

'Who is this man, Elric?' Count Smiorgan asked. 'You describe him as an ancestor – yet he lives in this world. What do you know of him?'

Elric weighed the large gold wheel in his hand before replacing it in his pouch. 'He was something of a legend in Melniboné. His story is part of our literature. He was a great sorcerer – one of the greatest – and he fell in love. It's rare enough for Melnibonéans to fall in love, as others understand the emotion, but rarer for one to have such feelings for a girl who was not even of our own race. She was half-Melnibonéan,

379

so I heard, but from a land which was, in those days, a Melnibonéan possession, a western province close to Dharijor. She was bought by him in a batch of slaves he planned to use for some sorcerous experiment, but he singled her out, saving her from whatever fate it was the others suffered. He lavished his attention upon her, giving her everything. For her, he abandoned his practices, retired to live quietly away from Imrryr, and I think she showed him a certain affection, though she did not seem to love him. There was another, you see, called Carolak, as I recall, and also half-Melnibonéan, who had become a mercenary in Shazar and risen in the favour of the Shazarian court. She had been pledged to this Carolak before her abduction . . . '

'She loved him?' Count Smiorgan asked.

'She was pledged to marry him, but let me finish my story . . . ' Elric continued: 'Well, at length Carolak, now a man of some substance, second only to the King in Shazar, heard of her fate and swore to rescue her. He came with raiders to Melniboné's shores and, aided by sorcery, sought out Saxif D'Aan's palace. That done, he sought the girl, finding her at last in the apartments Saxif D'Aan had set aside for her use. He told her that he had come to claim her as his bride, to rescue her from persecution. Oddly, the girl resisted, suggesting that she had been too long a slave in the Melnibonéan harem to readapt to the life of a princess in the Shazarian court. Carolak scoffed at this and seized her. He managed to escape the castle and had the girl over the saddle of his horse and was about to rejoin his men on the coast when Saxif D'Aan detected them. Carolak, I think, was slain, or else a spell was put on him, but Saxif D'Aan, in his terrible jealousy and certain that the girl had planned the escape with a lover, ordered her to die upon the Wheel of Chaos — a machine rather like that coin in design. Her limbs were broken slowly and Saxif D'Aan sat and watched, through long days, while she died. Her skin was peeled from her flesh, and Earl Saxif D'Aan observed every detail of her punishment. Soon it was evident that the drugs and sorcery used to sustain her life were failing and Saxif D'Aan ordered her taken from the Wheel of Chaos and laid upon a couch. 'Well,' he said, 'you have been punished for betraying me and I am glad. Now you may die.' And he saw that her lips, blood-caked and frightful, were moving, and he bent to hear her words.'

'Those words? Revenge? An oath?' asked Smiorgan.

'Her last gesture was an attempt to embrace him. And the words were those she had never uttered to him before, much as he had hoped that she would. Then she died.'

Smiorgan rubbed at his beard. 'Gods! What then? What did your ancestor do?'

'He knew remorse.'

'Of course!'

'Not so, for a Melnibonéan. Remorse is a rare emotion with us. Few have ever experienced it. Torn by guilt, Earl Saxif D'Aan left Melniboné, never to return. It was assumed that he had died in some remote land, trying to make amends for what he had done to the only creature he had ever loved. But now, it seems, he sought the Crimson Gate, perhaps thinking it an opening into Hell.'

'But why should he plague me!' the girl cried. 'I am not she! My name is Vassliss. I am a merchant's daughter, from Jharkor. I was voyaging to visit my uncle in Vilmir when our ship was wrecked. A few of us escaped in an open boat. More storms seized us. I was flung from the boat and was drowning when' – she shuddered – 'when *his* galley found me. I was grateful, then . . . '

'What happened?' Elric pushed the matted hair away from her face and offered her some of their wine. She drank gratefully.

'He took me to his palace and told me that he would marry me, that I should be his empress forever and rule beside him. But I was frightened. There was such pain in him – and such cruelty, too. I thought he must devour me, destroy me. Soon after my capture, I took the money and the boat and fled for the gateway, which he had told me about . . . '

'You could find this gateway for us?' Elric asked.

'I think so. I have some knowledge of seamanship, learned from my father. But what would be the use, sir? He would find us again and drag us back. And he must be very near, even now.'

'I have a little sorcery myself,' Elric assured her, 'and will pit it against Saxif D'Aan's, if I must.' He turned to Count Smiorgan. 'Can we get a sail aloft quickly?'

'Fairly quickly.'

'Then let's hurry, Count Smiorgan Baldhead. I might have the means of getting us through this Crimson Gate and free from any further involvement in the dealings of the dead!'

4

Visit of a White Horse

While Count Smiorgan and Vassliss of Jharkor watched, Elric lowered himself to the deck, panting and pale. His first attempt to work sorcery in this world had failed and had exhausted him.

'I am further convinced,' he told Smiorgan, 'that we are in another plane of existence, for I should have worked my incantations with less effort.'

'You have failed.'

Elric rose with some difficulty. 'I shall try again.'

He turned his white face skyward; he closed his eyes; he stretched out his arms and his body tensed as he began the incantation again, his voice growing louder and louder, higher and higher, so that it resembled the shrieking of a gale.

He forgot where he was; he forgot his own identity; he forgot those who were with him as his whole mind concentrated upon the summoning. He sent his call out beyond the confines of the world, into that strange plane where the elementals dwelled – where the powerful creatures of the air could still be found – the *sylphs* of the breeze, and the *sharnahs*, who lived in the storms, and the most powerful of all, the *h'Haarshanns*, creatures of the whirlwind.

And now at last some of them began to come at his summons, ready to serve him as, by virtue of an ancient pact, the elementals had served his forefathers. And slowly the sail of the ship began to fill, and the timbers creaked, and Smiorgan raised the anchor, and the ship was sailing away from the island, through the rocky gap of the harbour, and out into the open sea, still beneath a strange blue sun.

Soon a huge wave was forming around them, lifting up the ship and carrying it across the ocean, so that Count Smiorgan and the girl marvelled at the speed of their progress, while Elric, his crimson eyes open now, but blank and unseeing, continued to croon to his unseen allies.

Thus the ship progressed across the waters of the sea, and at last the island was out of sight and the girl, checking their position against the position of the sun, was able to give Count Smiorgan sufficient information for him to steer a course.

As soon as he could, Count Smiorgan went up to Elric, who straddled the deck, still as stiff-limbed as before, and shook him.

'Elric! You will kill yourself with this effort. We need your friends no longer!'

At once the wind dropped and the wave dispersed and Elric, gasping, fell to the deck.

'It is harder here,' he said. 'It is so much harder here. It is as if I have to call across far greater gulfs than any I have known before.'

And then Elric slept.

He lay in a warm bunk in a cool cabin. Through the porthole filtered diffused blue light. He sniffed. He caught the odour of hot food, and turning his head, saw that Vassliss stood there, a bowl of broth in her hands. 'I was able to cook this,' she said. 'It will improve your health. As far as I can tell, we are nearing the Crimson Gate. The seas are always rough around the gate, so you will need your strength.'

Elric thanked her pleasantly and began to eat the broth as she watched him.

'You are very like Saxif D'Aan,' she said. 'Yet harder in a way – and gentler, too. He is so remote. I know why that girl could never tell him that she loved him.'

Elric smiled. 'Oh, it's nothing more than a folktale, probably, the story I told you. This Saxif D'Aan could be another person altogether – or an impostor, even, who has taken his name – or a sorcerer. Some sorcerers take the names of other sorcerers, for they think it gives them more power.'

There came a cry from above, but Elric could not make out the words.

The girl's expression became alarmed. Without a word to Elric, she hurried from the cabin.

Elric, rising unsteadily, followed her up the companionway.

Count Smiorgan Baldhead was at the wheel of his ship and he was pointing towards the horizon behind them. 'What do you make of that, Elric?'

Elric peered at the horizon but could see nothing. Often his eyes were weak, as now. But the girl said in a voice of quiet despair:

'It is a golden sail.'

'You recognize it?' Elric asked her.

'Oh, indeed I do. It is the galleon of Earl Saxif D'Aan. He has found us. Perhaps he was lying in wait along our route, knowing we must come this way.'

'How far are we from the gate?'

'I am not sure.'

At that moment, there came a terrible noise from below, as if something sought to stave in the timbers of the ship.

'It's in the forward hatches!' cried Smiorgan. 'See what it is, friend Elric! But take care, man!'

Cautiously Elric prised back one of the hatch covers and peered into the murky fastness of the hold. The noise of stamping and thumping continued on, and as his eyes adjusted to the light, he saw the source.

The white horse was there. It whinnied as it saw him, almost in greeting.

'How did it come aboard?' Elric asked. 'I saw nothing. I heard nothing.'

The girl was almost as white as Elric. She sank to her knees beside the hatch, burying her face in her arms.

'He has us! He has us!'

'There is still a chance we can reach the Crimson Gate in time,' Elric reassured her. 'And once in my own world, why, I can work much stronger sorcery to protect us.'

'No,' she sobbed, 'it is too late. Why else would the white horse be here? He knows that Saxif D'Aan must soon board us.'

'He'll have to fight us before he shall have you,' Elric promised her.

'You have not seen his men. Cutthroats all. Desperate and wolfish! They'll show you no mercy. You would be best advised to hand me over to Saxif D'Aan at once and save yourselves. You'll gain nothing from trying to protect me. But I'd ask you a favour.'

'What's that?'

'Find me a small knife to carry, that I may kill myself as soon as I know you two are safe.'

Elric laughed, dragging her to her feet. 'I'll have no such melodramatics from you, lass! We stand together. Perhaps we can bargain with Saxif D'Aan.'

'What have you to barter?'

'Very little. But he is not aware of that.'

'He can read your thoughts, seemingly. He has great powers!'

'I am Elric of Melniboné. I am said to possess a certain facility in the sorcerous arts, myself.'

'But you are not as single-minded as Saxif D'Aan,' she said simply. 'Only one thing obsesses him – the need to make me his consort.'

'Many girls would be flattered by the attention – glad to be an

384

empress with a Melnibonéan emperor for a husband.' Elric was sardonic.

She ignored his tone. 'That is why I fear him so,' she said in a murmur. 'If I lost my determination for a moment, I could love him. I should be destroyed! It is what *she* must have known!'

5

A Melnibonéan
Nobleman

The gleaming galleon, sails and sides all gilded so that it seemed the sun itself pursued them, moved rapidly upon them while the girl and Count Smiorgan watched aghast and Elric desperately attempted to recall his elemental allies, without success.

Through the pale blue light the golden ship sailed relentlessly in their wake. Its proportions were monstrous, its sense of power vast, its gigantic prow sending up huge, foamy waves on both sides as it sped silently towards them.

With the look of a man preparing himself to meet death, Count Smiorgan Baldhead of the Purple Towns unslung his battle-axe and loosened his sword in its scabbard, setting his little metal cap upon his bald pate. The girl made no sound, no movement at all, but she wept.

Elric shook his head and his long, milk-white hair formed a halo around his face for a moment. His moody crimson eyes began to focus on the world around him. He recognized the ship; it was of a pattern with the golden battle-barges of Melniboné – doubtless the ship in which Earl Saxif D'Aan had fled his homeland, searching for the Crimson Gate. Now Elric was convinced that this must be that same Saxif D'Aan and he knew less fear than did his companions, but considerably greater curiosity. Indeed, it was almost with nostalgia that he noted the ball of fire, like a natural comet, glowing with green light, come hissing and spluttering towards them, flung by the ship's forward catapult. He half expected to see a great dragon wheeling in the sky overhead, for it was with dragons and gilded battle-craft like these that Melniboné had once conquered the world.

The fireball fell into the sea a few inches from their bow and was evidently placed there deliberately, as a warning.

'Don't stop!' cried Vassliss. 'Let the flames slay us! It will be better!'

Smiorgan was looking upward. 'We have no choice. Look! He has banished the wind, it seems.'

They were becalmed. Elric smiled a grim smile. He knew now what the folk of the Young Kingdoms must have felt when his ancestors had used these identical tactics against them.

'Elric?' Smiorgan turned to the albino. 'Are these your people? That ship's Melnibonéan without question!'

'So are the methods,' Elric told him. 'I am of the blood royal of Melniboné. I could be emperor, even now, if I chose to claim my throne. There is some small chance that Earl Saxif D'Aan, though an ancestor, will recognize me and, therefore, recognize my authority. We are a conservative people, the folk of the Dragon Isle.'

The girl spoke through dry lips, hopelessly: 'He recognizes only the authority of the Lords of Chaos, who give him aid.'

'All Melnibonéans recognize that authority,' Elric told her with a certain humour.

From the forward hatch, the sound of the stallion's stamping and snorting increased.

'We're besieged by enchantments!' Count Smiorgan's normally ruddy features had paled. 'Have you none of your own, Prince Elric, you can use to counter them?'

'None, it seems.'

The golden ship loomed over them. Elric saw that the rails, high overhead, were crowded not with Imrryrian warriors but with cut-throats equally as desperate as those he had fought on the island, and, apparently, drawn from the same variety of historical periods and nations. The galleon's long sweeps scraped the sides of the smaller vessel as they folded, like the legs of some water insect, to enable the grappling irons to be flung out. Iron claws bit into the timbers of the little ship and the brigandly crowd overhead cheered, grinning at them, menacing them with their weapons.

The girl began to run to the seaward side of the ship, but Elric caught her by the arm.

'Do not stop me, I beg you!' she cried. 'Rather, jump with me and drown!'

'You think that death will save you from Saxif D'Aan?' Elric said. 'If he has the power you say, death will only bring you more firmly into his grasp!'

'Oh!' The girl shuddered and then, as a voice called down to them from one of the tall decks of the gilded ship, she gave a moan and fainted into Elric's arms, so that, weakened as he was by his spell-working, it was all that he could do to stop himself falling with her to the deck.

The voice rose over the coarse shouts and guffaws of the crew. It was pure, lilting, and sardonic. It was the voice of a Melnibonéan,

387

though it spoke the common tongue of the Young Kingdoms, a corruption, in itself, of the speech of the Bright Empire.

'May I have the captain's permission to come aboard?'

Count Smiorgan growled back: 'You have us firm, sir! Don't try to disguise an act of piracy with a polite speech!'

'I take it I have your permission, then.' The unseen speaker's tone remained exactly the same.

Elric watched as part of the rail was drawn back to allow a gangplank, studded with golden nails to give firmer footing, to be lowered from the galleon's deck to theirs.

A tall figure appeared at the top of the gangplank. He had the fine features of a Melnibonéan nobleman, was thin, proud in his bearing, clad in voluminous robes of cloth-of-gold, an elaborate helmet in gold and ebony upon his long auburn locks. He had grey-blue eyes, pale, slightly flushed skin, and he carried, so far as Elric could see, no weapons of any kind.

With considerable dignity, Earl Saxif D'Aan began to descend, his rascals at his back. The contrast between this beautiful intellectual and those he commanded was remarkable. Where he walked with straight back, elegant and noble, they slouched, filthy, degenerate, unintelligent, grinning with pleasure at their easy victory. Not a man among them showed any sign of human dignity; each was overdressed in tattered and unclean finery, each had at least three weapons upon his person, and there was much evidence of looted jewellery, of nose-rings, earrings, bangles, necklaces, toe- and finger-rings, pendants, cloak-pins and the like.

'Gods! murmured Smiorgan. 'I've rarely seen such a collection of scum, and I thought I'd encountered most kinds in my voyages. How can such a man bear to be in their company?'

'Perhaps it suits his sense of irony,' Elric suggested.

Earl Saxif D'Aan reached their deck and stood looking up at them to where they still positioned themselves, in the poop. He gave a slight bow. His features were controlled and only his eyes suggested something of the intensity of emotion dwelling within him, particularly as they fell upon the girl in Elric's arms.

'I am Earl Saxif D'Aan of Melniboné, now of the Islands Beyond the Crimson Gate. You have something with you which is mine. I would claim it from you.'

'You mean the Lady Vassliss of Jharkor?' Elric said, his voice as steady as Saxif D'Aan's.

Saxif D'Aan seemed to note Elric for the first time. A slight frown crossed his brow and was quickly dismissed. 'She is mine,' he said.

'You may be assured that she will come to no harm at my hands.'

Elric, seeking some advantage, knew that he risked much when he next spoke, in the High Tongue of Melniboné, used between those of the blood royal. 'Knowledge of your history does not reassure me, Saxif D'Aan.'

Almost imperceptibly, the golden man stiffened and fire flared in his grey-blue eyes. 'Who are you, to speak the Tongue of Kings? Who are you, who claims knowledge of my past?'

'I am Elric, son of Sadric, and I am the four-hundred-and-twenty-eighth emperor of the folk of R'lin K'ren A'a, who landed upon the Dragon Isle ten thousand years ago. I am Elric, your emperor, Earl Saxif D'Aan, and I demand your fealty.' And Elric held up his right hand, upon which still gleamed a ring set with a single Actorios stone, the Ring of Kings.

Earl Saxif D'Aan now had firm control of himself again. He gave no sign that he was impressed. 'Your sovereignty does not extend beyond your own world, noble emperor, though I greet you as a fellow monarch.' He spread his arms so that his long sleeves rustled. 'This world is mine. All that exists beneath the blue sun do I rule. You trespass, therefore, in my domain. I have every right to do as I please.'

'Pirate pomp,' muttered Count Smiorgan, who had understood nothing of the conversation but had gathered something of what passed by the tone. 'Pirate braggadocio. What does he say, Elric?'

'He convinces me that he is not, in your sense, a pirate, Count Smiorgan. He claims that he is ruler of this plane. Since there is apparently no other, we must accept his claim.'

'Gods! Then let him behave like a monarch and let us sail safely out of his waters!'

'We may – if we give him the girl.'

Count Smiorgan shook his head. 'I'll not do that. She's my passenger, in my charge. I must die rather than do that. It is the Code of the Sea-lords of the Purple Towns.'

'You are famous for your adherence to that code,' Elric said. 'As for myself, I have taken this girl into my protection and, as hereditary emperor of Melniboné, I cannot allow myself to be browbeaten.'

They had conversed in a murmur, but, somehow, Earl Saxif D'Aan had heard them.

'I must let you know,' he said evenly, in the common tongue, 'that the girl is mine. You steal her from me. Is that the action of an emperor?'

'She is not a slave,' Elric said, 'but the daughter of a free merchant in Jharkor. You have no rights upon her.'

Earl Saxif D'Aan said, 'Then I cannot open the Crimson Gate for you. You must remain in my world forever.'

'You have closed the gate? Is it possible?'

'To me.'

'Do you know that the girl would rather die than be captured by you, Earl Saxif D'Aan? Does it give you pleasure to instill such fear?'

The golden man looked directly into Elric's eyes as if he made some cryptic challenge. 'The gift of pain has ever been a favourite gift among our folk, has it not? Yet it is another gift I offer her. She calls herself Vassliss of Jharkor, but she does not know herself. I know her. She is Gratyesha, Princess of Fwem-Omeyo, and I would make her my bride.'

'How can it be that she does not know her own name?'

'She is reincarnated – soul and flesh are identical – that is how I know. And I have waited, Emperor of Melniboné, for many scores of years for her. Now I shall not be cheated of her.'

'As you cheated yourself, two centuries past, in Melniboné?'

'You risk much with your directness of language, brother monarch!' There was a hint of a warning in Saxif D'Aan's tone, a warning much fiercer than any implied by the words.

'Well' – Elric shrugged – 'you have more power than we do. My sorcery works poorly in your world. Your ruffians outnumber us. It should not be difficult for you to take her from us.'

'You must give her to me. Then you may go free, back to your own world and your own time.'

Elric smiled. 'There is sorcery here. She is no reincarnation. You'd bring your lost love's spirit from the netherworld to inhabit this girl's body. Am I not right? That is why she must be given freely, or your sorcery will rebound upon you – or might – and you would not take the risk.'

Earl Saxif D'Aan turned his head away so that Elric might not see his eyes. 'She is the girl,' he said, in the High Tongue. 'I know that she is. I mean her soul no harm. I would merely give it back its memory.'

'Then it is stalemate,' said Elric.

'Have you no loyalty to a brother of the royal blood?' Saxif D'Aan murmured, still refusing to look at Elric.

'You claimed no such loyalty, as I recall, Earl Saxif D'Aan. If you accept me as your emperor, then you must accept my decisions. I keep the girl in my custody. Or you must take her by force.'

'I am too proud.'

'Such pride shall ever destroy love,' said Elric, almost in sympathy. 'What now, King of Limbo? What shall you do with us?'

Earl Saxif D'Aan lifted his noble head, about to reply, when from the hold the stamping and the snorting began again. His eyes widened. He looked questioningly at Elric, and there was something close to terror in his face.

'What's that? What have you in the hold?'

'A mount, my lord, that is all,' said Elric equably.

'A horse? An ordinary horse?'

'A white one. A stallion, with bridle and saddle. It has no rider.'

At once Saxif D'Aan's voice rose as he shouted orders for his men. 'Take those three aboard our ship. This one shall be sunk directly. Hurry! Hurry!'

Elric and Smiorgan shook off the hands which sought to seize them and they moved towards the gangplank, carrying the girl between them, while Smiorgan muttered, 'At least we are not slain, Elric. But what becomes of us now?'

Elric shook his head. 'We must hope that we can continue to use Earl Saxif D'Aan's pride against him, to our advantage, though the gods alone know how we shall resolve the dilemma.'

Earl Saxif D'Aan was already hurrying up the gangplank ahead of them.

'Quickly,' he shouted. 'Raise the plank!'

They stood upon the decks of the golden battle-barge and watched as the gangplank was drawn up, the length of rail replaced.

'Bring up the catapults,' Saxif D'Aan commanded. 'Use lead. Sink that vessel at once!'

The noise from the forward hold increased. The horse's voice echoed over ships and water. Hooves smashed at timber and then, suddenly, it came crashing through the hatch-covers, scrambling for purchase on the deck with its front hooves, and then standing there, pawing at the planks, its neck arching, its nostrils dilating, and its eyes glaring, as if ready to do battle.

Now Saxif D'Aan made no attempt to hide the terror on his face. His voice rose to a scream as he threatened his rascals with every sort of horror if they did not obey him with utmost speed. The catapults were dragged up and huge globes of lead were lobbed onto the decks of Smiorgan's ship, smashing through the planks like arrows through parchment so that almost immediately the ship began to sink.

'Cut the grappling hooks!' cried Saxif D'Aan, wrenching a blade from the hand of one of his men and sawing at the nearest rope. 'Cast loose – quickly!'

Even as Smiorgan's ship groaned and roared like a drowning beast, the ropes were cut. The ship keeled over at once, and the horse disappeared.

'Turn about!' shouted Saxif D'Aan. 'Back to Fhaligarn and swiftly, or your souls shall feed my fiercest demons!'

There came a peculiar, high-pitched neighing from the foaming water, as Smiorgan's ship, stern uppermost, gasped and was swallowed. Elric caught a glimpse of the white stallion, swimming strongly.

'Go below!' Saxif D'Aan ordered, indicating a hatchway. 'The horse can smell the girl and thus is doubly difficult to lose.'

'Why do you fear it?' Elric asked. 'It is only a horse. It cannot harm you.'

Saxif D'Aan uttered a laugh of profound bitterness. 'Can it not, brother monarch? Can it not?'

As they carried the girl below, Elric was frowning, remembering a little more of the legend of Saxif D'Aan, of the girl he had punished so cruelly, and of her lover, Prince Carolak. The last he heard of Saxif D'Aan was the sorcerer crying:

'More sail! More sail!'

And then the hatch had closed behind them and they found themselves in an opulent Melnibonéan day-cabin, full of rich hangings, precious metal, decorations of exquisite beauty and, to Count Smiorgan, disturbing decadence. But it was Elric, as he lowered the girl to a couch, who noticed the smell.

'Augh! It's the smell of a tomb – of damp and mould. Yet nothing rots. It is passing peculiar, friend Smiorgan, is it not?'

'I scarcely noticed, Elric.' Smiorgan's voice was hollow. 'But I would agree with you on one thing. We are entombed. I doubt we'll live to escape this world now.'

6

'I have the Key to The Crimson Gate'

An hour had passed since they had been forced aboard. The door had been locked behind them, and it seemed Saxif D'Aan was too preoccupied with escaping the white stallion to bother with them. Peering through the lattice of a porthole, Elric could look back to where their ship had been sunk. They were many leagues distant already; yet he still thought, from time to time, that he saw the head and shoulders of the stallion above the waves.

Vassliss had recovered and sat pale and shivering upon the couch.

'What more do you know of that horse?' Elric asked her. 'It would be helpful to me if you could recall anything you have heard.'

She shook her head. 'Saxif D'Aan spoke little of it, but I gather he fears the rider more than he does the horse.'

'Ah!' Elric frowned. 'I suspected it! Have you ever seen the rider?'

'Never. I think that Saxif D'Aan has never seen him, either. I think he believes himself doomed if that rider should ever sit upon the white stallion.'

Elric smiled to himself.

'Why do you ask so much about the horse?' Smiorgan wished to know.

Elric shook his head. 'I have an instinct, that is all. Half a memory. But I'll say nothing and think as little as I may, for there is no doubt Saxif D'Aan, as Vassliss suggests, has some power of reading the mind.'

They heard a footfall above, descending to their door.

A bolt was drawn and Saxif D'Aan, his composure fully restored, stood in the opening, his hands in his golden sleeves.

'You will forgive, I hope, the peremptory way in which I sent you here. There was danger which had to be averted at all costs. As a result, my manners were not all that they should have been.'

'Danger to us?' Elric asked. 'Or to you, Earl Saxif D'Aan?'

'In the circumstances, to all of us, I assure you.'

'Who rides the horse?' Smiorgan asked bluntly. 'And why do you fear him?'

Earl Saxif D'Aan was master of himself again, so there was no sign of a reaction. 'That is very much my private concern,' he said softly. 'Will you dine with me now?'

The girl made a noise in her throat and Earl Saxif D'Aan turned piercing eyes upon her. 'Gratyesha, you will want to cleanse yourself and make yourself beautiful again. I will see that facilities are placed at your disposal.'

'I am not Gratyesha,' she said. 'I am Vassliss, the merchant's daughter.'

'You will remember,' he said. 'In time, you will remember.' There was such certainty, such obsessive power, in his voice that even Elric experienced a frisson of awe. 'The things will be brought to you, and you may use this cabin as your own until we return to my palace on Fhaligarn. My lords . . . ' He indicated that they should leave.

Elric said, 'I'll not leave her, Saxif D'Aan. She is too afraid.'

'She fears only the truth, brother.'

'She fears you and your madness.'

Saxif D'Aan shrugged insouciantly. 'I shall leave first, then. If you would accompany me, my lords . . . ' He strode from the cabin and they followed.

Elric said, over his shoulder, 'Vassliss, you may depend upon my protection.' And he closed the cabin doors behind him.

Earl Saxif D'Aan was standing upon the deck, exposing his noble face to the spray which was flung up by the ship as it moved with supernatural speed through the sea.

'You called me mad, Prince Elric? Yet you must be versed in sorcery, yourself.'

'Of course. I am of the blood royal. I am reckoned knowledgeable in my own world.'

'But here? How well does your sorcery work?'

'Poorly, I'll admit. The spaces between the planes seem greater.'

'Exactly. But I have bridged them. I have time to learn how to bridge them.'

'You are saying that you are more powerful than am I?'

'It is a fact, is it not?'

'It is. But I did not think we were about to indulge in sorcerous battles, Earl Saxif D'Aan.'

'Of course. Yet, if you were to think of besting me by sorcery, you would think twice, eh?'

'I should be foolish to contemplate such a thing at all. It could cost

394

me my soul. My life, at least.'

'True. You are a realist, I see.'

'I suppose so.'

'Then we can progress on simpler lines, to settle the dispute between us.'

'You propose a duel?' Elric was surprised.

Earl Saxif D'Aan's laughter was light. 'Of course not – against your sword? That has power in all worlds, though the magnitude varies.'

'I'm glad that you are aware of that,' Elric said significantly.

'Besides,' added Earl Saxif D'Aan, his golden robes rustling as he moved a little nearer to the rail, 'you would not kill me – for only I have the means of your escaping this world.'

'Perhaps we'd elect to remain,' said Elric.

'Then you would be my subjects. But, no – you would not like it here. I am self-exiled. I could not return to my own world now, even if I wished to do so. It has cost me much, my knowledge. But I would found a dynasty here, beneath the blue sun. I must have my wife, Prince Elric. I must have Gratyesha.'

'Her name is Vassliss,' said Elric obstinately.

'She thinks it is.'

'Then it is. I have sworn to protect her, as has Count Smiorgan. Protect her we shall. You will have to kill us all.'

'Exactly,' said Earl Saxif D'Aan with the air of a man who has been coaching a poor student towards the correct answer to a problem. 'Exactly. I shall have to kill you all. You leave me with little alternative, Prince Elric.'

'Would that benefit you?'

'It would. It would put a certain powerful demon at my service for a few hours.'

'We should resist.'

'I have many men. I do not value them. Eventually, they would overwhelm you. Would they not?'

Elric remained silent.

'My men would be aided by sorcery,' added Saxif D'Aan. 'Some would die, but not too many, I think.'

Elric was looking beyond Saxif D'Aan, staring out to sea. He was sure that the horse still followed. He was sure that Saxif D'Aan knew, also.

'And if we gave up the girl?'

'I should open the Crimson Gate for you. You would be honoured guests. I should see that you were borne safely through, even taken safely to some hospitable land in your own world, for even if you passed through the gate there would be danger. The storms.'

Elric appeared to deliberate.

'You have only a little time to make your decision, Prince Elric. I had hoped to reach my palace, Fhaligarn, by now. I shall not allow you very much longer. Come, make your decision. You know I speak the truth.'

'You know that I can work some sorcery in your world, do you not?'

'You summoned a few friendly elementals to your aid, I know. But at what cost? Would you challenge me directly?'

'It would be unwise of me,' said Elric.

Smiorgan was tugging at his sleeve. 'Stop this useless talk. He knows that we have given our word to the girl and that we *must* fight him!'

Earl Saxif D'Aan sighed. There seemed to be genuine sorrow in his voice. 'If you are determined to lose your lives . . .' he began.

'I should like to know why you set such importance upon the speed with which we make up our minds,' Elric said. 'Why cannot we wait until we reach Fhaligarn?'

Earl Saxif D'Aan's expression was calculating, and again he looked full into Elric's crimson eyes. 'I think you know,' he said, almost inaudibly.

But Elric shook his head. 'I think you give me too much credit for intelligence.'

'Perhaps.'

Elric knew that Saxif D'Aan was attempting to read his thoughts; he deliberately blanked his mind, and suspected that he sensed frustration in the sorcerer's demeanour.

And then the albino had sprung at his kinsman, his hand chopping at Saxif D'Aan's throat. The earl was taken completely off guard. He tried to call out, but his vocal chords were numbed. Another blow, and he fell to the deck, senseless.

'Quickly, Smiorgan,' Elric shouted, and he had leaped into the rigging, climbing swiftly upward to the top yards. Smiorgan, bewildered, followed, and Elric had drawn his sword, even as he reached the crow's nest, driving upward through the rail so that the lookout was taken in the groin scarcely before he realized it.

Next, Elric was hacking at the ropes holding the mainsail to the yard. Already a number of Saxif D'Aan's ruffians were climbing after them.

The heavy golden sail came loose, falling to envelop the pirates and take several of them down with it.

Elric climbed into the crow's nest and pitched the dead man over the rail in the wake of his comrades. Then he had raised his sword over his head, holding it in his two hands, his eyes blank again, his head raised to the blue sun, and Smiorgan, clinging to the mast below, shuddered as he heard a peculiar crooning come from the albino's throat.

More of the cutthroats were ascending, and Smiorgan hacked at the rigging, having the satisfaction of seeing half a score go flying down to break their bones on the deck below, or be swallowed by the waves.

Earl Saxif D'Aan was beginning to recover, but he was still stunned.

'Fool!' he was crying. 'Fool!' But it was not possible to tell if he referred to Elric or to himself.

Elric's voice became a wail, rhythmical and chilling, as he chanted his incantation, and the strength from the man he had killed flowed into him and sustained him. His crimson eyes seemed to flicker with fires of another, nameless colour, and his whole body shook as the strange runes shaped themselves in a throat which had never been made to speak such sounds.

His voice became a vibrant groan as the incantation continued, and Smiorgan, watching as more of the crew made efforts to climb the mainmast, felt an unearthly coldness creep through him.

Earl Saxif D'Aan screamed from below:

'You would not dare!'

The sorcerer began to make passes in the air, his own incantation tumbling from his lips, and Smiorgan gasped as a creature made of smoke took shape only a few feet below him. The creature smacked its lips and grinned and stretched a paw, which became flesh even as it moved, towards Smiorgan. He hacked at the paw with his sword, whimpering.

'Elric!' cried Count Smiorgan, clambering higher so that he grasped the rail of the crow's nest. 'Elric! He sends demons against us now!'

But Elric ignored him. His whole mind was in another world, a darker, bleaker world even than this one. Through grey mists, he saw a figure, and he cried a name. 'Come!' he called in the ancient tongue of his ancestors. 'Come!'

Count Smiorgan cursed as the demon became increasingly substantial. Red fangs clashed and green eyes glared at him. A claw stroked his boot and no matter how much he struck with his sword, the demon did not appear to notice the blows.

There was no room for Smiorgan in the crow's nest, but he stood on the outer rim, shouting with terror, desperate for aid. Still Elric continued to chant.

'Elric! I am doomed!'

The demon's paw grasped Smiorgan by his ankle.

'Elric!'

Thunder rolled out at sea; a bolt of lightning appeared for a second and then was gone. From nowhere there came the sound of a horse's hooves pounding, and a human voice shouting in triumph.

Elric sank back against the rail, opening his eyes in time to see Smiorgan being dragged slowly downward. With the last of his strength he flung himself forward, leaning far out to stab downwards with Stormbringer. The runesword sank cleanly into the demon's right eye. It roared, letting go of Smiorgan, striking at the blade which drew its energy from it, and as that energy passed into the blade and thence to Elric, the albino grinned a frightful grin so that, for a second, Smiorgan became more frightened of his friend that he had been of the demon. The demon began to dematerialize, its only means of escape from the sword which drank its life-force, but more of Saxif D'Aan's rogues were behind it, and their blades rattled as they sought the pair.

Elric swung himself back over the rail, balanced precariously on the yard as he slashed at their attackers, yelling the old battle-cries of his people. Smiorgan could do little but watch. He noted that Saxif D'Aan was no longer on deck and he shouted urgently to Elric:

'Elric! Saxif D'Aan. He seeks out the girl.'

Elric now took the attack to the pirates, and they were more than anxious to avoid the moaning runesword, some even leaping into the sea rather than encounter it. Swiftly the two leaped from yard to yard until they were again upon the deck.

'What does he fear? Why does he not use more sorcery?' panted Count Smiorgan, as they ran towards the cabin.

'I have summoned the one who rides the horse,' Elric told him. 'I had so little time – and I could tell you nothing of it, knowing that Saxif D'Aan would read my intention in your mind, if he could not in mine!'

The cabin doors were firmly secured from the inside. Elric began to hack at them with the black sword.

But the door resisted as it should not have resisted. 'Sealed by sorcery and I've no means of unsealing it,' said the albino.

'Will he kill her?'

'I don't know. He might try to take her into some other plane. We must — '

Hooves clattered on the deck and the white stallion reared behind them, only now it had a rider, clad in bright purple and yellow armour. He was bareheaded and youthful, though there were several

398

old scars upon his face. His hair was thick and curly and blond and his eyes were a deep blue.

He drew tightly upon his reins, steadying the horse. He looked piercingly at Elric. 'Was it you, Melnibonéan, who opened the pathway for me?'

'It was.'

'Then I thank you, though I cannot repay you.'

'You have repaid me,' Elric told him, then drew Smiorgan aside as the rider leaned forward and spurred his horse directly at the closed doors, smashing through as though they were rotted cotton.

There came a terrible cry from within and then Earl Saxif D'Aan, hampered by his complicated robes of gold, rushed from the cabin, seizing a sword from the hand of the nearest corpse, darting Elric a look not so much of hatred but of bewildered agony, as he turned to face the blond rider.

The rider had dismounted now and came from the cabin, one arm around the shivering girl, Vassliss, one hand upon the reins of his horse, and he said, sorrowfully:

'You did me a great wrong, Earl Saxif D'Aan, but you did Gratyesha an infinitely more terrible one. Now you must pay.'

Saxif D'Aan paused, drawing a deep breath, and when he looked up again, his eyes were steady, his dignity had returned.

'Must I pay in full?' he said.

'In full.'

'It is all I deserve,' said Saxif D'Aan. 'I escaped my doom for many years, but I could not escape the knowledge of my crime. She loved me, you know. Not you.'

'She loved us both, I think. But the love she gave you was her entire soul and I should not want that from any woman.'

'You would be the loser, then.'

'You never knew how much she loved you.'

'Only – only afterward . . . '

'I pity you, Earl Saxif D'Aan.' The young man gave the reins of his horse to the girl, and he drew his sword. 'We are strange rivals, are we not?'

'You have been all these years in Limbo, where I banished you – in that garden on Melniboné?'

'All these years. Only my horse could follow you. The horse of Tendric, my father, also of Melniboné, and also a sorcerer.'

'If I had known that, then, I'd have slain you cleanly and sent the horse to Limbo.'

'Jealousy weakened you, Earl Saxif D'Aan. But now we fight as we should have fought then – man to man, with steel, for the hand of the one who loves us both. It is more than you deserve.'

'Much more,' agreed the sorcerer. And he brought up his sword to lunge at the young man who, Smiorgan guessed, could only be Prince Carolak himself.

The fight was predetermined. Saxif D'Aan knew that, if Carolak did not. Saxif D'Aan's skill in arms was up to the standard of any Melnibonéan nobleman, but it could not match the skill of a professional soldier, who had fought for his life time after time.

Back and forth across the deck, while Saxif D'Aan's rascals looked on in openmouthed astonishment, the rivals fought a duel which should have been fought and resolved two centuries before, while the girl they both plainly thought was the reincarnation of Gratyesha watched them with as much concern as might her original have watched when Saxif D'Aan first encountered Prince Carolak in the gardens of his palace, so long ago.

Saxif D'Aan fought well, and Carolak fought nobly, for on many occasions he avoided an obvious advantage, but at length Saxif D'Aan threw away his sword, crying: 'Enough. I'll give you your vengeance, Prince Carolak. I'll let you take the girl. But you'll not give me your damned mercy – you'll not take my pride.'

And Carolak nodded, stepped forward, and struck straight for Saxif D'Aan's heart.

The blade entered clean and Earl Saxif D'Aan should have died, but he did not. He crawled along the deck until he reached the base of the mast, and he rested his back against it, while the blood pumped from the wounded heart. And he smiled.

'It appears,' he said faintly, 'that I cannot die, so long have I sustained my life by sorcery. I am no longer a man.'

He did not seem pleased by this thought, but Prince Carolak, stepping forward and leaning over him, reassured him. 'You will die,' he promised, 'soon.'

'What will you do with her – with Gratyesha?'

'Her name is Vassliss,' said Count Smiorgan insistently. 'She is a merchant's daughter, from Jharkor.'

'She must make up her own mind,' Carolak said, ignoring Smiorgan.

Earl Saxif D'Aan turned glazed eyes on Elric. 'I must thank you,' he said. 'You brought me the one who could bring me peace, though I feared him.'

'Is that why, I wonder, your sorcery was so weak against me?' Elric said. 'Because you wished Carolak to come and release you from your guilt?'

400

'Possibly, Elric. You are wiser in some matters, it seems, than am I.'

'What of the Crimson Gate?' Smiorgan growled. 'Can that be opened? Have you still the power, Earl Saxif D'Aan?'

'I think so.' From the folds of his bloodstained garments of gold, the sorcerer produced a large crystal which shone with the deep colours of a ruby. 'This will not only lead you to the gate, it will enable you to pass through, only I must warn you . . . ' Saxif D'Aan began to cough. 'The ship — ' he gasped, 'the ship – like my body – has been sustained by means of sorcery – therefore . . . ' His head slumped forward. He raised it with a huge effort and stared beyond them at the girl who still held the reins of the white stallion. 'Farewell, Gratyesha, Princess of Fwem-Omeyo. I loved you.' The eyes remained fixed upon her, but they were dead eyes now.

Carolak turned back to look at the girl. 'How do you call yourself, Gratyesha?'

'They call me Vassliss,' she told him. She smiled up into his youthful, battle-scarred face. 'That is what they call me, Prince Carolak.'

'You know who I am?'

'I know you now.'

'Will you come with me, Gratyesha? Will you be my bride, at last, in the strange new lands I have found, beyond the world?'

'I will come,' she said.

He helped her up into the saddle of his white stallion and climbed so that he sat behind her. He bowed to Elric of Melniboné. 'I thank you again, Sir Sorcerer, though I never thought to be helped by one of the royal blood of Melniboné.

Elric's expression was not without humour. 'In Melniboné,' he said, 'I'm told it's tainted blood.'

'Tainted with mercy, perhaps.'

'Perhaps.'

Prince Carolak saluted them. 'I hope you find peace, Prince Elric, as I have found it.'

'I fear my peace will more resemble that which Saxif D'Aan found,' Elric said grimly. 'Nonetheless, I thank you for your good words, Prince Carolak.'

Then Carolak, laughing, had ridden his horse for the rail, leaped it, and vanished.

There was a silence upon the ship. The remaining ruffians looked uncertainly from one to the other. Elric addressed them:

'Know you this – I have the key to the Crimson Gate – and only I have the knowledge to use it. Help me sail the ship, and you'll have freedom from this world! What say you?'

'Give us our orders, Captain,' said a toothless individual, and he cackled with mirth. 'It's the best offer we've had in a hundred years or more!'

7

Passage To The Past

It was Smiorgan who first saw the Crimson Gate. He held the great red gem in his hand and pointed ahead.

'There! There, Elric! Saxif D'Aan has not betrayed us!'

The sea had begun to heave with huge, turbulent waves, and with the mainsail still tangled upon the deck, it was all that the crew could do to control the ship, but the chance of escape from the world of the blue sun made them work with every ounce of energy and, slowly, the golden battle-barge neared the towering crimson pillars.

The pillars rose from the grey, roaring water, casting a peculiar light upon the crests of the waves. They appeared to have little substance, and yet stood firm against the battering of the tons of water lashing around them.

'Let us hope they are wider apart than they look,' said Elric. 'It would be a hard enough task steering through them in calm waters, let alone this kind of sea.'

'I'd best take the wheel, I think,' said Count Smiorgan, handing Elric the gem, and he strode back up the tilting deck, climbing to the covered wheelhouse and relieving the frightened man who stood there.

There was nothing Elric could do but watch as Smiorgan turned the huge vessel into the waves, riding the tops as best he could, but sometimes descending with a rush which made Elric's heart rise to his mouth. All around them, then, the cliffs of water threatened, but the ship was taking another wave before the main force of water could crash onto her decks. For all this, Elric was quickly soaked through and, though sense told him he would be best below, he clung to the rail, watching as Smiorgan steered the ship with uncanny sureness towards the Crimson Gate.

And then the deck was flooded with red light and Elric was half blinded. Grey water flew everywhere; there came a dreadful scraping sound, then a snapping as oars broke against the pillars. The ship shuddered and began to turn, sideways to the wind, but Smiorgan forced her around and suddenly the quality of the light changed subtly, though the sea remained as turbulent as ever and Elric knew, deep within him, that overhead, beyond the heavy clouds, a yellow sun was burning again.

But now there came a creaking and a crashing from within the bowels of the battle-barge. The smell of mould, which Elric had noted earlier, became stronger, almost overpowering.

Smiorgan came hurrying back, having handed over the wheel. His face was pale again. 'She's breaking up, Elric,' he called out, over the noise of the wind and the waves. He staggered as a huge wall of water struck the ship and snatched away several planks from the deck. 'She's falling apart, man!'

'Saxif D'Aan tried to warn us of this!' Elric shouted back. 'As he was kept alive by sorcery, so was his ship. She was old before he sailed her to that world. While there, the sorcery which sustained her remained strong – but on this plane it has no power at all. Look!' And he pulled at a piece of the rail, crumbling the rotten wood with his fingers. 'We must find a length of timber which is still good.'

At that moment a yard came crashing from the mast and struck the deck, bouncing, then rolling towards them.

Elric crawled up the sloping deck until he could grasp the spar and test it. 'This one's still good. Use your belt or whatever else you can and tie yourself to it!'

The wind wailed through the disintegrating rigging of the ship; the sea smashed at the sides, driving great holes below the waterline.

The ruffians who had crewed her were in a state of complete panic, some trying to unship small boats which crumbled even as they swung them out, others lying flat against the rotted decks and praying to whatever gods they still worshipped.

Elric strapped himself to the broken yard as firmly as he could and Smiorgan followed his example. The next wave to hit the ship full on lifted them with it, cleanly over what remained of the rail and into the chilling, shouting waters of that terrible sea.

Elric kept his mouth tight shut against the water and reflected on the irony of his situation. It seemed that, having escaped so much, he was to die a very ordinary death, by drowning.

It was not long before his senses left him and he gave himself up to the swirling and somehow friendly waters of the ocean.

He awoke, struggling.

There were hands upon him. He strove to fight them off, but he was too weak. Someone laughed, a rough, good-humoured sound.

404

The water no longer roared and crashed around him. The wind no longer howled. Instead there was a gentler movement. He heard waves lapping against timber. He was aboard another ship.

He opened his eyes, blinking in warm, yellow sunlight. Red-cheeked Vilmirian sailors grinned down at him. 'You're a lucky man – if man you be!' said one.

'My friend?' Elric sought for Smiorgan.

'He was in better shape than were you. He's down in Duke Avan's cabin now.'

'Duke Avan?' Elric knew the name, but in his dazed condition could remember nothing to help him place the man. 'You saved us?'

'Aye. We found you both drifting, tied to a broken yard carved with the strangest designs I've ever seen. A Melnibonéan craft, was she?'

'Yes, but rather old.'

They helped him to his feet. They had stripped him of his clothes and wrapped him in woollen blankets. The sun was already drying his hair. He was very weak. He said:

'My sword?'

'Duke Avan has it, below.'

'Tell him to be careful of it.'

'We're sure he will.'

'This way,' said another. 'The duke awaits you.'

THREE
Sailing to the Past

1

What A Race Loses

Elric sat back in the comfortable, well-padded chair and accepted the wine-cup handed him by his host. While Smiorgan ate his fill of the hot food provided for them, Elric and Duke Avan appraised one another.

Duke Avan was a man of about forty, with a square, handsome face. He was dressed in a gilded silver breastplate, over which was arranged a white cloak. His britches, tucked into black knee-length boots, were of cream-coloured doeskin. On a small sea-table at his elbow rested his helmet crested with scarlet feathers.

'I am honoured, sir, to have you as my guest,' said Duke Avan. 'I know you to be Elric of Melniboné. I have been seeking you for several months, ever since news came to me that you had left your homeland (and your power) behind and were wandering, as it were, incognito in the Young Kingdoms.'

'You know much, sir.'

'I, too, am a traveller by choice. I almost caught up with you in Pikarayd, but I gather there was some sort of trouble there. You left quickly and then I lost your trail altogether. I was about to give up looking for your aid when, by the greatest of good fortune, I found you floating in the water!' Duke Avan laughed.

'You have the advantage of me,' said Elric, smiling. 'You raise many questions.'

'He's Avan Astran of Old Hrolmar,' grunted Count Smiorgan from the other side of a huge ham bone. 'He's well known as an adventurer – explorer – trader. His reputation's the best. We can trust him, Elric.'

'I recall the name now,' Elric told the duke. 'But why should you seek my aid?'

The smell of the food from the table had at last impinged and Elric got up. 'Would you mind if I ate something while you explained, Duke Avan?'

'Eat your fill, Prince Elric. I am honoured to have you as a guest.'

'You have saved my life, sir. I have never had it saved so courteously!'

Duke Avan smiled. 'I have never before had the pleasure of, let us say, catching so courteous a fish. If I were a superstitious man, Prince Elric, I should guess that some other force threw us together in this way.'

'I prefer to think of it as coincidence,' said the albino, beginning to eat. 'Now, sir, tell me how I can aid you.'

'I shall not hold you to any bargain, merely because I have been lucky enough to save your life,' said Duke Avan Astran, 'please bear that in mind.'

'I shall, sir.'

Duke Avan stroked the feathers of his helmet. 'I have explored most of the world, as Count Smiorgan rightly says. I have been to your own Melniboné and I have even ventured east, to Elwher and the Unknown Kingdoms. I have been to Myyrrhn, where the Winged Folk live. I have travelled as far as World's Edge and hope one day to go beyond. But I have never crossed the Boiling Sea and I know only a small stretch of coast along the western continent – the continent that has no name. Have you been there, Elric, in your travels?'

The albino shook his head. 'I seek experience of other cultures, other civilizations – that is why I travel. There has been nothing, so far, to take me there. The continent is inhabited only by savages, is it not?'

'So we are told.'

'You have other intelligence?'

'You know that there is some evidence,' said Duke Avan in a deliberate tone, 'that your own ancestors came originally from that mainland?'

'Evidence?' Elric pretended lack of interest. 'A few legends, that is all.'

'One of those legends speaks of a city older than dreaming Imrryr. A city that still exists in the deep jungles of the west.'

Elric recalled his conversation with Earl Saxif D'Aan, and he smiled to himself. 'You mean R'lin K'ren A'a?'

'Aye. A strange name.' Duke Avan Astran leaned forward, his eyes alight with delighted curiosity. 'You pronounce it more fluently than could I. You speak the secret tongue, the High Tongue, the Speech of Kings . . . '

'Of course.'

'You are forbidden to teach it to any but your own children, are you not?'

'You appear conversant with the customs of Melniboné, Duke Avan,' Elric said, his lids falling so that they half covered his eyes.

410

He leaned back in his seat as he bit into a piece of fresh bread with relish. 'Do you know what the words mean?'

'I have been told that they mean simply 'Where the High Ones Meet' in the ancient speech of Melniboné,' Duke Avan Astran told him.

Elric inclined his head. 'That is so. Doubtless only a small town, in reality. Where local chiefs gathered, perhaps once a year, to discuss the price of grain.'

'You believe that, Prince Elric?'

Elric inspected a covered dish. He helped himself to veal in a rich, sweet sauce. 'No,' he said.

'You believe, then, that there was an ancient civilization even before your own, from which your own culture sprang? You believe that R'lin K'ren A'a is still there, somewhere in the jungles of the west?'

Elric waited until he had swallowed. He shook his head.

'No,' he said. 'I believe that it does not exist at all.'

'You are not curious about your ancestors?'

'Should I be?'

'They were said to be different in character from those who founded Melniboné. Gentler . . . ' Duke Avan Astran looked deep into Elric's face.

Elric laughed. 'You are an intelligent man, Duke Avan of Old Hrolmar. You are a perceptive man. Oh, and indeed you are a cunning man, sir!'

Duke Avan grinned at the compliment. 'And you know much more of the legends than you are admitting, if I am not mistaken.'

'Possibly.' Elric sighed as the food warmed him. 'We are known as a secretive people, we of Melniboné.'

'Yet,' said Duke Avan, 'you seem untypical. Who else would desert an empire to travel in lands where his very race was hated?'

'An emperor rules better, Duke Avan Astran, if he has close knowledge of the world in which he rules.'

'Melniboné rules the Young Kingdoms no longer.'

'Her power is still great. But that, anyway, was not what I meant. I am of the opinion that the Young Kingdoms offer something which Melniboné has lost.'

'Vitality?'

'Perhaps.'

'Humanity!' grunted Count Smiorgan Baldhead. 'That is what your race has lost, Prince Elric. I say nothing of you – but look at Earl Saxif D'Aan. How can one so wise be such a simpleton? He lost everything – pride, love, power – because he had no humanity. And what humanity he had – why, it destroyed him.'

'Some say it will destroy me,' said Elric, 'but perhaps "humanity" is, indeed, what I seek to bring to Melniboné, Count Smiorgan.'

'Then you will destroy your kingdom!' said Smiorgan bluntly. 'It is too late to save Melniboné.'

'Perhaps I can help you find what you seek, Prince Elric,' said Duke Avan Astran quietly. 'Perhaps there is time to save Melniboné, if you feel such a mighty nation is in danger.'

'From within,' said Elric. 'But I speak too freely.'

'For a Melnibonéan, that is true.'

'How did you come to hear of this city?' Elric wished to know. 'No other man I have met in the Young Kingdoms has heard of R'lin K'ren A'a.'

'It is marked on a map I have.'

Deliberately, Elric chewed his meat and swallowed it. 'The map is doubtless a forgery.'

'Perhaps. Do you recall anything else of the legend of R'lin K'ren A'a?'

'There is the story of the Creature Doomed to Live.' Elric pushed the food aside and poured wine for himself. 'The city is said to have received its name because the Lords of the Higher Worlds once met there to decide the rules of the Cosmic Struggle. They were overheard by the one inhabitant of the city who had not flown when they came. When they discovered him, they doomed him to remain alive forever, carrying the frightful knowledge in his head . . . '

'I have heard that story, too. But the one that interests me is that the inhabitants of R'lin K'ren A'a never returned to their city. Instead they struck northward and crossed the sea. Some reached an island we now call Sorcerer's Isle while others went farther – blown by a great storm – and came at length to a large island inhabited by dragons whose venom caused all it touched to burn . . . to Melniboné, in fact.'

'And you wish to test the truth of that story. Your interest is that of a scholar?'

Duke Avan laughed. 'Partly. But my main interest in R'lin K'ren A'a is more materialistic. For your ancestors left a great treasure behind them when they fled their city. Particularly they abandoned an image of Arioch, the Lord of Chaos – a monstrous image, carved in jade, whose eyes were two huge, identical gems of a kind unknown anywhere else in all the lands of the Earth. Jewels from another plane of existence. Jewels which could reveal all the secrets of the Higher Worlds, of the past and the future, of the myriad planes of the cosmos . . . '

'All cultures have similar legends. Wishful thinking, Duke Avan, that is all . . . '

'But the Melnibonéans had a culture unlike any others. The Melnibonéans are not true men, as you well know. Their powers are superior, their knowledge far greater . . . '

'It was once thus,' Elric said. 'But that great power and knowledge is not mine. I have only a fragment of it . . . '

'I did not seek you in Bakshaan and later in Jadmar because I believed you could verify what I have heard. I did not cross the sea to Filkhar, then to Argimiliar and at last to Pikarayd because I thought you would instantly confirm all that I have spoken of – I sought you because I think you the only man who would wish to accompany me on a voyage which would give us the truth or falsehood to these legends once and for all.'

Elric tilted his head and drained his wine-cup.

'Cannot you do that for yourself? Why should you desire my company on the expedition? From what I have heard of you, Duke Avan, you are not one who needs support in his venturings . . . '

Duke Avan laughed. 'I went alone to Elwher when my men deserted me in the Weeping Waste. It is not in my nature to know physical fear. But I have survived my travels this long because I have shown proper foresight and caution before setting off. Now it seems I must face dangers I cannot anticipate – sorcery, perhaps. It struck me, therefore, that I needed an ally who had some experience of fighting sorcery. And since I would have no truck with the ordinary kind of wizard such as Pan Tang spawns, you were my only choice. You seek knowledge, Prince Elric, just as I do. Indeed, it could be said that if it had not been for your yearning for knowledge, your cousin would never have attempted to usurp the Ruby Throne of Melniboné . . . '

'Enough of that,' Elric said bitterly. 'Let's talk of this expedition. Where is the map?'

'You will accompany me?'

'Show me the map.'

Duke Avan drew a scroll from his pouch. 'Here it is.'

'Where did you find it?'

'On Melniboné.'

'You have been there recently?' Elric felt anger rise in him.

Duke Avan raised a hand. 'I went there with a group of traders and I gave much for a particular casket which had been sealed, it seemed, for an eternity. Within that casket was this map.' He spread out the scroll on the table. Elric recognized the style and the script – the old High Speech of Melniboné. It was a map of part of the western continent – more than he had ever seen on any other map. It showed a great river winding into the interior for a hundred miles or more. The river appeared to flow through a jungle and then divide into two rivers which later rejoined. The 'island' of land thus formed had a black circle marked on it. Against this circle, in the involved writing of ancient Melniboné, was the name R'lin K'ren A'a. Elric inspected the scroll carefully. It did not seem to be a forgery.

'Is this all you found?' he asked.

'The scroll was sealed and this was embedded in the seal,' Duke Avan said, handing something to Elric.

Elric held the object in his palm. It was a tiny ruby of a red so deep as to seem black at first, but when he turned it into the light he saw an image at the centre of the ruby and he recognized that image. He frowned, then he said, 'I will agree to your proposal, Duke Avan. Will you let me keep this?'

'Do you know what it is?'

'No. But I should like to find out. There is a memory somewhere in my head . . . '

'Very well, take it. I will keep the map.'

'When did you have it in mind to set off?'

Duke Avan's smile was sardonic. 'We are already sailing around the southern coast to the Boiling Sea.'

'There are few who have returned from that ocean,' Elric murmured bitterly. He glanced across the table and saw that Smiorgan was imploring with his eyes for Elric not to have any part of Duke Avan's scheme. Elric smiled at his friend. 'The adventure is to my taste.'

Miserably, Smiorgan shrugged. 'It seems it will be a little longer before I return to the Purple Towns.'

2

An Unnatural Heat

The coast of Lormyr had disappeared in warm mist and Duke Avan
Astran's schooner dipped its graceful prow towards the west and the
Boiling Sea.

The Vilmirian crew of the schooner were used to a less demanding
climate and more casual work than this and they went about their
tasks, it seemed to Elric, with something of an aggrieved air.

Standing beside Elric in the ship's poop, Count Smiorgan Baldhead
wiped sweat from his pate and growled: 'Vilmirians are a lazy lot,
Prince Elric. Duke Avan needs real sailors for a voyage of this kind. I
could have picked him a crew, given the chance . . . '

Elric smiled. 'Neither of us was given the chance, Count Smiorgan. It
was a fait accompli. He's a clever man, Duke Astran.'

'It is not a cleverness I entirely respect, for he offered us no real
choice. A free man is a better companion than a slave, says the old
aphorism.'

'Why did you not disembark when you had the chance, then, Count
Smiorgan?'

'Because of the promise of treasure,' said the black-bearded man
frankly. 'I would return with honour to the Purple Towns. Forget you
not that I commanded the fleet that was lost . . . '

Elric understood.

'My motives are straightforward,' said Smiorgan. 'Yours are much
more complicated. You seem to desire danger as other men desire
lovemaking or drinking – as if in danger you find forgetfulness.'

'Is that not true of many professional soldiers?'

'You are not a mere professional soldier, Elric. That you know as
well as I.'

'Yet few of the dangers I have faced have helped me forget,' Elric
pointed out. 'Rather they have strengthened the reminder of what I am
– of the dilemma I face. My own instincts war against the traditions of
my race.' Elric drew a deep, melancholy breath. 'I go where danger is

because I think that an answer might lie there – some reason for all this tragedy and paradox. Yet I know I shall never find it.'

'But it is why you sail to R'lin K'ren A'a, eh? You hope that your remote ancestors had the answer you need?'

'R'lin K'ren A'a is a myth. Even should the map prove genuine what shall we find but a few ruins? Imrryr has stood for ten thousand years and she was built at least two centuries after my people settled on Melniboné. Time will have taken R'lin K'ren A'a away.'

'And this statue, this Jade Man, Avan spoke of?'

'If the statue ever existed, it could have been looted at any time in the past hundred centuries.'

'And the Creature Doomed to Live?'

'A myth.'

'But you hope, do you not, that it is all as Duke Avan says . . .?' Count Smiorgan put a hand on Elric's arm. 'Do you not?'

Elric stared ahead, into the writhing steam which rose from the sea. He shook his head.

'No, Count Smiorgan. I *fear* that it is all as Duke Avan says.'

The wind blew whimsically and the schooner's passage was slow as the heat grew greater and the crew sweated still more and murmured fearfully. And upon each face, now, was a stricken look.

Only Duke Avan seemed to retain his confidence. He called to them all to take heart; he told them that they should all be rich soon; and he gave orders for the oars to be unshipped, for the wind could no longer be trusted. They grumbled at this, stripping off their shirts to reveal skins as red as cooked lobsters. Duke Avan made a joke of that. But the Vilmirians no longer laughed at his jokes as they had done in the milder seas of their home waters.

Around the ship the sea bubbled and roared, and they navigated by their few instruments, for the steam obscured everything.

Once a green thing erupted from the sea and glared at them before disappearing.

They ate and slept little and Elric rarely left the poop. Count Smiorgan bore the heat silently and Duke Avan, seemingly oblivious to any discomfort, went cheerfully about the ship, calling encouragement to his men.

Count Smiorgan was fascinated by the waters. He had heard of them, but never crossed them. 'These are only the outer reaches of this sea, Elric,' he said in some wonder. 'Think what it must be like at the middle.'

Elric grinned. 'I would rather not. As it is, I fear I'll be boiled to death before another day has passed.'

Passing by, Duke Avan heard him and clapped him on the shoulder. 'Nonsense, Prince Elric! The steam is good for you! There is nothing healthier!' Seemingly with pleasure, Duke Avan stretched his limbs. 'It cleans all the poisons from the system.'

Count Smiorgan offered him a glowering look and Duke Avan laughed. 'Be of better cheer, Count Smiorgan. According to my charts – such as they are – a couple of days will see us nearing the coasts of the western continent.'

'The thought fails to raise my spirits very greatly,' said Count Smiorgan, but he smiled, infected by Avan's good humour.

But shortly thereafter the sea grew slowly less frenetic and the steam began to disperse until the heat became more tolerable.

At last they emerged into a calm ocean beneath a shimmering blue sky in which hung a red-gold sun.

But three of the Vilmirian crew had died to cross the Boiling Sea, and four more had a sickness in them which made them cough a great deal, and shiver, and cry out in the night.

For a while they were becalmed, but at last a soft wind began to blow and fill the schooner's sails and soon they had sighted their first land – a little yellow island where they found fruit and a spring of fresh water. Here, too, they buried the three men who had succumbed to the sickness of the Boiling Sea, for the Vilmirians had refused to have them buried in the ocean on the grounds that the bodies would be 'stewed like meat in a pot.'

While the schooner lay at anchor, just off the island, Duke Avan called Elric to his cabin and showed him, for a second time, that ancient map.

Pale golden sunlight filtered through the cabin's ports and fell upon the old parchment, beaten from the skin of a beast long since extinct, as Elric and Duke Avan Astran of Old Hrolmar bent over it.

'See,' Duke Avan said, pointing. 'This island's marked. The map's scale seems reasonably accurate. Another three days and we shall be at the mouth of the river.'

Elric nodded. 'But it would be wise to rest here for a while until our strength is fully restored and the morale of the crew is raised higher. There are reasons, after all, why men have avoided the jungles of the west over the centuries.'

'Certainly there are savages there – some say they are not even human – but I'm confident we can deal with those dangers. I have much experience of strange territories, Prince Elric.'

'But you said yourself you feared other dangers.'

'True. Very well, we'll do as you suggest.'

On the fourth day a strong wind began to blow from the east and they raised anchor. The schooner leaped over the waves under only half her canvas and the crew saw this as a good omen.

'They are mindless fools,' Smiorgan said as they stood clinging to the rigging in the prow. 'The time will come when they will wish they were suffering the cleaner hardships of the Boiling Sea. This journey, Elric, could benefit none of us, even if the riches of R'lin K'ren A'a are still there.'

But Elric did not answer. He was lost in strange thoughts, unusual thoughts for him, for he was remembering his childhood, his mother and his father. They had been the last true rulers of the Bright Empire – proud, insouciant, cruel. They had expected him – perhaps because of his strange albinism – to restore the glories of Melniboné. Instead he threatened to destroy what was left of that glory. They, like himself, had had no real place in this new age of the Young Kingdoms, but they had refused to acknowledge it. This journey to the western continent, to the land of his ancestors, had a peculiar attraction for him. Here no new nations had emerged. The continent had, as far as he knew, re-mained the same since R'lin K'ren A'aa had been abandoned. The jungles would be the jungles his folk had known, the land would be the land that had given birth to his peculiar race, moulded the character of its people with their sombre pleasures, their melancholy arts, and their dark delights. Had his ancestors felt this agony of knowledge, this impotence in the face of the understanding that existence had no point, no purpose, no hope? Was this why they had built their civilization in that particular pattern, why they had disdained the more placid, spirit-ual values of mankind's philosophers? He knew that many of the intellectuals of the Young Kingdoms pitied the powerful folk of Melniboné as mad. But if they had been mad and if they had imposed a madness upon the world that had lasted a hundred centuries, what had made them so? Perhaps the secret did lie in R'lin K'ren A'a – not in any tangible form but in the ambience created by the dark jungles and the deep, old rivers. Perhaps here, at last, he would be able to feel at one with himself.

He ran his fingers through his milk-white hair and there was a kind of innocent anguish in his crimson eyes. He might be the last of his kind and yet he was unlike his kind. Smiorgan had been wrong. Elric knew that everything that existed had its opposite. In danger he might find peace. And yet, of course, in peace there was danger. Being an imperfect creature in an imperfect world he would always know paradox. And that was why in paradox there was always a kind of truth. That was why philosophers and soothsayers flourished. In a perfect world there would be no place for them. In an imperfect world the mysteries were always without solution and that was why there was always a great choice of solutions.

It was on the morning of the third day that the coast was sighted and the schooner steered her way through the sandbanks of the great delta and anchored, at last, at the mouth of the dark and nameless river.

3

Inhabitants of an Unhealthy Forest

Evening came and the sun began to set over the black outlines of the massive trees. A rich, ancient smell came from the jungle and through the twilight echoed the cries of strange birds and beasts. Elric was impatient to begin the quest up the river. Sleep – never welcome – was now impossible to achieve. He stood unmoving on the deck, his eyes hardly blinking, his brain barely active, as if expecting something to happen to him. The rays of the sun stained his face and threw black shadows over the deck and then it was dark and still under the moon and the stars. He wanted the jungle to absorb him. He wanted to be one with the trees and the shrubs and the creeping beasts. He wanted thought to disappear. He drew the heavily scented air into his lungs as if that alone would make him become what at that moment he desired to be. The drone of insects became a murmuring voice that called him into the heart of the old, old forest. And yet he could not move – could not answer. And at length Count Smiorgan came up on deck and touched his shoulder and said something and passively he went below to his bunk and wrapped himself in his cloak and lay there, still listening to the voice of the jungle.

Even Duke Avan seemed more introspective than usual when they upped anchor the next morning and began to row against the sluggish current. There were few gaps in the foliage above their heads and they had the impression that they were entering a huge, gloomy tunnel, leaving the sunlight behind with the sea. Bright plants twined among the vines that hung from the leafy canopy and caught in the ship's masts as they moved. Ratlike animals with long arms swung through the branches and peered at them with bright, knowing eyes. The river turned and the sea was no longer in sight. Shafts of sunlight filtered down to the deck and the light had a greenish tinge to it. Elric became more alert than he had ever been since he agreed to accompany Duke Avan. He took a keen interest in every detail of the jungle and the black river over which moved schools of insects like agitated clouds of mist and in which blossoms drifted like drops of blood in ink. Everywhere were rustlings, sudden squawks, barks and wet noises made by fish or river animals as they hunted the prey disturbed by the ship's oars which cut into the great clumps of weed and sent the things that hid there scurrying. The others began to complain of insect bites, but Elric was not troubled by them, perhaps because no insect could desire his deficient blood.

Duke Avan passed him on the deck. The Vilmirian slapped at his forehead. 'You seem more cheerful, Prince Elric.'

Elric smiled absently. 'Perhaps I am.'

'I must admit I personally find all this a bit oppressive. I'll be glad when we reach the city.'

'You are still convinced you'll find it?'

'I'll be convinced otherwise when I've explored every inch of the island we're bound for.'

So absorbed had he become in the atmosphere of the jungle that Elric was hardly aware of the ship or his companions. The ship beat very slowly up the river, moving at little more than walking speed.

A few days passed, but Elric scarcely noticed, for the jungle did not change – and then the river widened and the canopy parted and the wide, hot sky was suddenly full of huge birds crowding upwards as the ship disturbed them. All but Elric were pleased to be under the open sky again and spirits rose. Elric went below.

The attack on the ship came almost immediately. There was a whistling noise and a scream and a sailor writhed and fell over clutching at a grey thin semicircle of something which had buried itself in his stomach. An upper yard came crashing to the deck, bringing sail and rigging with it. A headless body took four paces towards the poop deck before collapsing, the blood pumping from the obscene hole that was its neck. And everywhere was the thin whistling noise. Elric heard the sounds from below and came back instantly, buckling on his sword. The first face he saw was Smiorgan's. The bald-pated man looked perturbed as he crouched against a rail on the starboard side. Elric had the impression of grey blurs whistling past, slashing into flesh and rigging, wood and canvas. Some fell to the deck and he saw that they were thin discs of crystalline rock, about a foot in diameter. They were being hurled from both banks of the river and there was no protection against them.

He tried to see who was throwing the discs and glimpsed something moving in the trees along the right bank. Then the discs ceased suddenly and there was a pause before some of the sailors dashed across the deck to seek better cover. Duke Avan suddenly appeared in the stern. He had unsheathed his sword.

'Get below. Get your bucklers and any armour you can find. Bring bows. Arm yourselves, men, or you're finished.'

And as he spoke their attackers broke from the trees and began to wade into the water. No more discs came and it seemed likely they had exhausted their supply.

'By Chardros!' Avan gasped. 'Are these real creatures or some sorcerer's conjurings?'

The things were essentially reptilian but with feathery crests and neck wattles, though their faces were almost human. Their forelegs were like the arms and hands of men, but their hindlegs were incredibly long and storklike. Balanced on these legs, their bodies towered over the water. They carried great clubs in which slits had been cut and doubtless these were what they used to hurl the crystalline discs. Staring at their faces, Elric was horrified. In some subtle way they reminded him of the characteristic faces of his own folk – the folk of Melniboné. Were these creatures his cousins? Or were they a species from which his people had evolved? He stopped asking the questions as an intense hatred for the creatures filled him. They were obscene: sight of them brought bile into his throat. Without thinking, he drew Stormbringer from its sheath.

The Black Sword began to howl and the familiar black radiance spilled from it. The runes carved into its blade pulsed a vivid scarlet which turned slowly to a deep purple and then to black once more.

The creatures were wading through the water on their stiltlike legs and they paused when they saw the sword, glancing at one another. And they were not the only ones unnerved by the sight, for Duke Avan and his men paled, too.

'Gods!' Avan yelled. 'I know not which I prefer the look of – those who attack us or that which defends us!'

'Stay well away from that sword,' Smiorgan warned. 'It has the habit of killing more than its master chooses.'

And now the reptilian savages were upon them, clutching at the ship's rails as the armed sailors rushed back on deck to meet the attack.

Clubs came at Elric from all sides, but Stormbringer shrieked and parried each blow. He held the sword in both hands, whirling it this way and that, plowing great gashes in the scaly bodies.

The creatures hissed and opened red mouths in agony and rage while their thick, black blood sank into the waters of the river. Although from the legs upward they were only slightly larger than a tall, well-built man, they had more vitality than any human and the deepest cuts hardly seemed to affect them, even when administered by Stormbringer. Elric was astonished at this resistance to the sword's power. Often a nick was enough for the sword to draw a man's soul from him. These things seemed immune. Perhaps they had no souls . . .

He fought on, his hatred giving him strength.

But elsewhere on the ship the sailors were being routed. Rails were torn off and the great clubs crushed planks and brought down more rigging. The savages were intent on destroying the ship as well as the crew. And there was little doubt, now, that they would be successful.

Avan shouted to Elric. 'By the names of all the gods, Prince Elric, can you not summon some further sorcery? We are doomed else!'

Elric knew Avan spoke truth. All around him the ship was being gradually pulled apart by the hissing reptilian creatures. Most of them had sustained horrible wounds from the defenders, but only one or two had collapsed. Elric began to suspect that they did, in fact, fight supernatural enemies.

He backed away and sought shelter beneath a half-crushed doorway as he tried to concentrate on a method of calling upon supernatural aid.

He was panting with exhaustion and he clung to a beam as the ship rocked back and forth in the water. He fought to clear his head.

And then the incantation came to him. He was not sure if it was appropriate, but it was the only one he could recall. His ancestors had made pacts, thousands of years before, with all the elementals who controlled the animal world. In the past he had summoned help from various of these spirits but never from the one he now sought to call. From his mouth began to issue the ancient, beautiful, and convoluted words of Melniboné's High Speech.

'King with Wings! Lord of all that work and are not seen, upon whose labours all else depends! Nnuuurrrr'c'c of the Insect Folk, I summon thee!'

Save for the motion of the ship, Elric ceased to be aware of all else happening around him. The sounds of the fight dimmed and were heard no more as he sent his voice out beyond his plane of the Earth into another – the plane dominated by King Nnuuurrrr'c'c of the Insects, paramount lord of his people.

In his ears now Elric heard a buzzing and gradually the buzzing formed itself in words.

'Who are thou, mortal? What right hast thee to summon me?'

'I am Elric, ruler of Melniboné. My ancestors aided thee, Nnuuurrrr'c'c.'

'Aye – but long ago.'

'And it is long ago that they last called on thee for thine aid!'

'True. What aid dost thou now require, Elric of Melniboné?'

'Look upon my plane. Thou wilt see that I am in danger. Canst thou abolish this danger, friend of the Insects?'

Now a filmy shape formed and could be seen as if through several layers of cloudy silk. Elric tried to keep his eyes upon it, but it kept leaving his field of vision and then returning for a few moments. He knew that he looked into another plane of the Earth.

'Canst thou help me, Nnuuurrrr'c'c?'

'Hast thou no patron of thine own species? Some Lord of Chaos who can aid thee?'

'My patron is Arioch and he is a temperamental demon at best. These days he aids me little.'

'Then I must send thee allies, mortal. But call upon me no more when this is done.'

'I shall not summon thee again, Nnuuurrrr'c'c.'

The layers of film disappeared and with them the shape.

The noise of the battle crashed once again on Elric's consciousness and he heard with sharper clarity than before the screams of the sailors and the hissing of the reptilian savages and when he looked out from his shelter he saw that at least half the crew were dead.

As he came on deck Smiorgan ran up. 'I thought you slain, Elric! What became of you?' He was plainly relieved to see his friend still lived.

'I sought aid from another plane – but it does not seem to have materialized.'

'I'm thinking we're doomed and had best try to swim downstream away from here and seek a hiding place in the jungle,' Smiorgan said.

'What of Duke Avan? Is he dead?'

'He lives. But those creatures are all but impervious to our weapons. This ship will sink ere long.' Smiorgan lurched as the deck tilted and he reached out to grab a trailing rope, letting his long sword dangle by its wrist-thong. 'They are not attacking the stern at present. We can slip into the water there . . . '

'I made a bargain with Duke Avan,' Elric reminded the islander. 'I cannot desert him.'

'Then we'll all perish!'

'What's that?' Elric bent his head, listening intently.

'I hear nothing.'

It was a whine which deepened in tone until it became a drone. Now Smiorgan heard it also and looked about him, seeking the source of the sound. And suddenly he gasped, pointing upward. 'Is that the aid you sought?'

There was a vast cloud of them, black against the blue of the sky. Every so often the sun would flash on a dazzling colour – a rich blue, green, or red. They came spiralling down towards the ship and now both sides fell silent, staring skyward.

The flying things were like huge dragonflies and the brightness and richness of their colouring was breathtaking. It was their wings which made the droning sound which now began to increase in loudness and heighten in pitch as the huge insects sped nearer.

Realizing that they were the object of the attack the reptile men stumbled backwards on their long legs, trying to reach the shore before the gigantic insects were upon them.

But it was too late for flight.

The dragonflies settled on the savages. Soon nothing could be seen of the bodies. The hissing increased and sounded almost pitiful as the insects bore their victims down to the surface and then inflicted on them whatever terrible death it was. Perhaps they stung with their tails – it was not possible for the watchers to see.

Sometimes a storklike leg would emerge from the water and thrash in the air for a moment. But soon, just as the reptiles were covered by the insect bodies, so were their cries drowned by the strange and blood-chilling humming that arose on all sides.

A sweating Duke Avan, sword still in hand, ran up the deck. 'Is this your doing, Prince Elric?'

Elric looked on with satisfaction, but the others were plainly disgusted. 'It was,' he said.

'Then I thank you for your aid. This ship is holed in a dozen places and is letting in water at a terrible rate. It's a wonder we have not yet sunk. I've given orders to begin rowing and I hope we make it to the island in time.' He pointed upstream. 'There, you can just see it.'

'What if there are more of those savages there?' Smiorgan asked.

Avan smiled grimly, indicating the farther shore. 'Look.' On their peculiar legs a dozen or more of the reptiles were fleeing into the jungle, having witnessed the fate of their comrades. 'They'll be reluctant to attack us again, I think.'

Now the huge dragonflies were rising into the air again and Avan turned away as he glimpsed what they had left behind. 'By the gods, you work fierce sorcery, Prince Elric! Ugh!'

Elric smiled and shrugged. 'It is effective, Duke Avan.' He sheathed his runesword. It seemed reluctant to enter the scabbard and it moaned as if in resentment.

Smiorgan glanced at it. 'That blade looks as if it will want to feast soon, Elric, whether you desire it or not.'

'Doubtless it will find something to feed on in the forest,' said the albino. He stepped over a piece of broken mast and went below.

Count Smiorgan Baldhead looked at the new scum on the surface of the water and he shuddered.

4

Nightfall on the Jungle

The wrecked schooner was almost awash when the crew clambered overboard with lines and began the task of dragging it up the mud that formed the banks of the island. Before them was a wall of foliage that seemed impenetrable. Smiorgan followed Elric, lowering himself into the shallows. They began to wade ashore.

As they left the water and set foot on the hard, baked earth, Smiorgan stared at the forest. No wind moved the trees and a peculiar silence had descended. No birds called from the trees, no insects buzzed, there were none of the barks and cries of animals they had heard on their journey upriver.

'Those supernatural friends of yours seem to have frightened more than the savages away,' the black-bearded man murmured. 'This place seems lifeless.'

Elric nodded. 'It is strange.'

Duke Avan joined them. He had discarded his finery – ruined in the fight, anyway – and now wore a padded leather jerkin and doeskin breeches. His sword was at his side. 'We'll have to leave most of our men behind with the ship,' he said regretfully. 'They'll make what repairs they can while we press on to find R'lin K'ren A'a.' He tugged his light cloak about him. 'Is it my imagination, or is there an odd atmosphere?'

'We have already remarked on it,' Smiorgan said. 'Life seems to have fled the island.'

Duke Avan grinned. 'If all we face is as timid, we have nothing further to fear. I must admit, Prince Elric, that had I wished you harm and then seen you conjure those monsters from thin air, I'd think twice about getting too close to you! Thank you, by the way, for what you did. We should have perished by now if it had not been for you.'

'It was for my aid that you asked me to accompany you,' Elric said wearily. 'Let's eat and rest and then continue with our expedition.'

A shadow passed over Duke Avan's face then. Something in Elric's manner had disturbed him.

Entering the jungle was no easy matter. Armed with axes the six members of the crew (all that could be spared) began to hack at the undergrowth. And still the unnatural silence prevailed . . .

By nightfall they were less than half a mile into the forest and completely exhausted. The forest was so thick that there was barely room to pitch their tent. The only light in the camp came from the small, sputtering fire outside the tent. The crewmen slept where they could in the open.

Elric could not sleep, but now it was not the jungle which kept him awake. He was puzzled by the silence, for he was sure that it was not their presence which had driven all life away. There was not a single small rodent, bird, or insect anywhere to be seen. There were no traces of animal life. The island had been deserted by all but vegetation for a long while – perhaps for centuries or tens of centuries. He remembered another part of the old legend of R'lin K'ren A'a. It had been said that when the gods came to meet there not only the citizens fled, but also all the wildlife. Nothing had dared see the High Lords or listen to their conversation. Elric shivered, turning his white head this way and that on the rolled cloak that supported it, his crimson eyes tortured. If there were dangers on this island, they would be subtler dangers than those they had faced on the river.

The noise of their passage through the forest was the only sound to be heard on the island as they forced their way on the next morning.

With lodestone in one hand and map in the other, Duke Avan Astran sought to guide them, directing his men where to cut their path. But the going became even slower and it was obvious that no creatures had come this way for many ages.

By the fourth day they had reached a natural clearing of flat volcanic rock and found a spring there. Gratefully they made camp. Elric began to wash his face in the cool water when he heard a yell behind him. He sprang up. One of the crewmen was reaching for an arrow and fitting it to his bow.

'What is it?' Duke Avan called.

'I saw something, my lord!'

'Nonsense, there are no — '

'Look!' The man drew back the string and let fly into the upper terraces of the forest. Something did seem to stir then and Elric thought he saw a flash of grey among the trees.

'Did you see what kind of creature it was?' Smiorgan asked the man.

'No, master. I feared at first it was those reptiles again.'

'They're too frightened to follow us onto this island,' Duke Avan reassured him.

'I hope you're right,' Smiorgan said nervously.

'Then what could it have been?' Elric wondered.

'I – I thought it was a man, master,' the crewman stuttered.

Elric stared thoughtfully into the trees. 'A man?'

Smiorgan asked, 'You were hoping for this, Elric?'

'I am not sure . . . '

Duke Avan shrugged. 'More likely the shadow of a cloud passing over the trees. According to my calculations we should have reached the city by now.'

'You think, after all, that it does not exist?' Elric said.

'I am beginning not to care, Prince Elric.' The duke leaned against the bole of a huge tree, brushing aside a vine which touched his face. 'Still there's naught else to do. The ship won't be ready to sail yet.' He looked up into the branches. 'I did not think I should miss those damned insects that plagued us on our way here . . . '

The crewman who had shot the arrow suddenly shouted again. 'There! I saw him! It is a man!'

While the others stared but failed to discern anything Duke Avan continued to lean against the tree. 'You saw nothing. There is nothing here to see.'

Elric turned towards him. 'Give me the map and the lodestone, Duke Avan. I have a feeling I can find the way.'

The Vilmirian shrugged, an expression of doubt on his square, handsome face. He handed the things over to Elric.

They rested the night and in the morning they continued, with Elric leading the way.

And at noon they broke out of the forest and saw the ruins of R'lin K'ren A'a.

5

A Confusion of Prisms

Nothing grew among the ruins of the city. The streets were broken and the walls of the houses had fallen, but there were no weeds flowering in the cracks and it seemed that the city had but recently been brought down by an earthquake. Only one thing still stood intact, towering over the ruins. It was a gigantic statue of white, grey, and green jade – the statue of a naked youth with a face of almost feminine beauty that turned sightless eyes towards the north.

'The eyes!' Duke Avan Astran said. 'They're gone!'

The others said nothing as they stared at the statue and the ruins surrounding it. The area was relatively small and the buildings had had little decoration. The inhabitants seemed to have been a simple, well-to-do folk – totally unlike the Melnibonéans of the Bright Empire. Elric could not believe that the people of R'lin K'ren A'a had been his ancestors. They had been too sane.

'The statue's already been looted,' Duke Avan continued. 'Our damned journey's been in vain!'

Elric laughed. 'Did you really think you would be able to prise the Jade Man's eyes from their sockets, my lord?'

The statue was as tall as any tower of the Dreaming City and the head alone must have been the size of a reasonably large building. Duke Avan pursed his lips and refused to listen to Elric's mocking voice. 'We may yet find the journey worth our while,' he said. 'There were other treasures in R'lin K'ren A'a. Come . . . '

He led the way into the city.

Very few of the buildings were even partially standing, but they were nonetheless fascinating if only for the peculiar nature of their building materials, which were of a kind the travellers had never seen before.

The colours were many, but faded by time – soft reds and yellows and blues – and they flowed together to make almost infinite combinations.

Elric reached out to touch one wall and was surprised at the cool feel of the smooth material. It was neither stone nor wood nor metal. Perhaps it had been brought here from another plane?

He tried to visualize the city as it had been before it was deserted. The streets had been wide, there had been no surrounding wall, the houses had been low and built around large courtyards. If this was, indeed, the original home of his people, what had happened to change them from the peaceful citizens of R'lin K'ren A'a to the insane builders of Imrryr's bizarre and dreaming towers? Elric had thought he might find a solution to a mystery here, but instead he had found another mystery. It was his fate, he thought, shrugging to himself.

And then the first crystal disc hummed past his head and smashed against a collapsing wall.

The next disc split the skull of a crewman and a third nicked Smiorgan's ear before they had thrown themselves flat among the rubble.

'They're vengeful, those creatures,' Avan said with a hard smile. 'They'll risk much to pay us back for their comrades' deaths!'

Terror was on the face of each surviving crewman and fear had begun to creep into Avan's eyes.

More discs clattered nearby, but it was plain that the party was temporarily out of sight of the reptiles. Smiorgan coughed as white dust rose from the rubble and caught in his throat.

'You'd best summon those monstrous allies of yours again, Elric.'

Elric shook his head. 'I cannot. My ally said he would not serve me a second time.' He looked to his left where the four walls of a small house still stood. There seemed to be no door, only a window.

'Then call something,' Count Smiorgan said urgently. 'Anything.'

'I am not sure . . . '

Then Elric rolled over and sprang for the shelter, flinging himself through the window to land on a pile of masonry that grazed his hands and knees.

He staggered upright. In the distance he could see the huge blind statue of the god dominating the city. This was said to be an image of Arioch – though it resembled no image of Arioch Elric had ever seen manifested. Did that image protect R'lin K'ren A'a – or did it threaten it? Someone screamed. He glanced through the opening and saw that a disc had chopped through a man's forearm.

He drew Stormbringer and raised it, facing the jade statue.

'Arioch!' he cried. 'Arioch – aid me!'

Black light burst from the blade and it began to sing, as if joining in Elric's incantation.

'Arioch!'

431

Would the demon come? Often the patron of the kings of Melniboné refused to materialize, claiming that more urgent business called him – business concerning the eternal struggle between Law and Chaos.

'Arioch!'

Sword and man were now wreathed in a palpitating black mist and Elric's white face was flung back, seeming to writhe as the mist writhed.

'Arioch! I beg thee to aid me! It is Elric who calls thee!'

And then a voice reached his ears. It was a soft, purring, reasonable voice. It was a tender voice.

'Elric, I am fondest of thee. I love thee more than any other mortal – but aid thee I cannot – not yet.'

Elric cried desperately: 'Then we are doomed to perish here!'

'Thou canst escape this danger. Flee alone into the forest. Leave the others while thou hast time. Thou hast a destiny to fulfill elsewhere and elsewhen . . . '

'I will not desert them.'

'Thou art foolish, sweet Elric.'

'Arioch – since Melniboné's founding thou hast aided her kings. Aid her last king this day!'

'I cannot dissipate my energies. A great struggle looms. And it would cost me much to return to R'lin K'ren A'a. Flee now. Thou shalt be saved. Only the others will die.'

And then the Duke of Hell had gone. Elric sensed the passing of his presence. He frowned, fingering his belt pouch, trying to recall something he had once heard. Slowly, he resheathed the reluctant sword. Then there was a thump and Smiorgan stood panting before him.

'Well, is aid on the way?'

'I fear not.' Elric shook his head in despair. 'Once again Arioch refuses me. Once again he speaks of a greater destiny – a need to conserve his strength.'

'Your ancestors could have picked a more tractable demon as their patron. Our reptilian friends are closing in. Look . . . ' Smiorgan pointed to the outskirts of the city. A band of about a dozen stilt-legged creatures were advancing, their huge clubs at the ready.

There was a scuffling noise from the rubble on the other side of the wall and Avan appeared, leading his men through the opening. He was cursing.

'No extra aid is coming, I fear,' Elric told him.

The Vilmirian smiled grimly. 'Then the monsters out there knew more than did we!'

'It seems so.'

'We'll have to try to hide from them,' Smiorgan said without much conviction. 'We'd not survive a fight.'

The little party left the ruined house and began to inch its way through what cover it could find, moving gradually nearer to the centre of the city and the statue of the Jade Man.

A sharp hiss from behind them told them that the reptile warriors had sighted them again and another Vilmirian fell with a crystal disc protruding from his back. They broke into a panicky run.

Ahead now was a red building of several storeys which still had its roof.

'In there!' Duke Avan shouted.

With some relief they dashed unhesitatingly up worn steps and through a series of dusty passages until they paused to catch their breath in a great, gloomy hall.

The hall was completely empty and a little light filtered through cracks in the wall.

'This place has lasted better than the others,' Duke Avan said. 'I wonder what its function was. A fortress, perhaps.'

'They seem not to have been a warlike race,' Smiorgan pointed out. 'I suspect the building had some other function.'

The three surviving crewmen were looking fearfully about them. They looked as if they would have preferred to have faced the reptile warriors outside.

Elric began to cross the floor and then paused as he saw something painted on the far wall.

Smiorgan saw it too. 'What's that, friend Elric?'

Elric recognized the symbols as the written High Speech of old Melniboné, but it was subtly different and it took him a short time to decipher its meaning.

'Know you what it says, Elric?' Duke Avan murmured, joining them.

'Aye – but it's cryptic enough. It says: "If thou hast come to slay me, then thou art welcome. If thou hast come without the means to awaken the Jade Man, then begone . . . "'

'Is it addressed to us, I wonder,' Avan mused, 'or has it been there for a long while?'

Elric shrugged. 'It could have been inscribed at any time during the past ten thousand years . . . '

Smiorgan walked up to the wall and reached out to touch it. 'I would say it was fairly recent,' he said. 'The paint still being wet.'

Elric frowned. 'Then there are inhabitants here still. Why do they not reveal themselves?'

'Could those reptiles out there be the denizens of R'lin K'ren A'a?'

Avan said. 'There is nothing in the legends that says they were humans who fled this place . . . '

Elric's face clouded and he was about to make an angry reply when Smiorgan interrupted.

'Perhaps there is just one inhabitant. Is that what you are thinking, Elric? The Creature Doomed to Live? Those sentiments could be his . . . '

Elric put his hands to his face and made no reply.

'Come,' Avan said. 'We've no time to debate on legends.' He strode across the floor and entered another doorway, beginning to descend steps. As he reached the bottom they heard him gasp.

The others joined him and saw that he stood on the threshold of another hall. But this one was ankle-deep in fragments of stuff that had been thin leaves of a metallic material which had the flexibility of parchment. Around the walls were thousands of small holes, rank upon rank, each with a character painted over it.

'What is it?' Smiorgan asked.

Elric stooped and picked up one of the fragments. This had half a Melnibonéan character engraved on it. There had even been an attempt to obliterate this.

'It was a library,' he said softly. 'The library of my ancestors. Some-one has tried to destroy it. These scrolls must have been virtually indestructible, yet a great deal of effort has gone into making them indecipherable.' He kicked at the fragments. 'Plainly our friend – or friends – is a consistent hater of learning.'

'Plainly,' Avan said bitterly. 'Oh, the *value* of those scrolls to the scholar! All destroyed!'

Elric shrugged. 'To Limbo with the scholar – their value to me was quite considerable!'

Smiorgan put a hand on his friend's arm and Elric shrugged it off. 'I had hoped . . . '

Smiorgan cocked his bald head. 'Those reptiles have followed us into the building, by the sound of it.'

They heard the distant sound of strange footsteps in the passages behind them.

The little band of men moved as silently as they could through the ruined scrolls and crossed the hall until they entered another corridor which led sharply upward.

Then, suddenly, daylight was visible.

Elric peered ahead. 'The corridor has collapsed ahead of us and is blocked, by the look of it. The roof has caved in and we may be able to escape through the hole.'

434

They clambered upward over the fallen stones, glancing warily behind them for signs of their pursuers.

At last they emerged in the central square of the city. On the far sides of this square were placed the feet of the great statue, which now towered high above their heads.

Directly before them were two peculiar constructions which, unlike the rest of the buildings, were completely whole. They were domed and faceted and were made of some glasslike substance which diffracted the rays of the sun.

From below they heard the reptile men advancing down the corridor.

'We'll seek shelter in the nearest of those domes,' Elric said. He broke into a trot, leading the way.

The others followed him through the irregularly shaped opening at the base of the dome.

Once inside, however, they hesitated, shielding their eyes and blinking heavily as they tried to discern their way.

'It's like a maze of mirrors!' Smiorgan gasped. 'By the gods, I've never seen a better. Was that its function, I wonder.'

Corridors seemed to go off in all directions – yet they might be nothing more than reflections of the passage they were in. Cautiously Elric began to continue further into the maze, the five others following him.

'This smells of sorcery to me,' Smiorgan muttered as they advanced. 'Have we been forced into a trap, I wonder.'

Elric drew his sword. It murmured softly – almost querulously.

Everything shifted suddenly and the shapes of his companions grew dim.

'Smiorgan! Duke Avan!'

He heard voices murmuring, but they were not the voices of his friends.

'Count Smiorgan!'

But then the burly sea-lord faded away altogether and Elric was alone.

6

The Jade Man's Eyes

He turned and a wall of red brilliance struck his eyes and blinded him.

He called out and his voice was turned into a dismal wail which mocked him.

He tried to move, but he could not tell whether he remained in the same spot or walked a dozen miles.

Now there was someone standing a few yards away, seemingly obscured by a screen of multicoloured transparent gems. He stepped forward and made to dash away the screen, but it vanished and he stopped suddenly.

He looked on a face of infinite sorrow.

And the face was his own face, save that the man's colouring was normal and his hair was black.

'What are you?' Elric said thickly.

'I have had many names. One is Erekosë. I have been many men. Perhaps I am all men.'

'But you are like me!'

'I am you.'

'No!'

The phantom's eyes held tears as it stared in pity at Elric.

'Do not weep for me!' Elric roared. 'I need no sympathy from you!'

'Perhaps I weep for myself, for I know our fate.'

'And what is that?'

'You would not understand.'

'Tell me.'

'Ask your gods.'

Elric raised his sword. Fiercely he said, 'No – I'll have my answer from you!'

And the phantom faded away.

Elric shivered. Now the corridor was populated by a thousand such phantoms. Each murmured a different name. Each wore different clothes. But each had his face, if not his colouring.

'Begone!' he screamed. 'Oh, Gods, what is this place?'

And at his command they disappeared.

'Elric?'

The albino whirled, sword ready. But it was Duke Avan Astran of Old Hrolmar. He touched his own face with trembling fingers, but said levelly, 'I must tell you that I believe I am losing my sanity, Prince Elric . . . '

'What have you seen?'

'Many things. I cannot describe them.'

'Where are Smiorgan and the others?'

'Doubtless each went his separate way, as we did.'

Elric raised Stormbringer and brought the blade crashing against a crystal wall. The Black Sword moaned, but the wall merely changed its position.

But through a gap now Elric saw ordinary daylight. 'Come, Duke Avan – there is escape!'

Avan, dazed, followed him and they stepped out of the crystal and found themselves in the central square of R'lin K'ren A'a.

But there were noises. Carts and chariots moved about the square. Stalls were erected on one side. People moved peacefully about. And the Jade Man did not dominate the sky above the city. Here, there was no Jade Man at all.

Elric looked at the faces. They were the eldritch features of the folk of Melniboné. Yet these had a different cast to them which he could not at first define. Then he reconized what they had. It was tranquillity. He reached out his hand to touch one of the people.

'Tell me, friend, what year . . .?'

But the man did not hear him. He walked by.

Elric tried to stop several of the passersby, but not one could see or hear him.

'How did they lose this peace?' Duke Avan asked wonderingly. 'How did they become like you, Prince Elric?'

Elric almost snarled as he turned sharply to face the Vilmirian. 'Be silent!'

Duke Avan shrugged. 'Perhaps this is merely an illusion.'

'Perhaps,' Elric said sadly, 'But I am sure this is how they lived – until the coming of the High Ones.'

'You blame the gods, then?'

'I blame the despair that the gods brought.'

Duke Avan nodded gravely. 'I understand.'

He turned back towards the great crystal and then stood listening. 'Do you hear that voice, Prince Elric? What is it saying?'

Elric heard the voice. It seemed to be coming from the crystal. It was speaking the old tongue of Melniboné, but with a strange accent. 'This way,' it said. 'This way.'

Elric paused. 'I have no liking to return there.'

Avan said, 'What choice have we?'

They stepped together through the entrance.

Again they were in the maze that could be one corridor or many and the voice was clearer. 'Take two paces to your right,' it instructed.

Avan glanced at Elric. 'What was that?' Elric told him. 'Shall we obey?' Avan asked.

'Aye.' There was resignation in the albino's voice.

They took two paces to their right.

'Now four to your left,' said the voice.

They took four paces to their left.

'Now one forward.'

They emerged into the ruined square of R'lin K'ren A'a.

Smiorgan and one Vilmirian crewman stood there.

'Where are the others?' Avan demanded.

'Ask him,' Smiorgan said wearily, gesturing with the sword in his right hand.

They stared at the man who was either an albino or a leper. He was completely naked and he bore a distinct likeness to Elric. At first Elric thought this was another phantom, but then he saw that there were also several differences in their faces. There was something sticking from the man's side, just above the third rib. With a shock, Elric recognized it as the broken shaft of a Vilmirian arrow.

The naked man nodded. 'Aye – the arrow found its mark. But it could not slay me, for I am J'osui C'reln Reyr . . . '

'You believe yourself to be the Creature Doomed to Live,' Elric murmured.

'I am he.' The man gave a bitter smile. 'Do you think I try to deceive you?'

Elric glanced at the arrow shaft and then shook his head.

'You are ten thousand years old?' Avan stared at him.

'What does he say?' asked J'osui C'reln Reyr of Elric. Elric translated.

'Is that all it has been?' The man sighed. Then he looked intently at Elric. 'You are of my race?'

'It seems so.'

'Of what family?'

'Of the royal line.'

'Then you have come at last. I, too, am of that line.'

438

'I believe you.'

'I notice that the Olab seek you.'

'The Olab?'

'Those primitives with the clubs.'

'Aye. We encountered them on our journey upriver.'

'I will lead you to safety. Come.'

Elric allowed J'osui C'reln Reyr to take them across the square to where part of a tottering wall still stood. The man then lifted a flag-stone and showed them steps leading down into darkness. They followed him, descending cautiously as he caused the flagstone to lower itself above their heads. And then they found themselves in a room lit by crude oil lamps. Save for a bed of dried grasses the room was empty.

'You live sparely,' Elric said.

'I have need for nothing else. My head is sufficiently furnished . . . '

'Where do the Olab come from?' Elric asked.

'They are but recently arrived in these parts. Scarcely a thousand years ago – or perhaps half that time – they came from further upriver after some quarrel with another tribe. They do not usually come to the island. You must have killed many of them for them to wish you such harm.'

'We killed many.'

J'osui C'reln Reyr gestured at the others who were staring at him in some discomfort. 'And these? Primitives, also, eh? They are not of our folk.'

'There are few of our folk left.'

'What does he say?' Duke Avan asked.

'He says that those reptile warriors are called the Olab,' Elric told him.

'And was it these Olab who stole the Jade Man's eyes?'

When Elric translated the question the Creature Doomed to Live was astonished. 'Did you not know, then?'

'Know what?'

'Why, you have been *in* the Jade Man's eyes! Those great crystals in which you wandered – that is what they are!'

The Irony of It

When Elric offered this information to Duke Avan, the Vilmirian burst into laughter. He flung his head back and roared with mirth while the others looked gloomily on. The cloud that had fallen across his features of late suddenly cleared and he became again the man whom Elric had first met.

Smiorgan was the next to smile and even Elric acknowledged the irony of what had happened to them.

'Those crystals fell from his face like tears soon after the High Ones departed,' continued J'osui C'reln Reyr.

'So the High Ones did come here.'

'Aye – the Jade Man brought the message and all the folk departed, having made their bargain with him.'

'The Jade Man was not built by your people?'

'The Jade Man is Duke Arioch of Hell. He strode from the forest one day and stood in the square and told the people what was to come about – that our city lay at the centre of some particular configuration and that it was only there that the Lords of the Higher Worlds could meet.'

'And the bargain?'

'In return for their city, our royal line might in the future increase their power with Arioch as their patron. He would give them great knowledge and the means to build a new city elsewhere.'

'And they accepted this bargain without question?'

'There was little choice, kinsman.'

Elric lowered his eyes to regard the dusty floor. 'And thus they were corrupted,' he murmured.

'Only I refused to accept the pact, I did not wish to leave this city and I mistrusted Arioch. When all others set off down the river, I remained here – where we are now – and I heard the Lords of the Higher Worlds arrive and I heard them speak, laying down the rules under which Law and Chaos would fight thereafter. When they had gone, I emerged. But Arioch – the Jade Man – was still here. He looked down on me through his crystal eyes and he cursed me. When that was done the crystals fell and landed where you now see them. Arioch's spirit departed, but his jade image was left behind.'

'And you still retain all memory of what transpired between the Lords of Law and Chaos?'

'That is my doom.'

'Perhaps your fate was less harsh than that which befell those who left,' Elric said quietly. 'I am the last inheritor of that particular doom . . . '

J'osui C'reln Reyr looked puzzled and then he stared into Elric's eyes and an expression of pity crossed his face. 'I had not thought there was a worse fate – but now I believe there might be . . . '

Elric said urgently, 'Ease my soul, at least. I must know what passed between the High Lords in those days. I must understand the nature of my existence – as you, at least, understand yours. Tell me, I beg you!'

J'osui C'reln Reyr frowned and he stared deeply into Elric's eyes. 'Do you not know all my story, then?'

'Is there more?'

'I can only *remember* what passed between the High Lords – but when I try to tell my knowledge aloud or try to write it down, I cannot . . . '

Elric grasped the man's shoulder. 'You must try! You must try!'

'I know that I cannot.'

Seeing the torture in Elric's face, Smiorgan came up to him. 'What is it, Elric?'

Elric's hand clutched his head. 'Our journey has been useless.' Unconsciously he used the old Melnibonéan tongue.

'It need not be,' said J'osui C'reln Reyr. 'For me, at least.' He paused. 'Tell me, how did you find this city? Was there a map?'

Elric produced the map. 'This one.'

'Aye, that is the one. Many centuries ago I put it into a casket which I placed in a small trunk. I launched the trunk into the river, hoping that it would follow my people and they would know what it was.'

'The casket was found in Melniboné, but no one had bothered to open it,' Elric explained. 'That will give you an idea of what happened to the folk who left here . . . '

The strange man nodded gravely. 'And was there still a seal upon the map?'

'There was, I have it.'

'An image of one of the manifestations of Arioch, embedded in a small ruby?'

'Aye. I thought I recognized the image, but I could not place it.'

'The Image in the Gem,' murmured J'osui C'reln Reyr. As I prayed, it has returned – borne by one of the royal line!'

'What is its significance?'

Smiorgan interrupted. 'Will this fellow help us to escape, Elric? We are becoming somewhat impatient . . . '

'Wait,' the albino said. 'I will tell you everything later.'

'The Image in the Gem could be the instrument of my release,' said the Creature Doomed to Live. 'If he who possesses it is of the royal line, then he can command the Jade Man.'

'But why did you not use it?'

'Because of the curse that was put on me. I had the power to command, but not to summon the demon. It was a joke, I understand, of the High Lords.'

Elric saw bitter sadness in the eyes of J'osui C'reln Reyr. He looked at the white, naked flesh and the white hair and the body that was neither old nor young, at the shaft of the arrow sticking out above the third rib on the left side.

'What must I do?' he asked.

'You must summon Arioch and then you must command him to enter his body again and recover his eyes so that he may see to walk away from R'lin K'ren A'a.'

'And when he walks away?'

'The curse goes with him.'

Elric was thoughful. If he did summon Arioch – who was plainly reluctant to come – and then commanded him to do something he did not wish to do, he stood the chance of making an enemy of that powerful, if unpredictable entity. Yet they were trapped here by the Olab warriors, with no means of escaping them. If the Jade Man walked, the Olab would almost certainly flee and there would be time to get back to the ship and reach the sea. He explained everything to his companions. Both Smiorgan and Avan looked dubious and the remaining Vilmirian crewman looked positively terrified.

'I must do it,' Elric decided 'for the sake of this man. I must call Arioch and lift the doom that is on R'lin K'ren A'a.'

'And bring a greater doom to us!' Duke Avan said, putting his hand automatically upon his sword-hilt. 'No. I think we should take our chances with the Olab. Leave this man – he is mad – he raves. Let's be on our way.'

'Go if you choose,' Elric said. 'But I will stay with the Creature Doomed to Live.'

'Then you will stay here forever. You cannot believe his story!'

'But I do believe it.'

'You must come with us. Your sword will help. Without it, the Olab will certainly destroy us.'

'You saw that Stormbringer has little effect against the Olab.'

'And yet it has some. Do not desert me, Elric!'

'I am not deserting you. I must summon Arioch. That summoning will be to your benefit, if not to mine.'

'I am unconvinced.'

'It was my sorcery you wanted on this venture. Now you shall have my sorcery.'

Avan backed away. He seemed to fear something more than the Olab, more than the summoning. He seemed to read a threat in Elric's face of which even Elric was unaware.

'We must go outside,' said J'osui C'reln Reyr. 'We must stand beneath the Jade Man.'

'And when this is done,' Elric asked suddenly, 'how will we leave R'lin K'ren A'a?'

'There is a boat. It has no provisions, but much of the city's treasure is on it. It lies at the west end of the island.'

'That is some comfort,' Elric said. 'And you could not use it yourself?'

'I could not leave.'

'Is that part of the curse?'

'Aye – the curse of my timidity.'

'Timidity has kept you here ten thousand years?'

'Aye . . . '

They left the chamber and went out into the square. Night had fallen and a huge moon was in the sky. From where Elric stood it seemed to frame the Jade Man's sightless head like a halo. It was completely silent. Elric took the Image in the Gem from his pouch and held it between the forefinger and thumb of his left hand. With his right he drew Stormbringer. Avan, Smiorgan, and the Vilmirian crewman fell back.

He stared up at the huge jade legs, the genitals, the torso, the arms, the head, and he raised his sword in both hands and screamed:

'Arioch!'

Stormbringer's voice almost drowned his. It pulled in his hands; it threatened to leave his grasp altogether as it howled.

'Arioch!'

All the watchers saw now was the throbbing, radiant sword, the white face and hands of the albino and his crimson eyes glaring through the blackness.

443

'*Arioch!*'

And then a voice which was not Arioch's came to Elric's ears and it seemed that the sword itself spoke.

'*Elric – Arioch must have blood and souls. Blood and souls, my lord . . .*'

'No. These are my friends and the Olab cannot be harmed by Stormbringer. Arioch must come without the blood, without the souls.'

'Only those can summon him for certain!' said a voice, more clearly now. It was sardonic and it seemed to come from behind him. He turned, but there was nothing there.

He saw Duke Avan's nervous face, and as his eyes fixed on the Vilmirian's countenance, the sword swung around, twisting against Elric's grip, and plunging towards the duke.

'No!' cried Elric. 'Stop!'

But Stormbringer would not stop until it had plunged deep into Duke Avan's heart and quenched its thirst. The crewman stood transfixed as he watched his master die.

Duke Avan writhed. 'Elric! What treachery do you . . .?' He screamed. 'Ah, no!'

He jerked. 'Please . . .'

He quivered. 'My soul . . .'

He died.

Elric withdrew the sword and cut the crewman down as he ran to his master's aid. The action had been without thought.

'Now Arioch has his blood and his souls,' he said coldly. 'Let Arioch come!'

Smiorgan and the Creature Doomed to Live had retreated, staring at the possessed Elric in horror. The albino's face was cruel.

'*Let Arioch come!*'

'I am here, Elric.'

Elric whirled and saw that something stood in the shadow of the statue's legs – a shadow within a shadow.

'Arioch – thou must return to this manifestation and make it leave R'lin K'ren A'a forever.'

'I do not choose to, Elric.'

'Then I must command thee, Duke Arioch.'

'Command? Only he who possesses the Image in the Gem may command Arioch – and then only once.'

'I have the Image in the Gem.' Elric held up the tiny object. 'See.'

The shadow within a shadow swirled for a moment as if in anger.

'If I obey your command, you will set in motion a chain of events which you might not desire,' Arioch said, speaking suddenly in Low

Melnibonéan as if to give extra gravity to his words.

'Then let it be. I command you to enter the Jade Man and pick up its eyes so that it might walk again. Then I command you to leave here and take the curse of the High Ones with you.'

Arioch replied, 'When the Jade Man ceases to guard the place where the High Ones meet, then the great struggle of the Upper Worlds begins on this plane.'

'I command thee, Arioch. Go into the Jade Man!'

'You are an obstinate creature, Elric.'

'Go!' Elric raised Stormbringer. It seemed to sing in monstrous glee and it seemed at that moment to be more powerful than Arioch himself, more powerful than all the Lords of the Higher Worlds.

The ground shook. Fire suddenly blazed around the form of the great statue. The shadow within a shadow disappeared.

And the Jade Man stooped.

Its great bulk bent over Elric and its hands reached past him and it groped for the two crystals that lay on the ground. Then it found them and took one in each hand, straightening its back.

Elric stumbled towards the far corner of the square where Smiorgan and J'osui C'reln Reyr already crouched in terror.

A fierce light now blazed from the Jade Man's eyes and the jade lips parted.

'It is done, Elric!' said a huge voice.

J'osui C'reln Reyr began to sob.

'Then go, Arioch.'

'I go. The curse is lifted from R'lin K'ren A'a and from J'osui C'reln Reyr — but a greater curse now lies upon your whole plane.'

'What is this, Arioch? Explain yourself!' Elric cried.

'Soon you will have your explanation. Farewell!'

The enormous legs of jade moved suddenly and in a single step had cleared the ruins and had begun to crash through the jungle. In a moment the Jade Man had disappeared.

Then the Creature Doomed to Live laughed. It was a strange joy that he voiced. Smiorgan blocked his ears.

'And now!' shouted J'osui C'reln Reyr. 'Now your blade must take my life. I can die at last!'

Elric passed his hand across his face. He had hardly been aware of any of the recent events. 'No,' he said in a dazed tone. 'I cannot . . . '

And Stormbringer flew from his hand — flew to the body of the Creature Doomed to Live and buried itself in its chest.

And as he died, J'osui C'reln Reyn laughed. He fell to the ground and his lips moved. A whisper came from them. Elric stepped nearer to hear.

'The sword has my knowledge now. My burden has left me.'

The eyes closed.

J'osui C'reln Reyr's ten-thousand-year life-span had ended.

Weakly, Elric withdrew Stormbringer and sheathed it. He stared down at the body of the Creature Doomed to Live and then he looked up, questioningly, at Smiorgan.

The burly sea-lord turned away.

The sun began to rise. Grey dawn came. Elric watched the corpse of J'osui C'reln Reyr turn to powder that was stirred by the wind and mixed with the dust of the ruins. He walked back across the square to where Duke Avan's twisted body lay and he fell to his knees beside it.

'You were warned, Duke Avan Astran of Old Hrolmar, that ill befell those who linked their fortunes with Elric of Melniboné. But you thought otherwise. Now you know.' With a sigh he got to his feet.

Smiorgan stood beside him. The sun was now touching the taller parts of the ruins. Smiorgan reached out and gripped his friend's shoulder.

'The Olab have vanished. I think they've had their fill of sorcery.'

'Another man has been destroyed by me, Smiorgan. Am I forever to be tied to this cursed sword? I must discover a way to rid myself of it or my heavy conscience will bear me down so that I cannot rise at all.'

Smiorgan cleared his throat, but was otherwise silent.

'I will lay Duke Avan to rest,' Elric said. 'You go back to where we left the ship and tell the men that we come.'

Smiorgan began to stride across the square towards the east.

Elric tenderly picked up the body of Duke Avan and went towards the opposite side of the square, to the underground room where the Creature Doomed to Live had lived out his life for ten thousand years.

It seemed so unreal to Elric now, but he knew that it had not been a dream, for the Jade Man had gone. His tracks could be seen through the jungle. Whole clumps of trees had been flattened.

He reached the place and descended the stairs and laid Duke Avan down on the bed of dried grasses. Then he took the duke's dagger and, for want of anything else, dipped it in the duke's blood and wrote on the wall above the corpse:

This was Duke Avan Astran of Old Hrolmar. He explored the world and brought much knowledge and treasure back to Vilmir, his land. He dreamed and became lost in the dream of another and so died. He enriched the Young Kingdoms – and thus encouraged another dream. He died so that the Creature Doomed to Live might die, as he desired . . .

Elric paused. Then he threw down the dagger. He could not justify his own feelings of guilt by composing a high-sounding epitaph for the man he had slain.

He stood there, breathing heavily, then once again picked up the dagger.

He died because Elric of Melniboné desired a peace and a knowledge he could never find. He died by the Black Sword.

Outside in the middle of the square, at noon, still lay the lonely body of the last Vilmirian crewman. Nobody had known his name. Nobody felt grief for him or tried to compose an epitaph for him. The dead Vilmirian had died for no high purpose, followed no fabulous dream. Even in death his body would fulfill no function. On this island there was no carrion-eater to feed. In the dust of the city there was no earth to fertilize.

Elric came back into the square and saw the body. For a moment, to Elric it symbolized everything that had transpired here and would transpire later.

'There is no purpose,' he murmured.

Perhaps his remote ancestors had, after all, realized that, but had not cared. It had taken the Jade Man to make them care and then go mad in their anguish. The knowledge had caused them to close their minds to much.

'Elric!'

It was Smiorgan returning. Elric looked up.

'The Olab dealt with the crew and the ship before they came after us. They're all slain. The boat is destroyed.'

Elric remembered something the Creature Doomed to Live had told him. 'There is another boat,' he said. 'On the east side of the island.'

It took them the rest of the day and all of that night to discover where J'osui C'reln Reyr had hidden his boat. They pulled it down to the water in the diffused light of the morning and they inspected it.

'It's a sturdy boat,' said Count Smiorgan approvingly. 'By the look of it, it's made of that same strange material we saw in the library of R'lin K'ren A'a.' He climbed in and searched through the lockers.

Elric was staring back at the city, thinking of a man who might have become his friend, just as Count Smiorgan had become his friend. He had no friends, save Cymoril, in Melniboné. He sighed.

Smiorgan had opened several lockers and was grinning at what he saw there. 'Pray the gods I return safe to the Purple Towns – we have what I sought! Look, Elric! Treasure! We have benefited from this

447

venture, after all!'

'Aye . . . ' Elric's mind was on other things. He forced himself to think of more practical matters. 'But the jewels will not feed us, Count Smiorgan,' he said. 'It will be a long journey home.'

'Home?' Count Smiorgan straightened his great back, a bunch of necklaces in either fist. 'Melniboné?'

'The Young Kingdoms. You offered to guest me in your house, as I recall.'

'For the rest of your life, if you wish. You saved my life, friend Elric now you have helped me save my honour.'

'These past events have not disturbed you? You saw what my blade can do – to friends as well as enemies.'

'We do not brood, we of the Purple Towns,' said Count Smiorgan seriously. 'And we are not fickle in our friendships. You know an anguish, Prince Elric, that I'll never feel – never understand – but I have already given you my trust. Why should I take it away again? That is not how we are taught to behave in the Purple Towns.' Count Smiorgan brushed at his black beard and he winked. 'I saw some cases of provisions among the wreckage of Avan's schooner. We'll sail around the island and pick them up.'

Elric tried to shake the black mood from himself, but it was hard, for he had slain a man who had trusted him, and Smiorgan's talk of trust only made the guilt heavier.

Together they launched the boat into the weed-thick water and Elric looked back once more at the silent forest and a shiver passed through him. He thought of all the hopes he had entertained on the journey upriver and he cursed himself for a fool.

He tried to think back, to work out how he had come to be in this place, but too much of the past was confused with those singularly graphic dreams to which he was prone. Had Saxif D'Aan and the world of the blue sun been real? Even now, it faded. Was this place real? There was something dreamlike about it. It seemed to him he had sailed on many fateful seas since he had fled from Pikarayd. Now the promise of the peace of the Purple Towns was very dear to him.

Soon the time must come when he must return to Cymoril and the Dreaming City, to decide if he was ready to take up the responsibilities of the Bright Empire of Melniboné, but until that moment he would guest with his new friend, Smiorgan, and learn the ways of the simpler, more direct folk of Menii.

As they raised the sail and began to move with the current, Elric said to Smiorgan suddenly, 'You trust me, then, Count Smiorgan?'

The sea-lord was a little surprised by the directness of the question.

He fingered his beard. 'Aye,' he said at length, 'as a man. But we live in cynical times, Prince Elric. Even the gods have lost their innocence, have they not?'

Elric was puzzled. 'Do you think that I shall ever betray you – as – as I betrayed Avan, back there?'

Smiorgan shook his head. 'It's not in my nature to speculate upon such matters. You are loyal, Prince Elric. You feign cynicism, yet I think I've rarely met a man so much in need of a little real cynicism.' He smiled. 'Your sword betrayed you, did it not?'

'To serve me, I suppose.'

'Aye. There's the irony of it. Man may trust man, Prince Elric, but perhaps we'll never have a truly sane world until men learn to trust mankind. That would mean the death of magic, I think.'

And it seemed to Elric, then, that his runesword trembled at his side, and moaned very faintly, as if it were disturbed by Count Smiorgan's words.

THE DREAMING CITY

For my mother

1

A Gathering of Wolves

'**W**hat's the hour?' The black-bearded man wrenched off his gilded helmet and flung it from him, careless of where it fell. He drew off his leathern gauntlets and moved closer to the roaring fire, letting the heat soak into his frozen bones.

'Midnight is long past,' growled one of the other armoured men who gathered around the blaze. 'Are you still sure he'll come?'

'It's said that he's a man of his word, if that comforts you.'

It was a tall, pale-faced youth who spoke. His thin lips formed the words and spat them out maliciously. He grinned a wolf-grin and stared the new arrival in the eyes, mocking him.

The newcomer turned away with a shrug. 'That's so – for all your irony, Yaris. He'll come.' He spoke as a man does when he wishes to reassure himself.

There were six men, now, around the fire. The sixth was Smiorgan – Count Smiorgan Baldhead of the Purple Towns. He was a short, stocky man of fifty years with a scarred face partially covered with a thick, black growth of hair. His morose eyes smouldered and his lumpy fingers plucked nervously at his rich-hilted longsword. His pate was hairless, giving him his name, and over his ornate, gilded armour hung a loose woollen cloak, dyed purple.

Smiorgan said thickly, 'He has no love for his cousin. He has become bitter. Yyrkoon sits on the Ruby Throne in his place and has proclaimed him an outlaw and a traitor. Elric needs us if he would take his throne and his bride back. We can trust him.'

'You're full of trust tonight, count,' Yaris smiled thinly, 'a rare thing to find in these troubled times. I say this – ' He paused and took a long breath, staring at his comrades, summing them up. His gaze flicked from lean-faced Dharmit of Jharkor to Fadan of Lormyr who pursed his podgy lips and looked into the fire.

'Speak up, Yaris,' petulantly urged the patrician-featured Vilmirian, Naclon. 'Let's hear what you have to say, lad, if it's worth hearing.'

Yaris looked towards Jiku the dandy, who yawned impolitely and scratched his long nose.

'Well!' Smiorgan was impatient. 'What d'you say, Yaris?'

'I say that we should start now and waste no more time waiting on Elric's pleasure! He's laughing at us in some tavern a hundred miles from here – or else plotting with the Dragon Princes to trap us. For years we have planned this raid. We have little time in which to strike – our fleet is too big, too noticeable. Even if Elric has not betrayed us, then spies will soon be running eastwards to warn the Dragons that there is a fleet massed against them. We stand to win a fantastic fortune – to vanquish the greatest merchant city in the world – to reap immeasurable riches – or horrible death at the hands of the Dragon Princes, if we wait overlong. Let's bide our time no more and set sail before our prize hears of our plan and brings up reinforcements!'

'You always were too ready to mistrust a man, Yaris.' King Naclon of Vilner spoke slowly, carefully – distastefully eyeing the taut-featured youth. 'We could not reach Imrryr without Elric's knowledge of the maze-channels which lead to its secret ports. If Elric will not join us – then our endeavour will be fruitless – hopeless. We need him. We must wait for him – or else give up our plans and return to our homelands.'

'At least I'm willing to take a risk,' yelled Yaris, anger lancing from his slanting eyes. 'You're getting old – all of you. Treasures are not won by care and forethought but by swift slaying and reckless attack.'

'Fool!' Dharmit's voice rumbled around the fire-flooded hall. He laughed wearily. 'I spoke thus in my youth – and lost a fine fleet soon after. Cunning and Elric's knowledge will win us Imrryr – that and the mightiest fleet to sail the Sighing Sea since Melniboné's banners fluttered over all the nations of the Earth. Here we are – the most powerful Sea Lords in the world, masters, every one of us, of more than a hundred swift vessels. Our names are feared and famous – our fleets ravage the coasts of a score of lesser nations. We hold *power*!' He clenched his great fist and shook it in Yaris' face. His tone became more level and he smiled viciously, glaring at the youth and choosing his words with precision.

'But all this is worthless – meaningless – without the power which Elric has. That is the power of knowledge – of sorcery, if I must use the cursed word. His fathers knew of the maze which guards Imrryr from sea-attack. And his fathers passed that secret on to him. Imrryr, the Dreaming City, dreams in peace – and will continue to do so unless we have a guide to help us steer a course through the treacherous waterways which lead to her harbours. We *need* Elric – we know it, and he knows it. That's the truth!'

454

'Such confidence, gentlemen, is warming to the heart.' There was irony in the heavy voice which came from the entrance to the hall. The heads of the six Sea Lords jerked towards the doorway.

Yaris' confidence fled from him as he met the eyes of Elric of Melniboné. They were old eyes in a fine featured, youthful face. Yaris shuddered, turned his back on Elric, preferring to look into the bright glare of the fire.

Elric smiled warmly as Count Smiorgan gripped his shoulder. There was a certain friendship between the two. He nodded condescendingly to the other four and walked with lithe grace towards the fire. Yaris stood aside and let him pass. Elric was tall, broad-shouldered and slim-hipped. He wore his long hair bunched and pinned at the nape of his neck and, for an obscure reason, affected the dress of a Southern barbarian. He had long, knee-length boots of soft doe-leather, a breastplate of strangely wrought silver, a jerkin of chequered blue and white linen, britches of scarlet wool and a cloak of rustling green velvet. At his hip rested his runesword of black iron – the feared Stormbringer, forged by ancient and alien sorcery.

His bizarre dress was tasteless and gaudy, and did not match his sensitive face and long-fingered, almost delicate hands, yet he flaunted it since it emphasized the fact that he did not belong in any company – that he was an outsider and an outcast. But, in reality, he had little need to wear such outlandish gear – for his eyes and skin were enough to mark him.

Elric, Last Lord of Melniboné, was a pure albino who drew his power from a secret and terrible source.

Smiorgan sighed. 'Well, Elric, when do we raid Imrryr?'

Elric shrugged. 'As soon as you like; I care not. Give me a little time in which to do certain things.'

'Tomorrow? Shall we sail tomorrow?' Yaris said hesitantly, conscious of the strange power dormant in the man he had earlier accused of treachery.

Elric smiled, dismissing the youth's statement. 'Three days' time,' he said, 'Three – or more.'

'Three days! But Imrryr will be warned of our presence by then!' Fat, cautious Fadan spoke.

'I'll see that your fleet's not found,' Elric promised. 'I have to go to Imrryr first – and return.'

'You won't do the journey in three days – the fastest ship could not make it.' Smiorgan gaped.

'I'll be in the Dreaming City in less than a day,' Elric said softly, with finality.

Smiorgan shrugged. 'If you say so, I'll believe it – but why this necessity to visit the city ahead of the raid?'

'I have my own compunctions, Count Smiorgan. But worry not – I shan't betray you. I'll lead the raid myself, be sure of that.' His dead-white face was lighted eerily by the fire and his red eyes smouldered. One lean hand firmly gripped the hilt of his runesword and he appeared to breathe more heavily. 'Imrryr fell, in spirit, five hundred years ago – she will fall completely soon – for ever! I have a little debt to settle. This is my only reason for aiding you. As you know I have made only a few conditions – that you raze the city to the ground and a certain man and woman are not harmed. I refer to my cousin Yyrkoon and his sister Cymoril . . . '

Yaris' thin lips felt uncomfortably dry. Much of his blustering manner resulted from the early death of his father. The old sea-king had died – leaving young Yaris as the new ruler of his lands and his fleets. Yaris was not at all certain that he was capable of commanding such a vast kingdom – and tried to appear more confident than he actually felt. Now he said: 'How shall we hide the fleet, Lord Elric?'

The Melnibonéan acknowledged the question. 'I'll hide it for you,' he promised. 'I go now to do this – but make sure all your men are off the ships first – will you see to it, Smiorgan?'

'Aye,' rumbled the stocky count.

He and Elric departed from the hall together, leaving five men behind; five men who sensed an air of icy doom hanging about the overheated hall.

'How could he hide such a mighty fleet when we, who know this fjord better than any, could find nowhere?' Dharmit of Jharkor said bewilderedly.

None answered him.

They waited, tensed and nervous, while the fire flickered and died untended. Eventually Smiorgan returned, stamping noisily on the boarded floor. There was a haunted haze of fear surrounding him; an almost tangible aura, and he was shivering, terribly. Tremendous, racking undulations swept up his body and his breath came short.

'Well? Did Elric hide the fleet – all at once? What did he do?' Dharmit spoke impatiently, choosing not to heed Smiorgan's ominous condition.

'He has hidden it.' That was all Smiorgan said, and his voice was thin, like that of a sick man, weak from fever.

Yaris went to the entrance and tried to stare beyond the fjord slopes where many campfires burned, tried to make out the outlines of ships' masts and rigging, but he could see nothing.

'The night mist's too thick,' he murmured, 'I can't tell whether our ships are anchored in the fjord or not.' Then he gasped involuntarily as a white face loomed out of the clinging fog. 'Greetings, Lord Elric,' he stuttered, noting the sweat on the Melnibonéan's strained features.

Elric staggered past him, into the hall. 'Wine,' he mumbled, 'I've done what's needed and it's cost me hard.'

Dharmit fetched a jug of strong Cadsandrian wine and with a shaking hand poured some into a carved wooden goblet. Wordlessly he passed the cup to Elric who quickly drained it. 'Now I will sleep,' he said, stretching himself into a chair and wrapping his green cloak around him. He closed his disconcerting crimson eyes and fell into a slumber born of utter weariness.

Fadan scurried to the door, closed it and pulled the heavy iron bar down.

None of the six slept much that night and, in the morning, the door was unbarred and Elric was missing from the chair. When they went outside, the mist was so heavy that they soon lost sight of one another, though scarcely two feet separated any of them.

Elric stood with his legs astride on the shingle of the narrow beach. He looked back at the entrance to the fjord and saw, with satisfaction, that the mist was still thickening, though it lay only over the fjord itself, hiding the mighty fleet. Elsewhere, the weather was clear and overhead a pale winter sun shone sharply on the black rocks of the rugged cliffs which dominated the coastline. Ahead of him the sea rose and fell monotonously, like the chest of a sleeping water-giant, grey and pure, glinting in the cold sunlight. Elric fingered the raised runes on the hilt of his black broadsword and a steady north wind blew into the voluminous folds of his dark green cloak, swirling it around his tall, lean frame.

The albino felt fitter than he had done on the previous night when he had expended all his strength in conjuring the mist. He was well-versed in the art of nature-wizardry, but he did not have the reserves of power which the Sorcerer Emperors of Melniboné had possessed when they had ruled the world. His ancestors had passed their knowledge down to him – but not their mystic vitality and many of the spells and secrets that he had were unusable, since he did not have the reservoir of strength, either of soul or of body, to work them. But for all that, Elric knew of only one other man who matched his knowledge – his cousin Yyrkoon. His hand gripped the hilt tighter as he thought of the cousin who had twice betrayed his trust, and he forced himself to concentrate on his present task – the speaking of spells to aid him on his voyage to the Isle of the Dragon Masters whose only city, Imrryr the Beautiful, was the object of the Sea Lords' massing.

Drawn up on the beach, a tiny sailing-boat lay – Elric's own small ship, sturdy and far stronger, far older, than it appeared. The brooding sea flung surf around its timbers as the tide withdrew, and Elric realized that he had little time in which to work his helpful sorcery.

His body tensed and he blanked his conscious mind, summoning secrets from the dark depths of his soul. Swaying, his eyes staring unseeingly, his arms jerking out ahead of him and making unholy signs in the air, he began to speak in a sibilant monotone. Slowly the pitch of his voice rose, resembling the scarcely heard shriek of a distant gale as it comes closer – then, quite suddenly, the voice rose higher until it was howling wildly to the skies and the air began to tremble and quiver. Shadow-shapes began slowly to form and they were never still but darted around Elric's body as, stiff-legged, he started forward towards his boat.

His voice was inhuman as it howled insistently, summoning the wind elementals – the *sylphs* of the breeze; the *sharnahs*, makers of gales; the *h'Haarshanns*, builders of whirlwinds – hazy and formless, they eddied around him as he summoned their aid with the alien words of his forefathers who had, ages before, made unthinkable pacts with the elementals in order to procure their services.

Still stiff-limbed, Elric entered the boat and, like an automaton, his fingers ran up the sail and set it. Then a great wave erupted out of the placid sea, rising higher and higher until it towered over the vessel. With a surging crash, the water smashed down on the boat, lifted it and bore it out to sea. Sitting blank-eyed in the stern, Elric still crooned his hideous song of sorcery as the spirits of the air plucked at the sail and sent the boat flying over the water faster than any mortal ship could speed. And all the while, the deafening, unholy shriek of the released elementals filled the air about the boat as the shore vanished and open sea was all that was visible.

2

Old Friends, Ancient Allies

So it was, with wind-demons for shipmates, that Elric, last Prince of the Royal line of Melniboné, returned to the last city still ruled by his own race – the last city and the final remnant of Melnibonéan architecture. The cloudy pink and subtle yellow tints of her nearer towers came into sight within a few hours of Elric's leaving the fjord and just off-shore of the Isle of the Dragon Masters the elementals left the boat and fled back to their secret haunts among the peaks of the highest mountains in the world. Elric awoke, then, from his trance, and regarded with fresh wonder the beauty of his own city's delicate towers which were visible even so far away, guarded still by the formidable sea-wall with its great gate, the five-doored maze and the twisting, high-walled channels, of which only one led to the inner harbour of Imrryr.

Elric knew that he dare not risk entering the harbour by the maze, though he knew the route perfectly. He decided, instead, to land the boat further up the coast in a small inlet of which he had knowledge. With sure, capable hands, he guided the little craft towards the hidden inlet which was obscured by a growth of shrubs loaded with ghastly blue berries of a type decidedly poisonous to men since their juice first turned one blind and then slowly mad. This berry, the *nodoil*, grew only on Imrryr, as did other rare and deadly plants.

Light, low-hanging cloud wisps streamed slowly across the sun-painted sky, like fine cobwebs caught by a sudden breeze. All the world seemed blue and gold and green and white, and Elric, pulling his boat up on the beach, breathed the clean, sharp air of winter and savoured the scent of decaying leaves and rotting undergrowth. Somewhere a bitch-fox barked her pleasure to her mate and Elric regretted the fact that his depleted race no longer appreciated natural beauty, preferring to stay close to their city and spend many of their days in drugged slumber. It was not the city which dreamed, but its overcivilised inhabitants. Elric, smelling the rich, clean winter-scents, was wholly glad that he had his birthright and did not rule the city as he had been born to do.

Instead, Yyrkoon, his cousin, sprawled on the Ruby Throne of Imrryr the Beautiful and hated Elric because he knew that the albino, for all his disgust with crowns and rulership, was still the rightful King of the Dragon Isle and that he, Yyrkoon, was an usurper, not elected by Elric to the throne, as Melnibonéan tradition demanded.

But Elric had better reasons for hating his cousin. For those reasons the ancient capital would fall in all its magnificent splendour and the last fragment of a glorious Empire would be obliterated as the pink, the yellow, the purple and white towers crumbled – if Elric had his way and the Sea Lords were successful.

On foot, Elric strode inland, towards Imrryr, and as he covered the miles of soft turf, the sun cast an ochre pall over the land and sank, giving way to a dark and moonless night, brooding and full of evil portent.

At last he came to the city. It stood out in stark black silhouette, a city of fantastic magnificence, in conception and in execution. It was the oldest city in the world, built by artists and conceived as a work of art rather than a functional dwelling place, but Elric knew that squalor lurked in many narrow streets and that the Lords of Imrryr left many of the towers empty and uninhabited rather than let the bastard population of the city dwell therein. There were few Dragon Masters left; few who would claim Melnibonéan blood.

Built to follow the shape of the ground, the city had an organic appearance, with winding lanes spiralling to the crest of the hill where stood the castle, tall and proud and many-spired, the final, crowning masterpiece of the ancient, forgotten artist who had built it. But there was no life-sound emanating from Imrryr the Beautiful, only a sense of soporific desolation. The city slept – and the Dragon Masters and their ladies and their special slaves dreamed drug-induced dreams of grandeur and incredible horror while the rest of the population, ordered by curfew, tossed on tawdry mattresses and tried not to dream at all.

Elric, his hand ever near his sword-hilt, slipped through an unguarded gate in the city wall and began to walk cautiously through the unlighted streets, moving upwards, through the winding lanes, towards Yyrkoon's great palace.

Wind sighed through the empty rooms of the Dragon towers and sometimes Elric would have to withdraw into places where the shadows were deeper when he heard the tramp of feet and a group of guards would pass, their duty being to see that the curfew was rigidly obeyed. Often he would hear wild laughter echoing from one of the towers, still ablaze with bright torchlight which flung strange, disturbing shadows on the walls; often, too, he would hear a chilling scream and a frenzied, idiot's yell as some wretch of a slave died in obscene agony to please his master.

Elric was not appalled by the sounds and the dim sights. He appreciated them. He was still a Melnibonéan – their rightful leader if he chose to regain his powers of kingship – and though he had an obscure urge to wander and sample the less sophisticated pleasures of the outside world, ten thousand years of a cruel, brilliant and malicious culture was behind him and the pulse of his ancestry beat strongly in his deficient veins.

Elric knocked impatiently upon the heavy, blackwood door. He had reached the palace and now stood by a small back entrance, glancing cautiously around him, for he knew that Yyrkoon had given the guards orders to slay him if he entered Imrryr.

A bolt squealed on the other side of the door and it moved silently inwards. A thin, seamed face confronted Elric.

'Is it the king?' whispered the man, peering out into the night. He was a tall, extremely thin individual with long, gnarled limbs which shifted awkwardly as he moved nearer, straining his beady eyes to get a glimpse of Elric.

'It's Prince Elric,' the albino said. 'But you forget, Tanglebones, my friend, that a new king sits on the Ruby Throne.'

Tanglebones shook his head and his sparse hair fell over his face. With a jerking movement he brushed it back and stood aside for Elric to enter. 'The Dragon Isle has but one king – and his name is Elric, whatever usurper would have it otherwise.'

Elric ignored this statement, but he smiled thinly and waited for the man to push the bolt back into place.

'She still sleeps, sire,' Tanglebones murmured as he climbed unlit stairs, Elric behind him.

'I guessed that,' Elric said. 'I do not underestimate my good cousin's powers of sorcery.'

Upwards, now, in silence, the two men climbed until at last they reached a corridor which was aflare with dancing torchlight. The marble walls reflected the flames and showed Elric, crouching with Tanglebones behind a pillar, that the room in which he was interested was guarded by a massive archer – a eunuch by the look of him – who was alert and wakeful. The man was hairless and fat, his blue-black gleaming armour tight on his flesh, but his fingers were curled round the string of his short, bone bow and there was a slim arrow resting on the string. Elric guessed that this man was one of the crack eunuch archers, a member of the Silent Guard, Elric's finest company of warriors.

Tanglebones, who had taught the young Elric the arts of fencing and archery, had known of the guard's presence and had prepared for it. Earlier he had placed a bow behind the pillar. Silently he picked it up and, bending it against his knee, strung it. He fitted an arrow to the string, aimed it at the right eye of the guard and let fly – just as the eunuch turned to face him. The shaft missed. It clattered against the man's gorget and fell harmlessly to the reed-strewn stones of the floor.

So Elric acted swiftly, leaping forward, his runesword drawn and its alien power surging through him. It howled in a searing arc of black steel and cut through the bone bow which the eunuch had hoped would deflect it. The guard was panting and his thick lips were wet as he drew breath to yell. As he opened his mouth, Elric saw what he had expected, the man was tongueless and was a mute. His own shortsword came out and he just managed to parry Elric's next thrust. Sparks flew from the iron and Stormbringer bit into the eunuch's finely edged blade; he staggered and fell back before the nigromantic sword which appeared to be endowed with a life of its own. The clatter of metal echoed loudly up and down the short corridor and Elric cursed the fate which had made the man turn at the crucial moment. Grimly, silently, he broke down the eunuch's clumsy guard.

The eunuch saw only a dim glimpse of his opponent behind the black, whirling blade which appeared to be so light and which was twice the length of his own stabbing sword. He wondered, frenziedly, who his attacker could be and he thought he recognized the face. Then a scarlet eruption obscured his vision, he felt searing agony at his face and then, philosophically, for eunuchs are necessarily given to a certain fatalism, he realized that he was to die.

Elric stood over the eunuch's bloated body and tugged his sword from the corpse's skull, wiping the mixture of blood and brains on his late opponent's cloak. Tanglebones had wisely vanished. Elric could hear the clatter of sandalled feet rushing up the stairs. He pushed the door open and entered the room which was lit by two small candles placed at either end of a wide, richly tapestried bed. He went to the bed and looked down at the raven-haired girl who lay there.

Elric's mouth twitched and bright tears leapt into his strange red eyes. He was trembling as he turned back to the door, sheathed his sword and pulled the bolts into place. He returned to the bedside and knelt down beside the sleeping girl. Her features were as delicate and of a similar mould as Elric's own, but she had an added, exquisite beauty. She was breathing shallowly, in a sleep induced not by natural weariness but by her own brother's evil sorcery.

Elric reached out and tenderly took one fine-fingered hand in his. He put it to his lips and kissed it.

'Cymoril,' he murmured, and an agony of longing throbbed in that name. 'Cymoril – wake up.'

The girl did not stir, her breathing remained shallow and her eyes remained shut. Elric's white features twisted and his red eyes blazed as he shook in terrible and passionate rage. He gripped the hand, so limp and nerveless, like the hand of a corpse; gripped it until he had to stop himself for fear that he would crush the delicate fingers.

A shouting soldier began to beat at the door.

Elric replaced the hand on the girl's breast and stood up. He glanced uncomprehendingly at the door.

A sharper, colder voice interrupted the soldier's yelling.

'What is happening – has someone tried to see my poor sleeping sister?'

'Yyrkoon, the black hellspawn,' said Elric to himself.

Confused babblings from the soldier and Yyrkoon's voice raised as he shouted through the door. 'Whoever is in there – you will be destroyed a thousand times when you are caught. You cannot escape. If my good sister is harmed in any way – then you will never die, I promise you that. But you will pray to your Gods that you could!'

'Yyrkoon, you paltry bombast – you cannot threaten one who is your equal in the dark arts. It is I, Elric – your rightful master. Return to your rabbit hole before I call down every evil power upon, above, and under the Earth to blast you!'

Yyrkoon laughed hesitantly. 'So you have returned again to try to waken my sister. Any such attempt will not only slay her – it will send her soul into the deepest hell – where you may join it, willingly!'

'By Arnara's six breasts – you it will be who samples the thousand deaths before long.'

'Enough of this.' Yyrkoon raised his voice. 'Soldiers – I command you to break this door down – and take that traitor alive. Elric – there are two things you will never again have – my sister's love and the Ruby Throne. Make what you can of the little time available to you, for soon you will be grovelling to me and praying for release from your soul's agony!'

Elric ignored Yyrkoon's threats and looked at the narrow window to the room. It was just large enough for a man's body to pass through. He bent down and kissed Cymoril upon the lips, then he went to the door and silently withdrew the bolts.

463

There came a crash as a soldier flung his weight against the door. It swung open, pitching the man forward to stumble and fall on his face. Elric drew his sword, lifted it high and chopped at the warrior's neck. The head sprang from its shoulders and Elric yelled loudly in a deep, rolling voice.

'*Arioch! Arioch*! I give you blood and souls – only aid me now! This man I give you, mighty King of Hell – aid your servant, Elric of Melniboné!'

Three soldiers entered the room in a bunch. Elric struck at one and sheared off half his face. The man screamed horribly.

'Arioch, Lord of the Darks – I give you blood and souls. Aid me, evil one!'

In the far corner of the gloomy room, a blacker mist began slowly, to form. But the soldiers pressed closer and Elric was hard put to hold them back.

He was screaming the name of Arioch, Lord of the Higher Hell, incessantly, almost unconsciously as he was pressed back further by the weight of the warriors' numbers. Behind them, Yyrkoon mouthed in rage and frustration, urging his men, still, to take Elric alive. This gave Elric some small advantage. The runesword was glowing with a strange black light and its shrill howling grated the ears of those who heard it. Two more corpses now littered the carpeted floor of the chamber, their blood soaking into the fine fabric.

'Blood and souls for my lord Arioch!'

The dark mist heaved and began to take shape, Elric spared a look towards the corner and shuddered despite his inurement to hell-born horror. The warriors now had their backs to the thing in the corner and Elric was by the window. The amorphous mass that was a less than pleasant manifestation of Elric's fickle patron God, heaved again and Elric made out its intolerably alien shape. Bile flooded into his mouth and as he drove the soldiers towards the thing which was sinuously flooding forward he fought against madness.

Suddenly, the soldiers seemed to sense that there was something behind them. They turned, four of them, and each screamed insanely as the black horror made one final rush to engulf them. Arioch crouched over them, sucking out their souls. Then, slowly, their bones began to give and snap and still shrieking bestially the men flopped like obnoxious invertebrates upon the floor: their spines broken, they still lived. Elric turned away, thankful for once that Cymoril slept, and leapt to the window ledge. He looked down and realized with despair that he was not going to escape by that route after all. Several hundred feet lay between him and the ground. He rushed to the door where

Yyrkoon, his eyes wide with fear, was trying to drive Arioch back. Arioch was already fading.

Elric pushed past his cousin, spared a final glance for Cymoril, then ran the way he had come, his feet slipping on blood. Tanglebones met him at the head of the dark stairway.

'What has happened, King Elric – what's in there?'

Elric seized Tanglebones by his lean shoulder and made him descend the stairs. 'No time,' he panted, 'but we must hurry while Yyrkoon is still engaged with his current problem. In five days' time Imrryr will experience a new phase in her history – perhaps the last. I want you to make sure that Cymoril is safe. Is that clear?'

'Aye, Lord, but . . . '

They reached the door and Tanglebones shot the bolts and opened it.

'There is no time for me to say anything else. I must escape while I can. I will return in five days – with companions. You will realize what I mean when that time comes. Take Cymoril to the Tower of D'a'rputna – and await me there.'

Then Elric was gone, soft-footed, running into the night with the shrieks of the dying still ringing through the blackness after him.

Of Revenge, Betrayal and Guilt

Elric stood unspeaking in the prow of Count Smiorgan's flagship. Since his return to the fjord and the fleet's subsequent sailing for open sea, he had spoken only orders, and those in the tersest of terms. The Sea Lords muttered that a great hate lay in him, that it festered his soul and made him a dangerous man to have as comrade or enemy; and even Count Smiorgan avoided the moody albino.

The reaver prows struck eastward and the sea was black with light ships dancing on the bright water in all directions; they looked like the shadow of some enormous sea-bird flung on the water. Nearly half a thousand fighting ships stained the ocean – all of them of similar form, long and slim and built for speed rather than battle, since they were for coast-raiding and trading. Sails were caught by the pale sun; bright colours of fresh canvas – orange, blue, black, purple, red, yellow, light green or white. And every ship had sixteen or more rowers – each rower a fighting man. The crews of the ships were also the warriors who would attack Imrryr – there was no wastage of good man-power since the sea-nations were underpopulated, losing hundreds of men each year in their regular raids.

In the centre of the great fleet, certain larger vessels sailed. These carried great catapults on their decks and were to be used for storming the sea wall of Imrryr. Count Smiorgan and the other Lords looked at their ships with pride, but Elric only stared ahead of him, never sleeping, rarely moving, his white face lashed by salt spray and wind, his white hand tight upon his swordhilt.

The reaver ships ploughed steadily eastwards – forging towards the Dragon Isle and fantastic wealth – or hellish horror. Relentlessly, doom-driven, they beat onwards, their oars splashing in unison, their sails bellying taut with a good wind.

Onwards they sailed, towards Imrryr the Beautiful, to rape and plunder the world's oldest city.

Two days after the fleet had set sail, the coastline of the Dragon

Isle was sighted and the rattle of arms replaced the sound of oars as the mighty fleet hove to and prepared to accomplish what sane men thought impossible.

Orders were bellowed from ship to ship and the fleet began to mass into battle formation, then the oars creaked in their grooves and ponderously, with sails now furled, the fleet moved forward again.

It was a clear day, cold and fresh, and there was a tense excitement about all the men, from Sea Lord to galley hand, as they considered the immediate future and what it might bring. Serpent prows bent towards the great stone wall which blocked off the first entrance to the harbour. It was nearly a hundred feet high and towers were built upon it – more functional than the lace-like spires of the city which shimmered in the distance, behind them. The ships of Imrryr were the only vessels allowed to pass through the great gate in the centre of the wall, and the route through the maze – the exact entrance even – was a well-kept secret from outsiders.

On the sea wall, which now loomed tall above the fleet, amazed guards scrambled frantically to their posts. To them, threat of attack was well-nigh unthinkable, yet here it was – a great fleet, the greatest they had ever seen – come against Imrryr the Beautiful! They took to their posts, their yellow cloaks and kilts rustling, their bronze armour rattling, but they moved with bewildered reluctance as if refusing to accept what they saw. And they went to their posts with desperate fatalism, knowing that even if the ships never entered the maze itself, they would not be alive to witness the reavers' failure.

Dyvim Tarkan, Commander of the Wall, was a sensitive man who loved life and its pleasures. He was highbrowed and handsome, with a thin wisp of beard and a tiny moustache. He looked well in the bronze armour and high-plumed helmet; he did not want to die. He issued terse orders to his men and, with well-ordered precision, they obeyed him. He listened with concern to the distant shouts from the ships and he wondered what the first move of the reavers would be. He did not wait long for his answer.

A catapult on one of the leading vessels twanged throatily and its throwing arm rushed up, releasing a great rock which sailed, with every appearance of leisurely grace, towards the wall. It fell short and splashed into the sea which frothed against the stones of the wall.

Swallowing hard and trying to control the shake in his voice. Dyvim Tarkan ordered his own catapult to discharge. With a thudding crash the release rope was cut and a retaliatory iron ball went hurtling towards the enemy fleet. So tight-packed were the ships that the ball could not miss – it struck full on the deck of the flagship of Dharmit of

Jharkor and crushed the timbers in. Within seconds, accompanied by the cries of maimed and drowning men, the ship had sunk and Dharmit with it. Some of the crew were taken aboard other vessels but the wounded were left to drown.

Another catapult sounded and this time a tower full of archers was squarely hit. Masonry erupted outwards and those who still lived fell sickeningly to die in the foam-tipped sea lashing the wall. This time, angered by the deaths of their comrades, Imrryrian archers sent back a stream of slim arrows into the enemy's midst. Reavers howled as red-fletched shafts buried themselves thirstily in flesh. But reavers returned the arrows liberally and soon only a handful of men were left on the wall as further catapult rocks smashed into towers and men, destroying their only war-machine and part of the wall besides.

Dyvim Tarkan still lived, though red blood stained his yellow tunic and an arrow shaft protruded from his left shoulder. He still lived when the first ram-ship moved intractably towards the great wooden gate and smashed against it, weakening it. A second ship sailed in beside it and, between them, they stove in the gate and glided through the entrance; the first non-Imrryrian ships ever to do such a thing. Perhaps it was outraged horror that tradition had been broken which caused poor Dyvim Tarkan to lose his footing at the edge of the wall and fall screaming down to break his neck on the deck of Count Smiorgan's flagship as it sailed triumphantly through the gate.

Now the ram-ships made way for Count Smiorgan's craft, for Elric had to lead the way through the maze. Ahead of them loomed five tall entrances, black gaping maws all alike in shape and size. Elric pointed to the third from the left and with short strokes the oarsmen began to paddle the ship into the dark mouth of the entrance. For some minutes, they sailed in darkness.

'Flares!' shouted Elric. 'Light the flares!'

Torches had already been prepared and these were now lighted. The men saw that they were in a vast tunnel hewn out of natural rock which twisted in all directions.

'Keep close,' Elric ordered and his voice was magnified a score of times in the echoing cavern. Torchlight blazed and Elric's face was a mask of shadow and frisking light as the torches threw up long tongues of flame to the bleak roof. Behind him, men could be heard muttering in awe and, as more craft entered the maze and lit their own torches, Elric could see some torches waver as their bearers trembled in superstitious fear. Elric felt some discomfort as he glanced through the flickering shadows and his eyes, caught by torchflare, gleamed fever-bright.

With dreadful monotony, the oars splashed onwards as the tunnel widened and several more cavemouths came into sight. 'The middle entrance,' Elric ordered. The steersman in the stern nodded and guided the ship towards the entrance Elric had indicated. Apart from the muted murmur of some men and the splash of oars, there was a grim and ominous silence in the towering cavern.

Elric stared down at the cold, dark water and shuddered.

Eventually they moved once again into bright sunlight and the men looked upwards, marvelling at the height of the great walls above them. Upon those walls squatted more yellow-clad, bronze-armoured archers and as Count Smiorgan's vessel led the way out of the black caverns, the torches still burning in the cool winter air, arrows began to hurtle down into the narrow canyon, biting into throats and limbs.

'Faster!' howled Elric. 'Row faster – speed is our only weapon now.'

With frantic energy the oarsmen bent to their sweeps and the ships began to pick up speed even though Imrryrian arrows took heavy toll of the reaver crewmen. Now the high-walled channel ran straight and Elric saw the quays of Imrryr ahead of him.

'Faster! Faster! Our prize is in sight!'

Then, suddenly, the ship broke past the walls and was in the calm waters of the harbour, facing the warriors drawn up on the quay. The ship halted, waiting for reinforcements to plunge out of the channel and join them. When twenty ships were through, Elric gave the command to attack the quay and now Stormbringer howled from its scabbard. The flagship's port side thudded against the quay as arrows rained down upon it. Shafts whistled all around Elric but, miraculously, he was unscathed as he led a bunch of yelling reavers on to land. Imrryrian axe-men bunched forward and confronted the reavers, but it was plain that they had little spirit for the fight – they were too disconcerted by the course which events had taken.

Elric's black blade struck with frenzied force at the throat of the leading axe-man and sheared off his head. Howling demoniacally now that it had again tasted blood, the sword began to writhe in Elric's grasp, seeking fresh flesh in which to bite. There was a hard, grim smile on the albino's colourless lips and his eyes were narrowed as he struck without discrimination at the warriors.

He planned to leave the fighting to those he had led to Imrryr, for he had other things to do – and quickly. Behind the yellow-garbed soldiers, the tall towers of Imrryr rose, beautiful in their soft and scintillating colours of coral pink and powdery blue, of gold and pale yellow, white and subtle green. One such tower was Elric's objective – the tower of D'a'rputna where he had ordered Tanglebones to take

Cymoril, knowing that in the confusion this would be possible.

Elric hacked a blood-drenched path through those who attempted to halt him and men fell back, screaming horribly as the runesword drank their souls.

Now Elric was past them, leaving them to the bright blades of the reavers who poured on to the quayside, and was running up through the twisting streets, his sword slaying anyone who attempted to stop him. Like a white-faced ghoul he was, his clothing tattered and bloody, his armour chipped and scratched, but he ran speedily over the cobble-stones of the twisting streets and came at last to the slender tower of hazy blue and soft gold – the Tower of D'a'rputna. Its door was open, showing that someone was inside, and Elric rushed through it and entered the large ground-floor chamber. No one greeted him.

'Tanglebones!' he yelled, his voice roaring loudly even in his own ears. 'Tanglebones – are you here?' He leapt up the stairs in great bounds, calling his servant's name. On the third floor he stopped suddenly, hearing a low groan from one of the rooms. 'Tanglebones – is that you?' Elric strode towards the room, hearing a strangled gasping. He pushed open the door and his stomach seemed to twist within him as he saw the old man lying upon the bare floor of the chamber, striving vainly to stop the flow of blood which gouted from a great wound in his side.

'What's happened man – where's Cymoril?'

Tanglebones' old face twisted in pain and grief. 'She – I – I brought her here, master, as you ordered. But – ' he coughed and blood dribbled down his wizened chin, 'but – Prince Yyrkoon – he – he apprehended me – must have followed us here. He – struck me down and took Cymoril back with him – said she'd be – safe in the Tower of B'aal'nezbett. Master – I'm sorry . . . '

'So you should be,' Elric retorted savagely. Then his tone softened. 'Do not worry, old friend – I'll avenge you and myself. I can still reach Cymoril now I know where Yyrkoon has taken her. Thank you for trying, Tanglebones – may your long journey down the last river be uneventful.'

He turned abruptly on his heel and left the chamber, running down the stairs and out into the street again.

The Tower of B'aal'nezbett was the highest tower in the Royal Palace. Elric knew it well, for it was there that his ancestors had studied their dark sorceries and conducted frightful experiments. He shuddered as he thought what Yyrkoon might be doing to his own sister.

The streets of the city seemed hushed and strangely deserted, but

Elric had no time to ponder why this should be so. Instead he dashed towards the palace, found the main gate unguarded and the main entrance to the building deserted. This too was unique, but it constituted luck for Elric as he made his way upwards, climbing familiar ways towards the topmost tower.

Finally, he reached a door of shimmering black crystal which had no bolt or handle to it. Frenziedly, Elric struck at the crystal with his sorcerous blade but the crystal appeared only to flow and re-form. His blows had no effect.

Elric racked his mind, seeking to remember the single alien word which would make the door open. He dared not put himself in the trance which would have, in time, brought the word to his lips, instead he had to dredge his subconscious and bring the word forth. It was dangerous but there was little else he could do. His whole frame trembled as his face twisted and his brain began to shake. The word was coming as his vocal chords jerked in his throat and his chest heaved.

He coughed the word out and his whole mind and body ached with the strain. Then he cried:

'I command thee – open!'

He knew that once the door opened, his cousin would be aware of his presence, but he had to risk it. The crystal expanded, pulsating and seething, and then began to flow *out*. It flowed into nothingness, into something beyond the physical universe, beyond time. Elric breathed thankfully and passed into the Tower of B'aal'nezbett. But now an eerie fire, chilling and mind-shattering, was licking around Elric as he struggled up the steps towards the central chamber. There was a strange music surrounding him, uncanny music which throbbed and sobbed and pounded in his head.

Above him he saw a leering Yyrkoon, a black runesword also in his hand, the mate of the one in Elric's own grasp.

'Hellspawn!' Elric said thickly, weakly, 'I see you have recovered Mournblade – well, test its powers against its brother if you dare. I have come to destroy you, cousin.'

Stormbringer was giving forth a peculiar moaning sound which sighed over the shrieking, unearthly music accompanying the licking, chilling fire. The runesword writhed in Elric's fist and he had difficulty in controlling it. Summoning all his strength he plunged up the last few steps and aimed a wild blow at Yyrkoon. Beyond the eerie fire bubbled yellow-green lava, on all sides, above and beneath. The two men were surrounded only by the misty fire and the lava which lurked beyond it – they were outside the Earth and facing one another for a final battle.

The lava seethed and began to ooze inwards, dispersing the fire.

The two blades met and a terrible shrieking roar went up. Elric felt his whole arm go numb and it tingled sickeningly. Elric felt like a puppet. He was no longer his own master – the blade was deciding his actions for him. The blade, with Elric behind it, roared past its brother sword and cut a deep wound in Yyrkoon's left arm. He howled and his eyes widened in agony. Mournblade struck back at Stormbringer, catching Elric in the very place he had wounded his cousin. He sobbed in pain, but continued to move upwards, now wounding Yyrkoon in the right side with a blow strong enough to have killed any other man. Yyrkoon laughed then – laughed like a gibbering demon from the foulest depths of Hell. His sanity had broken at last and Elric now had the advantage. But the great sorcery which his cousin had conjured was still in evidence and Elric felt as if a giant had grasped him, was crushing him as he pressed his advantage, Yyrkoon's blood spouting from the wound and covering Elric, also. The lava was slowly withdrawing and now Elric saw the entrance to the central chamber. Behind his cousin another form moved. Elric gasped. Cymoril had awakened and, with horror on her face, was shrieking at him.

The sword still swung in a black arc, cutting down Yyrkoon's brother blade and breaking the usurper's guard.

'Elric!' cried Cymoril desperately. 'Save me – save me now, else we are doomed for eternity.'

Elric was puzzled by the girl's words. He could not understand the sense of them. Savagely he drove Yyrkoon upwards towards the chamber.

'Elric – put Stormbringer away. Sheath your sword or we shall part again.'

But even if he could have controlled the whistling blade, Elric would not have sheathed it. Hate dominated his being and he would sheathe it in his cousin's evil heart before he put it aside.

Cymoril was weeping, now, pleading with him. But Elric could do nothing. The drooling, idiot thing which had been Yyrkoon of Imrryr, turned at its sister's cries and stared leeringly at her. It cackled and reached out one shaking hand to seize the girl by her shoulder. She struggled to escape, but Yyrkoon still had his evil strength. Taking advantage of his opponent's distraction Elric cut deep through his body, almost severing the trunk from the waist.

And yet, incredibly, Yyrkoon remained alive, drawing his vitality from the blade which still clashed against Elric's own rune-carved sword. With a final push he flung Cymoril forward and she died screaming on the point of Stormbringer.

472

Then Yyrkoon laughed one final cackling shriek and his black soul went howling down to hell.

The tower resumed its former proportions, all fire and lava gone. Elric was dazed – unable to marshal his thoughts. He looked down at the dead bodies of the brother and the sister. He saw them, at first, only as corpses – a man's and a woman's.

Then dark truth dawned on his clearing brain and he moaned in grief, like an animal. He had slain the girl he loved. The runesword fell from his grasp, stained by Cymoril's lifeblood, and clattered unheeded down the stairs. Sobbing now, Elric dropped beside the dead girl and lifted her in his arms.

'Cymoril,' he moaned, his whole body throbbing. 'Cymoril – I have slain you.'

4

A Dark Bond
Recognized

Elric looked back at the roaring, crumbling, tumbling, flame-spewing ruins of Imrryr and drove his sweating oarsmen faster. The ship, sail still unfurled, bucked as a contrary current of wind caught it and Elric was forced to cling to the ship's side lest he be tossed overboard. He looked back at Imrryr and felt a tightness in his throat as he realized that he was truly rootless, now; a renegade and a woman-slayer, though involuntarily the latter. He had lost the only woman he had loved in his blind lust for revenge. Now it was finished – everything was finished. He could envisage no future, for his future had been bound up with his past and now, effectively, that past was flaming in ruins behind him. Dry sobs eddied in his chest and he gripped the ship's rail yet more firmly.

His mind reluctantly brooded on Cymoril. He had laid her corpse upon a couch and had set fire to the Tower. Then he had gone back to find the reavers successful, straggling back to their ships loaded with loot and girl-slaves, jubilantly firing the tall and beautiful buildings as they went.

He had caused to be destroyed the last tangible sign that the grandiose, magnificent Bright Empire had ever existed. He felt that most of himself was gone with it.

Elric looked back at Imrryr and suddenly a greater sadness overwhelmed him as a tower, as delicate and as beautiful as fine lace, cracked and toppled with flames leaping about it.

He had shattered the last great monument to the earlier race – his own race. Men might have learned again, one day, to build strong, slender towers like those of Imrryr, but now the knowledge was dying with the thundering chaos of the fall of the Dreaming City and the fast-diminishing race of Melniboné.

But what of the Dragon Masters? Neither they nor their golden ships had met the attacking reavers – only their foot-soldiers had been there to defend the city. Had they hidden their ships in some secret

474

waterway and fled inland when the reavers overran the city? They had put up too short a fight to be truly beaten. It had been far too easy. Now that the ships were retreating, were they planning some sudden retaliation? Elric felt that they might have such a plan – perhaps a plan concerning dragons. He shuddered. He had told the others nothing of the beasts which Melnibonéans had controlled for centuries. Even now, someone might be unlocking the gates of the underground Dragon Caves. He turned his mind away from the unnerving prospect.

As the fleet headed towards open sea, Elric's eyes were still looking sadly towards Imrryr as he paid silent homage to the city of his fore-fathers and the dead Cymoril. He felt hot bitterness sweep over him again as the memory of her death upon his own sword-point came sharply to him. He recalled her warning, when he had left her to go adventuring in the Young Kingdoms, that by putting Yyrkoon on the Ruby Throne as Regent, by relinquishing his power for a year, he doomed them both. He cursed himself. Then a muttering, like a roll of distant thunder, spread through the fleet and he wheeled sharply, intent on discovering the cause of the consternation.

Thirty golden-sailed Melnibonéan battle barges had appeared on both sides of the harbour, issuing from two mouths of the maze. Elric realized that they must have hidden in the other channels, waiting to attack the fleet when they returned, satiated and depleted. Great war-galleys they were, the last ships of Melniboné and the secret of their building was unknown. They had a sense of age and slumbering might about them as they rowed swiftly, each with four or five banks of great sweeping oars, to encircle the raven ships.

Elric's fleet seemed to shrink before his eyes until it seemed as though it were a bobbing collection of wood-shavings against the towering splendour of the shimmering battle barges. They were well-equipped and fresh for a fight, whereas the weary reavers were intensely battle-tired. There was only one way to save a small part of the fleet, Elric knew. He would have to conjure a witch-wind for sailpower. Most of the flagships were around him and he now occupied that of Yaris, for the youth had got himself wildly drunk and had died by the knife of a Melnibonéan slave wench. Next to Elric's ship was Count Smiorgan's and the stocky Sea Lord was frowning, knowing full well that he and his ships, for all their superior numbers, would not stand up to a sea-fight.

But the conjuring of winds great enough to move many vessels was a dangerous thing, for it released colossal power and the elementals who controlled the winds were apt to turn upon the sorcerer himself if he was not more than careful. But it was the only chance, otherwise the rams which sent ripples from the golden prows would smash the reaver ships to driftwood.

Steeling himself, Elric began to speak the ancient and terrible, many-vowelled names of the beings who existed in the air. Again, he could not risk the trance-state, for he had to watch for signs of the elementals turning upon him. He called to them in a speech that was sometimes high like the cry of a gannet, sometimes rolling like the roar of shore-bound surf, and the dim shapes of the Powers of the Wind began to flit before his blurred gaze. His heart throbbed horribly in his ribs and his legs felt weak. He summoned all his strength and conjured a wind which shrieked wildly and chaotically about him, rocking even the huge Melnibonéan ships back and forth. Then he directed the wind and sent it into the sails of some forty of the reaver ships. Many he could not save for they lay outside even his wide range.

But forty of the craft escaped the smashing rams and, amidst the sound of howling wind and sundered timbers, leapt on the waves, their masts creaking as the wind cracked into their sails. Oars were torn from the hands of the rowers, leaving a wake of broken wood on the white salt trail which boiled behind each of the reaver ships.

Quite suddenly, they were beyond the slowly closing circle of Melnibonéan ships and careering madly across the open sea, while all the crews sensed a difference in the air and caught glimpses of strange, soft-shaped forms around them. There was a discomforting sense of evil about the beings which aided them, an awesome alienness.

Smiorgan waved to Elric and grinned thankfully.

'We're safe, thanks to you, Elric!' he yelled across the water. 'I knew you'd bring us luck!'

Elric ignored him.

Now the Dragon Lords, vengeance-bent, gave chase. Almost as fast as the magic-aided reaver fleet were the golden barges of Imrryr, and some reaver galleys, whose masts cracked and split beneath the force of the wind driving them, were caught.

Elric saw mighty grappling hooks of dully gleaming metal swing out from the decks of the Imrryrian galleys and thud with a moan of wrenched timber into those of the fleet which lay broken and power-less behind him. Fire leapt from catapults upon the Dragon Lords' ships and careered towards many a fleeing reaver craft. Searing, foul-stinking flame hissed like lava across the decks and ate into planks like vitriol into paper. Men shrieked, beating vainly at brightly burning clothes, some leaping into water which would not extinguish the fire. Some sank beneath the sea and it was possible to trace their descent as, flaming even below the surface, men and ships fluttered to the bottom like blazing, tired moths.

Reaver decks, untouched by fire, ran red with reaver blood as the enraged Imrryrian warriors swung down the grappling ropes and dropped among the raiders, wielding great swords and battle-axes and wreaking terrible havoc amongst the sea-ravens. Imrryrian arrows and Imrryrian javelins swooped from the towering decks of Imrryrian galleys and tore into the panicky men on the smaller ships.

All this Elric saw as he and his vessels began slowly to overhaul the leading Imrryrian ship, flag-galley of Admiral Magum Colim, commander of the Melnibonéan fleet.

Now Elric spared a word for Count Smiorgan. 'We've outrun them!' he shouted above the howling wind to the next ship where Smiorgan stood staring wide-eyed at the sky. 'But keep your ships heading westwards or we're finished!'

But Smiorgan did not reply. He still looked skyward and there was horror in his eyes; in the eyes of a man who, before this, had never known the quivering bite of fear. Uneasily, Elric let his own eyes follow the gaze of Smiorgan. Then he saw them.

They were dragons, without doubt! The great reptiles were some miles away, but Elric knew the stamp of the huge flying beasts. The average wingspan of these near-extinct monsters was some thirty feet across. Their snake-like bodies, beginning in a narrow-snouted head and terminating in a dreadful whip of a tail, were forty feet long and although they did not breathe the legendary fire and smoke, Elric knew that their venom was combustible and could set fire to wood or fabric on contact.

Imrryrian warriors rode the dragon backs. Armed with long, spear-like goads, they blew strangely shaped horns which sang out curious notes over the turbulent sea and calm blue sky. Nearing the golden fleet, now half-a-league away, the leading dragon sailed down and circled towards the huge golden flag-galley, its wings making a sound like the crack of lightning as they beat through the air.

The grey-green, scaled monster hovered over the golden ship as it heaved in the white-foamed turbulent sea. Framed against the cloudless sky, the dragon was in sharp perspective and it was possible for Elric to get a clear view of it. The goad which the Dragon Master waved to Admiral Magum Colim was a long, slim spear upon which the strange pennant of black and yellow zig-zag lines was, even at this distance, noticeable. Elric recognized the insignia on the pennant.

Dyvim Tvar, friend of Elric's youth, Lord of the Dragon Caves, was leading his charges to claim vengeance for Imrryr the Beautiful.

477

Elric howled across the water to Smiorgan. 'These are your main danger, now. Do what you can to stave them off!' There was a rattle of iron as the men prepared, near-hopelessly, to repel the new menace. Witch-wind would give little advantage over the fast-flying dragons. Now Dyvim Tvar had evidently conferred with Magum Colim and his goad lashed out at the dragon throat. The huge reptile jerked upwards and began to gain altitude. Eleven other dragons were behind it, joining it now.

With seeming slowness, the dragons began to beat relentlessly towards the reaver fleet as the crewmen prayed to their own Gods for a miracle.

They were doomed. There was no escaping the fact. Every reaver ship was doomed and the raid had been fruitless.

Elric could see the despair in the faces of the men as the masts of the reaver ships continued to bend under the strain of the shrieking witch-wind. They could do nothing, now, but die . . .

Elric fought to rid his mind of the swirling uncertainty which filled it. He drew his sword and felt the pulsating, evil power which lurked in rune-carved Stormbringer. But he hated that power now – for it had caused him to kill the only human he had cherished. He realized how much of his strength he owed to the black-iron sword of his fathers and how weak he might be without it. He was an albino and that meant that he lacked the vitality of a normal human being. Savagely, futilely, as the mist in his mind was replaced by red fear, he cursed the pretensions of revenge he had held, cursed the day when he had agreed to lead the raid on Imrryr and most of all he bitterly vilified dead Yyrkoon and his twisted envy which had been the cause of the whole doom-ridden course of events.

But it was too late now for curses of any kind. The loud slapping of beating dragon wings filled the air and the monsters loomed over the fleeing reaver craft. He had to make some kind of decision – though he had no love for life, he refused to die by the hands of his own people. When he died, he promised himself, it would be by his own hand. He made his decision, hating himself.

He called off the witch-wind as the dragon venom seared down and struck the last ship in line.

He put all his powers into sending a stronger wind into the sails of his own boat while his bewildered comrades in the suddenly becalmed ships called over the water, inquiring desperately the reason for his act. Elric's ship was moving fast, now, and might just escape the dragons. He hoped so.

He deserted the man who had trusted him, Count Smiorgan, and watched as venom poured from the sky and engulfed him in blazing green and scarlet flame. Elric fled, keeping his mind from thoughts of the future, and sobbed aloud, that proud prince of ruins; and he cursed the malevolent Gods for the black day when idly, for their amusement, they had spawned men.

Behind him, the last reaver ships flared into sudden appalling brightness and, although half-thankful that they had escaped the fate of their comrades, the crew looked at Elric accusingly. He sobbed on, not heeding them, great griefs racking his soul.

A night later, off the coast of an island called Pan Tang, when the ship was safe from the dreadful recriminations of the Dragon Masters and their beasts, Elric stood brooding in the stern while the men eyed him with fear and hatred, muttering betrayal and heartless cowardice. They appeared to have forgotten their own fear and subsequent safety.

Elric brooded and he held the black runesword in his two hands. Stormbringer was more than an ordinary battle-blade, this he had known for years, but now he realized that it was possessed of more sentience than he had imagined. Yet he was horribly dependent upon it; he realized this with soul-rending certainty. But he feared and resented the sword's power – hated it bitterly for the chaos it had wrought in his brain and spirit. In an agony of uncertainty he held the blade in his hands and forced himself to weigh the factors involved. Without the sinister sword, he would lose pride – perhaps even life – but he might know the soothing tranquillity of pure rest; with it he would have power and strength – but the sword would guide him into a doom-racked future. He would savour power – but never peace.

He drew a great, sobbing breath and, blind misgiving influencing him, threw the sword into the moon-drenched sea.

Incredibly, it did not sink. It did not even float on the water. It fell point forwards into the sea and *stuck* there, quivering as if it were embedded in timber. It remained throbbing in the water, six inches of its blade immersed, and began to give off a weird devil-scream – a howl of horrible malevolence.

With a choking curse Elric stretched out his slim, whitely gleaming hand, trying to recover the sentient hellblade. He stretched further, leaning far out over the rail. He could not grasp it – it lay some feet from him, still. Gasping, a sickening sense of defeat overwhelming him, he dropped over the side and plunged into the bone-chilling water, striking out with strained, grotesque strokes, towards the hovering sword. He was beaten – the sword had won.

He reached it and put his fingers around the hilt. At once it settled in his hand and Elric felt strength seep slowly back into his aching body. Then he realized that he and the sword were interdependent, for though he needed the blade, Stormbringer, parasitic, required a user – without a man to wield it, the blade was also powerless.

'We must be bound to one another then,' Elric murmured despairingly. 'Bound by hell-forged chains and fate-haunted circumstance. Well, then – let it be thus so – and men will have cause to tremble and flee when they hear the names of Elric of Melniboné and Stormbringer, his sword. We are two of a kind – produced by an age which has deserted us. Let us give this age *cause* to hate us!'

Strong again, Elric sheathed Stormbringer and the sword settled against his side; then, with powerful strokes, he began to swim toward the island while the men he left on the ship breathed with relief and speculated whether he would live or perish in the bleak waters of that strange and nameless sea . . .

WHILE THE GODS LAUGH

For my father

I, while the gods laugh, the world's vortex am;
Maelstrom of passions in that hidden sea
Whose waves of all-time lap the coasts of me,
And in small compass the dark waters cram.

Mervyn Peake, *Shapes and Sounds*, 1941

1

A Woman Who Would
Risk Grief to Her Soul

One night, as Elric sat moodily drinking alone in a tavern, a wingless woman of Myyrrhn came gliding out of the storm and rested her lithe body against him.

Her face was thin and frail-boned, almost as white as Elric's own albino skin, and she wore flimsy pale-green robes which contrasted well with her dark red hair.

The tavern was ablaze with candle-flame and alive with droning argument and gusty laughter, but the words of the woman of Myyrrhn came clear and liquid, carrying over the zesty din.

'I have sought you twenty days,' she said to Elric who regarded her insolently through hooded crimson eyes and lazed in a high-backed chair, a silver wine-cup in his long-fingered right hand and his left on the pommel of his sorcerous runesword Stormbringer.

'Twenty days,' murmured the Melnibonéan softly, speaking as if to himself, deliberately rude. 'A long time for a beautiful and lonely woman to be wandering the world.' He opened his eyes a trifle wider and spoke to her directly: 'I am Elric of Melniboné, as you evidently know. I grant no favours and ask none. Bearing this in mind, tell me why you have sought me for twenty days.'

Equably, the woman replied, undaunted by the albino's supercilious tone. 'You are a bitter man, Elric; I know this also – and you are grief-haunted for reasons which are already legend. I ask you no favours – but bring you myself and a proposition. What do you desire most in the world?'

'Peace,' Elric told her simply. Then he smiled ironically and said: 'I am an evil man, lady, and my destiny is hell-doomed, but I am not unwise, nor unfair. Let me remind you a little of the truth. Call this legend if you prefer – I do not care.

'A woman died a year ago, on the blade of my trusty sword.' He patted the blade sharply and his eyes were suddenly hard and self-mocking. 'Since then I have courted no woman and desired none. Why should I break such secure habits? If asked, I grant you that I could speak poetry to you, and that you have a grace and beauty which moves me to interesting speculation, but I would not load any part of my dark burden upon one as exquisite as you. Any relationship between us, other than formal, would necessitate my unwilling shifting of part of that burden.' He paused for an instant and then said slowly: 'I should admit that I scream in my sleep sometimes and am often tortured by incommunicable self-loathing. Go while you can, lady, and forget Elric for he can bring only grief to your soul.'

With a quick movement he turned his gaze from her and lifted the silver wine-cup, draining it and replenishing it from a jug at his side.

'No,' said the wingless woman of Myyrrhn calmly, 'I will not. Come with me.'

She rose and gently took Elric's hand. Without knowing why, Elric allowed himself to be led from the tavern and out into the wild, rain-less storm which howled around the Filkharian city of Raschil. A protective and cynical smile hovered about his mouth as she drew him towards the sea-lashed quayside where she told him her name. Shaarilla of the Dancing Mist, wingless daughter of a dead necromancer – a cripple in her own strange land, and an outcast.

Elric felt uncomfortably drawn to this calm-eyed woman who wasted few words. He felt a great surge of emotion well within him, emotion he had never thought to experience again, and he wanted to take her finely moulded shoulders and press her slim body to his. But he quelled the urge and studied her marble delicacy and her wild hair which flowed in the wind about her head.

Silence rested comfortably between them while the chaotic wind howled mournfully over the sea. Here, Elric could ignore the warm stink of the city and he felt almost relaxed. At last, looking away from him towards the swirling sea, her green robe curling in the wind, she said: 'You have heard, of course, of the Dead Gods' book?'

Elric nodded. He was interested, despite the need he felt to disassociate himself as much as possible from his fellows. The mythical book was believed to contain knowledge which could solve many problems that had plagued men for centuries – it held a holy and mighty wisdom which every sorcerer desired to sample. But it was believed destroyed, hurled into the sun when the Old Gods were dying in the cosmic wastes which lay beyond the outer reaches of the solar system. Another legend, apparently of later origin, spoke vaguely of the dark ones who had interrupted the Book's sunward coursing and had stolen it before it could be destroyed. Most scholars discounted this legend, arguing that, by this time, the book would have come to light if it did still exist.

Elric made himself speak flatly so that he appeared to be uninterested when he answered Shaarilla. 'Why do you mention the Book?'

'I know that it exists,' Shaarilla replied intensely, 'and I know where it is. My father acquired the knowledge just before he died. Myself — and the book — you may have if you will help me get it.'

Could the secret of peace be contained in the book? Elric wondered. Would he, if he found it, be able to dispense with Stormbringer?

'If you want it so badly that you seek my help,' he said eventually, 'why do you not wish to keep it?'

'Because I would be afraid to have such a thing perpetually in my custody — it is not a book for a woman to own, but you are possibly the last mighty nigromancer left in the world and it is fitting that you should have it. Besides, you might kill me to obtain it — I would never be safe with such a volume in my hands. I need only one small part of its wisdom.'

'What is that?' Elric inquired, studying her patrician beauty with a new pulse stirring within him.

Her mouth set and the lids fell over her eyes. 'When we have the book in our hands — then you will have your answer. Not before.'

'This answer is good enough,' Elric remarked quickly, seeing that he would gain no more information at that stage. 'And the answer appeals to me.' Then, half before he realized it, he seized her shoulders in his slim, pale hands and pressed his colourless lips to her scarlet mouth.

Elric and Shaarilla rode westwards, towards the Silent Land, across the lush plains of Shazaar where their ship had berthed two days earlier. The border country between Shazaar and the Silent Land was a lonely stretch of territory, unoccupied even by peasant dwellings; a no-man's land, though fertile and rich in natural wealth. The inhabitants of Shazaar had deliberately refrained from extending their borders further, for though the dwellers in the Silent Land rarely ventured beyond the Marshes of the Mist, the natural borderline between the two lands, the inhabitants of Shazaar held their unknown neighbours in almost superstitious fear.

The journey had been clean and swift, though ominous, with several persons who should have known nothing of their purpose warning the travellers of nearing danger. Elric brooded, recognizing the signs of doom but choosing to ignore them and communicate nothing to Shaarilla who, for her part, seemed content with Elric's silence. They spoke little in the day and so saved their breath for the wild love-play of the night.

The thud of the two horses' hooves on the soft turf, the muted creak and clatter of Elric's harness and sword, were the only sounds to break the stillness of the clear winter day as the pair rode steadily, nearing the quaking, treacherous trails of the Marshes of the Mist.

One gloomy night, they reached the borders of the Silent Land, marked by the marsh, and they halted and made camp, pitching their silk tent on a hill overlooking the mist-shrouded wastes.

Banked like black pillows against the horizon, the clouds were ominous. The moon lurked behind them, sometimes piercing them sufficiently to send a pale tentative beam down on to the glistening marsh or its ragged, grassy frontiers. Once, a moonbeam glanced off silver, illuminating the dark silhouette of Elric, but, as if repelled by the sight of a living creature on that bleak hill, the moon once again slunk behind its cloud-shield, leaving Elric thinking deeply. Leaving Elric in the darkness he desired.

Thunder rumbled over distant mountains, sounding like the laughter of far-off Gods. Elric shivered, pulled his blue cloak more tightly about him, and continued to stare over the misted lowlands.

Shaarilla came to him soon, and she stood beside him, swathed in a thick woollen cloak which could not keep out all the damp chill in the air.

'The Silent Land,' she murmured. 'Are all the stories true, Elric? Did they teach you of it in old Melniboné?'

Elric frowned, annoyed that she had disturbed his thoughts. He turned abruptly to look at her, staring blankly through his crimson-irised eyes for a moment and then saying flatly:

'The inhabitants are unhuman and feared. This I know. Few men ventured into their territory, ever. None have returned, to my knowledge. Even in the days when Melniboné was a powerful Empire, this was one nation my ancestors never ruled – nor did they desire to do so. The denizens of the Silent Land are said to be a dying race, far more evil than my ancestors ever were, who enjoyed dominion over the Earth long before men gained any sort of power. They rarely venture beyond the confines of their territory, nowadays, encompassed as it is by marshland and mountains.'

Shaarilla laughed, then, with little humour. 'So they are unhuman are they, Elric? Then what of my people, who are related to them? What of me, Elric?'

'You're human enough for me,' replied Elric insouciantly, looking her in the eyes. She smiled.

'No compliment,' she said, 'but I'll take it for one – until your glib tongue finds a better.'

That night they slept restlessly and, as he had predicted, Elric screamed agonizingly in his turbulent, terror-filled sleep and he called a name which made Shaarilla's eyes fill with pain and jealousy. Wide-eyed in his grim sleep, Elric seemed to be staring at the one he named, speaking other words in a sibilant language which made Shaarilla block her ears and shudder.

The next morning, as they broke camp, folding the rustling fabric of the yellow silk tent between them, Shaarilla avoided looking at Elric directly but later, since he made no move to speak, she asked him a question in a voice which shook somewhat.

It was a question which she needed to ask, but one which came hard to her lips. 'Why do you desire the Dead Gods' Book, Elric? What do you believe you will find in it?'

Elric shrugged, dismissing the question, but she repeated her words less slowly, with more insistence.

'Very well then,' he said eventually. 'But it is not easy to answer you in a few sentences. I desire, if you like, to know one of two things.'

'And what is that, Elric?'

The tall albino dropped the folded tent to the grass and sighed. His fingers played nervously with the pommel of his runesword. 'Can an ultimate God exist – or not? That is what I need to know, Shaarilla, if my life is to have any direction at all.

'The Lords of Law and Chaos now govern our lives. But is there some being greater than them?'

Shaarilla put a hand on Elric's arm. 'Why must you know?' she said.

'Despairingly, sometimes, I seek the comfort of a benign God, Shaarilla. My mind goes out, lying awake at night, searching through black barrenness for something – anything – which will take me to it, warm me, protect me, tell me that there is order in the chaotic tumble of the universe; that it is consistent, this precision of the planets, not simply a brief, bright spark of sanity in an eternity of malevolent anarchy.'

Elric sighed and his quiet tones were tinged with hopelessness. 'Without some confirmation of the order of things, my only comfort is to accept the anarchy. This way, I can revel in chaos and know, without fear, that we are all doomed from the start – that our brief existence is both meaningless and damned. I can accept then, that we are more than forsaken, because there was never anything there to forsake us. I have weighed the proof, Shaarilla, and must believe that anarchy prevails, in spite of all the laws which seemingly govern our

487

actions, our sorcery, our logic. I see only chaos in the world. If the Book we seek tells me otherwise, then I shall gladly believe it. Until then, I will put my trust only in my sword and myself.'

Shaarilla stared at Elric strangely. 'Could not this philosophy of yours have been influenced by recent events in your past? Do you fear the consequences of your murder and treachery? Is it not more comforting for you to believe in deserts which are rarely just?'

Elric turned on her, crimson eyes blazing in anger, but even as he made to speak, the anger fled him and he dropped his eyes towards the ground, hooding them from her gaze.

'Perhaps,' he said lamely. 'I do not know. That is the only *real* truth, Shaarilla. *I do not know.*'

Shaarilla nodded, her face lit by an enigmatic sympathy; but Elric did not see the look she gave him, for his own eyes were full of crystal tears which flowed down his lean, white face and took his strength and will momentarily from him.

'I am a man possessed,' he groaned, 'and without this devil-blade I carry I would not be a man at all.'

2

The Mist Giant, Bellbane

They mounted their swift, black horses and spurred them with abandoned savagery down the hillside towards the Marsh, their cloaks whipping behind them as the wind caught them, lashing them high into the air. Both rode with set, hard faces, refusing to acknowledge the aching uncertainty which lurked within them.

And the horses' hooves had splashed into quaking bogland before they could halt.

Cursing, Elric tugged hard on his reins, pulling his horse back on to firm ground. Shaarilla, too, fought her own panicky stallion and guided the beast to the safety of the turf.

'How do we cross?' Elric asked her impatiently.

'There was a map – ' Shaarilla began hesitantly.

'*Where is it?*'

'It – it was lost. I lost it. But I tried hard to memorise it. I think I'll be able to get us safely across.'

'How did you lose it – and why didn't you tell me of this before?' Elric stormed.

'I'm sorry, Elric – but for a whole day, just before I found you in that tavern, my memory was gone. Somehow, I lived through a day without knowing it – and when I awoke, the map was missing.'

Elric frowned. 'There is some force working against us, I am sure,' he muttered, 'but what it is, I do not know.' He raised his voice and said to her: 'Let us hope that your memory is not too faulty, now. These Marshes are infamous the world over, but by all accounts, only natural hazards wait for us.' He grimaced and put his fingers around the hilt of his runesword. 'Best go first, Shaarilla, but stay close. Lead the way.'

She nodded, dumbly, and turned her horse's head towards the north, galloping along the bank until she came to a place where a great, tapering rock loomed. Here, a grassy path, four feet or so across, led out into the misty marsh. They could only see a little distance ahead, because of the clinging mist, but it seemed that the trail remained firm for some way. Shaarilla walked her horse on to the path and jolted forward at a slow trot, Elric following immediately behind her.

Through the swirling, heavy mist which shone whitely, the horses moved hesitantly and their riders had to keep them on short, tight rein. The mist padded the marsh with silence and the gleaming, watery fens around them stank with foul putrescence. No animal scurried, no bird shrieked above them. Everywhere was a haunting, fear-laden silence which made both horses and riders uneasy.

With panic in their throats, Elric and Shaarilla rode on, deeper and deeper into the unnatural Marshes of the Mist, their eyes wary and even their nostrils quivering for scent of danger in the stinking morass.

Hours later, when the sun was long past its zenith, Shaarilla's horse reared, screaming and whinnying. She shouted for Elric, her exquisite features twisted in fear as she stared into the mist. He spurred his own bucking horse forwards and joined her.

Something moved, slowly, menacingly in the clinging whiteness. Elric's right hand whipped over to his left side and grasped the hilt of Stormbringer.

The blade shrieked out of its scabbard, a black fire gleaming along its length and alien power flowing from it into Elric's arm and through his body. A weird, unholy light leapt into Elric's crimson eyes and his mouth was wrenched into a hideous grin as he forced the frightened horse further into the skulking mist.

'Arioch, Lord of the Seven Darks, be with me now!' Elric yelled as he made out the shifting shape ahead of him. It was white, like the mist, yet somehow *darker*. It stretched high above Elric's head. It was nearly eight feet tall and almost as broad. But it was still only an outline, seeming to have no face or limbs – only movement: darting, malevolent movement! But Arioch, his patron god, chose not to hear.

Elric could feel his horse's great heart beating between his legs as the beast plunged forward under its rider's iron control. Shaarilla was screaming something behind him, but he could not hear the words. Elric hacked at the white shape, but his sword met only mist and it howled angrily. The fear-crazed horse would go no further and Elric was forced to dismount.

'Keep hold of the steed,' he shouted behind him to Shaarilla and moved on light feet towards the darting shape which hovered ahead of him, blocking his path.

Now he could make out some of its saliencies. Two eyes, the colour of thin, yellow wine, were set high in the thing's body, though it had no separate head. A mouthing, obscene slit, filled with fangs, lay just beneath the eyes. It had no nose or ears that Elric could see. Four appendages sprang from its upper parts and its lower body slithered along the ground, unsupported by any limbs. Elric's eyes ached as he looked at it. It was incredibly disgusting to behold and its amorphous body gave off a stench of death and decay. Fighting down his fear, the albino inched forward warily, his sword held high to parry any thrust the thing might make with its arms. Elric recognized it from a description in one of his grimoires. It was a Mist Giant – possibly the only Mist Giant, Bellbane. Even the wisest wizards were uncertain how many existed – one or many. It was a ghoul of the swamp-lands which fed off the souls and the blood of men and beasts. But the Marshes of this Mist were far to the east of Bellbane's reputed haunts.

Elric ceased to wonder why so few animals inhabited that stretch of the swamp. Overhead the sky was beginning to darken.

Stormbringer throbbed in Elric's grasp as he called the names of the ancient Demon-Gods of his people. The nauseous ghoul obviously recognized the names. For an instant, it wavered backwards. Elric made his legs move towards the thing. Now he saw that the ghoul was not white at all. But it had no colour to it that Elric could recognize. There was a suggestion of orangeness dashed with sickening greenish yellow, but he did not see the colours with his eyes – he only *sensed* the alien, unholy tinctures.

Then Elric rushed towards the thing, shouting the names which now had no meaning to his surface consciousness. *'Balaan – Marthim! Aesma! Alastor! Saebos! Verdelet! Nizilfkm! Haborym!* Haborym of the Fires Which Destroy!' His whole mind was torn in two. Part of him wanted to run, to hide, but he had no control over the power which now gripped him and pushed him to meet the horror. His sword blade hacked and slashed at the shape. It was like trying to cut through water – sentient, pulsating water. But Stormbringer had effect. The whole shape of the ghoul quivered as if in dreadful pain. Elric felt himself plucked into the air and his vision went. He could see nothing – do nothing but hack and cut at the thing which now held him.

Sweat poured from him as, blindly, he fought on.

Pain which was hardly physical – a deeper, horrifying pain, filled his being as he howled now in agony and struck continually at the yielding bulk which embraced him and was pulling him slowly towards its gaping maw. He struggled and writhed in the obscene grasp of the thing. With powerful arms, it was holding him, almost lasciviously, drawing him closer as a rough lover would draw a girl. Even the mighty power intrinsic in the runesword did not seem enough to kill the monster. Though its efforts were somewhat weaker than earlier, it still drew Elric nearer to the gnashing, slavering mouth-slit.

Elric cried the names again, while Stormbringer danced and sang an evil song in his right hand. In agony, Elric writhed, praying, begging and promising, but still he was drawn inch by inch towards the grinning maw.

Savagely, grimly, he fought and again he screamed for Arioch. A mind touched his – sardonic, powerful, evil – and he knew Arioch responded at last! Almost imperceptibly, the Mist Giant weakened. Elric pressed his advantage and the knowledge that the ghoul was losing its strength gave him more power. Blindly, agony piercing every nerve of his body, he struck and struck.

Then, quite suddenly, he was falling.

He seemed to fall for hours, slowly, weightlessly until he landed upon a surface which yielded beneath him. He began to sink.

Far off, beyond time and space, he heard a distant voice calling to him. He did not want to hear it; he was content to lie where he was as the cold, comforting stuff in which he lay dragged him slowly into itself.

Then, some sixth sense made him realize that it was Shaarilla's voice calling him and he forced himself to make sense out of her words.

'Elric – the marsh! You're in the marsh. Don't move!'

He smiled to himself. Why should he move? Down he was sinking, slowly, calmly – down into the welcoming marsh . . . *Had there been another time like this, another marsh?*

With a mental jolt, full awareness of the situation came back to him and he jerked his eyes open. Above him was mist. To one side a pool of unnameable colouring was slowly evaporating, giving off a foul odour. On the other side he could just make out a human form, gesticulating wildly. Beyond the human form were the barely discernible shapes of two horses. Shaarilla was there. Beneath him –

Beneath him was the marsh.

Thick, stinking slime was sucking him downwards as he lay spread-eagled upon it, half-submerged already. Stormbringer was still in his right hand. He could just see it if he turned his head. Carefully, he tried to lift the top half of his body from the sucking morass. He succeeded, only to feel his legs sink deeper. Sitting upright, he shouted to the girl.

'Shaarilla! Quickly – a rope!'

'There is no rope, Elric!' She was ripping off her top garment, frantically tearing it into strips.

Still Elric sank, his feet finding no purchase beneath them.

Shaarilla hastily knotted the strips of cloth. She flung the makeshift rope inexpertly towards the sinking albino. It fell short. Fumbling in her haste, she threw it again. This time his groping left hand found it. The girl began to haul on the fabric. Elric felt himself rise a little and then stop.

'It's no good, Elric – I haven't the strength.'

Cursing her, Elric shouted: 'The horse – tie it to the horse!'

She ran towards one of the horses and looped the cloth around the pommel of the saddle. Then she tugged at the beast's reins and began to walk it away.

Swiftly, Elric was dragged from the sucking bog and, still gripping Stormbringer was pulled to the inadequate safety of the strip of turf.

Gasping, he tried to stand, but found his legs incredibly weak beneath him. He rose, staggered, and fell. Shaarilla knelt down beside him.

'Are you hurt?'

Elric smiled in spite of his weakness. 'I don't think so.'

'It was dreadful. I couldn't see properly what was happening. You seemed to disappear and then – then you screamed that – that name!' She was trembling, her face pale and taut.

'What name?' Elric was genuinely puzzled. 'What name did I scream?'

She shook her head. 'It doesn't matter – but whatever it was – it saved you. You reappeared soon afterwards and fell into the marsh . . .'

Stormbringer's power was still flowing into the albino. He already felt stronger.

With an effort, he got up and stumbled unsteadily towards his horse.

'I'm sure that the Mist Giant does not usually haunt this marsh – it was sent here. By what – or whom – I don't know, but we must get to firmer ground while we can.'

Shaarilla said: 'Which way – back or forward?'

Elric frowned. 'Why, forward, of course. Why do you ask?'

She swallowed and shook her head. 'Let's hurry, then,' she said.

They mounted their horses and rode with little caution until the marsh and its cloak of mist was behind them.

Now the journey took on a new urgency as Elric realized that some force was attempting to put obstacles in their way. They rested little and savagely rode their powerful horses to a virtual standstill.

On the fifth day they were riding through barren, rocky country and a light rain was falling.

The hard ground was slippery so that they were forced to ride more slowly, huddled over the sodden necks of their horses, muffled in cloaks which only inadequately kept out the drizzling rain. They had ridden in silence for some time before they heard a ghastly cackling baying ahead of them and the rattle of hooves.

Elric motioned towards a large rock looming to their right. 'Shelter there,' he said. 'Something comes towards us – possibly more enemies. With luck, they'll pass us.' Shaarilla mutely obeyed him and together they waited as the hideous baying grew nearer.

'One rider – several other beasts,' Elric said, listening intently. 'The beasts either follow or pursue the rider.'

Then they were in sight – racing through the rain. A man frantically spurring an equally frightened horse – and behind him, the distance decreasing, a pack of what at first appeared to be dogs. But these were not dogs – they were half-dog and half-bird, with the lean, shaggy bodies and legs of dogs but possessing birdlike talons in place of paws and savagely curved beaks which snapped where muzzles should have been.

'The hunting dogs of the Dharzi!' gasped Shaarilla. 'I thought that they, like their masters, were long extinct!'

'I, also,' Elric said. 'What are they doing in these parts? There was never contact between the Dharzi and the dwellers of this Land.'

'Brought here – by *something*,' Shaarilla whispered. 'Those devil-dogs will scent us to be sure.'

Elric reached for his runesword. 'Then we can lose nothing by aiding their quarry,' he said, urging his mount forward. 'Wait here, Shaarilla.'

By this time, the devil-pack and the man they pursued were rushing past the sheltering rock, speeding down a narrow defile. Elric spurred his horse down the slope.

'Ho there!' he shouted to the frantic rider. 'Turn and stand, my friend – I'm here to aid you!'

His moaning runesword lifted high, Elric thundered towards the snapping, howling devil-dogs and his horse's hooves struck one with an impact which broke the unnatural beast's spine. There were some five or six of the weird dogs left. The rider turned his horse and drew a long sabre from a scabbard at his waist. He was a small man, with a broad ugly mouth. He grinned in relief.

'A lucky chance, this meeting, good master.'

This was all he had time to remark before two of the dogs were leaping at him and he was forced to give his whole attention to defending himself from their slashing talons and snapping beaks.

The other three dogs concentrated their vicious attention upon Elric. One leapt high, its beak aimed at Elric's throat. He felt foul breath on his face and hastily brought Stormbringer round in an arc which chopped the dog in two. Filthy blood spattered Elric and his horse and the scent of it seemed to increase the fury of the other dogs' attack. But the blood made the dancing black runesword sing an almost ecstatic tune and Elric felt it writhe in his grasp and stab at another of the hideous dogs. The point caught the beast just below its breastbone as it reared up at the albino. It screamed in terrible agony and turned its beak to seize the blade. As the beak connected with the lambent black metal of the sword, a foul stench, akin to the smell of burning, struck Elric's nostrils and the beast's scream broke off sharply.

Engaged with the remaining devil-dog, Elric caught a fleeting glimpse of the charred corpse. His horse was rearing high, lashing at the last alien animal with flailing hooves. The dog avoided the horse's attack and came at Elric's unguarded left side. The albino swung in the saddle and brought his sword hurtling down to slice into the dog's skull and spill brains and blood on the wetly gleaming ground. Still somehow alive, the dog snapped feebly at Elric, but the Melnibonéan ignored its futile attack and turned his attention to the little man who had dispensed with one of his adversaries, but was having difficulty with the second. The dog had grasped the sabre with its beak, gripping the sword near the hilt.

Talons raked towards the little man's throat as he strove to shake the dog's grip. Elric charged forward, his runesword aimed like a lance to where the devil-dog dangled in mid-air, its talons slashing, trying to reach the flesh of its former quarry. Stormbringer caught the beast in its lower abdomen and ripped upwards, slitting the thing's underparts from crutch to throat. It released its hold on the small man's sabre and fell writhing to the ground. Elric's horse trampled it into the rocky ground. Breathing heavily, the albino sheathed Stormbringer and warily regarded the man he had saved. He disliked unnecessary contact with anyone and did not wish to be embarrassed by a display of emotion on the little man's part.

He was not disappointed, for the wide, ugly mouth split into a cheerful grin and the man bowed in the saddle as he returned his own curved blade to its scabbard.

'Thanks, good sir,' he said lightly. 'Without your help, the battle might have lasted longer. You deprived me of good sport, but you meant well. Moonglum is my name.'

'Elric of Melniboné, I,' replied the albino, but saw no reaction on the little man's face. This was strange, for the name of Elric was now infamous throughout most of the world. The story of his treachery and the slaying of his cousin Cymoril had been told and elaborated upon in taverns throughout the Young Kingdoms. Much as he hated it, he was used to receiving some indication of recognition from those he met.

His albinism was enough to mark him.

Intrigued by Moonglum's ignorance, and feeling strangely drawn towards the cocky little rider, Elric studied him in an effort to discover from what land he came. Moonglum wore no armour and his clothes were of faded blue material, travel-stained and worn. A stout leather belt carried the sabre, a dirk and a woollen purse. Upon his feet, Moonglum wore ankle-length boots of cracked leather. His horse-furniture was much used but of obviously good quality. The man himself, seated high in the saddle, was barely more than five feet tall, with legs too long, in proportion, to the rest of his slight body. His nose was short and uptilted, beneath grey-green eyes, large and innocent-seeming. A mop of vivid red hair fell over his forehead and down his neck, unrestrained. He sat his horse comfortably, still grinning but looking now behind Elric to where Shaarilla rode to join them.

Moonglum bowed elaborately as the girl pulled her horse to a halt.

Elric said coldly, 'The Lady Shaarilla – Master Moonglum of – ?'

'Of Elwher,' Moonglum supplied, 'The mercantile capital of the East – the finest city in the world.'

Elric recognized the name. 'So you are from Elwher, Master Moonglum. I have heard of the place. A new city, is it not? Some few centuries old. You have ridden far.'

'Indeed I have, sir. Without knowledge of the language used in these parts, the journey would have been harder, but luckily the slave who inspired me with tales of his homeland taught me the speech thoroughly.'

'But why do you travel these parts – have you not heard the legends?' Shaarilla spoke incredulously.

'Those very legends were what brought me hence – and I'd begun to discount them, until those unpleasant pups set upon me. For what reason they decided to give chase, I will not know, for I gave them no cause to take a dislike to me. This is, indeed, a barbarous land.'

Elric was uncomfortable. Light talk of the kind which Moonglum seemed to enjoy was contrary to his own brooding nature. But in spite of this, he found that he was liking the man more and more.

It was Moonglum who suggested that they travel together for a while. Shaarilla objected, giving Elric a warning glance, but he ignored it.

'Very well then, friend Moonglum, since three are stronger than two, we'd appreciate your company. We ride towards the mountains.' Elric, himself, was feeling in a more cheerful mood.

'And what do you seek there?' Moonglum inquired.

'A secret,' Elric said, and his new-found companion was discreet enough to drop the question.

3

An Unnatural Ocean

So they rode, while the rainfall increased and splashed and sang among the rocks with a sky like dull steel above them and the wind crooning a dirge about their ears. Three small figures riding swiftly towards the black mountain barrier which rose over the world like a brooding God. And perhaps it was a God that laughed sometimes as they neared the foothills of the range, or perhaps it was the wind whistling through the dark mystery of canyons and precipices and the tumble of basalt and granite which climbed towards lonely peaks. Thunder clouds formed around those peaks and lightning smashed downwards like a monster finger searching the earth for grubs. Thunder rattled over the range and Shaarilla spoke her thoughts at last to Elric, spoke them as the mountains came in sight.

'Elric – let us go back, I beg you. Forget the Book – there are too many forces working against us. Take heed of the signs, Elric, or we are doomed!'

But Elric was grimly silent, for he had long been aware that the girl was losing her enthusiasm for the quest she had started.

'Elric – please. We will never reach the Book. Elric, turn back.'

She rode beside him, pulling at his garments until impatiently he shrugged himself clear of her grasp and said:

'I am intrigued too much to stop now. Either continue to lead the way – or tell me what you know and stay here. You desired to sample the Book's wisdom once – but now a few minor pitfalls on our journey have frightened you. What was it you needed to learn, Shaarilla?'

She did not answer him, but said instead: 'And what was it you desired, Elric? Peace, you told me. Well, I warn you, you'll find no peace in those grim mountains – if we reach them at all.'

'You have not been frank with me, Shaarilla,' Elric said coldly, still looking ahead of him at the black peaks. 'You know something of the forces seeking to stop us.'

She shrugged. 'It matters not – I know little. My father spoke a few vague warnings before he died, that is all.'

'What did he say?'

'He said that He who guards the Book would use all his power to stop mankind from using its wisdom.'

'What else?'

'Nothing else. But it is enough, now that I see that my father's warning was truly spoken. It was this guardian who killed him, Elric – or one of the guardian's minions. I do not wish to suffer that fate, in spite of what the Book might do for me. I had thought you powerful enough to aid me – but now I doubt it.'

'I have protected you so far,' Elric said simply. 'Now tell me what you seek from the Book?'

'I am too ashamed.'

Elric did not press the question, but eventually she spoke softly, almost whispering. 'I sought my wings,' she said.

'Your wings – you mean the Book might give you a spell so that you could grow wings!' Elric smiled ironically. 'And that is why you seek the vessel of the world's mightiest wisdom!'

'If you were thought deformed in your own land – it would seem important enough to you,' she shouted defiantly.

Elric turned his face towards her, his crimson-irised eyes burning with a strange emotion. He put a hand to his dead white skin and a crooked smile twisted his lips. 'I, too, have felt as you do,' he said quietly. That was all he said and Shaarilla dropped behind him again, shamed.

They rode on in silence until Moonglum, who had been riding discreetly ahead, cocked his overlarge skull on one side and suddenly drew rein.

Elric joined him. 'What is it, Moonglum?'

'I hear horses coming this way,' the little man said. 'And voices which are disturbingly familiar. More of those devil-dogs, Elric – and this time accompanied by riders!'

Elric, too, heard the sounds, now, and shouted a warning to Shaarilla.

'Perhaps you were right,' he called. 'More trouble comes towards us.'

'What now?' Moonglum said, frowning.

'Ride for the mountains,' Elric replied, 'and we may yet outdistance them.'

They spurred their steeds into a fast gallop and sped towards the hills.

But their flight was hopeless. Soon a black pack was visible on the horizon and the sharp birdlike baying of the devil-dogs drew nearer. Elric stared backward at their pursuers. Night was beginning to fall, and visibility was decreasing with every passing moment but he had a vague impression of the riders who raced behind the pack. They were swathed in dark cloaks and carried long spears. Their faces were invisible, lost in the shadow of the hoods which covered their heads.

Now Elric and his companions were forcing their horses up a steep incline, seeking the shelter of the rocks which lay above.

'We'll halt here,' Elric ordered, 'and try to hold them off. In the open they could easily surround us.'

Moonglum nodded affirmatively, agreeing with the good sense contained in Elric's words. They pulled their sweating steeds to a standstill and prepared to join battle with the howling pack and their dark-cloaked masters.

Soon the first of the devil-dogs were rushing up the incline, their beak-jaws slavering and their talons rattling on stone. Standing between two rocks, blocking the way between with their bodies Elric and Moonglum met the first attack and quickly dispatched three of the animals. Several more took the place of the dead and the first of the riders was visible behind them as night crept closer.

'Arioch!' swore Elric, suddenly recognizing the riders. 'These are the Lords of Dharzi – dead these ten centuries. We're fighting dead men, Moonglum, and the too-tangible ghosts of their dogs. Unless I can think of a sorcerous means to defeat them, we're doomed!'

The zombie-men appeared to have no intention of taking part in the attack for the moment. They waited, their dead eyes eerily luminous, as the devil-dogs attempted to break through the swinging network of steel with which Elric and his companion defended themselves. Elric was racking his brains – trying to dredge a spoken spell from his memory which would dismiss these living dead. Then it came to him, and hoping that the forces he had to invoke would decide to aid him, he began to chant:

> 'Let the Laws which govern all things
> Not so lightly be dismissed;
> Let the Ones who flaunt the Earth Kings
> With a fresher death be kissed.'

Nothing happened. 'I've failed.' Elric muttered hopelessly as he met the attack of a snapping devil-dog and spitted the thing on his sword.

But then – the ground rocked and seemed to *seethe* beneath the feet of the horses upon whose backs the dead men sat. The tremor lasted a few seconds and then subsided.

'The spell was not powerful enough,' Elric sighed.

The earth trembled again and small craters formed in the ground of the hillside upon which the dead Lords of Dharzi impassively waited. Stones crumbled and the horses stamped nervously. Then the earth rumbled.

'Back!' yelled Elric warningly. 'Back – or we'll go with them!' They retreated – backing towards Shaarilla and their waiting horses as the ground sagged beneath their feet. The Dharzi mounts were rearing and snorting and the remaining dogs turned nervously to regard their masters with puzzled, uncertain eyes. A low moan was coming from the lips of the living dead. Suddenly, a whole area of the surrounding hillside split into cracks, and yawning crannies appeared in the surface. Elric and his companions swung themselves on to their horses as, with a frightful multi-voiced scream, the dead Lords were swallowed by the earth, returning to the depths from which they had been summoned.

A deep unholy chuckle arose from the shattered pit. It was the mocking laughter of the Earth Kings taking their rightful prey back into their keeping. Whining, the devil-dogs slunk towards the edge of the pit, sniffing around it. Then, with one accord, the black pack hurled itself down into the chasm, following its masters to whatever cold doom awaited them.

Moonglum shuddered. 'You are on familiar terms with the strangest people, friend Elric,' he said shakily and turned his horse towards the mountains again.

They reached the black mountains on the following day and nervously Shaarilla led them along the rocky route she had memorised. She no longer pleaded with Elric to return – she was resigned to whatever fate awaited them. Elric's obsession was burning within him and he was filled with impatience – certain that he would find, at last, the ultimate truth of existence in the Dead Gods' Book. Moonglum was cheerfully sceptical, while Shaarilla was consumed with foreboding.

Rain still fell and the storm growled and crackled above them. And, as the driving rainfall increased with fresh insistence, they came, at last, to the black, gaping mouth of a huge cave.

'I can lead you no further,' Shaarilla said wearily. 'The Book lies somewhere beyond the entrance to this cave.'

Elric and Moonglum looked uncertainly at one another, neither of them sure what move to make next. To have reached their goal seemed somehow anticlimactic – for nothing blocked the cave entrance – and nothing appeared to guard it.

'It is inconceivable,' said Elric, 'that the dangers which beset us were not engineered by something, yet here we are – and no one seeks to stop us entering. Are you sure that this is the *right* cave, Shaarilla?'

The girl pointed upwards to the rock above the entrance. Engraved in it was a curious symbol which Elric instantly recognized.

'The sign of Chaos!' Elric exclaimed. 'Perhaps I should have guessed.'

'What does it mean, Elric?' Moonglum asked.

'That is the symbol of everlasting disruption and anarchy,' Elric told him. 'We are standing in territory presided over by the Lords of Entropy or one of their minions. So that is who our enemy is! This can only mean one thing – the Book is of extreme importance to the order of things on this plane – possibly all the myriad planes of the universe. It was why Arioch was reluctant to aid me – he, too, is a Lord of Chaos!'

Moonglum stared at him in puzzlement. 'What do you mean, Elric?'

'Know you not that two forces govern the world – fighting an eternal battle?' Elric replied. 'Law and Chaos. The upholders of Chaos state that in such a world as they rule, all things are possible. Opponents of Chaos – those who ally themselves with the forces of Law – say that without Law *nothing* material is possible.

'Some stand apart, believing that a balance between the two is the proper state of things, but we cannot. We have become embroiled in a dispute between the two forces. The Book is valuable to either faction, obviously, and I could guess that the minions of Entropy are worried what power we might release if we obtain this Book. Law and Chaos rarely interfere directly in Men's lives – that is why we have not been fully aware of their presence. Now perhaps, I will discover at last the answer to the one question which concerns me – does an ultimate force rule over the opposing factions of Law and Chaos?'

Elric stepped through the cave entrance, peering into the gloom while the others hesitantly followed him.

'The cave stretches back a long way. All we can do is press on until we find its far wall,' Elric said.

'Let's hope that its far wall lies not *downwards*,' Moonglum said ironically as he motioned Elric to lead on.

They stumbled forward as the cave grew darker and darker. Their voices were magnified and hollow to their own ears as the floor of the cave slanted sharply down.

'This is no cave,' Elric whispered, 'it's a *tunnel* – but I cannot guess where it leads.'

For several hours they pressed onwards in pitch darkness, clinging to one another as they reeled forward, uncertain of their footing and still aware that they were moving down a gradual incline. They lost all sense of time and Elric began to feel as if he were living through a dream. Events seemed to have become so unpredictable and beyond his control that he could no longer cope with thinking about them in ordinary terms. The tunnel was long and dark and wide and cold. It offered no comfort and the floor eventually became the only thing which had any reality. It was firmly beneath his feet. He began to feel that possibly he was not moving – that the floor, after all, was moving and he was remaining stationary. His companions clung to him but he was not aware of them. He was lost and his brain was numb. Sometimes he swayed and felt that he was on the edge of a precipice. Sometimes he fell and his groaning body met hard stone, disproving the proximity of the gulf down which he half-expected to fall.

All the while he made his legs perform walking motions, even though he was not at all sure whether he was actually moving forward. And time meant nothing – became a meaningless concept with relation to nothing.

Until, at last, he was aware of a faint, blue glow ahead of him and he knew that he had been moving forward. He began to run down the incline, but found that he was going too fast and had to check his speed. There was a scent of alien strangeness in the cool air of the cave tunnel and fear was a fluid force which surged over him, something separate from himself.

The others obviously felt it, too, for though they said nothing, Elric could sense it. Slowly they moved downward, drawn like automatons towards the pale blue glow below them.

And then they were out of the tunnel, staring awestruck at the unearthly vision which confronted them. Above them, the very air seemed of the strange blue colour which had originally attracted them. They were standing on a jutting slab of rock and, although it was still somehow *dark*, the eerie blue glow illuminated a stretch of glinting silver beach beneath them. And the beach was lapped by a surging dark sea which moved restlessly like a liquid giant in disturbed slumber. Scattered along the silver beach were the dim shapes of wrecks – the bones of peculiarly designed boats, each of a different pattern from the rest. The sea surged away into darkness and there was no horizon – only blackness. Behind them, they could see a sheer cliff which was also lost in darkness beyond a certain point. And it was cold – bitterly cold, with an unbelievable sharpness. For though the sea threshed beneath them, there was no dampness in the air – no smell of salt. It was a bleak and awesome sight and, apart from the sea, they were the only things that moved – the only things to make sound, for the sea was horribly silent in its restless movement.

'What now, Elric?' whispered Moonglum, shivering.

Elric shook his head and they continued to stand there for a long time until the albino – his white face and hands ghastly in the alien light said: 'Since it is impracticable to return – we shall venture over the sea.'

His voice was hollow and he spoke as one who was unaware of his words.

Steps, cut into the living rock, led down towards the beach and now Elric began to descend them. Staring around them, their eyes lit by a terrible fascination. The others allowed him to lead them.

4

Of Partings and Profits

Their feet profaned the silence as they reached the silver beach of
crystalline stones and crunched across it. Elric's crimson eyes fixed
upon one of the objects littering the beach and he smiled. He shook his
head savagely from side to side, as if to clear it. Trembling, he pointed
to one of the boats, and the pair saw that it was intact, unlike the
others. It was yellow and red – vulgarly gay in this environment and
nearing it they observed that it was made of wood, yet unlike any
wood they had seen. Moonglum ran his stubby fingers along its length.

'Hard as iron,' he breathed. 'No wonder it has not rotted as the
others have.' He peered inside and shuddered. 'Well the owner won't
argue if we take it,' he said wryly.

Elric and Shaarilla understood him when they saw the unnaturally
twisted skeleton which lay at the bottom of the boat. Elric reached
inside and pulled the thing out, hurling it on the stones. It rattled and
rolled over the gleaming shingle, disintegrating as it did so, scattering
bones over a wide area. The skull came to rest by the edge of the
beach, seeming to stare sightlessly out over the disturbing ocean.

As Elric and Moonglum strove to push and pull the boat down the
beach towards the sea, Shaarilla moved ahead of them and squatted
down, putting her hand into the wetness. She stood up sharply,
shaking the stuff from her hand.

'This is not water as I know it,' she said. They heard her, but said
nothing.

'We'll need a sail,' Elric murmured. The cold breeze was moving out
over the ocean. 'A cloak should serve.' He stripped off his cloak and
knotted it to the mast of the vessel. 'Two of us will have to hold this at
either edge,' he said. 'That way we'll have some slight control over the
direction the boat takes. It's makeshift – but the best we can manage.'

They shoved off, taking care not to get their feet in the sea.

The wind caught the sail and pushed the boat out over the ocean,
moving at a faster pace than Elric had at first reckoned. The boat

began to hurtle forward as if possessed of its own volition and Elric's and Moonglum's muscles ached as they clung to the bottom ends of the sail.

Soon the silver beach was out of sight and they could see little – the pale blue light above them scarcely penetrating the blackness. It was then that they heard the dry flap of wings over their heads and looked up.

Silently descending were three massive ape-like creatures, borne on great leathery wings. Shaarilla recognized them and gasped.

'Clakars!'

Moonglum shrugged as he hurriedly drew his sword – 'A name only – what are they?' But he received no answer for the leading winged ape descended with a rush, mouthing and gibbering, showing long fangs in a slavering snout. Moonglum dropped his portion of the sail and slashed at the beast but it veered away, its huge wings beating, and sailed upwards again.

Elric unsheathed Stormbringer – and was astounded. The blade remained silent, its familiar howl of glee muted. The blade shuddered in his hand and instead of the rush of power which usually flowed up his arm, he felt only a slight tingling. He was panic-stricken for a moment – without the sword, he would soon lose all vitality. Grimly fighting down his fear, he used the sword to protect himself from the rushing attack of one of the winged apes.

The ape gripped the blade, bowling Elric over, but it yelled in pain as the blade cut through one knotted hand, severing fingers which lay twitching and bloody on the narrow deck. Elric gripped the side of the boat and hauled himself upright once more. Shrilling its agony, the winged ape attacked again, but this time with more caution. Elric summoned all his strength and swung the heavy sword in a two-handed grip, ripping off one of the leathery wings so that the mutilated beast flopped about the deck. Judging the place where its heart should be, Elric drove the blade in under the breast-bone. The ape's movements subsided.

Moonglum was lashing wildly at two of the winged apes which were attacking him from both sides. He was down on one knee, vainly hacking at random. He had opened up the whole side of a beast's head but, though in pain, it still came at him. Elric hurled Stormbringer through the darkness and it struck the wounded beast in the throat, point first. The ape clutched with clawing fingers at the steel and fell overboard. Its corpse floated on the liquid but slowly began to sink. Elric grabbed with frantic fingers at the hilt of his sword, reaching far over the side of the boat. Incredibly, the blade was sinking with the beast; knowing Stormbringer's properties as he did, Elric was amazed. Now it was being dragged beneath the surface as any ordinary blade would be dragged. He gripped the hilt and hauled the sword out of the winged ape's carcass.

His strength was seeping swiftly from him. It was incredible. What alien laws governed this cavern world? He could not guess – and all he was concerned with was regaining his waning strength. Without the runesword's power, this was impossible!

Moonglum's curved blade had disembowelled the remaining beast and the little man was busily tossing the dead thing over the side. He turned, grinning triumphantly, to Elric.

'A good fight,' he said.

Elric shook his head. 'We must cross this sea speedily,' he replied, 'else we're lost – finished. My power is gone.'

'How? Why?'

'I know not – unless the forces of Entropy rule more strongly here. Make haste – there is no time for speculation.'

Moonglum's eyes were disturbed. He could do nothing but act as Elric said.

Elric was trembling in his weakness, holding the billowing sail with draining strength. Shaarilla moved to help him, her thin hands close to his, her deep-set eyes bright with sympathy.

'What *were* those things?' Moonglum gasped, his teeth naked and white beneath his back-drawn lips, his breath coming short.

'Clakars,' Shaarilla replied. 'They are the primeval ancestors of my people, older in origin than recorded time. My people are thought the oldest inhabitants of this planet.'

'Whoever seeks to stop us in this quest of yours had best find some – original means.' Moonglum grinned. 'The old methods don't work.' But the other two did not smile, for Elric was half-fainting and the woman was concerned only with his plight. Moonglum shrugged, staring ahead.

When he spoke again, sometime later, his voice was excited. 'We're nearing land!'

Land it was, and they were travelling fast towards it. Too fast. Elric heaved himself upright and spoke heavily and with difficulty. 'Drop the sail!' Moonglum obeyed him. The boat sped on, struck another stretch of silver beach and ground up it, the prow ploughing a dark scar through the glinting shingle. It stopped suddenly, tilting violently to one side so that the three were tumbled against the boat's rail.

Shaarilla and Moonglum pulled themselves upright and dragged the limp and nerveless albino on to the beach. Carrying him between them, they struggled up the beach until the crystalline shingle gave way to thick, fluffy moss, padding their footfalls. They laid the albino down and stared at him worriedly, uncertain of their next actions.

Elric strained to rise, but was unable to do so. 'Give me time,' he gasped. 'I won't die – but already my eyesight is fading. I can only hope that the blade's power will return on dry land.'

With a mighty effort, he pulled Stormbringer from its scabbard and he smiled in relief as the evil runesword moaned faintly and then, slowly, its song increased in power as black flame flickered along its length. Already the power was flowing into Elric's body, giving him renewed vitality. But even as strength returned, Elric's crimson eyes flared with terrible misery.

'Without this black blade,' he groaned, 'I am nothing, as you see. But what is it making of me? Am I to be bound to it for ever?'

The others did not answer him and they were both moved by an emotion they could not define – an emotion blended of fear, hate and pity – linked with something else . . .

Eventually, Elric rose, trembling, and silently led them up the mossy hillside towards a more natural light which filtered from above. They could see that it came from a wide chimney, leading apparently to the upper air. By means of the light, they could soon make out a dark, irregular shape which towered in the shadow of the gap.

As they neared the shape, they saw that it was a castle of black stone – a sprawling pile covered with dark green crawling lichen which curled over its ancient bulk with an almost sentient protectiveness. Towers appeared to spring at random from it and it covered a vast area. There seemed to be no windows in any part of it and the only orifice was a rearing doorway blocked by thick bars of a metal which glowed with dull redness, but without heat. Above this gate, in flaring amber, was the sign of the Lords of Entropy, representing eight arrows radiating from a central hub in all directions. It appeared to hang in the air without touching the black, lichen-covered stone.

'I think our quest ends here,' Elric said grimly. 'Here, or nowhere.'

'Before I go further, Elric, I'd like to know what it is you seek,' Moonglum murmured. 'I think I've earned the right.'

'A book,' Elric said carelessly. 'The Dead Gods' Book. It lies within those castle walls – of that I'm certain. We have reached the end of our journey.'

Moonglum shrugged. 'I might not have asked,' he smiled, 'for all your words mean to me. I hope that I will be allowed some small share of whatever treasure it represents.'

Elric grinned, in spite of the coldness which gripped his bowels, but he did not answer Moonglum.

'We need to enter the castle, first,' he said instead.

As if the gates had heard him, the metal bars flared to a pale green and then their glow faded back to red and finally dulled into non-existence. The entrance was unbarred and their way apparently clear.

'I like not *that*,' growled Moonglum. 'Too easy. A trap awaits us – are we to spring it at the pleasure of whoever dwells within the castle confines?'

'What else can we do?' Elric spoke quietly.

'Go back – or forward. Avoid the castle – do not tempt He who guards the Book!' Shaarilla was gripping the albino's right arm, her whole face moving with fear, her eyes pleading. 'Forget the Book, Elric!'

'*Now*?' Elric laughed humourlessly. 'Now – after this journey? No, Shaarilla, not when the truth is so close. Better to die than never to have tried to secure the wisdom in the Book when it lies so near.'

Shaarilla's clutching fingers relaxed their grip and her shoulders slumped in hopelessness. 'We cannot do battle with the minions of Entropy . . . '

'Perhaps we will not have to.' Elric did not believe his own words but his mouth was twisted with some dark emotion, intense and terrible. Moonglum glanced at Shaarilla.

'Shaarilla is right,' he said with conviction. 'You'll find nothing but bitterness, possibly death, inside those castle walls. Let us, instead, climb yonder steps and attempt to reach the surface.' He pointed to some twisting steps which led towards the yawning rent in the cavern roof.

Elric shook his head. 'No. You go if you like.'

Moonglum grimaced in perplexity. 'You're a stubborn one, friend Elric. Well, if it's all or nothing – then I'm with you. But personally, I have always preferred compromise.'

Elric began to walk slowly forward towards the dark entrance of the bleak and towering castle.

In a wide, shadowy courtyard a tall figure, wreathed in scarlet fire, stood awaiting them.

Elric marched on, passing the gateway. Moonglum and Shaarilla nervously followed.

Gusty laughter roared from the mouth of the giant and the scarlet fire fluttered about him. He was naked and unarmed, but the power which flowed from him almost forced the three back. His skin was scaly and of smoky purple colouring. His massive body was alive with rippling muscle as he rested lightly on the balls of his feet. His skull was long, slanting sharply backwards at the forehead and his eyes were like slivers of blue steel, showing no pupil. His whole body shook with mighty, malicious joy.

'*Greetings to you, Lord Elric of Melniboné – I congratulate you for your remarkable tenacity!*'

'Who are you?' Elric growled, his hand on his sword.

'*My name is Orunlu the Keeper and this is a stronghold of the Lords of Entropy.*' The giant smiled cynically. '*You need not finger your puny blade so nervously, for you should know that I cannot harm you now. I gained power to remain in your realm only by making a vow.*'

Elric's voice betrayed his mounting excitement. 'You cannot stop us?'

'*I do not dare to – since my oblique efforts have failed. But your foolish endeavours perplex me somewhat, I'll admit. The Book is of importance to us – but what can it mean to you? I have guarded it for three hundred centuries and have never been curious enough to seek to discover why my Masters place so much importance upon it – why they bothered to rescue it on its sunward course and incarcerate it on this boring ball of earth populated by the capering, briefly-lived clowns called Men.*'

'I seek in it the Truth,' Elric said guardedly.

'*There is no Truth but that of Eternal struggle,*' the scarlet-flamed giant said with conviction.

'What rules above the forces of Law and Chaos?' Elric asked. 'What controls your destinies as it controls mine?'

The giant frowned.

'*That question, I cannot answer. I do not know. There is only the Balance.*'

'Then perhaps the Book will tell us who holds it.' Elric said purposely. 'Let me pass – tell me where it lies.'

The giant moved back, smiling ironically. '*It lies in a small chamber in the central tower. I have sworn never to venture there, otherwise I might even lead the way. Go if you like – my duty is over.*'

Elric, Moonglum and Shaarilla stepped towards the entrance of the castle, but before they entered, the giant spoke warningly from behind them.

'*I have been told that the knowledge contained in the Book could swing the balance on the side of the forces of Law. This disturbs me – but, it appears, there is another possibility which disturbs me even more.*'

'What is that?' Elric said.

'*It could create such a tremendous impact on the multiverse that*' *complete entropy would result. My Masters do not desire that — for it could mean the destruction of all matter in the end. We exist only to fight — not to win, but to preserve the eternal struggle.'*

'I care not,' Elric told him. 'I have little to lose, Orunlu the Keeper.'

'Then go.' The giant strode across the courtyard into blackness.

Inside the tower, light of a pale quality illuminated winding steps leading upwards. Elric began to climb them in silence, moved by his own doom-filled purpose. Hesitantly, Moonglum and Shaarilla followed in his path, their faces set in hopeless acceptance.

On and upward the steps mounted, twisting tortuously towards their goal, until at last they came to the chamber, full of blinding light, many-coloured and scintillating, which did not penetrate outwards at all but remained confined to the room which housed it.

Blinking, shielding his red eyes with his arm, Elric pressed forward and, through slitted pupils saw the source of the light lying on a small stone dais in the centre of the room.

Equally troubled by the bright light, Shaarilla and Moonglum followed him into the room and stood in awe at what they saw.

It was a huge book — the Dead Gods' Book, its covers encrusted with alien gems from which the light sprang. It gleamed, it *throbbed* with light and brilliant colour.

'At last,' Elric breathed. 'At last — the Truth!'

He stumbled forward like a man made stupid with drink, his pale hands reaching for the thing he had sought with such savage bitterness. His hands touched the pulsating cover of the Book and, trembling, turned it back.

'Now, I shall learn,' he said, half-gloatingly.

With a crash, the cover fell to the floor, sending the bright gems skipping and dancing over the paving stones.

Beneath Elric's twitching hands lay nothing but a pile of yellowish dust.

'No!' His scream was anguished, unbelieving. 'No!' Tears flowed down his contorted face as he ran his hands through the fine dust. With a groan which racked his whole being, he fell forward, his face hitting the disintegrated parchment. Time had destroyed the Book — untouched, possibly forgotten, for three hundred centuries. Even the wise and powerful Gods who had created it had perished — and now its knowledge followed them into oblivion.

They stood on the slopes of the high mountain, staring down into the green valleys below them. The sun shone and the sky was clear and blue. Behind them lay the gaping hole which led into the stronghold of the Lords of Entropy.

Elric looked with sad eyes across the world and his head was lowered beneath a weight of weariness and dark despair. He had not spoken since his companions had dragged him sobbing from the chamber of the Book. Now he raised his pale face and spoke in a voice tinged with self-mockery, sharp with bitterness – a lonely voice: the calling of hungry seabirds circling cold skies above bleak shores.

'Now,' he said, 'I will live my life without ever knowing why I live it – whether it has purpose or not. Perhaps the Book could have told me. But would I have believed it, even then? I am the eternal sceptic – never *sure* that my actions are my own, never certain that an ultimate entity is not guiding me.

'I envy those who know. All I can do now is to continue my quest and hope, without hope, that before my span is ended, the truth will be presented to me.'

Shaarilla took his limp hands in hers and her eyes were wet.

'Elric – let me comfort you.'

The albino sneered bitterly. 'Would that we'd never met, Shaarilla of the Dancing Mist. For a while, you gave me hope – I had thought to be at last at peace with myself. But, because of you, I am left more hopeless than before. There is no salvation in this world – only malevolent doom. Goodbye.'

He took his hands away from her grasp and set off down the mountainside.

Moonglum darted a glance at Shaarilla and then at Elric. He took something from his purse and put it in the girl's hand.

'Good luck,' he said, and then he was running after Elric until he caught him up.

Still striding, Elric turned at Moonglum's approach and despite his brooding misery said: 'What is it, friend Moonglum? Why do you follow me?'

'I've followed you thus far, Master Elric, and I see no reason to stop,' grinned the little man. 'Besides, unlike yourself, I'm a materialist. We'll need to eat, you know.'

Elric frowned, feeling a warmth growing within him. 'What do you mean, Moonglum?'

Moonglum chuckled. 'I take advantage of situations of any kind, where I may,' he answered. He reached into his purse and displayed something on his outstretched hand which shone with a dazzling brilliancy. It was one of the jewels from the cover of the Book. 'There are more in my purse,' he said, 'And each one worth a fortune.' He took Elric's arm.

'Come Elric – what new lands shall we visit so that we may change these baubles into wine and pleasant company?'

Behind them, standing stock still on the hillside, Shaarilla stared miserably after them until they were no longer visible. The jewel Moonglum had given her dropped from her fingers and fell, bouncing and bright, until it was lost amongst the heather. Then she turned – and the dark mouth of the cavern yawned before her.

THE SINGING CITADEL

For E.J.

1

A Ship, Black-sailed
and Gilded

The turquoise sea was peaceful in the golden light of early evening, and the two men at the rail of the ship stood in silence, looking north to the misty horizon. One was tall and slim, wrapped in a heavy black cloak, its cowl flung back to reveal his long, milk-white hair; the other was short and red-headed.

'She was a fine woman and she loved you,' said the short man at length. 'Why did you leave her so abruptly?'

'She was a fine woman,' the tall one replied, 'but she would have loved me to her cost. Let her seek her own land and stay there. I have already slain one woman whom I loved, Moonglum. I would not slay another.'

Moonglum shrugged. 'I sometimes wonder, Elric, if this grim destiny of yours is the figment of your own guilt-ridden mood.'

'Perhaps,' Elric replied carelessly. 'But I do not care to test the theory. Let's speak no more of this.'

The sea foamed and rushed by as the oars disrupted the surface, driving the ship swiftly towards the port of Dhakos, capital of Jharkor, one of the most powerful of the Young Kingdoms. Less than two years previously Jharkor's king, Dharmit, had died in the ill-fated raid on Imrryr, and Elric had heard that the men of Jharkor blamed him for the young king's death, though this was not the case. He cared little whether they blamed him or not, for he was still disdainful of the greater part of mankind.

'Another hour will see nightfall, and it's unlikely we'll sail at night,' Moonglum said. 'I'll to bed, I think.'

Elric was about to reply when he was interrupted by a high-pitched shout from the crowsnest.

'Sail on larboard stern!'

The lookout must have been half asleep, for the ship bearing down on them could easily be made out from the deck. Elric stepped aside as the captain, a dark-faced Tarkeshite, came running along the deck.

'What's the ship, captain?' called Moonglum.

'A Pan Tang trireme – a warship. They're on ramming course.' The captain ran on, yelling orders to the helm to turn the ship aside.

Elric and Moonglum crossed the deck to see the trireme better. She was a black-sailed ship, painted black and heavily gilded, with three rowers to an oar as against their two. She was big and yet elegant, with a high curving stern and a low prow. Now they could see the waters broken by her big, brass-sheathed ram. She had two lateen-rigged sails, and the wind was in her favour.

The rowers were in a panic as they sweated to turn the ship according to the helmsman's orders. Oars rose and fell in confusion and Moonglum turned to Elric with a half-smile.

'They'll never do it. Best ready your blade, friend.'

Pan Tang was an isle of sorcerers, fully human, who sought to emulate the old power of Melniboné. Their fleets were among the best in the Young Kingdoms and raided with little discrimination. The Theocrat of Pan Tang, chief of the priest-aristocracy, was Jagreen Lern, who was reputed to have a pact with the powers of Chaos and a plan to rule the world.

Elric regarded the men of Pan Tang as upstarts who could never hope to mirror the glory of his ancestors, but even he had to admit that this ship was impressive and would easily win a fight with the Tarkeshite galley.

Soon the great trireme was bearing down on them and captain and helmsman fell silent as they realized they could not evade the ram. With a harsh sound of crushed timbers, the ram connected with the stern, holing the galley beneath the waterline.

Elric stood immobile, watching as the trireme's grappling irons hurtled towards their galley's deck. Somewhat half-heartedly, knowing they were no match for the well-trained and well-armoured Pan Tang crew, the Tarkeshites ran towards the stern, preparing to resist the boarders.

Moonglum cried urgently: 'Elric – we must help!'

Reluctantly Elric nodded. He was loathe to draw the runesword from its scabbard at his side. Of late its power seemed to have increased.

Now the scarlet-armoured warriors were swinging towards the waiting Tarkeshites. The first wave, armed with broadswords and battle-axes, hit the sailors, driving them back.

Now Elric's hand fell to the hilt of Stormbringer. As he gripped it and drew it, the blade gave an odd, disturbing moan, as if of anticipation, and a weird black radiance flickered along its length. Now it throbbed in Elric's hand like something alive as the albino ran forward to aid the Tarkeshite sailors.

Already half the defenders had been hewed down and as the rest retreated, Elric, with Moonglum at his heels, moved forward. The scarlet-armoured warriors' expressions changed from grim triumph to startlement as Elric's great black-blade shrieked up and down and clove through a man's armour from shoulder to lower ribs.

Evidently they recognized him and the sword, for both were legendary. Though Moonglum was a skilled swordsman, they all but ignored him as they realized that they must concentrate all their strength on bringing Elric down if they were to survive.

The old, wild killing-lust of his ancestors now dominated Elric as the blade reaped souls. He and the sword became one and it was the sword, not Elric, that was in control. Men fell on all sides, screaming more in horror than in pain as they realized what the sword had drawn from them. Four came at him with axes whistling. He sliced off one's head, cut a deep gash in another's midriff, lopped off an arm, and drove the blade point first into the heart of the last. Now the Tarkeshites were cheering, following after Elric and Moonglum as they cleared the sinking galley's decks of attackers.

Howling like a wolf, Elric grapped a rope – part of the black and golden trireme's rigging – and swung towards the enemy's decks.

'Follow him!' Moonglum yelled. 'This is our only chance – this ship's doomed!'

The trireme had raised decks fore and aft. On the foredeck stood the captain, splendid in scarlet and blue, his face aghast at this turn of events. He had expected to get his prize effortlessly; now it seemed *he* was to be the prize!

Stormbringer sang a wailing song as Elric pressed towards the fore-deck, a song that was at once triumphant and ecstatic. The remaining warriors no longer rushed at him, and concentrated on Moonglum, who was leading the Tarkeshite crew, leaving Elric's path to the captain clear.

The captain, a member of the theocracy, would be harder to vanquish than his men. As Elric moved towards him, he noted that the man's armour had a peculiar glow to it – it had been sorcerously treated.

The captain was typical of his kind – stocky, heavily-bearded, with malicious black eyes over a strong, hooked nose. His lips were thick and red and he was smiling a little as, with axe in one hand and sword in the other, he prepared to meet Elric, who was running up the steps.

Elric gripped Stormbringer in both hands and lunged for the

captain's stomach, but the man stepped sideways and parried with his sword, swinging the axe left-handed at Elric's unprotected head. The albino had to sway to one side, staggered, and fell to the deck, rolling as the broadsword thudded into the deck, just missing his shoulder. Stormbringer seemed to rise of its own accord to block a further axe blow and then chopped upwards to shear off the head near the handle. The captain cursed and discarded the handle, gripped his broadsword in both hands and raised it. Again Stormbringer acted a fraction sooner than Elric's own reactions. He drove the blade up towards the man's heart. The magic-treated armour stopped it for a second; but then Stormbringer shrilled a chilling, wailing song, shuddered as if summoning more strength, slipped on the armour again. And then the magic armour split like a nutshell, leaving Elric's opponent bare-chested, his arms still raised for the strike. His eyes widened. He backed away, his sword forgotten, his gaze fixed on the evil runeblade as it struck him under the breastbone and drove in. He grimaced, whimpered, and dropped his sword, clutching instead at the blade, which was sucking out his soul.

'By Chardros – not – not – aahhh!'

He died knowing that even his soul was not safe from the hell-blade borne by the wolf-faced albino.

Elric wrenched Stormbringer from the corpse, feeling his own vitality increase as the sword passed on its stolen energy, refusing to consider the knowledge that the more he used the sword, the more he needed it.

On the deck of the trireme, only the galley-slaves were left alive. But the deck was tilting badly, for the trireme's ram and grapples still tied it to the sinking Tarkeshite ship.

'Cut the grappling ropes and back water – quickly!' Elric yelled. Sailors, realizing what was happening, leapt forward to do as he ordered. The slaves backed water, and the ram came out with a groan of split wood. The grapples were cut and the doomed galley set adrift.

Elric counted the survivors. Less than half the crew were alive, and their captain had died in the first onslaught. He addressed the slaves.

'If you'd have your freedom, row well towards Dhakos,' he called. The sun was setting, but now that he was in command he decided to sail through the night by the stars.

Moonglum shouted incredulously: 'Why offer them their freedom? We could sell them in Dhakos and thus be paid for today's exertion!'

Elric shrugged. 'I offer them freedom because I choose to, Moonglum.'

The redhead sighed and turned to supervise the throwing of the dead and wounded overboard. He would never understand the albino, he decided. It was probably for the best.

And that was how Elric came to enter Dhakos in some style, when he had originally intended to slip into the city without being recognised.

Leaving Moonglum to negotiate the sale of the trireme and divide the money between the crew and himself, Elric drew his hood over his head and pushed through the crowd which had collected, making for an inn he knew of by the west gate of the city.

2

A Message For The White Wolf

Later that night, when Moonglum had gone to bed, Elric sat in the tavern room drinking. Even the most enthusiastic of the night's roisterers had left when they had noticed with whom they shared the room; and now Elric sat alone, the only light coming from a guttering reed torch over the outside door.

Now the door opened and a richly-dressed youth stood there, staring in.

'I seek the White Wolf,' he said, his head at a questioning angle. He could not see Elric clearly.

'I'm sometimes called that name in these parts,' Elric said calmly. 'Do you seek Elric of Melniboné?'

'Aye. I have a message.' The youth came in, keeping his cloak wrapped about him, for the room was cold though Elric did not notice it.

'I am Count Yolan, deputy-commander of the city guard,' the youth said arrogantly, coming up to the table at which Elric sat and studying the albino rudely. 'You are brave to come here so openly. Do you think the folk of Jharkor have such short memories they can forget that you led their king into a trap scarce two years since?'

Elric sipped his wine, then said from behind the rim of his cup: 'This is rhetoric, Count Yolan. What is your message?'

Yolan's assured manner left him; he made a rather weak gesture. 'Rhetoric to you, perhaps – but I for one feel strongly on the matter. Would not King Dharmit be here today if you had not fled from the battle that broke the power of the Sea Lords and your own folk? Did you not use your sorcery to aid you in your flight, instead of using it to aid the men who thought they were your comrades?'

Elric sighed. 'I know your purpose here was not to bait me in this manner. Dharmit died on board his flagship during the first attack on Imrryr's sea-maze, not in the subsequent battle.'

'You sneer at my questions and then proffer lame lies to cover your

522

own cowardly deed,' Yolan said bitterly. 'If I had my way you'd be fed to your hell-blade there – I've heard what happened earlier.'

Elric rose slowly. 'Your taunts tire me. When you feel ready to deliver your message, give it to the inn-keeper.'

He walked around the table, moving towards the stairs, but stopped as Yolan turned and plucked at his sleeve.

Elric's corpse-white face stared down at the young noble. His crimson eyes flickered with a dangerous emotion. 'I'm not used to such familiarity, young man.'

Yolan's hand fell away. 'Forgive me. I was self-indulgent and should not have let my emotions override diplomacy. I came on a matter of discretion – a message from Queen Yishana. She seeks your help.'

'I'm as disinclined to help others as I am to explain my actions,' Elric spoke impatiently. 'In the past my help has not always been to the advantage of those who've sought it. Dharmit, your queen's half-brother, discovered that.'

Yolan said sullenly: 'You echo my own warnings to the queen, sir. For all that, she desires to see you in private – tonight . . . ' he scowled and looked away. 'I would point out that I could have you arrested should you refuse.'

'Perhaps.' Elric moved again towards the steps. 'Tell Yishana that I stay the night here and move on at dawn. She may visit me if her request is so urgent.' He climbed the stairs, leaving a gape-mouthed Yolan sitting alone in the quiet of the tavern.

Theleb K'aarna scowled. For all his skill in the black arts, he was a fool in love; and Yishana sprawled on her fur-rich bed, knew it. It pleased her to have power over a man who could destroy her with a simple incantation if it were not for his love-weakness. Though Theleb K'aarna stood high in the hierarchy of Pan Tang, it was clear to her that she was in no danger from the sorcerer. Indeed, her intuition informed her that this man who loved to dominate others also needed to be dominated. She filled this need for him – with relish.

Theleb K'aarna continued to scowl at her. 'How can that decadent spell-singer help you where I cannot?' he muttered, sitting down on the bed and stroking her bejewelled foot.

Yishana was not a young woman, neither was she pretty. Yet there was an hypnotic quality about her tall, full body, her lush black hair, and her wholly sensuous face. Few of the men she had singled out for her pleasure had been able to resist her.

Neither was she sweet-natured, just, wise, nor self-sacrificing. The historians would append no noble soubriquet to her name. Still, there was something so self-sufficient about her, something denying the usual standards by which a person was judged, that all who knew her admired her, and she was well-loved by those she ruled – loved rather as a wilful child is loved, yet loved with firm loyalty.

Now she laughed quietly, mockingly at her sorcerer lover.

'You're probably right, Theleb K'aarna, but Elric is a legend – the most spoken-of, least-known man in the world. This is my opportunity to discover what others have only speculated on – his true character.'

Theleb K'aarna made a pettish gesture. He stroked his long black beard and got up, walking to a table bearing fruit and wine. He poured wine for them both. 'If you seek to make me jealous again, you are succeeding, of course. I hold little hope for your ambition. Elric's ancestors were half-demons – his race is not human and cannot be judged by our yardsticks. To us, sorcery is learned after years of study and sacrifice – to Elric's kind, sorcery is intuitive – natural. You may not live to learn his secrets. Cymoril, his beloved cousin, died on his blade – and she was his betrothed!'

'Your concern is touching.' She lazily accepted the goblet he handed to her. 'But I'll continue with my plan, none the less. After all, you can hardly claim to have had much success in discovering the nature of this citadel!'

'There are subtleties I have not properly plumbed as yet!'

'Then perhaps Elric's intuition will provide answers where you fail,' she smiled. Then she got up and looked through the window where the full moon hung in a clear sky over the spires of Dhakos. 'Yolan is late. If all went properly, he should have brought Elric here by now.'

'Yolan was a mistake. You should not have sent such a close friend of Dharmit's. For all we know, he's challenged Elric and killed him!'

Again she couldn't resist laughter. 'Oh, you wish too hard – it clouds your reason. I sent Yolan because I knew he would be rude to the albino and perhaps weaken his usual insouciance – arouse his curiosity. Yolan was a kind of bait to bring Elric to us!'

'Then possibly Elric sensed this?'

'I am not overly intelligent, my love – but I think my instincts rarely betray me. We shall see soon.'

A little later there was a discreet scratch at the door and a hand-maiden entered.

'Your Highness, Count Yolan has returned.'

'Only Count Yolan?' There was a smile on Theleb K'aarna's face. It was to disappear in a short while as Yishana left the room, garbed for the street.

524

'You are a fool!' he snarled as the door slammed. He flung down his goblet. Already he had been unsuccessful in the matter of the citadel and, if Elric displaced him, he could lose everything. He began to think very deeply, very carefully.

3

Maturing Vengeance

Though he claimed lack of conscience, Elric's tormented eyes belied the claim as he sat at his window, drinking strong wine and thinking on the past. Since the sack of Imrryr, he had quested the world, seeking some purpose to his existence, some meaning to his life.

He had failed to find the answer in the Dead God's Book. He had failed to love Shaarilla, the wingless woman of Myyrrhn, failed to forget Cymoril, who still inhabited his nightmares. And there were memories of other dreams – of a fate he dare not think upon.

Peace, he thought, was all he sought. Yet even peace in death was denied him. It was in this mood that he continued to brood until his reverie was broken by a soft scratching at the door.

Immediately his expression hardened. His crimson eyes took on a guarded look, his shoulders lifted so that when he stood up he was all cool arrogance. He placed the cup on the table and said lightly:

'Enter!'

A woman entered, swathed in a dark red cloak, unrecognizable in the gloom of the room. She closed the door behind her and stood there, motionless and unspeaking.

When at length she spoke, her voice was almost hesitant, though there was some irony in it, too.

'You sit in darkness, Lord Elric, I had thought to find you asleep . . .'

'Sleep, madam, is the occupation that bores me most. But I will light a torch if you find the darkness unattractive.' He went to the table and removed the cover from the small bowl of charcoal which lay there. He reached for a thin wooden spill and placed one end in the bowl, blowing gently. Soon the charcoal glowed, and the taper caught, and he touched it to a reed torch that hung in a bracket on the wall above the table.

The torch flared and sent shadows skipping around the small chamber. The woman drew back her cowl and the light caught her dark, heavy features and the masses of black hair which framed them.

She contrasted strongly with the slender, aesthetic albino who stood a head taller, looking at her impassively.

She was unused to impassive looks and the novelty pleased her.

'You sent for me, Lord Elric – and you see I am here.' She made a mock curtsey.

'Queen Yishana,' he acknowledged the curtsey with a slight bow. Now that she confronted him, she sensed his power – a power that perhaps attracted even more strongly than her own. And yet, he gave no hint that he responded to her. She reflected that a situation she had expected to be interesting might, ironically, become frustrating. Even this amused her.

Elric, in turn, was intrigued by this woman in spite of himself. His jaded emotions hinted that Yishana might restore their edge. This excited him and perturbed him at once.

He relaxed a little and shrugged. 'I have heard of you, Queen Yishana, in other lands than Jharkor. Sit down if you wish.' He indicated a bench and seated himself on the edge of the bed.

'You are more courteous than your summons suggested,' she smiled as she sat down, crossed her legs, and folded her arms in front of her. 'Does this mean that you will listen to a proposition I have?'

He smiled back. It was a rare smile for him, a little grim, but without the usual bitterness. 'I think so. You are an unusual woman, Queen Yishana. Indeed, I would suspect that you had Melnibonéan blood if I did not know better.'

'Not all your Young Kingdom "upstarts" are quite as unsophisticated as you believe, my lord.'

'Perhaps.'

'Now that I see you at last, face to face, I find your dark legend a little hard to credit in parts – and yet, on the other hand,' she put her head on one side and regarded him frankly, 'it would seem that the legends speak of a less subtle man than the one I see before me.'

'That is the way with legends.'

'Ah,' she half-whispered, 'what a force we could be together, you and I . . . '

'Speculation of that sort irritates me, Queen Yishana. What is your purpose in coming here?'

'Very well, I did not expect you to listen, even.'

'I'll listen – but expect nothing more.'

'Then listen. I think the story will be appreciated, even by you.'

Elric listened and, as Yishana had suspected, the tale she told began to catch his interest . . .

*

Several months ago, Yishana told Elric, peasants in the Gharavian province of Jharkor began to talk of some mysterious riders who were carrying off young men and women from the villages.

Suspecting bandits, Yishana had sent a detachment of her White Leopards, Jharkor's finest fighting men, to the province to put down the brigands.

None of the White Leopards had returned. A second expedition had found no trace of them but, in a valley close to the town of Thokora, they had come upon a strange citadel. Descriptions of the citadel were confused. Suspecting that the White Leopards had attacked and been defeated, the officer in charge had used discretion, left a few men to watch the citadel and report anything they saw, and returned at once to Dhakos. One thing was certain – the citadel had not been in the valley a few months before.

Yishana and Theleb K'aarna had led a large force to the valley. The men left behind had disappeared but, as soon as he saw the citadel, Theleb K'aarna had warned Yishana not to attack.

'It was a marvellous sight, Lord Elric,' Yishana continued. 'The citadel scintillated with shining, rainbow colours – colours that were constantly altering, changing. The whole building looked unreal – sometimes it stood out sharply; sometimes it seemed misty, as if about to vanish. Theleb K'aarna said its nature was sorcerous, and we did not doubt him. Something from the Realm of Chaos, he said, and that seemed likely.' She got up.

She spread her hands. 'We are not used to large-scale manifestations of sorcery in these parts. Theleb K'aarna was familiar enough with sorcery – he comes from the City of Screaming Statues on Pan Tang, and such things are seen frequently – but even he was taken aback.'

'So you withdrew,' Elric prompted impatiently.

'We were about to – in fact Theleb K'aarna and myself were already riding back at the head of the army when the music came . . . It was sweet, beautiful, unearthly, painful – Theleb K'aarna shouted to me to ride as swiftly as I could away from it. I dallied, attracted by the music, but he slapped the rump of my horse and we rode, fast as dragons in flight, away from there. Those nearest us also escaped – but we saw the rest turn and move back towards the citadel, drawn by the music. Nearly two hundred men went back – and vanished.'

'What did you do then?' Elric asked as Yishana crossed the floor and sat down beside him. He moved to give her more room.

'Theleb K'aarna has been trying to investigate the nature of the citadel – its purpose and its controller. So far, his divinations have told him little more than he guessed: that the Realm of Chaos has sent the citadel to the Realm of Earth and is slowly extending its range. More and more of our young men and women are being abducted by the minions of Chaos.'

'And these minions?' Yishana had moved a little closer, and this time Elric did not move away.

'None who has sought to stop them has succeeded – few have lived.'

'And what do you seek of me?'

'Help.' She looked closely into his face and reached out a hand to touch him. 'You have knowledge of both Chaos and Law – old knowledge, instinctive knowledge if Theleb K'aarna is right. Why, your very Gods are Lords of Chaos.'

'That is exactly true, Yishana – and because our patron Gods are of Chaos, it is not in my interest to fight against any one of them.'

Now he moved towards her and he was smiling, looking into her eyes. Suddenly, he took her in his arms. 'Perhaps you will be strong enough,' he said enigmatically, just before their lips met. 'And as for the other matter – we can discuss that later.'

In the deep greenness of a dark mirror, Theleb K'aarna saw something of the scene in Elric's room and he glowered impotently. He tugged at his beard as the scene faded for the tenth time in a minute. None of his mutterings could restore it. He sat back in his chair of serpent skulls and planned vengeance. That vengeance could take time maturing, he decided; for, if Elric could be useful in the matter of the citadel, there was no point in destroying him yet . . .

4

Favouring the Lords of Disorder

Next afternoon, three riders set off for the town of Thokora. Elric and Yishana rode close together; but the third rider, Theleb K'aarna, kept a frowning distance. If Elric was at all embarrassed by this display on the part of the man he had ousted in Yishana's affections, he did not show it.

Elric, finding Yishana more than attractive in spite of himself, had agreed at least to inspect the citadel and suggest what it might be and how it might be fought. He had exchanged a few words with Moonglum before setting off.

They rode across the beautiful grasslands of Jharkor, golden beneath a hot sun. It was two days' ride to Thokora, and Elric intended to enjoy it.

Feeling less than miserable, he galloped along with Yishana, laughing with her in her enjoyment. Yet, buried deeper than it would normally have been, there was a deep foreboding in his heart as they neared the mysterious citadel, and he noted that Theleb K'aarna occasionally looked satisfied when he should have looked disgruntled.

Sometimes Elric would shout to the sorcerer. 'Ho, old spell-maker, do you feel no joyful release from the cares of the court out here amidst the beauties of nature? Your face is long, Theleb K'aarna — breathe in the untainted air and laugh with us!' Then Theleb K'aarna would scowl and mutter, and Yishana would laugh at him and glance brightly at Elric.

So they came to Thokora and found it a smouldering pit that stank like a midden of hell.

Elric sniffed. 'This is Chaos work. You were right enough there, Theleb K'aarna. Whatever fire destroyed such a large town, it was not natural fire. Whoever is responsible for this is evidently increasing his power. As you know, sorcerer, the Lords of Law and Chaos are usually in perfect balance, neither tampering directly with our Earth. Evidently the balance has tipped a little way to one side, as it sometimes does, favouring the Lords of Disorder – allowing them access to our realm. Normally it is possible for an earthly sorcerer to summon aid from Chaos or Law for a short time, but it is rare for either side to establish itself so firmly as our friend in the citadel evidently has. What is more disturbing – for you of the Young Kingdoms, at least – is that, once such power is gained, it is possible to increase it, and the Lords of Chaos could in time conquer the Realm of Earth by gradual increase of their strength here.'

'A terrible possibility,' muttered the sorcerer, genuinely afraid. Even though he could sometimes summon help from Chaos, it was in no human being's interest to have Chaos ruling over him.

Elric climbed back into his saddle. 'We'd best make speed to the valley,' he said.

'Are you sure it is wise, after witnessing this?' Theleb K'aarna was nervous.

Elric laughed. 'What? And you a sorcerer from Pan Tang – that isle that claims to know as much of sorcery as my ancestors, the Bright Emperors! No, no – besides, I'm not in a cautious mood today!'

'Nor am I,' cried Yishana, clapping her steed's sides. 'Come, gentlemen – to the Citadel of Chaos!'

By late afternoon, they had topped the range of hills surrounding the valley and looked down at the mysterious citadel.

Yishana had described it well – but not perfectly. Elric's eyes ached as he looked at it, for it seemed to extend beyond the Realm of Earth into a different plane, perhaps several.

It shimmered and glittered and all Earthly colours were there, as well as many which Elric recognized as belonging to other planes. Even the basic outline of the citadel was uncertain. In contrast, the surrounding valley was a sea of dark ash, which sometimes seemed to eddy, to undulate and send up spurting geysers of dust, as if the basic elements of nature had been disturbed, and warped by the presence of the supernatural citadel.

'Well?' Theleb K'aarna tried to calm his nervous horse as it backed away from the citadel. 'Have you seen the like in the world before?'

Elric shook his head. 'Not in this world, certainly; but I've seen it before. During my final initiation into the arts of Melniboné, my father took me with him in astral form to the Realm of Chaos, there to receive the audience of my patron the Lord Arioch of the Seven Darks . . . '

Theleb K'aarna shuddered. 'You have been to Chaos? It is Arioch's citadel, then?'

Elric laughed in disdain. 'That! No, it is a hovel compared to the palaces of the Lords of Chaos.'

Impatiently, Yishana said: 'Then who dwells *there*?'

'As I remember, the one who dwelt in the citadel when I passed through the Chaos Realm in my youth – he was no Lord of Chaos, but a kind of servant to the Lords. 'Yet,' he frowned, 'not exactly a servant . . . '

'*Ach*! You speak in riddles.' Theleb K'aarna turned his horse to ride down the hills, away from the citadel. 'I know you Melnibonéans! Starving, you'd rather have a paradox than food!'

Elric and Yishana followed him some distance, then Elric stopped and pointed behind him.

'The one who dwells yonder is a paradoxical sort of fellow. He's a kind of Jester to the Court of Chaos. The Lords of Chaos respect him – perhaps fear him slightly – even though he entertains them. He delights them with cosmic riddles, with farcical satires purporting to explain the nature of the Cosmic Hand that holds Chaos and Law in balance, he juggles enigmas like baubles, laughs at what Chaos holds dear, takes seriously that which they mock at . . . ' He paused and shrugged. 'So I have heard, at least.'

'Why should he be here?'

'Why should he be anywhere? I could guess at the motives of Chaos or Law and probably be right. But not even the Lords of the Higher Worlds can understand the motives of Balo the Jester. It is said that he is the only one allowed to move between the Realms of Chaos and Law at will, though I have never heard of him coming to the Realm of Earth before. Neither, for that matter, have I ever heard him credited with such acts of destruction as that which we've witnessed. It is a puzzle to me – one which would no doubt please him if he knew.'

'There would be one way of discovering the purpose of his visit,' Theleb K'aarna said with a faint smile. 'If someone entered the citadel . . . '

'Come now, sorcerer,' Elric mocked. 'I've little love for life, to be sure, but there are some things of value to me – my soul, for one!'

Theleb K'aarna began to ride on down the hill, but Elric remained thoughtfully where he was, Yishana beside him.

'You seem more troubled by this than you should be, Elric,' she said.

'It *is* disturbing. There is a hint here that, if we investigate the citadel further, we should become embroiled in some dispute between Balo and his masters – perhaps even the Lords of Law, too. To become so involved could easily mean our destruction, since the forces at work are more dangerous and powerful than anything we are familiar with on Earth.'

'But we cannot simply watch this Balo laying our cities waste, carrying off our fairest, threatening to rule Jharkor himself within a short time!'

Elric sighed, but did not reply.

'Have you no sorcery, Elric, to send Balo back to Chaos where he belongs, to seal the breach he has made in our Realm?'

'Even Melnibonéans cannot match the power of the Lords of the Higher Worlds – and my forefathers knew much more of sorcery than do I. My best allies serve neither Chaos nor Law, they are elementals: lords of fire, earth, air, and water, entities with affinities with beasts and plants. Good allies in an earthly battle – but of no great use when matched against one such as Balo. I must think . . . At least, if I opposed Balo it would not necessarily incur the wrath of my patron Lords. Something, I suppose . . . '

The hills rolled green and lush to the grasslands at their feet, the sun beat down from a clear sky on the infinity of grass stretching to the horizon. Above them a large predatory bird wheeled; and Theleb K'aarna was a tiny figure, turning in the saddle to call to them in a thin voice, but his words could not be heard.

Yishana seemed dispirited. Her shoulders slightly slumped, and she did not look at Elric as she began to guide her horse slowly down towards the sorcerer of Pan Tang. Elric followed, conscious of his own indecision, yet half-careless of it. What did it matter to him if . . . ?

The music began, faintly at first, but beginning to swell with an attractive, poignant sweetnees, evoking nostalgic memories, offering peace and giving life a sharp meaning, all at once. If the music came from instruments, then they were not earthly. It produced in him a yearning to turn about and discover its source, but he resisted it. Yishana, on the other hand, was evidently not finding the music so easily resisted. She had wheeled completely round, her face radiant, her lips trembling and tears shining in her eyes.

Elric, in his wanderings in unearthly realms, had heard music like it before – it echoed many of the bizarre symphonies of old Melniboné – and it did not draw him as it drew Yishana. He recognized swiftly that she was in danger, and as she came past him, spurring her horse, he reached out to grab her bridle.

Her whip slashed at his hand and, cursing with unexpected pain, he dropped the bridle. She went past him, galloping up to the crest of the hill and vanishing over it in an instant.

'Yishana!' He shouted at her desperately, but his voice would not carry over the pulsing music. He looked back, hoping that Theleb K'aarna would lend help, but the sorcerer was riding rapidly away.

Evidently, on hearing the music, he had come to a swift decision.

Elric raced after Yishana, screaming for her to turn back. His own horse reached the top of the hill and he saw her bent over her steed's neck as she goaded it towards the shining citadel.

'*Yishana! You go to your doom!*'

Now she had reached the outer limits of the citadel, and her horse's feet seemed to strike off shimmering waves of colour as they touched the Chaos-disturbed ground surrounding the place. Although he knew it was too late to stop her, Elric continued to speed after her, hoping to reach her before she entered the citadel itself.

But, even as he entered the rainbow swirl, he saw what appeared to be a dozen Yishanas going through a dozen gateways into the citadel. Oddly refracted light created the illusion and made it impossible to tell which was the real Yishana.

With Yishana's disappearance the music stopped and Elric thought he heard a faint whisper of laughter following it. His horse was by this time becoming increasingly difficult to control, and he did not trust himself to it. He dismounted, his legs wreathed in radiant mist, and let the horse go. It galloped off, snorting its terror.

Elric's left hand moved to the hilt of his runesword, but he hesitated to draw it. Once pulled from its scabbard, the blade would demand souls before it allowed itself to be resheathed. Yet it was his only weapon. He withdrew his hand, and the blade seemed to quiver angrily at his side.

'Not yet, Stormbringer. There may be forces within who are stronger even than you!'

He began to wade through the faintly-resisting light swirls. He was half-blinded by the scintillating colours around him, which sometimes shone dark blue, silver, and red; sometimes gold, light green, amber. He also felt the sickening lack of any sort of orientation – distance, depth, breadth, were meaningless. He recognized what he had only experienced in an astral form – the odd, timeless, spaceless quality that marked a Realm of the Higher Worlds.

He drifted, pushing his body in the direction in which he guessed Yishana had gone, for by now he had lost sight of the gateway or any of its mirage images.

He realized that, unless he was doomed to drift here until he starved, he must draw Stormbringer, for the runeblade could resist the influence of Chaos.

This time, when he gripped the sword's hilt, he felt a shock run up his arm and infuse his body with vitality. The sword came free from the scabbard. From the huge blade, carved with strange old runes, a black radiance poured, meeting the shifting colours of Chaos and dispersing them.

Now Elric shrieked the age-old battle-ululation of his folk and pressed on into the citadel, slashing at the intangible images that swirled on all sides. The gateway was ahead, and Elric knew it now, for his sword had shown him which were the mirages. It was open as Elric reached the portal. He paused for a moment, his lips moving as he remembered an invocation that he might need later. Arioch, Lord of Chaos, patron god-demon of his ancestors, was a negligent power and whimful – he could not rely on Arioch to aid him here, unless . . .

In slow graceful strides, a golden beast with eyes of ruby-fire was loping down the passage that led from the portal. Bright though the eyes were, they seemed blind, and its huge, doglike muzzle was closed. Yet its path could only lead it to Elric and, as it neared him, the mouth suddenly gaped showing coral fangs. In silence it came to a halt, the blind eyes never once settling on the albino, and then sprang!

Elric staggered back, raising the sword in defence. He was flung to the ground by the beast's weight and felt its body cover him. It was cold, cold, and it made no attempt to savage him – just lay on top of him and let the cold permeate his body.

Elric began to shiver as he pushed at the chilling body of the beast. Stormbringer moaned and murmured in his hand, and then it pierced some part of the beast's body, and a horrible cold strength began to fill the albino. Reinforced by the beast's own life-force, he heaved upwards. The beast continued to smother him, though now a thin, barely audible sound was coming from it. Elric guessed that Stormbringer's small wound was hurting the creature.

Desperately, for he was shaking and aching with cold, he moved the sword and stabbed again. Again the thin sound from the beast; again cold energy flooded through him, and again he heaved. This time the beast was flung off and crawled back towards the portal. Elric sprang up, raised Stormbringer high, and brought the sword down on the golden creature's skull. The skull shattered as ice might shatter.

Elric ran forward into the passage and, once he was within, the place became filled with roars and shrieks that echoed and were magnified. It was as if the voice that the cold beast had lacked outside was shouting its death-agonies here.

Now the floor rose until he was running up a spiral ramp. Looking down, he shuddered, for he looked into an infinite pit of subtle, dangerous colours that swam about in such a way that he could hardly take his eyes from them. He even felt his body begin to leave the ramp and go towards the pit, but he strengthened his grip on the sword and disciplined himself to climb on.

Upwards, as he looked, was the same as downwards. Only the ramp had any kind of constancy, and this began to take on the appearance of a thinly-cut jewel, through which he could see the pit and in which it was reflected.

Greens and blues and yellows predominated, but there were also traces of dark red, black, and orange, and many other colours not in an ordinary human spectrum.

Elric knew he was in some province of the Higher Worlds and guessed that it would not be long before the ramp led him to new danger.

Danger did not seem to await him when at last he came to the end of the ramp and stepped on to a bridge of similar stuff, which led over the scintillating pit to an archway that shone with a steady blue light.

He crossed the bridge cautiously and as cautiously entered the arch. Everything was blue-tinged here, even himself; and he trod on, the blue becoming deeper and deeper as he progressed.

Then Stormbringer began to murmur and, either warned by the sword or by some sixth sense of his own, Elric wheeled to his right. Another archway had appeared there and from this there began to shine a light as deep red as the other was blue. Where the two met was a purple of fantastic richness and Elric stared at this, experiencing a similar hypnotic pull as he had felt when climbing the ramp. Again his mind was stronger, and he forced himself to enter the red arch. At once another arch appeared to his left, sending a beam of green light to merge with the red, and another to his left brought yellow light, one ahead brought mauve until he seemed trapped within the criss-cross of beams. He slashed at them with Stormbringer, and the black radiance reduced the beams for a moment to streamers of light, which reformed again. Elric continued to move forward.

Now, looming through the confusion of colour, a shape appeared and Elric thought it was that of a man.

Man it was in shape – but not in size it seemed. Yet, when it drew closer, it was no giant – less than Elric's height. Still it gave the *impression* of vast proportions, rather as if it *were* a giant and Elric had grown to its size.

It blundered towards Elric and went *through* him. It was not that the man was intangible – it was Elric who felt the ghost. The creature's mass seemed of incredible density. The creature was turning, its huge hands reaching out, its face a mocking grimace. Elric struck at it with Stormbringer and was astonished as the runesword was halted, making no impression on the creature's bulk.

Yet when it grasped Elric, its hands went through him. Elric backed away, grinning now in relief. Then he saw with some terror that the light was gleaming through him. He had been right – *he* was the ghost!

The creature reached out for him again, grabbed him again, failed to hold him.

Elric, conscious that he was in no physical danger from the monster, yet also highly conscious that his sanity was about to be permanently impaired, turned and fled.

Quite suddenly he was in a hall, the walls of which were of the same unstable, shifting colours as the rest of the place. But sitting on a stool in the centre of the hall, holding in his hands some tiny creatures that seemed to be running about on his palm, was a small figure who looked up at Elric and grinned merrily.

'Welcome, King of Melniboné. And how fares the last ruler of my favourite earthly race?'

The figure was dressed in shimmering motley. On his head was a tall, spiked crown – a travesty of and a comment upon the crowns of the mighty. His face was angular and his mouth wide.

'Greetings, Lord Balo,' Elric made a mock bow. 'Strange hospitality you offer in your welcome.'

'Ahaha – it did not amuse you, eh? Men are so much harder to please than gods – you would not think it, would you?'

'Men's pleasures are rarely so elaborate. Where is Queen Yishana?'

'Allow me my pleasure also, mortal. Here she is, I think.' Balo plucked at one of the tiny creatures on his palm. Elric stepped forward and saw that Yishana was indeed there, as were many of the lost soldiers. Balo looked up at him and winked. 'They are so much easier to handle in this size.'

'I do not doubt it, though I wonder if it is not we who are larger rather than they who are smaller . . . '

'You are astute, mortal. But can you guess how this came to be?'

'Your creature back there – your pits and colours and archways – somehow they warp – what?'

'*Mass*, King Elric. But you would not understand such concepts. Even the Lords of Melniboné, most godlike and intelligent of mortals, only learned how to manipulate the elements in ritual invocation and spell, but never understood what they manipulated – that is where the Lords of the Higher Worlds score, whatever their differences.'

'But I survived without need for spells. I survived by disciplining my mind!'

'That helped, for certain – but you forget your greatest asset – that disturbing blade there. You use it in your petty problems to aid you, and you never realize that it is like making use of a mighty war galley to catch a sprat. That sword represents power in *any* Realm, King Elric!'

'Aye, so it might. This does not interest me. Why are you here, Lord Balo?'

Balo chuckled, his laughter rich and musical. 'Oho, I am in disgrace. I quarrelled with my masters, who took exception to a joke of mine about their insignificance and egotism, about their destiny and their pride. Bad taste to them, King, is any hint of their own oblivion. I made a joke in bad taste. I fled from the Higher Worlds to Earth, where, unless invoked, the Lords of Law or Chaos can rarely interfere. You will like my intention, Elric, as would any Melnibonéan – I intend to establish my own Realm on Earth – the Realm of Paradox. A little from Law, a little from Chaos – a Realm of opposites, of curiosities and jokes.'

'I'm thinking we already have such a world as you describe, Lord Balo, with no need for you to create it!'

'Earnest irony, King Elric, for an insouciant man of Melniboné.'

'Ah, that it may be. I am a boor on occasions such as these. Will you release Yishana and myself?'

'But you and I are giants – I have given you the status and appearance of a god. You and I could be partners in this enterprise of mine!'

'Unfortunately, Lord Balo, I do not possess your range of humour and am unfitted for such an exalted role. Besides,' Elric grinned suddenly, 'it is in my mind that the Lords of the Higher Worlds will not easily let drop the matter of your ambition, since it appears to conflict so strongly with theirs.'

Balo laughed but said nothing.

Elric also smiled, but it was an attempt to hide his racing thoughts. 'What do you intend to do if I refuse?'

'Why, Elric, you would not refuse! I can think of many subtle pranks that I could play on you . . . '

'Indeed? And the Black Swords?'

'Ah, yes . . . '

'Balo, in your mirth and obsessions you have not considered everything thoroughly. You should have exerted more effort to vanquish me before I came here.'

Now Elric's eyes gleamed hot and he lifted the sword, crying:

'Arioch! Master! I invoke thee, Lord of Chaos!'

Balo started. 'Cease that, King Elric!'

'Arioch – here is a soul for you to claim!'

'Quiet, I say!'

'*Arioch! Hear me!*' Elric's voice was loud and desperate.

Balo let his tiny playthings fall and rose hurriedly, skipping towards Elric.

'Your invocation is unheeded!' He laughed, reaching out for Elric. But Stormbringer moaned and shuddered in Elric's hand and Balo withdrew his hand. His face became serious and frowning.

'*Arioch of the Seven Darks – your servant calls you!*'

The walls of flame trembled and began to fade. Balo's eyes widened and jerked this way and that.

'*Oh, Lord Arioch – come reclaim your straying Balo!*'

'You cannot!' Balo scampered across the room where one section of the flame had faded entirely, revealing darkness beyond.

'Sadly for you, little jester, he can . . . ' The voice was sardonic and yet beautiful. From the darkness stepped a tall figure, no longer the shapeless gibbering thing that had, until now, been Arioch's favoured manifestation when visiting the Realm of Earth. Yet the great beauty of the newcomer, filled as it was with a kind of compassion mingled with pride, cruelty, and sadness, showed at once that he could not be human. He was clad in doublet of pulsing scarlet, hose of ever-changing hue, a long golden sword at his hips. His eyes were large, but slanted high, his hair was long and as golden as the sword, his lips were full and his chin pointed like his ears.

'Arioch!' Balo stumbled backwards as the Lord of Chaos advanced.

'It was your mistake, Balo,' Elric said from behind the jester. 'Did you not realize only the Kings of Melniboné may invoke Arioch and bring him to the Realm of Earth? It has been their age-old privilege.'

'And much have they abused it,' said Arioch, smiling faintly as Balo grovelled. 'However, this service you have done us, Elric, will make up for past misuses. I was not amused by the matter of the Mist Giant . . .'

Even Elric was awed by the incredibly powerful presence of the Chaos Lord. He also felt much relieved, for he had not been sure that Arioch could be summoned in this way.

Now Arioch stretched an arm down towards Balo and lifted the jester by his collar so that he jerked and struggled in the air, his face writhing in fear and consternation.

Arioch took hold of Balo's head and squeezed it. Elric looked on in amazement as the head began to shrink. Arioch took Balo's legs and bent them in, folding Balo up and kneading him in his slender, inhuman hands until he was a small, solid ball. Arioch then popped the ball into his mouth and swallowed it.

'I have not eaten him, Elric,' he said with another faint smile. 'It is merely the easiest way of transporting him back to the Realms from which he came. He has transgressed and will be punished. All this' – he waved an arm to indicate the citadel – 'is unfortunate and contradicts the plans we of Chaos have for Earth – plans which will involve you, our servant, and make you mighty.'

Elric bowed to his master. 'I'm honoured, Lord Arioch, though I seek no favours.'

Arioch's silvery voice lost some of its beauty and his face seemed to cloud for a second. 'You are pledged to serve Chaos, Elric, as were your ancestors. You *will* serve Chaos! The time draws near when both Law and Chaos will battle for the Realm of Earth – and Chaos shall win! Earth will be incorporated into our Realm and you will join the hierarchy of Chaos, become immortal as we are!'

'Immortality offers little to me, my lord.'

'Ah, Elric, have the men of Melniboné become as the half-apes who now dominate Earth with their puny "civilizations"? Are you no better than those Young Kingdom upstarts? Think what we offer!'

'I shall, my lord, when the time you mention comes.' Elric's head was still lowered.

'You shall indeed,' Arioch raised his arms. 'Now to transport this toy of Balo's to its proper Realm, and redress the trouble he has caused, lest some hint reaches our opponents before the proper time.'

Arioch's voice swelled like the singing of a million brazen bells and Elric sheathed his sword and clapped his hands over his ears to stop the pain.

Then Elric felt his body seem to *shred* apart, swell and stretch until it became like smoke drifting on air. Then, faster, the smoke began to be drawn together, becoming denser and denser and he seemed to be shrinking now. All around him were rolling banks of colour, flashes and indescribable noises. Then came a vast blackness and he closed his eyes against the images that seemed reflected in the blackness.

When he opened them he stood in the valley and the singing citadel was gone. Only Yishana and a few surprised-looking soldiers stood there. Yishana ran towards him.

'Elric – was it you who saved us?'

'I must claim only part of the credit,' he said.

'Not all my soldiers are here,' she said, inspecting the men. Where are the rest – and the villagers abducted earlier?'

'If Balo's tastes are like his masters', then I fear they now have the honour of being part of a demi-god. The Lords of Chaos are not flesh-eaters, of course, being of the Higher Worlds, but there is something they savour in men which satisfies them . . .'

Yishana hugged her body as if in cold. 'He was huge – I cannot believe that his citadel could contain his bulk!'

'The citadel was more than a dwelling-place, that was obvious. Somehow it changed size, shape – and other things I cannot describe. Arioch of Chaos transported it and Balo back to where they belong.'

'Arioch! But he is one of the Greatest Six! How did he come to Earth?'

'An old pact with my remote ancestors. By calling him they allow him to spend a short time in our realm, and he repays them with some favour. This was done.'

'Come, Elric,' she took his arm. 'Let's away from the valley.'

Elric was weak and enfeebled by the efforts of summoning Arioch, and the experiences he had had before and since the episode. He could hardly walk; and soon it was Yishana who supported him as they made slow progress, the dazed warriors following in their wake, towards the nearest village, where they could obtain rest and horses to take them back to Dhakos.

5

A Reptile's Memories

As they staggered past the blasted ruins of Thokora, Yishana pointed suddenly at the sky.

'What is that?'

A great shape was winging its way towards them. It had the appearance of a butterfly, but a butterfly with wings so huge they blotted out the sun.

'Can it be some creature of Balo's left behind?' she speculated.

'Hardly likely,' he replied. 'This has the appearance of a monster conjured by a human sorcerer.'

'Theleb K'aarna!'

'He has surpassed himself,' Elric said wryly. 'I did not think him capable.'

'It is his vengeance on us, Elric!'

'That seems reasonable. But I am weak, Yishana – and Stormbringer needs souls if it is to replenish my strength.' He turned a calculating eye on the warriors behind him who were gaping up at the creature as it came nearer. Now they could see it had a man's body, covered with hairs or feathers hued like a peacock's.

The air whistled as it descended, its fifty-foot wings dwarfing the seven feet of head and body. From its head grew two curling horns, and its arms terminated in long talons.

'We are doomed, Elric!' cried Yishana. She saw that the warriors were fleeing and she cried after them to come back. Elric stood there passively, knowing that alone he could not defeat the butterfly-creature.

'Best go with them, Yishana,' he murmured. 'I think it will be satisfied with me.'

'No!'

He ignored her and stepped towards the creature as it landed and began to glide over the ground in his direction. He drew a quiescent Stormbringer, which felt heavy in his hand. A little strength flowed into him, but not enough. His only hope was to strike a good blow at the creature's vitals and draw some of its own life-force into himself.

The creature's voice shrilled at him, and the strange, insane face twisted as he approached. Elric realized that this was no true supernatural denizen of the nether worlds, but a once-human creature warped by Theleb K'aarna's sorcery. At least it was mortal, and he had only physical strength to contend with. In better condition it would have been easy for him – but now . . .

The wings beat at the air as the taloned hands grasped at him. He took Stormbringer in both hands and swung the runeblade at the thing's neck. Swiftly the wings folded in to protect its neck and Stormbringer became entangled in the strange, sticky flesh. A talon caught Elric's arm, ripping it to the bone. He yelled in pain and yanked the sword from the enfolding wing.

He tried to steady himself for another blow, but the monster grabbed his wounded arm and began drawing him towards its now lowered head – and the horns that curled from it.

He struggled, hacking at the thing's arms with the extra strength that came with the threat of death.

Then he heard a cry from behind him and saw a figure from the corner of his eye, a figure that leapt forward with two blades gleaming in either hand. The swords slashed at the talons and with a shriek the creature turned on Elric's would-be rescuer.

It was Moonglum. Elric fell backwards, breathing hard, as he watched his little red-headed friend engage the monster.

But Moonglum would not survive for long, unless aided.

Elric racked his brain for some spell that would help; but he was too weak, even if he could think of one, to raise the energy necessary to summon supernatural help.

And then it came to him! Yishana! She was not as exhausted as he. But could she do it?

He turned as the air moaned to the beating of the creature's wings. Moonglum was only just managing to hold it off, his two swords flashing rapidly as he parried every effort to grasp him.

'Yishana!' croaked the albino.

She came up to him and placed a hand on his. 'We could leave, Elric – perhaps hide from that thing.'

'No. I must help Moonglum. Listen – you realize how desperate our position is, do you not? Then keep that in mind while you recite this rune with me. Perhaps together we may succeed. There are many kinds of lizards in these parts, are there not?'

'Aye – many.'

'Then this is what you must say – and remember that we shall all perish by Theleb K'aarna's servant if you are not successful.'

In the half worlds, where dwelt the master-types of all creatures other than Man, an entity stirred, hearing its name. The entity was called Haaashaastaak; and it was scaly and cold, with no true intellect, such as men and gods possessed, but an *awareness* which served it as well if not better. It was brother, on this plane, to such entities as Meerclar, Lord of the Cats, Roofdrak, Lord of the Dogs, Nuru-ah, Lord of the Cattle, and many, many others. This was Haaashaastaak, Lord of the Lizards. It did not really hear words in the exact sense, but it heard rhythms which meant much to it, even though it did not know why. The rhythms were being repeated over and over again, but seemed too faint to be worth much attention. It stirred and yawned, but did nothing . . .

> '*Haaashaastaak, Lord of Lizards,*
> *Your children were fathers of men,*
> *Haaashaastaak, Prince of Reptiles,*
> *Come aid a grandchild now!*
>
> '*Haaashaastaak, Father of Scales,*
> *Cold-blooded bringer of life . . .*'

It was a bizarre scene, with Elric and Yishana desperately chanting the rune over and over again as Moonglum fought on, slowly losing strength.

Haaashaastaak quivered and became more curious. The rhythms were no stronger, yet they seemed more insistent. He would travel, he decided, to that place where those he watched over dwelt. He knew that if he answered the rhythms, he would have to obey whatever source they had. He was not, of course, aware that such decisions had been implanted into him in a far distant age – the time before the creation of Earth, when the Lords of Law and Chaos, then inhabitants of a single realm and known by another name, had watched over the forming of things and laid down the manner and logic in which things should behave, following their great edict from the voice of the Cosmic Balance – the voice which had never spoken since.

Haaashaastaak betook himself, a little slothfully, to Earth.

Elric and Yishana were still chanting hoarsely, as Haaashaastaak made his sudden appearance. He had the look of a huge iguana, and his eyes were many-coloured, many faceted jewels, his scales seeming of gold, silver, and other rich metals. A slightly hazy outline surrounded him, as if he had brought part of his own environment with him.

Yishana gasped and Elric breathed a deep sigh. As a child he had learned the languages of all animal-masters, and now he must recall the simple language of the lizard-master, Haaashaastaak.

His need fired his brain, and the words came suddenly.

'Haaashaastaak,' he cried pointing at the butterfly-creature, 'mokik ankkuh!'

The lizard lord turned its jewelled eyes on the creature and its great tongue suddenly shot out towards it, curling around the monster. It shrilled in terror as it was drawn towards the lizard lord's great maw. Legs and arms kicked as the mouth closed on it. Several gulps and Haaashaastaak had swallowed Theleb K'aarna's prize creation. Then it turned its head uncertainly about for a few moments and vanished.

Pain began to throb now through Elric's torn arm as Moonglum staggered towards him, grinning in relief.

'I followed behind you at a distance as you requested,' he said, 'since you suspected treachery from Theleb K'aarna. But then I spied the sorcerer coming this way and followed him to a cave in yonder hills,' he pointed. 'But when the deceased,' he laughed shakily, 'emerged from the cave, I decided that it would be best to chase *that*, for I had the feeling it was going in your direction.'

'I am glad you were so astute,' Elric said.

'It was your doing, really,' Moonglum replied. 'For, if you hadn't anticipated treachery from Theleb K'aarna, I might not have been here at the right moment.' Moonglum suddenly sank to the grass, leaned back, grinned, and fainted.

Elric felt very dazed himself. 'I do not think we need fear anything more from your sorcerer just yet, Yishana,' he said. 'Let us rest here and refresh ourselves. Perhaps then your cowardly soldiers will have returned, and we can send them to a village to get us some horses.'

They stretched out on the grass and, lying in each other's arms, went to sleep.

Elric was astonished to wake in a bed, a soft bed. He opened his eyes and saw Yishana and Moonglum smiling down at him.

'How long have I been here?'

'More than two days. You did not wake when the horses came, so we had the warriors construct a stretcher to bear you to Dhakos. You are in my palace.'

Elric cautiously moved his stiff, bandaged arm. It was still painful.

'Are my belongings still at the inn?'

'Perhaps, if they have not been stolen. Why?'

'I have a pouch of herbs there, which will heal this arm quickly and also supply me with a little strength, which I need badly.'

'I will go and see if they are still there,' Moonglum said and walked from the chamber.

Yishana stroked Elric's milk-white hair. 'I have much to thank you for, wolf,' said she. 'You have saved my kingdom – perhaps all the Young Kingdoms. In my eyes you are redeemed for my brother's death.'

'Oh, I thank you, madam,' said Elric with a mocking tone.

She laughed. 'You are still a Melnibonéan.'

'Still that, aye.'

'A strange mixture, however. Sensitive and cruel, sardonic and loyal to your little friend Moonglum. I look forward to knowing you better, my lord.'

'As to that, I am not sure if you will have the opportunity.'

She gave him a hard look. 'Why?'

'Your résumé of my character was incomplete, Queen Yishana – you should have added "careless of the world – and yet vengeful." I wish to be revenged on your pet wizard.'

'But he is spent, surely – you said so yourself.'

'I am, as you remarked, still a Melnibonéan! My arrogant blood calls vengeance on an upstart!'

'Forget Theleb K'aarna. I will have him hunted by my White Leopards. Even his sorcery will not win against such savages as they are!'

'Forget him? Oh, no!'

'Elric, Elric – I will give you my kingdom, declare you ruler of Jharkor, if you will let me be your consort.'

He reached out and stroked her bare arm with his good hand.

'You are unrealistic, queen. To take such an action would bring wholesale rebellion in your land. To your folk, I am still the Traitor of Imrryr.'

'Not now - now you are the Hero of Jharkor.'

'How so? They did not know of their peril and thus will feel no gratitude. It were best that I settled my debt with your wizard and went on my way. The streets must already be full of rumours that you have taken your brother's murderer to your bed. Your popularity with your subjects must be at its lowest, madam.'

'I do not care.'

'You will if your nobles lead the people in insurrection and crucify you naked in the city square.'

'You are familiar with our customs.'

'We Melnibonéans are a learned folk, queen.'

'Well versed in all the arts.'

'All of them.' Again he felt his blood race as she rose and barred the door. At that moment he felt no need for the herbs which Moonglum had gone to find.

When he tiptoed from the room that night, he found Moonglum waiting patiently in the antechamber. Moonglum proffered the pouch with a wink. But Elric's mood was not light. He took bunches of herbs from the pouch and selected what he needed.

Moonglum grimaced as he watched Elric chew and swallow the stuff. Then together they stole from the palace.

Armed with Stormbringer and mounted, Elric rode slightly behind his friend as Moonglum led the way towards the hills beyond Dhakos.

'If I know the sorcerers of Pan Tang,' murmured the albino, 'then Theleb K'aarna will be more exhausted than was I. With luck we will come upon him sleeping.'

'I shall wait outside the cave in that case,' said Moonglum, for he now had some experience of Elric's vengeance-taking and did not relish watching Theleb K'aarna's slow death.

They galloped speedily until the hills were reached and Moonglum showed Elric the cave mouth.

Leaving his horse, the albino went soft-footed into the cave, his runesword ready.

Moonglum waited nervously for Theleb K'aarna's first shrieks, but none came. He waited until dawn began to bring the first faint light and then Elric, face frozen with anger emerged from the cave.

Savagely he grasped his horse's reins and swung himself into the saddle.

'Are you satisfied?' Moonglum asked tentatively.

'Satisfied, no! The dog has vanished!'

'Gone – but . . . '

'He was more cunning than I thought. There are several caves and I sought him in all of them. In the farthest I discovered traces of sorcerous runes on the walls and floor. He has transported himself somewhere and I could not discover where, in spite of deciphering most of the runes! Perhaps he went to Pan Tang.'

'Ah, then our quest has been futile. Let us return to Dhakos and enjoy a little more of Yishana's hospitality.'

'No – we go to Pan Tang.'

'But, Elric, Theleb K'aarna's brother sorcerers dwell there in strength; and Jagreen Lern, the theocrat, forbids visitors!'

'No matter. I wish to finish my business with Theleb K'aarna.'

'You have no proof that he is there!'

'No matter!'

And then Elric was spurring his horse away, riding like a man possessed or fleeing from dreadful peril – and perhaps he was both possessed and fleeing. Moonglum did not follow at once but thoughtfully watched his friend gallop off. Not normally introspective, he wondered if Yishana had perhaps affected the albino more strongly than he would have wished. He did not think that vengeance on Theleb K'aarna was Elric's prime desire in refusing to return to Dhakos.

Then he shrugged and slapped his heels to his steed's flanks, racing to catch up with Elric as the cold dawn rose, wondering if they would continue towards Pan Tang once Dhakos was far enough behind.

But Elric's head contained no thoughts, only emotion flooded him – emotion he did not wish to analyse. His white hair streaming behind him, his dead-white, handsome face set, his slender hands tightly clutching the stallion's reins, he rode. And only his strange, crimson eyes reflected the misery and conflict within him.

In Dhakos that morning, other eyes held misery, but not for too long. Yishana was a pragmatic queen.